FLYING FINISH
AND
HOT MONEY

Also by Dick Francis

THE SPORT OF QUEENS
(autobiography)

LESTER: The Official
Biography

DEAD CERT

NERVE

FOR KICKS

ODDS AGAINST

BLOOD SPORT

FORFEIT

ENQUIRY

RAT RACE

BONECRACK

SMOKESCREEN

SLAY-RIDE

KNOCK DOWN

HIGH STAKES

IN THE FRAME

RISK

TRIAL RUN

WHIP HAND

REFLEX

TWICE SHY

BANKER

THE DANGER

PROOF

BREAK IN

BOLT

THE EDGE

STRAIGHT

LONGSHOT

COMEBACK

DRIVING FORCE

DECIDER

WILD HORSES

COME TO GRIEF

TO THE HILT

10lb PENALTY

FIELD OF THIRTEEN

SECOND WIND

SHATTERED

Dick Francis has written thirty-nine international bestsellers and is widely acclaimed as one of the world's finest thriller writers. His awards include the Crime Writers' Association's Cartier Diamond Dagger for his outstanding contribution to the crime genre, and an honorary Doctorate of Humane Letters from Tufts University of Boston. In 1996 Dick Francis was made a Mystery Writers of America Grand Master for a lifetime's achievement and in 2000 he received a CBE in the Queen's Birthday Honours list.

Dick Francis

FLYING FINISH
AND
HOT MONEY

PAN BOOKS

Flying Finish first published 1966 by Michael Joseph Ltd.
First published by Pan Books 1968
Hot Money first published 1987 by Michael Joseph Ltd.
First published by Pan Books 1988.

This omnibus edition published 2003 by Pan Books
an imprint of Pan Macmillan Ltd
Pan Macmillan, 20 New Wharf Road, London N1 9RR
Basingstoke and Oxford
Associated companies throughout the world
www.panmacmillan.com

ISBN 0 330 43672 4

Copyright © Dick Francis 1966, 1987

The right of Dick Francis to be identified as the
author of this work has been asserted by him in accordance
with the Copyright, Designs and Patents Act 1988.

All rights reserved. No part of this publication may be
reproduced, stored in or introduced into a retrieval system, or
transmitted, in any form, or by any means (electronic, mechanical,
photocopying, recording or otherwise) without the prior written
permission of the publisher. Any person who does any unauthorized
act in relation to this publication may be liable to criminal
prosecution and civil claims for damages.

1 3 5 7 9 8 6 4 2

A CIP catalogue record for this book is available from
the British Library.

Printed and bound in Great Britain by
Mackays of Chatham plc, Chatham, Kent

This book is sold subject to the condition that it shall not,
by way of trade or otherwise, be lent, re-sold, hired out,
or otherwise circulated without the publisher's prior consent
in any form of binding or cover other than that in which
it is published and without a similar condition including this
condition being imposed on the subsequent purchaser.

FLYING FINISH

With my thanks to
The British Bloodstock Agency
Bruce Dalglish of LEP Transport
Peter Palmer, Airline Captain
John Mercer of CSE Aviation, Oxford Airport
I assure them that everyone in this book is imaginary

CHAPTER ONE

'You're a spoilt bad-tempered bastard,' my sister said, and jolted me into a course I nearly died of.

I carried her furious unattractive face down to the station and into the steamed-up compartment of Monday gloom and half done crosswords and all across London to my unloved office.

Bastard I was not: not with parents joined by a bishop with half Debrett and Burke in the pews. And if spoilt, it was their doing, their legacy to an heir born accidentally at the last possible minute when earlier intended pregnancies had produced five daughters. My frail eighty-six-year-old father in his second childhood saw me chiefly as the means whereby a much hated cousin was to be done out of an earldom he had coveted: my father delighted in my existence and I remained to him a symbol.

My mother had been forty-seven at my birth and was now seventy-three. With a mind which had to all intents stopped developing round about Armistice Day 1918, she had been for as long as I could remember

1

completely batty. Eccentric, her acquaintances more kindly said. Anyway, one of the first things I ever learnt was that age had nothing to do with wisdom.

Too old to want a young child around them, they had brought me up and educated me at arm's length – nursemaids, prep school and Eton – and in my hearing had regretted the length of the school holidays. Our relationship was one of politeness and duty, but not of affection. They didn't even seem to expect me to love them, and I didn't. I didn't love anyone. I hadn't had any practice.

I was first at the office as usual. I collected the key from the caretaker's cubbyhole, walked unhurriedly down the long echoing hall, up the gritty stone staircase, down a narrow dark corridor, and at the far end of it unlocked the heavily brown varnished front door of the Anglia Bloodstock Agency. Inside, typical of the old London warren-type blocks of offices, comfort took over from barracks. The several rooms opening right and left from the passage were close carpeted, white painted, each with the occupant's name in neat black on the door. The desks ran to extravagances like tooled leather tops, and there were sporting prints on the wall. I had not yet, however, risen to this success bracket.

The room where I had worked (on and off) for nearly six years lay at the far end, past the reference room and the pantry. 'Transport' it said, on the half-open door. I pushed it wide. Nothing had changed from Friday. The three desks looked the same as usual:

Christopher's, with thick uneven piles of papers held down by cricket balls; Maggie's typewriter cover askew, carbons screwed up beside it, and a vase of dead chrysanthemums dropping petals into a scummy teacup; and mine, bare.

I hung up my coat, sat down, opened my desk drawers one by one and uselessly straightened the already tidy contents. I checked that it was precisely eight minutes to nine by my accurate watch, which made the office clock two minutes slow. After this activity I stared straight ahead unseeingly at the calendar on the pale green wall.

A spoilt bad-tempered bastard, my sister said.

I didn't like it. I was not bad-tempered, I assured myself defensively. I was not. But my thoughts carried no conviction. I decided to break with tradition and refrain from reminding Maggie that I found her slovenly habits irritating.

Christopher and Maggie arrived together, laughing, at ten past nine.

'Hullo,' said Christopher cheerfully, hanging up his coat. 'I see you lost on Saturday.'

'Yes,' I agreed.

'Better luck next time,' said Maggie automatically, blowing the sodden petals out of the cup on to the floor. I bit my tongue to keep it still. Maggie picked up the vase and made for the pantry, scattering petals as she went. Presently she came back with the vase, fumbled it, and left a dripping trail of Friday's tea across

3

my desk. In silence I took some white blotting paper from the drawer, mopped up the spots, and threw the blotting paper in the waste basket. Christopher watched in sardonic amusement, pale eyes crinkling behind thick spectacles.

'A short head, I believe?' he said, lifting one of the cricket balls and going through the motions of bowling it through the window.

'A short head,' I agreed. All the same if it had been ten lengths, I thought sourly. You got no present for losing, whatever the margin.

'My uncle had a fiver on you.'

'I'm sorry,' I said formally.

Christopher pivoted on one toe and let go: the cricket ball crashed into the wall, leaving a mark. He saw me frowning at it and laughed. He had come straight into the office from Cambridge two months before, robbed of a cricket blue through deteriorating eyesight and having failed his finals into the bargain. He remained always in better spirits than I, who had suffered no similar reverses. We tolerated each other. I found it difficult, as always, to make friends, and he had given up trying.

Maggie came back from the pantry, sat down at her desk, took her nail varnish out of the stationery drawer and began brushing on the silvery pink. She was a large assured girl from Surbiton with a naturally unkind tongue and a suspect talent for registering remorse immediately after the barbs were securely in.

The cricket ball slipped out of Christopher's hand and rolled across Maggie's desk. Lunging after it, he brushed one of his heaps of letters into a fluttering muddle on the floor, and the ball knocked over Maggie's bottle of varnish, which scattered pretty pink viscous blobs all over the 'We have received yours of the fourteenth ult.'

'God-damn,' said Christopher with feeling.

Old Cooper who dealt with insurance came into the room at his doddery pace and looked at the mess with cross disgust and pinched nostrils. He held out to me the sheaf of papers he had brought.

'Your pigeon, Henry. Fix it up for the earliest possible.'

'Right.'

As he turned to go he said to Christopher and Maggie in a complaining voice certain to annoy them, 'Why can't you two be as efficient as Henry? He's never late, he's never untidy, his work is always correct and always done in time. Why don't you try to be more like him?'

I winced inwardly and waited for Maggie's inevitable retaliation. She would be in good form: it was Monday morning.

'I wouldn't want to be like Henry in a thousand years,' she said sharply. 'He's a prim, dim, sexless *nothing*. He's not alive.'

Not my day, definitely.

'He rides those races, though,' said Christopher in mild defence.

'And if he fell off and broke both his legs, all he'd care about would be seeing they got the bandages straight.'

'The bones,' I said.

'What?'

'The bones straight.'

Christopher blinked and laughed. 'Well, well, what do you know? The still waters of Henry might just possibly be running deep.'

'Deep, nothing,' said Maggie. 'A stagnant pond, more like.'

'Slimy and smelly?' I suggested.

'No . . . oh dear . . . I mean, I'm sorry . . .'

'Never mind,' I said. 'Never mind.' I looked at the paper in my hand and picked up the telephone.

'Henry . . .' said Maggie desperately. 'I didn't mean it.'

Old Cooper tut-tutted and doddered away along the passage, and Christopher began sorting his varnished letters. I got through to Yardman Transport and asked for Simon Searle. 'Four yearlings from the Newmarket sales to go to Buenos Aires as soon as possible,' I said.

'There might be a delay.'

'Why?'

'We've lost Peters.'

'Careless,' I remarked.

'Oh, ha-ha.'

'Has he left?'

Simon hesitated perceptibly. 'It looks like it.'

'How do you mean?'

'He didn't come back from one of the trips. Last Monday. Just never turned up for the flight back, and hasn't been seen or heard of since.'

'Hospitals?' I said.

'We checked those, of course. And the morgue, and the gaol. Nothing. He just vanished. And as he hasn't done anything wrong the police aren't interested in finding him. No police would be, it isn't criminal to leave your job without notice. They say he fell for a girl, very likely, and decided not to go home.'

'Is he married?'

'No.' He sighed. 'Well, I'll get on with your yearlings, but I can't give you even an approximate date.'

'Simon,' I said slowly. 'Didn't something like this happen before?'

'Er . . . do you mean Ballard?'

'One of your liaison men,' I said.

'Yes. Well . . . I suppose so.'

'In Italy?' I suggested gently.

There was a short silence the other end. 'I hadn't thought of it,' he said. 'Funny coincidence. Well . . . I'll let you know about the yearlings.'

'I'll have to get on to Clarksons if you can't manage it.'

He sighed. 'I'll do my best. I'll ring you back tomorrow.'

I put down the receiver and started on a large batch of customs declarations, and the long morning disintegrated towards the lunch hour. Maggie and I said nothing at all to each other and Christopher cursed steadily over his letters. At one sharp I beat even Maggie in the rush to the door.

Outside, the December sun was shining. On impulse I jumped on to a passing bus, got off at Marble Arch, and walked slowly through the park to the Serpentine. I was still there, sitting on a bench, watching the sun ripple on the water, when the hands on my watch read two o'clock. I was still there at half past. At a quarter to three I threw some stones with force into the lake, and a park keeper told me not to.

A spoilt bad-tempered bastard. It wouldn't have been so bad if she had been used to saying things like that, but she was a gentle see-no-evil person who had been made to wash her mouth out with soap for swearing as a child and had never taken the risk again. She was my youngest sister, fifteen years my elder, unmarried, plain, and quietly intelligent. She had reversed roles with our parents: she ran the house and managed them as her children. She also to a great extent managed me, and always had.

A repressed, quiet, 'good' little boy I had been: and a quiet, withdrawn, secretive man I had become. I was almost pathologically tidy and methodical, early for every appointment, controlled alike in behaviour, handwriting and sex. A prim dim nothing, as Maggie said. The fact that for some months now I had not felt in the least like that inside was confusing, and getting more so.

I looked up into the blue gold-washed sky. Only there, I thought with a fleeting inward smile, only there am I my own man. And perhaps in steeplechases. Perhaps there too, sometimes.

She had been waiting for me as usual at breakfast, her face fresh from her early walk with the dogs. I had seen little of her over the weekend: I'd been racing on Saturday, and on Sunday I'd left home before breakfast and gone back late.

'Where did you go yesterday?' she asked.

I poured some coffee and didn't answer. She was used to that, however.

'Mother wanted to speak to you.'

'What about?'

'She has asked the Filyhoughs to lunch next Sunday.'

I tidily ate my bacon and egg. I said calmly, 'That coy spotty Angela. It's a waste of time. I won't be here anyway.'

'Angela will inherit half a million,' she said earnestly.

'And we have beetles in the roof,' I agreed dryly.

'Mother wants to see you married.'

'Only to a very rich girl.'

My sister acknowledged that this was true, but saw nothing particularly wrong in it. The family fortunes were waning: as my parents saw it, the swop of a future title for a future fortune was a suitable bargain. They

9

didn't seem to realize that a rich girl nowadays had more sense than to hand over her wealth to her husband, and could leave with it intact if she felt like it.

'Mother told Angela you would be here.'

'That was silly of her.'

'Henry!'

'I do not like Angela,' I said coldly. 'I do not intend to be here for lunch next Sunday. Is that quite clear?'

'But you must . . . you can't leave me to deal with them all alone.'

'You'll just have to restrain Mother from issuing these stupid invitations. Angela is the umpteenth unattractive heiress she's invited this year. I'm fed up with it.'

'We need . . .'

'I am not,' I said stiffly, 'a prostitute.'

She stood up, bitterly offended. 'That's unkind.'

'And while we are at it, I wish the beetles good luck. This damp decaying pile of a house eats up every penny we've got and if it fell down tomorrow we'd all be far better off.'

'It's our home,' she said, as if that was the final word.

When it was mine, I would get rid of it; but I didn't say that, and encouraged by my silence she tried persuasion. 'Henry, please be here for the Filyhoughs.'

'No,' I said forcefully. 'I won't. I want to do something else next Sunday. You can count me right out.'

She suddenly and completely lost her temper. Shaking she said, 'I cannot stand much more of your damned autistic behaviour. You're a spoilt, bad-tempered *bastard . . .*'

Hell, I thought by the Serpentine, was I really? And if so, why?

At three, with the air growing cold, I got up and left the park, but the office I went to was not the elegant suite of Anglia Bloodstock in Hanover Square. There, I thought, they could go on wondering why the ever-punctual Henry hadn't returned from lunch. I went instead by taxi to a small dilapidated rubbish-strewn wharf down in the Pool, where the smell of Thames mud at low tide rose earthily into my nostrils as I paid the fare.

At one end of the wharf, on an old bombed site, a small square concrete building had been thrown up shortly after the war and shoddily maintained ever since. Its drab walls, striped by rust from leaking gutters, badly needed a coat of 'Snowcem'; its rectangular metal windows were grimed and flaking. and no one had polished the brass door fittings since my previous visit six months ago. There was no need here to put on a plushy front for the customers; the customers were not expected to come.

I walked up the uncarpeted stairs, across the eight foot square of linoleumed landing and through the open door of Simon Searle's room. He looked up from some complicated doodling on a memo pad, lumbered to his feet and greeted me with a huge handshake and a wide grin. As he was the only person who ever gave me this sort of welcome I came as near to unbending with him as with anyone. But we had never done more than meet now and again on business and occasionally repair to a pub afterwards. There he was inclined to lots of beer and bonhomie, and I to a single whisky, and that was that.

'You haven't trekked all the way down here about those yearlings?' he protested. 'I told you . . .'

'No,' I said, coming to the point abruptly. 'I came to find out if Yardman would give me a job.'

'*You*,' said Simon, 'want to work *here*?'

'That's right.'

'Well I'm damned.' Simon sat down on the edge of his desk and his bulk settled and spread comfortably around him. He was a vast shambling man somewhere in the doldrums between thirty-five and forty-five, bald on top, bohemian in dress and broad of mind.

'Why, for God's sake?' he said, looking me up and down. A more thorough contrast than me in my charcoal worsted to him in his baggy green corduroys would have been hard to find.

'I need a change.'

'For the worse?' He was sardonic.

'Of course not. And I'd like the chance of a bit of globe-trotting now and then.'

'You can afford to do that in comfort. You don't have to do it on a horse transport.'

Like so many other people, he took it for granted that I had money. I hadn't. I had only my salary from

Anglia, and what I could earn by being frankly, almost notoriously, a shamateur jockey. Every penny I got was earmarked. From my father I took only my food and the beetle-infested roof over my head, and neither expected nor asked for anything else.

'I imagine I would like horse transport,' I said equably. 'What are the chances?'

'Oh,' Simon laughed. 'You've only to ask. I can't see him turning you down.'

But Yardman very nearly did turn me down, because he couldn't believe I really meant it.

'My dear boy, now think carefully, I do beg you. Anglia Bloodstock is surely a better place for you? However well you might do here, there isn't any power or any prestige . . . We must face facts, we must indeed.'

'I don't particularly care for power and prestige.'

He sighed deeply. 'There speaks one to whom they come by birth. Others of us are not so fortunate as to be able to despise them.'

'I don't despise them. Also I don't want them. Or not yet.'

He lit a dark cigar with slow care. I watched him, taking him in. I hadn't met him before, and as he came from a different mould from the top men of Anglia I found that I didn't instinctively know how his mind worked. After years of being employed by people of my own sort of background, where much that was understood never needed to be stated, Yardman was a foreign country.

He was being heavily paternal, which somehow came oddly from a thin man. He wore black-rimmed spectacles on a strong beaky nose. His cheeks were hollowed, and his mouth in consequence seemed to have to stretch to cover his teeth and gums. His lips curved downwards strongly at the corners, giving him at times a disagreeable and at times a sad expression. He was bald on the crown of his head, which was not noticeable at first sight, and his skin looked unhealthy. But his voice and his fingers were strong, and as I grew to acknowledge, his will and character also.

He puffed slowly at the cigar, a slim fierce-looking thing with an aroma to match. From behind the glasses his eyes considered me without haste. I hadn't a clue as to what he was thinking.

'All right,' he said at last. 'I'll take you on as an assistant to Searle, and we'll see how it goes.'

'Well . . . thank you,' I answered. 'But what I really came to ask for was Peters's job.'

'*Peters's* . . .' His mouth literally fell open, revealing a bottom row of regular false teeth. He shut it with a snap. 'Don't be silly, my boy. You can't have Peters's job.'

'Searle says he has left.'

'I dare say, but that's not the point, is it?'

I said calmly, 'I've been in the Transport Section of Anglia for more than five years, so I know all the technical side of it, and I've ridden horses all my life, so I know how to look after them. I agree that I haven't any practical experience, but I could learn very quickly.'

'Lord Grey,' he said, shaking his head, 'I don't think you realize just what Peters's job was.'

'Of course I do,' I said. 'He travelled on the planes with the horses and saw they arrived safely and well. He saw that they passed the Customs all right at both ends and that the correct people collected them, and where necessary saw that another load of horses was brought safely back again. It is a responsible job and it entails a lot of travelling and I am seriously applying for it.'

'You don't understand,' he said with some impatience. 'Peters was a travelling head groom.'

'I know.'

He smoked, inscrutable. Three puffs. I waited, quiet and still.

'You're not ... er ... in any trouble, at Anglia?'

'No. I've grown tired of a desk job, that's all.' I had been tired of it from the day I started, to be exact.

'How about racing?'

'I have Saturdays off at Anglia, and I take my three weeks annual holiday in separate days during the winter and spring. And they have been very considerate about extra half-days.'

'Worth it to them in terms of trade, I dare say.' He tapped off the ash absentmindedly into the inkwell. 'Are you thinking of giving it up?'

'No.'

'Mm . . . if you work for me, would I get any increase in business from your racing connections?'

'I'd see you did,' I said.

He turned his head away and looked out of the window. The river tide was sluggishly at the ebb, and away over on the other side a row of cranes stood like red meccano toys in the beginnings of dusk. I couldn't even guess then at the calculations clicking away at high speed in Yardman's nimble brain, though I've often thought about those few minutes since.

'I think you are being unwise, my dear boy. Youth . . . youth . . .' He sighed, straightened his shoulders and turned the beaky nose back in my direction. His shadowed greenish eyes regarded me steadily from deep sockets, and he told me what Peters had been earning: fifteen pounds a trip plus three pounds expenses for each overnight stop. He clearly thought that that would deter me; and it nearly did.

'How many trips a week?' I asked, frowning.

'It depends on the time of year. You know that of course. After the yearling sales, and when the brood mares come over, it might be three trips. To France, perhaps even four. Usually two, sometimes none.'

There was a pause. We looked at each other. I learned nothing.

'All right,' I said abruptly. 'Can I have the job?'

His lips twisted in a curious expression which I later came to recognize as an ironic smile.

'You can try it,' he said. 'If you like.'

16

CHAPTER TWO

A job is what you make it. Three weeks later, after Christmas, I flew to Buenos Aires with twelve yearlings, the four from Anglia and eight more from different bloodstock agencies, all mustered together at five o'clock on a cold Tuesday morning at Gatwick. Simon Searle had organized their arrival and booked their passage with a charter company; I took charge of them when they unloaded from their various horseboxes, installed them in the plane, checked their papers through the customs and presently flew away.

With me went two of Yardman's travelling grooms, both of them fiercely resenting that I had been given Peters's job over their heads. Each of them had coveted the promotion, and in terms of human relationships the trip was a frost-bitten failure. Otherwise, it went well enough. We arrived in Argentina four hours late, but the new owners' horseboxes had all turned up to collect the cargo. Again I cleared the horses and papers through the customs, and made sure that each of the five new owners had got the right horses and the certificates to go with them. The following day the plane picked up a load of crated furs for the return journey, and we flew back to Gatwick, arriving on Friday.

On Saturday I had a fall and a winner at Sandown Races, Sunday I spent in my usual way, and Monday I flew with some circus ponies to Germany. After a fortnight of it I was dying from exhaustion; after a month I was acclimatized. My body got used to long hours, irregular food, non-stop coffee, and sleeping sitting upright on bales of hay ten thousand feet up in the sky. The two grooms, Timmie and Conker, gradually got over the worst of their anger, and we developed into a quick, efficient, laconic team.

My family were predictably horrified by my change of occupation and did their best to pry me away from it. My sister anxiously retracted the words I knew I'd earned, my father foresaw the earldom going to the cousin after all, aeroplanes being entirely against nature and usually fatal, and my mother had hysterics over what her friends would say.

'It's a labourer's job,' she wailed.

'A job is what you make it.'

'What will the Filyhoughs think?'

'Who the hell cares what they think?'

'It isn't a *suitable* job for you.' She wrung her hands.

'It's a job I like. It suits me, therefore it *is* suitable.'

'You know that isn't what I mean.'

'I know exactly what you mean, Mother, and I profoundly disagree with you. People should do work they like doing; that's all that should decide them. Whether it is socially OK or not shouldn't come into it.'

'But it does,' she cried, exasperated.

'It has for me for nearly six years,' I admitted, 'but not any more. And ideas change. What I am doing now may be the top thing next year. If I don't look out half the men I know will be muscling in on the act. Anyway, it's right for me, and I'm going on with it.'

All the same she couldn't be won over, and could only face her own elderly convention-bound circle by pretending my job was 'for the experience, you know', and by treating it as a joke.

It was a joke to Simon Searle too, at first.

'You won't stick it, Henry,' he said confidently. 'Not you and all that dirt. You with your spotless dark suit and your snowy white shirts and not a hair out of place. One trip will be enough.'

After a month, looking exactly the same, I turned up for my pay packet late on Friday afternoon, and we sauntered along to his favourite pub, a tatty place with stained glass doors and a chronic smell of fug. He oozed on to a bar stool, his bulk drooping around him. A pint for him, he said. I bought it, and a half for me, and he drank most of his off with one much practised swallow.

'How's the globe-trotting, then?' He ran his tongue over his upper lip for the froth.

'I like it.'

'I'll grant you,' he said, smiling amicably, 'that you haven't made a mess of it yet.'

'Thanks.'

'Though of course since I do all the spade work for you at both ends, you bloody well shouldn't.'

'No,' I agreed. He was, in truth, an excellent organizer, which was mainly why Anglia often dealt with Yardman Transport instead of Clarkson Carriers, a much bigger and better known firm. Simon's arrangements were clear, simple, and always twice confirmed: agencies, owners and airlines alike knew exactly where they stood and at what hours they were expected to be where. No one else in the business, that I had come across at any rate, was as consistently reliable. Being so precise myself, I admired his work almost as a work of art.

He looked me over, privately amused. 'You don't go on trips dressed like that?'

'I do, yes, more or less.'

'What does more or less mean?'

'I wear a sweater instead of my jacket, in and around the aircraft.'

'And hang up your jacket on a hanger for when you land?'

'Yes, I do.'

He laughed, but without mockery. 'You're a rum sort of chap, Henry.' He ordered more beer, shrugged when I refused, and drank deep again. 'Why are you so methodical?'

'It's safer.'

'Safer.' He choked on his beer, coughing and laughing. 'I suppose it doesn't strike you that to many people steeplechasing and air transport might not seem especially safe?'

'That wasn't what I meant.'

'What, then?'

But I shook my head, and didn't explain.

'Tell me about Yardman,' I said.

'What about him?'

'Well, where he came from . . . anything.'

Simon hunched his great shoulders protectively around his pint, and pursed his lips.

'He joined the firm after the war, when he left the Army. He was a sergeant in an infantry regiment, I think. Don't know any details: never asked. Anyway he worked his way up through the business. It wasn't called Yardman Transport then, of course. Belonged to a family, the Mayhews, but they were dying out . . . nephews weren't interested, that sort of thing. Yardman had taken it over by the time I got there; don't know how really, come to think of it, but he's a bright lad, there's no doubt of that. Take switching to air, for instance. That was him. He was pressing the advantages of air travel for horses whilst all the other transport agencies were going entirely by sea.'

'Even though the office itself is on a wharf,' I remarked.

'Yes. Very handy once. It isn't used much at all now since they clamped down on exporting horses to the Continent for meat.'

'Yardman was in that?'

'Shipping agent,' he nodded. 'There's a big warehouse down the other end of the wharf where we used to collect them. They'd start being brought in three days before the ship came. Once a fortnight, on average. I can't say I'm sorry it's finished. It was a lot of work and a lot of mess and noise, and not much profit, Yardman said.'

'It didn't worry you, though, that they were going to be slaughtered?'

'No more than cattle or pigs.' He finished his beer. 'Why should it? Everything dies sometime.' He smiled cheerfully and gestured to the glasses. 'Another?' He had one, I didn't.

'Has anyone heard any more of Peters?' I asked.

He shook his head. 'Not a murmur.'

'How about his cards?'

'Still in the office, as far as I know.'

'It's a bit odd, isn't it?'

Simon shrugged. 'You never know, he might have wanted to duck someone, and did it thoroughly.'

'But did anyone ever come looking for him?'

'Nope. No police, no unpaid bookies, no rampaging females, no one.'

'He just went to Italy and didn't come back?'

'That's the size of it,' Simon agreed. 'He went with some brood mares to Milan and he should have come back the same day. But there was some trouble over an engine or something, and the pilot ran out of time and said he'd be in dead trouble if he worked too many hours. So they stayed there overnight and in the morning Peters didn't turn up. They waited nearly all day, then they came back without him.'

'And that's all?'

'That's the lot,' he agreed. 'Just one of life's little mysteries. What's the matter, are you afraid Peters will reappear and take back his job?'

'Something like that.'

'He was an awkward bastard,' he said thoughtfully. 'Stood on his rights. Always arguing; that sort of chap. Belligerent. Never stood any nonsense from foreign customs officers.' He grinned. 'I'll bet they're quite glad to see you instead.'

'I dare say I'll be just as cussed in a year or two.'

'A year or two?' He looked surprised. 'Henry, it's all very well you taking Peters's job for a bit of a giggle but you surely can't mean to go on with it permanently?'

'You think it would be more suitable if I was sitting behind a nice solid desk at Anglia?' I asked ironically.

'Yes,' he said seriously. 'Of course it would.'

I sighed. 'Not you too. I thought you at least might understand . . .' I stopped wryly.

'Understand what?'

'Well . . . that who one's father is has nothing to do with the sort of work one is best suited for. And I am not fitted for sitting behind a desk. I came to that conclusion my first week at Anglia, but I stayed there because I'd kicked up a fuss and insisted on getting an ordinary job, and I wasn't going to admit I'd made a mistake with it. I tried to like it. At any rate I got used to it, but now ... now ... I don't think I could face that nine-to-five routine ever again.'

'Your father's in his eighties, isn't he?' Simon said thoughtfully.

I nodded.

'And do you think that when he dies you will be allowed to go on carting horses round the world? And for how long *could* you do it without becoming an eccentric nut? Like it or not, Henry, it's easy enough to go up the social scale, but damn difficult to go down. And still be respected, that is.'

'And I could be respected sitting behind a desk at Anglia, transferring horses from owner to owner on paper, but not if I move about and do it on aeroplanes?'

He laughed. 'Exactly.'

'The world is mad,' I said.

'You're a romantic. But time will cure that.' He looked at me in a large tolerant friendship, finished his beer, and flowed down from the stool like a green corduroy amoeba.

'Come on,' he said, 'there's time for another along the road at the Saracen's Head.'

At Newbury Races the following afternoon I watched five races from the stands and rode in one.

This inactivity was not mine by choice, but thrust upon me by the Stewards. They had, by the time I was twenty, presented me with their usual ultimatum to regular amateur riders: either turn professional, or ride in only fifty open races each season. In other words, don't undercut the trade: stop taking the bread and butter out of the professionals' mouths. (As if jockeys *ate* much bread and butter, to start with.)

I hadn't turned professional when I was twenty because I had been both too conventional and not really good enough. I was still not good enough to be a top rank professional, but I had long been a fully employed amateur. A big fish in a small pond. In the new-found freedom of my Yardman's job I regretted that I hadn't been bolder at twenty. I liked steeplechasing enormously, and with full-time professional application I might just have made a decent success. Earthbound on the stands at Newbury I painfully accepted that my sister had brought me to my senses a lot too late.

The one horse I did ride was in the 'amateurs only' race. As there were no restrictions on the number of amateur events I could ride in, few were run without me. I rode regularly for many owners who grudged paying professional jockeys' fees, for some who reckoned their horses stood more chance in amateur races, and for a few who genuinely liked my work.

All of them knew very well that if I won either amateur or open races I expected ten per cent of the prize. The word had got around. Henry Grey rode for money, not love. Henry Grey was the shamateur to end all shamateurs. Because I was silent and discreet and they could trust my tongue, I had even been given cash presents by stewards: and solely because my father was the Earl of Creggan, my amateur permit survived.

In the changing room that afternoon I found that however different I might feel, I could not alter my long set pattern. The easy bantering chat flowed round me and as usual it was impossible to join in. No one expected me to. They were used to me. Half of them took my aloofness to be arrogant snobbery, and the rest shrugged it off as 'just Henry's way'. No one was actively hostile, and it was I, I who had failed to belong. I changed slowly into my racing clothes and listened to the jokes and the warm earthy language, and I could think of nothing, not one single thing, to say.

I won the race. The well pleased owner gave me a public clap on the shoulder and a drink in the members' bar, and surreptitiously, round a private corner, forty pounds.

On the following day, Sunday, I spent the lot.

I started my little Herald in the garage in the pre-dawn dark, and as quietly as possible opened the doors and drifted away down the drive. Mother had invited yet another well-heeled presumptive virgin for the weekend, together with her slightly forbidding parents, and having dutifully escorted them all to Newbury Races the day before and tipped them a winner – my own – I felt I had done quite enough. They would be gone, I thought coolly, before I got back late that evening, and with a bit of luck my bad manners in disappearing would have discouraged them for ever.

A steady two and a half hours' driving northwards found me at shortly before ten o'clock turning in through some inconspicuously signposted gates in Lincolnshire. I parked the car at the end of the row of others, climbed out, stretched, and looked up into the sky. It was a cold clear morning with maximum visibility. Not a cloud in sight. Smiling contentedly I strolled over to the row of white-painted buildings and pushed open the glass door into the main hall of the Fenland Flying Club.

The hall was a big room with several passages leading off it and a double door on the far side opening to the airfield itself. Round the walls hung framed charts, Air Ministry regulations, a large map of the surrounding area, do's and don'ts for visiting pilots, a thumb-tacked weather report and a list of people wanting to enter for a ping-pong tournament. There were several small wooden tables and hard chairs at one end, half occupied, and across the whole width of the other end stretched the reception-cum-operation-cum-everything else desk. Yawning behind it and scratching between his shoulder blades stood a plump sleepy man of about my own age, sporting a thick sloppy sweater and a fair-sized hangover. He held a cup of strong coffee and a cigarette in his free hand, and he was talking lethargically to a gay young spark who had turned up with a girl friend he wanted to impress.

'I've told you, old chap, you should have given us a ring. All the planes are booked today. I'm sorry, no can do. You can hang about if you like, in case someone doesn't turn up . . .'

He turned towards me, casually.

'Morning, Harry,' he said. 'How's things?'

'Very OK,' I said. 'And you?'

'Ouch,' he grinned, 'don't cut me. The gin would run out.' He turned round and consulted the vast timetable charts covering most of the wall behind him. 'You've got Kilo November today, it's out by the petrol pumps, I think. Cross country again; is that right?'

'Uh-huh,' I nodded.

'Nice day for it.' He put a tick on his chart where it said H. Grey, solo cross.

'Couldn't be better.'

The girl said moodily, 'How about this afternoon, then?'

'No dice. All booked. And it gets dark so early . . . there'll be plenty of planes tomorrow.'

I strolled away, out of the door to the airfield and round to the petrol pumps.

There were six single-engined aircraft lined up there in two rows of three, with a tall man in white overalls filling one up through the opening on the upper surface of the port wing. He waved when he saw me coming, and grinned.

'Just doing yours next, Harry. The boys have tuned her up special. They say you couldn't have done it better yourself.'

'I'm delighted to hear it,' I said smiling.

He screwed on the cap and jumped down.

'Lovely day,' he said, looking up. There were already two little planes in the air, and four more stood ready in front of the control tower. 'Going far?' he asked.

'Scotland,' I said.

'That's cheating.' He swung the hose away and began to drag it along to the next aircraft. 'The navigation's too easy. You only have to go west till you hit the A1 and then fly up it.'

'I'm going to Islay,' I smiled. 'No roads, I promise.'

'Islay. That's different.'

'I'll land there for lunch and bring you back a bit of heather.'

'How far is it?'

'Two seventy nautical miles, about.'

'You'll be coming back in the dark.' It was a statement, not a question. He unscrewed the cap of Kilo November and topped up the tanks.

'Most of the way, yes.'

I did the routine checks all round the aircraft, fetched my padded jacket and my charts from the car, filed my flight plan, checked with the control tower for taxi clearance, and within a short while was up in the sky and away.

Air is curious stuff. One tends to think that because it is invisible it isn't there. What you can't see don't exist, sort of thing. But air is tough, elastic and resistant; and the harder you dig into it the more solid it becomes. Air has currents stronger than tides and turbulences which would make Charybdis look like bath water running away.

When I first went flying I rationalized the invisibility thing by thinking of an aircraft being like a submarine: in both one went up and down and sideways in a medium one couldn't see but which was very palpably around. Then I considered that if human eyes had been constructed differently it might have been possible to see the mixture of nitrogen and oxygen we breathe as clearly as the hydrogen and oxygen we wash in. After that I took the air's positive plastic existence for granted, and thought no more about it.

The day I went to Islay was pure pleasure. I had flown so much by then that the handling of the little aircraft was as normal as driving a car, and with the perfect weather and my route carefully worked out and handy on the empty passenger seat behind me, there was nothing to do but enjoy myself. And that I did, because I liked being alone. Specifically I liked being alone in a tiny noisy efficient little capsule at 25,000 revs a minute, four thousand five hundred feet above sea level, speed over the ground one hundred and ten miles an hour, steady on a course 313 degrees, bound north-west towards the sea and a Scottish island.

I found Islay itself without trouble and tuned my radio to the frequency – 118.5 – of Port Ellen airfield.

I said, 'Port Ellen tower, this is Golf Alpha Romeo Kilo November, do you read?'

A Scots accent crackled back, 'Golf Kilo November, good afternoon, go ahead.'

'Kilo November is approaching from the south-east, range fifteen miles, request joining instructions, over.'

'Kilo November is cleared to join right base for runway zero four, QFE 998 millibars. Surface wind zero six zero, ten knots, call field in sight.'

Following his instructions I flew in and round the little airfield on the circuit, cut the engine, turned into wind, glided in at eighty, touched down, and taxied across to the control tower to report.

After eating in a snack bar I went for a walk by the sea, breathing the soft Atlantic air, and forgot to look for some heather to take back with me. The island lay dozing in the sun, shut up close because it was Sunday. It was peaceful and distant and slowed the pulse; soul's balm if you stayed three hours, devitalizing if you stayed for life.

The gold had already gone from the day when I started back, and I flew contentedly along in the dusk and the dark, navigating by compass and checking my direction by the radio beacons over which I passed. I dropped down briefly at Carlisle to refuel, and uneventfully returned to Lincolnshire, landing gently and regretfully on the well-known field.

As usual on Sunday the club room next to the main hall was bursting with amateur pilots like myself all talking at once about stalls and spins and ratings and side slips and allowances for deviations. I edged round the crowd to the bar and acquired some whisky and water, which tasted dry and fine on my tongue and reminded me of where I had been.

Turning round I found myself directly beside the reception desk man and a red-haired boy he was talking to. Catching my eye he said to the boy, 'Now here's someone you ought to have a word with. Our Harry here, he's dead quiet, but don't let that fool you . . . He could fly the pants off most of that lot.' He gestured round the room. 'You ask Harry, now. He started just like you, knowing nothing at all, only three or four years ago.'

'Four,' I said.

'There you are, then. Four years. Now he's got a commercial licence and enough ratings to fill a book and he can strip an engine down like a mechanic.'

'That's enough,' I interrupted mildly. The young man looked thoroughly unimpressed anyway, as he didn't understand what he was being told. 'I suppose the point is that once you start, you go on,' I said. 'One thing leads to another.'

'I had my first lesson today,' he said eagerly, and gave me a rev by rev account of it for the next fifteen minutes. I ate two thick ham sandwiches while he got it off his chest, and finished the whisky. You couldn't really blame him, I thought, listening with half an ear: if you liked it, your first flight took you by the throat and you were hooked good and proper. It had happened to him. It had happened to me, one idle day when I passed the gates of the airfield and then turned back and went in, mildly interested in going up for a spin in a baby aircraft just to see what it was like.

I'd been to visit a dying great-aunt, and was depressed. Certainly Mr . . .? 'Grey,' I said. Certainly Mr Grey could go up with an instructor, the air people said: and the instructor, who hadn't been told I only wanted a sight-seeing flip, began as a matter of course to teach me to fly. I stayed all day and spent a week's salary in fees; and the next Sunday I went back. Most of my Sundays and most of my money had gone the same way since.

The red-head was brought to a full stop by a burly tweed-suited man who said 'Excuse me' pleasantly but very firmly, and planted himself between us.

'Harry, I've been waiting for you to come back.'

'Have a drink?'

'Yes . . . all right, in a minute.'

His name was Tom Wells. He owned and ran a small charter firm which was based on the airfield, and on Sundays, if they weren't out on jobs, he allowed the flying club to hire his planes. It was one of his that I had flown to Islay.

'Have I done something wrong?' I asked.

'Wrong? Why should you, for God's sake? No, I'm in a spot and I thought you might be able to help me out.'

'If I can, of course.'

'I've overbooked next weekend and I'm going to be a pilot short. Will you do a flight for me next Sunday?'

'Yes,' I said; I'd done it before, several times.

He laughed. 'You never waste words, Harry boy. Well, thanks. When can I ring you to give you a briefing?'

I hesitated. 'I'd better ring you, as usual.'

'Saturday morning, then.'

'Right.'

We had a drink together, he talking discontentedly about the growing shortage of pilots and how it was now too expensive for a young man to take it up on his own account; it cost at least three thousand pounds to train a multi-engine pilot, and only the air lines could afford it. They trained their own men and kept them, naturally. When the generation who had learned flying in the RAF during the war got too old, the smaller charter firms were going to find themselves in very sticky straits.

'You know,' he said, and it was obviously what he'd been working round to all along, 'you're an oddity. You've got a commercial licence and all the rest, and you hardly use it. Why not? Why don't you give up that boring old desk job and come and work for me?'

34

I looked at him for a long, long moment. It was almost too tempting, but apart from everything else, it would mean giving up steeplechasing, and I wasn't prepared to do that. I shook my head slowly, and said not for a few years yet.

Driving home I enjoyed the irony of the situation. Tom Wells didn't know what my desk job was, only that I worked in an office. I hadn't got around to telling him that I no longer did, and I wasn't going to. He didn't know where I came from or anything about my life away from the airfield. No one there did, and I liked it that way. I was just Harry who turned up on Sundays and flew if he had any money and worked on the engines in the hangars if he hadn't.

Tom Wells had offered me a job on my own account, not, like Yardman, because of my father, and that pleased me very much. It was rare for me to be sure of the motive behind things which were offered to me. But if I took the job my anonymity on the airfield would vanish pretty soon, and all the old problems would crowd in, and Tom Wells might very well retract, and I would be left with nowhere to escape to on one day a week to be myself.

My family did not know I was a pilot. I hadn't told them I had been flying that first day because by the time I got home my great-aunt had died and I was ashamed of having enjoyed myself while she did it. I hadn't told them afterwards because I was afraid that they would make a fuss and stop me. Soon after that I realized what a release it was to lead two lives and I deliberately kept them separate. It was quite easy, as I had always been untalkative: I just didn't answer when asked where I went on Sundays, and I kept my books and charts, slide rules and computers, securely locked up in my bedroom. And that was that.

CHAPTER THREE

It was on the day after I went to Islay that I first met Billy.

With Conker and Timmie, once they had bitten down their resentment at my pinching their promotion, I had arrived at a truce. On trips they chatted exclusively to each other, not to me, but that was as usual my fault; and we had got as far as sharing things like sandwiches and chocolate – and the work – on a taken-for-granted level basis.

Billy at once indicated that with him it would be quite quite different. For Billy the class war existed as a bloody battlefield upon which he was the most active and tireless warrior alive. Within five seconds of our first meeting he was sharpening his claws.

It was at Cambridge Airport at five in the morning. We were to take two consignments of recently sold racehorses from Newmarket to Chantilly near Paris, and with all the loading and unloading at each end it would be a long day. Locking my car in the car park I was just thinking how quickly Conker and Timmie and

I were getting to be able to do things when Yardman himself drove up alongside in a dark Jaguar Mark 10. There were two other men in the car, a large indistinct shape in the back, and in the front, Billy.

Yardman stepped out of his car, yawned, stretched, looked up at the sky, and finally turned to me.

'Good morning, my dear boy,' he said with great affability. 'A nice day for flying.'

'Very,' I agreed. I was surprised to see him: he was not given to early rising or to waving us bon voyage. Simon Searle occasionally came if there were some difficulty with papers but not Yardman himself. Yet here he was with his black suit hanging loosely on his too thin frame and the cold early morning light making uncomplimentary shadows on his stretched coarsely pitted skin. The black-framed spectacles as always hid the expression in his deep-set eyes. After a month in his employ, seeing him at the wharf building two or three times a week on my visits for instructions, reports, and pay, I knew him no better than on that first afternoon. In their own way his defence barriers were as good as mine.

He told me between small shut-mouthed yawns that Timmie and Conker weren't coming, they were due for a few days' leave. He had brought two men who obligingly substituted on such occasions and he was sure I would do a good job with them instead. He had brought them, he explained, because public transport wasn't geared to five o'clock rendezvous at Cambridge Airport.

While he spoke the front passenger climbed out of his car.

'Billy Watkins,' Yardman said, casually, nodding between us.

'Good morning, Lord Grey,' Billy said. He was about nineteen, very slender, with round cold blue eyes.

'Henry,' I said automatically. The job was impossible on any other terms and these were in any case what I preferred.

Billy looked at me with eyes wide, blank, and insolent. He spaced his words, bit them out and hammered them down.

'Good ... morning ... Lord ... Grey.'

'Good morning then, Mr Watkins.'

His eyes flickered sharply and went back to their wide stare. If he expected any placatory soft soaping from me, he could think again.

Yardman saw the instant antagonism and it annoyed him.

'I warned you, Billy,' he began swiftly, and then as quickly stopped. 'You won't, I am sure, my dear boy,' he said to me gently, 'allow any personal ... er ... clash of temperaments to interfere with the safe passage of your valuable cargo.'

'No,' I agreed.

He smiled, showing his greyish regular dentures back to the molars. I wondered idly why, if he could afford such a car, he didn't invest in more natural-looking teeth. It would have improved his unprepossessing appearance one hundred per cent.

'Right then,' he said in brisk satisfaction. 'Let's get on.'

The third man levered himself laboriously out of the car. His trouble stemmed from a paunch which would have done a pregnant mother of twins proud. About him flapped a brown storeman's overall which wouldn't do up by six inches, and under that some bright red braces over a checked shirt did a load-bearing job on some plain dark trousers. He was about fifty, going bald, and looked tired, unshaven and sullen, and he did not then or at any time meet my eyes.

What a crew, I thought resignedly, looking from him to Billy and back. So much for a day of speed and efficiency. The fat man, in fact, proved to be even more useless than he looked, and treated the horses with the sort of roughness which is the product of fear. Yardman gave him the job of loading them from their own horse-boxes up the long matting-covered side-walled ramp into the aircraft, while Billy and I inside fastened them into their stalls.

John, as Yardman called him, was either too fat or too scared of having his feet trodden on to walk side by side with each horse up the ramp: he backed up it, pulling the horse after him, stretching its head forward uncomfortably. Not surprisingly they all stuck their toes in hard and refused to budge. Yardman advanced on them from behind, shouting and waving a pitch fork, and prodded them forward again. The net result was some thoroughly upset and frightened animals in no state to be taken flying.

After three of them had arrived in the plane sweating, rolling their eyes and kicking out, I went down the ramp and protested.

'Let John help Billy, and I'll lead the horses,' I said to Yardman. 'I don't suppose you'll want them to arrive in such an unnerved state that their owners won't use the firm again? Always supposing that they don't actually kick the aircraft to bits en route.'

He knew very well that this had really happened once or twice in the history of bloodstock transport. There was always the risk that a horse would go berserk in the air at the best of times: taking off with a whole planeload of het-up thoroughbreds would be a fair way to commit suicide.

He hesitated only a moment, then nodded.

'All right. Change over.'

The loading continued with less fuss but not more speed. John was as useless at installing the horses as he was at leading them.

Cargo on aeroplanes has to be distributed with even more care than on ships. If the centre of gravity isn't kept to within fairly close specific limits the plane won't fly at all, just race at high speed to the end of the runway and turn into scrap metal. If the cargo shifts radically in mid-air it keels the plane over exactly as it would a ship, but with less time to put it right, and no lifeboats handy as a last resort.

From the gravity point of view, the horses had to be stowed down the centre of the plane, where for their own comfort and balance they had to face forwards. This meant, in a medium sized aircraft such as Yardman's usually chartered, four pairs of horses standing behind each other. From the balance point of view, the horses had to be fairly immobile, and they also had to be accessible, as one had to be able to hold their heads and soothe them at take-off and landing. Each pair was therefore boxed separately, like four little islands down the centre of the plane. There were narrow gangways between the boxes and up both sides the whole length of the aircraft so that one could easily walk round and reach every individual horse to look after him.

The horses stood on large trays of peat which were bolted to the floor. The boxes of half inch thick wood panels had to be built up round the horses when each pair was loaded: one erected the forward end wall and the two sides, led in the horses and tied them up, added the back wall, and made the whole thing solid with metal bars banding the finished box. The bars were joined at each corner by lynch pins. There were three bars, at the top, centre and bottom. To prevent the boxes from collapsing inwards, each side of each box had to be separately fixed to the floor with chains acting as guy ropes. When the loading was complete, the result looked like four huge packing cases chained down, with the horses' backs and heads showing at the open tops.

As one couldn't afford to have a box fall apart in the air, the making of them, though not difficult, demanded attention and thoroughness. John conspicuously lacked both. He was also unbelievably clumsy at hooking on and tightening the guy chains, and he dropped two lynch pins which we couldn't find again: we had to use wire instead, which wouldn't hold if a strong-minded horse started kicking. By the end Billy and I were doing the boxes alone, while John stood sullenly by and watched: and Billy throughout made my share as difficult as he could.

It all took such a time that at least the three frightened horses had calmed down again before the pilot climbed aboard and started the engines. I closed the first of the big double doors we had loaded the horses through, and had a final view of Yardman on the tarmac, the slipstream from the propellers blowing his scanty hair up round the bald patch like a black sea anemone. The light made silver window panes of his glasses. He lifted his hand without moving his elbow, an awkward little gesture of farewell. I put my own hand up in acknowledgement and reply, and fastened the second door as the plane began to move.

As usual there was a crew of three flying the aircraft, pilot, co-pilot and engineer. The engineer, on all the trips I had so far made, was the one who got landed with brewing the coffee and who could also be reasonably asked to hold a pair of horses' heads during take-off. This one did so with far more familiarity than John.

The trip was a relatively short one and there was a helpful following wind, but we were over an hour late at the French end. When we had landed the airport staff rolled another ramp up to the doors and I opened them from inside. The first people through them were three unsmiling businesslike customs officials. With great thoroughness they compared the horses we had brought against our list and their own. On the papers for each horse were details of its physical characteristics and colour: the customs men checked carefully every star, blaze and sock, guarding against the possibility that some poorer animal had been switched for the good one bought. France proved more hard to satisfy and more suspicious than most other countries.

Content at length that no swindle had been pulled this time, the chief customs man politely gave me back the papers and said that the unloading could begin.

Four horseboxes from French racing stables had turned up to collect the new purchases. The drivers, phlegmatically resigned to all delays, were engaged in digging round their mouths with toothpicks in a solid little group. I went down the ramp and across to them and told them in which order the horses would be unloaded. My French vocabulary, which was shaky on many subjects, covered at least all horse jargon and was fairly idiomatic when it came to racing or bloodstock: at

Anglia I had done quite a bit of work on French horses, and after six years knew my way round the French stud book as well as I did the British.

The drivers nodded, sucked their teeth and drove up the boxes in the right order. The first horse off, the last loaded at Cambridge, was a nondescript brown filly who was led into the waiting horsebox by the driver himself. He took her casually from my hand, slapped her rump in a friendly fashion, and by the time I led out the second horse he had already loaded her up and was on his way.

The other drivers had, more usually, brought one or two grooms with them, as they were to collect more than one horse. Billy took over leading the horses from the ramp, and I dismantled the boxes with John. This very nearly meant, in effect, doing it by myself. He dropped the bars, tripped over the anchorage on the floor, caught his fingers in the chains, and because of the paunch could do nothing which entailed bending down. Why Yardman employed him at all, I thought in irritation, was an unfathomable mystery.

We were supposed to be taking four horses back on the return trip, but by the time the last of our cargo had departed, not one of the four had turned up. When they were more than half an hour overdue, I walked over to the airport buildings and rang up one of the trainers concerned. Certainly he was sending two horses today, he said, two four-year-old hurdlers which he had sold to an English stable, but they were not due at the airport until three o'clock. Fifteen hundred hours: it was typed clearly on his notice from Yardman Transport. A second trainer, consulted, said the same: and although I had no phone number for the third, I took it for granted that his notice had been identical. Either Simon, or more likely his typist, had written five instead of nought on all three. It was a bore, as it meant unloading at the end of the last trip when we would all be tired.

The day's troubles, however, had barely warmed up. On my way back to the plane I saw Billy and John standing beside it engaged in a furious argument, but they broke off before I was close enough to hear what they were saying. John turned his back and kicked moodily at the bottom of the ramp and Billy gave me his best insulting stare.

'What's the matter?' I said.

Billy pursed his lips into an expression which said clearly that it was none of my business, but after a visible inner struggle he did answer.

'He's got a headache,' he said, nodding at John. 'From the noise.'

A headache. That hardly explained the fat man's hopeless inefficiency, his sullenness, his shifty manner or his row with Billy. Nor, I realized in some surprise, did it explain why he hadn't spoken a single word to me the whole trip. But as repeating the question was unlikely to get a more fruitful answer, I shrugged and didn't bother.

'Get on board,' I said instead. 'We're going back empty. There's been a mix-up and we'll have to take the French horses back next time.'

'—' said Billy calmly. He used a word so obscene that I wondered what he used for when he was annoyed.

'I dare say,' I said dryly. 'Let's not waste any more time.'

John lumbered unwillingly and morosely up the ramp. Billy followed him after a pause, and I too let Billy get well ahead before I started after him. The spaces between us, I thought sardonically, were symbolic.

The airport staff removed the ramp, the plane's crew returned from their coffee break, and we proceeded back to Cambridge. On the way we sat on three separate bales of straw along the length of the aircraft and didn't even look at each other. John put his elbows on his knee and held his head in his hands, and Billy looked steadily and sightlessly at the cloud-dotted sky.

With all sides of the boxes lying flat and strapped down on the peat trays the body of the aircraft seemed large and empty. In that state it echoed and was much noisier than usual, and I had some small sympathy for John's head. The plane was adapted, by the charter company who owned it, for any purpose that was required. The regularly spaced anchorages on the floor were as often used for fastening passenger seats as boxes for animals, and the airline would fly sixty people on a coach tour holiday to Europe one day and a load of pigs or cattle the next. In between they merely bolted or unbolted the rows of seats and swept out the relevant debris, either farmyard manure and straw or cigarette packets and bags full of vomit.

One was not allowed to sweep out manure on to foreign soil. The whole lot had to be solemnly carted back to England to comply with quarantine regulations. The odd thing was, I reflected again, that the peat trays never seemed to smell. Not even now that there was no live horse smell to mask it. Of course this plane was unpressurized, so that fresh air continually found its way in, but all the same it smelled less than an ordinary stable, even after a whole day in a hot climate.

The first person on the plane at Cambridge was a cheerful underworked bareheaded excise officer who had come there especially to clear the horses. He bounced in as soon as the cockpit ladder was in position, made a loud rude comment to the pilot and came back through the galley into the main cabin.

'What have you done with them, then?' he said looking round at the emptiness. 'Dumped them in the Channel?'

I explained the situation.

'Damn,' he said. 'I wanted to get off early. Well, did any of you buy anything in France?'

John didn't answer. I shook my head. Billy said offensively, 'We weren't given a sodding minute to get off the sodding plane.'

The customs man in his navy blue suit glanced at

me sideways in amusement. I gathered that he had met Billy before.

'OK,' he said. 'See you this afternoon, then.'

He opened the big double doors, beckoned to the men outside who were wheeling up the ramp, and as soon as it was in position walked jauntily down it and back across the tarmac towards the airport building. As we were now more or less up to schedule through not having to load and unload the French hurdlers, John and Billy and I followed him in order to have lunch. I sat at one table and Billy and John ostentatiously moved to another as far away as they could get. But if Billy thought he could distress me in that way, he was wrong. I felt relieved to be alone, not shunned.

By one o'clock the horseboxes bringing the next consignment had arrived, and we started the loading all over again. This time I got the groom who had brought the horses to lead them up to the plane. Billy and I made the boxes, and John belched and got in the way.

When I had finished I went into the airport building, checked the horses' export papers with the customs man and persuaded the pilot away from his fourth cup of coffee. Up we went again into the clear wintry sky, across the grey sea, and down again in France. The same French customs men came on board, checked every horse as meticulously as before, and as politely let them go. We took down the boxes, led out the horses, saw them loaded into their horseboxes, and watched them depart.

This time the French hurdlers for the return journey had already arrived and without a pause we began getting them on board. As there were only four we had only two boxes to set up, which by that point I found quite enough. John's sole contribution towards the fourth journey was to refill and hang haynets for the hurdlers to pick from on their way, and even at that he was clumsy and slow.

With the horses at length unconcernedly munching in their boxes we went across to the airport buildings, Billy and John ahead, I following. The only word I heard pass between them as they left down the ramp was 'beer'.

There was a technical delay over papers in one of the airport offices. One of the things I had grown to expect in the racehorse export business was technical delays. A journey without one of some sort was a gift. With up to twenty horses sometimes carried on one aeroplane there only had to be a small query about a single animal for the whole load to be kept waiting for hours. Occasionally it was nothing to do with the horses themselves but with whether the airlines owed the airport dues for another plane or another trip: in which case the airport wouldn't clear the horse plane to leave until the dues were paid. Sometimes the quibbling was enough to get one near to jumping out of the window. I was growing very good indeed at keeping my temper when all around were losing theirs and blaming it on me. Kipling would have been proud.

This time it was some question of insurance which I could do nothing to smooth out as it involved the owner of one of the hurdlers, who was fighting a contested claim on a road accident it had been slightly hurt in. The insurance company didn't want the horse to leave France. I said it was a bit late, the horse was sold, and did the insurance company have the right to stop it anyway. No one was quite sure about that. A great deal of telephoning began.

I was annoyed, mainly because the horse in question was in the forward of the two boxes: if we had to take it off the plane it meant dismantling the rear box and unloading the back pair first in order to reach it, and then reloading those two again once we had got it off. And with Billy and John full of all the beer they were having plenty of time to ship, this was likely to be a sticky manoeuvre. The horses' own grooms and motor boxes had long gone home. The hurdlers were each worth thousands. Who, I wondered gloomily, was I going to trust not to let go of them if we had to have them standing about on the tarmac.

The pilot ran me to earth and said that if we didn't take off soon we would be staying all night as after six o'clock he was out of time. We had to be able to be back at Cambridge at six, or he couldn't start at all.

I relayed this information to the arguing officials. It produced nothing but some heavy Gallic shrugs. The pilot swore and told me that until twenty to five I would find him having coffee and after that he'd be en route for Paris. And I would have to get another pilot as he had worked the maximum hours for a long spell and was legally obliged now to have forty-eight hours' rest.

Looking morosely out of the window across to where the plane with its expensive cargo sat deserted on the apron, I reflected that this was the sort of situation I could do without. And if we had to stay all night, I was going to have to sleep with those horses. A delightful new experience every day, I thought in wry amusement. Join Yardman Transport and see the world, every discomfort thrown in.

With minutes to spare, the insurance company relented: the hurdler could go. I grabbed the papers, murmuring profuse thanks, raced to dig out the pilot, and ran Billy to earth behind a large frothy glass. It was clearly far from his first.

'Get John,' I said shortly. 'We've got to be off within ten minutes.'

'Get him yourself,' he said with sneering satisfaction. 'If you can.'

'Where is he?'

'Half way to Paris.' He drank unconcernedly. 'He's got some whore there. He said he'd come back tomorrow on a regular airline. There isn't a sodding thing you can do about it, so put that in your pipe and smoke it.'

John's presence, workwise, made little difference one

way or another. I really cared not a bent sou if he
wanted to pay his own fare back. He was free enough.
He had his passport in his pocket, as we all did. Mine
was already dog-eared and soft from constant use. We
had to produce them whenever asked, though they
were seldom stamped as we rarely went into the passengers' immigration section of airports. We showed
them more like casual passes than weighty official docu-
ments, and most countries were so tolerant of people
employed on aircraft that one pilot told me he had left
his passport in a hotel bedroom in Madrid and had
been going unhindered round the world for three weeks
without it while he tried to get it back.

'Ten minutes,' I said calmly to Billy. 'Fifteen, and
you'll be paying your own fare back too.'

Billy gave me his wide-eyed stare. He picked up his
glass of beer and poured it over my foot. The yellow
liquid ran away in a pool on the glossy stone floor,
froth bubbles popping round the edges.

'What a waste,' I said, unmoving. 'Are you coming?'

He didn't answer. It was too much to expect him to
get up meekly while I waited, and as I wanted to avoid
too decisive a clash with him if I could I turned away
and went back alone, squelching slightly, to the aircraft.
He came as I had thought he would, but with less than
two minutes in hand to emphasize his independence.
The engines were already running when he climbed
aboard, and we were moving as soon as the doors were
shut.

As usual during take-off and landing, Billy stood holding the heads of two horses and I of the other two. After that, with so much space on the half-loaded aircraft, I expected him to keep as far from me as he could, as he had done all day. But Billy by then was eleven hours away from Yardman's restraining influence and well afloat on airport beer. The crew were all up forward in the cockpit, and fat useless John was sexbent for Paris.

Billy had me alone, all to himself.

Billy intended to make the most of it.

CHAPTER FOUR

'Your kind ought not to be allowed,' he said, with charming directness. He had to say it very loudly, also, on account of the noise of the aircraft.

I sat on a hay bale with my back against the rear wall of the cabin and looked at him as he stood ten feet in front of me with his legs apart for balance.

'Your kind, of course,' I shouted back, 'are the salt of the earth.'

He took a step forward and the plane bumped hard in an air pocket. It lurched him completely off his balance and he fell rolling on his side. With sizzling fury, though it wasn't I who had pushed him, he raised himself up on one knee and thrust his face close to mine.'

'—you,' he said.

At close quarters I could see how very young he was. His skin was still smooth like a child's and he had long thick eyelashes round those vast pale blue-grey searchlight eyes. His hair, a fairish brown, curled softly close to his head and down the back of his neck, cut short and in the shape of a helmet. He had a soft, full lipped mouth and a strong straight nose. A curiously sexless face. Too unlined to be clearly male, too heavily boned to be female.

He wasn't so much a man, not even so much a person, as a force. A wild, elemental, poltergeist force trapped barely controllably in a vigorous steel-spring body. You couldn't look into Billy's cold eyes from inches away and not know it. I felt a weird unexpected primitive tingle away down somewhere in my gut, and at the same time realized on a conscious level that friendliness and reason couldn't help, that there would be no winning over, ever, of Billy.

He began mildly enough.

'Your sort,' he yelled. 'You think you own the bloody earth. You soft lot of out-of-date nincompoops, you and your lah-di-dah bloody Eton.'

I didn't answer. He put his sneering face even nearer.

'Think yourself something special, don't you? You and your sodding ancestors.'

'They aren't very usual,' I yelled in his ear.

'What aren't?'

'Sodding ancestors.'

He had no sense of humour. He looked blank.

'You didn't spring from an acorn,' I said resignedly. 'You've had as many ancestors as I have.'

He stood up and took a step back. 'Bloody typical,' he shouted, 'making fun of people you look down on.'

I shook my head, got to my feet, and went along the

plane to check the horses. I didn't care for useless arguments at the best of times, let alone those which strained the larynx. All four hurdlers were standing quietly in the boxes, picking peacefully at the haynets, untroubled by the noise. I patted their heads, made sure everything was secure, hesitated about going forward to the galley and cockpit for more friendly company, and had the matter settled for me by Billy.

'Hey,' he shouted. 'Look at this.' He was pointing downwards with one arm and beckoning me with sweeps of the other. There was anxiety in his face.

I walked back between the last box and the side wall of the aircraft, into the open space at the back, and across to Billy. As soon as I got near enough to see what he was pointing at, the anxiety on his faced changed to spite.

'Look at this,' he shouted again, and jabbed his clenched fist straight into my stomach.

The only flicker of talent I had shown in a thoroughly mediocre and undistinguished career at Eton had been for boxing. I hadn't kept it up afterwards, but all the same the defence reflex was still there even after eight years. Billy's unexpected blow landed on a twisting target and my head did not go forward to meet a punch on the jaw. Or more likely in this case, I thought fleetingly, a chop on the back of the neck. Instead, I gave him back as good as I got, a short hard jolt to the lower ribs. He was surprised, but it didn't stop him. Just the reverse. He seemed pleased.

There are better places for fighting than the back of an aircraft. The floor of that one was banded by the rows of seat anchorages, so that it was only a matter of time before one of us caught his foot in them and overbalanced, and it happened to be me, dodging away from a hand stretched at my throat. I went down flat on my back, unable to stop myself.

Billy fell deliberately and heavily on top of me, grinning fiercely with his own private pleasure, stabbing his elbows sharply into my chest and pressing me down hard on to the rigid anchorages. It hurt, and he meant it to. I kicked and rolled over, trying to get him underneath for a taste of it, but he was off like a cat at the crucial point and already aiming his boot as I stood up. I took that on the thigh and lunged accurately in return at his head. He just shook it briefly and went on punching, hard, quick, and with no respect for convention; but the pleasure left his face when he continued to get everything back with interest.

Thankful at least that he had produced no flick knife or bicycle chain I battled on, knowing in a cold detached part of my brain that I would gain nothing even if I won. Billy's resentment would be greater, not less, for being slogged by what he despised.

I did win in the end, if anyone did, but only because he had a belly full of beer and I hadn't. We were both near to a standstill. I hit him finally very hard just below the navel, my fist sinking in deep, and he fell against the aft box retching and clutching himself and sliding down on to his knees. I caught hold of one of his wrists and twisted his arm across his back.

'Now you listen, Billy,' I said loudly in his ear, panting to get enough breath, 'I don't see any point in fighting you, but I will if you make me. You can forget I'm an earl's son, Billy, and take me as I am, and this is what I am . . .' I jerked his arm. 'Hard, Billy, not soft. As tough as necessary. Remember it.'

He didn't answer, perhaps because he was showing signs of being sick. I yanked him to his feet, pushed him across to the lavatory compartment in the tail, opened the door for him, and shoved him through. As the only lock was on the inside I couldn't make sure he stayed there, but from the sounds which presently issued from the open door, he was in no state to leave.

My own body ached from head to foot from his punches and kicks and from brisk contact with many sharp and knobbed edges, not least those spaced regularly on the floor. I sat down weakly on a straw bale and rubbed a few places which didn't do much good, and was suddenly struck by something very odd indeed.

My face was completely unmarked.

I had bashed my head against one of the metal bars on the rear box and there was a tender swelling a little above my right ear. But Billy, I remembered distinctly, had not once even aimed at my face; not at any point higher than my throat.

For someone in the grip of obsessive fury, surely that was extraordinary, I thought. The usual impulse in

59

such a case was to 'smash his face in'. Billy had actually taken pains not to. I didn't understand why. I thought about it all the way to Cambridge.

It was dark when we landed and the cabin lights were on. The cheerful customs man made his way through the plane, raised his eyebrows, and asked where my two mates were.

'Billy is in there,' I nodded towards the lavatory, 'and John stayed in France. He said he was coming back tomorrow.'

'OK.' He checked through the horses' papers perfunctorily. 'All clear,' he said, and as an afterthought: 'Buy anything?'

I shook my head, and he grinned, helped me open the double doors, and whistled away down the ramp as soon as it was in position.

Billy had locked himself into the lavatory and refused to come out, so I had to get one of the box drivers who had arrived to collect the cargo to help me unload the horses. Unloading was always quicker and easier than loading, but I had begun to stiffen up all over with bruises, and I was glad when it was done. The helpful box driver led out the last horse, an undistinguished brown mare, and before turning back to tidy up I watched them step and slither down the ramp. That mare, I thought idly, was very like the one we had taken across in the morning, though the rug she wore might be misleading. But it couldn't of course be the same. No one would ship a horse out in the morning and back in the afternoon.

I turned away and began slowly to stack the box sides and the bars, wished painfully that Billy hadn't been quite so rough, and forgot about it.

The following day I went down to the wharf building and hooked Simon out for a liquid lunch. We shambled down the road to the usual hideous pub and he buried his face in a pint like a camel at an oasis.

'That's better,' he said, sighing, when a scant inch remained. 'How did yesterday's trip go?'

'All right.'

His eyes considered me thoughtfully. 'Did you have a fall on Saturday?'

'No. A winner. Why?'

'You're moving a bit carefully, that's all.'

I grinned suddenly. 'You should see the other fellow.'

His face melted in comprehension and he laughed. 'I imagine I have,' he said. 'Billy has a sunset of a black eye.'

'You've seen him?' I was surprised.

Simon nodded. 'He was in the office this morning, talking to Yardman.'

'Getting his version in first I suppose.'

'What happened?' he asked interestedly.

'Billy picked a fight.' I shrugged. 'He resents my

existence. It's ridiculous. No one can help what his father is. You can't choose your birth.'

'You feel strongly about it,' Simon observed, ordering another pint. I shook my head to his invitation.

'So would you, if you had to live with it. I mostly get treated as a villain or a nit or a desirable match, and not much else.' I was exaggerating, but not unduly.

'That last doesn't sound too bad.' He grinned.

'You haven't had half the debs' mums in London trying to net you for their daughters,' I said gloomily, 'with your own mother egging them on.'

'It sounds a wow.' He had no sympathy for such a fate.

'It isn't me they want,' I pointed out. 'It's only my name. Which is no fun at all. And on the other end from the wedding ring I get bashed around for exactly the same reason.'

'Very few can feel as strongly as Billy.'

I looked at him. 'There were the French in seventeen eighty-nine, remember? And the Russians in nineteen-seventeen. They all felt as strongly as Billy.'

'The English like their aristocrats.'

'Don't you believe it. They don't mind them from the social point of view because titles make the scandal sheets juicier. But they make damn sure they have no effective power. They say we are a joke, an anachronism, out of date, and weak and silly. They pretend we are these things so that we are kept harmless, so that no one will take us seriously. Think of the modern attitude to the House of Lords, for example. And you – you still think it funny that I want this sort of job, but you wouldn't think so if my father was a ... a farmer, or a pubkeeper, or a schoolmaster. But I'm me, here and now, a man of now, not of some dim glorious past. I am not an anachronism. I'm Henry Grey, conceived and born like everyone else, into this present world. Well, I insist on living in it. I am not going to be shoved off into an unreal playboy existence where my only function is to sire the next in line, which is what my parents want.'

'You could renounce your title, when you get it,' Simon pointed out calmly. He spotted a pin on the bar counter and absentmindedly tucked it into his lapel. It was such a habit with him that he sported a whole row of them, like a dressmaker.

'I could,' I said, 'but I won't. The only good reason for doing that is to stay in the House of Commons, and I'll never be a politician, I'm not the type. Renouncing for any other reason would be just a retreat. What I want is for people to acknowledge that an earl is as good as the next man, and give him an equal chance.'

'But if you get on, they say it's because of your title, not because you have talent.'

'You are so right. But there's a prince or two, a few dukes' sons, and some others like me, all in the same boat just now, and I reckon that our generation, if we try hard enough, might in the end be treated on our own terms. Have some more beer.'

He laughed and agreed.

'I've never heard you say so much,' he said.

'It's Billy's fault. Forget it.'

'I don't think I will.'

'You know something odd? I'm covered with bruises, and there isn't a single one on my face.'

He considered, drinking.

'He'd have got into trouble if he'd marked you for all to see.'

'I suppose so.'

'I gather you haven't told Yardman?'

'No.'

'Why not?'

I shrugged. 'I think he expected it, or something like it. He was ironic when he gave me the job. He must have known that sooner or later I would come up against Billy. And yesterday, he knew Billy would be after me. He warned me, in his way.'

'What are you going to do about it?'

'Nothing.'

'But what if you find yourself on another trip with Billy? I mean, you're bound to, sometime.'

'Yes, I know. Well, it's up to him entirely. I wouldn't start anything. I didn't yesterday. But I did tell him plainly that I'd fight back any time. And I am not, repeat *not*, leaving here because of him.'

'And you look so quiet and mild.' He smiled one-sidedly, looking down into his again empty glass. 'I think,' he said slowly, almost it seemed to me sadly, 'that one or two people in Yardman Transport have miscalculated about you, Henry.'

But when I pressed him to explain, he wouldn't.

With no more export trips to be flown until Thursday, I went the next day, Wednesday, to the races. Someone offered me a spare ride in the novice chase and for some reason it fretted me more than ever to have to refuse. 'I can't,' I said, explaining thoroughly so that he wouldn't think I was being rude. 'I'm only allowed to ride in fifty open races a season, and I'm already over the forty mark, and I've got mounts booked for Cheltenham and the Whitbread and so on. And if I ride too much now I'll be out of those, but thank you very much for asking me.'

He nodded understandingly and hurried off to find someone else, and in irritation two hours later I watched his horse canter home to a ten lengths' win. It was some consolation, however, when immediately afterwards I was buttonholed by a large shrewd-faced man I knew very slightly, the father of another well occupied amateur jockey. Between them, father and son owned and trained half a dozen good hunter 'chasers which they ran only in amateur events with notoriously satisfactory results. But on this particular afternoon Mr Thackery, a large-scale farmer from Shropshire, showed signs both of worry and indecision.

'Look,' he said, 'I'll not beat about the bush, I'm a

blunt man, so I'm told. Now, what do you say to riding all my horses until the end of the season?'

I was astonished. 'But surely Julian . . . I mean, he hasn't had a bad fall or anything, has he?'

He shook his head. The worry stayed in placed. 'Not a fall. He's got jaundice. Got it pretty badly, poor chap. He won't be fit again for weeks. But we've a grand lot of horses this year and he won't hear of them not running just because he can't ride them. He told me to ask you, it's his idea.'

'It's very good of him,' I said sincerely. 'And thank you, I'd like to ride for you very much, whenever I can.'

'Good, then.' He hesitated, and added, 'Er . . . Julian told me to tell you, to ask you, if ten per cent of the prize money would be in order?'

'Thank you,' I said. 'That will be fine.'

He smiled suddenly, his heavy face lightening into wrinkles which made him look ten years younger. 'I wasn't sure about asking you, I'll tell you that, only Julian insisted on it. There's no nonsense about Henry, he said, and I can see he's right. He said Henry don't drink much, don't talk much, gets on with the job and expects to be paid for it. A pro at heart, he says you are. Do you want expenses?'

I shook my head. 'Ten per cent for winning. Nothing else.'

'Fair enough.' He thrust out his hand and I shook it.

'I'm sorry about Julian's jaundice,' I said.

Mr Thackery's lips twitched. 'He said if you said that, that he hoped for the sake of our horses you were being hypothetical.'

'Oh, subtle stuff.' I pondered. 'Tell him to get up too soon and have a relapse.'

The next afternoon I went on a flight to New York.

With Billy.

The ice between us was as cold as the rarefied air outside the pressurized stratocruiser which took us. Yardman, I reflected, wasn't showing much sense in pushing us off together so soon, and on a two-day journey at that.

The wide cold stare was somewhat marred by the blackish streaks and yellow smudges left by my fist, and Billy was distinctly warier than he had been on the French journeys. There were no elementary taunts this time; but at the end of everything he said to me he tacked on the words 'Lord Grey', and made them sound like an insult.

He tried nothing so crude as punching to make my trip memorable; instead he smashed down one of the metal bars as I was fixing a guy chain during the loading. I looked up angrily, squeezing four squashed right fingers in my left hand, and met his watchful waiting eyes. He was looking down at me with interest, with faintly sneering calculation, to see what I would do.

If anyone else had dropped the bar, I would have

known it was accidental. With Billy, apart from the force with which it had landed, I knew it wasn't. But the day had barely begun, and the cargo was much too valuable to jeopardize for personal reasons, which I dare say he was counting on. When he saw that I was not going to retaliate, or at least not instantly, he nodded in satisfaction, picked up the bar with a small cold private smile, and calmly began putting it into place.

The loading was finished and the plane took off. There were thick dark red marks across my fingers an inch below the nails, and they throbbed all the way to America.

With us on that trip, looking after a full load of twelve horses, we took two other grooms, an elderly deaf one supplied by Yardman, and another man travelling privately with one particular horse. Owners occasionally sent their own grooms to Yardman's and far from resenting it I had learned from Timmie and Conker to be glad of the extra help.

The horse involved on this occasion had come from Norway, stayed in England overnight, and was bound for a racing stable in Virginia. The new owner had asked for the Norwegian groom to go all the way, at his expense, so that the horse should have continuous care on the journey. It didn't look worth it, I reflected, looking over it idly while I checked the horses in the next box. A weak-necked listless chestnut, it had a straggle of hair round the fetlocks which suggested

68

there had been a cart horse not far enough back in its ancestry, and the acute-angled hocks didn't have the best conformation for speed. Norway was hardly famed for the quality of its racing any more, even though it was possibly the Vikings who had invented the whole sport. They placed heaps of valued objects (the prizes) at varying distances from the starting point: then all the competitors lined up, and with wild whoops the race began. The prizes nearest the start were the smallest, the farthest away the richest, so each rider had to decide what suited his mount best, a quick sprint or a shot at stamina. Choosing wrong meant getting no prize at all. Twelve hundred years ago fast sturdy racing horses had been literally worth a fortune in Norway, but the smooth skinned long legged descendants of those tough shaggy ponies didn't count for much in the modern thoroughbred industry. It was sentiment, I supposed, which caused an American to pay for such an inferior looking animal to travel so far from home.

I asked the middle-aged Norwegian groom if he had everything he wanted, and he said, in halting, heavily accented English that he was content. I left him sitting on his hay bale staring mindlessly into space, and went on with my rounds. The horses were all travelling quietly, munching peacefully at their haynets, oblivious to rocketing round the world at six hundred miles an hour. There is no sensation of speed if you can't see an environment rushing past.

We arrived without incident at Kennedy airport,

where a gum-chewing customs man came on board with three helpers. He spoke slowly, every second word an 'uh', but he was sharply thorough with the horses. All their papers were in order, however, and we began the unloading without more ado. There was the extra job of leading all the horses through a tray of disinfectant before they could set foot on American soil, and while I was seeing to it I heard the customs man asking the Norwegian groom about a work permit, and the halting reply that he was staying for a fortnight only, for a holiday, the kindness of the man who owned the horse.

It was the first time I too had been to the States, and I envied him his fortnight. Owing to the five hours' difference, it was only six in the morning, local time, when we landed at Kennedy and we were due to leave again at six next morning; which gave me about nine free hours in which to see New York. Although to my body mechanism it was already bedtime, I didn't waste any of them in sleeping.

The only snag to this was having to start another full day's work with eyes requiring matchsticks. Billy yawned over making the boxes as much as I did and only the third member of the team, the deaf elderly Alf, had had any rest. Since even if one shouted he could hear very little, the three of us worked in complete silence like robots, isolated in our own thoughts, with gaps as unbridgeable between us as between like poles of magnets. Unlike poles attract, like poles repel. Billy and I were a couple of cold Norths.

There was a full load going back again, as was usual on Yardman trips from one continent to another. He hated wasting space, and was accustomed to telephone around the studs when a long flight was on the books, to find out if they had anything to send or collect. The customers all liked it, for on full long distance loads Yardman made a reduction in the fares. Timmie and Conker had less cheerful views of this practice, and I now saw why. One's body didn't approve of tricks with the clock. But at the point of no return way out over the Atlantic I shed my drowsiness in one leaping heartbeat, and with horror had my first introduction to a horse going berserk in mid-air.

Old Alf shook my shoulder, and the fright in his face brought me instantly to my feet. I went where he pointed, up towards the nose of the aircraft.

In the second to front box a solidly muscled three-year-old colt had pulled his head collar to pieces and was standing free and untied in the small wooden square. He had his head down, his forelegs straddled, and he was kicking out with his hind feet in a fixed, fearful rhythm. White foamy sweat stood out all over him, and he was squealing. The companion beside him was trying in a terrified way to escape, his eyes rolling and his body pushing hard against the wooden side of the box.

The colt's hooves thudded against the back wall of

the box like battering rams. The wooden panels shook
and rattled and began to splinter. The metal bars banding the sides together strained at the corner lynch pins,
and it only needed one to break for the whole thing to
start disintegrating.

I found the co-pilot at my elbow, yelling urgently.

'Captain says how do you expect him to fly the
aircraft with all this thumping going on. He says to
keep that horse still, it's affecting the balance.'

'How?' I asked.

'That's your affair,' he pointed out. 'And for God's
sake do something about it quickly.'

The back wall of the colt's box cracked from top to
bottom. The pieces were still held in place by the guy
chains, but at the present rate they wouldn't hold more
than another minute, and then we should have on our
minds a maddened animal loose in a pressurized aircraft with certain death to us all if he got a hoof through
a window.

'Have you got a humane killer on board?' I said.

'No. This is usually a passenger craft. Why don't you
bring your own?'

There were no rules to say one had to take a humane
killer in animal transport. There should be. But it was
too late to regret it.

'We've got drugs in the first aid kit,' the co-pilot
suggested.

I shook my head. 'They're unpredictable. Just as
likely to make him worse.' It might even have been a

tranquillizer which started him off, I thought fleetingly. They often backfired with horses. And it would be quite impossible in any case to inject even a safe drug through a fine needle designed for humans into a horse as wild as this.

'Get a carving knife or something from the galley,' I said. 'Anything long and sharp. And quick.'

He turned away, stumbling in his haste. The colt's hind feet smashed one broken half of the back wall clean out. He turned round balefully, thrust his head between the top and centre banding bars, and tried to scramble through. The panic in his eyes was pitiful.

From inside his jerkin Billy calmly produced a large pistol and pointed it towards the colt's threshing head.

'Don't be a bloody fool,' I shouted. 'We're thirty thousand feet up.'

The co-pilot came back with a white-handled saw-edged bread knife, saw the gun, and nearly fainted.

'D . . . don't,' he stuttered. 'D . . . d . . . don't.'

Billy's eyes were very wide. He was looking fixedly at the heaving colt and hardly seemed to hear. All his mind seemed to be concentrated on aiming the gun that could kill us all.

The colt smashed the first of the lynch pins and lunged forwards, bursting out of the remains of the box like flood water from a dam. I snatched the knife from the co-pilot and as the horse surged towards me stuck the blade into the only place available, the angle where the head joined the neck.

I hit by some miracle the carotid artery. But I couldn't get out of his way afterwards. The colt came down solidly on top of me, pouring blood, flailing his legs and rolling desperately in his attempts to stand up again.

His mane fell in my mouth and across my eyes, and his heaving weight crushed the breath in and out of my lungs like some nightmare form of artificial respiration. He couldn't right himself over my body, and as his struggles weakened he eventually got himself firmly wedged between the remains of his own box and the one directly aft of it. The co-pilot bent down and put his hands under my armpits and in jerks dragged me out from underneath.

The blood went on pouring out, hot sticky gallons of it, spreading down the gangways in scarlet streams. Alf cut open one of the hay bales and began covering it up, and it soaked the hay into a sodden crimson brown mess. I don't know how many pints of blood there should be in a horse: the colt bled to death and his heart pumped out nearly every drop.

My clothes were soaked in it, and the sweet smell made me feel sick. I stumbled down the plane into the lavatory compartment and stripped to the skin, and washed myself with hands I found to be helplessly trembling. The door opened without ceremony, and the co-pilot thrust a pair of trousers and a sweater into my arms. His overnight civvies.

'Here,' he said. 'Compliments of the house.'

I nodded my thanks, put them on, and went back up the plane, soothing the restive frightened cargo on the way.

The co-pilot was arguing with Billy about whether Billy would really have pulled the trigger and Billy was saying a bullet from a revolver wouldn't make a hole in a metal aircraft. The co-pilot cursed, said you couldn't risk it, and mentioned richochets and glass windows. But what I wanted to know, though I didn't ask, was what was Billy doing carrying a loaded pistol round with him in an underarm holster as casually as a wallet.

CHAPTER FIVE

I slept like the dead when I finally got home, and woke with scant time the next morning to reach Kempton for the amateurs' chase. After such a mangling week I thought it highly probable I would crown the lot by falling off the rickety animal I had in a weak moment promised to ride. But though I misjudged where it was intending to take off at the last open ditch and practically went over the fence before it while it put in an unexpected short one, I did in fact cling sideways like a limpet to the saddle, through sheer disinclination to hit the ground.

Though I scrambled back on top, my mount, who wouldn't have won anyway, had lost all interest, and I trotted him back and apologized to his cantankerous owner, who considered I had spoilt his day and was churlish enough to say so. As he outranked my father by several strawberry leaves he clearly felt he had the right to be as caustic as he chose. I listened to him saying I couldn't ride in a cart with a pig-net over it and wondered how he treated the professionals.

Julian Thackery's father caught the tail end of these remarks as he was passing, and looked amused: and when I came out of the weighing room after changing he was leaning against the rails waiting for me. He had brought the list of entries of his horses, and at his suggestion we adjourned to the bar to discuss them. He bought me some lemon squash without a quiver, and we sat down at a small table on which he spread out several sheets of paper. I realized, hearing him discussing his plans and prospects, that the year by year success of his horses was no accident: he was a very able man.

'Why don't you take out a public licence?' I said finally.

'Too much worry,' he smiled. 'This way it's a hobby. If I make mistakes, I have no one on my conscience. No one to apologize to or smooth down. No need to worry about owners whisking their horses away at an hour's notice. No risk of them not paying my fees for months on end.'

'You know the snags,' I agreed dryly.

'There's no profit in training,' he said. 'I break even most years, maybe finish a little ahead. But I work the stable in with the farm, you see. A lot of the overheads come into the farm accounts. I don't see how half these public trainers stay in business, do you? They either have to be rich to start with, or farmers like me, or else they have to bet, if they want a profit.'

'But they don't give it up,' I pointed out mildly. 'And they all drive large cars. They can't do too badly.'

He shook his head and finished his whisky. 'They're good actors, some of them. They put on a smiling not-a-care-in-the-world expression at the races when they've got the bank manager camping on their door-step back home. Well, now,' he shuffled the papers together, folded them, and tucked them into a pocket, 'you think you can get next Thursday off to go to Stratford?'

'I'm pretty sure of it, yes.'

'Right. I'll see you there then.'

I nodded and we stood up to go. Someone had left an *Evening Standard* on the next table, and I glanced at it casually. Then I stopped and went back for a closer look. A paragraph on the bottom of the front page started 'Derby Hope Dead', and told in a few bald words that Okinawa, entered for the Derby, had died on the flight from the United States, and was consequently scratched from all engagements.

I smiled inwardly. From the lack of detail or excitement, it was clear the report had come from someone like the trainer to whom Okinawa had been travelling, not from airport reporters sniffing a sensational story. No journalist who had seen or even been told of the shambles on that plane could have written so starkly. But the horse had been disposed of now, and I had helped wash out the plane myself, and there was nothing to see any more. Okinawa had been well insured, a vet had certified that destroying him was essential, and I had noticed that my name on the crew list was spelled wrongly: H. Gray. With a bit of luck, and if Yardman himself had his way, that was the end of it. 'My dear boy,' he'd said in agitation when hurriedly summoned to the airport, 'it does no good to have horses go crazy on our flights. We will not broadcast it, will we?'

'We will not,' I agreed firmly, more for my sake than for his.

'It was unfortunate . . .' he sighed and shrugged, obviously relieved.

'We should have a humane killer,' I said, striking the hot iron.

'Yes. Certainly. All right. I'll get one.'

I would hold him to that, I thought. Standing peacefully in the bar at Kempton I could almost feel the weight of Okinawa and the wetness of his blood, the twenty-four-hour-old memory of lying under a dying horse still much too vivid for comfort. I shook myself firmly back into the present and went out with Julian's father to watch a disliked rival ride a brilliant finish.

Saturday night I did my level best to be civil to Mother's youngest female weekend guest, while avoiding all determined manoeuvres to leave me alone with her, and Sunday morning I slid away before dawn northwards to Lincolnshire.

Tom Wells was out on the apron when I arrived, giving his planes a personal check. He had assigned me, as I had learned on the telephone the previous morning, to fly three men to Glasgow for a round of golf. I was to take them in an Aztec and do exactly what they wanted. They were good customers. Tom didn't want to lose them.

'Good morning, Harry,' he said as I reached him. 'I've given you Quebec Bravo. You planned your route?'

I nodded.

'I've put Scotch and champagne on board, in case they forget to bring any,' he said. 'You're fetching them from Coventry – you know that – and taking them back there. They may keep you late at Gleneagles until after dinner. I'm sorry about that.'

'Expensive game of golf,' I commented.

'Hm,' he said shortly. 'That's an alibi. They are three tycoons who like to compare notes in private. They stipulate a pilot who won't repeat what he hears, and I reckon you fit that bill, Harry my lad, because you've been coming here for four years and if a word of gossip has passed your lips in that time I'm a second class gas fitter's mate.'

'Which you aren't.'

'Which I'm not.' He smiled, a pleasant solid sturdy man of forty plus, a pilot himself who knew chartering

backwards and ran his own little firm with the minimum
of fuss. Ex-RAF, of course, as most flyers of his age
were: trained on bombers, given a love for the air, and
let down with a bang when the Service chucked them
out as redundant. There were too many pilots chasing
too few jobs in the post-war years, but Tom Wells had
been good, persistent and lucky, and had converted a
toe-hold co-pilot's job in a minor private airline into
a seat on the board, and finally, backed by a firm of
light aircraft manufacturers, had started his present
company as his own.

'Give me a ring when you're leaving Gleneagles,' he
said. 'I'll be up in the Tower myself when you come
back.'

'I'll try not to keep you too late.'

'You won't be the last.' He shook his head. 'Joe
Wilkins is fetching three couples from a weekend in Le
Touquet. A dawn job, that'll be, I shouldn't wonder . . .'

I picked up the three impressive business men as
scheduled and conveyed them to Scotland. On the way
up they drank Tom Wells' Black and White and talked
about dividend equalization reserves, unappropriated
profits, and contingent liabilities: none of which I found
in the least bit interesting. They moved on to exports
and the opportunities available in the European
market. There was some discussion about 'whether the
one and three quarters was any positive inducement',
which was the only point of their conversation I really
understood.

The one and three quarters, as I had learned at Anglia Bloodstock, was a percentage one could claim from the Government on anything one sold for export. The three tycoons were talking about machine tools and soft drinks, as far as I could gather, but the mechanism worked for bloodstock also. If a stud sold a horse abroad for say twenty thousand pounds, it received not only that sum from the buyer, but also one and three quarters per cent of it – three hundred and fifty pounds – from the Government. A carrot before the export donkey. A bonus. A pat on the head for helping the country's economy. In effect, it did influence some studs to prefer foreign buyers. But racehorses were simple to export: they needed no after sales service, follow-up campaign or multi-lingual advertising, which the tycoons variously argued were or were not worth the trouble. Then they moved on to taxation and I lost them again, the more so as there were some lowish clouds ahead over the Cheviots and at their request I was flying them below three thousand feet so that they could see the countryside.

I went up above the cloud into the quadrantal system operating above three thousand feet, where to avoid collision one had to fly on a steady regulated level according to the direction one was heading: in our case, going north west, four thousand five hundred or six thousand five hundred or eight thousand five hundred, and so on up.

One of the passengers commented on the climb and asked the reason for it, and wanted to know my name.

'Grey.'

'Well, Grey, where are we off to? Mars?'

I smiled. 'High hills, low clouds.'

'My God,' said the weightiest and oldest tycoon, patting me heavily on the shoulder. 'What wouldn't I give for such succinctness in my boardroom.'

They were in good form, enjoying their day as well as making serious use of it. The smell of whisky in the warm luxurious cabin overcame even that of hot oil, and the expensive cigar smoke swirled huskily in my throat. I enjoyed the journey, and for Tom's sake as well as my own pride, knowing my passengers were connoisseurs of private air travel, put them down on the Gleneagles strip like a whisper on a lake.

They played golf and drank and ate; and repeated the programme in the afternoon. I walked on the hills in the morning, had lunch, and in the late afternoon booked a room in the hotel, and went to sleep. I guess it was a satisfactory day all round.

It was half past ten when the reception desk woke me by telephone and said my passengers were ready to leave, and eleven before we got away. I flew back on a double dogleg, making for the St Abbs radio beacon on the Berwickshire coast and setting a course of one sixty degrees south south east from there on a one five two nautical mile straight course to Ottringham, and then south west across country to

Coventry, coming in finally on their 122,70 homer signal.

The tycoons, replete, talked in mellow, rumbling, satisfied voices, no longer about business but about their own lives. The heaviest was having trouble over currency regulations with regard to a villa he had bought on the Costa del Sol: the Government had slapped a two thousand pound ceiling on pleasure spending abroad, and two thousand would hardly buy the bath taps . . .

The man sitting directly behind me asked about decent yachts available for charter in the Aegean, and the other two told him. The third said it was really time his wife came back from Gstaad, she had been there for two months, and they were due to go to Nassau for Easter. They made me feel poverty-stricken, listening to them.

We landed safely at Coventry, where they shook my hand, yawning, thanked me for a smooth trip, and ambled off to a waiting Rolls, shivering in the chilly air. I made the last small hop back to Fenland and found Tom, as good as his word, on duty in the control tower to help me down. He yelled out of the window to join him, and we drank coffee out of a thermos jug while he waited for his Le Touquet plane to come back. It was due in an hour: earlier than expected. Apparently the client had struck a losing steak and the party had fizzled out.

'Everything go all right with your lot?' Tom said.

'They seemed happy,' I nodded, filling in the flight details on his record chart and copying them into my own log book.

'I suppose you want your fee in flying hours, as usual?'

I grinned. 'How did you guess?'

'I wish you'd change your mind and work for me permanently.'

I put down the pen and stretched, lolling back on the wooden chair with my hands laced behind my head. 'Not yet. Give it three or four years; perhaps then.'

'I need you now.'

Need. The word was sweet. 'I don't know ... I'll think it over again, anyway.'

'Well, that's something I suppose.' He ruffled his thinning light brown hair and rubbed his hands down over his face, his skin itching with tiredness. 'Sandwich?'

'Thanks.' I took one. Ham, with French mustard, made in their bungalow by Tom's capable wife Janie, not from the airport canteen. The ham was thick and juicy, home cooked in beer. We ate in silence and drank the hot strong coffee. Outside the glass-walled high up square room the sky grew a thick matt black, with clouds drifting in to mask the stars. The wind was slowly backing, the atmospheric pressure falling. It was getting steadily colder. Bad weather on its way.

Tom checked his instruments, frowned, leaned back

on his chair and twiddled his pencil. 'The forecast was
right,' he said gloomily. 'Snow tomorrow.'

I grunted sympathetically. Snow grounded his planes
and caused a hiatus in his income.

'Have to expect it in February, I suppose,' he sighed.

I nodded in agreement. I wondered if Stratford races
would be snowed off on Thursday. I wondered if
weather interfered much with Yardman's trips. I
reflected that Janie Wells made good coffee, and that
Tom was a sound sensible man. Untroubled, organized
surface thoughts. And it was the last night I ever spent
in my calm emotional deep-freeze.

The sky was a sullen orange grey when we took off at
eight the next morning from Gatwick, the as yet unshed
snow hanging heavily as spawn in a frog's belly. We
were carrying eight brood mares in an old unpressurized DC4, flying away from the incoming storm, en
route to Milan. Timmie and Conker were back, to my
relief, but neither had had a scintillating holiday, by the
sound of it. I overheard Conker, a much harassed small
father of seven large hooligans, complaining as he
loaded the cargo that he'd done nothing but cook and
wash up while his wife curled up in bed with what
was, in his opinion, opportunist malingering influenza.
Timmie showed his sympathy in his usual way: a hearty
gear-changing sniff. A thick-set black haired square
little Welshman, he suffered from interminable catarrh

and everyone around him suffered also. It had been his sinuses, he unrepentantly said after one particularly repulsive spitting session, which had stopped him going down the mines like his pa. The February holiday, Timmie agreed, was not much cop.

'How many holidays do you have?' I asked, fixing chains.

'A week off every two months,' Conker said. 'Blimey mate, don't tell me you took this job without asking that.'

'I'm afraid I did.'

'You'll be exploited,' Conker said seriously. 'When you start a job, you want your terms cut and dried, wages, overtime, holidays with pay, bonuses, superannuation, the lot. If you don't stand up for your rights, no one else will, there isn't a union for us, you know, bar the agricultural workers, if you care for that which I don't. And old Yardman, he don't give nothing away you know. You want to make sure about your weeks off, mate, or you won't get any. I'm telling you.'

'Well . . . thank you. I'll ask him.'

'Aw, look man,' said Timmie in his soft Welsh voice, 'we get other times off too. You don't want to work yourself to death. Mr Yardman don't hold you to more than two trips a week, I'll say that for him. If you don't want to go, that is.'

'I see,' I said. 'And if you don't go, Billy and Alf do?'

'That's about it,' agreed Conker. 'I reckon.' He fitted

the last lynch pin on the last box and rubbed his hands down the sides of his trousers.

I remembered Simon saying that my predecessor Peters had been a belligerent stand-on-your-rights man, and I supposed that Conker had caught his anti-exploitation attitude from him, because it seemed to me, from what they'd said, that Conker and Timmie both had free time positively lavished upon them. A day's return trip certainly meant working a continuous stretch of twelve hours or more, but two of those in seven days wasn't exactly penal servitude. Out of interest I had added up my hours on duty some weeks, and even at the most they had never touched forty. They just don't know when they are well off, I thought mildly, and signalled to the airport staff to take the ramp away.

The DC4 was noisy and very cramped. The gangways between and alongside the horses were too narrow for two people to pass, and in addition one had to go forward and backward along the length of the plane bent almost double. It was, as usual, normally a passenger ship, and it had low-hung luggage shelves along its length on both sides. There were catches to hold the racks up out of the way, but they were apt to shake open in flight and it was more prudent to start with all the racks down than have them fall on one's head. This, added to the angled guy chains cutting across at shin level, made walking about a tiresome process and provided the worst working conditions I had yet struck.

But Conker, I was interested to notice, had no complaints. Peters, maybe, hadn't been with him on a DC4.

After take-off, the horses all being quiet and well behaved, we went forward into the galley for the first cup of coffee. The engineer, a tall thin man with a habit of raising his right eyebrow five or six times rather fast when he asked a question, was already dispensing it into disposable mugs. Two full ones had names pencilled on: Patrick and Bob. The engineer picked them up and took them forward to the pilot and co-pilot in the cockpit. Coming back, the engineer asked our names and wrote us each a mug.

'There aren't enough on board for us to throw them away every time,' he explained, handing me 'Henry'. 'Sugar?' He had a two-pound bag of granulated, and red plastic spoon. 'I know the way you lot drink coffee. The skipper, too.'

We drank the scalding brown liquid: it didn't taste of coffee, but if you thought of it as a separate unnamed thirst quencher, it wasn't too bad. In the galley the engine noise made it necessary to shout loudly to be heard, and the vibration shook concentric ripples in the coffee. The engineer sipped his gingerly over the scrawled word 'Mike'.

'You've got a right load there,' he commented. 'A ship full of expectant mums, aren't they?'

Conker, Timmie and I nodded in unison.

'Are they Italian?'

Together we shook our heads. Music hall stuff.

'What are they going for, then?'

'They are English mares going to be mated with Italian sires,' explained Conker, who had once worked in a stud and would be positively happy if one of the mares foaled down prematurely on the flight.

'Pull the other one, it's got bells on,' said the engineer.

'No, it's right,' said Conker. 'They have to have the foals they are carrying now in the stud where their next mate is.'

'Why?' The agile eyebrow worked overtime.

'Ah,' said Conker seriously. 'The gestation period for horses is eleven months, right? And a brood mare has a foal every twelve months, right? So there's only four weeks left between production and – er – reproduction, do you see? And in those four weeks the new foal isn't fit for travelling hundreds of miles in the freezing cold, so the mares have to have the foals in the stud of their next mate. Get?'

'I get,' agreed the engineer. 'I get indeed.'

'That one,' said Conker admiringly, pointing out in the foremost box an elegant brown silky head which owing to the general lack of space was almost in the galley, 'that one's going to Molvedo.'

'How do you know?' asked Timmie interestedly.

'Horsebox driver told me.'

The co-pilot came back from the cockpit and said the skipper wanted a refill.

'Already? That man's a tank.' The engineer poured into the Patrick mug.

'Here,' said the co-pilot, handing it to me. 'Take it to him, will you? I'm off to see a man about a dog.' He brushed under Molvedo's future wife's inquisitive nose and bent down for the obstructed walk down to the john.

I took the steaming mug forward into the cockpit. The pilot, flying in whiter-than-white shirtsleeves despite the zero temperature outside, stretched out a languid hand and nodded his thanks. I stayed for a second looking round at the banked instruments, and he glanced up at me and gestured to me to put my ear down to his mouth. The noise there made even ordinary shouting impossible.

'Are you the head chap with the horses?'

'Yes.'

'Like to sit there for a bit?' He pointed to the empty co-pilot's seat.

'Yes, I would.' He gestured permissively, and I edged sideways into the comfortable bucket seat beside him. The cockpit was tiny, considering how much had to be packed into it, and battered and dented with age. It was also, to me, very much my home.

I studied the instruments with interest. I had never flown a four engined craft, only one and two, for the excellent reason that there were no four engined planes at Fenland. As even small two engined jobs like the Aztec I had taken to Gleneagles the day before cost nearly thirty-five pounds per flying hour to hire from Tom, I thought it unlikely I would ever raise enough cash for a course on the really big stuff, even if I could use the qualification once I got it. You couldn't just go up alone for an afternoon's jolly in an airliner; they simply weren't to be had. None of which stopped me for a moment being intent on learning everything I could.

The pilot, Patrick, indicated that I should put on the combined set of earphones and mouthpiece which was hanging over the semicircular wheel. I slid it on to my head, and through it he began to explain to me what all the switches and dials were for. He was the first pilot I'd flown with on Yardman's trips who had taken such trouble, and I listened and nodded and felt grateful, and didn't tell him I knew already most of what he was saying.

Patrick was a big striking looking man of about thirty, with straight dark auburn hair cut a bit theatrically in duck tails, and light amber eyes like a cat. His mouth turned naturally up at the corners so that even in repose he seemed to be smiling, as if everything in the world was delightful, with no evil to be found anywhere. Nor, I later proved, did the implication of that curve lie: he persisted in believing the best of everybody, even with villainy staring him in the face. He had the illogical faith in human goodness of a probation officer, though in that first half-hour all I learned about him was that he was a gentle, careful, self-assured and eminently safe pilot.

He tuned in to the frequency of the radio beacon at Dieppe, explaining it to me as he went, and took a weather report there before turning on to the course to Paris.

'We'll go down to the Med and fly along the coast,' he said. 'There's too much cloud over the Alps to go straight across. Not being pressurized we ought not to go above ten thousand feet but fourteen thousand or so doesn't hurt unless you've got a bad heart. Even that doesn't give us enough in hand over the Alps in the present conditions, so I'm going the long way round.'

I nodded, thoroughly approving.

He checked the de-icing equipment for a second time in ten minutes and said, 'This bird won't fly with more than a quarter of a ton of ice on her, and the de-icers were *us* last week.' He grinned. 'It's OK, I've checked them six times since they were repaired, they're doing all right.'

He peeled and ate one of a large bunch of bananas lying on the ledge over the instrument panel, then calmly unhinged the window beside him a few inches and threw the skin out. I laughed to myself in appreciation and began to like Patrick a good deal.

The co-pilot returned to claim his place, and I went back to the horses for the rest of the journey. Uneventfully we went down across France to Dijon, turned south down the Rhone valley, east at Saint Tropez, and north again at Albenga, landing at Malpensa Airport, Milan, in exactly four hours from Gatwick.

Italy was cold. Shivering as the open doors let in air thirty degrees below the cabin temperature we watched about ten airport men in royal blue battle dress push the wide top-class ramp into position, and waited while three customs men made their way over from the building. They came up the ramp, and the eldest of them said something in his own language.

'*Non parlo italiano*,' I said apologetically, which useful sentence was all I knew.

'*Non importa*,' he said. He took from me the mares' temporary import permits which had been made out in both English and Italian, and his two assistants began going from horse to horse calling out their descriptions.

All was in order. He gave me back the papers with a courteous nod of the head, and led his shadows away down the ramp. Again we went through the familiar routine of transferring the cargo from the plane to the waiting horseboxes, Conker making a great fuss of the mare going to Molvedo.

With an hour to spare before we set about loading another cargo of mares bound in the opposite direction for the same reason, Conker, Timmie and I walked across a quarter of a mile of tarmac to the airport building to have lunch. We were met at the door by Patrick, looking very official with gold-braided shoulder tabs on his navy uniform jacket, and wearing an expression of resignation.

'We can't go back today,' he said, 'so you chaps don't need to hurry over your beer.'

'What's up, then?' asked Timmie, sniffing loudly.

'A blizzard. Came down like a burst eiderdown in a wind tunnel after we left this morning. It's raging all over the south and halfway across the Channel and snowing clear up to John O'Groats. The bottom's dropped out of the barometer and . . . well, anyway, my instructions are not to go back.'

'All that pasta,' said Conker philosophically. 'It does my tripes no good.'

He and Timmie went off to the snack bar and Patrick showed me the telegraph office to send 'no go' messages to Yardman and the expectant studs. After that we went back to the aircraft, where he collected his overnight bag and I turned homewards the arriving convoy of Italian mares. He waited for me to finish and helped me shut the big double doors from inside at the top of the ramp, and we walked forward across the flattened dismantled boxes, through the galley, and down the staircase which had been wheeled up to the door just behind the cockpit.

'Where will you stay?' he said.

'Hotel, I suppose,' I said vaguely.

'If you like, you could come with me. There's a family in Milan I berth with when I'm stranded, and there's room for two.'

I had a strong inclination, as usual, to be by myself, but principally because I couldn't even ask for a hotel room in Italian let alone find entertainment except looking at architecture for the rest of the day, I accepted his offer, and thanked him.

'You'll like them,' he said.

We went two hundred yards in silence.

'Is it true,' he said, 'that you're a viscount?'

'No,' I said casually. 'A Boeing 707.'

He chuckled. 'A bleeding viscount, that little Welshman said you were, to be precise.'

'Would it make any difference to you if I were?'

'None whatever.'

'That's all right, then.'

'So you are?'

'On and off.'

We went through the glass doors into the hall of the airport. It was spacious, airy, glass-walled, stone floored. Along one side stretched a long gift counter with souvenir presents crowded in a row of display cases and stacked on shelves at the back. There were silk ties on a stand, and dolls in local dress scattered on the counter, and trays of paper-backed books and local view postcards. In charge of this display stood a tall dark-haired girl in a smooth black dress. She saw us coming and her coolly solemn face lit into a delicious smile.

'Patrick,' she said. 'Hullo, Patrick, *come sta*?'

He answered her in Italian, and as an afterthought waved his hand at me and said 'Gabriella ... Henry.'

He asked her a question, and she looked at me carefully and nodded.

'*Si*,' she said. '*Henry anche.*'

'That's fixed, then,' said Patrick cheerfully.

'You mean,' I said incredulously, 'that we are going to stay with – er – Gabriella?'

He stiffened slightly. 'Do you object?'

I looked at Gabriella, and she at me.

'I think,' I said slowly, 'that it is too good to be true.'

It wasn't for another ten minutes, during which time she talked to Patrick while looking at me, that I realized that I spoke no Italian and the only English word that she knew was 'Hullo'.

CHAPTER SIX

You couldn't say it was reasonable, it was just electric. I found out between one heartbeat and the next what all poets throughout the ages had been going on about. I understood at last why Roman Antony threw away his honour for Egyptian Cleopatra, why Trojan Paris caused a ten years' war abducting Greek Helen, why Leander drowned on one of his risky nightly swims across the Dardenelles to see Hero. The distance from home, the mystery, the unknownness, were a part of it: one couldn't feel like that for the girl next door. But that didn't explain why it hadn't happened before: why it should be this girl, this one alone who fizzed in my blood.

I stood on the cool stone airport floor and felt as if I'd been struck by lightning: the world had tilted, the air was crackling, the grey February day blazed with light, and all because of a perfectly ordinary girl who sold souvenirs to tourists.

The same thing, fantastically, had happened to her as well. Perhaps it had to be mutual, to happen at all.

I don't know. But I watched the brightness grow in her eyes, the excitement and gaiety in her manner, and I knew that against all probability it was for me. Girls were seldom moved to any emotion by my brown-haired tidy unobtrusive self, and since I rarely set out to make an impression on them, I even more rarely did so. Even the ones who wanted to marry my title were apt to yawn in my face. Which made Gabriella's instant reaction doubly devastating.

'For God's sake,' said Patrick in amusement, when she didn't answer a twice repeated question, 'will you two stop gawping at each other?'

'Gabriella,' I said.

'*Si?*'

'Gabriella . . .'

Patrick laughed. 'You're not going to get far like that.'

'*Parla francese?*' she said anxiously.

Patrick translated. 'Do you speak French?'

'Yes.' I laughed with relief. 'Yes, more or less.'

'*E bene,*' she sighed smiling. '*E molto molto bene.*'

Perhaps because we were unburdened by having to observe any French proprieties and because we both knew already that we would need it later on, we began right away using the intimate form *tu* instead of *vous*, for 'you'. Patrick raised his eyebrows and laughed again and said in three languages that we were nuts.

I *was* nuts, there was no getting away from it. Patrick endured the whole afternoon sitting at a table in the snack bar drinking coffee and telling me about Gabriella and her family. We could see her from where we sat, moving quietly about behind her long counter, selling trinkets to departing travellers. She was made of curves, which after all the flat hips, flat stomachs, and more or less flat chests of the skinny debs at home, was as warming as a nightwatchman's fire on a snowy night. Her oval pale olive-skinned face reminded me of medieval Italian paintings, a type of bone structure which must have persisted through centuries, and her expression, except when she smiled, was so wholly calm as to be almost unfriendly.

It struck me after a while, when I had watched her make two or three self-conscious customers nervous by her detached manner, that selling wasn't really suited to her character, and I said so, idly, to Patrick.

'I agree,' he said dryly. 'But there are few places better for a smuggler to work than an airport.'

'A . . . *smuggler*? I don't believe it.' I was aghast.

Patrick enjoyed his effect. 'Smuggler,' he nodded. 'Definitely.'

'No,' I said.

'So am I,' he added smiling,

I looked down at my coffee, very disturbed. 'Neither of you is the type.'

'You're wrong, Henry. I'm only one of many who brings . . . er . . . goods . . . in to Gabriella.'

'What,' I said slowly, fearing the answer, 'are the goods?'

He put his hand into his jacket pocket, pulled out a flat bottle about five inches high, and handed it to me. A printed chemist's label on the front said 'Two hundred aspirin tablets BP', and the brown glass bottle was filled to the brim with them. I unscrewed the top, pulled out the twist of cotton wool, and shook a few out on to my hand.

'Don't take one,' said Patrick, still smiling. 'It wouldn't do you any good at all.'

'They're not aspirins.' I tipped them back into the bottle and screwed on the cap.

'No.'

'Then what?'

'Birth control pills,' he said.

'*What?*'

'Italy is a Roman Catholic country,' he observed. 'You can't buy these pills here. But that doesn't stop women wanting to avoid being in a constant state of baby production, does it? And the pills are marvellous for them, they can take them without the devoutest husbands knowing anything about it.'

'Good God,' I said.

'My brother's wife collects them at home from her friends and so on, and when she has a bottleful I bring it to Gabriella and she passes them on at this end. I know for a fact that at least four other pilots do the same, not to mention a whole fleet of air hostesses, and she admitted to me once that a day seldom goes by without some supplies flying in.'

'Do you . . . well . . . sell . . . them to Gabriella?'

He was quite shocked, which pleased me. 'Of course not. She doesn't sell them, either. They are a gift, a service if you like, from the women of one country to the women of another. My sister-in-law and her friends are really keen on it, they don't see why any woman in the world should have to risk having a child if she doesn't want one.'

'I've never thought about it,' I said, fingering the bottle.

'You've never had a sister who's borne six children in six years and collapsed into a shattering nervous breakdown when she started the seventh.'

'Gabriella's sister?'

He nodded. 'That's why she got some pills in the first place. And the demand just grew and grew.'

I gave him back the bottle and he put it back in his pocket. 'Well?' he said, with a hint of challenge.

'She must be quite a girl,' I said, 'to do something like this.'

His curving mouth curved wider. 'If she smuggled the Crown Jewels you'd forgive her. Confess it.'

'Whatever she did,' I said slowly.

The amusement died right out of his face and he looked at me soberly. 'I've heard of this sort of thing,' he said. 'But I've never seen it happen before. And you didn't even need to speak to each other. In fact, it's just damn lucky you *can* speak to each other . . .'

Three times during the afternoon I made sure of

that. She would get into trouble, she said, if she just talked to me when she should be working, so I bought presents, separately, for my father, mother and sister, taking a long time over each choice. Each time she spoke and looked at me in a kaleidoscopic mixture of excitement, caution and surprise, as if she too found falling helplessly in love with a complete stranger an overwhelming and almost frightening business.

'I like that one.'

'It costs six thousand lire.'

'That is too dear.'

'This one is cheaper.'

'Show me some others.'

We began like that, like school-day text books, in careful stilted French, but by the end of the afternoon, when she locked the display cases and left with Patrick and me through the employees' entrance, we could talk with some ease. I perhaps knew most French of the three of us, then Gabriella, then Patrick; but his Italian was excellent, so between us everything could in one language or another be understood.

We left the airport in a taxi, and as soon as we were on the move Patrick gave her the aspirin bottle. She thanked him with a flashing smile and asked him if they were all the same sort. He nodded, and explained they'd come from some RAF wives whose husbands were away on a three months' overseas course.

From her large shoulder-sling bag of black leather she produced some of the bright striped wrapping paper from her airport gift shop and a large packet of sweets. The sweets and aspirin bottle were expertly whisked into a ball shaped parcel with four corners sticking up on top like leaves on a pineapple, and a scrap of sticky tape secured them.

The taxi stopped outside a dilapidated narrow terrace house in a poor looking street. Gabriella climbed out of the taxi, but Patrick waved me back into my seat.

'She doesn't live here,' he said. 'She's just delivering the sweets.'

She was already talking to a tired looking young woman whose black dress accentuated the pallor of her skin, and whose varicose veins were the worst I had seen, like great dark blue knobbed worms networking just under the surface of her legs. Round her clung two small children with two or three more behind in the doorway, but she had a flat stomach in her skimpy dress and no baby in her arms. The look she gave Gabriella and her pretty present were all the reward that anyone would need. The children knew that there were sweets in the parcel. They were jumping up trying to reach it as their mother held it above their heads, and as we left she went indoors with them, and she was laughing.

'Now,' said Patrick, turning away from the window, 'we had better show Henry Milan.'

It was getting dark and was still cold, but not for us. I couldn't have noticed if it had been raining ice. They began by marching me slowly around the Piazza del

Duomo to see the great Gothic cathedral and the Palazzo Reale, and along the high glass arcade into the Piazza della Scala to gaze at the opera house, which Gabriella solemnly told me was the second largest theatre in Europe, and could hold three thousand six hundred people.

'Where is the largest?' said Patrick.

'In Naples,' she said smiling. 'It is ours too.'

'I suppose Milan has the biggest cathedral, then,' he teased her.

'No,' she laughed, showing an unsuspected dimple, 'Rome.'

'An extravagant nation, the Italians.'

'We were ruling the world while you were still painting yourselves blue.'

'Hey, hey,' said Patrick.

'Leonardo da Vinci lived in Milan,' she said.

'Italy is undoubtedly the most beautiful country in the world and Milan is its pearl.'

'Patrick, you are a great idiot,' she said affectionately. But she was proud indeed of her native city, and before dinner that evening I learned that nearly a million and a half people lived there and that there were dozens of museums, and music and art schools, and that it was the best manufacturing town in the country, and the richest, and its factories made textiles and paper and railway engines and cars. And, in fact, aeroplanes.

We ate in a quiet warmly lit little restaurant which

looked disconcertingly like Italian restaurants in London but smelled quite different, spicy and fragrant. I hardly noticed what I ate: Gabriella chose some sort of veal for us all, and it tasted fine, like everything else that evening. We drank two bottles of red local wine which fizzed slightly on the tongue, and unending little gold cups of black coffee. I knew even then that it was because we were all speaking a language not of our own that I felt liberated from my usual self. It was so much easier to be uninhibited away from everything which had planted the inhibitions: another sky, another culture, a time out of time. But that only made the way simpler, it didn't make the object less real. It meant I didn't have chains on my tongue; but what I had said wasn't said loosely, it was still rooted in some unchanging inner core. On that one evening in Milan I learned what it was like to be gay deep into the spirit, and if for nothing else I would thank Gabriella for that all my life.

We talked for hours; not profoundly, I dare say, but companionably: at first about the things we had done and seen that day, then of ourselves, our childhood. Then of Fellini's films, and a little about travel, and then, in ever widening ripples, of religion, and our own hopes, and the state the world was in. There wasn't an ounce of natural reforming zeal among the three of us, as perhaps there ought to have been when so much needed reforming; but faith didn't move mountains any more, it got bogged down by committees, Patrick said, and the saints of the past would be smeared as psychological misfits today.

'Could you imagine the modern French Army allowing itself to be inspired and led into battle by a girl who saw visions?' he said. 'You could not.'

It was true. You could not.

'Psychology,' Patrick said, with wine and candlelight in his yellow eyes, 'is the death of courage.'

'I don't understand,' protested Gabriella.

'Not for girls,' he said. 'For men. It is now not considered sensible to take physical risks unless you can't avoid them. Ye gods, there's no quicker way to ruin a nation than to teach its young men it's foolish to take risks. Or worse than foolish, they would have you believe.'

'What do you mean?' she said.

'Ask Henry. He'll cheerfully go out and risk his neck on a racehorse any day of the week. Ask him why.'

'Why?' she said, half-serious, half-laughing, the glints of light in her dark eyes outpointing the stars.

'I like it,' I said. 'It's fun.'

Patrick shook his red head. 'You look out, pal, you mustn't go around admitting that sort of thing these days. You've got to say you do it only for the money, or you'll be labelled as a masochistic guilt complex before you can say ... er ... masochistic guilt complex.'

'Oh yeah?' I said, laughing.

'Yeah, damn it, and it's not funny. It's deadly serious.

The knockers have had so much success and now it's fashionable to say you're a coward. You may not *be* one, mind, but you've got to *say* so, just to prove you're normal. Historically, it's fantastic. What other nation ever went around saying on television and in the Press and at parties and things that cowardice is normal and courage is disgusting? Nearly all nations used to have elaborate tests for young men to prove they were brave. Now in England they are taught to settle down and want security. But bravery is built in somewhere in human nature and you can't stamp it out any more than the sex urge. So if you outlaw ordinary bravery it bursts out somewhere else, and I reckon that's what the increase in crime is due to. If you make enjoying danger seem perverted, I don't see how you can complain if it becomes so.'

This was too much for his French; he said it to me in hot English, and repeated it, when Gabriella protested, in cooler Italian.

'But,' she said wonderingly, 'I do not like a man to say he is a coward. Who wants that? A man is for hunting and for defending, for keeping his wife safe.'

'Back to the caves?' I said.

'Our instincts are still the same,' agreed Patrick. 'Basically good.'

'And a man is for loving,' Gabriella said.

'Yes, indeed,' I agreed with enthusiasm.

'If you like to risk your neck, I like that. If you risk it for me, I like it better.'

'You mustn't say so,' said Patrick smiling. 'There's probably some vile explanation for that too.'

We all laughed, and some fresh coffee came, and the talk drifted away to what girls in Italy wanted of life as opposed to what they could have. Gabriella said the gap was narrowing fast, and that she was content, particularly as she was an orphan and had no parental pressure to deal with. We discussed for some time the pros and cons of having parents after adolescence, and all maintained that what we had was best: Gabriella her liberty, Patrick a widowed mother who spoiled him undemandingly, and I, free board and lodging. Patrick looked at me sharply when I said that, and opened his mouth to blow the gaff.

'Don't tell her,' I said in English. 'Please don't.'

'She would like you even more.'

'No.'

He hesitated, but to my relief he left it, and when Gabriella asked, told her we had been arguing as to who should pay the bill. We shared it between us, but we didn't leave for some time after that. We talked, I remember, about loyalty: at first about personal loyalty, and then political.

Gabriella said that Milan had many communists, and she thought that for a Roman Catholic to be a communist was like an Arab saying he wanted to be ruled by Israel.

'I wonder who they would be loyal to, if Russia invaded Italy?' Patrick said.

'That's a big if,' I said smiling. 'Pretty impossible with Germany, Austria and Switzerland in between, not to mention the Alps.'

Gabriella shook her head. 'Communists begin at Trieste.'

I was startled and amused at the same time, hearing an echo of my die-hard father. 'Wogs begin at Calais.'

'Of course they do,' Patrick said thoughtfully. 'On your doorstep.'

'But cheer up,' she said laughing. 'Yugoslavia also has mountains, and the Russians will not be arriving that way either.'

'They won't invade any more countries with armies,' I agreed mildly. 'Only with money and technicians. Italian and French and British communists can rely on never having to choose which side to shoot at.'

'And can go on undermining their native land with a clear conscience,' Patrick nodded smiling.

'Let's not worry about it,' I said, watching the moving shadows where Gabriella's smooth hair fell across her cheek. 'Not tonight.'

'It will never touch us, anyway,' Patrick agreed. 'And if we stay here much longer Gabriella's sister will lock us out.'

Reluctantly we went out into the cold street. When we had gone ten paces Patrick exclaimed that he had left his overnight bag behind, and went back for it, striding quickly.

I turned to Gabriella, and she to me. The street

lights were reflected in her welcoming eyes, and the solemn mouth trembled on the edge of that transfiguring smile. There wasn't any need to say anything. We both knew. Although I stood with my body barely brushing hers and put my hands very gently on her arms just below the shoulders, she rocked as if I'd pushed her. It was the same for me. I felt physically shaken by a force so primitive and volcanic as to be frightening. How could just touching a girl, I thought confusedly, just touching a girl I'd been longing to touch all afternoon and all evening, sweep one headlong into such an uncivilized turbulence. And on a main street in Milan, where one could do nothing about it.

She let her head fall forward against my shoulder, and we were still standing like that, with my cheek on her hair, when Patrick came back with his bag. Without a word, smiling resignedly, he pulled her round, tucked her arm into his, and said briefly, 'Come on. You'll get run in if you stay here much longer like that.' She looked at him blindly for a moment, and then laughed shakily. 'I don't understand why this has happened,' she said.

'Struck by the gods,' said Patrick ironically. 'Or chemistry. Take your pick.'

'It isn't sensible.'

'You can say that again.'

He began to walk down the road, pulling her with him. My feet unstuck themselves from the pavement and re-attached themselves to my watery legs and I caught them up. Gabriella put her other arm through mine, and we strolled the mile and a half to where her sister lived, gradually losing the heavy awareness of passion and talking normally and laughing, and finally ending up on her doorstep in a fit of giggles.

Lisabetta, Gabriella's sister, was ten years older and a good deal fatter, though she had the same smooth olive skin and the same shaped fine dark eyes. Her husband, Giulio, a softly flabby man approaching forty with a black moustache, bags under his eyes, and less hair than he'd once had, lumbered ungracefully out of his armchair when we went into his sitting-room and gave us a moderately enthusiastic welcome.

Neither he nor Lisabetta spoke English or French so while the two girls made yet more coffee, and Patrick talked to Giulio, I looked around with some interest at Gabriella's home. Her sister had a comfortable four bedroomed flat in a huge recently built tower, and all the furnishings and fabrics were uncompromisingly modern. The floors were some sort of reconstituted stone heated from underneath and without carpet or rugs, and there were blinds, not curtains, to cover the windows. I thought the total effect rather stark, but reflected idly that Milan in mid-summer must be an oven, and the flat had been planned for the heat.

Several children came and went, all indistinguishable to my eyes. Seven of them, there should be, I remembered. Four boys, three girls, Patrick had said. Although it was nearly midnight, none of them seemed to have gone to bed. They had all been waiting to see Patrick and tumbled about him like puppies.

When Lisabetta had poured the coffee and one of the children had handed it round Giulio asked Patrick a question, looking at me.

'He wants to know what your job is,' Patrick said.

'Tell him I look after the horses.'

'Nothing else?'

'Nothing else.'

Giulio was unimpressed. He asked another question.

Smiling faintly, Patrick said, 'He wants to know how much you earn?'

'My pay for a single trip to Milan is about one fifth of yours.'

'He won't like that.'

'Nor do I.'

He laughed. When he translated Giulio scowled.

Patrick and I slept in a room which normally belonged to two of the boys, now doubling with the other two. Gabriella shared a third bedroom with the two elder girls, while the smallest was in with her parents. There were toys all over the place in our room, and small shoes kicked off and clothes dumped in heaps, and the unchanged sheets on the boys' beds were wrinkled like elephant skins from their restless little bodies. Patrick had from long globe trotting habit come equipped with pyjamas, slippers, washing things, and a clean shirt for the morning. I eyed this splendour with some envy, and slept in my underpants.

'Why,' said Patrick in the dark, 'won't you tell them you have a title?'

'It isn't important.'

'It would be to Giulio.'

'That's the best reason for not telling him.'

'I don't see why you're so keen to keep it a secret.'

'Well, you try telling everyone you're an earl's son, and see what happens.'

'I'd love it. Everyone would be bowing and scraping in all directions. Priorities galore. Instant service. A welcome on every mat.'

'And you'd never be sure if anyone liked you for yourself.'

'Of course you would.'

'How many head grooms have you brought here before?' I asked mildly.

He drew in a breath audibly and didn't answer.

'Would you have offered me this bed if Timmie had kept his big mouth shut?'

He was silent.

I said, 'Remind me to kick your teeth in in the morning.'

But the morning, I found, was a long way off. I simply couldn't sleep. Gabriella's bed was a foot away from me on the far side of the wall, and I lay and sweated for her with a desire I hadn't dreamed possible. My body literally ached. Cold controlled Henry Grey, I thought helplessly. Grey by name and grey by nature. Cold controlled Henry Grey lying in a child's bed in a foreign city biting his arm to stop himself crying out. You could laugh at such hunger: ridicule it away. I tried that, but it didn't work. It stayed with me hour after wretched hour, all the way to the dawn, and I would have been much happier if I'd been able to go to sleep and dream about her instead.

She had kissed me good-night in the passage outside her door, lightly, gaily, with Patrick and Lisabetta and about six children approvingly looking on. And she had stopped and retreated right there because it was the same as in the street outside the restaurant; even the lightest touch could start an earthquake. There just wasn't room for an earthquake in that crowded flat.

Patrick lent me his razor without a word when we got up.

'I'm sorry,' I said.

'You were quite right. I would not have offered to take you with me if the Welshman hadn't said . . .'

'I know.' I put on my shirt and buttoned the cuffs.

'All the same I still wouldn't have asked you if I hadn't thought you looked all right.'

I turned towards him, surprised.

'What you need, Henry, is a bit more self-confidence. Why ever shouldn't people like you for yourself? Gabriella obviously does. So do I.'

'People often don't.' I pulled on my socks.

'You probably don't give them half a chance.' With which devastatingly accurate shot he went out of the door, shrugging his arms into his authoritative captain's uniform.

Subdued by the raw steely morning, the three of us went back to the airport. Gabriella had dark shadows under her eyes and wouldn't look at me, though I could think of nothing I had done to offend her. She spoke only to Patrick, and in Italian, and he, smiling briefly, answered her in the same language. When we arrived at the airport, she asked me, hurriedly, not to come and talk to her at the gift counter, and almost ran away from me without saying goodbye. I didn't try to stop her. It would be hours before we got the horses loaded, and regardless of what she asked, I intended to see her again before I left.

I hung around the airport all the morning with Conker and Timmie, and about twelve Patrick came and found me and with a wide grin said I was in luck, traffic at Gatwick was restricted because of deep snow, and unessential freight flights were suspended for another day.

'You'd better telephone the studs again, and tell them we are taking the mares to England tomorrow at eight,' he said. 'Weather permitting.'

Gabriella received the news with such a flash of delight that my spirits rose to the ionosphere. I hesitated over the next question, but she made it easy for me.

'Did you sleep well?' she asked gravely, studying my face.

'I didn't sleep at all.'

She sighed, almost blushing. 'Nor did I.'

'Perhaps,' I said tentatively, 'if we spent the evening together, we could sleep tonight.'

'Henry!' She was laughing. 'Where?'

Where proved more difficult than I had imagined, as she would not consider a hotel, as we must not sleep there, but go back to her sister's before midnight. One must not be shameless, she said. She could not stay out all night. We ended up, of all unlikely places, inside the DC4, lying in a cosy nest hollowed in a heap of blankets stacked in the luggage bay alongside the galley.

There, where no one would ever find us, and with a good deal of the laughter of total happiness, we spent the whole of the evening in the age-old way: and were pleased and perhaps relieved to find that we suited each other perfectly.

Lying quietly cradled in my arms, she told me hesitantly that she had had a lover before, which I knew anyway by then, but that it was odd making love anywhere except in bed. She felt the flutter in my chest and lifted her head up to peer at my face in the dim reflected moonlight.

'Why are you laughing?' she said.

'It so happens that I have never made love *in* bed.'

'Where then?'

'In the grass.'

'Henry! Is that the custom in England?'

'Only at the end of parties in the summer.'

She smiled and put her head down contentedly again, and I stroked her hair and thought how wholesome she was, and how dreadful in comparison seemed the half-drunk nymphs taken casually down the deb-dance garden path. I would never do that again, I thought. Never again.

'I was ashamed, this morning,' she said, 'of wanting this so much. Ashamed of what I had been thinking all night.'

'There is no shame in it.'

'Lust is one of the seven deadly sins.'

'Love is a virtue.'

'They get very mixed up. Are we this evening being virtuous or sinful?' She didn't sound too worried about it.

'Doing what comes naturally.'

'Then it's probably sinful.'

She twisted in my arms, turning so that her face was close to mine. Her eyes caught a sheen in the soft near-darkness. Her teeth rubbed gently against the bare skin on the point of my shoulder.

'You taste of salt,' she said.

I moved my hand over her stomach and felt the deep muscles there contract. Nothing, I thought, shaken by an echoing ripple right down my spine, nothing was so impossibly potent as being wanted in return. I kissed her, and she gave a long soft murmuring sigh which ended oddly in a laugh.

'Sin,' she said, with a smile in her voice, 'is OK.'

We went back to her sister's and slept soundly on each side of the wall. Early in the morning, in her dressing-gown, with tousled hair and dreaming eyes, she made coffee for Patrick and me before we set off for the airport.

'You'll come back?' she said almost casually, pouring my cup.

'As soon as I can.'

She knew I meant it. She kissed me goodbye without clinging, and Patrick also. 'For bringing him,' she said.

In the taxi on the way to the airport Patrick said, 'Why don't you just stay here with her? You easily could.'

I didn't answer him until we were turning into the airport road.

'Would you? Stay, I mean.'

'No. But then, I need to keep my job.'

'So do I. For different reasons, perhaps. But I need to keep it just the same.'

'It's none of my business,' he said, 'but I'm glad.'

We loaded the Italian mares and flew them to snowy England without another hitch. I soothed them on their way and thought about Gabriella, who seemed to have established herself as a warming knot somewhere under my diaphragm.

I thought about her with love and without even the conventional sort of anxiety, for as she had said with a giggle, it would be a poor smuggler who couldn't swallow her own contraband.

CHAPTER SEVEN

Stratford Races were off because of snow, which was just as well as Yardman squeezed in an extra trip on that day at very short notice. Seven three-year-olds to France, he said; but at loading time there were eight.

I was held up on the way to Cambridge by a lorry which had skidded sideways and blocked the icy road, and when I reached the airport all the cargo had already arrived, with the box drivers stamping their feet to keep warm and cursing me fluently. Billy, and it was Billy again, not Conker and Timmie, stood about with his hands in his pocket and a sneer permanently fixed like epoxy resin, enjoying the disapproval I had brought on myself. He had not, naturally, thought of beginning the work before I arrived.

We loaded the horses, he, I, and deaf old Alf, whom Billy had brought with him, and we worked in uncompanionable silence. There was a fourth groom on the trip, a middle-aged characterless man with a large straggly moustache and a bad cold, but he had come with one particular horse from an upper crust stud, and he refrained from offering to help with any others. Neither did he lend a hand on the journey, but sat throughout beside his own protegee guarding it carefully from no visible danger. Billy dropped a handful of peat in my coffee and later poured his own, which was half full of sugar, over my head. I spent the rest of the journey in the washroom, awkwardly rinsing the stickiness out of my hair and vowing to get even with Billy one day when I hadn't thousands of pounds' worth of bloodstock in my care.

During the unloading I looked closely at one inconspicuous brown mare, trying to memorize her thoroughly unmemorable appearance. She was definitely not a three-year-old, like all the others on the trip, and she was, I was sure, almost identical to the one we had taken to France the first day I flew with Billy. And very like the one we had brought back that afternoon on the second trip. Three mares, all alike . . . well, it was not impossible, especially as they had no distinct markings between them, none at all.

The special groom left us in Paris, escorting his own horse right through to its new home. He had been engaged, he said, to bring another horse back, a French stallion which his stud had bought, and we would be collecting him again the next week. We duly did collect him, the next Tuesday, complete with the stallion, a tight-muscled butty little horse with a fiery eye and a restless tail. He was squealing like a colt when we stored him on board, and this time there was some point in his straggly moustached keeper staying beside him all the way.

Among the cargo there was yet another undistinguished brown mare. I was leaning on the starboard side of her box, gazing over and down at her, not able to see her very clearly against the peat she stood on and the brown horse on her other side, when Billy crept up behind me and hit me savagely across the shoulders with a spare tethering chain. I turned faster than he expected and got in two hard quick kicks on his thigh. His lips went back with the pain and he furiously swung his arm, the short chain flickering and bending like an angry snake. I dodged it by ducking into one of the crossway alleys between the boxes, and the chain wrapped itself with a vicious clatter round the corner where I had been standing. Unhesitatingly I skipped through to the port side of the plane and went forward at top speed to the galley. Hiding figuratively under the engineer's skirts may not have been the noblest course, but in the circumstances by far the most prudent, and I stayed with him, drinking coffee, until we were on the final approach to Cambridge.

I did a good deal of hard thinking that night and I didn't like my thoughts.

In the morning I waited outside Yardman's office, and fell into step with Simon as he shambled out to lunch.

'Hullo,' he said, beaming. 'Where did you spring from? Come and have a warmer up at the Angel.'

I nodded and walked beside him, shuffling on the thawing remains of the previous week's snow. Our breaths shot out in small sharp clouds. The day was misty and overcast; the cold, raw, damp, and penetrating, exactly matched my mood.

Simon pushed the stained glass and entered the fug; swam on to his accustomed stool, tugged free his disreputable corduroy jacket and hustled the willing barmaid into pouring hot water on to rum and lemon juice, a large glass each. There was a bright new modern electric fire straining at its kilowatts in the old brick fireplace, and the pulsating light from its imitation coal base lit warmly the big smiling face opposite me, and shone brightly on the friendliness in his eyes.

I had so few friends. So few.

'What's the matter then?' he said, sipping his steaming drink. 'You're excessively quiet today, even for you.'

I watched the fake flames for a while, but it couldn't be put off for ever.

'I have found out,' I said slowly, 'about the brown mare.'

He put down his glass with a steady hand but the smile drained completely away.

'What brown mare?'

I didn't answer. The silence lengthened hopelessly.

'What do you mean?' he said at last.

'I escorted a brown mare to France and back twice in a fortnight. The same brown mare every time.'

'You must be mistaken.'

'No.'

There was a pause. Then he said again, but without conviction, 'You are mistaken.'

'I noticed her the day she went over in the morning and came back the same afternoon. I wondered when she went over again last Thursday . . . and I was certain it was the same horse yesterday, when she came back.'

'You've been on several other trips. You couldn't remember one particular mare out of all those you dealt with . . .'

'I know horses,' I said.

'You're too quick,' he said, almost to himself. 'Too quick.'

'No,' I shook my head. 'You were. You shouldn't have done it again so soon; then I might not have realized . . .'

He shook himself suddenly, the bulk quivering in folds. 'Done what?' he said more firmly. 'What if a horse did go over and back twice? And what's it got to do with me?'

'There's no point in telling you what you already know.'

'Henry,' he leaned forward, 'I know what I know, but I don't know what you think you know. You've got some damn-fool notion in your head and I want to hear what it is.'

I watched the steam rise gently from my untouched drink and wished I hadn't come.

'Nice little fiddle,' I sighed. 'A sweet, neat little fraud. Easy as shelling peas. A few hundred quid every time you send the mare to France.'

He looked at me without speaking, waiting, making me say it all straight out.

'All right then. You sell a horse – the brown mare – to an accomplice in France. He arranges for his bank to transfer the purchase price to England and the bank over here certifies that it has been received. You put in a claim to the government that one thoroughbred has been exported for x thousand francs: part of the great bloodstock industry. The grateful government pays you the bonus, the one and three quarters per cent bonus on exports, and you put it in your pocket. Meanwhile you bring the horse back here and smuggle the money back as cash to France and you're ready to start again.'

Simon sat like a stone, staring at me.

'All you really need is the working capital,' I said. 'A big enough sum to make the one and three quarters per cent worth the trouble. Say twenty thousand pounds, for argument's sake. Three hundred and fifty pounds every time the mare goes across. If she went only once a month that would make an untaxed dividend of over 20 per cent on the year. Four thousand or more, tax free. You'd have a few expenses, of course, but even so . . .'

'Henry!' His voice was low and stunned.

'It's not a big fraud,' I said. 'Not big. But pretty safe. And it had to be you, Simon, because it's all a matter of filling up the right forms, and you fill the forms at Yardman's. If anyone else, an outsider, tried it, he'd have to pay the horse's air passage each way, which would make the whole business unprofitable. No one would do it unless they could send the horse for nothing. You can send one for nothing, Simon. You just put one down on the flying list, but not on the office records. Every time there's room on a flight to France, you send the mare. Yardman told me himself there would be seven three-year-olds going over last Thursday, but we took eight horses, and the eighth wasn't a three-year-old, it was the brown mare.

'The day we did two trips, when we took her over in the morning and brought her back in the afternoon, that day it was no accident the return horses weren't at the airport to come back on the first trip. Not even you could risk unloading the mare and promptly loading her up again straight away. So you made a "mistake" and put fifteen hundred hours on the trainers' travelling instructions instead of ten hundred hours, you, who never make such mistakes, whose accuracy is so phenomenal usually that no one queries or checks up on what you do . . .'

'How,' he said dully, 'how did you work it out?'

'I came from Anglia Bloodstock,' I said gently. 'Don't you remember? I used to fill up the same export forms as you do. I used to send them to you from the transport section. But I might not have remembered about the government bonus if I hadn't heard three business men discussing it ten days ago, and last night while I was wondering how anyone could gain from shuffling that mare over and back, the whole thing just clicked.'

'Clicked,' he said gloomily.

I nodded. 'No markings on the mare, either. You couldn't keep sending her in her own name, someone would have noticed at once. I would have done, for a start. But all you had to do was go through the stud book, and choose other unmarked mares of approximately the same age and fill up the export forms accordingly. The customs certify a brown mare was actually exported from here, and the French customs certify it was imported there. No trouble at all. No one bothers to check with an owner that he has sold his horse. Why ever should they? And coming back, you go through the same process with the French stud book, only this time you have to be a bit careful your faked mare isn't too well bred because you can't spend more than two thousand in sterling abroad without searching enquiries, which you couldn't risk.'

'Got it all buttoned up, haven't you?' he said bitterly.

'I was thinking about it nearly all night.'

'Who are you going to tell?'

I glanced at him and away, uncomfortably.

'Yardman?' he asked.

I didn't answer.

'The police?'

I looked at the flickering fire. I wouldn't have told anyone had it not been for . . .

'Did you,' I said painfully, 'did you *have* to get Billy to knock me about?'

'Henry!' He looked shattered. 'I didn't. How can you think I did that?'

I swallowed. 'He's been on all the trips with the mare, and he's never given me a moment's peace on any of them, except perhaps the first. He's punched me and poured syrupy coffee on my hair, and yesterday when I was looking at the mare he hit me with a chain. He's not doing it because he dislikes me . . . or not only. It's a smoke screen to keep me away from looking too closely at the horses. That's why he didn't smash my face in . . . he was fighting for a purpose, not from real fury.'

'Henry, I promise you, it isn't true.' He seemed deeply distressed. 'I wouldn't hurt you, for God's sake.'

He put out his hand for his drink and took a long swallow. There was no more steam: drink and friendship were both cold.

'Don't look like that,' he said shivering. 'Like an iceberg.' He drank again. 'All right, you've got it right about the mare. I'll admit that, but as God's my judge, I didn't put Billy on to you. I can't stand him. He's a young thug. Whatever he's been doing to you, it's from his own bloody nature. I promise you, Henry, I promise you . . .'

I looked at him searchingly, wanting very much to believe him, and feeling I'd merely be fooling myself if I did.

'Look,' he said anxiously, leaning forward, 'would you have sicked him on to me?'

'No.'

'Well, then.' He leaned back again. 'I didn't either.'

There was a long, long pause.

'What do you do with the money?' I asked, shelving it.

He hesitated. 'Pay my gambling debts.'

I shook my head. 'You don't gamble.'

'I do.'

'No.'

'You don't know everything.'

'I know that,' I said tiredly. 'I know that very well. You're not interested in racing. You never ask me for tips, never even ask me if I expect to win myself. And don't say you gamble at cards or something feeble like that . . . if you gambled enough to have to steal to pay your debts, you'd gamble on anything, horses as well. Compulsively.'

He winced. 'Steal is a hard word.' He leaned forward, picked up my untasted drink, and swallowed the lot.

'There's no pension at Yardman's,' he said.

I looked into his future, into his penurious

retirement. I would have the remains of the Creggan fortune to keep me in cars and hot rums. He would have what he'd saved.

'You've banked it?'

'Only a third,' he said. 'A third is my cousin's. He's the one who keeps the mare on his smallholding and drives her to the airport at this end. And a third goes to a chap with a horse dealing business in France. He keeps the mare when she is over there, and drives her back and forth to the planes. They put up most of the stake, those two, when I thought of it. I hadn't anything like enough on my own.'

'You don't really make much out of it, then, yourself, considering the risks.'

'Double my salary,' he observed dryly. 'Tax free. And you underestimate us. We have two horses, and they each go about fifteen times a year.'

'Have I seen the other one?'

'Yes,' he nodded. 'There and back.'

'Once?'

'Once.'

'And how do you get the money back to France?'

'Send it in magazines. Weeklies. The *Horse and Hound*, things like that.'

'English money?'

'Yes. The chap in France has a contact who exchanges it.'

'Risky, sending it by post.'

'We've never lost any.'

'How long have you been doing it?'

'Since they invented the bonus. Shortly after, anyway.'

There was another long silence. Simon fiddled with his empty glass and didn't look like an embezzler. I wondered sadly if it was priggish to want one's friends to be honest, and found that I did still think of him as a friend, and could no longer believe that he had paid Billy to give me a bad time. Billy quite simply hated my pedigreed guts: and I could live with that.

'Well,' he said in the end. 'What are you going to do about it?'

He knew as well as I did that he'd have no chance in an investigation. Too many records of his transaction would still exist in various government and banking files. If I started any inquiry he would very likely end up in gaol. I stood up stiffly off the bar stool and shook my head.

'Nothing . . .' I hesitated.

'Nothing . . . as long as we stop?'

'I don't know.'

He gave me a twisted smile. 'All right, Henry. We'll pack it in.'

We went out of the pub and walked together through the slush back to the office, but it wasn't the same. There was no trust left. He must have been wondering whether I would keep my mouth shut permanently, and I knew, and hated the knowledge, that he could probably go on with his scheme in spite of saying he wouldn't. The brown mare wouldn't go again, but he could change her for another, and there was his second horse, which I hadn't even noticed. If he was careful, he could go on. And he was a careful man.

The travel schedules in the office, checked again, still showed no more trips to Milan till the Wednesday of the following week. Nor, as far as I could see, were there any flights at all before then; only a couple of sea passages booked for polo ponies, which weren't my concern. I knocked on Yardman's door, and went in and asked him if I could have the rest of the week off; my rights, Conker would have said.

'Milan next Wednesday,' he repeated thoughtfully. 'And there's nothing before that? Of course, my dear boy, of course you can have the time off. If you don't mind if I bring you back should an urgent trip crop up?'

'Of course not.'

'That's good, that's good!' The spectacles flashed as he glanced out of the window, the tight skin around his mouth lifting fleetingly into a skeletal smile. 'You still like the job then?'

'Yes, thank you,' I said politely.

'Well, well, my dear boy, and I won't say that you're not good at it, I won't say that at all. Very reliable, yes, yes. I admire you for it, dear boy, I do indeed.'

'Well . . . thank you, Mr Yardman.' I wasn't sure that

underneath he wasn't laughing at me, and wondered how long it would be before he understood that I didn't look on my job as the great big joke everyone else seemed to think it.

I wrote to Gabriella to tell her I would be coming back the following week, and drove moderately home, thinking alternately of her and Simon in an emotional see-saw.

There was a message for me at home to ring up Julian Thackery's father, which I did. The weather forecast was favourable, he said, and it looked as though there would be racing on Saturday. He was planning to send a good 'hunter chaser up to Wetherby, and could I go and ride it.

'I could,' I said. 'Yes.'

'That's fine. She's a grand little mare, a real trier, with the shoulders of a champion and enough behind the saddle to take you over the best.'

'Wetherby fences are pretty stiff,' I commented.

'She'll eat them,' he said with enthusiasm. 'And she's ready. We gave her a mile gallop this morning, thinking she'd be backward after the snow, and she was pulling like a train at the end of it. Must thrive on being held up.'

'Sounds good.'

'A snip,' he said. 'I'll see you in the weighing room, just before the first. Right?'

I assured him I would be there, and was glad to be going, as I learned from a letter of acceptance lying beside the telephone that the Filyhoughs were again expected for the weekend. My sister Alice came along while I held the letter in my hand.

'I'm going up to Wetherby on Saturday,' I said, forestalling her.

'Sunday . . .' she began.

'No, Alice dear, no. I have no intention whatsoever of marrying Angela Filyhough and there's no point in seeing her. I thought that we had agreed that Mother should stop this heiress hunting.'

'But you must marry someone, Henry,' she protested.

I thought of Gabriella, and smiled. Maybe her, once I was sure she'd be a friend for life, not just a rocket passion with no embers.

'I'll marry someone, don't you worry.'

'Well,' Alice said, 'if you're going as far north as Wetherby you might as well go on and see Louise and cheer her up a bit.'

'Cheer her up?' I said blankly. Louise was the sister just older than Alice. She lived in Scotland, nearly twice as far from Wetherby, as it happened, as Wetherby from home, but before I could point that out Alice replied.

'I told you yesterday evening,' she said in exasperation. 'Weren't you listening?'

'I'm afraid not.' I'd been thinking about brown mares.

'Louise has had an operation. She goes home from

hospital today and she'll be in bed for two or three weeks more.'

'What's wrong with her?' But Alice either didn't know or wouldn't tell me, and though I hardly knew Louise in any deep sense I thought she would be far preferable to Angela Filyhough, and I agreed to go. Deciding, as I would be driving a long way after the races, to go up to Yorkshire on the Friday and spend the Saturday morning lazily, I set off northward at lunchtime and made a detour out of habit to Fenland.

'Hey, Harry, you're just the man I want. A miracle.' Tom Wells grabbed my arm as I walked in. 'Do me a short flight tomorrow? Two trainers and a jockey from Newmarket to Wetherby races.'

I nearly laughed. 'I'm awfully sorry. I can't, Tom. I really called in to cancel my booking for Sunday. I can't come then either. Got to go and visit a sick sister in Scotland. I'm on my way now.'

'Blast,' he said forcibly. 'Couldn't you put it off?'

'Afraid not.'

'You can have a plane to fly up, on Sunday.' He was cunning, looking at me expectantly. 'Free.'

I did laugh then. 'I can't.'

'I'll have to tell the trainers I can't fix them up.'

'I'm really sorry.'

'Yeah. Damn it all. Well, come and have a cup of coffee.'

We sat in the canteen for an hour and talked about aircraft, and I continued my journey to Wetherby thinking in amusement that my life was getting more and more like a juggling act, and that it would need skill to keep the racing, flying, horse-ferrying and Gabriella all spinning round safely in separate orbits.

At Wetherby the struggling sunshine lost to a fierce wind, but the going was perfect, a surprise after the snow. Mr Thackery's mare was all that he had promised, a tough workmanlike little chestnut with a heart as big as a barn, a true racer who didn't agree with giving up. She took me over the first two fences carefully, as she'd not been on the course before, but then with confidence attacked the rest. I'd seldom had a more solid feeling ride and enjoyed it thoroughly, finding she needed the barest amount of help when meeting a fence wrong and was not too pigheaded to accept it. Coming round the last bend into the straight she was as full of running as when she started, and with only a flicker of encouragement from me she began working her way up smoothly past the four horses ahead of us. She reached the leader coming to the last, pecked a bit on landing, recovered without breaking up her stride, and went after the only horse in sight with enviable determination. We caught him in time, and soared past the winning post with the pleasure of winning coursing like wine in the blood.

'Not bad,' said Julian's father beaming. 'Not bad at all,' and he gave me a sealed envelope he'd had the faith to prepare in advance.

With about three hundred and fifty miles to go I left

soon after the race, and on the empty northern roads made good time to Scotland. My sister Louise lived in a dreary baronial hall near Elgin, a house almost as big as ours at home and just as inadequately heated. She had pleased our parents by marrying for money, and hadn't discovered her husband's fanatical tightfist-edness until afterwards. For all she'd ever had to spend since, she'd have been better off in a semi-detached in Peckham. Her Christmas gifts to me as a child had been Everyman editions of the classics. I got none at all now.

Even so, when I went in to see her in the morning, having arrived after she was sleeping the night before, it was clear that some of her spirit had survived. We looked at each other as at strangers. She, after a seven-year gap, was much older looking than I remembered, older than forty-three, and pale with illness, but her eyes were bright and her smile truly pleased.

'Henry, my little brother, I'm so glad you've come . . .'

One had to believe her. I was glad too, and suddenly the visit was no longer a chore. I spent all day with her, looking at old photographs and playing Chinese chequers, which she had taught me as a child, and listening to her chat about the three sons away at boarding school and how poor the grouse had been this winter and how much she would like to see London again, it was ten years since she had been down. She asked me to do various little jobs for her, explaining that 'dear James' was apt to be irritated, and the maids had too much else to do, poor things. I fetched things for her, packed up a parcel, tidied her room, filled her hot water bottle and found her some more toothpaste. After that she wondered if we couldn't perhaps turn out her medicine drawer while we had the opportunity.

The medicine drawer could have stocked a dispensary. Half of them, she said with relief, she would no longer need. 'Throw them away.' She sorted the bottles and boxes into two heaps. 'Put all those in the waste-paper basket.' Obediently I picked up a handful. One was labelled 'Conovid', with some explanatory words underneath, and it took several seconds before the message got through. I picked that box out of the rubbish and looked inside. There was a strip of foil containing pills, each packed separately. I tore one square open and picked out the small pink tablet.

'Don't you want these?' I asked.

'Of course not. I don't need them any more, after the operation.'

'Oh . . . I see. No, of course not. Then may I have them?'

'What on earth for?'

'Don't be naïve, Louise.'

She laughed. 'You've got a girl friend at last? Of course you can have them. There's a full box lying around somewhere too, I think. In my top drawer, perhaps? Maybe some in the bathroom too.'

I collected altogether enough birth control pills to

fill a bottle nearly as big as the one Patrick had given Gabriella, a square cornered brown bottle four inches high, which had held a prescription for penicillin syrup for curing the boys' throat infections. Louise watched with amusement while I rinsed it out, baked it dry in front of her electric fire, and filled it up, stuffing the neck with cotton wool before screwing on the black cap.

'Marriage?' she said. As bad as Alice.

'I don't know.' I put the drawer she had tidied back into the bedside table. 'And don't tell Mother.'

Wednesday seemed a long time coming, and I was waiting at Gatwick a good hour before the first horses turned up. Not even the arrival of Billy and Alf could damp my spirits, and we loaded the horses without incident and faster than usual, as two of the studs had sent their own grooms as well, and for once they were willing.

It was one of the mornings that Simon came with last minute papers, and he gave them to me warily in the charter airline office when the plane was ready to leave.

'Good morning, Henry.'

'Good morning.'

One couldn't patch up a friendship at seven-thirty in the morning in front of yawning pilots and office staff. I took the papers with a nod, hesitated, and went out across the tarmac, bound for the aircraft and Milan.

There were running steps behind me and a hand on my arm.

'Lord Grey? You're wanted on the telephone. They say it's urgent.'

I picked up the receiver and listened, said 'All right,' and slowly put it down again. I was not, after all, going to see Gabriella. I could feel my face contract into lines of pain.

'What is it?' Simon said.

'My father . . . my father has died . . . sometime during the night. They have just found him . . . he was very tired, yesterday evening . . .'

There was a shocked silence in the office. Simon looked at me with great understanding, for he knew how little I wanted this day.

'I'm sorry,' he said, his voice thick with sincerity.

I spoke to him immediately, without thinking, in the old familiar way. 'I've got to go home.'

'Yes, of course.'

'But the horses are all loaded, and there's only Billy . . .'

'That's easy. I'll go myself.' He fished in his briefcase and produced his passport.

It was the best solution. I gave him back the papers and took the brown bottle of pills out of my pocket. With a black ball point I wrote on the label, 'Gabriella Barzini, Souvenir Shop, Malpensa Airport'.

'Will you give this to the girl at the gift counter, and tell her why I couldn't come, and say I'll write?'

He nodded.

'You won't forget?' I said anxiously.

'No, Henry.' He smiled as he used to. 'I'll see she gets it, and the message. I promise.'

We shook hands, and after a detour through the passport office he shambled across the tarmac and climbed up the ramp into the plane. I watched the doors shut. I watched the aircraft fly away, taking my job, my friend and my gift, but not me.

Simon Searle went to Italy instead of me, and he didn't come back.

CHAPTER EIGHT

It was over a week before I found out. I went straight up to his room when I reached the wharf, and it was empty and much too tidy.

The dim teenage secretary next door, in answer to my questions, agreed that Mr Searle wasn't in today, and that no one seemed to know when he would be in at all – or whether.

'What do you mean?'

'He hasn't been in for a week. We don't know where he's got to.'

Disturbed, I went downstairs and knocked on Yardman's door.

'Come in.'

I went in. He was standing by the open window, watching colliers' tugs pulling heavy barges up the river. A Finnish freighter, come up on the flood, was manoeuvring alongside across the river under the vulture-like meccano cranes. The air was alive with hooter signals and the bang and clatter of dock work, and the tide was carrying the garbage from the lower docks steadily upstream to the Palace of Westminster. Yardman turned, saw me, carefully closed the window, and came across the room with both hands outstretched.

'My dear boy,' he said, squeezing one of mine. 'My condolences on your sad loss, my sincere condolences.'

'Thank you,' I said awkwardly. 'You are very kind. Do you ... er ... know where Simon Searle is?'

'Mr Searle?' He raised his eyebrows so that they showed above the black spectacle frames.

'He hasn't been in for a week, the girl says.'

'No ...' he frowned. 'Mr Searle, for reasons best known to himself, chose not to return to this country. Apparently he decided to stay in Italy, the day he went to Milan in your place.'

'But why?' I said.

'I really have no idea. It is very inconvenient. Very. I am having to do his work until we hear from him.'

He shook his head. 'Well, my dear boy, I suppose our troubles no longer concern you. You'd better have your cards, though I don't expect you'll be needing them.' He smiled the twisted ironic smile and stretched out his hand to the inter-office phone.

'You're giving me the sack, then?' I said bluntly.

He paused, his hand in mid-air. 'My dear boy,' he protested. 'My dear boy. It simply hadn't occurred to me that you would want to stay on.'

'I do.'

He hesitated, and then sighed. 'It's against my better judgement, it is indeed. But with Searle and you both away, the agency has had to refuse business, and we can't afford much of that. No, we certainly can't. Very well then, if you'll see us through at least until I hear from Searle, or find someone to replace him, I shall be very grateful, very grateful indeed.'

If that was how he felt, I thought I might as well take advantage of it. 'Can I have three days off for Cheltenham races in a fortnight? I've got a ride in the Gold Cup.'

He nodded calmly. 'Let me have the exact dates, and I'll avoid them.'

I gave them to him then and there, and went back to Simon's room thinking that Yardman was an exceptionally easy employer, for all that I basically understood him as little as on our first meeting. The list of trips on Simon's wall showed that the next one scheduled was for the following Tuesday, to New York. Three during the past and present week had been crossed out, which as Yardman had said, was very bad for business. The firm was too small to stand much loss of its regular customers.

Yardman confirmed on the intercom that the Tuesday trip was still on, and he sounded so pleased that I guessed that he had been on the point of cancelling it when I turned up. I confirmed that I would fetch the relevant papers from the office on Monday afternoon, and be at Gatwick on the dot on Tuesday morning. This gave me a long weekend free and unbeatable ideas on how to fill it. With some relief the next day I drove determinedly away from the gloomy gathering of relations at home, sent a cable, picked up a stand-by afternoon seat with Alitalia, and flew to Milan to see Gabriella.

Three weeks and three days apart had changed nothing. I had forgotten the details of her face, shortened her nose in my imagination and lessened the natural solemnity of her expression, but at the sight of her again, my heart instantly did its levitation act. She looked momentarily anxious that I wouldn't feel the same, and then smiled with breathtaking brilliance when she saw that I did.

'I got your cable,' she said. 'One of the girls has changed her free day with me, and now I don't have to keep the shop tomorrow or Sunday.'

'That's marvellous.'

She hesitated, almost blushing. 'And I went home at lunchtime to pack some clothes, and I have told my sister I am going to stay for two days with a girl friend near Genoa.'

'Gabriella!'

'Is that all right?' she asked anxiously.

'It's a miracle,' I said fervently, having expected only snatched unsatisfactory moments by day, and nights spent each side of a wall. 'It's unbelievable.'

When she had finished for the day we went to the station and caught a train, and on the principle of not telling more lies than could be helped, we did in fact go to Genoa. We booked separately into a large impersonal hotel full of incurious business men, and found our rooms were only four doors apart.

Over dinner in a warm obscure little restaurant she said, 'I'm sorry about your father, Henry.'

'Yes . . .' Her sympathy made me feel a fraud. I had tried to grieve for him, and had recognized that my only strong emotion was an aversion to being called by his name. I wished to remain myself. Relations and family solicitors clearly took it for granted, however, that having sown a few wild oats I would now settle down into his pattern of life. His death, if I wasn't careful, would be my destruction.

'I was pleased to get your letter,' Gabriella said, 'because it was awful when you didn't come with the horses. I thought you had changed your mind about me.'

'But surely Simon explained?'

'Who is Simon?'

'The big fat bald man who went instead of me. He promised to tell you why I couldn't come, and give you a bottle . . .' I grinned, 'a bottle of pills.'

'So they were from you!'

'Simon gave them to you. I suppose he couldn't explain why I hadn't come, because he doesn't know Italian. I forgot to tell him to speak French.'

She shook her head.

'One of the crew gave them to me. He said he'd found them in the toilet compartment just after they had landed, and he brought them across to see if I had lost them. He is a tall man, in uniform. I've seen him often. It was not your bald, fat Simon.'

'And Simon didn't try to talk to you at all?'

'No.' She shook her head. 'I don't think so. I see hundreds of bald, fat travellers, but no one tried to speak to me about you.'

'A friendly big man, with kind eyes,' I said. 'He was wearing a frightful old green corduroy jacket, with a row of pins in one lapel. He has a habit of picking them up.'

She shook her head again. 'I didn't see him.'

Simon had promised to give her my message and the bottle. He had done neither, and he had disappeared. I hadn't liked to press Yardman too hard to find out where Simon had got to because there was always the chance that too energetic spadework would turn up the export bonus fraud, and I had vaguely assumed that it was because of the fraud that Simon had chosen not to come back. But even if he had decided on the spur of the moment to duck out, he would certainly have kept his promise to see Gabriella. Or didn't a resuscitated friendship stretch that far?

'What's the matter?' Gabriella asked.

I explained.

'You are worried about him?'

'He's old enough to decide for himself . . .' But I was remembering like a cold douche that my predecessor Peters hadn't come back from Milan, and before him the liaison man Ballard.

'Tomorrow morning,' she said firmly, 'you will go back to Milan and find him.'

'I can't speak Italian.'

'Undoubtedly you will need an interpreter,' she nodded. 'Me.'

'The best,' I agreed, smiling.

We walked companionably back to the hotel.

'Were the pills all right?' I asked.

'Perfect, thank you very much. I gave them to the wife of our baker ... She works in the bakery normally, but when she gets pregnant she's always sick for months, and can't stand the sight of dough, and he gets bad-tempered because he has to pay a man to help him instead. He is not a good Catholic.' She laughed. 'He makes me an enormous cake oozing with cream when I take the pills.'

No one took the slightest notice of us in the hotel. I went along the empty passage in my dressing-gown and knocked on her door, and she opened it in hers to let me in. I locked it behind me.

'If my sister could see us,' she said smiling, 'she'd have a fit.'

'I'll go away ... if you like.'

'Could you?' She put her arms round my neck.

'Very difficult.'

'I don't ask it.'

I kissed her. 'It would be impossible to go now,' I said.

She sighed happily. 'I absolutely agree. We will just have to make the best of it.'

We did.

We went back to Milan in the morning sitting side by side in the railway carriage and holding hands surreptitiously under her coat, as if by this tiny area of skin contact we could keep alive the total union of the night. I had never wanted to hold hands with anyone before: never realized that it could feel like being plunged into a small electric current, warm, comforting, and vibrant, all at the same time.

Apart from being together, it was a depressing day. No one had seen Simon.

'He couldn't just vanish,' I said in exasperation, standing late in the afternoon in a chilly wind outside the last of the hospitals. We had drawn a blank there as everywhere else, though they had gone to some trouble to make sure for us. No man of his description had been admitted for any illness or treated for any accident during the past ten days.

'Where else can we look?' she said, the tiredness showing in her voice and in the droop of her rounded body. She had been splendid all day, asking questions unendingly from me and translating the replies, calm and businesslike and effective. It wasn't her fault the answers had all been negative. Police, government departments, undertakers, we had tried them all. We had rung up every hotel in Milan and asked for him: he had stayed in none.

'I suppose we could ask the taxi drivers at the airport...' I said finally.

'There are so many... and who would remember one passenger after so long?'

'He had no luggage,' I said as I'd said a dozen times before. 'He didn't know he was coming here until fifteen minutes before he took off. He couldn't have made any plans. He doesn't speak Italian. He hadn't any Italian money. Where did he go? What did he do?'

She shook her head dispiritedly. There was no answer. We took a tram back to the station and with half an hour to wait made a few last enquiries from the station staff. They didn't remember him. It was hopeless.

Over dinner at midnight in the same cafe as the night before we gradually forgot the day's frustration; but the fruitless grind, though it hadn't dug up a trace of Simon, had planted foundations beneath Gabriella and me.

She drooped against me going back to the hotel, and I saw with remorse how exhausted she was. 'I've tired you too much.'

She smiled at the anxiety in my voice. 'You don't realize how much energy you have.'

'Energy?' I repeated in surprise.

'Yes. It must be that.'

'What do you mean?'

'You don't look energetic. You're quiet, and you move like machinery, oiled and smooth. No effort. No jerks. No awkwardness. And inside somewhere is a dynamo. It doesn't run down. I can feel its power. All day I've felt it!'

I laughed. 'You're too fanciful.'

'No, I'm right.'

I shook my head. There were no dynamos ticking away inside me. I was a perfectly ordinary and not too successful man, and the smoothness she saw was only tidiness.

She was already in bed and half asleep when I went along to her room. I locked the door and climbed in beside her, and she made a great effort to wake up for my sake.

'Go to sleep,' I said, kissing her lightly. 'There is always the morning.'

She smiled contentedly and snuggled into my arms, and I lay there cradling her sweet soft body, her head on my chest and her hair against my mouth, and felt almost choked by the intensity with which I wanted to protect her and share with her everything I had. Henry Grey, I thought in surprise in the dark, was suddenly more than halfway down the untried track to honest-to-goodness love.

Sunday morning we strolled aimlessly round the city, talking and looking at the mountains of leather work in the shops in the arcades; Sunday afternoon we went improbably to a football match, an unexpected passion of Gabriella's; and Sunday night we went to bed early because, as she said with her innocent giggle, we would have to be up at six to get her back to start work in the shop on time. But there was something desperate in the way she clung to me during that night, as if it were our last for ever instead of only a week or two, and when I kissed her there were tears on her cheeks.

'Why are you crying?' I said, wiping them away with my fingers. 'Don't cry.'

'I don't know why.' She sniffed, half laughing. 'The world is a sad place. Beauty bursts you. An explosion inside. It can only come out as tears.'

I was impossibly moved. I didn't deserve her tears. I kissed them away in humility and understood why people said love was painful, why Cupid was invented with arrows. Love did pierce the heart, truly.

It wasn't until we were on the early train to Milan the next morning that she said anything about money, and from her hesitation in beginning I saw that she didn't want to offend me.

'I will repay you what you lent me for my bill,' she said matter of factly, but a bit breathlessly. I had pushed the notes into her hand on the way downstairs, as she hadn't wanted me to pay for her publicly, and she hadn't enough with her to do it herself.

'Of course not,' I said.

'It was a much more expensive place than I'd thought of . . .'

'Big hotels ignore you better.'

She laughed. 'All the same . . .'

'No.'

'But you don't earn much. You can't possibly afford it all. The hotel and the train fares, and the dinners.'

'I earned some money winning a race.'

'Enough?'

'I'll win another race . . .' then it will be enough.'

'Giulio doesn't like it that you work with horses.' She laughed. 'He says that if you were good enough to be a jockey you'd do it all the time instead of being a groom.'

'What does Giulio do?'

'He works for the government in the taxation office.'

'Ah,' I said, smiling. 'Would it help if you told him my father has left me some money? Enough to come to see you, anyway, when I get it.'

'I'm not sure I'll tell him. He judges people too much by how much money they've got.'

'Do you want to marry a rich man?'

'Not to please Giulio.'

'To please yourself?'

'Not rich necessarily. But not too poor. I don't want to worry about how to afford shoes for the children.'

I smoothed her fingers with my own.

'I think I will have to learn Italian,' I said.

She gave me the flashing smile. 'Is English very difficult?'

'You can practise on me.'

'If you come back often enough. If your father's money should not be saved for the future.'

'I think,' I said slowly, smiling into her dark eyes, 'that there will be enough left. Enough to buy the children's shoes.'

I went to New York with the horses the following day in the teeth of furious opposition from the family. Several relatives were still staying in the house, including my three sharp tongued eldest sisters, none of whom showed much reserve in airing their views. I sat through a depressing lunch, condemned from all sides. The general opinion was, it seemed, that my unexplained absence over the weekend was disgraceful enough, but that continuing with my job was scandalous. Mother cried hysterical tears and Alice was bitterly reproving.

'Consider your *position*,' they all wailed, more or less in chorus.

I considered my position and left for Yardman's and Gatwick three hours after returning from Milan.

Mother had again brought up the subject of my early marriage to a suitable heiress. I refrained from telling her I was more or less engaged to a comparatively penniless Italian girl who worked in a gift shop, smuggled birth control pills, and couldn't speak English. It wasn't exactly the moment.

The outward trip went without a hitch. Timmie and

Conker were along, together with a pair of grooms with four Anglia Bloodstock horses, and in consequence the work went quickly and easily. We were held up for thirty-six hours in New York by an engine fault, and when I rang up Yardman to report our safe return on the Friday morning he asked me to stay at Gatwick, as another bunch of brood mares was to leave that afternoon.

'Where for?'

'New York again,' he said briskly. 'I'll come down with the papers myself, early in the afternoon. You can send Timms and Chestnut home. I'm bringing Billy and two others to replace them.'

'Mr Yardman . . .' I said.

'Yes?'

'If Billy tries to pick a fight, or molests me at all on the way, my employment with you ceases the instant we touch down in New York, and I will not help unload the horses or accept any responsibility for them.'

There was a short shocked silence. He couldn't afford to have me do what I threatened, in the present sticky state of the business.

'My dear boy . . .' he protested sighing. 'I don't want you to have troubles. I'll speak to Billy. He's a thoughtless boy. I'll tell him not everyone is happy about his little practical jokes.'

'I'd appreciate it,' I said with irony at his view of Billy's behaviour.

Whatever Yardman said to him worked. Billy was

sullen, unhelpful, and calculatingly offensive, but for once I completed a return trip with him without a bruise to show for it.

On the way over I sat for a time on a hay bale beside Alf and asked him about Simon's last trip to Milan. It was hard going, as the old man's deafness was as impenetrable as seven eighths cloud.

'Mr Searle,' I shouted. 'Did he say where he was going?'

'Eh?'

After about ten shots the message got through, and he nodded.

'He came to Milan with us.'

'That's right, Alf. Where did he go then?'

'Eh?'

'Where did he go then?'

'I don't rightly know,' he said. 'He didn't come back.'

'Did he *say* where he was going?'

'Eh?'

I yelled again.

'No. He didn't say. Perhaps he told Billy. He was talking to Billy, see?'

I saw. I also saw that it was no use my ever asking Billy anything about anything. Yardman would have asked him, anyway, so if Simon had told Billy where he was going Yardman would have known. Unless, of course, Simon had asked Billy not to tell, and he hadn't. But Simon didn't like Billy and would never trust him with a secret.

'Where did Mr Searle go, when you left the plane?'

I was getting hoarse before he answered.

'I don't know where he went. He was with Billy and the others. I went across on my own, like, to get a beer. Billy said they were just coming. But they never came.'

'None of them came?'

There had been the two grooms from the stud beside Simon and Billy, on that trip.

Eventually Alf shook his head. 'I finished my beer and went back to the plane. There was no one there as I ate my lunch.'

I left it at that because my throat couldn't stand any more.

Coming back we were joined by some extra help in the shape of a large pallid man who didn't know what to do with his hands and kept rubbing them over the wings of his jodhpurs as if he expected to find pockets there. He was ostensibly accompanying a two-year-old, but I guessed tolerantly he was some relation of the owner or trainer travelling like that to avoid a trans-atlantic fare. I didn't get around to checking on it, because the double journey had been very tiring, and I slept soundly nearly all the way back. Alf had to shake me awake as we approached Gatwick. Yawning, I set about the unloading – it was by then well into Sunday morning – and still feeling unusually tired, drove home afterwards in a bee line to bed. A letter from Gabriella stopped me in the hall, and I went slowly upstairs reading it.

She had, she said, asked every single taxi driver and all the airport bus drivers if they had taken anywhere a big fat Englishman who couldn't speak Italian, had no luggage, and was wearing a green corduroy jacket. None of them could remember anyone like that. Also, she said, she had checked with the car hire firms which had agencies at the airport, but none of them had dealt with Simon. She had checked with all the airlines' passenger lists for the day he went to Milan, and the days after: he had not flown off to anywhere.

I lay in a hot bath and thought about whether I should go on trying to find him. Bringing in any professional help, even private detectives, would only set them searching in England for a reason for his disappearance, and they'd all too soon dig it up. A warrant out for his arrest was not what I wanted. It would effectively stop him coming back at all. Very likely he didn't want to be found in the first place, or he wouldn't have disappeared so thoroughly, or stayed away so long. But supposing something had happened to him ... though what, I couldn't imagine. And I wouldn't have thought anything could have happened at all were it not for Peters and Ballard.

There were Simon's partners in the fraud. His cousin, and the man in France. Perhaps I could ask them if they had heard from him ... I couldn't ask them, I thought confusedly: I didn't know their names. Simon had an elderly aunt somewhere, but I didn't know her name either ... the whole thing was too much ... and I was going to sleep in the bath.

I went to the wharf building the next morning at nine thirty to collect my previous week's pay and see what was on the schedule for the future. True to his word, Yardman had arranged no air trips for the following three days of Cheltenham races. There was a big question mark beside a trip for six circus horses for Spain that same afternoon, but no question mark, I was glad to see, about a flight to Milan with brood mares on Friday.

Yardman, when I went down to see him, said the circus horses were postponed until the following Monday owing to their trainer having read in his stars that it was a bad week to travel. Yardman was disgusted. Astrology was bad for business.

'Milan on Friday, now,' he said, sliding a pencil to and fro through his fingers. 'I might come on that trip myself, if I can get away. It's most awkward, with Searle's work to be done. I've advertised for someone to fill his place ... anyway, as I was saying, if I can get away I think I'd better go and see our opposite numbers out there. It always pays you know, my dear boy. I go to all the countries we export to. About once a year. Keeps us in touch, you know.'

I nodded. Good for business, no doubt.

'Will you ask them ... our opposite numbers ... if they saw Simon Searle any time after he landed?'

He looked surprised, the taut skin stretched over his jaw.

'I could, yes. But I shouldn't think he told them where he was going, if he didn't have the courtesy to tell me.'

'It's only an outside chance,' I agreed.

'I'll ask, though.' He nodded. 'I'll certainly ask.'

I went upstairs again to Simon's room, shut his door, sat in his chair, and looked out of his window. His room, directly over Yardman's, had the same panoramic view of the river, from a higher angle. I would-like to live there, I thought idly. I liked the shipping, the noise of the docks, the smell of the river, the coming and going. Quite simply, I supposed, I liked the business of transport.

The Finnish ship had gone from the berth opposite and another small freighter had taken her place. A limp flag swung fitfully at her mast head, red and white horizontal stripes with a navy blue triangle and a white star. I looked across at the nationality chart on Simon's wall. Puerto Rico. Well, well, one lived and learned. Three alphabetical flags lower down, when checked, proved to be E, Q and M. Mildly curious, I turned them up in the international code of signals. 'I am delivering.' Quite right and proper. I shut the book, twiddled my thumbs, watched a police launch swoop past doing twenty knots on the ebb, and reflected not for the first time that the London river was a fast rough waterway for small boats.

After a while I picked up the telephone and rang up Fenland to book a place for Sunday.

'Two o'clock?'

'That'll do me fine,' I said. 'Thanks.'

'Wait a minute, Harry. Mr Wells said if you rang that he wanted a word with you.'

'OK.'

There were some clicks, and then Tom's voice.

'Harry? Look, for God's sake, what is this job of yours?'

'I work for . . . a travel agency.'

'Well, what's so special about it? Come here, and I'll pay you more.' He sounded worried and agitated, not casually inviting as before.

'What's up?' I said.

'Everything's up except my planes. I've landed an excellent contract with a car firm in Coventry ferrying their executives, technicians, salesmen and so on all round the shop. They've a factory in Lancashire and tie-ups all over Europe, and they're fed up with the airfield they've been using. They're sending me three planes. I'm to maintain them, provide pilots and have them ready when wanted.'

'Sounds good,' I said. 'So what's wrong?'

'So I don't want to lose them again before I've started. And not only can I not find any out-of-work pilots worth considering, but one of my three regulars went on a ski-ing holiday last week and broke his leg, the silly bastard. So how about it?'

'It's not as easy as you make it sound,' I said reluctantly.

'What's stopping you?'

'A lot of things . . . if you'll be around on Sunday, anyway, we could talk it over.'

He sighed in exasperation. 'The planes are due here at the end of the month, in just over a fortnight.'

'Get someone else, if you can,' I said.

'Yeah . . . if I can.' He was depressed. 'And if I can't?'

'I don't know. I could do a day a week to help out, but even then . . .'

'Even then, what?'

'There are difficulties.'

'Nothing to mine, Harry. Nothing to mine. I'll break you down on Sunday.'

Everyone had troubles, even with success. The higher the tougher, it seemed. I wiggled the button, and asked for another number, the charter airline which Patrick worked for. The Gatwick office answered, and I asked them if they could tell me how to get hold of him.

'You're in luck. He's actually here, in the office. Who's speaking?'

'Henry Grey, from Yardman Transport.'

I waited, and he came on the line.

'Hullo . . . how's things? How's Gabriella?'

'She,' I said, 'is fine. Other things are not. Could you do me a favour?'

'Shoot.'

'Could you look up for me the name of the pilot who flew a load of horses to Milan for us a fortnight last Thursday? Also the names of the co-pilot and engineer, and could you also tell me how or when I could talk to one or all of them?'

'Trouble?'

'Oh, no trouble for your firm, none at all. But one of our men went over on that trip and didn't come back, and hasn't got in touch with us since. I just wanted to find out if the crew had any idea what became of him. He might have told one of them where he was going . . . anyway, his work is piling up here and we want to find out if he intends to come back.'

'I see. Hang on then. A fortnight last Thursday?'

'That's it.'

He was away several minutes. The cranes got busy on the freighter from Puerto Rico. I yawned.

'Henry? I've got them. The pilot was John Kyle, co-pilot G. L. Rawlings, engineer V. N. Brede. They're not here, though; they've just gone to Arabia, ferrying mountains of luggage from London after some oil chieftain's visit. He brought about six wives, and they all went shopping.'

'Wow,' I said. 'When do they get back?'

He consulted someone in the background.

'Sometime Wednesday. They have Thursday off, then another trip to Arabia on Friday.'

'Some shopping,' I said gloomily. 'I can't get to see them on Wednesday or Thursday. I'm racing at Cheltenham. But I could ring them up on Wednesday night, if you can give me their numbers.'

'Well . . .' said Patrick slowly. 'John Kyle likes his flutter on the horses.'

'You don't think he'd come to Cheltenham, then?'

'He certainly might, if he isn't doing anything else.'

'I'll get him a member's badge, and the others too, if they'd like.'

'Fair enough. Let's see. I'm going to Holland twice tomorrow. I should think I could see them on Wednesday, if we all get back reasonably on schedule. I'll tell them what you want, and ring you. If they go to Cheltenham you'll see them, and if not you can ring them. How's that?'

'Marvellous. You'll find me at the Queen's Hotel at Cheltenham. I'll be staying there.'

'Right . . . and oh, by the way, I see I'm down for a horse transport flight on Friday to Milan. Is that your mob, or not?'

'Our mob,' I agreed. 'What's left of it.'

We rang off, and I leaned back in Simon's chair, pensively biting my thumbnail and surveying the things on his desk: telephone, tray of pens, blank notepad, and a pot of paper clips and pins. Nothing of any help. Then slowly, methodically, I searched through the drawers. They were predictably packed with export forms of various sorts, but he had taken little of a personal nature to work. Some indigestion tablets, a screwdriver, a pair of green socks, and a plastic box labelled 'spare keys'. That was the lot. No letters, no bills, no private papers of any sort.

I opened the box of keys. There were about twenty or more, the silt of years. Suitcase keys, a heavy old iron key, car keys. I stirred them up with my finger. A Yale key. I picked it out and looked at it. It was a duplicate, cut for a few shillings from a blank, and had no number. The metal had been dulled by time, but not smoothed, from use. I tapped it speculatively on the edge of the desk, thinking that anyway there would be no harm in trying.

CHAPTER NINE

Simon's home address, obtained off his insurance card via the dim typist, proved to be located in a dingy block of flats in the outer reaches of St John's Wood. The grass on patchy lawns had remained uncut from about the previous August, which gave the graceless building a mournful look of having been thoughtlessly dumped in a hayfield. I walked through spotted glass entrance doors, up an uninspiring staircase, met no one, and came to a halt outside number fifteen in white two-penny plastic letters screwed on to cheap green painted deal.

The Yale key slid raspingly into the lock as if it had never been there before, but it turned under my pressure and opened the door. There was a haphazard foot-high pile of newspapers and magazines just inside. When I pushed the door against them they slithered away, and I stepped in and round them, and shut the door behind me.

The flat consisted only of a tiny entrance hall, a small bedroom, poky kitchen and bathroom and a slightly larger sitting-room. The prevailing colour was maroon, which I found depressing, and the furniture looked as if it had been bought piece by piece from second-class second-hand shops. The total effect could have been harmonious, but it wasn't: not so much through lack of taste as lack of imagination. He had spent the minimum of trouble on his surroundings, and the result was gloomy. Cold dead air and a smell of mustiness seeped up my nose. There were unwashed, mould-growing dishes on the draining board in the kitchen, and crumpled thrown-back bedclothes on the bed. He had left his shaving water in the washbasin and the scum had dried into a hard grey line round the edge. Poor Simon, I thought forlornly, what an existence. No wife, no warmth: no wonder he liked pubs.

One wall in the sitting-room was lined with book-cases, and the newest, most obviously luxurious object in the flat was a big stereophonic radiogram standing behind the door. No television. No pictures on the dull coffee walls. Not a man of visual pleasures. Beside a large battered armchair, handy to perpetual reach, stood a wooden crate of bottled beer.

Wandering round his flat I realized what a fearful comment it was on myself that I had never been there before. The big tolerant dishonest man I would have counted my only friend, yet I'd never seen where he lived. Never been asked; never thought of asking him to my own home. Even where I had wanted friendship, I hadn't known how to try. I felt as cold inside as

Simon's flat, as uninhabited. Gabriella seemed very far away.

I picked up the heap of papers inside the front door and carried them into the sitting-room. Sorted into piles, they consisted of sixteen dailies, three Sundays, three *Horse and Hounds*, three *Sporting Life* weeklies and one *Stud and Stable*. Several letters in brown unstuck envelopes looked unpromising, and with very little hesitation I opened all the rest. There were none from France, and none from the accomplice cousin. The only one of any help was written in spiky black hand on dark blue paper. It began 'Dear Simon,' thanked him for a birthday present, and was signed 'your loving aunt Edna'. The handwritten address at the top said 3 Gordon Cottages, East Road, Potter's Green, Berks, and there was no telephone number.

There was no desk as such in his flat. He kept his bills and papers clipped into labelled categories in the top drawer of a scratched chest in his bedroom, but if his cousin's name and address was among them, I couldn't recognize them. Alongside the papers lay a *Horse and Hound* rolled tightly into a tube and bound with wide brown sticky paper, ready to be posted. I picked it up and turned it round in my hands. It bore no address. The thick layers of brown sticky paper were tough, and even though I was careful with my penknife it looked as though a tiger had been chewing it when I finally hacked my way through. The magazine unrolled reluctantly, and I picked it up and shook it. Nothing happened. It wasn't until one looked at it page by page that the money showed, five-pound notes stuck on with sellotape. They were used notes, not new and there were sixty of them. I rolled the *Horse and Hound* up again and laid it back in the drawer, seeing a vivid mental picture, as I picked up the brown pieces of gummed strips and put them in the wastebasket, of Simon listening to his radiogram and sticking his money into journals, night after night, an endless job, working for his old age.

Potter's Green turned out to be a large village spreading out into tentacles of development around the edges. East Road was a new one, and Gordon Cottages proved to be one of several identical strips of council-built bungalows for old people. Number three like all the rest still looked clean and fresh, with nothing growing yet in the bathmat sized flower bed under the front window. There was bright yellow paint clashing with pale pink curtains and a bottle of milk standing on the concrete doorstep.

I rang the bell. The pink curtains twitched, and I turned my head to see myself being inspected by a pair of mournful, faded eyes set in a large pale face. She flapped a hand at me in a dismissing movement, shooing me away, so I put my finger on the bell and rang again.

I heard her come round to the other side of the door.

'Go away,' she said. 'I don't want anything.'

'I'm not selling,' I said through the letter-box. 'I'm a friend of Simon's, your nephew Simon Searle.'

'Who are you? I don't know you.'

'Henry Grey ... I work with Simon at Yardman's. Could I please talk to you inside, it's very difficult like this, and your neighbours will wonder what's going on.' There were in truth several heads at the front windows already, and it had its effect. She opened the door and beckoned me in.

The tiny house was crammed with the furniture she must have brought with her from a much larger place, and every available surface was covered with useless mass-produced ornaments. The nearest to me as I stood just inside the doorway was a black box decorated with 'A present from Brighton' in shells. And next to that a china donkey bore panniers of dried everlasting flowers. Pictures of all sorts crowded the walls, interspersed by several proverbs done in poker-work on wood. 'Waste not, Want not' caught my eye, and farther round there was 'Take care of the pence and the pounds will take care of you'; an improvement on the original.

Simon's stout aunt had creaking corsets and wheezing breath and smelled of mentholated cough pastilles. 'Simon isn't here, you know. He lives in London, not here.'

'I know, yes.' Hesitatingly, I told her about Simon

170

going away and not coming back. 'I wondered,' I finished, 'if by any chance he has written to you. Sent you a picture postcard. That sort of thing.'

'He will do. He's sure to.' She nodded several times. 'He always does, and brings me a little souvenir when he's been away. Very considerate is Simon.'

'But you haven't had a postcard yet.'

'Not yet. Soon, I expect.'

'If you do, would you write to me and let me know? You see, he hasn't said when he'll be back, and Mr Yardman is advertising for someone to fill his job.'

'Oh, dear.' She was troubled. 'I hope nothing has happened to him.'

'I don't expect so; but if you hear from him, you will let us know?'

'Yes, yes, of course. Dear oh dear, I wonder what he is up to.'

Her choice of phrase reminded me of what in fact he was up to, and I asked her if she knew Simon's cousin's name and address. Unhesitatingly she reeled it off. 'He's my poor dead sister's son,' she said. 'But a surly man. I don't get on with him at all. Not easy, like Simon, now. Simon stayed with me a lot when he was little, when I kept the village shop. He never forgets my birthday, and always brings me nice little mementoes like these.' She looked proudly round her overflowing possessions. 'Simon's very kind. I've only my old age pension, you know, and a little bit put by, and Simon's the only one who bothers with me much. Oh,

I've got my two daughters, of course, but one's married in Canada and the other's got enough troubles on her own. Simon's given me a hundred pounds for my birthday every year for the last three years; what do you think of that?'

'Absolutely splendid.' A hundred pounds of tax payers' money. Robin Hood stuff. Oh well.

'You'll let me know, then,' I said, turning to go. She nodded, creaking as she moved round me to open the street door. Facing me in the little hall hung more time-worn poker-work. 'See a pin and pick it up, all the day you'll have good luck. See a pin and let it lie, you will want before you die.' So there, I thought, smiling to myself, was the origin of Simon's pin tidying habit, a proverb stretching back to childhood. He didn't intend to want before he died.

The accomplice cousin farmed in Essex, reasonably handy for Cambridge airport, but a long haul for Gatwick. It was evident at once, however, that I could expect no easy help from him.

'You,' he said forcefully, 'you're the interfering bastard who's fouled up the works, aren't you? Well you can damn well clear off, that's what you can do. It's no business of yours where Simon's gone and in future you keep your bloody nose out of things that don't concern you.'

'If,' I said mildly, 'you prefer me to ask the police to find him, I will.'

He looked ready to explode, a large red faced man

in khaki clothes and huge gum boots, standing four square in a muddy yard. He struggled visibly between the pleasure of telling me to go to hell and fear of the consequences if he did so. Prudence just won.

'All right. All right. I don't know where he is and that's straight. He didn't tell me he was going, and I don't know when he's coming back.'

Depressed, I drove home to Bedfordshire. The bulk and grandeur of the great house lay there waiting as I rolled slowly up the long drive. History in stone; the soul of the Creggans. Earl upon earl had lived there right back to the pirate who brought Spanish gold to Queen Bess, and since my father died I had only to enter to feel the chains fall heavily on me like a net. I stopped in the sweep of gravel in front instead of driving round to the garages as usual, and looked at what I had inherited. There was beauty, I admitted, in the great façade with its pillars and pediments and the two wide flights of steps sweeping up to meet at the door. The Georgian Palladian architect who had grafted a whole new mansion on to the Elizabethan and Stuart one already existing had produced a curiously satisfactory result, and as a Victorian incumbent had luckily confined his Gothic urges to a ruined folly in the garden, the only late addition had been a square red-bricked block of Edwardian plumbing. But for all its splendid outer show it had those beetles in the roof, miles of draughty passages, kitchens in the basement, and twenty bedrooms mouldering into dust. Only a multi-millionaire could maintain and fill such a place now with servants and guests, whereas after death duties I would be hard put to it to find a case of champagne once the useless pile had voraciously gulped what it cost just to keep standing.

Opening it to the public might have been a solution if I had been any sort of a showman. But to someone solitary by nature that way meant a lifetime of horrifying square-peggery. Slavery to a building. Another human sacrifice on the altar of tradition. I simply couldn't face it. The very idea made me wilt.

Since it was unlikely anyone would simply let me pull the whole thing down, the National Trust, I thought, was the only hope. They could organize the sight-seeing to their heart's content and they might let Mother live there for the rest of her life, which she needed.

Mother usually used the front entrance while Alice and I drove on and went in through one of the doors at the side, near the garages. That early evening, however, I left my little car on the gravel and walked slowly up the shallow steps. At the top I leaned against the balustrade and looked back over the calm wide fields and bare branched trees just swelling into bud. I didn't really own all this, I thought. It was like the baton in a relay race, passed on from one, to be passed on to the next, belonging to none for more than a lap. Well, I wasn't going to pass it on. I was the last runner. I would escape from the track at a tangent and give the baton away. My son, if I ever had one, would have to lump it.

I pushed open the heavy front door and stepped into the dusk-filled house. I, Henry Grey, descendant of the sea pirate, of warriors and explorers and empire builders and of a father who'd been decorated for valour on the Somme, I, the least of them, was to bring their way of life to an end. I felt one deep protesting pang for their sakes, and that was all. If they had anything of themselves to pass on to me, it was already in my genes. I carried their inheritance in my body, and I didn't need their house.

Not only did John Kyle and his engineer come to Cheltenham, but Patrick as well.

'I've never been before,' he said, his yellow eyes and auburn hair shining as he stood in the bright March sun. 'These two are addicts. I just came along for the ride.'

'I'm glad you did,' I said, shaking hands with the other two. John Kyle was a bulky battered looking young man going prematurely thin on top. His engineer, tall and older, had three racing papers and a form sheet tucked under his arm.

'I see,' he said, glancing down at them, 'th . . . that you won the United Hunts Ch . . . Challenge Cup yesterday.' He managed his stutter unselfconsciously. 'W . . . w . . . well done.'

'Thank you,' I said. 'I was a bit lucky. I wouldn't have won if Century hadn't fallen at the last.'

'It d . . . d . . . does say that, in the p . . . p . . . paper,' he agreed disarmingly.

Patrick laughed and said, 'What are you riding in today?'

'The Gold Cup and the Mildmay of Flete Challenge Cup.'

'Clobber and Boathook,' said John Kyle readily.

'I'll back you,' Patrick said.

'M . . . m . . . money down the drain b . . . backing Clobber,' said the engineer seriously.

'Thanks very much,' I said with irony.

'F . . . form's all haywire. V . . . v . . . very inconsistent,' he explained.

'Do you think you've got a chance?' Patrick asked.

'No, not much. I've never ridden him before. The owner's son usually rides him, but he's got jaundice.'

'N . . . not a b . . . betting proposition,' nodded the engineer.

'For God's sake don't be so depressing, man,' protested Kyle.

'How about Boathook?' I asked, smiling.

The engineer consulted the sky. The result wasn't written there, as far as I could see.

'B . . . B . . . Boathook,' he remarked, coming back to earth, 'm . . . m . . . might just do it. G . . . good for a p . . . place anyway.'

'I shall back both, just the same,' said Patrick firmly.

I took them all to lunch and sat with them while they ate.

'Aren't you having any?' said Patrick.

'No. It makes you sick if you fall after eating.'

'How often do you fall, then?' asked Kyle curiously, cutting into his cold red beef.

'On average, once in a dozen rides, I suppose. It varies. I've never really counted.'

'When did you fall last?'

'Day before yesterday.'

'Doesn't it bother you?' asked Patrick, shaking salt. 'The prospect of falling?'

'Well, no. You never think you're going to, for a start. And a lot of falls are easy ones; you only get a bruise, if that. Sometimes when the horse goes right down you almost step off.'

'And sometimes you break your bones,' Kyle said dryly.

I shook my head. 'Not often.'

Patrick laughed. I passed him the butter for his roll, looked at my watch, and said, 'I'll have to go and change soon. Do you think we could talk about the day you took Simon Searle to Milan?'

'Shoot,' said Kyle. 'What do you want to know?'

'Everything you can think of that happened on the way there and after you landed.'

'I don't suppose I'll be much help,' he said apologetically. 'I was in the cockpit most of the time, and I hardly spoke to him at all. I went aft to the karzy once, and he was sitting in one of those three pairs of seats that were bolted on at the back.'

I nodded. I'd bolted the seats on to the anchorage myself, after we had loaded all the horses. There was usually room for a few seats, and they made a change from hay bales.

'Was he alone?'

'No, there was a young fellow beside him. Your friend Searle was on the inside by the window, I remember, because this young chap had his legs sprawled out in the gangway and I had to step over them. He didn't move.'

'Billy,' I nodded.

'After I came out I asked them if they were OK and said we'd be landing in half an hour. The young one said "Thanks, Dad," as if he was bored to death, and I had to step over his legs again to get past. I can't say I took to him enormously.'

'You surprise me,' I said sardonically. 'Did Simon say anything?'

He hesitated. 'It's three weeks ago. I honestly can't remember, but I don't think so. Nothing special, anyway.'

I turned to the engineer. 'How about you?'

He chewed, shook his head, swallowed, and took a sip of beer.

'D . . . d . . . don't think I'm much better. I w . . . w . . . was talking to him q . . . q . . . quite a lot at the beginning. In the g . . . g . . . galley. He said he'd come

178

at the l . . . l . . . last minute instead of you. He t . . . t . . . talked about you quite a lot.'

The engineer took a mouthful of salad and stuttered through it without embarrassment. A direct man, secure in himself. 'He s . . . said you were ice on a v . . . volcano. I said th . . . th . . . that didn't make sense, and he said it w . . . was the only w . . . way to describe you.'

Without looking up from his plate Patrick murmured, 'In a nutshell.'

'That's no help at all,' I said, disregarding him. 'Didn't he say anything about where he was going, or what he might do, when you got to Milan?'

The engineer shook his head. 'He m . . . m . . . meant to come straight back with us, in the afternoon, I'm sure of th . . . th . . . that.'

'We didn't come straight back, of course,' said Kyle matter-of-factly.

'You didn't?' I was surprised. 'I didn't know that.'

'We were supposed to. They got the return load of horses loaded up and then discovered there were no papers for one of the two they'd put in first. They had to get the whole lot out again, and they weren't very quick because there were only two of them, and by that time I said it was pointless loading again, as it would be too late to start, I'd be out of hours.'

'They should have checked they had all the papers before they loaded,' I said.

'Well, they didn't.'

'Only two of them,' I said, frowning.

'That's right. The young one – Billy, did you say? – and one other. Not your friend Simon. A deaf old fellow.'

'Alf,' I said. 'That's Alf. What about the two others who went over? They were two specials going with horses from the studs they worked in.'

'From what I could make out from the old man, those two were going on with their horses right to their destination, somewhere farther south.'

I thought it over. Simon obviously hadn't intended to come back at all, and it hadn't been the unexpected overnight stop which had given him the idea.

'You didn't see where Simon was headed, I suppose, when you got to Milan?' I spoke without much hope, and they both shook their heads.

'We got off the plane before him,' Kyle said.

I nodded. The crew didn't have Customs and unloading to see to.

'Well . . . that's that. Thank you for coming today, anyway. And thank you,' I said directly to the engineer, 'for delivering that bottle of pills to the girl in the souvenir shop.'

'P . . . pills? Oh yes, I remember.' He was surprised. 'How on earth d . . . d . . . did you know about that?'

'She told me a tall crew member brought them over for her.'

'I f . . . f . . . found them on the plane, standing on the w . . . w . . . washbasin in the k . . . k . . . karzy. I th . . . th . . . thought I might as well give them to her, as I was g . . . going across anyway. I did . . . didn't see how they got there, b . . . b . . . but they had her name on them.'

'Simon was taking them to her from me,' I explained.

'Oh, I s . . . see.'

Patrick said, grinning, 'Were they . . .?'

'Yes, they were.'

'He didn't go over to the airport building at all, then,' said Patrick flatly. 'He left the pills on board, hoping they would get to Gabriella somehow, and scooted from there.'

'It looks like it,' I agreed gloomily.

'You can get off that end of the airfield quite easily, of course. It's only that scrubland and bushes, and if you walk down that road leading away from the unloading area, the one the horseboxes often use, you're off the place in no time. I should think that explains pretty well why no one saw him.'

'Yes,' I sighed, 'that's what he must have done.'

'But it doesn't explain why he went,' said Patrick gently.

There was a pause.

'He had . . . troubles,' I said at last.

'*In* trouble?' said Kyle.

'Looming. It might be because of something I discovered, that he went. I wanted to find him, and tell him it was . . . safe . . . to come back.'

'On your conscience,' said Patrick.

'You might say so.'

They all nodded, acknowledging their final under-standing of my concern for a lost colleague. The waiter brought their cheese and asked whether they would like coffee. I stood up.

'I'll see you again,' I said. 'How about after the fifth, outside the weighing room? After I've changed.'

'Sure thing,' said Patrick.

I ambled off to the weighing room and later got dressed in Mr Thackery's red and blue colours. I'd never ridden in the Gold Cup before, and although I privately agreed with the engineer's assessment of the situation, there was still something remarkably stirring in going out in the best class race of the season. My human opponents were all handpicked professionals and all Clobber's bunch looked to have the beating of him, but nevertheless my mouth grew dry and my heart thumped.

I suspected Mr Thackery had entered Clobber more for the prestige of having a Gold Cup runner than from any thought that he would win, and his manner in the parade ring confirmed it. He was enjoying himself enormously, untouched by the sort of anxious excitement characteristic of the hopeful.

'Julian's regards,' he said, beaming and shaking hands vigorously. 'He'll be watching on TV.'

TV. There was always the fair chance that one of the people I knew at Fenland might be watching television, though none that I'd heard of was interested in racing. I turned my back on the cameras, as usual.

'Just don't disgrace me,' said Mr Thackery happily. 'Don't disgrace me, that's all I ask.'

'You could have got a professional,' I pointed out.

'Oh, eh, I could. But frankly, it hasn't done me any harm, here and there, for folks to know you're riding my horses.'

'A mutually satisfactory arrangement, then,' I said dryly.

'Yes,' said Mr Thackery contentedly. 'That's about it.'

I swung up on his horse, walked out in the parade, and cantered down to the start. Clobber, an eight-year-old thoroughbred chestnut hunter, had only once won (thanks to being low in the handicap) in the company he was taking on now at level weights, but he shone with condition and his step was bursting with good feeling. Like so many horses, he responded well to spring air and sun on his back and my own spirits lifted with his. It was not, after all, going to be a fiasco.

We lined up and the tapes went up, and Clobber set off to the first fence pulling like a train. As he hadn't a snowball's hope in hell of winning, I thought Mr Thackery might as well enjoy a few moments in the limelight, and I let Clobber surge his way to the front. Once he got there he settled down and stopped trying to run away with me and we stayed there, surprisingly leading the distinguished field for over two and a half of the three and a quarter miles.

Clobber had never been run in front before, according to the form book, but from his willingness it was evidently to his liking. Holding him up against his inclination, I thought, probably accounted for his inconsistency: he must have lost interest on many occasions when thwarted, and simply packed up trying.

The others came up to him fast and hard going into the second last fence, and three went ahead before the last; but Clobber jumped it cleanly and attacked the hill with his ears still pricked good temperedly, and he finished fourth out of eight with some good ones still behind him. I was pleased with the result myself, having thoroughly enjoyed the whole race, and so it appeared was Mr Thackery.

'By damn,' he said, beaming, 'that's the best he's ever run.'

'He likes it in front.'

'So it seems, yes. We've not tried that before, I must say.'

A large bunch of congratulating females advanced on him and I rolled the girths round my saddle and escaped to the weighing room to change for the next race. The colours were those of Old Strawberry Leaves, who had commented sourly that it was disgraceful of me to ride in public only three weeks after my father's death, but had luckily agreed not to remove me from his horse. The truth was he begrudged paying professionals when he could bully the sons of his friends and acquaintances for nothing. Boathook was his best horse, and for the pleasure of winning on him I could easily put up with the insults I got from losing on the others. On that day, however, there was one too good for him from Ireland, and for being beaten by half a length I got the customary bawling out. Not a good loser by any means, Old Strawberry Leaves.

All in all I'd had a good Cheltenham, I thought, as I changed into street clothes: a winner, a second, an also ran, one harmless fall, and fourth in the Gold Cup. I wouldn't improve on it very easily.

Patrick and the other two were waiting for me outside, and after we'd watched the last race together, I drove them down to the station to catch the last train to London. They had all made a mint out of the engineer's tips and were in a fine collective state of euphoria.

'I can see why you like it,' Patrick said on the way. 'It's a magnificent sport. I'll come again.'

'Good,' I said, stopping at the station to let them out. 'I'll see you tomorrow, then.'

He grinned. 'Milan first stop.'

'Arabia again for us,' said Kyle, resignedly, shutting the door.

They waved their thanks and began to walk away into the station. An elderly man tottered across in front of my car, and as I was waiting for him to pass the engineer's voice floated back to me, clear and unmistakable.

'It's f . . . funny,' he said, 'you qu . . . quite forget he's a l . . . lord.'

I turned my head round to them, startled. Patrick

looked over his shoulder and saw that I had heard, and laughed. I grinned sardonically in return, and drove off reflecting that I was much in favour of people like him who could let me forget it too.

CHAPTER TEN

Fire can't burn without air. Deprived of an oxygen supply in a sealed space, it goes out. There existed a state of affairs like a smouldering room which had been shuttered and left to cool down in safety. Nothing much would have happened if I hadn't been trying to find Simon; but when I finally came on a trace of him, it was like throwing wide the door. Fresh air poured in and the whole thing banged into flames.

The fine Cheltenham weather was still in operation on the Friday, the day after the Gold Cup. The met. reports in the charter company's office showed clear skies right across Europe, with an extended high pressure area almost stationary over France. No break up of the system was expected for at least twenty-four hours. Someone tapped me on the shoulder and I half turned to find Patrick reading over my shoulder.

'Trouble free trip,' he commented with satisfaction. 'Piece of cake.'

'We've got that old DC4 again, I see,' I said, looking

out of the window across to where it stood on the tarmac.

'Nice reliable old bus.'

'Bloody uncomfortable old bus.'

Patrick grinned. 'You'll be joining a union next.'

'Workers unite,' I agreed.

He looked me up and down. 'Some worker. You remind me of Fanny Craddock.'

'Of *who*?' I said.

'That woman on television who cooks in a ball gown without marking it.'

'Oh.' I looked down at my neat charcoal worsted, my black tie, and the fraction of white showing at the cuffs. Beside me, in the small overnight bag I now carried everywhere, was the high necked black jersey I worked in, and a hanger for my jacket. Tidiness was addictive: one couldn't kick it, even when it was inappropriate.

'You're no slouch yourself,' I pointed out defensively. He wore his navy gold-braided uniform with the air of authority, his handsome good natured face radiating confidence. A wonderful bedside manner for nervous passengers, I thought. An inborn conviction that one only had to keep to the rules for everything to be all right. Fatal.

'Eight each way, today?' he said.

'Eight out, four back. All brood mares.'

'Ready to drop?'

'Let's hope not too ready.'

'Let's indeed.' He grinned and turned away to check over his flight plan with one of the office staff. 'I suppose,' he said over his shoulder, 'you'd like me to organize an overnight delay at Milan?'

'You suppose correctly.'

'You could do it yourself.'

'How?'

'Load up all the horses and then "lose" the papers for a front one. Like John Kyle said, by the time they'd unloaded and reloaded, it was too late to take off.'

I laughed. 'An absolutely brilliant idea. I shall act on it immediately.'

'That'll be the day.' He smiled over his papers, checking the lists.

The door opened briskly and Yardman came in, letting a blast of cold six-thirty air slip past him.

'All set?' he said, impressing on us his early hour alertness.

'The horses haven't arrived yet,' I said mildly. 'They're late again.'

'Oh.' He shut the door behind him and came in, putting down his briefcase and rubbing his thin hands together for warmth. 'They were due at six.' He frowned and looked at Patrick. 'Are you the pilot?'

'That's right.'

'What sort of trip are we going to have?'

'Easy,' said Patrick. 'The weather's perfect.'

Yardman nodded in satisfaction. 'Good, good.' He pulled out a chair and sat down, lifting and opening his brief case. He had brought all the brood mares' papers with him, and as he seemed content to check them with the airline people himself. I leaned lazily against the office wall and thought about Gabriella. The office work went steadily on, regardless of the hour. No nine-to-five about an airline. As usual, some of the flying staff were lying there fast asleep, one on a canvas bed under the counter Patrick was leaning on, another underneath the big table where Yardman sat, and a third on my right, stretched along the top of a row of cupboards. They were all wrapped in blankets, heads and all, and were so motionless that one didn't notice them at first. They managed to sleep solidly through the comings and goings and telephoning and typing, and even when Yardman inadvertently kicked the one under the table he didn't stir.

The first of the horseboxes rolled past the window and drove across to the waiting plane. I peeled myself off the wall, temporarily banished Gabriella, and touched Yardman's arm.

'They're here,' I said.

He looked round and glanced through the window. 'Ah, yes. Well here you are, my dear boy, here's the list. You can load the first six, they are all checked. There's just one more to do . . . it seems there's some query of insurance on this one . . .' He bent back to his work, rifling through his briefcase for more papers.

I took the list and walked across to the plane. I had expected Timmie and Conker to arrive in a horsebox as they lived near the stud one lot of horses had come from, but when I got over there I found it was to be Billy and Alf again. They had come with Yardman, and were already sitting on the stacked box sides in the plane, eating sandwiches. With them sat a third man in jodhpurs and a grubby tweed jacket a size too small. He was wearing an old greenish cap and he didn't bother to look up.

'The horses are here,' I said.

Billy turned his wide insolent glare full on and didn't answer. I bent down and touched Alf's knee, and pointed out of the oval window. He saw the horseboxes, nodded philosophically, and began to wrap up his remaining sandwiches. I left them and went down the ramp again, knowing very well that Billy would never obey an instruction of mine if I waited over him to see he did it.

The horsebox drivers said they'd had to make a detour because of roadworks. A detour into a transport cafe, more like.

Two grooms who had travelled with the mares gave a hand with the loading, which made it easy. The man who had come with Billy and Alf, whose name was John, was more abstracted than skilful, but with six of us it was the quickest job I had done when Billy was along. I imagined that it was because he knew Yardman was within complaining distance that he left me alone.

Yardman came across with the all clear for the other two mares, and we stowed them on board. Then as always we trooped along to the Immigration Office in the main passenger building where a bored official collected our dog-eared passports, flipped through them, and handed them back. Mine still had Mr on it, because I'd originally applied for it that way, and I intended to put off changing it as long as possible.

'Four grooms and you,' he said to Yardman. 'That's the lot?'

'That's the lot.' Yardman stifled a yawn. Early starts disagreed with him.

A party of bleary-eyed passengers from a cut rate night flight shuffled past in an untidy crocodile.

'OK then.' The passport man flicked the tourists a supercilious glance and retired into his office. Not everyone was at his best before breakfast.

Yardman walked back to the plane beside me.

'I've arranged to meet our opposite numbers for lunch,' he said. 'You know what business lunches are, my dear boy. I'm afraid it may drag on a little, and that you'll be kicking your heels about the airport for a few hours. Don't let any of them get ... er ... the worse for wear.'

'No,' I agreed insincerely. The longer his lunch, the better I'd be pleased. Billy drunk couldn't be worse than Billy sober, and I didn't intend to waste my hours at Malpensa supervising his intake.

Patrick and his crew were ready out by the plane, and had done their checks. The mobile battery truck stood by the nose cone with its power lead plugged into the aircraft: Patrick liked always to start his engines from the truck, so that he took off with the plane's own batteries fully charged.

Yardman and I followed Billy, Alf and John up the ramp at the rear, and Patrick with his co-pilot Bob, and the engineer, Mike, climbed the forward stairs into the nose. The airport staff wheeled away the stairs and unfastened and removed the two long sections of ramp. The inner port propeller began to grind slowly round as I swung shut the double doors, then sparked into life with a roar, and the plane came alive with vibration. The moment of the first engine firing gave me its usual lift of the spirits and I went along the cabin checking the horses with a smile in my mind.

Patrick moved down the taxi track and turned on to the apron set aside for power checks, the airframe quivering against the brakes as he pushed the throttles open. Holding two of the horses by their head collars I automatically followed him in imagination through the last series of checks before he closed the throttles, released the brakes and rolled round on to Gatwick's large single runway. The engine's note deepened and the plane began to move, horses and men leaning against the thrust as the speed built up to a hundred over the tarmac. We unstuck as per schedule and climbed away in a great wheeling turn, heading towards the Channel on course to the radio beacon at Dieppe. The heavy mares took the whole thing philosophically, and having checked round the lot of them I went forward into the galley, bending under the luggage racks and stepping over the guy chains as always in the cramped DC4.

Mike, the engineer, was already writing names on disposable cups with a red felt pen.

'All OK?' he asked, the eyebrow going up and down like a yo-yo.

'All fine,' I said.

He wrote 'Patrick' and 'Bob' and 'Henry' and asked me the names of the others. 'Mr Y', 'Billy', 'Alf' and 'John' joined the roll. He filled the crew's cups and mine, and I took Patrick's and Bob's forward while he went to ask the others if they were thirsty. The rising sun blazed into the cockpit, dazzling after the comparative gloom of the cabin. Both pilots were wearing dark glasses, and Patrick already had his jacket off, and had started on the first of his attendant bunch of bananas. The chart lay handy, the usual unlikely mass of half-inch circles denoting radio stations connected by broad pale blue areas of authorized airlines, with the normal shape of the land beneath only faintly drawn in and difficult to distinguish. Bob pulled a tuft of cotton wool off a shaving cut, made it bleed again, and swore, his exact words inaudible against the racket of the engines. Both of them were wearing head-sets, earphones combined with a microphone mounted on a metal band which curved round in front of the mouth. They spoke to each other by means of a transmitting switch set into the wheel on the control column, since normal speech in that noise was impossible. Giving me a grin and a thumbs up sign for the coffee, they went on with their endless attention to the job in hand. I watched for a bit, then strolled back through the galley, picking up 'Henry' en route, and relaxed on a hay bale to drink, looking down out of the oval window and seeing the coast of France tilt underneath as we passed the Dieppe beacon and set course for Paris.

A day like any other day, a flight like any other flight. And Gabriella waiting at the other end of it. Every half hour or so I checked round the mares, but they were a docile lot and travelled like veterans. Mostly horses didn't eat much in the air, but one or two were picking at their haynets, and a chestnut in the rearmost box was fairly guzzling. I began to untie her depleted net to fill it again for her from one of the bales when a voice said in my ear, 'I'll do that.'

I looked round sharply and found Billy's face two feet from my own.

'You?' The surprise and sarcasm got drowned by the engine noise.

He nodded, elbowed me out of the way, and finished untying the haynet. I watched with astonishment as he carried it away into the narrow starboard gangway and began to stuff it full again. He came back pulling the drawstring tight round the neck, slung it over to hang inside the box, and re-tied the rope on to the cleat. Wordlessly he treated me to a wide sneering glare from his searchlight eyes, pushed past, and flung himself with what suddenly looked like pent-up fury into one of the seats at the back.

In the pair of seats immediately behind him Yardman and John sat side by side. Yardman was frowning crossly at Billy, though to my mind he should have been giving him a pat on the head and a medal for self control.

Yardman turned his head from Billy to me and gave me his graveyard smile. 'What time do we arrive?' he shouted.

'About half an hour.'

He nodded and looked away through the window. I glanced at John and saw that he was dozing, with his grubby cap pushed back on his head and his hands lying limp on his lap. He opened his eyes while I was looking at him, and his relaxed facial muscles sharply contracted so that suddenly he seemed familiar to me, though I was certain I hadn't met him before. It puzzled me for only a second because Billy, getting up again, managed to kick my ankle just out of Yardman's sight. I turned away from him, lashed backwards with my heel, and felt a satisfactory clunking jar as it landed full on his shin. One day, I thought, smiling to myself as I squeezed forward along the plane, one day he'll get tired of it.

We joined the circuit at Malpensa four hours from Gatwick; a smooth, easy trip. Holding the mares' heads I saw the familiar red and white chequered huts near the edge of the airfield grow bigger and bigger as we

196

descended, then they were suddenly behind us at eye level as Patrick levelled out twenty feet from the ground at about a hundred and ten miles an hour. The bump from the tricycle undercarriage as we touched down with full flaps at a fraction above stalling speed wasn't enough to rock the mares on their feet. Top of the class, I thought.

The customs man and his two helpers came on board, and Yardman produced the mares' papers from his briefcase. The checking went on without a hitch, brisk but thorough. The customs man handed the papers back to Yardman with a small bow and signed that the unloading could begin.

Yardman ducked out of any danger of giving a hand with that by saying that he'd better see if the opposite numbers were waiting for him inside the airport. As it was barely half past eleven, it seemed doubtful, but all the same he marched purposefully down the ramp and away across the tarmac, a gaunt black figure with sunshine flashing on his glasses.

The crew got off at the sharp end and followed him, a navy blue trio in peaked caps. A large yellow Shell tanker pulled up in front of the aircraft, and three men in white overalls began the job of refuelling.

We unloaded into the waiting horseboxes in record time, Billy seemingly being as anxious as me to get it done quickly, and within half an hour of landing I had changed my jersey for my jacket and was pushing open the glass doors of the airport. I stood just inside, watching Gabriella. She was selling a native doll, fluffing up the rich dark skirt to show the petticoats underneath, her face solemn and absorbed. The heavy dark club-cut hair swung forward as she leaned across the counter, and her eyes were cool and quiet as she shook her head gently at her customer, the engineer Mike. My chest constricted at the sight of her, and I wondered how I was possibly going to bear leaving again in three hours' time. She looked up suddenly as if she felt my gaze, and she saw me and smiled, her soft mouth curving sweet and wide.

Mike looked quite startled at the transformation and turned to see the reason.

'Henry,' said Gabriella, with welcome and gaiety shimmering in her voice. 'Hullo, darling.'

'Darling?' exclaimed Mike, the eyebrow doing its stuff.

Gabriella said in French, 'I've doubled my English vocabulary, as you see. I know two words now.'

'Essential ones, I'm glad to say.'

'Hey,' said Mike. 'If you can talk to her, Henry, ask her about this doll. It's my elder girl's birthday tomorrow, and she's started collecting these things, but I'm damned if I know whether she'll like this one.'

'How old is she?'

'Twelve.'

I explained the situation to Gabriella, who promptly produced a different doll, much prettier and more colourful, which she wrapped up for him while he sorted out some lire. Like Patrick's his wallet was stuffed with several different currencies, and he scattered a day's pay in deutschmarks over the merchandise before finding what he wanted. Collecting his cash in an untidy handful he thanked her cheerfully in basic French, picked up his parcel and walked off upstairs into the restaurant. There were always lunches provided for us on the planes, tourist class lunches packed in boxes, but both Mike and Bob preferred eating on the ground, copiously and in comfort.

I turned back to Gabriella and tried to satisfy my own sort of hunger by looking at her and touching her hand. And I could see in her face that to her too this was like a bowl of rice to the famine of India.

'When do you go?' she said.

'The horses arrive at two-thirty. I have to go then to load them. I might get back for a few minutes afterwards, if my boss dallies over his coffee.'

She sighed, looking at the clock. It was ten past noon. 'I have an hour off in twenty minutes. I'll make it two hours ...' She turned away into a swift chatter with the girls along in the duty free shop, and came back smiling. 'I'm doing her last hour today, and she'll do the gift shop in her lunch hour.'

I bowed my thanks to the girl and she laughed back with a flash of teeth, very white against the gloom of her bottle shop.

'Do you want to have lunch up there?' I suggested to Gabriella, pointing where Mike and Bob had gone.

She shook her head. 'Too public. Everyone knows me so well. We've time to go in to Milan, if you can do that?'

'If the horses get here early, they can wait.'

'Serve them right.' She nodded approvingly, her lips twitching.

A crowd of outgoing passengers erupted into the hall and swarmed round the gift counter. I retired to the snack bar at the far end to wait out the twenty minutes, and found Yardman sitting alone at one of the small tables. He waved me to join him, which I would just as soon not have done, and told me to order myself a double gin and tonic, like his.

'I'd really rather have coffee.'

He waved a limp hand permissively. 'Have whatever you like, my dear boy.'

I looked casually round the big airy place, at the glass, the polished wood, the terrazza. Along one side, next to a stall of sweets and chocolates, stretched the serving counter with coffee and beer rubbing shoulders with milk and gin. And down at the far end, close-grouped round another little table and clutching pint glasses, sat Alf and Billy, and with his back to us, John. Two and a half hours of that, I thought wryly, and we'd have a riotous trip home.

'Haven't your people turned up?' I asked Yardman.

'Delayed,' he said resignedly. 'They'll be here about one, though.'

'Good,' I said, but not for his sake. 'You won't forget to ask them about Simon?'

'Simon?'

'Searle.'

'Searle . . . oh yes. Yes, all right, I'll remember.'

Patrick walked through the hall from the office department, exchanged a greeting with Gabriella over the heads of her customers and came on to join us.

'Drink?' suggested Yardman, indicating his glass. He only meant to be hospitable, but Patrick was shocked.

'Of course not.'

'Eh?'

'Well . . . I thought you'd know. One isn't allowed to fly within eight hours of drinking alcohol.'

'Eight hours,' repeated Yardman in astonishment.

'That's right. Twenty-four hours after a heavy party, and better not for forty-eight if you get paralytic.'

'I didn't know,' said Yardman weakly.

'Air Ministry regulations,' Patrick explained. 'I'd like some coffee, though.'

A waitress brought him some, and he unwrapped four sugars and stirred them in. 'I enjoyed yesterday,' he said, smiling at me with his yellow eyes. 'I'll go again. When do you race next?'

'Tomorrow.'

'That's out for a start. When else?'

I glanced at Yardman. 'It depends on the schedules.'

Patrick turned to him in his usual friendly way. 'I

went to Cheltenham yesterday and saw our Henry here come fourth in the Gold Cup. Very interesting.'

'You know each other well, then?' Yardman asked. His deep set eyes were invisible behind the glasses, and the slanting sunlight showed up every blemish in his sallow skin. I still had no feeling for him either way, not liking, not disliking. He was easy to work for. He was friendly enough. He was still an enigma.

'We know each other,' Patrick agreed. 'We've been on trips together before.'

'I see.'

Gabriella came down towards us, wearing a supple brown suede coat over her black working dress. She had flat black round-toed patent leather shoes and swung a handbag with the same shine. A neat, composed, self-reliant, nearly beautiful girl who took work for granted and a lover for fun.

I stood up as she came near, trying to stifle a ridiculous feeling of pride, and introduced her to Yardman. He smiled politely and spoke to her in slow Italian, which surprised me a little, and Patrick translated for me into one ear.

'He's telling her he was in Italy during the war. Rather tactless of him, considering her grandfather was killed fighting off the invasion of Sicily.'

'Before she was born,' I protested.

'True.' He grinned. 'She's pro-British enough now, anyway.'

'Miss Barzini tells me you are taking her to lunch in Milan,' Yardman said.

'Yes,' I agreed. 'If that's all right with you? I'll be back by two-thirty when the return mares come.'

'I can't see any objection,' he said mildly. 'Where do you have in mind?'

'Trattoria Romana,' I said promptly. It was where Gabriella, Patrick and I had eaten on our first evening together.

Gabriella put her hand in mine. 'Good. I'm very hungry.' She shook hands with Yardman and waggled her fingers at Patrick. '*Arrivederci.*'

We walked away up the hall, the voltage tingling gently through our joined palms. I looked back once, briefly, and saw Yardman and Patrick watching us go. They were both smiling.

CHAPTER ELEVEN

Neither of us had much appetite, when it came to the point. We ate half our lasagne and drank coffee, and needed nothing else but proximity. We didn't talk a great deal, but at one point, clairvoyantly reading my disreputable thoughts, she said out of the blue that we couldn't go to her sister's flat as her sister would be in, complete with two or three kids.

'I was afraid of that,' I said wryly.

'It will have to be next time.'

'Yes.' We both sighed deeply in unison, and laughed.

A little later, sipping her hot coffee, she said, 'How many pills were there in the bottle you sent with Simon Searle?'

'I don't know. Dozens. I didn't count them. The bottle was over three-quarters full.'

'I thought so.' She sighed. 'The baker's wife rang up last night to ask me whether I could let her have some more. She said the bottom of the bottle was all filled up with paper, but if you ask me she's given half of them away to a friend, or something, and now regrets it.'

'There wasn't any paper in the bottle. Only cotton wool on top.'

'I thought so.' She frowned, wrinkling her nose in sorrow. 'I wish she'd told me the truth.'

I stood up abruptly. 'Come on,' I said. 'Leave the coffee.'

'Why?' She began to put on her coat.

'I want to see that bottle.'

She was puzzled. 'She'll have thrown it away.'

'I hope to God she hasn't,' I said urgently, paying the bill. 'If there's paper in the bottle, Simon put it there.'

'You mean ... it could matter?'

'He thought I was giving the pills to you. He didn't know they'd go to someone else. And I forgot to tell him you didn't speak English. Perhaps he thought when you'd finished the pills you'd read the paper and tell me what it said. Heaven knows. Anyway, we must find it. It's the first and only trace of him we've had.'

We hurried out of the restaurant, caught a taxi, and sped to the bakery. The baker's wife was fat and motherly and looked fifty, though she was probably only thirty-five. Her warm smile for Gabriella slowly turned anxious as she listened, and she shook her head and spread her hands wide.

'It's in the dustbin,' Gabriella said. 'She threw it away this morning.'

'We'll have to look. Ask her if I can look for it.'

The two women consulted.

'She says you'll dirty your fine suit.'

'Gabriella . . .'

'She says the English are mad, but you can look.'

There were three dustbins in the backyard, two luckily empty and one full. We turned this one out and I raked through the stinking contents with a broom handle. The little brown bottle was there, camouflaged by wet coffee grounds and half a dozen noodles. Gabriella took it and wiped it clean on a piece of newspaper while I shovelled the muck back into the dustbin and swept the yard.

'The paper won't come out,' she said. She had the cap off and was poking down the neck of the bottle with her finger. 'It's quite right. There is some in there.' She held it out to me.

I looked and nodded, wrapped the bottle in newspaper, put it on the ground, and smashed it with the shovel. She squatted beside me as I unfolded the paper and watched me pick out from the winking fragments of brown glass the things which had been inside.

I stood up slowly, holding them. A strip torn off the top of a piece of Yardman's stationery. A bank note of a currency I did not recognize, and some pieces of hay. The scrap of writing paper and the money were pinned together, and the hay had been folded up inside them.

'They are nonsense,' said Gabriella slowly.

'Do you have any idea where this comes from?' I touched the note. She flicked it over to see both sides.

'Yugoslavia. One hundred dinars.'

'Is that a lot?'

'About five thousand one hundred lire.'

Three pounds. Wisps of hay. A strip of paper. In a bottle.

Gabriella took the money out of my hands and removed the pin which joined them.

'What do they mean?' she asked.

'I don't know.'

A message in a bottle.

'There are some holes in the paper.'

'Where he put the pin.'

'No. More holes than that. Look.' She held it up to the sky. 'You can see the light through.'

The printed heading said in thick red letters 'Yardman Transport Ltd, Carriers'. The strip of paper was about six inches across and two inches deep from the top smooth edge to the jagged one where it had been torn off the page. I held it up to the light.

Simon had pinpricked four letters. S M E N. I felt the first distant tremor of cold apprehension.

'What is it?' she asked. 'What does it say?'

'Yardman Transport.' I showed her. 'See where he has added to it. If you read it with the pin hole letters tacked on, it says: "Yardman Transports MEN".'

She looked frightened by the bleakness in my voice,

as if she could feel the inner coldness growing. 'What does it mean?'

'It means he didn't have a pencil,' I said grimly, evading the final implication. 'Only pins in his coat.'

A message in a bottle, washed ashore.

'I've got to think it out,' I said. 'I've got to remember.'

We perched on a pile of empty boxes stacked in one corner of the baker's yard, and I stared sightlessly at the whitewashed wall opposite and at the single bush in a tub standing in one corner.

'Tell me,' Gabriella said. 'Tell me. You look so . . . so terrible.'

'Billy,' I said. 'Billy put up a smoke screen, after all.'

'Who is Billy?'

'A groom. At least, he works as one. Men . . . Every time Billy has been on a trip, there has been a man who didn't come back.'

'Simon?' she said incredulously.

'No, I don't mean Simon, though he went with Billy . . . No. Someone who went as a groom, but wasn't a groom at all. And didn't come back. I can't remember any of their faces, not to be sure, because I never talked to any of them much. Billy saw to that.'

'How?'

'Oh, by insults and . . .' I stopped, concentrating hard. 'The first time I went with Billy, there was a very fat man called John. At least, that was what I was told he was called. He was absolutely useless. Didn't know how to handle horses at all. We did two trips to France that day, and I think he wanted to vanish after the first. I saw him arguing furiously with Billy just before we came back the first time. But Billy made him do the double journey . . . and when he told me John had gone to Paris instead of coming back with us, he poured beer over my foot, so that I'd think about that, and not about John. And he made sure of it by picking a fight on the plane coming back . . .'

'But who is this John?'

I shook my head. 'I've no idea.'

'And were there others?'

'Yes . . . we went to New York next, he and I. There was a groom travelling with a half-bred Norwegian horse. He hardly talked at all, said he didn't speak English much. I understood he was staying in the States for a fortnight; but who knows if he came back? And on that trip Billy smashed a bar across my fingers so that they hurt all the way across, and I thought about them, not the Norwegian groom.'

'Are you sure?' She was frowning.

'Oh, yes, I'm sure. I thought once before that Billy had done it for a purpose. I just got the purpose wrong.' I pondered. 'There was a day we took a man with a large bushy moustache to France, and a fortnight later we brought a man with a large moustache back again. I never looked beyond the moustache . . . I think it could have been two different men.'

'What did Billy do, those times?'

'On the way he poured syrupy coffee on my head, and I spent nearly all the time in the washroom getting it out. And on the way back he hit me with a chain, and I went up into the galley all the way with the engineer to avoid any more.'

She looked at me very gravely. 'Is that . . . is that the lot?'

I shook my head. 'We went to New York last week. I told Yardman if Billy didn't leave me alone I'd quit. The journey out went quite all right, but coming back . . . there was a man who was plainly not a horseman. He wasn't even comfortable in the riding clothes he had on. I thought at the time he was the owner's nephew or something, cadging a free ride, but again I didn't talk to him much. I slept all the way back. All ten hours . . . I don't usually get tired like that, but I thought it was only because it was my fourth Atlantic crossing in six days . . .'

'A sleeping pill?' she said slowly.

'It might have been. Alf brought some coffee back for me soon after we left. There was a restive colt in the aft box and I was trying to soothe him . . . It could have been that.'

'Alf?'

'An old deaf man, who always goes with Billy.'

'Do you think it *was* a sleeping pill?'

'It could . . . I was still tired long after I got home. I even went to sleep in the bath.'

'It's serious,' she said.

'Today,' I said. 'There's a stranger with us today. His name is John too. I've never met him before, but there's something about him ... I was looking at him on the plane and wondering what it was, and Billy kicked me on the ankle. I kicked him back, but I went away, and stopped thinking about that man.'

'Can you think now?'

'Well ... his hands are wrong for one thing. Stablemen's hands are rough and chafed from being wet so often in cold weather, with washing tack and so on, but his are smooth, with well shaped nails.'

She picked up one of my hands and looked at it, running the tips of her fingers over the roughnesses which had developed since I left my desk job.

'They are not like yours, then.'

'Not like mine. But it's his expression really. I watched him wake up. It was what came into his face with consciousness ...' I could remember that moment vividly, in spite of Billy's kick. I knew that expression very well ... so what was it? 'Oh,' I exclaimed in enlightenment, half laughing at my own stupidity, 'I know what it is ... he went to the same school as I did.'

'You do know him then, I mean, you've seen him before, if you were at school together.'

'Not together. He's older. He must have left about five years before I went. No, I've never seen him before, but the look he has is typical of some of the boys there. Not the nicest ones ... only the ones who think they are God's gift to mankind and everyone else is a bit inferior. He's one of those. Definitely *not* a groom. He looked as if wearing the grubby riding clothes he's got on was a kick in the dignity.'

'But you don't wear riding clothes,' she pointed out. 'It isn't necessary for him if he doesn't like them.'

'It is though. Alf wears jodhpurs, Billy wears jeans. The two grooms who travel about with these two, Timmie and Conker, they both wear breeches to work in. It's a sort of badge of office ... No one would think twice about a man arriving on a horse transport dressed in breeches or jodhpurs.'

'No, I see that.'

'No one bothers much about our passports,' I said. 'Look how simply I came out into Milan today, through the airport staff door. Hardly any airports, especially the very small ones, take much notice of you, if you work on aeroplanes. It's dead easy just to walk off most airfields round at the loading bays without ever being challenged. The Americans are strictest, but even they are used to comings and goings.'

'But people do look at your passports sometimes, surely,' she protested.

I produced mine, battered and dogeared in the last three months after several years of dark blue stiffness. 'Look at it. It gets like that from always being in my pocket, but it doesn't get stamped much.' I turned through the pages. 'American visa, certainly. But look, the only stamp from Milan is the time I came on a scheduled flight and went through immigration with the other passengers. Hardly a mark for France, and I've been over several times . . . of course it gets looked at, but never very thoroughly. It must be easy to fake one in this condition, and even travelling without one wouldn't be impossible. A pilot told me he'd done it for three weeks once, all over the world.'

'People who work on aircraft would go mad if everyone started checking their passports thoroughly every time they walked in or out.'

'Well . . . normally there's no need for it. It isn't all that easy to get on a single one way flight as a worker. Impossible, if you haven't a strong pull somewhere or other. Just any odd person who fancies a quiet trip to foreign parts wouldn't have a hope of getting himself into a horse transport. But if the transport agency itself, or someone working for it, is ready to export people illegally along with the horses, then it's easy.'

'But . . . what people?'

'What indeed! Billy can hardly advertise his service in the daily Press. But he had no shortage of customers.'

'Crooks, do you think?' Gabriella asked frowning.

I fingered the banknote and twisted the small pieces of hay.

'Hay,' I said. 'Why hay?'

Gabriella shrugged. 'Perhaps he found the money in some hay.'

'Of course!' I exclaimed. 'You're dead right. Haynets. Carried openly on and off the planes and never searched by customs officers. Perhaps they're

213

transporting currency as well as men.' I told her about Billy refilling the net for me on the trip over, and how astonished I had been.

'But, Henry darling, what I really do not understand is why you were not astonished all along at the unpleasant things Billy has been doing to you. I would have thought it utterly extraordinary, and I would have made a very big fuss about it.' She looked solemn and doubtful.

'Oh, I thought it was simply because I . . .' I stopped.

'Because you what?'

I smiled slightly. 'Because I belong to a sort of people he thinks should be exterminated.'

'Henry!' Her mouth lost its severity. 'What sort of people?'

'Well . . . you have counts and countesses still in Italy . . .'

'But you're not . . . you're not, are you . . . a count?'

'Sort of. Yes.'

She looked at me doubtfully, halfway to laughing, not sure that I was not teasing her.

'I don't believe you.'

'The reason I wasn't astonished at Billy knocking me about was that I knew he hated my guts for having a title.'

'That makes sense, I suppose.' She managed to frown and smile at the same time, which looked adorable. 'But if you have a title, Henry, why are you working in a horse transport?'

'You tell me why,' I said.

She looked at me searchingly for a moment, then she put her arms round my neck and her cheek on mine, with her mouth against my ear.

'It isn't enough for you to have a title,' she said. 'It isn't enough for anyone. It is necessary to show also that you are . . .' She fished around in her French vocabulary, and came up with a word: '. . . *veritable*. Real.'

I took a deep breath of relief and overspilling love, and kissed her neck where the dark hair swung below her ear.

'My wife will be a countess,' I said. 'Would you mind that?'

'I could perhaps bear it.'

'And me? Could you bear me? For always?'

'I love you,' she said in my ear. 'Yes. For always. Only, Henry . . .'

'Only what?'

'You won't stop being real?'

'No,' I said sadly.

She pulled away from me, shaking her head.

'I'm stupid. I'm sorry. But if even I can doubt you . . . and so quickly . . . you must always be having to prove . . .'

'Always,' I agreed.

'Still, you don't have to go quite so far.'

My heart sank.

'It's not everyone,' she said, 'who gets proposed to

in a baker's backyard surrounded by dustbins.' Her mouth trembled and melted into a heart-wrenching smile.

'You wretch, my love.'

'Henry,' she said. 'I'm so happy I could burst.'

I kissed her and felt the same, and lived another half minute of oblivion before I thought again of Simon.

'What is it?' she said, feeling me straighten.

'The time . . .'

'Oh.'

'And Simon . . .'

'I fear for him,' she said, half under her breath.

'I too.'

She took the piece of paper out of my hand and looked at it again.

'We've been trying to avoid realizing what this means.'

'Yes,' I said softly.

'Say it, then.'

'This was the only message he had a chance of sending. The only way he could send it.' I paused, looking into her serious dark eyes. After ten silent seconds I finished it. 'He is dead.'

She said in distress, 'Perhaps he is a prisoner.'

I shook my head. 'He's the third man who's disappeared. There was a man called Ballard who used to arrange trips from this end, and the man who used to have my job, a man called Peters. They both vanished. Ballard over a year ago, and no one's heard of them since.'

'This Billy . . .' she said slowly, her eyes anxious.

'This Billy,' I said, 'is young and heartless, and carries a loaded revolver under his left arm.'

'Please . . . don't go back with him.'

'It will be quite safe as long as I keep quiet about this.' I took the hurried, desperate, pinpricked message back, folded it up with the banknote and the hay, and put them all in my wallet. 'When I get back to England, I'll find out who I have to tell.'

'The police,' she said, nodding.

'I'm not sure . . .' I thought about the Yugoslav currency and remembered Gabriella saying on our first evening 'Communists begin at Trieste.' I felt like someone who had trodden through a surface into a mole run underneath, and had suddenly realized that it was part of a whole dark invisible network. I thought it very unlikely that the men I'd flown with were ordinary crooks. They were couriers, agents . . . heaven knew what. It seemed fantastic to me to have brushed so closely with people I had known must exist but never expected to see; but I supposed the suburban people who lived next door to Peter and Helen Kroger in Cranley Drive, Ruislip, had been pretty astonished too.

'Billy must have unloaded whatever he brought over in the haynet today,' I said. 'But going back . . .'

'No,' Gabriella said vehemently. 'Don't look. That's

what Simon must have done. Found the money. And Billy saw him.'

It might have been like that. And there had been two extra grooms on that trip, men I'd never seen before. Somehow, on the way, Simon had come across something I'd been blind to: perhaps because there was one more man than he'd arranged for; perhaps because Billy couldn't distract his attention by the methods he'd used on me; perhaps because of other happenings in the past which I didn't know about. In any case, Simon had found Billy out, and had let Billy know it. I thought drearily of Simon suddenly realizing towards the end of that flight that Ballard and Peters had never come back, and that he wouldn't get a chance to put Billy in gaol. Billy the young thug, with his ready gun. A few minutes in the lavatory, that was all the time he'd had. No pencil. Only his pins, and the little bottle I'd given him in the privacy of the airline office; the bottle Billy didn't know existed, with Gabriella's name on it. Pills into loo. Banknote and paper with its inadequate message into bottle. Simon into eternity.

'Please don't search the haynets,' Gabriella said again.

'No,' I agreed. 'Someone official had better do it, next time Billy goes on a trip.'

She relaxed with relief. 'I'd hate you to disappear.'

I smiled. 'I won't do that. I'll go back most of the way up front with the crew, with Patrick and the man who bought the doll. And when I get to England I'll telephone you to let you know I arrived safely. How's that?'

'It would be wonderful. I could stop worrying.'

'Don't start,' I said confidently. 'Nothing will go wrong.'

How the local gods must have laughed their Roman heads off.

CHAPTER TWELVE

We went through the baker's shop and out into the street. I looked somewhat anxiously at my watch and calculated a dead heat with the brood mares.

'We need a taxi,' I said.

Gabriella shook her head. 'Very unlikely to find one in this quarter. We'd better catch a tram back to the centre, and take one on from there.'

'All right,' I agreed. 'Tram or taxi, whichever comes first.'

The trams ran along the busy street at the end of the quiet empty road where the baker lived, and we began to walk towards them with some dispatch.

'I didn't realize how late it is,' Gabriella said, catching sight of a clock with the hands together pointing north-east.

'And that one's slow. It's a quarter past.'

'Oh dear.'

One of the long green and cream single decker trams rolled across the end of the road, not far ahead.

'Run,' Gabriella said. 'The stop's just around the corner. We must catch it.'

We ran, holding hands. It couldn't have been more than ten strides to the corner. Not more.

Gabriella cried out suddenly and stumbled, whirling against me as I pulled her hand. There was a sharp searing stab in my side and we fell down on the pavement, Gabriella's weight pulling me over as I tried to save her from hurting herself.

Two or three passers by stopped to help her up, but she didn't move. She was lying face down, crumpled. Without belief, I stared at the small round hole near the centre of the back of her coat. Numbly, kneeling beside her, I put my left hand inside my jacket against my scorching right side, and when I brought it out it was covered in blood.

'Oh no,' I said in English. 'Oh dear God, no.'

I bent over her and rolled her up and on to her back in my arms. Her eyes were open. They focused on my face. She was alive. It wasn't much.

'Henry,' her voice was a whisper. 'I can't . . . breathe.'

The three passers by had grown to a small crowd. I looked up desperately into their enquiring faces.

'Doctor,' I said. '*Medico.*' That was Spanish. 'Doctor.'

'*Si si,*' said a small boy by my elbow. '*Un dottore, si.*'

There was a stir in the crowd and a great deal of speculation of which I understood only one word. '*Inglese,*' they said and I nodded, '*Inglese.*'

I opened gently the front of Gabriella's brown suede

221

coat. There was a jagged tear in the right side, nearest me, and the edges of it were dark. Underneath, the black dress was soaking. I waved my arm wildly around at the people to get them to stand back a bit, and they did take one pace away. A motherly looking woman produced a pair of scissors from her handbag and knelt down on Gabriella's other side. She pointed at me to open the coat again, and when I'd tucked it back between Gabriella's body and my own she began to cut away the dress. Gentle as she was, Gabriella moved in my arms and gave a small gasping cry.

'Hush,' I said, 'my love, it's all right.'

'Henry . . .' She shut her eyes.

I held her in anguish while the woman with the scissors carefully cut and peeled away a large piece of dress. When she saw what lay underneath her big face filled with overwhelming compassion, and she begun to shake her head. '*Signor,*' she said to me, '*mi dispiace molto. Molto.*'

I took the clean white handkerchief out of my top pocket, folded it inside out, and put it over the terrible wound. The bullet had smashed a rib on its way out. There were splinters of it showing in the bleeding area just below her breast. The bottom edge of her white bra had a new scarlet border. I gently untucked the coat and put it over her again to keep her warm and I thought in utter agony that she would die before the doctor came.

A *carabiniere* in glossy boots and greenish khaki

breeches appeared beside us, but I doubt if I could have spoken to him even if he'd known the same language. The crowd chattered to him in subdued voices and he left me alone.

Gabriella opened her eyes. Her face was grey and wet with the sweat of appalling pain.

'Henry . . .'

'I'm here.'

'I can't . . . breathe.'

I raised her a little more so that she was half sitting, supported by my arm and my bent knee. The movement was almost too much for her. Her pallor became pronounced. The short difficult breaths passed audibly through her slackly open mouth.

'Don't . . . leave me.'

'No,' I said. 'Hush, my dearest love.'

'What . . . happened?'

'You were shot,' I said.

'Shot . . .' She showed no surprise. 'Was it . . . Billy?'

'I don't know. I didn't see. Don't talk, my sweet love, don't talk. The doctor will be here soon.'

'Henry . . .' She was exhausted, her skin the colour of death. 'Henry . . . I love you.'

Her eyes flickered shut again, but she was still conscious, her left hand moving spasmodically and restlessly on the ground beside her and the lines of suffering deepening in her face.

I would have given anything, anything on earth, to have had her whole again, to have taken that pain away.

The doctor, when at last he came, was young enough to have been newly qualified. He had thick black curly hair and thin clever hands: this was what I most saw of him as he bent over Gabriella, and all I remembered. He looked briefly under my white handkerchief and turned to the policeman.

I heard the words '*auto ambulanza*' and '*pallota*', and eager information from the crowd.

The young doctor went down on one knee and felt Gabriella's pulse. She opened her eyes, but only a fraction.

'Henry . . .'

'I'm here. Don't talk.'

'Mm . . .'

The young doctor said something soothing to her in Italian and she said faintly '*Si*'. He opened his case behind him on the ground and with quick skilful fingers prepared an injection, made a hole in her stocking, swabbed her skin with surgical spirit, and pushed the needle firmly into her thigh. Again he spoke to her gently, and again felt her pulse. I could read nothing but reassurance in his manner, and the reassurance was for her, not me.

After a while she opened her eyes wider and looked at me, and a smile struggled to her damp face.

'That's better,' she said. Her voice was so weak as to be scarcely audible, and she was growing visibly more breathless. Nothing was better, except the pain.

I smiled back. 'Good. You'll be all right soon, when they get you to hospital.'

She nodded a fraction. The doctor continued to hold her pulse, checking it on his watch.

Two vehicles drove up and stopped with a screech of tyres. A Citroen police car and an ambulance like a large estate car. Two *carabinieri* of obvious seniority emerged from one, and stretcher bearers from the other. These last, and the doctor, lifted Gabriella gently out of my arms and on to the stretcher. They piled blankets behind her to support her, and I saw the doctor take a look at what he could see of the small hole in her back. He didn't try to take off her coat.

One of the policemen said, 'I understand you speak French.'

'Yes,' I said standing up. I hadn't felt the hardness of the pavement until that moment. The leg I'd been kneeling on was numb.

'What are the young lady's name and address?'

I told him. He wrote them down.

'And your own?'

I told him.

'What happened?' he said, indicating the whole scene with a flickering wave of the hand.

'We were running to catch the tram. Someone shot at us, from back there.' I pointed down the empty street towards the baker's.

'Who?'

'I didn't see.' They were lifting Gabriella into the ambulance. 'I must go with her,' I said.

The policeman shook his head. 'You can see her later. You must come with us, and tell us exactly what happened.'

'I said I wouldn't leave her . . .' I couldn't bear to leave her. I took a quick stride and caught the doctor by the arm. 'Look,' I said, pulling open my jacket.

He looked. He tugged my bloodstained shirt out of my trousers to inspect the damage more closely. A ridged furrow five inches along my lowest rib. Not very deep. It felt like a burn. The doctor told the policeman who also looked.

'All right,' said the one who spoke French, 'I suppose you'd better go and have it dressed.' He wrote an address on a page of his notebook, tore it off and gave it to me. 'Come here afterwards.'

'Yes.'

'Have you your passport with you?'

I took it out of my pocket and gave it to him, and put the address he'd given me in my wallet. The doctor jerked his head towards the ambulance to get in, and I did.

'Wait,' said the policeman as they were shutting the door. 'Did the bullet go through the girl into you?'

'No,' I said. 'Two bullets. She was hit first, me after.'

'We will look for them,' he said.

*

Gabriella was still alive when we reached the hospital.
Still alive when they lifted her, stretcher and all, on to
a trolley. Still alive while one of the ambulance men
explained rapidly to a doctor what had happened, and
while that doctor and another took in her general condition, left my handkerchief undisturbed, and whisked
her away at high speed.

One doctor went with her. The other, a thick set
man with the shoulders of a boxer, stayed behind and
asked me a question.

'*Inglese.*' I shook my head. '*Non parlo italiano.*'

'Sit down,' he said in English. His accent was thick,
his vocabulary tiny, but it was a relief to be able to talk
to him at all. He led me into a small white cubicle
containing a hard, high narrow bed and a chair. He
pointed to the chair and I sat on it. He went away and
returned with a nurse carrying some papers.

'The name of the miss?'

I told him. The nurse wrote it down, name, address
and age, gave me a comforting smile, took the papers
away and came back with a trolley of equipment and
a message.

She told it to the doctor, and he translated, as it was
for me.

'Telephone from *carabinieri*. Please go to see them
before four.'

I looked at my watch, blank to the time. It was still
less than an hour since Gabriella and I had run for the
tram. I had lived several ages.

227

'I understand,' I said.

'Please now, remove your coat,' the doctor said.

I stood up, took off my jacket and slid my right arm out of my shirt. He put two dressings over the bullet mark, an impregnated gauze one and a slightly padded one with adhesive tape. He pressed the tapes firmly into my skin and stood back. I put my arm back into my shirt sleeve.

'Don't you feel it?' he said. He seemed surprised.

'No.'

His rugged face softened. '*E sua moglie?*'

I didn't understand.

'I am sorry . . . is she your wife?'

'I love her,' I said. The prospect of losing her was past bearing. There were tears suddenly in my eyes and on my cheeks. 'I love her.'

'Yes.' He nodded, sympathetic and unembarrassed, one of a nation who saw no value in stiff upper lips. 'Wait here. We will tell you . . .' He left the sentence unfinished and went away, and I didn't know whether it was because he didn't want to tell me she was dying or because he simply didn't know enough English to say what he meant.

I waited an hour I couldn't endure again. At the end of it another doctor came, a tall, grey-haired man with a fine boned face.

'You wish to know about Signorina Barzini?' His English was perfect, his voice quiet and very precise.

I nodded, unable to ask.

'We have cleaned and dressed her wound. The bullet passed straight through her lung, breaking a rib on the way out. The lung was collapsed. The air from it, and also a good deal of blood, has passed in to the chest cavity. It was necessary to remove the air and blood at once so that the lung would have room to inflate again, and we have done that.' He was coolly clinical.

'May I . . . may I see her?'

'Later,' he said, without considering it. 'She is unconscious from the anaesthetic and she is in the post-operative unit. You may see her later.'

'And . . . the future?'

He half smiled. 'There is always danger in such a case, but with good care she could certainly recover. The bullet itself hit nothing immediately fatal; none of the big blood vessels. If it had, she would have died soon, in the street. The longer she lived, the better were her chances.'

'She seemed to get worse,' I said, not daring to believe him.

'In some ways that was so,' he explained patiently. 'Her injury was very painful, she was bleeding internally, and she was suffering from the onset of shock, which as you may know is a physical condition often as dangerous as the original damage.'

I nodded, swallowing.

'We are dealing with all those things. She is young and healthy, which is good, but there will be more pain and there may be difficulties. I can give you no assurances. It is too soon for that. But hope, yes definitely, there is considerable hope.'

'Thank you,' I said dully, 'for being so honest.'

He gave his small smile again. 'Your name is Henry?' I nodded.

'You have a brave girl,' he said.

If I couldn't see her yet, I thought, I would have to go and talk to the police. They had said to be with them by four and it was already twenty past; not that that mattered a jot.

I was so unused to thinking in the terms of the strange half world into which I had stumbled that I failed to take the most elementary precautions. Distraught about Gabriella, it didn't even cross my mind that if I had been found and shot at in a distant back street I was equally vulnerable outside the hospital.

There was a taxi standing in the forecourt, the driver reading a newspaper. I waved an arm at him, and he folded the paper, started the engine and drove over. I gave him the paper with the address the policeman had written out for me, and he looked at it in a bored sort of way and nodded. I opened the cab door and got in. He waited politely till I was settled, his head half turned, and then drove smoothly out of the hospital gates. Fifty yards away he turned right down a tree-lined secondary road beside the hospital, and fifty yards down there he stopped. From a tree one yard from the kerb a lithe figure peeled itself, wrenched open the nearest door, and stepped inside.

He was grinning fiercely, unable to contain his triumph. The gun with the silencer grew in his hand as if born there. I had walked right into his ambush.

Billy the Kid.

'You took your bloody time, you stinking bastard,' he said.

I looked at him blankly, trying to keep the shattering dismay from showing. He sat down beside me and shoved his gun into my ribs, just above the line it had already drawn there.

'Get cracking, Vittorio,' he said. 'His effing lordship is late.'

The taxi rolled smoothly away and gathered speed.

'Four o'clock we said,' said Billy, grinning widely. 'Didn't you get the message?'

'The police . . .' I said weakly.

'Hear that, Vittorio?' Billy laughed. 'The hospital thought you were the police. Fancy that. How extraordinary.'

I looked away from him, out of the window on my left.

'You just try it,' Billy said. 'You'll have a bullet through you before you get the door open.'

I looked back at him.

'Yeah,' he grinned. 'Takes a bit of swallowing, don't it, for you to have to do what I say. Sweet, I call it. And believe me, matey, you've hardly bloody started.'

I didn't answer. It didn't worry him. He sat sideways, the gloating grin fixed like a rictus.

'How's the bird ... Miss what's her name?' He flicked his finger. 'The girl friend.'

I did some belated thinking.

I said stonily, 'She's dead.'

'Well, well,' said Billy gleefully. 'How terribly sad. Do you hear that, Vittorio? His Lordship's bit of skirt has passed on.'

Vittorio's head nodded. He concentrated on his driving, mostly down side streets, avoiding heavy traffic. I stared numbly at the greasy back of his neck and wondered what chance I had of grabbing Billy's gun before he pulled the trigger. The answer to that, I decided, feeling its steady pressure against my side, was none.

'Come on now, come on,' said Billy. 'Don't you think I'm clever?'

I didn't answer. Out of the corner of my eye I sensed the grin change from triumph to vindictiveness.

'I'll wipe that bloody superior look off your face,' he said. 'You sodding blue-arsed—'

I said nothing. He jerked the gun into my ribs.

'You just wait, your high and mighty lordship, you just bloody well wait.'

There didn't in fact seem to be much else I could do. The taxi bowled steadily on, leaving the city centre behind.

'Hurry it up, Vittorio,' said Billy. 'We're late.'

Vittorio put his foot down and we drove away from the town and out into an area of scrubland. The road twisted twice and then ran straight, and I stared in astonishment and disbelief at what lay ahead at the end of it. It was the broad open sweep of Malpensa Airport. We had approached it from the side road leading away from the loading bay, the road the horse-boxes sometimes took.

The DC4 stood there on the tarmac less than a hundred yards away, still waiting to take four mares back to England. Vittorio stopped the taxi fifty yards from the loading area. 'Now,' said Billy to me, enjoying himself again. 'You listen and do as you are told, otherwise I'll put a hole in you. And it'll be the breadbasket, not the heart. That's a promise.' I didn't doubt him. 'Walk down the road, straight across to the plane, up the ramp and into the toilet. Get it? I'll be two steps behind you, all the way.'

I was puzzled, but greatly relieved. I had hardly expected such a mild end to the ride. Without a word I opened the door and climbed out. Billy wriggled agilely across and stood up beside me, the triumphant sneer reasserting itself on his babyish mouth.

'Go on,' he said.

There was no one about at that side of the airfield. Four hundred yards ahead there were people moving round the main building, but four hundred yards across open tarmac looked a very long way. Behind lay scrubland and the taxi. Mentally shrugging, I followed Billy's

233

instructions: walked down the short stretch of road, across to the plane, and up the ramp. Billy stalked a steady two paces behind me, too far to touch, too near to miss.

At the top of the ramp stood Yardman. He was frowning heavily, though his eyes were as usual inscrutable behind the glasses, and he was tapping his watch.

'You've cut it very fine,' he said in annoyance. 'Another quarter of an hour and we'd have been in trouble.'

My chief feeling was still of astonishment and unreality. Billy broke the bubble, speaking over my shoulder.

'Yeah, he was dead late coming out of the hospital. Another five minutes, and we'd have had to go in for him.'

My skin rose in goose pimples. The ride had after all led straight to the heart of things. The pit yawned before me.

'Get in then,' Yardman said. 'I'll go and tell the pilot our wandering boy has at last returned from lunch and we can start back for England.' He went past us and down the ramp, hurrying.

Billy sniggered. 'Move, your effing lordship,' he said. 'Open the toilet door and go in. The one on the left.' The pistol jabbed against the bottom of my spine. 'Do as you're told.'

I walked the three necessary steps, opened the left hand door, and went in.

'Put your hands on the wall,' said Billy. 'Right there in front of you, so that I can see them.'

I did as he said. He swung the door shut behind him and leaned against it. We waited in silence. He sniggered complacently from time to time, and I considered my blind stupidity.

Yardman. Yardman transports men. Simon had fought through to a conclusion, where I had only gone halfway. Billy's smoke screen had filled my eyes. I hadn't seen beyond it to Yardman. And instead of grasping from Simon's message and my own memory that it had to be Yardman too, I had kissed Gabriella and lost the thread of it. And five minutes later she had been bleeding on the pavement . . .

I shut my eyes and rested my forehead momentarily against the wall. Whatever the future held it meant nothing to me if Gabriella didn't live.

After a while Yardman returned. He rapped on the door and Billy moved to give him room to come in.

'They're all coming across, now,' he said. 'We'll be away shortly. But before we go . . . how about the girl?'

'Croaked,' said Billy laconically.

'Good,' Yardman said. 'One less job for Vittorio.'

My head jerked.

'My dear boy,' said Yardman. 'Such a pity. Such a nice girl too.' In quite a different voice he said to Billy, 'Your shooting was feeble. You are expected to do better than that.'

'Hey.' There was a suspicion of a whine in Billy's reply. 'They started running.'

'You should have been closer.'

'I *was* close. Close enough. Ten yards at the most. I was waiting in a doorway, ready to pump it into them just after they'd passed me. And then they just suddenly started running. I got the girl all right, though, didn't I? I mean, I got her, even if she lingered a bit, like. As for him, well, granted I did miss him, but she sort of swung round and knocked him over just as I pulled the trigger.'

'If Vittorio hadn't been with you,' Yardman began coldly.

'Well, he was with me, then, wasn't he?' Billy defended himself. 'After all, it was me that told him to worm into that crowd around the girl and keep his ears flapping. Granted it was Vittorio who heard the police telling this creep to go and see them straight from the hospital, but it was me that thought of ringing up the hospital and winkling him out. And anyway, when I rang you up the second time, didn't you say it was just as well, you could do with him back here alive as you'd got a use for him?'

'All right,' said Yardman. 'It's worked out all right, but it was still very poor shooting.'

He opened the door, letting in a brief murmur of people moving the ramp away, and closed it behind him. Billy sullenly delivered a long string of obscenity, exclusively concerned with the lower part of the body. Not one to take criticism sweetly.

The aircraft trembled as the engines started one after the other. I glanced at my watch, on a level with my eyes. If it had been much later, Patrick would have refused to take off that day. As it was, there was little enough margin for him to get back to Gatwick within fifteen hours of going on duty that morning. It was the total time which mattered, not just flying hours, with inquiries and fines to face for the merest minutes over.

'Kneel down,' Billy said, jabbing me in the spine. 'Keep your hands on the wall. And don't try lurching into me accidental like when we take off. It wouldn't do you an effing bit of good.'

I didn't move.

'You'll do as you're ruddy well told, matey,' said Billy, viciously kicking the back of one of my knees. 'Get down.'

I knelt down on the floor. Billy said 'There's a good little earl,' with a pleased sneer in his voice, and rubbed the snout of his pistol up and down the back of my neck.

The plane began to taxi, stopped at the perimeter for power checks, rolled forward on to the runway, and gathered speed. Inside the windowless lavatory compartment it was impossible to tell the exact moment of unstick, but the subsequent climb held me close anyway against the wall, as I faced the tail, and Billy stopped himself from overbalancing on to me by putting his gun between my shoulder blades and leaning on it. I hoped remotely that Patrick wouldn't strike an air pocket.

Up in the cockpit, as far away in the plane as one could get and no doubt furious with me for coming back so late, he would be drinking his first coffee, and peeling his first banana, a mile from imagining I could need his help. He completed a long climbing turn and after a while levelled off and reduced power. We were well on the first leg south to the Mediterranean.

The Mediterranean. A tremor as nasty as the one I'd had on finding Yardman at the heart of things fluttered through my chest. The DC4 was unpressurized. The cabin doors could be opened in flight. Perhaps Billy had simply opened the door and pushed Simon out.

The traceless exit. Ten thousand feet down to the jewel blue sea.

CHAPTER THIRTEEN

Yardman came back, edging round the door.

'It's time,' he said.

Billy sniggered. 'Can't be too soon.'

'Stand up, stand up, my dear boy,' Yardman said. 'You look most undignified down there. Face the wall all the time.'

As I stood up he reached out, grasped my jacket by the collar, and pulled it backwards and downwards. Two more jerks and it was off.

'I regret this, I do indeed,' he said. 'But I'm afraid we must ask you to put your hands together behind your back.'

I thought that if I did that I was good as dead. I didn't move. Billy squeezed round into the small space between me and the washbasin and put the silencer against my neck.

Yardman's unhurried voice floated into my ear. 'I really must warn you, my dear boy, that your life hangs by the merest thread. If Billy hadn't clumsily missed you in the street you would be in the Milan morgue by now. If you do not do as we ask, he will be pleased to rectify his mistake immediately.'

I put my hands behind my back.

'That's right,' Yardman said approvingly. He tied them together with a rough piece of rope.

'Now, my dear boy,' he went on. 'You are going to help us. We have a little job for you.'

Billy's searchlight eyes were wide and bright, and I didn't like his smile.

'You don't ask us what it is,' Yardman said. 'So I will tell you. You are going to persuade your friend the pilot to alter course.'

Alter course. Simple words. Premonition shook me to the roots. Patrick wasn't strong enough.

I said nothing. After a moment Yardman continued conversationally, 'We were going to use the engineer originally, but as I find you and the pilot are good friends I am sure he will do as you ask.'

I still said nothing.

'He doesn't understand,' Billy sneered.

I understood all right. Patrick would do what they told him. Yardman opened the washroom door. 'Turn round,' he said.

I turned. Yardman's eyes fell immediately to the dried bloodstains on my shirt. He reached out a long arm, pulled the once white poplin out of my trousers and saw the bandage underneath.

'You grazed him,' he said to Billy, still critical.

'Considering he was running and falling at the same time that isn't bad, not with a silencer.'

'Inefficient.' Yardman wasn't letting him off the hook.

'I'll make up for it,' Billy said viciously.

'Yes, you do that.'

Yardman turned his head back to me. 'Outside, dear boy.'

I followed him out of the washroom into the cabin, and stopped. It looked utterly normal. The four mares stood peacefully in the two middle boxes, installed, I presumed, by Yardman and Alf. The foremost and aft boxes were strapped down flat. There were the normal bales of hay dotted about. The noise was the normal noise, the air neither hotter nor colder than usual. All familiar. Normal. As normal as a coffin.

Yardman walked on.

'This way,' he said. He crossed the small area at the back of the plane, stepped up on to the shallow platform formed by the flattened rear box, walked across it, and finished down again on the plane's floor, against the nearest box containing mares. Billy prodded his gun into my back. I joined Yardman.

'So wise, my dear boy,' nodded my employer. 'Stand with your back to the box.'

I turned round to face the tail of the aircraft. Yardman took some time fastening my tied hands to the centre banding bar round the mare's box. Billy stood up on the flattened box and amused himself by pointing

241

his gun at various parts of my anatomy. He wasn't going to fire it. I took notice of his antics but looked beyond him, to the pair of seats at the back. There was a man sitting there, relaxed and interested. The man who had flown out with us, whose name was John. Milan hadn't been the end of his journey, I thought. Yardman wanted to land him somewhere else.

He stood up slowly, his pompous manner a complete contradiction to his grubby ill-fitting clothes.

'Is this sort of thing really necessary?' he asked, but with curiosity, not distress. His voice was loud against the beat of the engine.

'Yes,' said Yardman shortly. I turned my head to look at him. He was staring gravely at my face, the bones of his skull sharp under the stretched skin. 'We know our business.'

Billy got tired of waving his gun about to an unappreciative audience. He stepped off the low platform and began dragging a bale of hay into the narrow alleyway between the standing box and the flattened one, settling it firmly longways between the two. On top of that bale he put another and on top of that another and another. Four bales high. Jammed against these, on top of the flattened box, he raised three more, using all the bales on the plane. Together, they formed a solid wall three feet away on my left. Yardman, John and I watched him in silence.

'Right,' Yardman said when he'd finished it. He

checked the time and looked out of the window. 'Ready?'

Billy and John said they were. I refrained from saying that I wasn't, and never would be.

All three of them went away up the plane, crouching under the luggage racks and stumbling over the guy chains. I at once discovered by tugging that Yardman knew his stuff with a rope. I couldn't budge my hands. Jerking them in vain, I suddenly discovered Alf watching me. He had come back from somewhere up front, and was standing on my right with his customary look of missing intelligence.

'Alf,' I shouted. 'Untie me.'

He didn't hear. He simply stood and looked at me without surprise. Without feeling. Then he slowly turned and went away. Genuinely deaf; but it paid him to be blind too, I thought bitterly. Whatever he saw he didn't tell. He had told me nothing about Simon.

I thought achingly of Gabriella hanging on to her life in Milan. She must still be alive, I thought. She must. Difficulties, the doctor had said. There might be difficulties. Like infection. Like pneumonia. Nothing would matter if she died . . . but she wouldn't . . . she couldn't. Anxiety for her went so deep that it pretty well blotted out the hovering knowledge that I should spare some for myself. The odds on her survival were about even: I wouldn't have taken a hundred to one on my own.

After ten eternal minutes Yardman and Billy came

back, with Patrick between them. Patrick stared at me, his face tight and stiff with disbelief. I knew exactly how he felt. Billy pushed him to the back with his gun, and Yardman pointed to the pair of seats at the back. He and Patrick sat down on them, side by side, fifteen feet away. A captive audience, I reflected sourly. Front row of the stalls.

Billy put his mouth close to my ear. 'He doesn't fancy a detour, your pilot friend. Ask him to change his mind.'

I didn't look at Billy, but at Patrick. Yardman was talking to him unhurriedly, but against the engine noise I couldn't hear what he said. Patrick's amber eyes looked dark in the gauntness of his face, and he shook his head slightly, staring at me beseechingly. Beseech all you like, I thought, but don't give in. I knew it was no good. He wasn't tough enough.

'Ask him,' Billy said.

'Patrick,' I shouted.

He could hear me. His head tilted to listen. It was difficult to get urgency and conviction across when one had to shout to be heard at all, but I did my best. 'Please ... fly back to Milan.'

Nothing happened for three seconds. Then Patrick tried to stand up and Yardman pulled him back, saying something which killed the beginning of resolution in his shattered face. Patrick, for God's sake, I thought, have some sense. Get up and go.

Billy unscrewed the silencer from his gun and put it

in his pocket. He carefully unbuttoned my shirt, pulled the collar back over my shoulders, and tucked the fronts round into the back of my trousers. I felt very naked and rather silly. Patrick's face grew, if anything, whiter.

Billy firmly clutched the dressing over the bullet mark and with one wrench pulled the whole thing off.

'Hey,' he shouted to Yardman. 'I don't call that a miss.'

Yardman's reply got lost on the way back.

'Want to know something?' Billy said, thrusting his sneering face close to mine. 'I'm enjoying this.'

I saved my breath.

He put the barrel of his revolver very carefully against my skin, laying it flat along a rib just above the existing cut. Then he pushed me round until I was half facing the wall he had made of the hay bales. 'Keep still,' he said. He drew the revolver four inches backwards with the barrel still touching me and pulled the trigger. At such close quarters, without the silencer, the shot was a crashing explosion. The bullet sliced through my skin over my ribs and embedded itself in the wall of hay. The spit of flame from the barrel scorched in its wake. In the box behind me, the startled mares began making a fuss. It would create a handy diversion, I thought, if they were frightened into dropping their foals.

Patrick was on his feet, aghast and swaying. I heard

him shouting something unintelligible to Billy, and Billy shouting back, 'Only you can stop it, mate.'

'Patrick,' I yelled. 'Go to Milan.'

'That's bloody enough,' Billy said. He put his gun back on my side, as before. 'Keep still.'

Yardman couldn't afford me dead until Patrick had flown where they wanted. I was all for staying alive as long as possible, and jerking around in the circumstances could cut me off short. I did as Billy said, and kept still. He pulled the trigger.

The flash, the crash, the burn, as before.

I looked down at myself, but I couldn't see clearly because of the angle. There were three long furrows now, parallel and fiery. The top two were beginning to bleed.

Patrick sat down heavily as if his knees had given way and put his hands over his eyes. Yardman was talking to him, clearly urging him to save me any more. Billy wasn't for waiting. He put his gun in position, told me to keep still, and shot.

Whether he intended it or not, that one went deeper, closer to the bone. The force of it spun me round hard against the mares' box and wrenched my arms, and my feet stumbled as I tried to keep my balance. The mares whinnied and skittered around, but on the whole they were getting less agitated, not more. A pity.

I had shut my eyes, that time. I opened them slowly to see Patrick and Yardman much nearer, only eight feet away on the far side of the flattened box. Patrick was staring with unreassuring horror at Billy's straight lines. Too soft-hearted, I thought despairingly. The only chance we had was for him to leave Billy to get on with it and go and turn back to Milan. We weren't much more than half an hour out. In half an hour we could be back. Half an hour of this . . .

I swallowed and ran my tongue round my dry lips.

'If you go where they say,' I said urgently to Patrick, 'they will kill us all.'

He didn't believe it. It wasn't in his nature to believe it. He listened to Yardman instead.

'Don't be silly, my dear boy. Of course we won't kill you. You will land, we will disembark, and you can all fly off again, perfectly free.'

'Patrick,' I said desperately. 'Go to Milan.'

Billy put his gun along my ribs.

'How long do you think you can keep still?' he asked, as if with genuine interest. 'What'll you bet?'

I tried to say, 'They shot Gabriella,' but Billy was waiting for that. I got the first two words out but he pulled the trigger as I started her name, and the rest of it got lost in the explosion and my own gasping breath.

When I opened my eyes that time, Patrick and Yardman had gone.

For a little while I clung to a distant hope that Patrick would turn back, but Billy merely blew across the top of his hot revolver and laughed at me, and when the plane banked it was to the left, and not a

one eighty degree turn. After he had straightened out
I looked at the acute angle of the late afternoon sun
as it sliced forwards in narrow slivers of brilliance
through the row of oval windows on my right.

No surprise, I thought drearily.

We were going east.

Billy had a pocket full of bullets. He sat on the flattened
box, feeding his gun. The revolving cylinder broke out
sideways with its axis still in line with the barrel, and
an ejector rod, pushed back towards the butt, had lifted
the spent cartridges out into his hand. The empty cases
now lay beside him in a cluster, rolling slightly on their
rims. When all the chambers were full again he snapped
the gun shut and fondled it. His eyes suddenly switched
up to me, the wide stare full of malice.

'Stinking earl,' he said.

A la lanterne, I thought tiredly. And all that jazz.

He stood up suddenly and spoke fiercely, with some
sort of inner rage.

'I'll make you,' he said.

'What?'

'Ask.'

'Ask what?'

'Something . . . anything. I'll make you bloody well
ask me for something.'

I said nothing.

'Ask,' he said savagely.

I stared past him as if he wasn't there. Fights, I thought with some chill, weren't always physical.

'All right,' he said abruptly. 'All right. You'll ask in the end. You bloody sodding well will.'

I didn't feel sure enough to say I bloody sodding well wouldn't. The taunting sneer reappeared on his face, without the same infallible confidence perhaps, but none the less dangerous for that. He nodded sharply, and went off along the alleyway towards the nose, where I hoped he'd stay.

I watched the chips of sunshine grow smaller and tried to concentrate on working out our course, more for distraction than from any hope of needing the information for a return journey. The bullets had hurt enough when Billy fired them, but the burns, as burns do, had hotted up afterwards. The force generated inside the barrel of a pistol was, if I remembered correctly, somewhere in the region of five tons. A bullet left a revolver at a rate of approximately seven hundred feet per second and if not stopped carried about five hundred yards. The explosion which drove the bullet spinning on its way also shot out flames, smoke, hot propulsive gases and burning particles of gunpowder, and at close quarters they made a very dirty mess. Knowing these charming facts was of no comfort at all. The whole ruddy area simply burnt and went on burning, as if someone had stood an electric iron on it and had forgotten to switch off.

After Billy went away it was about an hour before

I saw anyone again, and then it was Alf. He shuffled into my sight round the corner of the box I was tied to, and stood looking at me with one of the disposable mugs in his hand. His lined old face was, as usual, without expression.

'Alf,' I shouted. 'Untie me.'

There wasn't anywhere to run to. I just wanted to sit down. But Alf either couldn't hear, or wouldn't. He looked unhurriedly at my ribs, a sight which as far as I could see produced no reaction in him at all. But something must have stirred somewhere, because he took a slow step forward, and being careful not to touch me, lifted his mug. It had 'Alf' in red where Mike had written it that morning, in that distant sane and safe lost world of normality.

'Want some?' he said.

I nodded, half afraid he'd pour it out on the floor, as Billy would have done, but he held it up to my mouth, and let me finish it all. Lukewarm, oversweet neo-coffee. The best drink I ever had.

'Thank you,' I said.

He nodded, produced the nearest he could do to a smile, and shuffled away again. Not an ally. A non-combatant, rather.

More time passed. I couldn't see my watch or trust my judgement, but I would have guessed it was getting on for two hours since we had turned. I had lost all sense of direction. The sun had gone, and we were travelling into dusk. Inside the cabin the air grew colder. I would have liked to have had my shirt on properly, not to mention a jersey, but the mares behind my back provided enough warmth to keep me from shivering. On a full load in that cramped plane eight horses generated a summer's day even with icy conditions outside, and we seldom needed the cabin heaters. It was far too much to hope in the circumstances that Patrick would think of switching them on.

Two hours' flying. We must, I thought, have been down near Albenga when we turned, which meant that since then, if we were still going east and the winds were the same as in the morning, we could have been crossing Italy somewhere north of Florence. Ahead lay the Adriatic, beyond that, Yugoslavia, and beyond that, Romania.

It didn't matter a damn where we went, the end would be the same.

I shifted wearily, trying to find some ease, and worried for the thousandth time whether Gabriella was winning, back in Milan. The police there, I supposed, wrenching my mind away from her, would be furious I hadn't turned up. They still had my passport. There might at least be a decent investigation if I never went back for it, and Gabriella knew enough to explain what I'd inadvertently got caught up in. If she lived. If she lived . . .

The plane banked sharply in a steep turn to the left. I leant against the roll and tried to gauge its extent. Ninety degrees turn, I thought. No, more. It didn't seem to make much sense. But if – if – we had reached the Adriatic I supposed it was possible we were now going up it, north west, back towards Venice . . . and Trieste. I admitted gloomily to myself that it was utter guesswork; that I was lost, and in more than one sense.

Ten minutes later the engine note changed and the volume of noise decreased. We had started going down. My heart sank with the plane. Not much time left. Oncoming night and a slow descent, the stuff of death.

There were two rows of what looked like car headlights marking each side of a runway. We circled once so steeply that I caught a glimpse of them through the tipped window, and then we levelled out for the approach and lost speed, and the plane bumped down on to a rough surface. Grass, not tarmac. The plane taxied round a bit, and then stopped. One by one the four engines died. The plane was quiet and dark, and for three long deceptive minutes at my end of it there was peace.

The cabin lights flashed on, bright overhead. The mares behind me kicked the box. Farther along, the other pair whinnied restlessly. There was a clatter in the galley, and the noise of people coming back through the plane, stumbling over the chains.

Patrick came first, with Billy after. Billy had screwed the silencer back on his gun.

Patrick went past the flattened box into the small area in front of the two washroom doors. He moved stiffly, as if he couldn't feel his feet on the floor, as if he were sleep walking.

Billy had stopped near me, on my right.

'Turn round, pilot,' he said.

Patrick turned, his body first and his legs untwisting after. He staggered slightly, and stood swaying. If his face had been white before, it was leaden grey now. His eyes were stretched and glazed with shock, and his good-natured mouth trembled.

He stared at me with terrible intensity.

'He ... shot ... them,' he said. 'Bob ... and Mike. Bob and Mike.' His voice broke on the horror of it.

Billy sniggered quietly.

'You said ... they would kill us all.' A tremor shook him. 'I didn't ... believe it.'

His eyes went down to my side. 'I couldn't ...' he said. 'They said they'd go on and on ...'

'Where are we?' I asked sharply.

His eyes came back in a snap, as if I'd kicked his brain.

'Italy,' he began automatically. 'South west of ...'

Billy raised his gun, aiming high for the skull.

'No.' I yelled at him in rage and horror at the top of my voice. 'No.'

He jumped slightly, but he didn't even pause. The gun coughed through the silencer and the bullet hit its target. Patrick got both his hands halfway to his head before the blackness took him. He spun on his collapsing legs and crashed headlong, face down, his long body still and silent, the auburn hair brushing against the washroom door. The soles of his feet were turned mutely up, and one of his shoes needed mending.

CHAPTER FOURTEEN

Yardman and John edged round Billy and the flattened box and stood in the rear area, looking down at Patrick's body.

'Why did you do it back here?' John said.

Billy didn't answer. His gaze was fixed on me.

Yardman said mildly, 'Billy, Mr Rous-Wheeler wants to know why you brought the pilot here to shoot him?'

Billy smiled and spoke to me. 'I wanted you to watch,' he said.

John – Rous-Wheeler – said faintly, 'My God,' and I turned my head and found him staring at my ribs.

'Pretty good shooting,' said Billy complacently, following the direction of his eyes and taking his tone as a compliment. 'There's no fat on him and the skin over his ribs is thin. See where I've got every shot straight along a bone? Neat, that's what it is. A bit of craftsmanship I'd say. These lines are what I'm talking about,' – he was anxious to make his point – 'not all that black and red around them. That's only dried blood and powder burn.'

Rous-Wheeler, to do him justice, looked faintly sick.

'All right, Billy,' Yardman said calmly. 'Finish him off.'

Billy lifted his gun. I had long accepted the inevitability of that moment, and I felt no emotion but regret.

'He's not afraid,' Billy said. He sounded disappointed.

'What of it?' Yardman asked.

'I want him to be afraid.'

Yardman shrugged. 'I can't see what difference it makes.'

To Billy it made all the difference in the world. 'Let me take a little time over him, huh? We've got hours to wait.'

Yardman sighed. 'All right, Billy, if that's what you want. Do all the other little jobs first, eh? Shut all the curtains on the plane first, we don't want to advertise ourselves. And then go down and tell Giuseppe to turn those landing lights off, the stupid fool's left them on. He'll have ladders and paint waiting for us. He and you and Alf can start straight away on painting out the airline's name and the plane's registration letters.'

'Yeah,' said Billy. 'OK. And while I'm doing it I'll think of something.' He put his face close to mine, mocking. 'Something special for your effing lordship.'

He put the gun in its holster and the silencer in his pocket, and drew all the curtains in the back part of the plane, before starting forward to do the rest.

Rous-Wheeler stepped over Patrick's body, sat down

in one of the seats, and lit a cigarette. His hands were shaking.

'Why do you let him?' he said to Yardman. 'Why do you let him do what he likes?'

'He is invaluable.' Yardman sighed. 'A natural killer. They're not at all common, you know. That combination of callousness and enjoyment, it's unbeatable. I let him have his way if I can as a sort of reward, because he'll kill anyone I tell him to. I couldn't do what he does. He kills like stepping on a beetle.'

'He's so young,' Rous-Wheeler protested.

'They're only any good when they're young,' Yardman said. 'Billy is nineteen. In another seven or eight years, I wouldn't trust him as I do now. And there's a risk a killer will turn maudlin any time after thirty.'

'It sounds,' Rous-Wheeler cleared his throat, trying to speak as unconcernedly as Yardman, 'it sounds rather like keeping a pet tiger on a leash.'

He began to cross his legs and his shoes knocked against Patrick's body. With an expression of distaste he said, 'Can't we cover him up?'

Yardman nodded casually and went away up the plane. He came back with a grey blanket from the pile in the luggage bay, opened it out, and spread it over, covering head and all. I spent the short time that he was away watching Rous-Wheeler refuse to meet my eyes and wondering just who he was, and why he was so important that taking him beyond Milan was worth the lives of three totally uninvolved and innocent airmen.

An unremarkable looking man of about thirty-five, with incipient bags under his eyes, and a prim mouth. Unused to the violence surrounding him, and trying to wash his hands of it. A man with his fare paid in death and grief.

When Yardman had covered Patrick, he perched himself down on the edge of the flattened box. The overhead lights shone on the bald patch on his skull and the black spectacle frames made heavy bars of shadow on his eyes and cheeks.

'I regret this, my dear boy, believe me, I regret it sincerely,' he said, eyeing the result of Billy's target practice. Like Rous-Wheeler he took out a cigarette and lit it. 'He really has made a very nasty mess.'

But only skin deep, if one thought about it. I thought about it. Not much good.

'Do you understand what Billy wants?' Yardman said, shaking out his match.

I nodded.

He sighed. 'Then couldn't you ... er ... satisfy him, my dear boy? You will make it so hard for yourself, if you don't.'

I remembered the stupid boast I'd made to Billy the first day I'd met him, that I could be as tough as necessary. Now that I looked like having to prove it, I had the gravest doubts.

When I didn't answer Yardman shook his head

sorrowfully. 'Foolish boy, whatever difference would it make, after you are dead?'

'Defeat . . .' I cleared my throat and tried again. 'Defeat on all levels.'

He frowned. 'What do you mean?'

'Communists are greedy,' I said.

'Greedy,' he echoed. 'You're wandering, my dear boy.'

'They like to . . . crumble . . . people, before they kill them. And that's . . . gluttony.'

'Nonsense,' said Rous-Wheeler in a vintage Establishment voice.

'You must have read newspaper accounts of trials in Russia,' I said, raising an eyebrow. 'All those "confessions".'

'The Russians,' he said stiffly, 'are a great warmhearted simple people.'

'Oh, sure,' I agreed. 'And some are like Billy.'

'Billy is English.'

'So are you,' I said. 'And where are you going?'

He compressed his lips and didn't answer.

'I hope,' I said, looking at the blanket which covered Patrick, 'that your travel agents have confirmed your belief in the greatness, warm-heartedness and simplicity of the hemisphere you propose to join.'

'My dear boy,' interrupted Yardman smoothly, 'what eloquence!'

'Talking,' I explained, 'takes the mind off . . . this and that.'

A sort of recklessness seemed to be running in my blood, and my mind felt clear and sharp. To have even those two to talk to was suddenly a great deal more attractive than waiting for Billy on my own.

'The end justifies the means,' said Rous-Wheeler pompously, as if he'd heard it somewhere before.

'Crap,' I said inelegantly. 'You set yourself too high.'

'I am . . .' he began angrily, and stopped.

'Go on,' I said. 'You are what? Feel free to tell me. Moriturus, and all that.'

It upset him, which was pleasant. He said stiffly, 'I am a civil servant.'

'Were,' I pointed out.

'Er, yes.'

'Which ministry?'

'The Treasury,' he said, with the smugness of those accepted in the inner of inner sanctums.

The Treasury. It was a stopper, that one.

'What rank?' I asked.

'Principal.' There was a grudge in his voice. He hadn't risen.

'And why are you defecting?'

The forthcomingness vanished. 'It's none of your business.'

'Well it is rather,' I said in mock apology, 'since your change of allegiance looks like having a fairly decisive effect on my future.'

He looked mulish and kept silent.

'I suppose,' I said with mild irony, 'you are going where you think your talents will be appreciated.'

For a second he looked almost as spiteful as Billy. A petty-minded man I thought, full of imagined slights, ducking the admission that he wasn't as brilliant as he thought he was. None of that lessened one jot the value of the information he carried in his head.

'And you,' I said to Yardman. 'Why do you do it? All this.'

He looked back gravely, the tight skin pulling over his shut mouth.

'Ideology?' I suggested.

He tapped ash off his cigarette, made a nibbling movement with his lip, and said briefly, 'Money.'

'The brand of goods doesn't trouble you, as long as the carriage is paid?'

'Correct,' he said.

'A mercenary soldier. Slaughter arranged. Allegiance always to the highest bidder?'

'That,' he said, inclining his head, 'is so.'

It wasn't so strange, I thought inconsequentially, that I'd never been able to understand him.

'But believe me, my dear boy,' he said earnestly, 'I never really intended you any harm. Not you.'

'Thanks,' I said dryly.

'When you asked me for a job I nearly refused you ... but I didn't think you'd stay long, and your name gave my agency some useful respectability, so I agreed.' He sighed. 'I must admit, you surprised me.

You were very good at that job, if it's of any comfort to you. Very good. Too good. I should have stopped it when your father died, when I had the chance, before you stumbled on anything ... it was selfish of me. Selfish.'

'Simon Searle stumbled,' I reminded him. 'Not me.'

'I fear so,' he agreed without concern. 'A pity. He too was invaluable. An excellent accurate man. Very hard to replace.'

'Would you be so good as to untuck my shirt?' I said. 'I'm getting cold.'

Without a word he stood up, came round, tugged the bunched cloth out of the back of my trousers and pulled the collar and shoulders back to their right place. The shirt fronts fell together edge to edge, the light touch of the cloth on the burns being more than compensated by the amount of cool air shut out.

Yardman sat down again where he had been before and lit another cigarette from the stub of the first, without offering one to Rous-Wheeler.

'I didn't mean to bring you on this part of the trip,' he said. 'Believe me, my dear boy, when we set off from Gatwick I intended to organize some little delaying diversion for you in Milan, so that you wouldn't embark on the trip back.'

I said bleakly, 'Do you call sh ... shooting my girl a little diversion?'

He looked distressed. 'Of course not. Of course not. I didn't know you had a girl until you introduced her.

But then I thought it would be an excellent idea to tell you to stay with her a day or two, that we could easily manage without you on the way back. He' – he nodded at Patrick's shrouded body – 'told me you were ... er ... crazy about her. Unfortunately for you, he also told me how assiduous you had been in searching for Searle. He told me all about that bottle of pills. Now, my dear boy, that was a risk we couldn't take.'

'Risk,' I said bitterly.

'Oh yes, my dear boy, of course. Risk is something we can't afford in this business. I always act on risk. Waiting for certain knowledge may be fatal. And I was quite right in this instance, isn't that so? You had told me yourself where you were going to lunch, so I instructed Billy to go and find you and follow you from there, and make sure it was all love's young dream and no excitement. But you went bursting out of the restaurant and off at high speed to an obscure little bakery. Billy followed you in Vittorio's cab and rang me up from near there.' He spread his hands. 'I told him to kill you both and search you under cover of helping, as soon as you came out.'

'Without waiting to find out if there was anything in the bottle except pills?'

'Risk,' he nodded. 'I told you. We can't afford it. And that reminds me; where is Searle's message?'

'No message,' I said wearily.

'Of course there was, my dear boy,' he chided. 'You've shown so little surprise, asked so few questions.

It was clear to me at once that you knew far too much when Billy brought you back to the plane. I have experience in these things, you see.'

I shrugged a shoulder. 'In my wallet,' I said.

He drew on his cigarette, gave me an approving look, stepped over Patrick, and fetched my jacket from the washroom. He took everything out of the wallet and spread them beside him on the flattened box. When he picked out the hundred dinar note and unfolded it, the pieces of writing paper and hay fell out.

He fingered the note. 'It was plain carelessness on Billy's part,' he said. 'He didn't hide the canisters properly.'

'There was a lot of money, then, on the plane?'

'Wheels have to be oiled,' Yardman said reasonably, 'and it's no good paying Yugoslavs in sterling. All agents insist on being paid in the currency they can spend without arousing comment. I do, myself.'

I watched him turn the scrap of his stationery over and over, frowning. He saw the pin holes in the end, and held them up to the light. After a few seconds he put it down and looked from me to Rous-Wheeler.

'Men,' he said without inflection. 'And when you read that, my dear boy, you understood a great deal.' A statement, not a question.

Gabriella, I thought dumbly, for God's sake, live. Live and tell. I shut my eyes and thought of her as she had been at lunch. Gay and sweet and vital. Gabriella my dearest love ...

'Dear boy,' said Yardman in his dry unconcerned voice, 'are you feeling all right?'

I opened my eyes and shut Gabriella away out of reach of his frightening intuition.

'No,' I said with truth.

Yardman actually laughed. 'I like you, my dear boy, I really do. I shall miss you very much in the agency.'

'Miss . . .' I stared at him. 'You are going back?'

'Of course.' He seemed surprised, then smiled his bony smile. 'How could you know, I was forgetting. Oh yes, of course we're going back. My transport system . . . is . . . er . . . much needed, and much appreciated. Yes. Only the plane and Mr Rous-Wheeler are going on.'

'And the horses?' I asked.

'Those too,' he nodded. 'They carry good blood lines, those mares. We expected to have to slaughter them, but we have heard they will be acceptable alive, on account of their foals. No, my dear boy, Billy and I go back by road, halfway with Giuseppe, the second half with Vittorio.'

'Back to Milan?'

'Quite so. And tomorrow morning we learn the tragic news that the plane we missed by minutes this afternoon has disappeared and must be presumed lost with all souls, including yours, my dear boy, in the Mediterranean.'

'There would be a radar trace . . .' I began.

'My dear boy, we are professionals.'

'Oiled wheels?' I said ironically.

'So quick,' he said nodding. 'A pity I can't tempt you to join us.'

'Why can't you?' said Rous-Wheeler truculently.

Yardman answered with slightly exaggerated patience. 'What do I offer him?'

'His life,' Rous-Wheeler said with an air of triumph.

Yardman didn't even bother to explain why that wouldn't work. The Treasury, I thought dryly, really hadn't lost much.

Billy's voice suddenly spoke from the far end of the plane.

'Hey, Mr Yardman,' he called. 'Can't you and Mr Rous-flipping-Wheeler come and give us a hand? This ruddy aeroplane's bloody covered with names and letters. We're practically having to paint the whole sodding crate.'

Yardman stood up. 'Yes, all right,' he said.

Rous-Wheeler didn't want to paint. 'I don't feel . . .' he began importantly.

'And you don't want to be late,' Yardman said flatly.

He stood aside to let the deflated Rous-Wheeler pass, and they both made their way up past the two boxes, through the galley, and down the telescopic ladder from the forward door.

Desperation can move mountains. I'd never hoped to have another minute alone to put it to the test, but I'd thought of a way of detaching myself from the mare's box, if I had enough strength. Yardman had had difficulty squeezing the rope down between the banding bar and the wooden box side when he'd tied me there: he'd had to push it through with the blade of his pen-knife. It wouldn't have gone through at all, I thought, if either the box side wasn't a fraction warped or the bar a shade bent. Most of the bars lay flat and tight along the boxes, with no space at all between them.

I was standing less than two feet from the corner of the box, and along at the corner the bar was fastened by a lynch pin.

I got splinters in my wrists, and after I'd moved along six inches I thought I'd never manage it. The bar and the box seemed to come closer together the farther I went, and jerking the rope along between them grew harder and harder, until at last it was impossible. I shook my head in bitter frustration. Then I thought of getting my feet to help, and bending my knee put my foot flat on the box as high behind me as I could get leverage. Thrusting back with my foot, pulling forward on the bar with my arms, and jerking my wrists side-ways at the same time, I moved along a good inch. It worked. I kept at it grimly and finally arrived at the last three inches. From there, twisting, I could reach the lynch pin with my fingers. Slowly, agonizingly slowly, I pushed it up from the bottom, transferred my weak grip to the rounded top, slid it fraction by fraction up in my palm, and with an enormous sense of triumph felt it come free. The iron bands parted at the corner, and it required the smallest of jerks to tug the rope out through the gap.

Call that nothing, I said to myself with the beginnings of a grin. All that remained was to free my hands from each other.

Yardman had left my jacket lying on the flattened box, and in my jacket pocket was a small sharp penknife. I sat down on the side of the shallow platform, trying to pretend to myself that it wasn't because my legs were buckling at the knees but only the quickest way to reach the jacket. The knife was there, slim and familiar. I clicked open the blade, gripped it firmly, and sawed away blindly at some unseen point between my wrists. The friction of dragging the rope along had frayed it helpfully, and before I'd begun to hope for it I felt the strands stretch and give, and in two more seconds my hands were free. With stiff shoulders I brought them round in front of me. Yardman had no personal brutality and hadn't tied tight enough to stop the blood. I flexed my fingers and they were fine.

Scooping up wallet and jacket I began the bent walk forward under the luggage rack and over the guy chains, stepping with care so as not to make a noise and fetch the five outdoor decorators in at the double. I reached the galley safely and went through it. In the space behind the cockpit I stopped dead for a moment. The body of Mike the engineer lay tumbled in a heap against the left hand wall.

Tearing both mind and eyes away from him I edged

towards the way out. On my immediate right I came first to the luggage bay, and beyond that lay the door. The sight of my overnight bag in the bay made me remember the black jersey inside it. Better than my jacket, I thought. It had a high neck, was easier to move in, and wouldn't be so heavy on my raw skin. In a few seconds I had it on, and had transferred my wallet to my trousers.

Five of them round the plane, I thought. The exit door was ajar, but when I opened it the light would spill out, and for the time it took to get on to the ladder they would be able to see me clearly. Unless by some miracle they were all over on the port side, painting the tail. Well, I thought coldly, I would just be unlucky if the nearest to me happened to be Billy with his gun.

It wasn't Billy, it was the man I didn't know, Giuseppe. He was standing at the root of the starboard wing painting out the airline's name on the fuselage, and he saw me as soon as I opened the door not far below him. I pulled the door shut behind me and started down the ladder, hearing Giuseppe shouting and warning all the others. They had ladders to get down too, I thought. I could still make it.

Giuseppe was of the hard core, a practising militant communist. He was also young and extremely agile. Without attempting to reach a ladder he ran along the wing to its tip, put his hands down, swung over the edge, and dropped ten feet to the ground. Seeing his running form outlined on the wing against the stars I veered away to the left as soon as I had slid down the ladder, and struck out forwards, more or less on the same axis as the plane.

My eyes weren't accustomed to the light as theirs were. I couldn't see where I was going. I heard Giuseppe shouting in Italian, and Yardman answering. Billy tried a shot which missed by a mile. I scrambled on, holding my arms up defensively and hoping I wouldn't run into anything too hard. All I had to do, I told myself, was to keep going. I was difficult to see in black and moved silently over the grass of the field. If I got far enough from the plane they wouldn't be able to find me, not five of them with Alf no better than a snail. Keep going and get lost. After that I'd have all night to search out a bit of civilization and someone who could speak English.

The field seemed endless. Endless. And running hurt. What the hell did that matter, I thought dispassionately, with Billy behind me. I had also to refrain from making a noise about it in case they should hear me, and with every rib-stretching breath that got more difficult. In the end I stopped, went down on my knees, and tried to get air in shallow silent gulps. I could hear nothing behind but a faint breeze, see nothing above but the stars, nothing ahead but the dark. After a few moments I stood up again and went on, but more slowly. Only in nightmares did fields go on for ever. Even airfields.

At the exact second that I first thought I'd got away

with it, bright white lights blazed out and held me squarely in their beams. A distant row of four in front, a nearer row of four behind, and I a black figure in the flarepath. Sick devastating understanding flooded through me. I had been trying to escape down the runway.

Sharply, almost without missing a step, I wheeled left and sprinted; but Giuseppe wasn't very far behind after all. I didn't see or hear him until the last moment when he closed in from almost in front. I swerved to avoid him, and he threw out his leg at a low angle and tripped me up.

Even though I didn't fall very heavily, it was enough. Giuseppe very slickly put one of his feet on each side of my head and closed them tight on my ears. Grass pressed into my eyes, nose and mouth, and I couldn't move in the vice.

Billy came up shouting as if with intoxication, the relief showing with the triumph.

'What you got there then, my friend? A bleeding aristocrat, then? Biting the dust, too, ain't that a gas?'

I guessed with a split second to spare what he would do, and caught his swinging shoe on my elbow instead of my ribs.

Yardman arrived at a smart military double.

'Stop it,' he said. 'Let him get up.'

Giuseppe stepped away from my head and when I put my hands up by my shoulders and began to push myself up, Billy delivered the kick I had avoided before.

I rolled half over, trying not to care. The beams from the runway lights shone through my shut eyelids, and the world seemed a molten river of fire, scarlet and gold.

Without, I hoped, taking too long about it I again started to get up. No one spoke. I completed the incredibly long journey to my feet and stood there, quiet and calm. We were still on the runway between the distant lights, Yardman close in front of me, Giuseppe and Billy behind, with Rous-Wheeler struggling breathlessly up from the plane. Yardman's eyes, level with mine, were lit into an incandescent greenness by the glow. I had never clearly seen his eyes before. It was like drawing back curtains and looking into a soul.

A soldier without patriotism. Strategy, striking power and transport were skills he hired out, like any other craftsman. His pride was to exercise his skill to the most perfect possible degree. His pride overrode all else.

I think he probably meant it when he said he liked me. In a curious way, though I couldn't forgive him Gabriella, I felt respect for him, not hatred. Battle against him wasn't personal or emotional, as with Billy. But I understood that in spite of any unexpected warmth he might feel, he would be too prudent to extend foolish mercy to the enemy.

We eyed each other in a long moment of cool appraisal. Then his gaze slid past me, over my shoulder, and he paid me what was from his point of view a compliment.

'You won't crack him, Billy. Kill him now. One shot, nice and clean.'

CHAPTER FIFTEEN

I owed my life to Billy's greed. He was still hungry, still unsatisfied, and he shook his head to Yardman's request. Seeing the way Yardman delicately deferred to Billy's wishes it struck me that Rous-Wheeler's simile of a tiger on a leash might not be too far off the mark. In any case for the first time I was definitely glad of Billy's lust to spill my blue blood ounce by ounce, as I really was most averse to being shot down on the spot; and I acknowledge that I already had him to thank that I was still breathing at all. If I'd been anyone but who I was I would have died with the crew.

We walked back up the runway, I in front, the other four behind. I could hear Rous-Wheeler puffing, the only one not physically fit. Fit . . . It was only yesterday, I thought incredulously, that I rode in the Gold Cup.

The plane was a faintly lit shape to the left of the end of the runway. A hundred yards short of it Yardman said, 'Turn left, dear boy. That's it. Walk straight on. You will see a building. Go in.'

There was, in fact, a building. A large one. It

resembled an outsize prefabricated garage, made of asbestos sheets on a metal frame. The door was ajar and rimmed by light. I pushed it open, and with Billy's gun touching my back, walked in.

The right-hand two-thirds of the concrete floor space was occupied by a small four-seater single-engined aeroplane, a new looking high-winged Cessna with an Italian registration. On its left stood a dusty black Citroen, its bonnet towards me. Behind the car and the plane the whole far wall consisted of sliding doors. No windows anywhere. Three metal girders rose from floor to ceiling on the left of the car, supporting the flat roof and dividing the left hand part of the hangar into a kind of bay. In that section stood Alf.

'Right,' said Yardman briskly. 'Well done, Alf, turn them off now.' His voice echoed hollowly in space.

Alf stared at him without hearing.

Yardman went up to him and shouted in his ear. 'Turn the runway lights off.'

Alf nodded, walked up to the wall on the left of the door I had come in by, and pushed up a heavy switch beside a black fuse box. A second similar box worked, I supposed, the fluorescent strips across the ceilings and the low-powered radiant heaters mounted high on both side walls. Beside the switches stood a mechanic's bench with various tools and a vice, and farther along two sturdy brackets held up a rack of gardening implements: spades, fork, rake, hoe and shears. Filling all the back of the bay was a giant motor mower with a seat for the driver, and dotted about there were some five gallon petrol cans, funnels, tins of paint, an assortment of overalls and several greasy looking metal chairs.

That Cessna, I thought briefly: I could fly it like riding a bicycle. And the car ... if only I had known they were there.

Yardman searched among the clutter on the bench and produced a length of chain and two padlocks, one large, one small. Billy had shut the door and was standing with his back to it, the gun pointing steadily in my direction. Alf, Rous-Wheeler and Giuseppe had prudently removed themselves from his line of fire.

Yardman said, 'Go over to that first girder, my dear boy, and sit down on the floor.'

To say I was reluctant to be tied again is to put it mildly. It wasn't only that it was the end of any hope of escape, but I had a strong physical repugnance to being attached to things, the result of having been roped to a fir in a Scottish forest one late afternoon in a childhood game by some cousins I was staying with: they had run away to frighten me and got lost themselves, and it had been morning before the subsequent search had found me.

When I didn't obey at once, Yardman, Giuseppe and Billy all took a step forward as if moved by the same mind. There was no percentage in having them jump on me: I was sore enough already. I walked over to the girder and sat down facing them, leaning back idly against the flat metal surface.

'That's better,' Yardman said. He came round and knelt down on the ground at my back. 'Hands behind, my dear boy.'

He twined the chain round my wrists and clicked on both padlocks. Tossing the keys on his palm he stood up and came round in front of me. All five of them stared down with varying degrees of ill-feeling and I stared glassily back.

'Right,' said Yardman after a pause. 'We'd better get out and finish the painting. But this time we must leave someone with him, just in case.' He reviewed his available troops, and alighted on Rous-Wheeler. 'You sit here,' he said to him, picking up a chair and taking it over beside the switches, 'and if he does anything you aren't sure about, switch on the runway lights and we'll come at once. Clear?'

Rous-Wheeler was delighted to avoid any more painting and accepted his new task with enthusiasm.

'Good.' Yardman looked at his watch. 'Go on then, Billy.' Billy, Alf and Giuseppe filed out and Yardman stopped as he followed them to say to Rous-Wheeler, 'The cargo will be arriving soon. Don't be alarmed.'

'Cargo?' said Rous-Wheeler in surprise.

'That's right,' Yardman said. 'Cargo. The reason for this ... um ... operation.'

'But I thought I ...' began Rous-Wheeler.

'My dear Rous-Wheeler, no,' said Yardman. 'Had it

been just you, I could have sent you down the usual discreet pipeline from Milan. Your journey would have been just as secret as it is now. No, we needed the plane for a rather special cargo, and as you know, my dear boy,' – he swung round to speak directly to me with a small ironic smile – 'I do hate wasting space on flights. I always try to make up a full load, so as not to neglect an opportunity.'

'What is this cargo, then?' asked Rous-Wheeler with a damaged sense of self-importance.

'Mm?' said Yardman, putting the padlock keys down on the bench. 'Well now, it's the brain child of a brilliant little research establishment near Brescia. A sort of machine. An interesting little development, one might say. Broadly speaking, it's a device for emitting ultrasonic rays on the natural frequency of any chosen mineral substance.'

'Ultrasonics have been extensively researched,' Rous-Wheeler said testily.

Yardman smiled tightly. 'Take it from me, dear fellow, this particular development has great possibilities. Our friends have been trying to arrange photographs of the drawings and specifications, but these have been too well guarded. It proved easier in the end to . . . er . . . remove some vital parts of the device itself. But that of course presented a transport problem, a difficult transport problem, requiring my own personal supervision.' He was talking for my benefit as much as Rous-Wheeler's: letting me know how expert he was at his job. 'Once we were committed to the plane, of course it was the easiest way to take you too.'

No opportunity wasted. But he hadn't originally intended to take me as well, to give him his due.

Yardman went out of the hangar. Rous-Wheeler sat on his hard chair and I on the hard concrete and again my presence and/or predicament embarrassed him.

'Played any good wall games lately?' I said at length.

A hit, a palpable hit. He hadn't expected any needling school chums on his little trip. He looked offended.

'Have you been to ... er ... wherever you're going ... before?' I asked.

'No,' he said shortly. He wouldn't look at me.

'And do you speak the language?'

He said stiffly, 'I am learning.'

'What are they offering you?'

Some heavy smugness crept into his manner. 'I am to have a flat and a car, and a better salary. I will of course be in an important advisory position.'

'Of course,' I said dryly.

He flicked me his first glance. Disapproving.

'I am to be a consultant interpreter of the British way of life ... I pride myself that in my own small way I shall be promoting better understanding between two great peoples and making a positive contribution to the establishment of fruitful relations.'

He spoke as if he really meant it; and if he were as self-satisfied as that, he wouldn't consider turning

round and going back. But Yardman had left the padlock keys on the bench . . .

'Your actions may be misunderstood, back home,' I
said.

'At first. That has been explained to me. But in
time . . .'

'You're wrong,' I said roughly. 'They'll call you a
traitor. A plain stinking common or garden traitor.'

'No,' he said uneasily.

'What you need is someone to put your views forward, to explain what you are doing, so that your
former colleagues admire you, and wish they had made
more use of your undoubted abilities while they had
the chance . . .' I thought I'd laid it on too thick, but
not so. He was looking seriously pensive.

'You mean . . . you? You would represent me?' He
pursed his lips.

'I don't always look so dirty,' I said earnestly. 'I could
pull a certain amount of weight with my father's friends,
and . . . er . . . I have an uncle who more or less lives in
the Reform Club.'

He was nodding, taking it all in.

'A word in the right ear,' he said judiciously.

'Recognition,' I put in gently.

He looked modest. 'That's too much to hope for.'

'In time,' I insinuated.

'Do you really think so?'

'Well, of course.' I paused. 'I would be happy to

clear up any... er... bad feelings which your...
move ... may have left.'

'Uncommonly kind of you,' he said pompously.

'At the moment, however, I don't look like being
able to.'

He looked disappointed. 'I suppose not.' He
frowned. 'You could have done me an excellent... as
I see it now, an essential... service.'

I said casually, 'A great pity, yes. Of course ... the
keys are just beside you ... if you felt like it.'

He looked at the keys and at me. He stood up. He
took the keys into his hand. I could feel my heart
thudding as I tried to look unconcerned. He took a
step in my direction. Then, looking uneasily round, his
glance fell on the runway lights switch. He stared at it,
transfixed.

'Yardman said to put the lights on, if you tried anything.' There was consternation in his voice. He turned
and put the keys back on the bench as if they were
suddenly hot. 'Yardman considered it essential for you
to remain here. It would not be an auspicious start for
me with my new friends if the first thing I did was so
exactly contrary to their wishes.'

'Yardman's wishes.'

He used a modicum of brain. 'If I let you go back to
England, Yardman wouldn't be able to. His invaluable
transport service would have come to an end...' He
looked horrified at the abyss he had almost stepped
into. 'I would have been most unpopular.'

I didn't say anything. Down the snakes and back to square one. I tried again without success to do a Houdini on Yardman's chain job, and Rous-Wheeler sat down again and watched me with a mixture of anxiety and annoyance.

'What branch of the Treasury?' I said, giving it up.

'Initial finance,' he replied stiffly.

'What does that mean?'

'Grants.'

'You mean, your department settles who gets grants of public money, and how much?'

'That is so.'

'Development, research, defence, and so on?'

'Precisely.'

'So that you personally would know what projects are in hand . . . or contemplated?'

'Yes.'

They wouldn't have bothered with him, I supposed, for any less.

After a pause, I said, 'What about this ultrasonic transmitter?'

'What about it? It isn't a British project, if that's what you mean.'

'Did I get it right . . . that it will emit waves on the natural frequency of any mineral substance?'

'I believe that's what Yardman said,' he agreed stiffly.

'It would break things . . . like sound breaks glass?'

'I am not a scientist. I've no idea.' And from the tone of his voice he didn't care.

I stared gloomily at the floor and wondered what made a man change his allegiance. Rous-Wheeler might have been self-important and disappointed and have refused to face his own limitations, but thousands of men were like that, and thousands of men didn't give away a slice of their nation's future in return for a flat, a car, and a pat on the back. There had to be more to it. Deep obsessive murky convoluted motives I couldn't guess at, pushing him irresistibly over. But he would be the same man wherever he went: in five years or less, again disgruntled and passed over. A useless dispensable piece of flotsam.

He, it appeared, took as pessimistic a view of my future as I of his.

'Do you think – ' he cleared his throat. 'Do you think Billy will really kill you?'

'Be your age,' I said. 'You saw what he did to the crew.'

'He keeps putting it off,' he said.

'Saving the icing till last.'

'How can you be so frivolous?' he exclaimed. 'Your position is very serious.'

'So is yours,' I said. 'And I wouldn't swop.'

He gave me a small pitying smile of contemptuous disbelief, but it was true enough. Everyone dies sometime, as Simon had once said, and one was probably as little eager at eighty as at twenty-six. And there really were, I reflected with a smile for Victorian melodramas, fates worse than death.

A heavy van or lorry of some sort pulled up with a squeak of brakes somewhere near the door and after a few moments its driver came into the hangar. He was like Giuseppe, young, hard, cold-eyed and quick. He looked at me without apparent surprise and spoke to Rous-Wheeler in rapid Italian, of which the only intelligible word as far as I was concerned was Brescia.

Rous-Wheeler held up a hand, palm towards the driver. 'I don't understand you, my good fellow. Wait until I fetch Yardman.'

This proved unnecessary as my ex-employer had already seen the lorry's arrival. Followed by his entourage carrying ladders, paint pots, brushes and overalls, Yardman came forward into the hangar and exchanged some careful salutations with the driver.

'Right,' Yardman said in English to Billy. 'There should be several small light cases and one large heavy one. It will be easiest to load the light cases up through the forward door and stow them in the luggage bay. Then we will open the back doors, haul the heavy case in on the block and tackle, and stand it in the peat tray of the last box, the one that's now flattened. Clear?'

Billy nodded.

I opened my mouth to speak, and shut it again.

Yardman noticed. 'What is it?' he said sharply.

'Nothing.' I spoke listlessly.

He came over to me and looked down. Then he squatted on his haunches to peer on a level with my face.

'Oh yes, my dear boy, there is something. Now what, what?'

He stared at me as if he could read my thoughts while the calculations ticked over in his own. 'You were going to tell me something, and decided not to. And I feel I really should know what it is. I feel it must be to my disadvantage, something definitely to my disadvantage, as things stand between us.'

'I'll shoot it out of him,' Billy offered.

'It'll be quicker if I guess it . . . Now, what is wrong with stowing the cases the way I suggested? Ah yes, my dear boy, you know all about loading aeroplanes, don't you? You know what I said was wrong . . .' He snapped his fingers and stood up. 'The heavy case at the back is wrong. Billy, move the mares forward so that they occupy the two front boxes, and put the heavy case in the second to back box, and leave the rear one as it is.'

'Move the mares?' Billy complained.

'Yes, certainly. The centre of gravity is all-important, isn't that right, my dear boy?' He was pleased with himself, smiling. Quick as lightning. If I gave him even a thousandth of a second of suspicion that Gabriella was still alive . . .

Billy came over and stood looking down at me with a revoltingly self-satisfied smile.

'Not long now,' he promised.

'Load the plane first,' Yardman said. 'The van has to go back as soon as possible. You can . . . er . . . have your fun when I go to fetch the pilot. And be sure he's dead by the time I get back.'

'OK,' Billy agreed. He went away with Alf, Giuseppe and the driver, and the van ground away on the short stretch to the DC4.

'What pilot?' Rous-Wheeler asked.

'My dear Rous-Wheeler,' Yardman explained with a touch of weary contempt. 'How do you think the plane is going on?'

'Oh ... Well, why did you kill the other one? He would have flown on to wherever you said.'

Yardman sighed. 'He would have done no such thing without Billy at hand to shoot pieces off our young friend here. And frankly, my dear fellow, quite apart from the problem of Billy's and my return journey, it would have been embarrassing for us to kill the crew in your new country. Much better here. Much more discreet, don't you think?'

'Where exactly ... where are we?' asked Rous-Wheeler. A good question if ever there was one.

'A private landing field,' Yardman said. 'An elderly respected nobleman lets us use it from time to time.'

Elderly and respected: Yardman's voice held some heavy irony.

'The usual sort of blackmail?' I asked. 'Filmed in a bed he had no right in?'

Yardman said 'No,' unconvincingly.

'What's he talking about?' Rous-Wheeler asked testily.

'I'm talking about the methods employed by your new friends,' I said. 'If they can't get help and information by bamboozling and subverting people like you, they do it by any form of blackmail or intimidation that comes to hand.'

Rous-Wheeler was offended. 'I haven't been bamboozled.'

'Nuts,' I said. 'You're a proper sucker.'

Yardman took three threatening steps towards me with the first anger he had shown. 'That's enough.'

'Nothing's enough,' I said mildly. 'What the hell do you think I have to lose?'

Yardman's glasses flashed in the light, and Rous-Wheeler said self-righteously, 'He tried to get me to free him, while you were painting the plane. He asked me to unlock him. I didn't, of course.'

'You nearly did,' I said. 'Anyone can reach you; your overgrown self-esteem makes you permanently gullible.'

Yardman looked from me to him with a taut mouth. 'I have to go over to the plane, Mr Rous-Wheeler, and I think it would be best if you came with me.'

'But I wouldn't let him go,' he said, like a scolded schoolboy.

'All the same . . .' Yardman came behind me and bent down to check that his chains were still effective, which unfortunately they were. 'You look so gentle, dear boy,' he said into my ear. 'So misleading, isn't it?'

They went away and left me alone. I had another go

at the chains, tantalized by the Cessna standing so close behind me, but this time Yardman had been more careful. The girder was rooted in concrete, the chain wouldn't fray like rope, and try as I might I couldn't slide my hands out.

Little time to go, I thought. And no questions left. There wasn't much profit in knowing the answer, since in a very short while I would know nothing at all. I thought about that too. I didn't believe in any form of afterlife. To die was to finish. I'd been knocked out several times in racing falls, and death was just a knock-out from which one didn't awake. I couldn't honestly say that I much feared it. I never had. Undoubtedly on my part a defect of the imagination, a lack of sensitivity. All I felt was a strong reluctance to leave the party so soon when there was so much I would have liked to do. But there was the messy business of Billy to be got through first . . . and I admitted gloomily to myself that I would have avoided that if I could have dredged up the smallest excuse.

Alf shuffled into the hangar, went across to the rack of gardening tools and took down a spade. I shouted to him, but he showed no sign of having heard, and disappeared as purposefully as he'd come.

More minutes passed. I spent them thinking about Gabriella. Gabriella alive and loving, her solemnity a crust over depths of warmth and strength. A girl for always. For what was left of always.

The lorry came back, halted briefly outside, and

rumbled away into the distance. Yardman and all his crew except Alf trooped into the hangar. Giuseppe walked past me across to the sliding doors at the back and opened a space behind the Citroen. A cool draught blew in and sent the dust round in little squirls on the concrete floor, and outside the sky was an intense velvety black.

Yardman said, 'Right Billy. If the new crew are on time, we'll be back with them in a little over an hour. I want you ready to go then, immediately the plane has taken off. All jobs done. Understand?'

'OK.' Billy nodded. 'Relax.'

Yardman walked over and paused in front of me, looking down with a mixture of regret and satisfaction.

'Goodbye, my dear boy.'

'Goodbye,' I answered politely.

His taut mouth twisted. He looked across at Billy. 'Take no chances, Billy, do you understand? You underestimate this man. He's not one of your fancy nitwits, however much you may want him to be. You ought to know that by now. And Billy, I'm warning you, I'm warning you my dear Billy, that if you should let him escape at this stage, knowing everything that he does, you may as well put one of your little bullets through your own brain, because otherwise, rest assured, my dear Billy, I will do it for you.'

Even Billy was slightly impressed by the cold menace in Yardman's usually uninflected voice. 'Yeah,' he said uneasily. 'Well he won't bloody escape, not a chance.'

'Make sure of it.' Yardman nodded, turned, and went and sat in the front passenger seat of the Citroen. Giuseppe beside him started the engine, reversed the car out of the hangar, and drove smoothly away, Yardman facing forwards and not looking back. Billy slid the door shut again behind them and came slowly across the concrete, putting his feet down carefully and silently like a stalker. He stopped four paces away, and the silence slowly thickened.

Rous-Wheeler cleared his throat nervously, and it sounded loud.

Billy flicked him a glance. 'Go for a walk,' he said.

'A . . . walk?'

'Yeah, a walk. One foot in front of the other.' He was offensive. 'Down the runway and back should just about do it.'

Rous-Wheeler understood. He wouldn't meet my eyes and he hadn't even enough humanity to plead for me. He turned his back on the situation and made for the exit. So much for the old school tie.

'Now,' said Billy. 'Just the two of us.'

CHAPTER SIXTEEN

He walked cat-footed round the hangar in his quiet shoes, looking for things. Eventually he came back towards me carrying an old supple broken bicycle chain and a full flat five gallon tin of petrol. I looked at these objects with what I hoped was fair impassiveness and refrained from asking what he intended to do with them. I supposed I would find out soon enough.

He squatted on his haunches and grinned at me, his face level with mine, the bicycle chain in one hand and the petrol can on the floor in the other. His gun was far away, on the bench.

'Ask me nicely,' he said. 'And I'll make it easy.'

I didn't believe him anyway. He waited through my silence and sniggered.

'You will,' he said. 'You'll ask all right, your sodding lordship.'

He brought forward the bicycle chain, but instead of hitting me with it as I'd expected he slid it round my ankle and tied it there into two half hitches. He had difficulty doing this but once the knots were tied the links looked like holding for ever. The free end he fed through the handle of the petrol can and again bent it back on itself into knots. When he had finished there was a stalk of about six inches between the knots on my ankle and those on the can. Billy picked up the can and jerked it. My leg duly followed, firmly attached. Billy smiled, well satisfied. He unscrewed the cap of the can and let some of the petrol run out over my feet and make a small pool on the floor. He screwed the cap back on, but looser.

Then he went round behind the girder and unlocked both the padlocks on my wrists. The chain fell off, but owing to a mixture of surprise and stiffened shoulders I could do nothing towards getting my hands down to undo the bicycle chain before Billy was across the bay for his gun and turning with it at the ready.

'Stand up,' he said. 'Nice and easy. If you don't, I'll throw this in the petrol.' This, in his left hand, was a cigarette lighter: a gas lighter with a top which stayed open until one snapped it shut. The flame burned bright as he flicked his thumb.

I stood up stiffly, using the girder for support, the sick and certain knowledge of what Billy intended growing like a lump of ice in my abdomen. So much for not being afraid of death. I had changed my mind about it. Some forms were worse than others.

Billy's mouth curled. 'Ask, then,' he said.

I didn't. He waved his pistol slowly towards the floor. 'Outside, matey. I've a little job for you to do. Careful now, we don't want a bleeding explosion in here if we can help it.' His face was alight with greedy enjoyment. He'd never had such fun in his life. I found it definitely irritating.

The can was heavy as I dragged it along with slow steps to the door and through on to the grass outside. Petrol slopped continuously in small amounts through the loosened cap, leaving a highly inflammable trail in my wake. The night air was sweet and the stars were very bright. There was no moon. A gentle wind. A beautiful night for flying.

'Turn right,' Billy said behind me. 'That's Alf along there where the light is. Go there, and don't take too bloody long about it, we haven't got all night.' He sniggered at his feeble joke.

Alf wasn't more than a tennis court away, but I was fed up with the petrol can before I got there. He had been digging, I found. A six or seven foot square of grass had been cut out, the turf lying along one edge in a tidy heap, and about a foot of earth had been excavated into a crumbling mound. A large torch standing on the pile of turf shone on Alf's old face as he stood in the shallow hole. He held the spade loosely and looked at Billy enquiringly.

'Go for a walk,' Billy said loudly. Alf interpreted the meaning if not the words, nodded briefly, leaned the spade against the turf, stepped up on to the grass and shuffled away into the engulfing dark.

'OK, then,' said Billy. 'Get in there and start digging.

Any time you want to stop, you've only got to ask. Just ask.'

'And if I do?'

The light shone aslant on Billy's wide bright eyes and his jeering delighted mouth. He lifted the pistol a fraction. 'In the head,' he said. 'And I'll have bloody well beaten you, your effing bloody lordship. And it's a pity I haven't got the whole lot like you here as well.'

'We don't do any harm,' I said, and wryly knew that history gave me the lie. There'd been trampling enough done in the past, and resentment could persist for centuries.

'Keep both hands on the spade,' he said. 'You try and untie the bicycle chain, and you've had it.'

He watched me dig, standing safely out of reach of any slash I might make with the spade and snapping his lighter on and off. The smell of petrol rose sharply into my nostrils as it oozed drop by drop through the leaking cap and soaked into the ground I stood on. The earth was soft and loamy, not too heavy to move, but Billy hadn't chosen this task without careful malice aforethought. Try as I might, I found I could scarcely shift a single spadeful without in some way knocking or rubbing my arm against my side. Jersey and shirt were inadequate buffers, and every scoop took its toll. The soreness increased like a geometrical progression.

Billy watched and waited. The hole grew slowly deeper. I told myself severely that a lot of other people had had to face far worse than this, that others before me had dug what they knew to be their own graves, that others had gone up in flames for a principle ... that it was possible, even if not jolly.

Billy began to get impatient. 'Ask,' he said. I threw a spadeful of earth at him in reply and very nearly ended things there and then. The gun barrel jerked up fiercely at my head, and then slowly subsided. 'You'll be lucky,' he said angrily. 'You'll have to go down on your bloody knees.'

When I was sure my feet must be below his line of sight I tugged my foot as far away from the petrol can as the chain would allow, and jammed the spade down hard on the six inches of links between the knots. It made less noise than I'd feared on the soft earth. I did it again and again with every spadeful, which apart from being slightly rough on my ankle produced no noticeable results.

'Hurry up,' Billy said crossly. He flicked the lighter. 'Hurry it up.'

Excellent advice. Time was fast running out and Yardman would be back. I jammed the spade fiercely down and with a surge of long dead hope felt the battered links begin to split. It wasn't enough. Even if I got free of the petrol can I was still waist deep in a hole, and Billy still had his revolver; but even a little hope was better than none at all. The next slice of the spade split the chain further. The one after that severed it, but I had hit it with such force that when it broke I fell over, sprawling on hands and knees.

'Stand up,' Billy said sharply. 'Or I'll . . .'

I wasn't listening to him. I was acknowledging with speechless horror that the grave which was big enough for Patrick and Mike and Bob as well as myself was already occupied. My right hand had closed on a piece of cloth which flapped up through the soil. I ran my fingers along it, burrowing, and stabbed them into something sharp. I felt, and knew. A row of pins.

I stood up slowly and stared at Billy. He advanced nearly to the edge of the hole, looked briefly down, and back at me.

'Simon,' I said hopelessly. 'It's . . . Simon.'

Billy smiled. A cold, terrible, satisfied smile.

There was no more time. Time was only the distance from his gun to my head, from his gas lighter to my petrol-soaked shoes and the leaking can at my feet. He'd only been waiting for me to find Simon. His hunger was almost assuaged.

'Well,' he said, his eyes wide. 'Ask. It's your last chance.'

I said nothing.

'Ask,' he repeated furiously. 'You must.'

I shook my head. A fool, I thought. I'm a bloody fool. I must be mad.

'All right,' he said, raging. 'If I had more time you'd ask. But if you won't . . .' His voice died, and he seemed suddenly almost as afraid as I was at what he was going to do. He hesitated, half lifting the gun instead: but the moment passed and his nerve came back, renewed and pitiless.

He flicked the lighter. The flame shot up, sharp and blazing against the night sky. He poised it just for a second so as to be sure to toss it where I couldn't catch it on the way; and in that second I bent down, picked up the petrol can, and flung it at him. The loose cap unexpectedly came right off on the way up, and the petrol splayed out in a great glittering volatile stream, curving round to meet the flame.

A split second for evasion before the world caught fire.

The flying petrol burnt in the air with a great rushing noise and fell like a fountain over both the spots where Billy and I had just been standing. The can exploded with a gust of heat. The grave was a square blazing pit and flames flickered over the mound of dug out soil like brandy on an outsize plum pudding. Five gallons made dandy pyrotechnics.

I rolled out on my back over the lip of the grave with nothing to spare before it became a crematorium, and by some blessed miracle my feet escaped becoming part of the general holocaust. More than I had hoped.

Billy was running away screaming with his coat on fire along the left shoulder and down his arm. He was making frantic efforts to get it off but he was still clinging to his gun and this made it impossible. I had to have the gun and would have fought for it, but as I went after him I saw him drop it and stagger on, tearing at his jacket buttons in panic and agony: and my spine and scalp shuddered at the terror I had escaped.

With weak knees I half stumbled, half ran for the place where the revolver had fallen. The light of the flames glinted on it in the grass, and I bent and took it into my hand, the bulbous silencer heavy on the barrel and the butt a good fit in my palm.

Billy had finally wrenched his jacket off and it lay on the ground ahead in a deserted smouldering heap. Billy himself was still on his feet and making for the hangar, running and staggering and yelling for Alf.

I went after him.

Alf wasn't in the hangar. When I reached it Billy was standing with his back to me in the place where the car had been, rocking on his feet and still yelling. I stepped through the door and shut it behind me.

Billy swung round. The left sleeve of his shirt had burned into ribbons and his skin was red and glistening underneath. He stared unbelievingly at me and then at his gun in my hand. His mouth shut with a snap; and even then he could still raise a sneer.

'You won't do it,' he said, panting.

'Earls' sons,' I said, 'learn to shoot.'

'Only birds.' He was contemptuous. 'You haven't the guts.'

'You're wrong, Billy. You've been wrong about me from the start.'

I watched the doubt creep in and grow. I watched his eyes and then his head move from side to side as he looked for escape. I watched his muscles bunch to run for it. And when I saw that he finally realized in a moment of stark astonishment that I was going to, I shot him.

CHAPTER SEVENTEEN

The Cessna had full tanks. Hurriedly I pressed the master switch in the cockpit and watched the needles swing round the fuel gauges. All the instruments looked all right, the radio worked, and the latest date on the maintenance card was only three days old. As far as I could tell from a cursory check, the little aircraft was ready to fly. All the same . . .

Alf and Rous-Wheeler came bursting in together through the door, both of them startled and wild looking and out of breath. Back from their little walks and alarmed by the bonfire. Alf gave an inarticulate cry and hurried over to Billy's quiet body. Rous-Wheeler followed more slowly, not liking it.

'It's Billy,' he said, as if stupefied. 'Billy.'

Alf gave no sign of hearing. They stood looking down at Billy as he lay on his back. There was a small scarlet star just left of his breastbone, and he had died with his eyes wide open, staring sightlessly up to the roof. Alf and Rous-Wheeler looked lost and bewildered.

I climbed quickly and quietly out of the Cessna and walked round its tail. They turned after a moment or two and saw me standing there not six paces away, holding the gun. I wore black. I imagine my face was grim. I frightened them.

Alf backed away two steps, and Rous-Wheeler three. He pointed a shaking arm at Billy.

'You . . . you killed him.'

'Yes.' My tone gave him no comfort. 'And you too, if you don't do exactly as I say.'

He had less difficulty in believing it than Billy. He made little protesting movements with his hands, and when I said, 'Go outside. Take Alf,' he complied without hesitation.

Just outside the door I touched Alf's arm, pointed back at Billy and then down to where the grave was. The flames had burnt out.

'Bury Billy,' I shouted in his ear.

He heard me, and looked searchingly into my face. He too found no reassurance, and he was used to doing what I said. Accepting the situation with only a shade more dumb resignation than usual he went slowly back across the concrete. I watched him shut the glazing eyes with rough humane fingers, and remembered the cup of coffee he'd given me when I badly needed it. He had nothing to fear from me as long as he stayed down by the grave. He picked Billy up, swung him over his shoulder in a fireman's lift, and carried him out and away across the grass, a sturdy old horseman who should never have got caught up in this sort of thing. Any more than I should.

I stretched an arm back into the hangar and pulled down the lever which controlled the runway lights. At each end of the long strip the four powerful beams sprang out, and in that glow Alf could see where he was going and what he was going to do.

That Cessna, I thought, glancing at it, probably had a range of about six or seven hundred miles . . .

'You,' I said abruptly to Rous-Wheeler. 'Go and get into the plane we came in. Go up the forward steps, back through the galley, right back through the cabin, and sit down on those seats. Understand?'

'What . . .?' He began nervously.

'Hurry up.'

He gave me another frightened glance and set off to the plane, a lumbering grey shape behind the runway lights. I walked three steps behind him and unsympathetically watched him stumble in his fear.

'Hurry,' I said again, and he stumbled faster. The thought of the Citroen returning was like a devil on my tail. I was just not going to be taken again. There were five bullets left in the gun. The first for Rous-Wheeler, the next for Yardman, and after that . . . he would have Giuseppe with him, and at least two others. Not nice.

'Faster,' I said.

Rous-Wheeler reached the ladder and stumbled up it, tripping over half the steps. He went awkwardly back through the plane just as I had said and flopped down panting on one of the seats. I followed him. Someone, Alf I supposed, had given the mares some hay, and one of the bales from Billy's now dismantled wall had been clipped open and split. The binding wire from it lay handy on the flattened aft box. I picked it up to use on Rous-Wheeler, but there was nothing on the comfortable upholstered double seat I could tie him to.

He made no fuss when I bound his wrists together. His obvious fear made him flabby and malleable, and his eyes looked as if he could feel shock waves from the violence and urgency which were flowing through me.

'Kneel down,' I said, pointing to the floor in front of the seats. He didn't like that. Too undignified.

'Kneel,' I said. 'I haven't time to bother about your comfort.'

With a pained expression that at any other time would have been funny he lowered himself on to his knees. I slid the ends of the wire through one of the holes in the seat anchorages on the floor, and fastened him there securely by the wrists.

'I ss . . . say,' he protested.

'You're bloody lucky to be alive at all, so shut up.'

He shut up. His hands were tied only a couple of feet away from the blanket which covered Patrick. He stared at the quiet mound and he didn't like that either. Serve him right, I thought callously.

'What . . . what are you going to do?' he said.

I didn't answer. I went back up the cabin, looking at the way they'd re-stored the cargo. Aft box still flat. The walls of the next one, dismantled, had been stacked in the starboard alley. On the peat tray now stood a giant packing case six feet long, four feet wide, and nearly five feet tall. Chains ran over it in both directions, fastening it down to the anchorages. It had rope handles all the way round, and Yardman had said something about using a block and tackle, but all the same manoeuvring it into its present position must have been a tricky business. However, for the sake of forwarding the passage of this uninformative crate Yardman had also been prepared to steal a plane and kill three airmen. Those who had no right to it wanted it very badly.

I went up farther. The four mares were unconcernedly munching at full haynets and paid me scant attention. Through the galley and into the space behind the cockpit, where Mike's body still lay. Burial had been the last of the jobs. Uncompleted.

The luggage compartment held four more crates, the size of tea chests. They all had rope handles and no markings.

Beyond them was the open door. It represented to me a last chance of not going through with what I had in mind. Yardman hadn't yet come back, and the Cessna was ready. If I took it, with its radio and full tanks, I would undoubtedly be safe, and Yardman's transport business would be busted. But he'd still have the DC4 and the packing cases . . .

Abruptly I pulled up the telescopic ladder and shut the door with a clang. Too much trouble, I told myself, to change my mind now. I'd have to take Rous-Wheeler all the way back to the Cessna or shoot him, and neither course appealed. But the situation I found in the cockpit nearly defeated me before I began.

Billy had shot Bob as he sat, through the back of the head. The upper part of him had fallen forward over the wheel, the rest held firmly in the seat by the still fastened safety strap across his thighs. In the ordinary way even stepping into the co-pilot's seat in the cramped space was awkward enough, and lifting a dead man out of it bodily was beyond me. Blacking my mind to the sapping thought that this was a man I had known, and considering him solely as an object which spelled disaster to me if I didn't move it, I undid the seat belt, heaved the pathetic jack-knifed figure round far enough to clear his feet and head from the controls, and fastened the belt tight across him again in his new position, his back half towards me.

With the same icy concentration I sat in Patrick's place and set about starting the plane. Switches. Dozens of switches everywhere: on the control panel, on the roof, in the left side wall and in the bank of throttles on my right. Each labelled in small metal letters, and too many having to be set correctly before the plane would fly.

Patrick had shown me how. Quite different from doing it. I pared the pre-starting checks down to the barest minimum: fuel supply on, mixture rich, propeller revs maximum, throttle just open, brakes on, trimmer central, direction indicator synchronized with the compass.

My boats were burned with the first ignition switch, because it worked. The three bladed propeller swung and ground and the inner port engine roared into action with an earsplitting clatter. Throttle too far open. Gently I pulled the long lever with its black knob down until the engine fell back to warming up speed, and after that in quick succession and with increasing urgency I started the other three. Last, I switched on the headlights: Alf might not have heard the engines, but he would certainly see the lights. It couldn't be helped. I had to be able to see where I was going. With luck he wouldn't know what to do, and do nothing.

I throttled back a bit and took the brakes off and the plane began to roll. Too fast. Too fast. I was heading straight for the runway lights and could smash them, and I needed them alight. I pulled the two starboard throttles back for a second and the plane slewed round in a sort of skid and missed the lights and rolled forward on to the runway.

The wind was behind me, which meant taxiing to the far end and turning back to take off. No one ever taxied a DC4 faster. And at the far end I skipped all the power checks and everything else I'd been taught and swung the plane round facing the way I'd come and without a pause pushed forward all the four throttles wide open.

The great heavy plane roared and vibrated and began to gather speed with what seemed to me agonizing slowness. The runway looked too short. Grass was slower than tarmac, the strip was designed for light aircraft, and heaven alone knew the weight of that packing case ... For short runways, lower flaps. The answer came automatically from the subconscious, not as a clear coherent thought. I put my hand on the lever and lowered the trailing edges of the wings. Twenty degrees. Just under halfway. Full flaps were brakes ...

Yardman came back.

Unlike Alf, he knew exactly what to do, and wasted no time doing it. Towards the far end the Citroen was driven straight out on to the centre line of the runway, and my headlights shone on distant black figures scrambling out and running towards the hangar. Swerve wide enough to miss the car, I thought, and I'll get unbalanced on rough ground and pile up. Go straight up the runway and not be able to lift off in time, and I'll hit it either with the wheels or the propellers ...

Yardman did what Alf hadn't. He switched off the runway lights. Darkness clamped down like a sack over the head. Then I saw that the plane's bright headlights raised a gleam on the car now frighteningly close ahead and at least gave me the direction to head for. I was going far too fast to stop, even if I'd felt like it. Past the point of no return, and still on the ground. I eased gently back on the control column, but she wouldn't come. The throttles were wide; no power anywhere in reserve. I ground my teeth and with the car coming back to me now at a hundred miles an hour hung on for precious moments I couldn't spare, until it was then or never. No point in never. I hauled back on the control column and at the same time slammed up the lever which retracted the undercarriage. Belly flop or car crash; I wasn't going to be around to have second thoughts. But the DC4 flew. Unbelievably there was no explosive finale, just a smooth roaring upward glide. The plane's headlights slanted skywards, the car vanished beneath, the friction of the grass fell away. Airborne was the sweetest word in the dictionary.

Sweat was running down my face: part exertion, part fear. The DC4 was heavy, like driving a fully loaded pantechnicon after passing a test on empty Minis, and the sheer muscle power needed to hold it straight on the ground and get it into the air was in the circumstances exhausting. But it was up and climbing steadily at a reasonable angle, and the hands were circling reassuringly round the clock face of the altimeter. Two thousand, three thousand, four thousand feet. I levelled out at that and closed the throttles a little as the airspeed increased to two twenty knots. A slow old plane, built in nineteen forty-five. Two twenty was the most it could manage.

The little modern Cessna I'd left behind was just

about as fast. Yardman had brought a pilot. If he too took off without checks, he could be only scant minutes behind.

Get lost, I thought. I'd the whole sky to get lost in. The headlights were out, but from habit I'd switched on the navigation lights on the wing tips and tail and also the revolving beacon over the cockpit. The circling red beam from it washed the wings alternately with pale pink light. I switched it out, and the navigation lights too. Just one more broken law in a trail of others.

The runway had been laid out from due east to west. I had taken off to the west and flown straight on, urgent to get out, regardless of where. Too easy for them. I banked tentatively to the left and felt the plane respond cumbrously, heavy on my arms. South-west, into the wind. I straightened up and flew on, an invisible shell in the darkness, and after five minutes knew they wouldn't find me. Not with the Cessna, anyway.

The tight-strung tension of my nerves relaxed a little: with most uncomfortable results. I was suddenly far too aware of the wicked square of burn over my ribs, and realized that I hadn't really felt it since the moment I found Simon. Under the pressure of events its insistent message hadn't got through. Now it proceeded to rectify that with enthusiasm.

Weakness seeped down my limbs. I shivered, although I was still sweating from exertion. My hands started trembling on the wheel, and I began to realize the extent to which I was unfit to fly anything, let alone take a first try at an airliner way out of my normal class. But far worse than the physical stress was the mental let-down which accompanied it. It was pride which had got me into that plane and up into the air. Nothing but pride. I was still trying to prove something to Billy, even though he was dead. I hadn't chosen the DC4 because of any passionate conviction that the ultrasonic gadget needed saving at all costs, but simply to show them, Yardman and Billy's ghost, that there wasn't much I couldn't do. Childish, vainglorious, stupid, ridiculous: I was the lot.

And now I was stuck with it. Up in the air in thundering tons of metal, going I didn't know where.

I wiped the sleeve of my jersey over my face and tried to think. Direction and height were vital if I were ever to get down again. Four thousand feet, I thought, looking at the altimeter; at that height I could fly straight into a mountain . . . if there were any. South west steady: but south west from where? I hunted round the cockpit for a map of any sort, but there wasn't one to be found.

Patrick had said we were in Italy, and Giuseppe was Italian, and so was the registration on the Cessna, and the ultrasonic device had been driven straight from Brescia. Conclusive, I thought. Northern Italy, probably somewhere near the east coast. Impossible to get closer than that. If I continued south-west, in the end I'd be over the Mediterranean. And before that . . . new sweat broke out on my forehead. Between the northern plain and the Mediterranean lay the Apennines, and I couldn't remember at all how high they were. But four thousand was much too low . . . and for all I knew they were only a mile ahead . . .

I put the nose up and opened the throttles and slowly gained height. Five thousand, six thousand, seven thousand, eight. That ought to be enough . . . The Alps only reached above twelve thousand at the peaks, and the Apennines were a good deal lower. I was guessing. They might be higher than I thought. I went up again to ten thousand.

At that height I was flying where I had no business to be, and at some point I'd be crossing the airways to Rome. Crossing a main road in the dark, without lights. I switched the navigation lights on again, and the revolving beacon too. They wouldn't give much warning to a jetliner on a collision course, but possibly better than none.

The thunderous noise of the engines was tiring in itself. I stretched out a hand for Patrick's headset and put it on, the padded earphone reducing the din to a more manageable level. I had taken it for granted from the beginning that Yardman would have put the radio out of order before ever asking Patrick to change course, and some short tuning with the knobs confirmed it. Not a peep or crackle from the air. There had been just a chance that he wouldn't have disconnected the VOR – Very high frequency Omni-range – by which one navigated from one radio beacon to the next: it worked independently of two-way ground to air communication, and he might have needed to use it to find the airfield we had landed on. But that too was dead.

Time, I thought. If I didn't keep track of the time I'd be more lost than ever. I looked at my watch. Half past eleven. I stared at the hands blankly. If they'd said half nine or half one it would have felt the same. The sort of time one measured in minutes and hours had ceased to exist in a quiet street in Milan. I shook myself. Half past eleven. From now on it was important. Essential. Without maps or radio, time and the compass were going to decide my fate. Like all modern pilots I had been taught to stick meticulously to using all the aids and keeping all the regulations. The 'seat of the pants' stuff of the pioneers was held to be unscientific and no longer necessary. This was a fine time to have to learn it from scratch.

If I'd been up for a quarter of an hour, I thought, and if I'd started from the northern plain, and if I could only remember within a hundred miles how broad Italy was, then I might have some idea of when I'd be over the sea. Not yet, anyway. There were pinpricks of lights below me, and several small clusters of towns. Not conveniently lit airports with welcoming runways.

If I'd taken the Cessna, I thought wretchedly, it would have been easy. Somewhere, by twiddling the knobs, I'd have raised radio contact with the ground. The international air language was English. A piece of cake. They'd have told me my position, what course to set, how to get down, everything. But if I'd taken the Cessna, I would have had to leave the DC4 intact, because of the mares. I'd thought at first of piling a couple more five gallon cans under the big plane and putting a match to it, and then remembered the living half of the cargo. Yardman might be cold-bloodedly prepared to kill three airmen, but I balked at roasting alive four horses. And I couldn't get them out, because the plane carried no ramp. With time I could have put the engines out of action ... and with time they could have mended them again. But I hadn't had time. If I'd done that, I couldn't have got the Cessna out and away before Yardman's return.

I could have taken Rous-Wheeler in the Cessna and landed safely and put Yardman Transport out of business. But I was as greedy as Billy: half wasn't enough. It had to be all. I could choke on all, as Billy had.

The useless thoughts squirrelled round and round, achieving nothing. I wiped my face again on the sleeve of my jersey and understood why Patrick had nearly always flown in shirt sleeves, even though it was winter.

Italy couldn't be much wider than England. If as wide. A hundred and twenty, a hundred and forty nautical miles. Perhaps more. I hadn't looked at the time when I took off. I should have done. It was routine. I hadn't a hope if I couldn't concentrate better than that. A hundred and forty miles at two twenty knots ... say a hundred and sixty miles to be sure ... it would take somewhere between forty and forty-five minutes. If I'd had the sense to look at my watch earlier I would have known how far I'd gone.

The lights below grew scarcer and went out. It was probably too soon to be the sea . . . it had to be mountains. I flew on for some time, and then checked my watch. Midnight. And still no lights underneath. The Apennines couldn't be so broad . . . but if I went down too soon, I'd hit them. I gave it another five minutes and spent them wishing Billy's burns would let up again. They were a five star nuisance.

Still no lights. I couldn't understand it. I couldn't possibly still be over the narrow Apennines. It was no good. I'd have to go down for a closer look. I throttled back, let the nose go down, and watched the altimeter hands go anti-clockwise through seven, six, five, four. At four thousand feet I levelled out again, and the night was as black as ever. I'd certainly hit no mountains, but for all I could see I was a lost soul in Limbo. It wasn't a safe feeling, not at all.

When at last I saw lights ahead I was much more uneasy than reassured. It was twelve fifteen by my watch, which meant I had come nearly two hundred miles already, and Italy couldn't be as wide as that. Or at least I wouldn't have thought so.

The lights ahead resolved themselves into little clusters strung out in a horizontal line. I knew the formation too well to mistake it. I was approaching a coastline. Incredulity swamped me. I was approaching *from the sea.*

Nightmares weren't in it. I felt a great sense of unreality, as if the world had spun and rearranged its face, and nothing was ever going to be familiar again. I must be somewhere, I thought, taking a fierce grip on my escaping imagination. But where on earth, where literally on earth, was I?

I couldn't go on flying blindly south-west for ever. The coastline must have a shape. About three miles short of it I banked to the right, wheeling northwards, guided by nothing more rational than instinct, and flew along parallel with the few and scattered lights on the shore. The sea beneath was black but the land was blacker. The line where they met was like ebony against coal, a shadowy change of texture, a barely perceptible rub of one mass against another.

I couldn't, I thought, bullying my mind into some sort of order, I couldn't possibly have flown straight across the Gulf of Genoa and now be following the Italian coast northwards from Alassio. There weren't enough lights, even for that time of night. And I knew that coastline well. This one, I didn't. Moreover, it ran due north for far too long. I had already been following it for fifteen minutes: fifty-five miles.

It had to be faced that I'd been wrong about where I started from. Or else the directional gyro was jammed. It couldn't be ... I'd checked it twice against the remote reading compass, which worked independently. I checked again: they matched. They couldn't both be wrong. But I *must* have started in Italy. I went right back in my mind to the flight out, when Patrick had first turned east. It had been east. I was still sure of that: and that was all.

There was a flashing light up ahead, on the edge of the sea. A lighthouse. Very useful if I'd had a nautical chart, which I hadn't. I swept on past the lighthouse and stopped dead in my mental tracks. There was no land beyond.

I banked the plane round to the left and went back. The lighthouse stood at the end of a long narrow finger of land pointing due north. I flew southwards along the western side of it for about twenty miles until the sporadic lights spread wider and my direction swung again to the south-west. A fist pointing north.

Supposing I'd been right about starting from Italy, but wrong about being so far east. Then I would have been over the sea when I thought I was over mountains. Supposing I'd been going for longer than a quarter of an hour when I first looked at my watch: then I would have gone farther than I guessed. All the same, there simply wasn't any land this shape in the northern Mediterranean, not even an island.

An island of this size . . .

Corsica.

It couldn't be, I thought. I couldn't be so far south. I wheeled the plane round again and went back to the lighthouse. If it was Corsica and I flew north-west I'd reach the south of France and be back on the map. If it was Corsica I'd started from right down on the southern edge of the northern plain, not near Trieste or Venice as I'd imagined. It wasn't impossible. It made sense. The world began to fall back into place. I flew north-west over the black invisible sea. Twenty-seven minutes. About a hundred miles.

The strings and patterns of lights along the French coast looked like lace sewn with diamonds, and were just as precious. I turned and followed them westwards, looking for Nice airport. It was easy to spot by day: the runways seemed to be almost on the beach, as the airfield had been built on an outward curve of the shoreline. But either I was farther west than I thought, or the airport had closed for the night, because I missed it. The first place I was sure of was Cannes with its bay of embracing arms, and that was so close to Nice that if the runway had been lit I must have seen it.

A wave of tiredness washed through me, along with a numb feeling of futility. Even if I could find one, which was doubtful, I couldn't fly into a major airport without radio, and all the minor ones had gone to bed. I couldn't land anywhere in the dark. All I looked like being able to do was fly around in circles until it got light again and land at Nice . . . and the fuel would very likely give out before then.

It was at that depressing point that I first thought about trying to go all the way to England. The homing instinct in time of trouble. Primitive. I couldn't think of a thing against it except that I was likely to go to sleep from tiredness on the way, and I could do that even more easily going round in circles outside Cannes.

Committed from the moment I'd thought of it, I followed the coast until it turned slightly north again and the widespread lights of Marseilles lay beneath. The well-known way home from there lay up the Rhone Valley over the beacons at Montelimar and Lyons, with a left wheel at Dijon to Paris. But though the radio landmarks were unmistakable the geographical ones weren't, and I couldn't blindly stumble into the busy Paris complex without endangering every other plane in the area. North of Paris was just as bad, with the airlanes to Germany and the East. South, then. A straight line across France south of Paris. It would be unutterably handy to have known where Paris lay; what precise bearing. I had to guess again . . . and my first guesses hadn't exactly been a riotous triumph.

Three-twenty degrees, I thought. I'd try that. Allow ten degrees for wind drift from the south-west. Three ten. And climb a bit . . . the centre of France was occupied by the Massif Central and it would be fairly inefficient to crash into it. I increased the power and went back up to ten thousand feet. That left fuel, the worst problem of all.

I'd taken off on the main tanks and the gauges now stood at half full. I switched over to the auxiliaries and they also were half full. And half empty too. The plane had been refuelled at Milan that morning, ten centuries ago. It carried . . . I thought searchingly back to Patrick's casually thrown out snippets of information the first day I flew with him ... it carried twelve hundred United States gallons, giving a range of approximately eighteen hundred miles in normal conditions with a normal load. The load, though unconventional, was normal enough in weight. The condition of the weather was perfect, even if the condition of the pilot wasn't. Nine hundred miles from Marseilles would see me well over England, but it wouldn't take much more than four hours at the present speed until the tanks ran dry and it would still be too dark ...

There was just one thing to be done about that. I put my hand on the throttle levers and closed them considerably. The airspeed fell back from two-twenty back through two hundred, one-eighty, steadied on one-fifty. I didn't dare go any slower than that because one thing Patrick hadn't told me was the stalling speed, and a stall I could do without. The nose wanted to go down heavily with the decreased airspeed and I was holding it up by brute strength, the wheel of the control column lodged against my whole left forearm. I stretched my right hand up to the trimmer handle in the roof and gave it four complete turns, and cursed as a piece of shirt which was sticking to the furrows and burns unhelpfully unstuck itself. The nose of the plane steadied; ten thousand feet at one-fifty knots; and blood oozed warmly through my jersey.

A hundred and fifty knots should reduce the petrol consumption enough for me to stay in the air until long enough after dawn to find an airfield. I hoped. It also meant not four hours ahead, but more than five: and I'd had enough already. Still, now that I knew roughly where I was going, the plane could fly itself. I made small adjustments to the trimmer until the needle on the instrument which showed whether she was climbing or descending pointed unwaveringly to level, and then switched in the automatic pilot. I took my hands off the wheel and leaned back. The DC4 flew straight on. Very restful.

Nothing happened for several minutes except that I developed a thirst and remembered Rous-Wheeler for the first time since takeoff. Still on his knees, I supposed, and extremely uncomfortable. His bad luck.

There was water in the galley only five or six steps behind me, cold and too tempting. Gingerly I edged out of my seat. The plane took no notice. I took two steps backwards. The instruments didn't quiver. I went into the galley and drew a quick cup of water, and went back towards the cockpit drinking it. Clearly the plane was doing splendidly without me. I returned to the galley for a refill of the cold delicious liquid, and when I'd got it, nearly dropped it.

Even above the noise of the engines I could hear Rous-Wheeler's scream. Something about the raw terror in it raised the hair on my neck. That wasn't pain, I thought, not the sort he'd get from cramp anyway. It was fear.

He screamed again, twice.

One of the horses, I thought immediately. If Billy hadn't boxed them properly ... my newly irrigated mouth went dry again. A loose horse was just too much.

I went back to the cockpit, hurrying. Nothing had moved on the instrument panel. I'd have to risk it.

The plane had never seemed longer, the chains and racks more obstructing. And none of the mares was loose. They weren't even fretting, but simply eating hay. Half relieved, half furious, I went on past the packing case. Rous-Wheeler was still there, still kneeling. His eyes protruded whitely and his face was wet. The last of his screams hung like an echo in the air.

'What the hell's the matter?' I shouted to him angrily.

'He ...' his voice shrieked uncontrollably. 'He ... moved.'

'Who moved?'

'Him.' His eyes were staring fixedly at the blanket covering Patrick.

He couldn't have moved. Poor, poor Patrick. I went across and pulled the rug off and stood looking down at him, the tall silent body, the tumbled hair, the big pool of blood under his downturned face.

Pool of blood.

It was impossible. He hadn't had time to bleed as much as that. I knelt down beside him and rolled him over, and he opened his yellow eyes.

CHAPTER EIGHTEEN

He'd been out cold for six hours and he was still unconscious. Nothing moved in his eyes, and after a few seconds they fell slowly shut again.

My fingers were clumsy on his wrist and for anxious moments I could feel nothing; but his pulse was there. Slow and faint, but regular. He was on his way up from the depths. I was so glad that he wasn't dead that had Rous-Wheeler not been there I would undoubtedly have wept. As it was, I fought against the flooding back of the grief I'd suppressed when Billy shot him. Odd that I should be tumbled into such intense emotion only because the reason for it was gone.

Rous-Wheeler stuttered 'What . . . what is it?' with a face the colour and texture of putty, and I glanced at him with dislike.

'He's alive,' I said tersely.

'He can't be.'

'Shut up.'

Billy's bullet had hit Patrick high, above the hairline and at a rising angle, and instead of penetrating his skull had slid along outside it. The long, swollen and clotted wound looked dreadful, but was altogether beautiful in comparison with a neat round hole. I stood up and spread the blanket over him again, to keep him warm. Then, disregarding Rous-Wheeler's protest, I went away up the plane.

In the cockpit nothing had changed. The plane roared steadily on its three ten heading and all the instruments were like rocks. I touched the back of the co-pilot, awake again to his presence. The silence in him was eternal: he wouldn't feel my sympathy, but he had it.

Turning back a pace or two, I knelt down beside Mike. He too had been shot in the head, and about him too there was no question. The agile eyebrow was finished. I straightened him out from his crumpled position and laid him flat on his back. It wouldn't help any, but it seemed to give him more dignity. That was all you could give the dead, it seemed; and all you could take away.

The four packing cases in the luggage bay were heavy and had been thrust in with more force than finesse, pushing aside and crushing most of the things already there. Shifting the first case a few inches I stretched a long arm past it and tugged out a blanket, which I laid over Mike. Armed with a second one I went back to the galley. Sometime in the past I'd seen the first aid box in one of the cupboards under the counter, and to my relief it was still in the same place.

Lying on top of it was a gay parcel wrapped in the striped paper of Malpensa Airport. The doll for Mike's daughter. I felt the jolt physically. Nothing could soften the facts. I was taking her a dead father for her birthday.

And Gabriella . . . anxiety for her still hovered in my mind like a low ceiling, thick, threatening and unchanged. I picked up the parcel she had wrapped and put it on the counter beside the plastic cups and the bag of sugar. People often did recover from bullets in the lungs: I knew they did. But the precise Italian doctor had only offered hope, and hope had tearing claws. I was flying home to nothing if she didn't live.

Taking the blanket and the first aid kit I went back to Patrick. In the lavatory compartment I washed my filthy hands and afterwards soaked a chunk of cotton wool with clean water to wipe his bloodstreaked face. Dabbing dry with more cotton wool I found a large hard lump on his forehead where it had hit the floor: two heavy concussing shocks within seconds, his brain had received. His eyelids hadn't flickered while I cleaned him, and with a new burst of worry I reached for his pulse: but it was still there, faint but persevering.

Sighing with relief I broke open the wrapping of a large sterile wound dressing, laid it gently over the deep gash in his scalp, and tied it on with tape. Under his head I slid the second blanket, folded flat, to shield him a little from the vibration in the aircraft's metal skin. I loosened his tie and undid the top button of his shirt and also the waistband of his trousers; and beyond that there was no help I could give him. I stood up slowly with the first aid kit and turned to go.

With anxiety bordering on hysteria Rous-Wheeler shouted, 'You aren't going to leave me like this again, are you?'

I looked back at him. He was half sitting, half kneeling, with his hands still fastened to the floor in front of him. He'd been there for nearly three hours, and his flabby muscles must have been cracking. It was probably too cruel to leave him like that for the rest of the trip. I put the first aid kit down on the flattened box, pulled a bale of hay along on the starboard side and lodged it against the ultrasonic packing case. Then with Alf's cutter I clipped through the wire round his wrists and pointed to the bale.

'Sit there.'

He got up slowly and stiffly, crying out. Shuffling, half falling, he sat where I said. I picked up another piece of wire and in spite of his protests bound his wrists together again and fastened them to one of the chains anchoring the crate. I didn't want him bumbling all over the plane and breathing down my neck.

'Where are we going?' he said, the pomposity reawakening now that he'd got something from me.

I didn't answer.

'And who is flying the plane?'

'George,' I said, finishing his wrists with a twirl he'd never undo. 'Naturally.'

'George who?'

'A good question,' I said nodding casually.

He was beautifully disconcerted. I left him to stew in it, picked up the first aid kit, checked again that Patrick's pulse was plodding quietly along, and made my way back to the galley.

There were a number of dressings in the first aid box, including several especially for burns, and I wasn't keen on my shirt sticking and tearing away again. Gingerly I pulled my jersey up under my arms and tucked the side of the shirt away under it. No one except Billy would have found the view entertaining, and the air at once started everything going again at full blast. I opened one of the largest burn dressings and laid it in place with that exquisite kind of gentleness you only give to yourself. Even so, it was quite enough. After a moment I fastened it on and pulled my shirt and jersey down on top. It felt so bad for a bit that I really wished I hadn't bothered.

I drank another cup of water, which failed to put out the fire. The first aid kit, on further inspection, offered a three-way choice in pain killers: a bottle each of aspirin and codeine tablets, and six ampoules of morphine. I shook out two of the codeines, and swallowed these. Then I packed everything back into the box, shut the lid, and left it on the counter.

Slowly I went up to the cockpit and stood looking at the instruments. All working fine. I fetched a third blanket from the luggage bay and tucked it over and round the body of Bob. He became immediately less of a harsh reality, and I wondered if that was why people always covered the faces of the dead.

I checked the time. An hour from Marseilles. Only a hundred and fifty miles, and a daunting way still to go. I leaned against the metal wall and shut my eyes. It was no good feeling the way I did with so much still to do. Parts of Air Ministry regulations drifted ironically into my mind . . . 'Many flying accidents have occurred as a result of pilots flying while medically unfit . . . and the more exacting the flying task the more likely are minor indispositions to be serious . . . so don't go up at all if you are ill enough to need drugs . . . and if coffee isn't enough to keep you awake you are not fit to fly.'

Good old Air Ministry I thought: they'd hit the nail on the head. Where they would have me be was down on the solid earth, and I wholeheartedly agreed.

The radio, I thought inconsequentially. Out of order. I opened my eyes, pushed myself off the wall, and set about finding out why. I hadn't far to look. Yardman had removed all the circuit breakers, and the result was like an electric light system with no fuses in the fuse box. Every plane carried spares, however. I located the place where the spares should have been, and there weren't any. The whole lot in Yardman's pockets, no doubt.

Fetching a fresh cup of water, I climbed again into Patrick's seat and put on the headset to reduce the noise. I leaned back in the comfortable leather upholstery and rested my elbows on the stubby arms, and after a while the codeine and the bandage turned in a reasonable job.

Outside the sky was still black and dotted with brilliant stars, and the anti-collision beacon still skimmed pinkly over the great wide span of the wings, but there was also a new misty greyish quality in the light. Not dawn. The moon coming up. Very helpful of it, I thought appreciatively. Although it was well on the wane I would probably be able to see what I was doing the next time I flew out over the coastline. I began to work out what time I would get there. More guesses. North-west across France coast to coast had to be all of five hundred miles. It had been one-forty when I left Marseilles; was three-ten now. ETA English Channel somewhere about five.

Patrick's being alive made a lot of difference to everything. I was now thankful without reservation that I had taken the DC4 however stupid my motive at the time, for if I'd left it, and Yardman had found him alive, they would simply have pumped another bullet into him, or even buried him as he was. The tiring mental merry-go-round of whether I should have taken the Cessna troubled me no more.

I yawned. Not good. Of all things I couldn't afford to go to sleep. I shouldn't have taken those pills, I thought: there was nothing like the odd spot of agony for keeping you awake. I rubbed my hand over my face and it felt as if it belonged to someone else.

I murdered Billy, I thought.

I could have shot him in the leg and left him to Yardman, and I'd chosen to kill him myself. Choice and those cold-blooded seconds of revenge . . . they made it murder. An interesting technical point, where self-defence went over the edge into something else. Well . . . no one would ever find out; and my conscience didn't stir.

I yawned again more deeply, and thought about eating one of Patrick's bananas. A depleted bunch of them lay on the edge by the windscreen, with four blackening stalks showing where he had fended off starvation on the morning trip. But I imagined the sweet pappiness of them in my mouth, and left them alone. I wasn't hungry enough. The last thing I'd eaten had been the lasagne with Gabriella.

Gabriella . . .

After a while I got up and went through the plane to look at Patrick. He lay relaxed and unmoving, but his eyes were open again. I knelt beside him and felt his pulse. Unchanged.

'Patrick,' I said. 'Can you hear?'

There was no response of any sort.

I stood up slowly and looked at Rous-Wheeler sitting on the bale of hay. He seemed to have shrunk slightly as if the gas had leaked out, and there was a defeated sag to his whole body which showed that he realized his future was unlikely to be rosy. I left him without speaking and went back to the cockpit.

Four o'clock. France had never seemed so large. I checked the fuel gauges for the hundredth time and saw that the needles on the auxiliary tanks were knocking uncomfortably near zero. The plane's four engines used a hundred and fifty gallons an hour at normal speed and even with the power reduced they seemed to be drinking the stuff. Fuel didn't flow automatically from the main tanks when the auxiliaries were empty: one had to switch over by hand. And I simply couldn't afford to use every drop in the auxiliaries, because the engines would stop without warning the second the juice dried up. My fingers hovered on the switch until I hadn't the nerve to wait any longer, and then flipped it over to the mains.

Time passed, and the sleeping country slipped by underneath. When I got to the coast, I thought wearily, I was going to have the same old problem. I wouldn't know within two hundred miles where I was, and the sky was ruthless to the lost. One couldn't stop to ask the way. One couldn't stop at all. A hundred and fifty an hour might be slow in terms of jetliners, but it was much too fast in the wrong direction.

In Patrick's briefcase there would be not only a thick book of radio charts but also some topographical ground maps; they weren't needed for ordinary aerial navigation, but they had to be carried in case of radio failure. The briefcase was almost certainly somewhere under or behind the four packing cases in the luggage bay. I went to have a look, but I already knew. The heavy cases were jammed in tight, and even if there had been room to pull them all out into the small area behind the cockpit I hadn't enough strength to do it.

At about half past four I went back for another check on Patrick, and found things very different. He had thrown off the blanket covering him and was plucking with lax uncoordinated hands at the bandage on his head. His eyes were open but unfocused still, and his breath came out in short regular groans.

'He's dying,' Rous-Wheeler shouted unhelpfully.

Far from dying, he was up close to the threshold of consciousness, and his head was letting him know it. Without answering Rous-Wheeler I went back along the alley and fetched the morphine from the first aid kit.

There were six glass ampoules in a flat box, each with its own built-in hypodermic needle enclosed in a glass cap. I read the instruction leaflet carefully and Rous-Wheeler shouted his unasked opinion that I had no right to give an injection, I wasn't a doctor, I should leave it for someone who knew how.

'Do you?' I said.

'Er, no.'

'Then shut up.'

He couldn't. 'Ask the pilot, then.'

I glanced at him. 'I'm the pilot.'

That did shut him up. His jaw dropped to allow a clear view of his tonsils and he didn't say another word.

While I was rolling up his sleeve Patrick stopped

groaning. I looked quickly at his face and his eyes moved slowly round to meet mine.

'Henry,' he said. His voice didn't reach me, but the lip movement was clear.

I bent down and said, 'Yes, Patrick. You're OK. Just relax.'

His mouth moved. I put my ear to his lips, and he said 'My bloody head hurts.'

I nodded, smiling. 'Not for long.'

He watched me snap the glass to uncover the needle and didn't stir when I pushed it into his arm, though I'd never been on the delivering end of an injection before and I must have been clumsy. When I'd finished he was talking again. I put my head down to hear.

'Where . . . are . . . we?'

'On your way to a doctor. Go to sleep.'

He lay looking vaguely at the roof for a few minutes and then gradually shut his eyes. His pulse was stronger and not so slow. I put the blanket over him again and tucked it under his legs and arms and with barely a glance for Rous-Wheeler went back to the cockpit.

A quarter to five. Time to go down. I checked all the gauges, found I was still carrying the box of ampoules, and put it up on the ledge beside the bananas and the cup of water. I switched out the cockpit lights so that I could see better outside, leaving the round dial faces illuminated only by rims of red, and finally unlocked the automatic pilot.

It was when I'd put the nose down and felt again the great weight of the plane that I really doubted that I could ever land it, even if I found an airfield. I wasn't a mile off exhaustion and my muscles were packing up, and not far beyond this point I knew the brain started missing on a cylinder or two, and haze took the place of thought. If I couldn't think in crystalline terms and at reflex speed I was going to make an irretrievable mistake, and for Patrick's sake, quite apart from my own, I couldn't afford it.

Four thousand feet. I levelled out and flew on, looking down through the moonlit blackness, searching for the sea. Tiredness was insidious and crept up like a tide, I thought, until it drowned you. I shouldn't have taken that codeine, it was probably making me sleepy . . . though I'd had some at other times after racing injuries, and never noticed it. But that was on the ground, with nothing to do but recover.

There. There was the sea. A charcoal change from black, the moonlight just reflecting enough to make certain. I flew out a little way, banked the plane to the right and began to follow the shore. Compass heading, east-south-east. This seemed extraordinary, but it certainly had to be the north-east coast of France somewhere, and I wasn't going to lose myself again. There were lighthouses, flashing their signals. No charts to interpret them. The biggest port along that coast, I thought, was Le Havre. I couldn't miss that. There would be a lot of lights even at five in the morning. If

I turned roughly north from there I couldn't help but reach England. Roughly was just the trouble. The map in my head couldn't be trusted. Roughly north could find me barging straight into the London Control Zone, which would be even worse than Paris.

It wouldn't be light until six at the earliest. Sunrise had been about a quarter to seven, the day before.

The lights of Le Havre were ahead and then below me before I'd decided a thing. Too slow, I thought numbly, I was already too slow. I'd never get down.

The coast swung northwards, and I followed. Five twenty a.m. The fuel gauges looked reasonable with dawn not far ahead. But I'd got to decide where I was going. I'd got to.

If I simply went on for a bit I'd reach Calais. It still wouldn't be light. Somewhere over in Kent were Lympne, Lydd and Manston airports. Somewhere. My mind felt paralysed.

I went on and on along the French coast like an automaton until at last I knew I'd gone too far. I hadn't watched the compass heading closely enough and it had crept round from north to nearly east. That light I'd passed a while back, I thought vaguely, the light flashing at five second intervals, that must have Gris Nez. I'd gone past Calais. I was nearly round to Belgium. I'd simply got to decide . . .

The sky was definitely lighter. With surprise I realized that for several minutes the coastline had been easier to see, the water beneath lightening to a flat dark grey. Soon I could look for an airport: but not in Belgium. The explanations would be too complicated. Back to Kent, perhaps . . .

In a way, the solution when it came was simple. I would go to the place I knew best. To Fenland. In daylight I could find my way unerringly there from any direction, which meant no anxious circling around, and familiarity would cancel out a good deal of the tiredness. The flying club used grass runways which were nothing like long enough for a DC4, but its buildings had once been part of an old Air Force base, and the concrete runways the bombers had used were still there. Grass grew through the cracks in them and they weren't maintained, but they were marked at the ends with a white cross over a white bar, air traffic signal for a safe enough landing in an emergency.

My mental fog lifted. I banked left and set off North Seawards, and only after five decisive minutes remembered the fuel.

The burns were hurting again and my spirits fell to zero. Would I never get it right? I was an amateur, I thought despairingly. Still an amateur. The jockey business all over again. I had never achieved anything worthwhile and I certainly hadn't built the solid life I wanted. Simon had been quite right, I couldn't have gone on carting racehorses all my life; and now that Yardman Transport no longer existed I wouldn't look for the same job again.

It was a measure of my exhausted state that having

once decided to go to Fenland I hadn't the will to plunge back into uncertainty. The fuel margin was far too small for it to be prudent to go so far. Prudence in the air was what kept one alive. If I went to Fenland I'd be landing on a thimbleful, and if the engines stopped five miles away it would be too late to wish I hadn't.

Streaks of faint red crept into the sky and the sea turned to grey pearl. The sky wasn't so clear any more: there were layers of hazy cloud on the horizon, shading from dark grey-blue to a wisp of silver. The moment before dawn had always seemed to me as restoring as sleep, but that time when I really needed it, it had no effect. My eyes felt gritty and my limbs trembled under every strain. And the codeine had worn off.

The coast of East Anglia lay like a great grey blur ahead on my left. I would follow it round, I thought, and go in over the Wash . . .

A swift dark shape flashed across in front of the DC4 and my heart jumped at least two beats. A fighter, I thought incredulously. It had been a jet fighter. Another came over the top of me ridiculously close and screamed away ahead leaving me bumping horribly in the turbulence he left in his wake. They both turned a long way ahead and roared back towards me, flying level together with their wing tips almost touching. Expert formation pilots: and unfriendly. They closed at something like the speed of sound and swept over the DC4 with less than a hundred feet between. To them

I must have seemed to be standing still. To me, the trail they left me was very nearly the clincher.

Yardman couldn't have found me, I thought desperately. Not after the wavering roundabout route I'd taken. They couldn't have followed me and wouldn't have guessed I'd go up the North Sea ... it couldn't be Yardman's doing. So who?

I looked out at East Anglia away on my left, and didn't know whether to laugh or die of fear. Americans. East Anglia was stiff with American air bases. They would have picked me up on their radar, an unidentified plane flying in at dawn and not answering to radio. Superb watchdogs, they would send someone to investigate ... and they'd found a plane without registration numbers or markings of any sort. A plane like that couldn't be up to any good ... had to be hostile. One could almost hear them think it.

They wouldn't start shooting, not without making sure ... not yet. If I just went straight on and could deal with the buffeting, what would they do? I wouldn't let them force me down ... I had only to plod straight on ... They swept past on each side and threw the DC4 about like a cockleshell.

I couldn't do it, I thought, not this on top of everything else. My hands were slipping on the wheel with sweat. If the fighters went on much longer the sturdy old plane would shake to bits. They came past twice more and proved me wrong. They also reduced me to a dripping wreck. But after that they vanished somewhere above me, and when I looked up I saw them still circling overhead like angry bees. They were welcome to accompany me home, I thought weakly, if that was only where they'd stay.

I could see the lightship off Cromer still flashing its group of four every fifteen seconds. The first real sign of home. Only sixty miles to go. Fifteen minutes to the lightship in the Wash, and the sun rose as I went over it. I turned the plane on to the last leg to Fenland, and up above the escorts came with me.

The fuel gauges looked horrible. I drove what was left of my mind into doing some vital checks. Pitch fully fine, brakes off, mixture rich, fuel pumps on. There must have been a list somewhere but heaven knew where. I had no business to be flying the plane at all, I didn't know its drill ... The Air Ministry could take away my licence altogether and I was liable for a prison sentence as well. Except, I thought suddenly with a flicker of amusement, that Patrick was qualified to fly it, and he might be said to be technically in charge. Resident, anyway.

I throttled back and began to go down. If I managed it, I thought, I would be a professional. The decision was suddenly standing there full-blown like a certainty that had been a long time growing. This time it wasn't too late. I would take Tom Wells' job and make him stick to it when he inevitably found out my name. I would fly his car firm executives around and earn the sort of life I wanted, and if it meant giving up racing . . . I'd do that too.

The airspeed indicator stood at a hundred and thirty knots on the slow descent, and I could see the airfield ahead. The fighters were there already, circling high. The place would be crawling with investigators before my wheels stopped rolling. Questions, when I could do with sleep.

The distant orange wind sock blew out lazily, still from the south west. There wasn't enough fuel for frills like circuits, the gauges registered empty. I'd have to go straight in, and get down first time . . . get down. If I could.

I was close now. The club building developed windows, and there was Tom's bungalow . . .

A wide banking turn to line up with the old concrete runway . . . It looked so narrow, but the bombers had used it. Six hundred feet. My arms were shaking. I pushed down the lever of the undercarriage and the light went green as it locked. Five hundred . . . I put on full flap, maximum drag . . . retrimmed . . . felt the plane get slower and heavier, soft on the controls . . . I could stall and fall out of the sky . . . a shade more power . . . still some fuel left . . . the end of the runway ahead with its white cross coming up to meet me, rushing up . . . two hundred feet . . . I was doing a hundred and twenty . . . I'd never landed a plane with a cockpit so high off the ground . . . allow for that . . . One hundred . . . lower . . . I seemed to be holding the whole plane up ... I closed the throttles completely and levelled out as the white cross and the bar slid underneath, and waited an agonized few seconds while the air speed fell down and down until there was too little lift to the wings and the whole mass began to sink ...

The wheels touched and bounced, touched and stayed down, squeaking and screeching on the rough surface. With muscles like jelly, with only tendons, I fought to keep her straight. I couldn't crash now ... I wouldn't. The big plane rocketed along the bumpy concrete ... I'd never handled anything so powerful ... I'd misjudged the speed and landed too fast and she'd never stop ...

A touch of brake ... agonizing to be gentle with them and fatal if I wasn't ... They gripped and tugged and the plane stayed straight ... more brake, heavier ... it was making an impression ... she wouldn't flip over on to her back, she had a tricycle undercarriage with a nose wheel ... I'd have to risk it ... I pulled the brakes on hard and the plane shuddered with the strain, but the tyres didn't burst and I hadn't dipped and smashed a wing or bent the propellers and there wasn't going to be a scratch on the blessed old bus ... She slowed to taxiing speed with a hundred yards to spare before the runway tapered off into barbed wire and gorse bushes. Anything would have been enough. A hundred yards was a whole future.

Trembling, feeling sick, I wheeled round in a circle and rolled slowly back up the runway to where it ran closest to the airport buildings. There I put the brakes full on and stretched out a hand which no longer seemed part of me, and stopped the engines. The roar died to a whisper, and to nothing. I slowly pulled off the headset and listened to the cracking noises of the hot metal cooling.

It was done. And so was I. I couldn't move from my seat. I felt disembodied. Burnt out. Yet in a sort of exhausted peace I found myself believing that against all probability I had survived the night, so had Gabriella ... that away back in Milan she would be breathing safely through her damaged lung. I had to believe it. Nothing else would do.

Through the window I saw Tom Wells come out of his bungalow, staring first up at the circling fighters and then down at the DC4. He shrugged his arms into his old sheepskin jacket and began to run towards me over the grass.

HOT MONEY

With love and thanks as usual
to
MERRICK and FELIX

THE PEMBROKES

MALCOLM PEMBROKE

HIS WIVES	1	**Vivien**
	2	**Joyce**
	3	**Alicia**
	4	**Coochie**
	5	**Moira**

VIVIEN'S CHILDREN	1	**Donald**, married to Helen
	2	**Lucy**, married to Edwin
	3	**Thomas**, married to Berenice

JOYCE'S CHILD	1	**Ian**, unmarried

ALICIA'S CHILDREN	1	**Gervase**, married to Ursula
	2	**Ferdinand**, married to Debs
	3	**Serena**, unmarried

COOCHIE'S CHLDREN	1	**Robin**
	2	**Peter**, dead

CHAPTER ONE

I intensely disliked my father's fifth wife, but not to the point of murder.

I, the fruit of his second ill-considered gallop up the aisle, had gone dutifully to the next two of his subsequent nuptials, the changes of 'mother' punctuating my life at six and fourteen.

At thirty however I'd revolted: wild horses couldn't have dragged me to witness his wedding to the sharp-eyed honey-tongued Moira, his fifth choice. Moira had been the subject of the bitterest quarrel my father and I ever had and the direct cause of a non-speaking wilderness which had lasted three years.

After Moira was murdered, the police came bristling with suspicion to my door, and it was by the merest fluke that I could prove I'd been geographically elsewhere when her grasping little soul had left her carefully tended body. I didn't go to her funeral, but I wasn't alone in that. My father didn't go either.

A month after her death he telephoned me, and it

1

was so long since I'd heard his voice that it seemed that of a stranger.

'Ian?'

'Yes,' I said.

'Malcolm.'

'Hello,' I said.

'Are you doing anything?'

'Reading the price of gold.'

'No, dammit,' he said testily. 'In general, are you busy?'

'In general,' I said, 'fairly.'

The newspaper lay on my lap, an empty wine glass at my elbow. It was late evening, after eleven, growing cold. I had that day quit my job and put on idleness like a comfortable coat.

He sighed down the line. 'I suppose you know about Moira?'

'Front page news,' I agreed. 'The price of gold is on ... er ... page thirty-two.'

'If you want me to apologize,' he said, 'I'm not going to.'

His image stood sharp and clear in my mind: a stocky, grey-haired man with bright blue eyes and a fizzing vitality that flowed from him in sparks of static electricity in cold weather. He was to my mind stubborn, opinionated, rash and often stupid. He was also financially canny, intuitive, quick-brained and courageous, and hadn't been nicknamed Midas for nothing.

'Are you still there?' he demanded.

2

'Yes.'

'Well . . . I need your help.'

He said it as if it were an everyday requirement, but I couldn't remember his asking anyone for help ever before, certainly not me.

'Er . . .' I said uncertainly. 'What sort of help?'

'I'll tell you when you get here.'

'Where is "here"?'

'Newmarket,' he said. 'Come to the sales tomorrow afternoon.'

There was a note in his voice which couldn't be called entreaty but was far from a direct order, and I was accustomed only to orders.

'All right,' I said slowly.

'Good.'

He disconnected immediately, letting me ask no questions: and I thought of the last time I'd seen him, when I'd tried to dissuade him from marrying Moira, describing her progressively, in the face of his implacable purpose, as a bad misjudgement on his part and as a skilful, untruthful manipulator and, finally, as a rapacious blood-sucking tramp. He'd knocked me down to the floor with one fast, dreadful blow, which he'd been quite capable of at sixty-five, three years ago. Striding furiously away, he'd left me lying dazed on my carpet and had afterwards behaved as if I no longer existed, packing into boxes everything I'd left in my old room in his house and sending them by public carrier to my flat.

3

Time had proved me right about Moira, but the unforgivable words had remained unforgiven to her death and, it had seemed, beyond. On this October evening, though, perhaps they were provisionally on ice.

I, Ian Pembroke, the fourth of my father's nine children, had from the mists of infancy loved him blindly through thunderous years of domestic infighting which had left me permanently impervious to fortissimo voices and slammed doors. In a totally confused chaotic upbringing, I'd spent scattered unhappy periods with my bitter mother but had mostly been passed from wife to wife in my father's house as part of the furniture and fittings, treated by him throughout with the same random but genuine affection he gave to his dogs.

Only with the advent of Coochie, his fourth wife, had there been peace, but by the time she took over I was fourteen and world-weary, cynically expecting a resumption of hostilities within a year of the honeymoon.

Coochie, however, had been different. Coochie of all of them had been my only real mother, the only one who'd given me a sense of worth and identity, who'd listened and encouraged and offered good advice. Coochie produced twin boys, my half-brothers Robin and Peter, and it had seemed that at last Malcolm Pembroke had achieved a friendly family unit, albeit a sort of sunny clearing surrounded by jungle thickets of ex-wives and discontented siblings.

I grew up and left home but went back often, never feeling excluded. Coochie would have seen Malcolm into a happy old age but, when she was forty and the twins eleven, a hit-and-run driver swerved her car off the road and downhill onto rocks. Coochie and Peter had been killed outright. Robin, the elder twin, suffered brain damage. I had been away. Malcolm was in his office: a policeman went to him to tell him, and he let me know soon after. I'd learned the meaning of grief on that drizzly afternoon, and still mourned them all, their loss irreparable.

On the October evening of Malcolm's telephone call, I glanced at them as usual as I went to bed, their three bright faces grinning out from a silver frame on my chest of drawers. Robin lived – just – in serene twilight in a nursing home. I went to see him now and again. He no longer looked like the boy in the photograph, but was five years older, growing tall, empty-eyed.

I wondered what Malcolm could possibly want. He was rich enough to buy anything he needed, maybe – only maybe – excluding the whole of Fort Knox. I couldn't think of anything I could do for him that he couldn't get from anyone else.

Newmarket, I thought. The sales.

Newmarket was all very well for me because I'd been working as an assistant to a racehorse trainer. But Newmarket for Malcolm? Malcolm never gambled on horses, only on gold. Malcolm had made several immense consecutive fortunes from buying and selling the hard yellow stuff, and had years ago reacted to my stated choice of occupation by saying merely, 'Horses? Racing? Good Lord! Well, if that's what you want, my boy, off you go. But don't expect me to know the first thing about anything.' And, as far as I knew, he was still as ignorant of the subject as he'd been all along.

Malcolm and Newmarket bloodstock sales simply didn't mix. Not the Malcolm I'd known, anyway.

I drove the next day to the isolated Suffolk town whose major industry was the sport of kings, and among the scattered purposeful crowd found my father standing bareheaded in the area outside the sale-ring building, eyes intently focused on a catalogue.

He looked just the same. Brushed grey hair, smooth brown vicuna knee-length overcoat, charcoal business suit, silk tie, polished black shoes; confidently bringing his City presence into the casual sophistication of the country.

It was a golden day, crisp and clear, the sky a cold cloudless blue. I walked across to him in my own brand of working clothes: cavalry twill trousers, checked wool shirt, padded olive-green jacket, tweed cap. A surface contrast that went personality deep.

'Good afternoon,' I said neutrally.

He raised his eyes and gave me a stare as blue as the sky.

'So you came.'

'Well . . . yes.'

He nodded vaguely, looking me over. 'You look older,' he said.

'Three years.'

'Three years and a crooked nose.' He observed it dispassionately. 'I suppose you broke that falling off a horse?'

'No . . . You broke it.'

'Did I?' He seemed only mildly surprised. 'You deserved it.'

I didn't answer. He shrugged. 'Do you want some coffee?'

'OK.'

We hadn't touched each other, I thought. Not a hug, not a handshake, not a passing pat on the arm. Three years' silence couldn't easily be bridged.

He set off not in the direction of the regular refreshment room, but towards one of the private rooms set aside for the privileged. I followed in his footsteps, remembering wryly that it took him roughly two minutes any time to talk himself into the plushest recesses, wherever.

The Newmarket sales building was in the form of an amphitheatre, sloping banks of seats rising all round from the ground-level ring where each horse was led round while being auctioned. Underneath the seating and in a large adjacent building were rooms used as offices by auctioneers and bloodstock agents, and as entertainment rooms by commercial firms, such as Ebury Jewellers, Malcolm's present willing hosts.

I was used only to the basic concrete boxes of the bloodstock agents' offices. Ebury's space was decorated in contrast as an expensive showroom, with well-lit glass display cases round three walls shining with silver and sparkling with baubles, everything locked away safely but temptingly visible. Down the centre of the room, on brown wall-to-wall carpeting, stood a long polished table surrounded with armed, leather-covered dining chairs. Before each chair was neatly laid a leather-edged blotter alongside a gold-tooled tub containing pens, suggesting that all any client needed to provide here was his cheque book.

A smooth young gentleman welcomed Malcolm with enthusiastic tact and offered drinks and goodies from the well-stocked buffet table which filled most of the fourth wall. Lunch, it seemed, was an all-day affair. Malcolm and I took cups of coffee and sat at the table, I, at any rate, feeling awkward. Malcolm fiddled with his spoon. A large loud lady came in and began talking to the smooth young man about having one of her dogs modelled in silver. Malcolm raised his eyes to them briefly and then looked down again at his cup.

'What sort of help?' I said.

I suppose I expected him to say he wanted help in

some way with horses, in view of the venue he'd chosen, but it seemed to be nothing as straightforward.

'I want you beside me,' he said.

I frowned, puzzled. 'How do you mean?'

'Beside me,' he said. 'All the time.'

'I don't understand.'

'I don't suppose you do,' he said. He looked up at my face. 'I'm going to travel a bit. I want you with me.'

I made no fast reply and he said abruptly, explosively, 'Dammit, Ian, I'm not asking the world. A bit of your time, a bit of your attention, that's all.'

'Why now, and why me?'

'You're my son.' He stopped fiddling with the spoon and dropped it onto the blotter where it left a round stain. He leaned back in his chair. 'I trust you.' He paused. 'I need someone I can trust.'

'Why?'

He didn't tell me why. He said, 'Can't you get some time off from work? Have a holiday?'

I thought of the trainer I'd just left, whose daughter had made my job untenable because she wanted it for her fiancé. There was no immediate need for me to find another place, save for paying the rent. At thirty-three, I'd worked for three different trainers, and had lately come to feel I was growing too old to carry on as anyone's assistant. The natural progression was towards becoming a trainer myself, a dicey course without money.

'What are you thinking?' Malcolm asked.

'Roughly whether you would lend me half a million quid.'

'No,' he said.

I smiled. 'That's what I thought.'

'I'll pay your fares and your hotel bills.'

Across the room the loud lady was giving the smooth young man her address. A waitress had arrived and was busy unpacking fresh sandwiches and more alcohol onto the white-clothed table. I watched her idly for a few seconds, then looked back to Malcolm's face, and surprised there an expression that could only be interpreted as anxiety.

I was unexpectedly moved. I'd never wanted to quarrel with him: I'd wanted him to see Moira as I did, as a calculating, sweet-talking honeypot who was after his money, and who had used the devastation of Coochie's death to insinuate herself with him, turning up constantly with sympathy and offers to cook. Malcolm, deep in grief, had been helpless and grateful and seemed hardly to notice when she began threading her arm through his in company, and saying 'we'. I had for the whole three silent years wanted peace with my father, but I couldn't bear to go to his house and see Moira smirking in Coochie's place, even if he would have let me in through the door.

Now that Moira was dead, peace was maybe possible, and it seemed now as though he really wanted it also. I thought fleetingly that peace wasn't his prime object, that peace was only a preliminary necessary for some other purpose, but all the same it was enough.

'Yes,' I said, 'all right. I can take time off.'

His relief was visible. 'Good! Good! Come along then, I may as well buy a horse.' He stood up, full of sudden energy, waving his catalogue. 'Which do you suggest?'

'Why on earth do you want a horse?'

'To race, of course.'

'But you've never been interested . . .'

'Everyone should have a hobby,' he said briskly, though he'd never had one in his life. 'Mine is racing.' And, as an afterthought, he added, 'Henceforth,' and began to walk to the door.

The smooth young man detached himself from the dog lady and begged Malcolm to come back any time. Malcolm assured him he would, then wheeled round away from him again and marched across to one of the display cabinets.

'While I was waiting for you, I bought a cup,' he said to me over his shoulder. 'Want to see? One rather like that.' He pointed. 'It's being engraved.'

The cup in question was a highly-decorated and graceful elongated jug, eighteen inches tall and made undoubtedly of sterling silver.

'What's it for?' I asked.

'I don't know yet. Haven't made up my mind.'

'But . . . the engraving?'

'Mm. The Coochie Pembroke Memorial Challenge Trophy. Rather good, don't you think?'

'Yes,' I said.

He gave me a sidelong glance. 'I thought you'd think so.' He retraced his steps to the door. 'Right, then, a horse.'

Just like old times, I thought with half-forgotten pleasure. The sudden impulses which might or might not turn out to be thoroughly sensible, the intemperate enthusiasms needing instant gratification . . . and sometimes, afterwards, the abandoning of a débâcle as if it didn't exist. The Coochie Pembroke Memorial Challenge Trophy might achieve worldwide stature in competition or tarnish unpresented in an attic: with Malcolm it was always a toss-up.

I called him Malcolm, as all his children did, on his own instructions, and had grown up thinking it natural. Other boys might have Dad: I had my father, Malcolm.

Outside Ebury's room, he said, 'What's the procedure, then? How do we set about it?'

'Er . . .' I said. 'This is the first day of the Highflyer Sales.'

'Well?' he demanded as I paused. 'Go on.'

'I just thought you ought to know . . . the minimum opening bid today is twenty thousand guineas.'

It rocked him only slightly. 'Opening bid? What do they sell them for?'

'Anything from a hundred thousand up. You'll be lucky today to get a top-class yearling for under a quarter of a million. This is generally the most expensive day of the year.'

He wasn't noticeably deterred. He smiled. 'Come on, then,' he said. 'Let's go and start bidding.'

'You need to look up the breeding first,' I said. 'And then look at the animals, to see if you like them, and then get the help and advice of an agent . . .'

'Ian,' he said with mock sorrow, 'I don't know anything about the breeding, I can just about tell if a thing's got four legs, and I don't trust agents. So let's get on and bid.'

It sounded crazy to me, but it was his money. We went into the sale-ring itself where the auction was already in progress, and Malcolm asked me where the richest bidders could be found, the ones that really meant business.

'In those banks of seats on the left of the auctioneers, or here, in the entrance, or just round there to the left . . .'

He looked and listened and then led the way up to a section of seats from where we could watch the places I'd pointed out. The amphitheatre was already more than three-quarters full, and would later at times be crammed, especially whenever a tip-top lot came next.

'The very highest prices will probably be bid this evening,' I said, half teasing him, but all he said was, 'Perhaps we should wait, then.'

'If you buy ten yearlings,' I said, 'six might get to a

racecourse, three might win a race and one might be pretty good. If you're lucky.'

'Cautious Ian.'

'You,' I said, 'are cautious with gold.'

He looked at me with half-shut eyes. 'Not many people say that.'

'You're fast and flamboyant,' I said, 'but you sit and wait for the moment.'

He merely grunted and began paying attention to the matter in hand, intently focusing not on the merchandise but on the bidders on the far side of the ring. The auctioneers in the box to our left were relaxed and polished, the one currently at the microphone elaborately unimpressed by the fortunes passing. 'Fifty thousand, thank you, sir; sixty thousand, seventy . . . eighty? Shall I say eighty? Eighty, thank you, sir. Against you, sir. Ninety? Ninety. One hundred thousand. Selling now. I'm selling now. Against you, sir? No? All done? All done?' A pause for a sweep round to make sure no new bidder was frantically waving. 'Done, then. Sold to Mr Siddons. One hundred thousand guineas. The next lot . . .'

'Selling now,' Malcolm said. 'I suppose that means there was a reserve on it?'

I nodded.

'So until the fellow says "selling now", it's safe to bid, knowing you won't have to buy?'

'Yours might be the bid that reaches the reserve.'

He nodded. 'Russian roulette.'

We watched the sales for the rest of the afternoon, but he aimed no bullets at his own head. He asked who people were. 'Who is that Mr Siddons? That's the fourth horse he's bought.'

'He works for a bloodstock agency. He's buying for other people.'

'And that man in navy, scowling. Who's he?'

'Max Jones. He owns a lot of horses.'

'Every time that old woman bids, he bids against her.'

'It's a well-known feud.'

He sniffed. 'It must cost them fortunes.' He looked around the amphitheatre at the constantly changing audience of breeders, trainers, owners and the simply interested. 'Whose judgement would you trust most?'

I mentioned several trainers and the agents who might be acting on their behalf, and he told me to tell him when someone with good judgement was bidding, and to point them out. I did so many times, and he listened and passed no comment.

After a while, we went out for a break, an Ebury scotch, a sandwich and fresh air.

'I suppose you know,' Malcolm said casually, watching yearlings skittering past in the grasp of their handlers, 'that Moira and I were divorcing?'

'Yes, I heard.'

'And that she was demanding the house and half my possessions?'

'Mm.'

'And half my future earnings?'

'Could she?'

'She was going to fight for it.'

I refrained from saying that whoever had murdered Moira had done Malcolm a big favour, but I'd thought it several times.

I said instead, 'Still no clues?'

'No, nothing new.'

He spoke without regret. His disenchantment with Moira, according to his acid second wife, my own mother Joyce, had begun as soon as he'd stopped missing Coochie; and as Joyce was as percipient as she was catty, I believed it.

'The police tried damned hard to prove I did it,' Malcolm said.

'Yes, so I heard.'

'Who from? Who's your grapevine?'

'All of them,' I said.

'The three witches?'

I couldn't help smiling. He meant his three living ex-wives, Vivien, Joyce and Alicia.

'Yes, them. And all of the family.'

He shrugged.

'They were all worried that you might have,' I said.

'And were you worried?' he asked.

'I was glad you weren't arrested.'

He grunted noncommittally. 'I suppose you do know that most of your brothers and sisters, not to mention the witches, told the police you hated Moira?'

'They told me they'd told,' I agreed. 'But then, I did.'

'Lot of stinkers I've fathered,' he said gloomily.

Malcolm's personal alibi for Moira's death had been as unassailable as my own, as he'd been in Paris for the day when someone had pushed Moira's retroussé little nose into a bag of potting compost and held it there until it was certain she would take no more geranium cuttings. I could have wished her a better death, but it had been quick, everyone said. The police still clung to the belief that Malcolm had arranged for an assassin, but even Joyce knew that that was nonsense. Malcolm was a creature of tempest and volatility, but he'd never been calculatingly cruel.

His lack of interest in the horses themselves didn't extend to anything else at the sales: inside the sale-ring he had been particularly attentive to the flickering electronic board which lit up with the amount as each bid was made, and lit up not only in English currency but in dollars, yen, francs, lire and Irish punts at the current exchange rates. He'd always been fascinated by the workings of money, and had once far more than doubled a million pounds simply by banking it in the United States at two dollars forty cents to the pound, waiting five years, and bringing it back when the rate stood at one dollar twenty cents, which neatly gave him twice the capital he'd started with and the interest besides. He thought of the money market, after gold, as a sort of help-yourself cornucopia.

17

None of his children had inherited his instinct for timing and trends, a lack he couldn't understand. He'd told me directly once or twice to buy this or sell that, and he'd been right, but I couldn't make money the way he did without his guidance.

He considered that the best years of his talent had been wasted: all the years when, for political reasons, the free movement of capital had been restricted and when gold bullion couldn't be bought by private Britons. Always large, Malcolm's income, once the controls were lifted, went up like a hot air balloon, and it was at the beginning of that period, when he'd woken to the possibilities and bought his first crock of gold for sixty pounds an ounce to sell it presently for over a hundred, that he'd first been called Midas.

Since then, he'd ridden the yellow roller-coaster several times, unerringly buying when the price sank ever lower, selling as it soared, but before the bubble burst, always seeming to spot the wobbling moment when the market approached trough or peak.

Coochie had appeared wearing ever larger diamonds. The three witches, Vivien, Joyce and Alicia, each with a nice divorce settlement agreed in less sparkling days, unavailingly consulted their lawyers.

There was a second electronic board outside the sale-ring showing the state of the sale inside. Malcolm concentrated on the flickering figures until they began to shine more brightly in the fading daylight, but he still paid no close attention to the merchandise itself.

'They all look very small,' he said reprovingly, watching a narrow colt pass on its way from stable to sale-ring.

'Well, they're yearlings.'

'One year old, literally?'

'Eighteen months, twenty months: about that. They race next year, when they're two.'

He nodded and decided to return to the scene of the action, and again found us seats opposite the big-money crowd. The amphitheatre had filled almost to capacity while we'd been outside, and soon, with every seat taken, people shoved close-packed into the entrance and the standing-room sections: the blood of Northern Dancer and Nijinsky and of Secretariat and Lyphard was on its regal way to the ring.

A hush fell in the building at the entrance of the first of the legend-bred youngsters, the breath-held expectant hush of the knowledgeable awaiting a battle among financial giants. A fat cheque on this sales evening could secure a Derby winner and found a dynasty, and it happened often enough to tempt belief each time that this . . . *this* . . . was the one.

The auctioneer cleared his throat and managed the introduction without a quiver. 'Ladies and gentlemen, we now have Lot No 76, a bay colt by Nijinsky . . .' He recited the magical breeding as if bored, and asked for an opening bid.

Malcolm sat quiet and watched while the numbers flew high on the scoreboard, the price rising in jumps

19

of fifty thousand; watched while the auctioneer scanned the bidding faces for the drop of an eyelid, the twitch of a head, the tiny acknowledgements of intent.

' . . . against you, sir. No more, then? All done?' The auctioneer's eyebrows rose with his gavel, remained poised in elevation, came smoothly, conclusively down. 'Sold for one million seven hundred thousand guineas to Mr Siddons . . .'

The crowd sighed, expelling collective breath like a single organism. Then came rustling of catalogues, movement, murmuring and rewound expectation.

Malcolm said, 'It's a spectator sport.'

'Addictive,' I agreed.

He glanced at me sideways. 'For one million . . . five million . . . there's no guarantee the colt will ever race, isn't that what you said? One could be throwing one's cash down the drain?'

'That's right.'

'It's a perfectly blameless way of getting rid of a lot of money very fast, wouldn't you say?'

'Well . . .' I said slowly, 'is that what you're at?'

'Do you disapprove?'

'It's your money. You made it. You spend it.'

He smiled almost secretively at his catalogue and said, 'I can hear the "but" in your voice.'

'Mm. If you want to enjoy yourself, buy ten next-best horses instead of one super-colt, and get interested in them.'

'And pay ten training fees instead of one?'

I nodded. 'Ten would drain the exchequer nicely.'

He laughed in his throat and watched the next half-grown blue-blood reach three million guineas before Mr Siddons shook his head. ' . . . sold for three million and fifty thousand guineas to Mrs Terazzini . . .'

'Who's she?' Malcolm asked.

'She owns a worldwide bloodstock empire.'

He reflected. 'Like Robert Sangster?'

'Yep. Like him.'

He made a noise of understanding. 'An industry.'

'Yes.'

The following lot, a filly, fetched a more moderate sum, but the hush of expectancy returned for the next offering. Malcolm, keenly tuned by now to the atmosphere, watched the bidders as usual, not the nervous chestnut colt.

The upward impetus stopped at a fraction over two million and the auctioneer's eyebrows and gavel rose. 'All done?'

Malcolm raised his catalogue.

The movement caught the eye of the auctioneer, who paused with the gavel raised, using his eyebrows as a question, looking at Malcolm with surprise. Malcolm sat in what could be called the audience, not with the usual actors.

'You want to bid, sir?' asked the auctioneer.

'And fifty,' Malcolm said clearly, nodding.

There was a fluttering in the dovecot of auctioneers as head bent to head among themselves, consulting. All

21

round the ring, necks stretched to see who had spoken, and down in the entrance-way the man who'd bid last before Malcolm shrugged, shook his head and turned his back to the auctioneer. His last increase had been for twenty thousand only: a last small raise over two million, which appeared to have been his intended limit.

The auctioneer himself seemed less than happy. 'All done, then?' he asked again, and with no further replies, said, 'Done then. Sold for two million and seventy thousand guineas to ... er ... the bidder opposite.'

The auctioneer consulted with his colleagues again and one of them left the box, carrying a clipboard. He hurried down and round the ring to join a minion on our side, both of them with their gaze fastened on Malcolm.

'Those two auctioneers won't let you out of their sight,' I observed. 'They suffered badly from a vanishing bidder not so long ago.'

'They look as if they're coming to arrest me,' Malcolm said cheerfully; and both of the auctioneers indeed made their way right to his side, handing him the clipboard and politely requiring him to sign their bill of sale, in triplicate and without delay. They retired to ground level but were still waiting for us with steely intent when, after three further sales had gone through as expected, we made our way down.

They invited Malcolm civilly to the quieter end of their large office, and we went. They computed what he owed and deferentially presented the total. Malcolm wrote them a cheque.

They politely suggested proof of identity and a reference. Malcolm gave them an American Express card and the telephone number of his bank manager. They took the cheque gingerly and said that although Mr . . . er . . . Pembroke should if he wished arrange insurance on his purchase at once, the colt would not be available for removal until . . . er . . . tomorrow.

Malcolm took no offence. He wouldn't have let anyone he didn't know drive off with a horsebox full of gold. He said tomorrow would be fine, and in high good spirits told me I could ferry him back to his Cambridge hotel, from where he'd come that morning in a taxi, and we would have dinner together.

After we'd called in at an insurance agent's office and he'd signed some more papers and another cheque, we accordingly walked together to the car park from where people were beginning to drift home. Night had fallen, but there were lights enough to see which car was which, and as we went I pointed out the row ahead where my wheels stood.

'Where are you going to send your colt?' I asked, walking.

'Where would you say?'

'I should think,' I said . . . but I never finished the answer, or not at that actual moment.

A car coming towards us between two rows of parked cars suddenly emitted two headlight beams, blinding us; and at the same moment it seemed to accelerate fiercely, swerving straight towards Malcolm.

I leaped ... flung myself ... at my father, my flying weight spinning him off balance, carrying him off his feet, knocking him down. I fell on top of him, knowing that the pale speeding bulk of the car had caught me, but not sure to what extent. There was just a bang and a lot of lights curving like arcs, and a whirling view of gleams on metal, and a fast crunch into darkness.

We were on the ground then between two silent parked cars, our bodies heavy with shock and disorientation, in a sort of inertia.

After a moment, Malcolm began struggling to free himself from under my weight, and I rolled awkwardly onto my knees and thankfully thought of little but bruises. Malcolm pushed himself up until he was sitting with his back against a car's wheel, collecting his wits but looking as shaken as I felt.

'That car,' he said eventually, between deep breaths, 'was aiming ... to kill me.'

I nodded speechlessly. My trousers were torn, thigh grazed and bleeding.

'You always had ... quick reactions,' he said. 'So now ... now you know ... why I want you beside me ... all the time.'

CHAPTER TWO

It was the second time someone had tried to kill him, he said.

I was driving towards Cambridge a shade more slowly than usual, searching anxiously in the rear-view mirror for satanically-minded followers but so far thankfully without success. My right leg was stiffening depressingly from the impact of twenty minutes ago, but I was in truth fairly used to that level of buffet through having ridden over the years in three or four hundred jump races, incurring consequent collisions with the ground.

Malcolm didn't like driving for reasons Coochie had deftly diagnosed as impatience. Coochie hadn't liked his driving either, for reasons (she said) of plain fear, and had taken over as family chauffeur. I too had been used to driving Malcolm from the day I gained my licence: I would need to have been delirious to ask him to take the wheel just because of some grazed skin.

The second time someone had tried to kill him . . .

'When was the first time?' I asked.

'Last Friday.'

It was currently Tuesday evening. 'What happened?' I said.

He took a while over answering. When he did there was more sadness in his voice than anger, and I listened to his tone behind the words and slowly understood his deepest fears.

'One moment I was walking the dogs... well, I think I was, but that's it, I don't really remember.' He paused. 'I think I had a bang on the head... Anyway, the last thing I remember is calling the dogs and opening the kitchen door. I meant to take them through the garden to that field with the stream and the willows. I don't know how far I went. I shouldn't think far. Anyway, I woke up in Moira's car in the garage... it's still there... and it's damn lucky I woke up at all... the engine was running...' He stopped for a few moments. 'It's funny how the mind works. I knew absolutely at once that I had to switch off the engine. Extraordinary. Like a flash. I was in the back seat, sort of tumbled... toppled over... half lying. I got up and practically fell through between the front seats to reach the key in the ignition, and when the engine stopped I just lay there, you know, thinking that I was bloody uncomfortable but not having any more energy to move.'

'Did anyone come?' I said, when he paused.

'No... I felt better after a while. I stumbled out of the car and was sick.'

'Did you tell the police?'

'Sure, I told them.' His voice sounded weary at the recollection. 'It must have been about five when I set off with the dogs. Maybe seven by the time I called the police. I'd had a couple of stiff drinks by then and stopped shaking. They asked me why I hadn't called them sooner. Bloody silly. And it was the same lot who came after Moira. They think I did it, you know. Had her killed.'

'I know.'

'Did the witches tell you that too?'

'Joyce did. She said you couldn't have. She said you might have ... er ...' I baulked from repeating my mother's actual words, which were 'throttled the little bitch in a rage', and substituted more moderately, ' ... been capable of killing her yourself, but not of paying someone else to do it.'

He made a satisfied noise but no comment, and I added, 'That seems to be the family concensus.'

He sighed. 'It's not the police concensus. Far from it. I don't think they believed anyone had tried to kill me. They made a lot of notes and took samples ... I ask you ... of my vomit, and dusted over Moira's car for fingerprints, but it was obvious they were choked with doubts. I think they thought I'd been going to commit suicide and thought better of it ... or else that I'd staged it in the hope people would believe I couldn't have killed Moira if someone was trying to kill *me* ...'

He shook his head. 'I'm sorry I told them at all, and that's why we're not reporting tonight's attempt either.'

He had been adamant, in the sales car park, that we shouldn't.

'What about the bump on your head?' I asked.

'I had a swelling above my ear. Very tender, but not very big. The word I heard the police use about that was "inconclusive".'

'And if you'd died . . .' I said thoughtfully.

He nodded. 'If I'd died, it would have wrapped things up nicely for them. Suicide. Remorse. Implicit admission of guilt.'

I drove carefully towards Cambridge, appalled and also angry. Moira's death hadn't touched me in the slightest, but the attacks on my father showed me I'd been wrong. Moira had had a right to live. There should have been rage, too, on her behalf.

'What happened to the dogs?' I said.

'What? Oh, the dogs. They came back . . . they were whining at the kitchen door. I let them in while I was waiting for the police. They were muddy . . . heaven knows where they'd been. They were tired anyway. I fed them and they went straight to their baskets and went to sleep.'

'Pity they couldn't talk.'

'What? Yes, I suppose so. Yes.' He fell into silence, sighing occasionally as I thought over what he'd told me.

'Who,' I said eventually, 'knew you were going to Newmarket Sales?'

'Who?' He sounded surprised at the question, and then understood it. 'I don't know.' He was puzzled. 'I've no idea. I didn't know myself until yesterday.'

'Well, what have you been doing since the police left you last Friday night?'

'Thinking.' And the thoughts, it was clear, had been melancholic: the thoughts now saddening his voice.

'Mm,' I said, 'along the lines of why was Moira killed?'

'Along those lines.'

I said it plainly. 'To stop her taking half your possessions?'

He said unwillingly, 'Yes.'

'And the people who had a chief interest in stopping her were your likely heirs. Your children.'

He was silent.

I said, 'Also perhaps their husbands and wives, also perhaps even the witches.'

'I don't want to believe it,' he said. 'How could I have put a murderer into the world.'

'People do,' I said.

'*Ian*!'

The truth was that, apart from poor Robin, I didn't know my half-brothers and half-sisters well enough to have any certainty about any of them. I was usually on speaking terms with them all, but didn't seek them out. There had been too much fighting, too many rows:

Vivien's children disliked Alicia's, Alicia's disliked them and me, Vivien hated Joyce and Joyce hated Alicia very bitterly indeed. Under Coochie's reign, the whole lot had been banned from sleeping in the house, if not from single-day visits, with the result that a storm of collective resentment had been directed at me whom she had kept and treated as her own.

'Apart from thinking,' I said, 'what have you been doing since Friday night?'

'When the police had gone, I . . . I . . .' he stopped.

'The shakes came back?' I suggested.

'Yes. Do you understand that?'

'I'd have been scared silly,' I said. 'Stupid not to be. I'd have felt that whoever had tried to kill me was prowling about in the dark waiting for me to be alone so he could have another go.'

Malcolm audibly swallowed. 'I telephoned to the hire firm I use now and told them to send a car to fetch me. Do you know what panic feels like?'

'Not that sort, I guess.'

'I was sweating, and it was cold. I could feel my heart thumping . . . banging away at a terrible rate. It was awful. I packed some things . . . I couldn't concentrate.'

He shifted in his seat as the outskirts of Cambridge came up in the headlights and began to give me directions to the hotel where he said he'd spent the previous four nights.

'Does anyone know where you're staying?' I asked,

turning corners. 'Have you seen any of your old chums?'

Malcolm knew Cambridge well, had been at university there and still had friends at high tables. It must have seemed to him a safe city to bolt to, but it was where I would have gone looking for him, if not much else failed.

'Of course I have,' he said in answer to my question. 'I spent Sunday with the Rackersons, dined with old Digger in Trinity last night ... it's nonsense to think they could be involved.'

'Yes,' I agreed, pulling up outside his hotel. 'All the same, go and pack and check out of here, and we'll go somewhere else.'

'It's not necessary,' he protested.

'You appointed me as minder, so I'm minding,' I said.

He gave me a long look in the dim light inside the car. The doorman of the hotel stepped forward and opened the door beside me, an invitation to step out.

'Come with me,' my father said.

I was both astounded by his fear and thought it warranted. I asked the doorman where I should park, and turned at his suggestion through an arch into the hotel's inner courtway. From there, through a back door and comfortable old-fashioned hallways, Malcolm and I went up one flight of red-carpeted stairs to a lengthy winding corridor. Several people we passed glanced down at my torn trouser-leg with the dried-blood scenery inside, but no one said anything: was it still British politeness, I wondered, or the new creed of not getting involved? Malcolm, it seemed, had forgotten the problem existed.

He brought his room key out of his pocket and, with it raised, said abruptly, 'I suppose *you* didn't tell anyone I would be at the sales.'

'No, I didn't.'

'But you knew.' He paused. 'Only you knew.'

He was staring at me with the blue eyes and I saw all the sudden fear-driven question marks rioting through his mind.

'Go inside,' I said. 'The corridor isn't the place for this.'

He looked at the key, he looked wildly up and down the now empty corridor, poised, almost, to run.

I turned my back on him and walked purposefully away in the direction of the stairs.

'*Ian*,' he shouted.

I stopped and turned round.

'Come back,' he said.

I went back slowly. 'You said you trusted me,' I said.

'I haven't seen you for three years . . . and I broke your nose . . .'

I took the key out of his hand and unlocked the door. I supposed I might have been suspicious of me if I'd been attacked twice in five days, considering I came into the high-probability category of son. I switched on the light and went forward into the room which was free from lurking murderers that time at least.

Malcolm followed, only tentatively reassured, closing the door slowly behind him. I drew the heavy striped curtains across the two windows and briefly surveyed the spacious but old-fashioned accommodation: reproduction antique furniture, twin beds, pair of armchairs, door to bathroom.

No murderer in the bathroom.

'Ian . . .' Malcolm said.

'Did you bring any scotch?' I asked. In the old days, he'd never travelled without it.

He waved a hand towards a chest of drawers where I found a half-full bottle nestling among a large number of socks. I fetched a glass from the bathroom and poured him enough to tranquillize an elephant.

'For God's sake . . .' he said.

'Sit down and drink it.'

'You're bloody arrogant.'

He did sit down, though, and tried not to let the glass clatter against his teeth from the shaking of his hand.

With much less force, I said, 'If I'd wanted you dead, I'd have let that car hit you tonight. I'd have jumped the other way . . . out of trouble.'

He seemed to notice clearly for the first time that there had been any physical consequences to our escape.

'Your leg,' he said, 'must be all right?'

'Leg is. Trousers . . . can I borrow a pair of yours?'

He pointed to a cupboard where I found a second suit almost identical to the one he was wearing. I was three inches taller than he and a good deal thinner but, belted and slung round the hips, whole cloth was better than holey.

He silently watched me change and made no objection when I telephoned down to the reception desk and asked them to get his bill ready for his departure. He drank more of the scotch, but nowhere was he relaxed.

'Shall I pack for you?' I asked.

He nodded, and watched some more while I fetched his suitcase, opened it on one of the beds and began collecting his belongings. The things he'd brought spoke eloquently of his state of mind when he'd packed them: about ten pairs of socks but no other underwear, a dozen shirts, no pyjamas, two towelling bath-robes, no extra shoes. The clearly new electric razor in the bathroom still bore a stick-on price tag, but he had brought his antique gold-and-silver-backed brushes, all eight of them, including two clothes brushes. I put everything into the case, and closed it.

'Ian,' he said.

'Mm?'

'People can pay assassins . . . You could have decided not to go through with it tonight . . . at the last moment . . .'

34

'It wasn't like that,' I protested. Saving him had been utterly instinctive, without calculation or counting of risks: I'd been lucky to get off with a graze.

He said almost beseechingly, with difficulty, 'It wasn't you, was it, who had Moira . . . Or me, in the garage . . .? Say it wasn't you.'

I didn't know really how to convince him. He'd known me better, lived with me longer than with any of his other children, and if his trust was this fragile then there wasn't much future between us.

'I didn't have Moira killed,' I said. 'If you believe it of me, you could believe it of yourself.' I paused. 'I don't want you dead, I want you alive. I could never do you harm.'

It struck me that he really needed to hear me say I loved him, so although he might scoff at the actual words, and despite the conditioned inhibitions of my upbringing, I said, feeling that desperate situations needed desperate remedies, 'You're a great father . . . and . . . er . . . I love you.'

He blinked. Such a declaration pierced him, one could see. I'd probably overdone it, I thought, but his distrust had been a wound for me too.

I said much more lightly, 'I swear on the Coochie Pembroke Memorial Challenge Trophy that I would never touch a hair on your head . . . nor Moira's either, though I did indeed loathe her.'

I lifted the suitcase off the bed.

'Do I go on with you or not?' I said. 'If you don't trust me, I'm going home.'

He was looking at me searchingly, as if I were a stranger, which I suppose in some ways I was. He had never before, I guessed, had to think of me not as a son but as a man, as a person who had led a life separate from his, with a different outlook, different desires, different values. Sons grew from little boys into their own adult selves: fathers tended not to see the change clearly. Malcolm, I was certain, thought of me basically as still having the half-formed personality I'd had at fifteen.

'You're different,' he said.

'I am the same. Trust your instinct.'

Some of the tension at last slackened in his muscles. His instinct had been trust, an instinct strong enough to carry him to the telephone after three silent years. He finished the scotch and stood up, filling his lungs with a deep breath as if making resolves.

'Come with me, then,' he said.

I nodded.

He went over to the chest of drawers and from the bottom drawer, which I hadn't checked, produced a briefcase. I might have guessed it would be there somewhere: even in the direst panic, he wouldn't have left behind the lists of his gold shares or his currency exchange calculator. He started with the briefcase to the door, leaving me to bring the suitcase, but on impulse I went over again to the telephone and asked for a taxi to be ready for us.

'But your car's here,' Malcolm said.

'Mm. I think I'll leave it here, for now.'

'But why?'

'Because if I didn't tell anyone you were going to Newmarket Sales, and nor did you, then it's probable you were followed there, from ... er ... here. If you think about it ... the car that tried to kill you was waiting in the sales car park, but you didn't have a car. You went there by taxi. Whoever drove at you must have seen you and me together, and known who I was, and guessed you might leave with me, so although I didn't see anyone following us tonight from New-market, whoever-it-was probably knew we would come here, to this hotel, so ... well ... so they might be hanging about in the courtyard where we parked, where it's nice and dark outside the back door, waiting to see if we come out again.'

'My God!'

'It's possible,' I said. 'So we'll leave through the front with the doorman in attendance, don't you think?'

'If you say so,' he said weakly.

'From now on,' I said, 'we take every exaggerated precaution we can think of.'

'Well, where are we going in this taxi?'

'How about somewhere where we can rent a car?'

The taxi-driver, however, once we'd set off without incident from the hotel, bill paid, luggage loaded, doorman tipped, informed us doubtfully that nine o'clock on a Tuesday night wasn't going to be easy. All the car-hire firms' offices would be closed.

'Chauffeur-driven car, then,' Malcolm said. 'Fellows who do weddings, that sort of thing. Twenty quid in it for you if you fix it.'

Galvanized by this offer, the taxi-driver drove us down some back streets, stopped outside an unpromising little terraced house and banged on the door. It opened, shining out a melon-slice of light, and gathered the taxi-driver inside.

'We're going to be mugged,' Malcolm said.

The taxi-driver returned harmlessly, however, accompanied by a larger man buttoning the jacket of a chauffeur's uniform and carrying a reassuring peaked cap.

'The firm my brother-in-law works for does mostly weddings and funerals,' the taxi-driver said. 'He wants to know where you want to go.'

'London,' I said.

London appeared to be no problem at all. The driver and his brother-in-law climbed into the front of the taxi which started off, went round a corner or two, and pulled up again outside a lock-up garage. We sat in the taxi as asked while the two drivers opened the garage, disclosing its contents. Which was how Malcolm and I proceeded to London in a very large, highly-polished black Rolls-Royce, the moonlighting chauffeur separated from us discreetly by a glass partition.

'Why did you go to the sales at all?' I asked Malcolm. 'I mean, why Newmarket? Why the sales?'

Malcolm frowned. 'Because of Ebury's, I suppose.'

'The jewellers?'

'Yes ... well ... I knew they were going to have a showroom there. They told me so last week when I went to see them about Coochie's jewellery. I mean, I know them pretty well, I bought most of her things from there. I was admiring a silver horse they had, and they said they were exhibiting this week at Newmarket Sales. So then yesterday when I was wondering what would fetch you ... where you would meet me ... I remembered the sales were so close to Cambridge, and I decided on it not long before I rang you.'

I pondered a bit. 'How would you set about finding where someone was, if you wanted to, so to speak?'

To my surprise he had a ready answer. 'Get the fellow I had for tailing Moira.'

'Tailing ...'

'My lawyer said to do it. It might save me something, he said, if Moira was having a bit on the side, see what I mean?'

'I do indeed,' I agreed dryly. 'But I suppose she wasn't?'

'No such luck.' He glanced at me. 'What do you have in mind?'

'Well ... I just wondered if he could check where everyone in the family was last Friday and tonight.'

'Everyone!' Malcolm exclaimed. 'It would take weeks.'

'It would put your mind at rest.'

He shook his head gloomily. 'You forget about assassins.'

'Assassins aren't so frightfully easy to find, not for ordinary people. How would you set about it, for instance, if you wanted someone killed? Put an ad in *The Times*?'

He didn't seem to see such a problem as I did, but he agreed that 'the fellow who tailed Moira' should be offered the job of checking the family.

We discussed where we should stay that night: in which hotel, in fact, as neither of us felt like returning home. Home, currently, to me, was a rather dull suburban flat in Epsom, not far from the stable I'd been working for. Home for Malcolm was still the house where I'd been raised, from which Moira had apparently driven him, but to which he had returned immediately after her death. 'Home' for all the family was that big house in Berkshire which had seen all five wives come and go: Malcolm himself had been brought up there, and I could scarcely imagine what he must have felt at the prospect of losing it.

'What happened between you and Moira?' I said.

'None of your goddam business.'

We travelled ten miles in silence. Then he shifted, sighed, and said, 'She wanted Coochie's jewellery and I wouldn't give it to her. She kept on and on about it, rabbit, rabbit. Annoyed me, do you see? And then . . . well . . .' he shrugged, 'she caught me out.'

'With another woman?' I said without surprise.

He nodded, unashamed. He'd never been monogamous and couldn't understand why it should be expected. The terrible rows in my childhood had all been centred on his affairs: while he'd been married to Vivien and then to Joyce, he had maintained Alicia all the time as his mistress. Alicia bore him two children while he was married to Vivien and Joyce, and also one subsequently, when he'd made a fairly honest woman of her, at her insistence.

I liked to think he had been faithful finally to Coochie, but on the whole it was improbable, and I was never going to ask.

Malcolm favoured our staying at the Dorchester, but I persuaded him he was too well known there, and we settled finally on the Savoy.

'A suite,' Malcolm said at the reception desk. 'Two bedrooms, two bathrooms and a sitting room, and send up some Bollinger right away.'

I didn't feel like drinking champagne, but Malcolm did. He also ordered scrambled eggs and smoked salmon for us both from room service, with a bottle of Hine Antique brandy and a box of Havana cigars for comforts.

Idly I totted up the expenses of his day: one solid silver trophy, one two-million-guinea thoroughbred, insurance for same, Cambridge hotel bill, tip for the taxi-driver, chauffeured Rolls-Royce, jumbo suite at the Savoy with trimmings. I wondered how much he was really worth, and whether he intended to spend the lot.

We ate the food and drank the brandy still not totally in accord with each other. The three years' division had been, it seemed, a chasm not as easy to cross as I'd thought. I felt that although I'd meant it when I said I loved him, it was probably the long memories of him that I really loved, not his physical presence here and now, and I could see that if I was going to stay close to him, as I'd promised, I would be learning him again and from a different viewpoint; that each of us, in fact, would newly get to know the other.

'Any day now,' Malcolm said, carefully dislodging ash from his cigar, 'we're going to Australia.'

I absorbed the news and said, 'Are we?'

He nodded. 'We'll need visas. Where's your passport?'

'In my flat. Where's yours?'

'In the house.'

'Then I'll get them both tomorrow,' I said, 'and you stay here.' I paused. 'Are we going to Australia for any special reason?'

'To look at gold mines,' he said. 'And kangaroos.'

After a short silence, I said, 'We don't just have to escape. We do have to find out who's trying to kill you, in order to stop them succeeding.'

'Escape is more attractive,' he said. 'How about a week in Singapore on the way?'

'Anything you say. Only . . . I'm supposed to ride in a race at Sandown on Friday.'

'I've never understood why you like it. All those cold wet days. All those falls.'

'You get your rush from gold,' I said.

'Danger?' His eyebrows rose. 'Quiet, well-behaved, cautious Ian? Life is a bore without risk, is that it?'

'It's not so extraordinary,' I said.

I'd ridden always as an amateur, unpaid, because something finally held me back from the total dedication needed for turning professional. Race riding was my deepest pleasure, but not my entire life, and in consequence I'd never developed the competitive drive necessary for climbing the pro ladder. I was happy with the rides I got, with the camaraderie of the changing room, with the wide skies and the horses themselves, and yes, one had to admit it, with the risk.

'Staying near me,' Malcolm said, 'as you've already found out, isn't enormously safe.'

'That's why I'm staying,' I said.

He stared. He said, 'My God,' and he laughed. 'I thought I knew you. Seems I don't.'

He finished his brandy, stubbed out his cigar and decided on bed; and in the morning he was up before me, sitting on a sofa in one of the bathrobes and reading the *Sporting Life* when I ambled out in the underpants and shirt I'd slept in.

'I've ordered breakfast,' he said. 'And I'm in the paper – how about that?'

I looked where he pointed. His name was certainly there, somewhere near the end of the detailed lists of yesterday's sales. 'Lot 79, ch. colt, 2,070,000 gns. Malcolm Pembroke'.

He put down the paper, well pleased. 'Now, what do we do today?'

'We summon your private eye, we fix a trainer for the colt, I fetch our passports and some clothes, and you stay here.'

Slightly to my surprise, he raised no arguments except to tell me not to be away too long. He was looking rather thoughtfully at the healing graze down my right thigh and the red beginnings of bruising around it.

'The trouble is,' he said, 'I don't have the private eye's phone number. Not with me.'

'We'll get another agency, then, from the yellow pages.'

'Your mother knows it, of course. Joyce knows it.'

'How does she know it?'

'She used him,' he said airily, 'to follow me and Alicia.'

There was nothing, I supposed, which should ever surprise me about my parents.

'When the lawyer fellow said to have Moira tailed, I got the private eye's name from Joyce. After all, he'd done a good job on me and Alicia all those years ago. Too bloody good, when you think of it. So get through to Joyce, Ian, and ask her for the number.'

Bemused, I did as he said.

'Darling,' my mother shrieked down the line. 'Where's your father?'

'I don't know,' I said.

'Darling, do you know what he's bloody *done*?'

'No . . . what?'

'He's given a *fortune*, darling, I mean literally *hundreds* of *thousands*, to some wretched little film company to make some absolutely *ghastly* film about tadpoles or something. Some bloody fool of a man telephoned to find out where your father was, because it seems he promised them even *more* money which they'd like to have . . . I ask you! I know you and Malcolm aren't talking, but you've got to do something to stop him.'

'Well,' I said, 'it's his money.'

'Darling, don't be so *naive*. Someone's going to inherit it, and if only you'd swallow all that bloody pride, as I've told you over and over, it would be *yours*. If you go on and on with this bloody quarrel, he'll leave it all to Alicia's beastly brood, and I cannot *bear* the prospect of her gloating for ever more. So make it up with Malcolm *at once*, darling, and get him to see sense.'

'Calm down,' I said. 'I have.'

'*What?*'

45

'Made it up with him.'

'Thank God, at *last*!' my mother shrieked. 'Then, darling, what are you waiting for? Get onto him *straight* away and stop him spending your inheritance.'

CHAPTER THREE

Malcolm's house, after three years of Moira's occupancy, had greatly changed.

Malcolm's Victorian house was known as 'Quantum' because of the Latin inscription carved into the lintel over the front door. QUANTUM IN ME FUIT – roughly, 'I did the best I could.'

I went there remembering the comfortable casualness that Coochie had left and not actually expecting that things would be different: and I should have known better, as each wife in turn, Coochie included, had done her best to eradicate all signs of her predecessor. Marrying Malcolm had, for each wife, involved moving into his house, but he had indulged them all, I now understood, in the matter of ambience.

I let myself in through the kitchen door with Malcolm's keys and thought wildly for a moment that I'd come to the wrong place. Coochie's pinewood and red-tiled homeliness had been swept away in favour of glossy yellow walls, glittering white appliances and shelves crowded with scarlet and deep pink geraniums cascading from white pots.

Faintly stunned, I looked back through time to the era before Coochie, to Alicia's fluffy occupancy of broderie anglaise frills on shimmering white curtains with pale blue work-tops and white floor tiles; and back further still to the starker olive and milk-coffee angularities chosen by Joyce. I remembered the day the workmen had torn out my mother's kitchen, and how I'd gone howling to Malcolm: he'd packed me off to Joyce immediately for a month, which I didn't like either, and when I returned I'd found the white frills installed, and the pale blue cupboards, and I thought them all sissy, but I'd learned not to say so.

For the first time ever, I wondered what the kitchen had looked like in Vivien's time, when forty-five or so years ago young Malcolm had brought her there as his first bride. Vivien had been dispossessed and resentful by the time I was born, and I'd seldom seen her smiling. She seemed to me the least positive of the five wives and the least intelligent but, according to her photographs, she had been in her youth by streets the most beautiful. The dark sweep of her eyebrows and the high cheekbones remained, but the thick black hair had thinned now in greying, and entrenched bitterness had soured the once sweet mouth. Vivien's marriage, I'd guessed, had died through Malcolm's boredom with her, and although they now still met occasionally at events to do with their mutual children and grandchildren, they were more apt to turn their backs than to kiss.

Vivien disliked and was plaintively critical of almost everybody while at the same time unerringly interpreting the most innocent general remarks of others as being criticism of herself. It was impossible to please her often or for long, and I, like almost all the extended family, had long ago stopped trying. She had indoctrinated her three offspring with her own dissatisfactions to the point where they were nastily disparaging of Malcolm behind his back, though not to his face, hypocrites that they were.

Malcolm had steadfastly maintained them through young adulthood and then cast them loose, each with a trust fund that would prevent them from actually starving. He had treated all seven of his normally surviving children in the same way; his eighth child, Robin, would be looked after for ever. None of us seven could have any complaints: he had given us all whatever vocational training we'd chosen and afterwards the cushion against penury, and at that point in each of our lives had considered his work done. Whatever became of us in the future, he said, had to be in our own hands.

With the family powerfully in mind, I went from the kitchen into the hall where I found that Moira had had the oak panelling painted white. Increasingly amused, I thought of the distant days when Alicia had painstakingly bleached all the old wood, only to have Coochie stain it dark again: and I supposed that perhaps Malcolm enjoyed change around him in many ways, not just in women.

His own private room, always called the office although more like a comfortable cluttered sitting room, seemed to have escaped the latest refit except in the matter of gold velvet curtains replacing the old green. Otherwise, the room as always seemed filled with his strong personality, the walls covered with dozens of framed photographs, the deep cupboards bulging with files, the bookshelves crammed, every surface bearing mementoes of his journeyings and achievements, nothing very tidy.

I went over to the desk to find his passport and half-expected to hear his voice at any minute even though I'd left him forty miles away persuasively telephoning to 'the fellow who tailed Moira'.

His passport, he'd said, was in the second drawer down on the right-hand side, and so it was, among a large clutter of bygone travel arrangements and expired medical insurances. Malcolm seldom threw much away, merely building another cupboard for files. His filing system was such that no one but he had the slightest idea where any paper or information could be found, but he himself could put his finger on things unerringly. His method, he'd told me once long ago, was always to put everything where he would first think of looking for it; and as a child, I'd seen such sense in that that I had copied him ever since.

Looking around again, it struck me that although

the room was crammed with objects, several familiar ones were missing. The gold dolphin, for instance, and the gold tree bearing amethysts, and the Georgian silver candelabras. Perhaps at last, I thought, he had stored them prudently in the bank.

Carrying the passport, I went upstairs to fetch clothes to add to his sketchy packing and out of irresistible curiosity detoured into the room which had been mine. I expected a bright Moira-style transformation, but in fact nothing at all had been changed, except that nothing of me remained.

The room was without soul; barren. The single bed, stripped, showed a bare mattress. There were no cobwebs, no dust, no smell of neglect, but the message was clear: the son who had slept there no longer existed.

Shivering slightly, I closed the door and wondered whether the absolute rejection had been Malcolm's or Moira's and, shrugging, decided I didn't now mind which.

Moira's idea of the perfect bedroom turned out to be plum and pink with louvred doors everywhere possible. Malcolm's dressing room next door had received the same treatment, as had their joint bathroom, and I set about collecting his belongings with a strong feeling of intruding upon strangers.

I found Moira's portrait only because I kicked it while searching for pyjamas: it was underneath Malcolm's chest of drawers in the dressing room. Looking to see what I'd damaged, I pulled out a square gold frame which fitted a discoloured patch on the wall and, turning it over, found the horrible Moira smiling at me with all her insufferable complacency.

I had forgotten how young she had been, and how pretty. Thirty years younger than Malcolm; thirty-five when she'd married him and, in the painting anyway, unlined. Reddish-gold hair, pale unfreckled skin, pointed chin, delicate neck. The artist seemed to me to have caught the calculation in her eyes with disconcerting clarity, and when I glanced at the name scrawled at the bottom I understood why. Malcolm might not have given her diamonds, but her portrait had been painted by the best.

I put her back face down under the chest of drawers as I'd found her, where Malcolm, I was sure, had consigned her.

Fetching a suitcase from the boxroom (no decor changes there), I packed Malcolm's things and went downstairs, and in the hall came face to face with a smallish man carrying a large shotgun, the business end pointing my way.

I stopped abruptly, as one would.

'Put your hands up,' he said hoarsely.

I set the suitcase on the floor and did as he bid. He wore earth-stained dark trousers and had mud on his hands, and I asked him immediately, 'Are you the gardener?'

'What if I am? What are you doing here?'

'Collecting clothes for my father . . . er . . . Mr Pembroke. I'm his son.'

'I don't know you. I'm getting the police.' His voice was belligerent but quavery, the shotgun none too steady in his hands.

'All right,' I said.

He was faced then with the problem of how to telephone while aiming my way.

I said, seeing his hesitation, 'I can prove I'm Mr Pembroke's son, and I'll open the suitcase to show you I'm not stealing anything. Would that help?'

After a pause, he nodded. 'You stay over there, though,' he said.

I judged that if I alarmed him there would be a further death in my father's house, so I very slowly and carefully opened the suitcase, removed the underpants and the rest, and laid them out on the hall floor. After that, I equally slowly took my own wallet out of my pocket, opened it, removed a credit card and laid it on the floor face upwards. Then I retreated backwards from the exhibits, ending with my back against the closed and locked front door.

The elderly gardener came suspiciously forward and inspected the show, dropping his eyes only in split seconds, raising them quickly, giving me no chance to jump him.

'That's his passport,' he said accusingly.

'He asked me to fetch it.'

'Where is he?' he said. 'Where's he gone?'

53

'I have to meet him with his passport. I don't know where he's going.' I paused. 'I really am his son. You must be new here. I haven't seen you before.'

'Two years,' he said defensively. 'I've worked here two years.' He seemed to come quite suddenly to a decision to believe me, and almost apologetically lowered the gun. 'This house is supposed to be locked up,' he said. 'Then I see you moving about upstairs.'

'Upsetting,' I agreed.

He gestured to Malcolm's things. 'You'd better pack them again.'

I began to do so under his still watchful eye.

'It was brave of you to come in here,' I said, 'if you thought I was a burglar.'

He braced his shoulders in an old automatic movement. 'I was in the army once.' He relaxed and shrugged. 'Tell you the truth, I was coming in quietly-like to phone the police, then you started down the stairs.'

'And . . . the gun?'

'Brought it with me just in case. I go after rabbits . . . I keep the gun handy.'

I nodded. It was the gardener's own gun, I thought. Malcolm had never owned one, as far as I knew.

'Has my father paid you for the week?' I said.

His eyes at once brightened hopefully. 'He paid me last Friday, same as usual. Then Saturday morning he phoned my house to tell me to come round here to see to the dogs. Take them home with me, same as I always do when he's away. So I did. But he was gone off the line before I could ask him how long he'd be wanting me to have them.'

I pulled out my cheque-book and wrote him a cheque for the amount he specified. Arthur Bellbrook, he said his name was. I tore out the cheque and gave it to him and asked him if there was anyone else who needed wages.

He shook his head. 'The cleaner left when Mrs Pembroke was done in ... er ... murdered. Said she didn't fancy the place any more.'

'Where exactly was Mrs Pembroke ... er ... murdered?'

'I'll show you if you like.' He stored the cheque away in a pocket. 'Outside in the greenhouse.'

He took me, however, not as I'd imagined to the rickety old familiar greenhouse sagging against a mellowed wall in the kitchen garden, but to a bright white octagonal wrought-iron construction like a fancy birdcage set as a summer-house on a secluded patch of lawn. From far outside, one could clearly see the flourishing geraniums within.

'Well, well,' I said.

Arthur Bellbrook uttered 'Huh' as expressing his disapproval and opened the metal-and-glass door.

'Cost a fortune to heat, will this place,' he observed. 'And it got too hot in the summer. The only thing as will survive in it is geraniums. Mrs Pembroke's passion, geraniums.'

An almost full sack of potting compost lay along one of the work surfaces, the top side of it slit from end to end to make the soil mixture easy to reach. A box of small pots stood nearby, some of them occupied by cuttings.

I looked at the compost with revulsion. 'Is that where . . .?' I began.

'Yes,' he said. 'Poor lady. There's no one ought to die like that, however difficult they could be.'

'No,' I agreed. A thought struck me. 'It was you who found her, wasn't it?'

'I went home like always at four o'clock, but I was out for a stroll about seven, and I thought I would just come in to see what state she'd left the place in. See, she played at gardening. Never cleaned the tools, things like that.' He looked at the boarded floor as if still seeing her there. 'She was lying face down, and I turned her over. She was dead all right. She was white like always but she had these little pink dots in her skin. They say you get those dots from asphyxiation. They found potting compost in her lungs, poor lady.' He had undoubtedly been shocked and moved at the time, but there was an echo of countless repetitions in his voice now and precious little feeling.

'Thank you for showing me,' I said.

He nodded and we both went out, shutting the door behind us.

'I don't think Mr Pembroke liked this place much,' he said unexpectedly. 'Last spring, when she chose it, he said she could have it only if he couldn't see it from the house. Otherwise he wouldn't pay the bill. I wasn't supposed to hear, of course, but there you are, I did. They'd got to shouting, you see.'

'Yes,' I said, 'I do see.' Shouting, slammed doors, the lot.

'They were all lovey-dovey when I first came here,' he said, 'but then I reckon her little ways got to him, like, and you could see it all going downhill like a runaway train. I'm here all day long, see, and in and out of the house, and you couldn't miss it.'

'What little ways?' I asked casually.

He glanced at me sideways with reawakening suspicions. 'I thought you were his son. You must have known her.'

'I didn't come here. I didn't like her.'

He seemed to find that easily believable.

'She could be as sweet as sugar . . .' He paused, remembering. 'I don't know what you'd call it, really, what she was. But for instance last year, as well as the ordinary vegetables for the house, I grew a special little patch separately . . . fed them, and so on . . . to enter in the local show. Just runner beans, carrots and onions, for one of the produce classes. I'm good at that, see? Well, Mrs Pembroke happened to spot them a day or two before I was ready to harvest. On the Thursday, with the show on the Saturday. "What huge vegetables," she says, and I tell her I'm going to exhibit them on Saturday. And she looks at me sweet as syrup and says, "Oh no, Arthur. Mr Pembroke and I both like vegetables, as you know. We'll have some of these for dinner tomorrow and I'll freeze the rest. They are *our* vegetables, aren't they, Arthur? If you want to grow vegetables to show, you must do it in your own garden in your own time." And blow me, when I came to work the next morning, the whole little patch had been picked over, beans, carrots, onions, the lot. She'd taken them, right enough. Pounds and pounds of them, all the best ones. Maybe they ate some, but she never did bother with the freezing. On the Monday, I found a load of the beans in the dustbin.'

'Charming,' I said.

He shrugged. 'That was her sort of way. Mean, but within her rights.'

'I wonder you stayed,' I said.

'It's a nice garden, and I get on all right with Mr Pembroke.'

'But after he left?'

'He asked me to stay on to keep the place decent. He paid me extra, so I did.'

Walking slowly, we arrived back at the kitchen door. He smelled faintly of compost and old leaves and the warm fertility of loam, like the gardener who'd reigned in this place in my childhood.

'I grew up here,' I said, feeling nostalgia.

He gave me a considering stare. 'Are you the one who built the secret room?'

Startled, I said, 'It's not really a room. Just a sort of triangular-shaped space.'

'How do you open it?'

'You don't.'

'I could use it,' he said obstinately, 'for an apple store.'

I shook my head. 'It's too small. It's not ventilated. It's useless, really. How do you know of it?'

He pursed his lips and looked knowing. 'I could see the kitchen garden wall looked far too thick from the back down at the bottom corner and I asked old Fred about it, who used to be gardener here before he retired. He said Mr Pembroke's son once built a sort of shed there. But there's no door, I told him. He said it was the son's business, he didn't know anything about it himself, except that he thought it had been bricked up years ago. So if it was you who built it, how do you get in?'

'You can't now,' I said. 'I did brick it up soon after I built it to stop one of my half-brothers going in there and leaving dead rats for me to find.'

'Oh.' He looked disappointed. 'I've often wondered what was in there.'

'Dead rats, dead spiders, a lot of muck.'

He shrugged. 'Oh well, then.'

'You've been very helpful,' I said. 'I'll tell my father.'

His lined face showed satisfaction. 'You tell him I'll keep the dogs and everything in good nick until he comes back.'

'He'll be grateful.'

I picked up the suitcase from inside the kitchen door, gave a last look at Moira's brilliant geraniums, vibrantly alive, shook the grubby hand of Arthur Bellbrook, and (in the car hired that morning in London) drove away towards Epsom.

Collecting my own things from my impersonal suburban flat took half the time. Unlike Malcolm, I liked things bare and orderly and, meaning always to move to somewhere better but somehow never going out to search, I hadn't decked the sitting room or the two small bedrooms with anything brighter than new patterned curtains and a Snaffles print of Sergeant Murphy winning the 1923 Grand National.

I changed from Malcolm's trousers into some of my own, packed a suitcase and picked up my passport. I had no animals to arrange for, nor any bills pressing. Nothing anywhere to detain me.

The telephone answering machine's button glowed red, announcing messages taken. I rewound the tape and listened to the disembodied voices while I picked out of the fridge anything that would go furry and disgusting before my return.

Something, since I'd left the day before, had galvanized the family into feverish activity, like stirring an anthill with a stick.

A girlish voice came first, breathless, a shade anxious. 'Ian, this is Serena. Why are you always out? Don't you sleep at home? Mummy wants to know where Daddy is. She knows you and he aren't speaking, she's utterly thick to expect you to know, but anyway she insisted I ask you. So if you know, give me a ring back, OK?'

Serena, my half-sister, daughter of Alicia, the one child born to Alicia in wedlock. Serena, seven years my junior, lay in my distant memory chiefly as a small fair-haired charmer who'd followed me about like a shadow, which had flattered my twelve-year-old ego disgracefully. She liked best to sit on Malcolm's lap, his arms protectively around her, and from him, it had seemed to me, she could conjure a smile when he was angry and pretty dresses when she had a cupboardful.

Alicia, in sweeping out of the house when Serena was six, taking with her not only Serena but her two older boys, had left me alone in the suddenly quiet house, alone in the frilly kitchen, alone and untormented in the garden. There had been a time then when I would positively have welcomed back Gervase, the older boy, despite his dead rats and other rotten tricks; and it had actually been in the vacuum after his departure that I contrived the bricking up of my kitchen-wall room, not while he was there to jeer at it.

Grown up, Gervase still displayed the insignia of a natural bully: mean tightening of the mouth, jabbing forefinger, cold patronizing stare down the nose, visible enjoyment of others' discomfiture. Serena, now tall and slim, taught aerobic dancing for a living, bought clothes still by the cartload and spoke to me only when she wanted something done.

'Mummy wants to know where Daddy is ...' The childish terms sat oddly in the ear, somehow, coming from someone now twenty-six; and she alone of all his children had resisted calling Malcolm, Malcolm.

The next caller was Gervase himself. He started crossly, 'I don't like these message contraptions. I tried to get you all evening yesterday and I hear nothing but your priggish voice telling me to leave my name and telephone number, so this time I'm doing it, but under protest. This is your brother Gervase, as no doubt you realize, and it is imperative we find Malcolm at once. He has gone completely off his rocker. It's in your own interest to find him, Ian. We must all bury our differences and stop him spending the family money in this reckless way.' He paused briefly. 'I suppose you do know he has given half a million ... *half a million ...* to a busload of retarded children? I got a phone call from some stupid gushing female who said, "Oh Mr Pembroke, however can we thank you?" and when I asked her what for, she said wasn't I *the* Mr Pembroke who had solved all their problems, Mr Malcolm Pembroke? Madam, I said, what are you talking about? So she told me. *Half a million pounds.* Are you listening, Ian? He's irresponsible. It's out of proportion. He's got to be prevented from giving way to such ridiculous impulses. If you ask me, it's the beginning of senility. You must find him and tell us where he's got to, because so far as I can discover he hasn't answered his telephone since last Friday morning when I rang him to say Alicia's alimony had not been increased by the rate of inflation in this last quarter. I expect to hear from you without delay.'

His voice stopped abruptly on the peremptory order and I pictured him as he was now, not the muscular thick-set black-haired boy but the flabbier, overweight thirty-five-year-old stockbroker, over-bearingly pompous beyond his years. In a world increasingly awash with illegitimate children, he increasingly resented his own illegitimacy, referring to it illtemperedly on inappropriate occasions and denigrating the father who, for all his haste into bed with Alicia, had accepted Gervase publicly always as his son, and given him his surname with legal adoption.

Gervase had nonetheless been taunted early on by cruel schoolmates, developing an amorphous hatred then which later focused itself on me, Ian, the halfbrother who scarcely valued or understood the distinction between his birth and mine. One could understand why he'd lashed out in those raw adolescent days, but it was a matter of regret, I thought, that he'd never outgrown his bitterness. It remained with him, festering, colouring his whole personality, causing people often to wriggle away from his company, erupting in didactic outbursts and wretched unjustified jealousies.

Yet his wife appeared to love him forgivingly, and had produced two children, both girls, the first of them appearing a good three years after the well-attended marriage. Gervase had said a little too often that he himself would never in any circumstances have burdened a child with what he had suffered. Gervase, to my mind, would spend his last-ever moments worrying that the word 'illegitimate' would appear on his death certificate.

Ferdinand, his brother, was quite different, taking illegitimacy as of little importance, a matter of paperwork, no more.

Three years younger than Gervase, a year younger than myself, Ferdinand looked more like Malcolm than any of us, a living testimony to his parentage. Along with the features, he'd inherited the financial agility but lacking Malcolm's essential panache had carved himself a niche in an insurance company, not a multi-million fortune.

Ferdinand and I had been friends while we both lived in the house as children, but Alicia had thoroughly soured all that when she'd taken him away, dripping into all her children's ears the relentless spite of her dispossession. Ferdinand now looked at me with puzzlement as if he couldn't quite remember why he disliked me, and then Alicia would remind him sharply that if he wasn't careful I would get my clutches on his, Gervase's and Serena's rightful shares of Malcolm's money, and his face would darken again into unfriendliness.

It was a real pity about Ferdinand, I thought, but I never did much about it.

After Gervase on my answering machine came my mother, Joyce, very nearly incoherent with rage. Someone, it appeared, had already brought the *Sporting Life* to her notice. She couldn't *believe* it, she said. Words failed her. (They obviously didn't.) How *could* I have done anything as stupid as taking Malcolm to Newmarket Sales, because obviously I would have been there with him, it wasn't his scene otherwise, and why had I been so *deceitful* that morning when I'd talked to her, and would I without fail ring her *immediately*, this was a *crisis*, Malcolm had got to be stopped.

The fourth and last message, calmer after Joyce's hysteria, was from my half-brother Thomas, the third of Malcolm's children, born to his first wife, Vivien.

Thomas, rising forty, prematurely bald, pale skinned, sporting a gingerish moustache, had married a woman who acidly belittled him every time she opened her mouth. ('Of course, Thomas is absolutely useless when it comes to . . .' [practically anything] and 'if only poor Thomas was capable of commanding a suitable salary' and 'Dear Thomas is one of life's failures, aren't you, darling?') Thomas bore it all with hardly a wince, though after years of it I observed him grow less effective and less decisive, not more, almost as if he had come to believe in and to act out his Berenice's opinion of him.

'Ian,' Thomas said in a depressed voice, 'this is

Thomas. I've been trying to reach you since yesterday lunchtime but you seem to be away. When you've read my letter, please will you ring me up.'

I'd picked up his letter from my front doormat but hadn't yet opened it. I slit the envelope then and found that he too had a problem. I read:

Dear Ian,

Berenice is seriously concerned about Malcolm's wicked selfishness. She, well, to be honest, she keeps on and on about the amounts he's throwing away these days, and to be honest the only thing which has pacified her for a long time now is the thought of my eventual share of Malcolm's money, and if he goes on spending at this rate, well my life is going to be pretty *intolerable*, and I wouldn't be telling you this if you weren't my brother and the best of the bunch, which I suppose I've never said until now, but sometimes I think you're the only sane one in the family even if you do ride in those dangerous races, and, well, can you do anything to reason with Malcolm, as you're the only one he's likely to listen to, even though you haven't been talking for ages, which is unbelievable considering how you used to be with each other, and I blame that money-grubbing Moira, I really do, though Berenice used to think that anything or anyone who came between you and Malcolm could only be to my benefit, because Malcolm might with luck cut you out of his will.

Well, I didn't mean to say that, old chap, but it's what Berenice thought, to be honest, until Moira was going to take half of everything in the divorce settlement, and I really thought Berenice would have a seizure when she heard that, she was so furious. It really would save my sanity, Ian, if you could make Malcolm see that we all *NEED* that money. I don't know what will happen if he goes on spending it at this rate. I do *BEG* you, old chap, to stop him.

Your brother Thomas.

I looked at the letter's general incoherence and at the depth of the plea in the last few sentences with their heavily underlined words and thought of the non-stop barrage of Berenice's disgruntlement, and felt more brotherly towards Thomas than ever before. True, I still thought he should tell his wife to swallow her bile, not spill it all out on him, corroding his self-confidence and undermining his prestige with everyone within earshot; but I did at least and perhaps at last see how he could put up with it, by soothing her with the syrup of prosperity ahead.

I understood vaguely why he didn't simply ditch her and decamp: he couldn't face doing what Malcolm had done, forsaking wife and children when the going got rough. He had been taught from a very young age to despise Malcolm's inconstancy. He stayed grimly glued to Berenice and their two cheeky offspring and suffered for his virtue; and it was from fear of making the same calamitous mistake, I acknowledged, that I had married no one at all.

Thomas's was the last message on the tape. I took it out of the machine and put it in my pocket, inserting a fresh tape for future messages. I also, after a bit of thought, sorted through a boxful of family photographs, picking out groups and single pictures until I had a pretty comprehensive gallery of Pembrokes. These went into my suitcase along with a small cassette player and my best camera.

I did think of answering some of the messages, but decided against it. The arguments would all have been futile. I did truly believe in Malcolm's absolute right to do what he liked with the money he had made by his own skill and diligence. If he chose to give it in the end to his children, that was our good luck. We had no rights to it; none at all. I would have had difficulty in explaining that concept to Thomas or Joyce or Gervase or Serena, and apart from not wanting to, I hadn't the time.

I put my suitcase in the car, along with my racing saddle, helmet, whip and boots and drove back to the Savoy, being relieved to find Malcolm still there, unattacked and unharmed.

He was sitting deep in an armchair, dressed again as for the City, drinking champagne and smoking an oversize cigar. Opposite him, perched on the front edge of an identical armchair, sat a thin man of much Malcolm's age but with none of his presence.

'Norman West,' Malcolm said to me, waving the cigar vaguely at his visitor; and to the visitor he said, 'My son, Ian.'

Norman West rose to his feet and shook my hand briefly. I had never so far as I knew met a private detective before, and it wouldn't have been the occupation I would have fitted to this damp-handed nervous threadbare individual. Of medium height, he had streaky grey hair overdue for a wash, dark-circled brown eyes, greyish unhealthy skin and a day's growth of greying beard. His grey suit looked old and uncared for and his shoes had forgotten about polish. He looked as much at home in a suite in the Savoy as a punk rocker in the Vatican.

As if unerringly reading my mind he said, 'As I was just explaining to Mr Pembroke, I came straight here from an all-night observation job, as he was most insistent that it was urgent. This rig fitted my observation point. It isn't my normal gear.'

'Clothes for all seasons?' I suggested.

'Yes, that's right.'

His accent was the standard English of bygone radio announcers, slightly plummy and too good to be true. I gestured to him to sit down again, which he did as before, leaning forward from the front edge of the seat cushion and looking enquiringly at Malcolm.

'Mr West had just arrived when you came,'

Malcolm said. 'Perhaps you'd better explain to him what we want.'

I sat on the spindly little sofa and said to Norman West that we wanted him to find out where every single member of our extended family had been on the previous Friday from, say, four o'clock in the afternoon onwards, and also on Tuesday, yesterday, all day.

Norman West looked from one to the other of us in obvious dismay.

'If it's too big a job,' Malcolm said, 'bring in some help.'

'It's not really *that*,' Norman West said unhappily. 'But I'm afraid there may be a conflict of interest.'

'What conflict of interest?' Malcolm demanded.

Norman West hesitated, cleared his throat and hummed a little. Then he said, 'Last Saturday morning I was hired by one of your family to find *you*, Mr Pembroke. I've already been working, you see, for one of your family. Now you want me to check up on *them*. I don't think I should, in all conscience, accept your proposition.'

'*Which* member of my family?' Malcolm demanded.

Norman West drummed his fingers on his knee, but decided after inner debate to answer.

'Mrs Pembroke,' he said.

CHAPTER FOUR

Malcolm blinked. 'Which one?' he asked.

'Mrs Pembroke,' Norman West repeated, puzzled.

'There are nine of them,' I said. 'So which one?'

The detective looked uncomfortable. 'I spoke to her only on the telephone. I thought ... I assumed ... it was the Mrs Malcolm Pembroke for whom I worked once before, long ago. She referred me to that case, and asked for present help. I looked up my records ...' He shrugged helplessly. 'I imagined it was the same lady.'

'Did you find Mr Pembroke,' I asked, 'when you were looking for him?'

Almost unwillingly, West nodded. 'In Cambridge. Not too difficult.'

'And you reported back to Mrs Pembroke?'

'I really don't think I should be discussing this any further.'

'At least, tell us how you got back in touch with Mrs Pembroke to tell her of your success.'

'I didn't,' he said. 'She rang me two or three times

a day, asking for progress reports. Finally on Monday evening, I had news for her. After that, I proceeded with my next investigation, which I have now concluded. This left me free for anything Mr Pembroke might want.'

'I want you to find out which Mrs Pembroke wanted to know where I was.'

Norman West regretfully shook his unkempt head. 'A client's trust . . .' he murmured.

'A client's trust, poppycock!' Malcolm exploded. 'Someone who knew where to find me damn near killed me.'

Our detective looked shocked but rallied quickly. 'I found you, sir, by asking Mrs Pembroke for a list of places you felt at home in, as in my experience missing people often go to those places, and she gave me a list of five such possibilities, of which Cambridge was number three. I didn't even go to that city looking for you. As a preliminary, I was prepared to telephone to all the hotels in Cambridge asking for you, but I tried the larger hotels first, as being more likely to appeal to you, sir, and from only the third I got a positive response. If it was as easy as that for me to find you, it was equally easy for anyone else. And, sir, if I may say so, you made things easy by registering under your own name. People who want to stay lost shouldn't do that.'

He spoke with a touching air of dignity ill-matched to his seedy appearance and for the first time I thought he might be better at his job than he looked. He must have been pretty efficient, I supposed, to have stayed in the business so long, even if catching Malcolm with his trousers off couldn't have taxed him sorely years ago.

He finished off the glass of champagne that Malcolm had given him before my arrival, and refused a refill.

'How is Mrs Pembroke paying you?' I asked.

'She said she would send a cheque.'

'When it comes,' I said, 'you'll know which Mrs Pembroke.'

'So I will.'

'I don't see why you should worry about a conflict of interests,' I said. 'After all, you've worked pretty comprehensively for various Pembrokes. You worked for my mother, Joyce Pembroke, to catch my father with the lady who gave her grounds for divorce. You worked for my father, to try to catch his fifth wife having a similar fling. You worked for the unspecified Mrs Pembroke to trace my father's whereabouts. So now he wants you to find out where all his family were last Friday and yesterday so as to be sure it was none of his close relatives who tried to kill him, as it would make him very unhappy if it were. If you can't square that with your conscience, of course with great regret he'll have to retain the services of someone else.'

Norman West eyed me with a disillusionment which again encouraged me to think him not as dim as he looked. Malcolm was glimmer-eyed with amusement.

'Pay you well, of course,' he said.

'Danger money,' I said, nodding.

Malcolm said, 'What?'

'We don't want him to step on a rattlesnake, but in fairness he has to know he might.'

Norman West looked at his short and grimy nails. He didn't seem unduly put out, nor on the other hand eager.

'Isn't this a police job?' he asked.

'Certainly,' I said. 'My father called them in when someone tried to kill him last Friday, and he'll tell you all about it. And you have to bear in mind that they're also enquiring into the murder of Moira Pembroke, whom you followed through blameless days. But you would be working for my father, not for the police, if you take his cash.'

'Pretty decisive, aren't you, sir?' he said uneasily.

'Bossy,' Malcolm agreed, 'in his quiet way.'

All those years, I thought, of getting things done in a racing stable, walking a tightrope between usurping the power of the head lad on one hand and the trainer himself on the other, like a lieutenant between a sergeant-major and a colonel. I'd had a lot of practice, one way and another, at being quietly bossy.

Malcolm unemotionally told West about his abortive walk with the dogs and the brush with carbon monoxide, and after that described also the near-miss at Newmarket.

Norman West listened attentively with slowly

blinking eyes and at the end said, 'The car at New-market could have been accidental. Driver looking about for cigarettes, say. Not paying enough attention. Seeing you both at the last minute... swerving desperately.'

Malcolm looked at me. 'Did it seem like that to you?'

'No.'

'Why not?' West asked.

'The rate of acceleration, I suppose.'

'Foot on accelerator going down absent-mindedly during search for cigarettes?'

'Headlights, full beam,' I said.

'A sloppy driver? Had a few drinks?'

'Maybe.' I shook my head. 'The real problem is that if the car *had* hit us – or Malcolm – there might have been witnesses. The driver might have been stopped before he could leave the sales area. The car number might have been taken.'

West smiled sorrowfully. 'It's been done successfully before now, in broad daylight in a crowded street.'

'Are you saying,' Malcolm demanded of me, 'that the car *wasn't* trying to kill me?'

'No, only that the driver took a frightful risk.'

'Did any witnesses rush to pick us up?' Malcolm asked forcefully. 'Did anyone so much as pass a sympathetic remark? No, they damned well didn't. Did anyone try to stop the driver or take his number? The hell they did.'

'All the same,' West said, 'your son is right. Hit-and-run in a public place has its risks. If it was tried here, and, sirs, I'm not saying it wasn't, the putative gain must have outweighed the risk, or, er, in other words – '

'In other words,' Malcolm interrupted with gloom, 'Ian is right to think they'll try again.'

Norman West momentarily looked infinitely weary, as if the sins of the world were simply too much to contemplate. He had seen, I supposed, as all investigators must, a lifetime's procession of sinners and victims; and, moreover, he looked roughly seventy and hadn't slept all night.

'I'll take your job,' he said without enthusiasm, radiating minimum confidence, and I glanced at Malcolm to see if he really thought this was the best we could do in detectives, signs of intelligence or not. Malcolm appeared to have no doubts, however, and spent the next five minutes discussing fees which seemed ominously moderate to me.

'And I'll need a list,' West said finally, 'of the people you want checked. Names and addresses and normal habits.'

Malcolm showed unexpected discomfort, as if checking that amorphous entity 'the family' was different from checking each individual separately, and it was I who found a piece of Savoy writing paper to draw up the list.

'OK,' I said, 'first of all there's Vivien, my father's first wife. Mrs Vivien Pembroke.'

'Not her,' Malcolm objected. 'It's ridiculous.'

'Everyone,' I said firmly. 'No exceptions. That makes it fair on everyone ... because there are going to be some extremely angry relations when they all realize what's happening.'

'They won't find out,' Malcolm said.

Fat chance, I thought.

To West, I said, 'They all telephone each other all the time, not by any means always out of friendship but quite often out of spite. They won't gang up against you because they seldom form alliances among themselves. Some of them are pretty good liars. Don't believe everything they say about each other.'

'*Ian*!' Malcolm said protestingly.

'I'm one of them, and I know,' I said.

After Vivien's name on the list I wrote the names of her children:

Donald

Lucy

Thomas

'Thomas,' I said, 'is married to Berenice.' I added her name beside his. 'He is easy to deal with, she is not.'

'She's a five-star cow,' Malcolm said.

West merely nodded.

'Lucy,' I said, 'married a man called Edwin Bugg. She didn't like that surname, and persuaded him to change it to hers, and she is consequently herself a Mrs Pembroke.'

West nodded.

'Lucy is a poet,' I said. 'People who know about poetry say her stuff is the real thing. She makes a big production of unworldliness which Edwin, I think, has grown to find tiresome.'

'Huh,' Malcolm said. 'Edwin's an out-and-out materialist, always tapping me for a loan.'

'Do you give them to him?' I said interestedly.

'Not often. He never pays me back.'

'Short of money, are they?' West asked.

'Edwin Bugg,' Malcolm said, 'married Lucy years ago because he thought she was an heiress, and they've scraped along ever since on the small income she gets from a trust fund I set up for her. Edwin's never done a stroke of work in his parasitic life and I can't stand the fellow.'

'They have one teenage schoolboy son,' I said, smiling, 'who asked me the last time I saw him how to set about emigrating to Australia.'

West looked at the list and said to Malcolm, 'What about Donald, your eldest?'

'Donald,' said his father, 'married a replica of his mother, beautiful and brainless. A girl called Helen. They live an utterly boring virtuous life in Henley-on-Thames and are still billing and cooing like newlyweds although Donald must be nearly forty-five, I suppose.'

No one commented. Malcolm himself, rising sixty-nine, could bill and coo with the best, and with a suppressed shiver I found myself thinking for the first time about the *sixth* marriage, because certainly, in the future, if Malcolm survived, there would be one. He had never in the past lived long alone. He liked rows better than solitude.

'Children?' Norman West asked into the pause.

'Three,' Malcolm said. 'Pompous little asses.'

West glanced at me questioningly, and yawned.

'Are you too tired to take all this in?' I asked.

'No, go ahead.'

'Two of Donald's children are too young to drive a car. The eldest, a girl at art school, is five foot two and fragile, and I cannot imagine her being physically capable of knocking Malcolm out and carrying his body from garden to garage and inserting him into Moira's car.'

'She hasn't the courage either,' Malcolm said.

'You can't say that,' I disagreed. 'Courage can pop up anywhere and surprise you.'

West gave me a noncommittal look. 'Well,' he said, taking the list himself and adding to it, 'this is what we have so far. Wife number one: Vivien Pembroke. Her children: Donald (44), wife Helen, three offspring. Lucy, husband Edwin (née Bugg), school-age son. Thomas, wife Berenice . . .?'

'Two young daughters.'

'Two young daughters,' he repeated, writing.

'My grandchildren,' Malcolm protested, 'are all too young to have murdered anybody.'

'Psychopaths start in the nursery,' West said laconically. 'Any sign in any of them of abnormal violent behaviour? Excessive cruelty, that sort of thing? Obsessive hatreds?'

Malcolm and I both shook our heads but with a touch of uncertainty; his maybe because of something he did know, mine because of all I didn't know, because of all the things that could be hidden.

'Does greed, too, begin in the nursery?' I said.

'I wouldn't say so, would you?' West answered.

I shook my head again. 'I'd say it was nastily adult and grows with opportunity. The more there is to grab, the greedier people get.'

Malcolm said, only half as a question, 'My fortune corrupts . . . geometrically?'

'You're not alone,' I said dryly. 'Just think of all those multi-billionaire families where the children have already had millions settled on them and still fight like cats over the pickings when their father dies.'

'Bring it down to thousands,' West said unexpectedly. 'Or to hundreds. I've seen shocking spite over hundreds. And the lawyers rub their hands and syphon off the cream.' He sighed, half disillusionment, half weariness. 'Wife number two?' he asked, and answered his own question, 'Mrs Joyce Pembroke.'

'Right,' I said. 'I'm her son. She had no other children. And I'm not married.'

West methodically wrote me down.

'Last Friday evening,' I said, 'I was at work in a racing stable at five o'clock with about thirty people as witnesses, and last night I was certainly not driving the car that nearly ran us over.'

West said stolidly, 'I'll write you down as being cleared of primary involvement. That's all I can do with any of your family, Mr Pembroke.' He finished the sentence looking at Malcolm who said, 'Hired assassin' between his teeth, and West nodded. 'If any of them hired a good professional, I doubt if I'll discover it.'

'I thought good assassins used rifles,' I said.

'Some do. Most don't. They pick their own way. Some use knives. Some garotte. I knew of one who used to wait at traffic lights along his victim's usual route to work. One day, the lights would be red, the victim would stop. The assassin tapped on the window, asking a question . . . or so it's supposed. The victim wound down the window and the assassin shot him point blank in the head. By the time the lights turned green and the cars behind started tooting their horns, the assassin had long gone.'

'Did they ever catch him?' I asked.

West shook his head. 'Eight prominent businessmen were killed that way within two years. Then it stopped. No one knows why. My guess is the assassin lost his nerve. It happens in every profession.'

I thought of jump jockeys to whom it had happened

almost overnight, and I supposed it occurred in stock-brokers also. Any profession, as he said.

'Or someone bumped him off because he knew too much,' Malcolm said.

'That too is possible.' West looked at the list. 'After Mrs Joyce?'

Malcolm said sourly, 'The lady you so artfully photo-graphed me with at the instigation of, as you call her, Mrs Joyce.'

The West eyebrows slowly rose. 'Miss Alicia Sand-ways? With, if I remember, two little boys?'

'The little boys are now thirty-five and thirty-two,' I said.

'Yes.' He sighed. 'As I said, I recently dug out that file. I didn't realize that ... er ... Well, so we have wife number three, Mrs Alicia Pembroke. And her children?'

Malcolm said, 'The two boys, Gervase and Ferdi-nand. I formally adopted them when I married their mother, and changed their surname to Pembroke. Then we had little Serena,' his face softened, 'and it was for her I put up with Alicia's tantrums the last few years we were together. Alicia was a great mistress but a rotten wife. Don't ask me why. I indulged her all the time, let her do what she liked with my house, and in the end nothing would please her.' He shrugged. 'I gave her a generous divorce settlement, but she was very bitter. I wanted to keep little Serena ... and Alicia screamed that she supposed I didn't want the boys because they were illegitimate. She fought in the courts for Serena, and she won . . . She filled all her children's heads with bad feelings for me.' The old hurt plainly showed. 'Serena did suggest coming back to look after me when Coochie was killed, but it wasn't necessary because Moira was there. When Moira was killed, she offered again. It was kind of Serena. She's a nice girl, really, but Alicia tries to set her against me.'

West, in a pause that might or might not have been sympathetic, wrote after Alicia's name:

Gervase. Illegitimate at birth, subsequently adopted

Ferdinand. The same

Serena. Legitimate

'Are they married?' he asked.

'Gervase has a wife called Ursula,' I said. 'I don't know her well, because when I see them they're usually together and it's always Gervase who does the talking. They too, like Thomas, have two little girls.'

West wrote it down.

'Ferdinand,' I said, 'has married two raving beauties in rapid succession. The first, American, has gone back to the States. The second one, Deborah, known as Debs, is still in residence. So far, no children.'

West wrote.

'Serena,' I said, 'is unmarried.'

West completed that section of the list. 'So we have wife number three, Mrs Alicia Pembroke. Her children are Gervase, wife Ursula, two small daughters.

Ferdinand, current wife Debs, no children. Serena, unmarried ... er ... a fiancé, perhaps? Live-in-lover?'

'I don't know of one,' I said, and Malcolm said he didn't know either.

'Right,' West said. 'Wife number four?'

There was a small silence. Then I said, 'Coochie. She's dead. She had twin sons. One was killed with her in a car crash, the other is brain-damaged and lives in a nursing home.'

'Oh.' The sound carried definite sympathy this time. 'And wife number five, Mrs Moira Pembroke, did she perhaps have any children from a previous marriage?'

'No,' Malcolm said. 'No previous marriage, no children.'

'Right.' West counted up his list. 'That's three ex-wives ... er, by the way, did any of them remarry?'

I answered with a faint smile, 'They would lose their alimony if they did. Malcolm was pretty generous in their settlements. None of them has seen any financial sense in remarrying.'

'They all should have done,' Malcolm grumbled. 'They wouldn't be so warped.'

West said merely, 'Right. Then, er, six sons, two daughters. Four current daughters-in-law, one son-in-law. Grandchildren ... too young. So, er, discounting the invalid son and Mr Ian here, there are fourteen adults to be checked. That will take me a week at least. Probably more.'

'As fast as you can,' I said.

84

He looked actually as if he had barely enough strength or confidence to get himself out of the door let alone embark on what was clearly an arduous task.

'Can I tell them all why I'm making these enquiries?' he asked.

'Yes, you damned well can,' Malcolm said positively. 'If it's one of them, and I hope to God it isn't, it might put the wind up them and frighten them off. Just don't tell them where to find me.'

I looked down at the list. I couldn't visualize any of them as being criminally lethal, but then greed affected otherwise rational people in irrational ways. All sorts of people . . . I knew of a case when two male relatives had gone into a house where an old woman had been reported newly dead, and taken the bedroom carpet off the floor, rolling it up and making off with it and leaving her lying alone in her bed above bare boards, all to seize her prize possession before the rest of the family could get there. Unbelievable, I'd thought it. The old woman's niece, who cleaned my flat every week, had been most indignant, but not on her aunt's account. 'It was the only good carpet in the house,' she vigorously complained. 'Nearly new. The only thing worth having. It should have come to me, by rights. Now I'll never get it.'

'I'll need all their addresses,' West said.

Malcolm waved a hand. 'Ian can tell you. Get him to write them down.'

Obediently I opened my suitcase, took out my

address book and wrote the whole list, with telephone numbers. Then I got out the pack of photographs and showed them to West.

'Would they help you?' I asked. 'If they would, I'll lend them to you, but I want them back.'

West looked through them one by one, and I knew that he could see, if he were any detective at all, all the basic characters of the subjects. I liked taking photographs and preferred portraits, and somehow taking a camera along gave me something positive to do whenever the family met. I didn't like talking to some of them; photography gave me a convincing reason for disengagements and drifting around.

If there was one common factor in many of the faces it was discontent, which I thought was sad. Only in Ferdinand could one see real lightheartedness, and even in him, as I knew, it could come and go; and Debs, his second wife, was a stunning blonde, taller than her husband, looking out at the world quizzically as if she couldn't quite believe her eyes, not yet soured by disappointment.

I'd caught Gervase giving his best grade-one bullying down-the-nose stare, and saw no good purpose in ever showing him the reflection of his soul. Ursula merely looked indeterminate and droopy and somehow guilty, as if she thought she shouldn't even have her photo taken without Gervase's permission.

Berenice, Thomas's wife, was the exact opposite, staring disapprovingly straight into the lens, bold and sarcastic, unerringly destructive every time she uttered. And Thomas, a step behind her, looking harried and anxious. Another of Thomas alone, smiling uneasily, defeat in the sag of his shoulders, desperation in his eyes.

Vivien, Joyce and Alicia, the three witches, dissimilar in features but alike in expression, had been caught when they weren't aware of the camera, each of them watching someone else with disfavour.

Alicia, fluffy and frilly, still wore her hair brought youthfully high to a ribbon bow on the crown, from where rich brown curls tumbled in a cascade to her shoulders. Nearly sixty, she looked in essence younger than her son Gervase, and she would still have been pretty but for the pinched hardness of her mouth.

She had been a fair sort of mother to me for the seven years of her reign, seeing to my ordinary needs like food and new clothes and treating me no different from Gervase and Ferdinand, but I'd never felt like going to her for advice or comfort. She hadn't loved me, nor I her, and after the divorce we had neither felt any grief in separation. I'd detested what she'd done afterwards to Gervase, Ferdinand and Serena, twisting their minds with her own spite. I would positively have liked to have had friendly brothers and sisters as much as Malcolm would have valued friendly children. After nearly twenty years, Alicia's intense hurt still spread suffering outward in ripples.

Serena's picture showed her as she had been a year

earlier, before aerobic dancing had slimmed her further to a sexless-looking leanness. The fair hair of childhood had slightly darkened, and was stylishly cut in a short becoming cap-shape which made her look young for her twenty-six years. A leggy Peter Pan, I thought, not wanting to grow up: a girl-woman with a girlish voice saying 'Mummy and Daddy', and an insatiable appetite for clothes. I wondered briefly whether she were still a virgin and felt faintly surprised to find that I simply didn't know and, moreover, couldn't tell.

'These are very interesting,' West said, glancing at me. 'I should certainly like to borrow them.' He shuffled them around and sorted them out. 'Who are these? You haven't put their names on the back, like the others.'

'That's Lucy and Edwin, and that's Donald and Helen.'

'Thanks.' He wrote the identification carefully in small neat letters.

Malcolm stretched out a hand for the photographs which West gave him. Malcolm looked through them attentively and finally gave them back.

'I don't remember seeing any of these before,' he said.

'They're all less than three years old.'

His mouth opened and shut again. He gave me a brooding look, as if I'd just stabbed him unfairly in the ribs.

'What do you think of them?' I asked.

'A pity children grow up.'

West smiled tiredly and collected the lists and photographs together.

'Right, Mr Pembroke. I'll get started.' He stood up and swayed slightly, but when I took a step forward to steady him he waved me away. 'Just lack of sleep.' On his feet, he looked even nearer to exhaustion, as if the outer greyness had penetrated inwards to the core. 'First thing in the morning, I'll be checking the Pembrokes.'

It would have been churlish to expect him to start that afternoon, but I can't say I liked the delay. I offered him another drink and a reviving lunch, which he declined, so I took him to the hotel's front door and saw him safely into a taxi, watching him sink like a collapsing scarecrow into the seat cushions.

Returning to the suite, I found Malcolm ordering vodka and Beluga caviar from room service with the abandon to which I was becoming accustomed. That done, he smoothed out the *Sporting Life* and pointed to one section of it.

'It says the Arc de Triomphe race is due to be run this Sunday in Paris.'

'Yes, that's right.'

'Then let's go.'

'All right,' I said.

Malcolm laughed. 'We may as well have some fun. There's a list here of the runners.'

I looked where he pointed. It was a bookmaker's advertisement showing the ante-post prices on offer.

'What are the chances,' Malcolm said, 'of my buying one of these horses?'

'Er,' I said. 'Today, do you mean?'

'Of course. No good buying one *after* the race, is there?'

'Well . . .'

'No, of course not. The winner will be worth millions and the others peanuts. *Before* the race, that's the thing.'

'I don't suppose anyone will sell,' I said, 'but we can try. How high do you want to go? The favourite won the Epsom Derby and is reported to be going to be syndicated for ten million pounds. You'd have to offer a good deal more than that before they'd consider selling him now.'

'Hm,' Malcolm said. 'What do you think of him as a horse?'

I smothered a gasp or two and said with a deadpan face, 'He's a very good horse but he had an exceptionally exhausting race last time out. I don't think he's had enough time to recover, and I wouldn't back him this time.'

'Have you backed him before?' Malcolm asked curiously.

'Yes, when he won the Derby, but he was favourite for that, too.'

'What do you think will win the Arc de Triomphe, then?'

'Seriously?' I said.

'Of course seriously.'

'One of the French horses, Meilleurs Voeux.'

'Can we buy him?'

'Not a hope. His owner loves his horses, loves winning more than profit and is immensely rich.'

'So am I,' Malcolm said simply. 'I can't help making money. It used to be a passion, now it's a habit. But this business about Moira jolted me, you know. It struck me that I may not have a hell of a lot of time left, not with enough health and strength to enjoy life. I've spent all these years amassing the stuff, and for what? For my goddam children to murder me for it? Sod that for a sad story. You buy me a good horse in this race on Sunday and we'll go and yell it home, boy, at the top of our lungs.'

It took all afternoon and early evening to get even a tinge of interest from anyone. I telephoned to the trainers of the English – or Irish – runners, asking if they thought their owners might sell. I promised each trainer that he would go on training the horse, and that my father would send him also the two-million-guinea colt he'd bought yesterday. Some of the trainers were at the Newmarket Sales and had to be tracked down to hotels, and once tracked, had to track and consult with their owners. Some simply said no, forget it.

Finally, at seven forty-five, a trainer from Newmarket rang back to say his owner would sell a half-share if his price was met. I relayed the news and the price to Malcolm.

'What do you think?' he said.

'Um . . . the horse is quite good, the price is on the high side, the trainer's in the top league.'

'OK.' Malcolm said. 'Deal.'

'My father accepts,' I said. 'And, er, the colt is still in the sales stables. Can you fetch it tomorrow, if we clear it with the auctioneers?'

Indeed he could. He sounded quite cheerful altogether. He would complete his paperwork immediately if Malcolm could transfer the money directly to his bloodstock account, bank and account number supplied. I wrote the numbers to his dictation. Malcolm waved a hand and said, 'No problem. First thing in the morning. He'll have it by afternoon.'

'Well,' I said, breathing out as I put the receiver down, 'you now own half of Blue Clancy.'

'Let's drink to it,' Malcolm said. 'Order some Bollinger.'

I ordered it from room service, and while we waited for it to arrive I told him about my encounter with his gardener, Arthur Bellbrook.

'Decent chap,' Malcolm said, nodding. 'Damned good gardener.'

I told him wryly about Moira and the prize vegetables, which he knew nothing about.

'Silly bitch,' he said. 'Arthur lives in a terrace house

with a pocket handkerchief garden facing north. You couldn't grow prize stuff there. If she'd asked me I'd have told her that, and told her to leave him alone. Good gardeners are worth every perk they get.'

'He seemed pretty philosophical,' I said, 'and, incidentally, pretty bright. He'd spotted that the kitchen garden wall is thicker than it should be at the corner. He'd asked old Fred, and heard about the room I built there. He wanted to know how to get in, so he could use it as an apple store.'

Malcolm practically ejected from his armchair, alarm widening his eyes, his voice coming out strangled and hoarse. 'My God, you didn't tell him, did you?'

'No, I didn't,' I said slowly. 'I told him it was empty and was bricked up twenty years ago.' I paused. 'What have you put in there?'

Malcolm subsided into his chair, not altogether relieved of anxiety.

'Never you mind,' he said.

'You forget that I could go and look.'

'I don't forget it.'

He stared at me. He'd been interested, all those summers ago, when I'd designed and built the pivoting brick door. He'd come down the garden day after day to watch, and had patted me often on the shoulder, and smiled at the secret. The resulting wall looked solid, felt solid, *was* solid. But at one point there was a thick vertical steel rod within it, stretching from a concrete underground foundation up into the beam supporting the roof. Before I'd put the new roof on, I'd patiently drilled round holes in bricks (breaking many) and slid them into the rod, and arranged and mortared the door in neat courses, so that the edges of it dovetailed into the fixed sections next to it.

To open the room, when I'd finished everything, one had first to remove the wedge-like wooden sill which gave extra support to the bottom course of the door when it was closed, and then to activate the spring latch on the inner side by poking a thin wire through a tiny hole in the mortar at what had been my thirteen-year-old waist height. The design of the latch hadn't been my own, but something I'd read in a book: at any rate, when I'd installed it, it worked obligingly at once.

It had pleased me intensely to build a door that Gervase would never find. No more dead rats. No more live birds, shut in and fluttering with fright. No more invasions of my own private place.

Gervase had never found the door and nor had anyone else and, as the years passed, grass grew long in front of the wall, and nettles, and although I'd meant to give the secret to Robin and Peter some day, I hadn't done so by the time of the crash. Only Malcolm knew how to get in – and Malcolm had used the knowledge.

'What's in there?' I repeated.

He put on his airiest expression. 'Just some things I didn't want Moira to get her hands on.'

I remembered sharply the objects missing from his study.

'The gold dolphin, the amethyst tree, the silver candelabra . . . those?'

'You've been looking,' he accused.

I shook my head. 'I noticed they were gone.'

The few precious objects, all the same, hardly accounted for the severity of his first alarm.

'What else is in there?' I said.

'Actually,' he said, calmly now, 'quite a lot of gold.'

CHAPTER FIVE

'Some people buy and sell gold without ever seeing it,' he said. 'But I like possessing the actual stuff. There's no fun in paper transactions. Gold is beautiful on its own account, and I like to see it and feel it. But it's not all that easy to store it in banks or safety deposits. Too heavy and bulky. And insurance is astronomical. Takes too much of the profit. I never insure it.'

'You're storing it there in the wall . . . waiting for the price to rise?'

'You know me, don't you?' He smiled. 'Buy low, bide your time, sell high. Wait a couple of years, not often more. The price of gold itself swings like a pendulum, but there's nothing, really, like gold shares. When gold prices rise, gold shares often rise by two or three times as much. I sell the gold first and the shares a couple of months later. Psychological phenomenon, you know, that people go on investing in gold mines, pushing the price up, when the price of gold itself is static or beginning to drop. Illogical, but invaluable to people like me.'

He sat looking at me with the vivid blue eyes, teaching his child.

'Strategic Minerals, now. There never was anything like the Strategic Minerals Corporation of Australia. This year, the price of gold itself rose twenty-five per cent, but Strats – shares in Strategic Minerals – rose nearly a thousand per cent before they dropped off the top. Incredible, I got in near the beginning of those and sold at nine hundred and fifty per cent profit. But don't be fooled, Strats happen only once or twice in a lifetime.'

'How much,' I said, fascinated, 'did you invest in Strats?'

After a brief pause he said, 'Five million. I had a feeling about them ... they just smelled right. I don't often go in so deep, and I didn't expect them to fly so high, no one could, but there you are, all gold shares rose this year, and Strats rose like a skylark.'

'How are they doing now?' I asked.

'Don't know. I'm concerned with the present. Gold mines, you see, don't go on for ever. They have a life: exploration, development, production, exhaustion. I get in, wait a while, take a profit, forget them. Never stay too long with a rising gold share. Fortunes are lost by selling too late.'

He did truly trust me, I thought. If he'd doubted me still, he wouldn't have told me there was gold behind the brick door, nor that even after tax he had made approximately thirty million pounds on one deal. I stopped worrying that he was overstretching himself in buying the colt and a half-share in Blue Clancy. I stopped worrying about practically everything except how to keep him alive and spending.

I'd talked to someone once whose father had died when she was barely twenty. She regretted that she hadn't ever known him adult to adult, and wished she could meet him again, just to talk. Watching Malcolm, it struck me that in a way I'd been given her wish: that the three years' silence had been a sort of death, and that I could talk to him now adult to adult, and know him as a man, not as a father.

We spent a peaceful evening together in the suite, talking about what we'd each done during the hiatus, and it was difficult to imagine that outside, somewhere, a predator might be searching for the prey.

At one point I said, 'You gave Joyce's telephone number on purpose to the film man, didn't you? And Gervase's number to the retarded-children lady? You wanted me with you to see you buy the colt ... You made sure that the family knew all about your monster outlays as soon as possible, didn't you?'

'Huh,' he said briefly, which after a moment I took as admission. One misdirected telephone call had been fairly possible: two stretched credibility too far.

'Thomas and Berenice,' I said, 'were pretty frantic over some little adventure of yours. What did you do to stir *them* up?'

'How the hell do you know all this?'

I smiled and fetched the cassette player, and re-ran for him the message tape from my telephone. He listened grimly but with an undercurrent of amusement to Serena, Gervase and Joyce and then read Thomas's letter, and when he reached Thomas's intense closing appeal I waited for explosions.

They didn't come. He said wryly, 'I suppose they're what I made them.'

'No,' I said.

'Why not?'

'Personality is mysterious, but it's born in you, not made.'

'But it can be brainwashed.'

'Yes, OK,' I said. 'But you didn't do it.'

'Vivien and Alicia did . . . because of me.'

'Don't wallow in guilt so much. It isn't like you.'

He grinned. 'I don't feel guilty, actually.'

Joyce, I thought, had at least played fair. A screaming fury she might have been on the subject of Alicia, but she'd never tried to set me against Malcolm. She had agreed in the divorce settlement when I was six that he should have custody of me: she wasn't basically maternal, and infrequent visits from her growing son were all she required. She'd never made great efforts to bind me to her, and it had always been clear to me that she was relieved every time at my departure. Her life consisted of playing, teaching, and writing about bridge, a game she played to international tournament standard, and she was often abroad. My visits had always disrupted the acute concentration she needed for winning, and as winning gave her the prestige essential for lecture tours and magazine articles, I had more often raised impatience in her than comradeship, a feeling she had dutifully tried to stifle.

She had given me unending packs of cards to play with and had taught me a dozen card games, but I'd never had her razor memory of any and every card played in any and every game, a perpetual disappointment to her and a matter for impatience in itself. When I veered off to make my life in a totally different branch of the entertainment industry, she had been astonished at my choice and at first scornful, but had soon come round to checking the racing pages during the steeplechase season to see if I was listed as riding.

'What did you tell Thomas and Berenice?' I asked Malcolm again, after a pause.

With satisfaction he said, 'I absentmindedly gave their telephone number to a wine merchant who was to let me know the total I owed him for the fifty or so cases of 1979 Pol Roger he was collecting for me to drink.'

'And, er, roughly how much would that cost?'

'The 1979, the Winston Churchill vintage, is quite exceptional, you know.'

'Of course it would be,' I said.

'Roughly twenty-five thousand pounds, then, for fifty cases.'

Poor Thomas, I thought.

'I also made sure that Alicia knew I'd given about a quarter of a million pounds to fund scholarships for bright girls at the school Serena went to. Alicia and I haven't been talking recently. I suppose she's furious I gave it to the school and not to Serena herself.'

'Well, why did you?'

He looked surprised. 'You know my views. You must all carve your own way. To make you all rich too young would rob you of incentive.'

I certainly did know his views, but I wasn't sure I always agreed with them. I would have had bags of incentive to make a success of being a racehorse trainer if he'd lent, advanced or given me enough to start, but I also knew that if he did, he'd have to do as much for the others (being ordinarily a fair man), and he didn't believe in it, as he said.

'Why did you want them all to know how much you've been spending?' I asked. 'Because of course they all will know by now. The telephone wires will have been red hot.'

'I suppose I thought . . . um . . . if they believed I was getting rid of most of it there would be less point in killing me . . . do you see?'

I stared at him. 'You must be crazy,' I said. 'It sounds to me like an invitation to be murdered without delay.'

'Ah well, that too has occurred to me of late.' He smiled vividly. 'But I have you with me now to prevent that.'

After a speechless moment I said, 'I may not always be able to see the speeding car.'

'I'll trust your eyesight.'

I pondered. 'What else have you spent a bundle on, that I haven't heard about?'

He drank some champagne and frowned, and I guessed that he was trying to decide whether or not to tell me. Finally he sighed and said, 'This is for your ears only. I didn't do it for the same reason, and I did it earlier ... several weeks ago, in fact, before Moira was murdered.' He paused. 'She was angry about it, though she'd no right to be. It wasn't her money. She hated me to give anything to anyone else. She wanted everything for herself.' He sighed. 'I don't know how you knew right from the beginning what she was like.'

'Her calculator eyes,' I said.

He smiled ruefully. He must have seen that look perpetually, by the end.

'The nursing home where Robin is,' he said unexpectedly, 'needed repairs. So I paid for them.'

He wasn't talking, I gathered, in terms of a couple of replaced window-frames.

'Of course, you know it's a private nursing home?' he said. 'A family business, basically.'

'Yes.'

'They needed a new roof. New wiring. A dozen urgent upgradings. They tried raising the residential fees too high and lost patients, familiar story. They asked my advice about fund-raising. I told them not to bother. I'd get estimates, and all I'd want in return was that they'd listen to a good business consultant who I'd send them.' He shifted comfortably in his armchair. 'Robin's settled there. Calm. Any change upsets him, as you know. If the whole place closed and went out of business, which was all too likely, I'd have to find somewhere else for him, and he's lost enough . . .'

His voice tapered off. He had delighted in Robin and Peter when they'd been small, playing with them on the carpet like a young father, proud of them as if they were his first children, not his eighth and ninth. Good memories: worth a new roof.

'I know you still go to visit him,' he said. 'The nurses tell me. So you must have seen the place growing threadbare.'

I nodded, thinking about it. 'They used to have huge vases of fresh flowers everywhere.'

'They used to have top quality everything, but they've had to compromise to patch up the building. Country houses are open money drains when they age. I can't see the place outliving Robin, really. You will look after him, when I've gone?'

'Yes,' I said.

He nodded, taking it for granted. 'I appointed you his trustee when I set up the fund for him, do you remember? I've not altered it.'

I was glad that he hadn't. At least, somewhere, obscurely, things had remained the same between us.

'Why don't we go and see him tomorrow?' he said. 'No one will kill me there.'

'All right,' I agreed: so we went in the hired car in the morning, stopping in the local town to buy presents of chocolate and simple toys designed for three-year-olds, and I added a packet of balloons to the pile while Malcolm paid.

'Does he like balloons?' he asked, his eyebrows rising.

'He gets frustrated sometimes. I blow the balloons up, and he bursts them.'

Malcolm looked surprised and in some ways disturbed. 'I didn't know he could feel frustration.'

'It seems like that. As if sometimes he half remembers us . . . but can't quite.'

'Poor boy.'

We drove soberly onwards and up the drive of the still splendid-looking Georgian house which lay mellow and symmetrical in the autumn sunshine. Inside, its near fifty rooms had been adapted and transformed in the heyday of private medicine into a highly comfortable hospital for mostly chronic, mostly old, mostly rich patients. Short-stay patients came and went, usually convalescing after major operations performed elsewhere, but in general one saw the same faces month after month: the same faces ageing, suffering, waiting for release. Dreadfully depressing, I found it, but for Robin, it was true, it seemed the perfect haven, arrived at after two unsuccessful stays in more apparently suitable homes involving other children, bright colours, breezy nurses and jollying atmospheres. Robin seemed better with peace, quiet and no demands, and Malcolm had finally acted against professional advice to give them to him.

Robin had a large room on the ground floor with French doors opening on to a walled garden. He seldom went out into the garden, but he preferred the doors open in all weathers, including snow-storms. Apart from that, he was docile and easy to deal with, and if anyone had speculated on the upheavals that might happen soon if puberty took its natural course, they hadn't mentioned it in my hearing.

He looked at us blankly, as usual. He seldom spoke, though he did retain the ability to make words: it was just that he seemed to have few thoughts to utter. Brain damage of that magnitude was idiosyncratic, we'd been told, resulting in behaviour individual to each victim. Robin spoke rarely and then only to himself, in private, when he didn't expect to be overheard: the nurses sometimes heard him, and had told us, but said he stopped as soon as he saw them.

I'd asked them what he said, but they didn't know, except for words like 'shoes' and 'bread' and 'floor': ordinary words. They didn't know why he wouldn't speak at other times. They were sure, though, that he understood a fair amount of what others said, even if in a haze.

We gave him some pieces of chocolate which he ate,

and unwrapped the toys for him which he fingered but didn't play with. He looked at the balloon packet without emotion. It wasn't a frustration day: on those, he looked at the packet and made blowing noises with his mouth.

We sat with him for quite a while, talking, telling him who we were while he wandered around the room. He looked at our faces from time to time, and touched my nose once with his finger as if exploring that I was really there, but there was no connection with our minds. He looked healthy, good looking, a fine boy: heart-breaking, as always.

A nurse came in the end, middle-aged, kind-faced, to take him to a dining room for lunch, and Malcolm and I transferred to the office where my father was given a saviour's welcome and offered a reviving scotch.

'Your son, slow progress, I'm afraid.' Earnest, dedicated people.

Malcolm nodded. No progress would have been more accurate.

'We do our best for him always.'

'Yes, I know.' Malcolm drank the scotch, shook their hands, made our farewells. We left, as I always left, in sadness, silence and regret.

'So bloody unfair,' Malcolm said halfway back to London. 'He ought to be laughing, talking, roaring through life.'

'Yes.'

'I can't bear to see him, and I can't bear not to. I'd give all my money to have him well again.'

'And make a new fortune afterwards,' I said.

'Well, yeah, why not?' He laughed, but still with gloom. 'It would have been better if he'd died with the others. Life's a bugger, sometimes, isn't it?'

The gloom lasted back to the Savoy and through the next bottle of Bollinger, but by afternoon Malcolm was complaining of the inactivity I'd thrust upon him and wanting to visit cronies in the City. Unpredictability be our shield, I prayed, and kept my eyes open for speeding cars; but we saw the day out safely in offices, bars, clubs and a restaurant, during which time Malcolm increased his wealth by gambling a tenner at evens on the day's closing price of gold which fell by two pounds when the trend was upwards. 'It'll shoot right up next year, you watch.'

On Friday, despite my pleas for sanity, he insisted on accompanying me to Sandown Park races.

'You'll be safer here,' I protested, 'in the suite.'

'I shan't *feel* safer.'

'At the races, I can't stay beside you.'

'Who's to know I'll be there?'

I gazed at him. 'Anyone who guesses we are now together could know. They'll know how to find *me*, if they look in the papers.'

'Then don't go.'

'I'm going. You stay here.'

I saw, however, that the deep underlying apprehension which he tried to suppress most of the time would erupt into acute nervous anxiety if I left him alone in the suite for several hours, and that he might, out of boredom, do something much sillier than going to the races, like convincing himself that anyone in his family would keep a secret if he asked it.

Accordingly I drove him south of London and took him through the jockeys' entrance gate to the weighing room area where he made his afternoon a lot safer by meeting yet another crony and being instantly invited to lunch in the holy of holies.

'Do you have cronies all over the world?' I asked.

'Certainly,' he said, smiling broadly. 'Anyone I've known for five minutes is a crony, if I get on with them.'

I believed him. Malcolm wasn't easy to forget, nor was he hard to like. I saw the genuine pleasure in his immediate host's face as they walked away together, talking, and reflected that Malcolm would have been a success in whatever career he had chosen, that success was part of his character, like generosity, like headlong rashness.

I was due to ride in the second race, a steeplechase for amateurs, and as usual had arrived two prudent hours in advance. I turned away from watching Malcolm and looked around for the owner of the horse I was about to partner, and found my path blocked by a substantial lady in a wide brown cape. Of all the

members of the family, she was the last I would have
expected to see on a racecourse.

'Ian,' she said accusingly, almost as if I'd been pretending to be someone else.

'Hello.'

'Where have you been? Why don't you answer your
telephone?'

Lucy, my elder half-sister. Lucy, the poet.

Lucy's husband Edwin was, as always, to be found
at her side, rather as if he had no separate life. The
leech, Malcolm had called him unkindly in the past.
From a Bugg to a leech.

Lucy was blessed with an unselfconsciousness about
her weight which stemmed both from unworldliness
and an overbelief in health foods. 'But nuts and raisins
are *good* for you,' she would say, eating them by the
kilo. 'Bodily vanity, like intellectual arrogance, is a sick-
ness of the soul.'

She was forty-two, my sister, with thick straight
brown hair uncompromisingly cut, large brown eyes,
her mother's high cheek-bones and her father's strong
nose. She was as noticeable in her own way as Malcolm
was himself, and not only because of her shapeless
clothes and dedicated absence of cosmetics. Malcolm's
vitality ran in her too, though in different directions,
expressing itself in vigour of thought and language.

I had often, in the past, wondered why someone as
talented and strongminded as she shouldn't have made
a marriage of equal minds, but in recent years had

come to think she had settled for a nonentity like Edwin because the very absence of competition freed her to be wholly herself.

'Edwin is concerned,' she said, 'that Malcolm is leaving his senses.'

For Edwin, read Lucy, I thought. She had a trick of ascribing her own thoughts to her husband if she thought they would be unwelcome to her audience.

Edwin stared at me uneasily. He was a good-looking man in many ways, but mean spirited, which if one were tolerant one would excuse because of the perpetual knife-edge state of his and Lucy's finances. I wasn't certain any more whether it was he who had actually failed to achieve employment, or whether Lucy had in some way stopped him from trying. In any event, she earned more prestige than lucre for her writing, and Edwin had grown tired of camouflaging the frayed elbows of his jackets with oval patches of thin leather badly sewn on.

Edwin's concern, it seemed, was real enough although if it had been his alone they wouldn't have come.

'It isn't fair of him,' he said, meaning Malcolm. 'Lucy's trust fund was set up years ago before inflation and doesn't stretch as far as it used to. He really ought to put that right. I've told him so several times, and he simply ignores me. And now he's throwing his money away in this profligate way as if his heirs had no rights at all.' Indignation shook in his voice, along with, I could see, a very definite fear of a rocky future if the fortune he'd counted on for so long should be snatched away in the last furlong, so to speak.

I sighed and refrained from saying that I thought that Malcolm's heirs had no rights while he was alive. I said merely, soothingly, 'I'm sure he won't let you starve.'

'That's not the point,' Edwin said with thin fury. 'The point is that he's given an *immense* amount of money to Lucy's old college to establish post-graduate scholarships for poets.'

I looked from his pinch-lipped agitated mouth to Lucy's face and saw shame where there should perhaps have been pride. Shame, I thought, because she found herself sharing Edwin's views when they ran so contrary to her normal disdain for materialism. Perhaps even Lucy, I thought, had been looking forward to a comfortably off old age.

'You should be honoured,' I said.

She nodded unhappily. 'I am.'

'No,' Edwin said. 'It's disgraceful.'

'The Lucy Pembroke Scholarships,' I said slowly.

'Yes. How did you know?' Lucy asked.

And there would be the Serena Pembroke Scholarships, of course. And the Coochie Pembroke Memorial Challenge Trophy . . .

'What are you smiling at?' Lucy demanded. 'You can't say you've made much of a success of your life so far, can you? If Malcolm leaves us all nothing, you'll end up carting horse-muck until you drop from senility.'

'There are worse jobs,' I said mildly.

There were horses around us, and racecourse noises, and a skyful of gusty fresh air. I could happily spend my life, I knew, in almost any capacity that took me to places like Sandown Park.

'You've wasted every talent you have,' Lucy said.

'My only talent is riding horses.'

'You're blind and stupid. You're the only male Pembroke with decent brains and you're too lazy to use them.'

'Well, thanks,' I said.

'It's not a compliment.'

'No, so I gathered.'

'Joyce says you're sure to know where Malcolm is as you've finally made up your quarrel, though you'll lie about it as a matter of course,' Lucy said. 'Joyce said you would be here today on this spot at this time, if I wanted to reach you.'

'Which you did, rather badly.'

'Don't be so obtuse. You've got to stop him. You're the only one who can, and Joyce says you're probably the only one who won't try ... and you *must* try, Ian, and succeed, if not for yourself, then for the rest of the family.'

'For you?' I asked.

'Well ...' She couldn't openly abandon her principles, but they were bending, it seemed. 'For the others,' she said stalwartly.

I looked at her with new affection. 'You're a hypocrite, my dear sister,' I said.

In smarting retaliation, she said sharply, 'Vivien thinks you're trying to cut the rest of us out and ingratiate yourself again with Malcolm.'

'I expect she would,' I said. 'I expect Alicia will think it also, when Vivien has fed it to her.'

'You really are a bastard.'

'No,' I said, my lips twitching, 'that's Gervase.'

'*Ian!*'

I laughed. 'I'll tell Malcolm you're concerned. I promise I will, somehow. And now I've got to change my clothes and ride in a race. Are you staying?'

Lucy hesitated but Edwin said, 'Will you win?'

'I don't think so. Save your money.'

'You're not taking it seriously,' Lucy said.

I looked straight at her eyes. 'Believe me,' I said, 'I take it very seriously indeed. No one had a right to murder Moira to stop her taking half Malcolm's money. No one has a right to murder Malcolm to stop him spending it. He is fair. He will leave us all provided for, when the time comes, which I hope may be twenty years from now. You tell them all to stop fretting, to ease off, to have faith. Malcolm is teasing you all and I think it's dangerous, but he is dismayed by everyone's greed, and is determined to teach us a lesson. So you tell them, Lucy, tell Joyce and Vivien and everyone, that the more we try to grab, the less we will get. The more we protest, the more he will spend.'

She looked back silently. Eventually she said, 'I am ashamed of myself.'

'Rubbish,' Edwin said to me vehemently. 'You must stop Malcolm. You must.'

Lucy shook her head. 'Ian's right.'

'Do you mean Ian won't even try?' Edwin demanded incredulously.

'I'm positive he won't,' Lucy said. 'Didn't you hear what he said? Weren't you listening?'

'It was all rubbish.'

Lucy patted my arm. 'We may as well see you race, while we're here. Go and get changed.'

It was a more sisterly gesture and tone than I was used to, and I reflected with a shade of guilt that I'd paid scant attention to her own career for a couple of years.

'How is the poetry going?' I asked. 'What are you working on?'

The question caught her unprepared. Her face went momentarily blank and then filled with what seemed to be an odd mixture of sadness and panic.

'Nothing just now,' she said. 'Nothing for quite a while,' and I nodded almost apologetically as if I had intruded, and went into the weighing room and through to the changing room reflecting that poets, like mathematicians, mostly did their best work when young. Lucy wasn't writing; had maybe stopped altogether.

And perhaps, I thought, the frugality she had for so long embraced had begun to seem less worthy and less worth it, if she were losing the inner sustaining comfort of creative inspiration.

Poor Lucy, I thought. Life could be a bugger, as Malcolm said. She had already begun to value the affluence she had long despised or she wouldn't have come on her mission to Sandown Park, and I could only guess at the turmoil in her spiritual life. Like a nun losing her faith, I thought. But no, not a nun. Lucy, who had written explicitly of sex in a way I could never believe had anything to do with Edwin (though one could be wrong), wouldn't ever have been a nun.

With such random thoughts, I took off my ordinary clothes and put on white breeches and a scarlet jersey with blue stripes on the sleeves, and felt the usual battened-down excitement which made me breathe deeply and feel intensely happy. I rode in about fifty races a year, if I was lucky ... and I would have to get another job fairly soon, I reflected, if I were to ride exercise regularly and stay fit enough to do any good.

Going outside, I talked for a while to the trainer and owner of the horse I was to ride, a husband and wife who had themselves ridden until twenty years earlier in point-to-point races and who liked to re-live it all vicariously through me. The husband, George, was now a public trainer on a fairly grand scale, but the wife, Jo, still preferred to run her own horses in amateur races. She currently owned three steeplechasers, all pretty good. It did me no harm at all to be seen on them and to be associated in racing minds with that stable.

'Young Higgins is jumping out of his skin,' Jo said.

Young Higgins was the name of that day's horse. Young Higgins was thirteen, a venerable gentleman out to disprove rumours of retirement. We all interpreted 'jumping out of his skin' as meaning fit, sound and pricking his ears with enthusiasm, and at his age one couldn't ask for much more. Older horses than he had won the Grand National, but Young Higgins and I had fallen in the great race the only time we'd tried it, and to my regret Jo had decided on no more attempts.

'We'll see you in the parade ring, then, Ian, before the race,' George said, and Jo added, 'And give the old boy a good time.'

I nodded, smiling. Giving all of us a good time was the point of the proceedings. Young Higgins was definitely included.

The minute George and Jo turned away to go off towards the grandstands, someone tapped me on the back of the shoulder. I turned round to see who it was and to my total astonishment found myself face to face with Lucy's older brother, Malcolm's first child, my half-brother Donald.

'Good heavens,' I said. 'You've never been to the races in your life.'

He often told me he hadn't, saying rather superciliously that he didn't approve of the sordid gambling.

'I haven't come for the races,' he said crossly. 'I've come to see you about Malcolm's taking leave of his senses.'

'How ... er ...?' I stopped. 'Did Joyce send you?' I said.

'What if she did? We are all concerned. She told us where to find you, certainly.'

'Did she tell the whole family?' I asked blankly.

'How do I know? She telephoned us. I daresay she telephoned everyone she could get hold of. You know what she's like. She's your mother, after all.'

Even so late in his life, he couldn't keep out of his voice the old resentments, and perhaps also, I reflected, they were intensifying with age. My mother had supplanted his, he was saying, and any indiscretion my mother ever committed was in some way my fault. He had thought in that illogical way for as long as I'd been aware of him, and nothing had changed.

Donald was, in the family's opinion, the brother nearest in looks to myself, and I wasn't sure I liked it. Irrefutably, he was the same height and had blue eyes less intense in colour than Malcolm's. Agreed, Donald had middling brown curly hair and shoulders wider than his hips. I didn't wear a bushy moustache though, and I just hoped I didn't walk with what I thought of as a self-important strut; and I sometimes tried to make sure, after I'd been in Donald's company, that I absolutely didn't.

Donald's life had been so disrupted when Malcolm

117

had ousted Vivien, Donald always told us, that he had never been able to decide properly on a career. It couldn't have been easy, I knew, to survive such an upheaval, but Donald had only been nine at the time, a bit early for life decisions. In any event, as an adult he had drifted from job to job in hotels, coming to harbour at length as secretary of a prestigious golf club near Henley-on-Thames, a post which I gathered had proved ultimately satisfactory in social standing, which was very important to his self-esteem.

I didn't either like or dislike Donald particularly. He was eleven years older than I was. He was *there*.

'Everyone insists you stop Malcolm squandering the family money,' he said, predictably.

'It's *his* money, not the family's,' I said.

'What?' Donald found the idea ridiculous. 'What you've got to do is explain that he owes it to us to keep the family fortune intact until we inherit it. Unfortunately we know he won't listen to any of us except you, and now that you appear to have made up your quarrel with him, you are elected to be our spokesman. Joyce thinks we have to convince you first of the need to stop Malcolm, but I told her it was ridiculous. You don't need convincing, you want to be well off one day just the same as the rest of us, of course you do, it's only natural.'

I was saved from both soul-searching and untrue disclaimers by the arrival of Helen, Donald's wife, who had apparently been buying a racecard.

'We're not staying,' Donald said disapprovingly, eyeing it.

She gave him a vague smile. 'You never know,' she said.

Beautiful and brainless, Malcolm had said of her, and perhaps he was right. Tall and thin, she moved with natural style and made cheap clothes look expensive: I knew they were cheap because she had a habit of saying where they'd come from and how much she'd paid for them, inviting admiration of her thriftiness. Donald always tried to shut her up.

'Do tell us where to watch the races from,' she said.

'We're not here for that,' Donald said.

'No, dear, we're here because we need money now that the boys have started at Eton.'

'No, dear,' Donald said sharply.

'But you know we can't afford . . .'

'Do be quiet, dear,' Donald said.

'Eton costs a bomb,' I said mildly, knowing that Donald's income would hardly stretch to one son there, let alone two. Donald had twin boys, which seemed to run in the family.

'Of course it does,' Helen said, 'but Donald puts such store by it. "My sons are at Eton," that sort of thing. Gives him *standing* with the people he deals with in the golf club.'

'Helen, dear, do be quiet.' Donald's embarrassment showed, but she was undoubtedly right.

'We thought Donald might have inherited before the

119

boys reached thirteen,' she said intensely. 'As he hasn't, we're borrowing every penny we can to pay the fees, the same as we borrowed for the prep school and a lot of other things. But we've borrowed against Donald's expectations . . . so you see it's essential for us that there really is plenty to inherit, as there are so many people to share it with. We'll be literally bankrupt if Malcolm throws too much away . . . and I don't think Donald could face it.'

I opened my mouth to answer her but no sound came out. I felt as if I'd been thrust into a farce over which I had no control.

Walking purposefully to join us came Serena, Ferdinand and Debs.

CHAPTER SIX

'Stay right here,' I said to all of them. 'I have to go into the weighing room to deal with a technicality. Stay right here until I come out.'

They nodded with various frowns, and I dived into privacy in a desperate search for a sheet of paper and an envelope.

I wrote to Malcolm:

Half the family have turned up here, sent by Joyce. For God's sake stay where you are, keep out of sight and wait until I come to fetch you.

I stuck the note into the envelope, wrote Malcolm's name on the outside, and sought out an official who had enough rank to send someone to deliver it.

'My father is lunching in the Directors' dining room,' I said. 'And it's essential that he gets this note immediately.'

The official was obliging. He was going up to the Stewards' room anyway, he said, and he would take it

DICK FRANCIS

himself. With gratitude and only a minor lessening of despair – because it would be just like Malcolm to come down contrarily to confront the whole bunch – I went out again into the sunlight and found the five of them still faithfully waiting exactly where I'd left them.

'I say,' Debs said, half mocking, 'you do look dashing in all that kit.'

Donald looked at her in surprise, and I had a vivid impression of his saying soon in his golf club, 'My brother, the amateur jockey . . .' knowing that if I'd been a professional he would have hushed it up if he could. A real snob, Donald: but there were worse sins.

Debs, Ferdinand's second wife, had come to the races in a black leather coat belted at the waist, with shoulder-length blonde hair above and long black boots below. Her eyelids were purple, like her fingernails. The innocence I'd photographed in her a year ago was in danger of disappearing.

Ferdinand, shorter than Debs and more like Malcolm than ever, appeared to be in his usual indecision over whether I was to be loved or hated. I smiled at him cheerfully and asked what sort of a journey he'd had.

'A lot of traffic,' he said lamely.

'We didn't come here to talk about traffic,' Serena said forbiddingly. 'We want to know where Daddy is.'

Malcolm's little Serena, now taller than he, was dressed that day in royal blue with white frills at neck and wrists, a white woollen hat with a pompom on top covering her cap of fair hair. She looked a leggy sixteen, not ten years older. Her age showed only in the coldness of her manner towards me, which gave no sign of thawing.

In her high-pitched, girlish voice she said, 'We want him to settle very substantial sums on us all right now. Then he can go to blazes with the rest.'

I blinked. 'Who are you quoting?' I asked.

'Myself,' she said loftily, and then more probably added, 'Mummy too. And Gervase.'

It had Gervase's thuggish style stamped all over it.

Donald and Helen looked distinctly interested in the proposal. Ferdinand and Debs had of course heard it before.

'Gervase thinks it's the best solution,' Ferdinand said, nodding.

I doubted very much that Malcolm would agree, but said only, 'I'll pass on your message next time he gets in touch with me.'

'But Joyce is sure you know where he is,' Donald objected.

'Not exactly,' I said. 'Do you know that Lucy and Edwin are here too?'

They were satisfactorily diverted, looking over their shoulders to see if they could spot them in the growing crowds.

'Didn't Joyce tell you she was sending so many of you here?' I asked generally, and it was Ferdinand, sideways, his face turned away, who answered.

'She told Serena to come here. She told Serena to tell me, which she did, so we came together. I didn't know about Donald and Helen or Lucy and Edwin. I expect she wanted to embarrass you.'

His eyes swivelled momentarily to my face, wanting to see my reaction. I don't suppose my face showed any. Joyce might call me 'darling' with regularity but could be woundingly unkind at the same time, and I'd had a lifetime to grow armour.

Ferdinand happened to be standing next to me. I said on impulse into his ear, 'Ferdinand, who killed Moira?'

He stopped looking for Lucy and Edwin and transferred his attention abruptly and wholly to me. I could see calculations going on in the pause before he answered, but I had no decoder for his thoughts. He was the most naturally congenial to me of all my brothers, yet the others were open books compared with him. He was secretive, as perhaps I was myself. He had wanted to build his own kitchen-wall hidey-hole when I'd built mine, only Malcolm had said we must share, that one was enough. Ferdinand had sulked and shunned me for a while, and smirked at Gervase's dead rats. I wondered to what extent people remained the same as they'd been when very young: whether it was safe to assume they hadn't basically changed, to believe that if one could peel back the layers of living one would come to the known child. I wanted Ferdinand to be as I had known him at ten, eleven, twelve

– a boy dedicated to riding a bicycle while standing on his head on the saddle – and not in a million years a murderer.

'I don't know who killed Moira,' he said finally. 'Alicia says you did. She told the police it *had* to be you.'

'I couldn't have.'

'She says the police could break your alibi if they really tried.'

I knew that they had really tried: they'd checked every separate five minutes of my day, and their manner and their suspicions had been disturbing.

'And what do *you* think?' I asked curiously.

His eyelids flickered. 'Alicia says . . .'

I said abruptly, 'Your mother says too damned much. Can't you think for yourself?'

He was offended, as he would be. He hooked his arms through those of Debs and Serena and made an announcement. 'We three are going to have a drink and a sandwich. If you fall off and kill yourself, no one will miss you.'

I smiled at him, though his tone had held no joke.

'And don't be so bloody forgiving,' he said.

He whirled the girls away from me and marched them off. I wondered how he'd got the day off from work, though I supposed most people could if they tried. He was a statistician, studying to be an actuary in his insurance company. What were the probabilities, I wondered, of a thirty-two-year-old statistician whose wife had purple fingernails being present when his brother broke his neck at Sandown Park?

Donald and Helen said that they too would run a sandwich to earth (Donald's words) and Helen added earnestly that *she* would care that I finished the race safely, whatever Ferdinand said.

'Thanks,' I said, hoping I could believe her, and went back into the changing room for an interval of thought.

Lucy and Edwin might leave before the end of the afternoon, and so might Donald and Helen, but Ferdinand wouldn't. He liked going racing. He'd said on one mellow occasion that he'd have been quite happy being a bookmaker; he was lightning fast at working out relative odds.

The problem of how to extract Malcolm unseen from the racecourse didn't end, either, with those members of the family I'd talked to. If they were all so certain I knew where Malcolm was, one of the others, more cunning, could be hiding behind trees, waiting to follow me when I left.

There were hundreds of trees in Sandown Park.

The first race came and went, and in due course I went out to partner Young Higgins in the second.

Jo as usual had red cheeks from pleasure and hope. George was being gruffly businesslike, also as usual, telling me to be especially careful at the difficult first fence and to go easy up the hill past the stands the first time.

I put Malcolm out of my mind, and also murder,

and it wasn't difficult. The sky was a clear distant blue, the air crisp with the coming of autumn. The leaves on all those trees were yellowing, and the track lay waiting, green and springy, with the wide fences beckoning to be flown. Simple things; and out there one came starkly face to face with oneself, which I mostly found more exhilarating than frightening. So far, anyway.

Jo said, 'Only eight runners, just a perfect number,' and George said, as he always did, 'Don't lie too far back coming round the last long bend.'

I said I would try not to.

Jo's eyes were sparkling like a child's in her sixty-year-old face, and I marvelled that she had never in all that time lost the thrill of expectation in moments like these. There might be villains at every level in horse racing, but there were also people like Jo and George whose goodness and goodwill shone out like search-lights, who made the sport overall good fun and wholesome.

Life and death might be serious in the real world, but life and death on a fast steeplechaser on a Friday afternoon in the autumn sunshine was a lighthearted toss-up, an act of health on a sick planet.

I fastened the strap of my helmet, was thrown up on Young Higgins and rode him out onto the track. Perhaps if I'd been a professional and ridden up to ten times as often I would have lost the swelling joy that that moment always gave me: one couldn't grin like a maniac, even to oneself, at a procession of bread-and-butter rides on cold days, sharp tracks, bad horses.

Young Higgins was living up to his name, bouncing on his toes and tossing his head in high spirits. We lined up with the seven others, all of whose riders I happened to know from many past similar occasions. Amateurs came in all guises: there was a mother, an aunt and a grandfather riding that afternoon, besides a journalist, an earl's son, a lieutenant colonel, a showjumper and myself. From the stands, only a keen eye could have told one from the other without the guidance of our colours, and that was what amateur racing was all about: the equality, the levelling anonymity of the starting gate.

The tapes went up and we set off with three miles to go, almost two whole circuits, twenty-two jumps and an uphill run to the winning post.

The aunt's horse, too strong for her, took hold of the proceedings and opened up an emphatic lead, which no one else bothered to cut down. The aunt's horse rushed into the difficult downhill first fence and blundered over it, which taught him a lesson and let his rider recover control, and for about a mile after that there were no dramatic excitements. The first race I'd ever ridden in had seemed to pass in a whirling heaving flurry leaving me breathless and exhausted, but time had stretched out with experience until one could watch and think and even talk.

'Give me room, blast you,' shouted the lieutenant colonel on one side of me.

'Nice day,' said the earl's son chattily on the other, always a clown who enlivened his surroundings.

'Shift your *arse*!' yelled the mother to her horse, giving him a crack round that part of his anatomy. She was a good rider, hated slow horses, hated not to win, weighed a muscular ten stone and was scornful of the showjumper, whom she had accused often of incompetence.

The showjumper, it was true, liked to set his horse right carefully before jumps, as in the show ring, and hadn't managed to speed up in the several steeplechase races he'd ridden so far. He wasn't in consequence someone to follow into a fence and I avoided him whenever possible.

The journalist was the best jockey in the race, a professional in all but status, and the grandfather was the worst but full of splendid reckless courage. More or less in a bunch, the whole lot of us came round the bottom bend and tackled the last three jumps of the first circuit. The aunt was still in front, then came the lieutenant colonel, myself and the earl's son in a row, then the mother just behind, with the showjumper and the grandfather beside her. I couldn't see the journalist: somewhere in the rear, no doubt, biding his wily time.

The lieutenant colonel's mount made a proper hash of the last of the three fences, jogging both of his rider's feet out of the irons and tipping the military backside into the air somewhere in the region of the horse's mane. Landing alongside and gathering my reins, I saw that the lieutenant colonel's balance was hopelessly progressing down the horse's galloping shoulder as he fought without success to pull himself back into the saddle.

I put out an arm, grasped his jersey and yanked him upwards and backwards, shifting his disastrous centre of gravity into a more manageable place and leaving him slowing and bumping in my wake as he sat down solidly in the saddle, trying to put his feet back into his flying stirrups, which was never very easy at thirty miles an hour.

He had breathing space to collect things going up the hill, though, as we all did, and we swept round the top bend and down to the difficult fence again with not much change in order from the first time.

Someone had once long ago pulled me back into the saddle in that same way: it was fairly common in jump racing. Someone had also once tipped me straight into the air with an upward wrench of my heel, but that was another story. The lieutenant colonel was saying 'Thanks' and also 'Move over, you're crowding me,' more or less in the same breath.

After crossing the water jump for the second time over on the far side of the track, the showjumper made a spurt to the front and then slowed almost to a stand-still on landing over the next fence, having jumped especially pedantically, and the aunt crashed into the back of him with some singularly un-aunt-like language.

'Lovely lady,' said the earl's son, appreciatively, as we passed the débâcle. 'How are you going yourself?'

'Not bad,' I said. 'How are you?'

We jumped the last of the seven far-side fences together and in front, and put all our energies into staying there round the long last bend and over the three last fences. I could hear horses thudding behind me and the mother's voice exhorting her slowcoach. Approaching the Pond fence, I could sense the earl's son's horse beginning to tire, I could see that precious winning post far ahead and the way to it clear, and for at least a few moments I thought I might win. But then the lieutenant colonel reappeared fast at my elbow, still shouting for room, and between the last two fences, as I'd feared he would, the journalist materialized from the outback and made it look easy, and Young Higgins tired into Middle-Aged Higgins on the hill.

He and I finished third, which wasn't too bad, with the earl's son, persevering, not far away fourth.

'A nice afternoon out,' he said happily as we trotted back together, and I looked at the lights in his eyes and saw it was the same for him as for me, a high that one couldn't put into words, an adventure of body and spirit that made of dismounting and walking on the ground a literal coming down to earth.

Jo was pleased enough, patting Young Higgins hard.

'Ran a great race, didn't you, old boy? Jumped like a stag.'

'You'd have been second,' said George, who had good binoculars, 'if you'd let the lieutenant colonel fall off.'

'Yeah, well,' I said, unbuckling the girths, 'there were a lot of hooves down there.'

George smiled. 'Don't forget to weigh in.' (He said it every time.) 'Come for a drink in the Owners' bar when you've changed.'

I accepted. It was part of the ritual, part of the bargain. They liked to re-live Young Higgins' outing fence for fence in return for having given me the ride. They were still standing in the unsaddling enclosure talking to friends when I went out again in street clothes, and with welcoming smiles waved me into their group. None of my own family being in sight, I went with them without problems and, over glasses of Jo's favourite brandy and ginger ale, earned my afternoon's fun by describing it.

I returned to the weighing room area afterwards and found that not only were all the same family members still on the racecourse, but that they had coalesced into an angry swarm and had been joined by one of the queen bees herself, my mother Joyce.

Joyce, in fur and a green hat, was a rinsed blonde with greenish eyes behind contact lenses which seldom missed a trick in life as in cards. Dismayed but blank-faced, I gave her a dutiful peck on her smooth cheek which, it seemed, she was in no mood to receive.

'Darling,' she said, the syllables sizzling with displeasure, 'did you or did you not send that weasel Norman West to check up on my whereabouts last Friday?'

'Er,' I said.

'Did you or did you not send him sniffing round Vivien on the same errand?'

'Well,' I said, half smiling, 'I wouldn't have put it as crudely, but I suppose so, yes.'

The battery of eyes from the others was as friendly as napalm.

'Why?' Joyce snapped.

'Didn't Norman West tell you?'

She said impatiently, 'He said something nonsensical about Malcolm being attacked. I told him if Malcolm had been attacked, I would have heard of it.'

'Malcolm was very nearly killed,' I said flatly. 'He and I asked Norman West to make sure that none of you could have done it.'

Joyce demanded to be told what had happened to Malcolm, and I told her. She and all the others listened with open mouths and every evidence of shock, and if there was knowledge, not ignorance, behind any of the horrified eyes, I couldn't discern it.

'Poor Daddy!' Serena exclaimed. 'How *beastly*.'

'A matter for the police,' Donald said forcefully.

'I agree,' I said. 'I'm surprised they haven't been to see all of you already, as they did when Moira died.'

Edwin said, with a shake of the head, 'How near, how near,' and then, hearing the regret in his voice as clearly as I did, added hurriedly, 'What a blessing he woke up.'

'When the police make their enquiries,' I said, 'they don't exactly report the results to Malcolm. He wants to make sure for himself that none of the family was at Quantum last Friday afternoon. If you cooperate with Norman West when he gets to you, you'll set Malcolm's mind at rest.'

'And what if we can't prove where we were?' Debs asked.

'Or even remember?' Lucy said.

'Malcolm will have to live with it,' Joyce said crisply.

'Living with it would present him less problem,' I said dryly. 'It's dying he wants to avoid.'

They stared at me in silence. The reality of Moira's murder had been to them, I guessed, as to me, a slow-burning fuse, with seemingly no bad consequences at first, but with accelerating worries as time passed. Perhaps they, as I had done, had clung to the motive-less-intruder-from-outside theory at first because the alternative was surely unthinkable, but in the weeks since then, they must at least have begun to wonder. The fuse would heat soon into active suspicions, I saw, which might tear apart and finally scatter for ever the fragile family fabric.

Would I mind, I thought? Not if I still had Malcolm . . . and perhaps Ferdinand . . . and Joyce . . . and maybe Lucy, or Thomas . . . Serena . . . would I care if I never again laid eyes on Gervase?

The answer, surprisingly enough, was yes, I would mind. Imperfect, quarrelsome, ramshackle as it was, the family were origins and framework, the geography of living. Moira, ungrieved, was already rewriting that map, and if her murderer remained for ever undiscovered, if Malcolm himself – I couldn't think of it – were killed, there would be no healing, no reforming, no telephone network for information, no contact, just a lot of severed galaxies moving inexorably apart.

The big bang, I thought, still lay ahead. The trick was to smother the fuse before the explosion, and that was all very well, but where was the burning point, and how long had we got?

'Buy me a drink, darling,' Joyce commanded. 'We're in deep trouble.'

She began to move off, but the others showed no signs of following. I looked at the seven faces all expressing varying degrees of anxiety and saw them already begin to move slightly away from each other, not one cohesive group, but Donald and Helen as a couple, Lucy and Edwin, a pair, and Ferdinand, Debs and Serena, the youngest trio.

'I'll tell Malcolm your fears,' I said. 'And your needs.'

'Oh yes, please do,' Helen said intensely.

'And Gervase's plan,' Ferdinand added.

'Do come on, darling,' Joyce said peremptorily over her shoulder. 'Which way is the bar?'

'Run along, little brother,' Lucy said with irony. Serena said, 'Mumsie's waiting,' and Debs fairly tittered. I thought of sticking my toes in and making Joyce come back, but what did it matter? I could put up with the jibes, I'd survived them for years, and I understood what prompted them. I shrugged ruefully and went after Joyce, and could feel the pitying smiles on the back of my neck.

I steered Joyce into the busy Members' bar which had a buffet table along one side with salads and breads and a large man in chef's clothes carving from turkeys, haunches of beef and hams on the bone. I was hungry after riding and offered Joyce food, but she waved away the suggestion as frivolity. I bought her instead a large vodka and tonic with a plain ginger ale for myself, and we found spare seats at a table in a far corner where, after the merest glance around to make sure she wouldn't be overheard among the general hubbub, she leaned forward until the brim of the green hat was practically touching my forehead and launched into her inquisition.

'Where is your father?' she said.

'When did you last see your father?' I amended.

'What on earth are you talking about?'

'That picture by Orchardson.'

'Stop playing games. Where is Malcolm?'

'I don't know,' I said.

'You're lying.'

'Why do you want to find him?'

'*Why?*' She was astonished. 'Because he's out of his mind.' She dug into her capacious handbag and brought out an envelope, which she thrust towards me. 'Read that.'

I opened the envelope and found a small piece of newspaper inside, a snipped paragraph without headline or provenance.

It said:

Second-string British contender is Blue Clancy, second in last year's Derby and winner this year of Royal Ascot's King Edward VII Stakes. Owner Ramsey Osborn yesterday hedged his Arc bets by selling a half-share in his four-year-old colt to arbitrageur Malcolm Pembroke, who launched into bloodstock only this week with a two million guineas yearling at the Premium Sales.

Ouch, I thought.

'Where did it come from?' I asked.

'What does it matter where it came from? That new "Racing Patter" column in the *Daily Towncrier*, as a matter of fact. I was drinking coffee this morning when I read it and nearly choked. The point is, is it true?'

'Yes,' I said.

'*What?*'

'Yes,' I said again. 'Malcolm bought half of Blue Clancy. Why shouldn't he?'

'Sometimes,' my mother said forcefully, 'you are so stupid I could hit you.' She paused for breath. 'And what exactly is an arbitrageur?'

'A guy who makes money by buying low and selling high.'

'Oh. Gold.'

'And foreign currencies. And shares. And maybe racehorses.'

She was unmollified. 'You know perfectly well he's just throwing his money away to spite everybody.'

'He didn't like Moira being killed. He didn't like being attacked himself. I shouldn't think he'll stop spending until he knows whether we have or haven't a murderer in the family, and even then . . .' I smiled, 'he's getting a taste for it.'

Joyce stared. 'Moira was murdered by an intruder,' she said.

I didn't answer.

She took a large swallow of her vodka and tonic and looked at me bleakly. She had been barely twenty when I was born, barely nineteen when Malcolm had whisked her headlong from an antique shop in Kensington and within a month installed her in his house with a new wedding ring and too little to do.

Malcolm, telling me now and again about those days, had said, 'She understood figures, you see. And she could beat me at cards. And she looked so damned demure. So young. Not bossy at all, like she was later. Her people thought me an upstart, did you know? Their ancestors traced back to Charles II, mine traced back to a Victorian knife-grinder. But her people weren't rich, you know. More breeding than boodle. It was an impulse, marrying Joyce. There you are, I admit it. Turned out she didn't like sex much, more's the pity. Some women are like that. No hormones. So I went on seeing Alicia. Well, I would, wouldn't I? Joyce and I got on all right, pretty polite to each other and so on, until she found out about Alicia. Then we had fireworks, all hell let loose for months on end, do you remember? Don't suppose you remember, you were only four or five.'

'Five and six, actually.'

'Really? Joyce liked being mistress of the house, you know. She learned about power. Grew up, I suppose. She took up bridge seriously, and started voluntary work. She hated leaving all that, didn't much mind leaving me. She said Alicia had robbed her of her self-esteem and ruined her position in the local community. She's never forgiven her, has she?'

Joyce had returned to the small Surrey town where her parents had lived and later died, their social mantle falling neatly onto her able shoulders. She bullied the local people into good works, made continual bridge-tournament forays, earned herself a measure of celebrity, and no, had never forgiven Alicia.

In the bar at Sandown she was dressed, as always,

with a type of businesslike luxury: mink jacket over grey tailored suit, neat white silk shirt, long strings of pearls, high-heeled shoes, green felt hat, polished calf handbag. 'A well-dressed, well-bred, brassy blonde' Alicia had once called her, which was both accurate and unfair, as was Joyce's tart tit-for-tat opinion of Alicia as 'White meat of chicken aboard the gravy train'.

Joyce drank most of the rest of her vodka and said, 'Do you really think one of the family is capable of murder?'

'I don't know.'

'But *who*?'

'That's the question.'

'It isn't possible,' she insisted.

'Well,' I said. 'Take them one by one. Tell me why it's impossible in each individual case, according to each person's character. Start at the beginning, with Vivien.'

'No, Ian,' she protested.

'Yes,' I said. 'Help me. Help Malcolm. Help us all.'

She gave me a long worried look, oblivious to the movement and noise going on all around us. The next race was already in progress but without noticeable thinning of the crowd who were watching it on closed circuit television above our heads.

'Vivien,' I prompted.

'Impossible, just impossible. She's practically dim-witted. If she was ever going to murder anybody, it

140

would have been long ago and it would have been Alicia. Alicia ruined Vivien's marriage, just like mine. Vivien's a sniffler, full of self-pity. And why would she do it? For those three wimpish offspring?'

'Perhaps,' I said. 'They all need money. She hasn't enough herself to bail them out of their holes.'

'It's still impossible.'

'All right,' I said. 'How about Donald? And Helen?'

Donald had been ten, more than half Joyce's age, when she had married Malcolm, and he had been in and out of Quantum, as had Lucy and Thomas, whenever Malcolm had exercised his joint-custody rights and had them to stay. Joyce's lack of interest in children had definitely extended to her step-children, whom she'd found noisy, bad tempered and foul mannered, though Malcolm disagreed.

'Donald's a pompous, snobbish ass,' she said now, 'and as insecure as hell under the bluster. Malcolm thinks Helen's as brainless as she's pretty, but I'd say you don't need brains to murder, rather the opposite. I'd think Helen would fight like a fury to save her cubs from physical harm. But Moira wasn't threatening her cubs, not directly. I'd think Helen could be only a hot-blood killer, but so could most people, driven hard enough to defend themselves or their young.'

I wondered if she knew about the school-fees crisis: if they hadn't directly told her, she had got them remarkably right.

'Lucy?' I said.

141

'Lucy thinks everyone is inferior to herself, especially if they have more money.'

Poor Lucy, I thought. 'And Edwin?' I said.

Joyce frowned. 'Edwin . . .'

'Edwin isn't impossible?' I asked.

'He never gets time off from running errands. Not enough time anyway for waiting around to catch Moira alone in her glass house.'

'But in character?'

'I don't know enough about him,' Joyce confessed. 'He yearns for money, that's for sure, and he's earned it, picking up after Lucy all these years. I don't know his impatience level.'

'All right then,' I said, 'what about Thomas?'

'Thomas!' Joyce's face looked almost sad. 'He wasn't as insufferable as Donald and Lucy when he was little. I liked him best of the three. But that damned Vivien screwed him up properly, didn't she? God knows why he married Berenice. She'll badger him into the grave before he inherits, and then where will she be?'

Joyce finished the vodka and said, 'I don't like doing this, Ian, and I'm stopping right here.'

Thomas, I thought. She wasn't sure about Thomas, and she doesn't want to say so. The analysis had all of a sudden come to an unwelcome, perhaps unexpected, abyss.

'Another drink?' I suggested.

'Yes. Gervase is drinking, did you know?'

'He always drinks.'

'Ursula telephoned me to ask for advice.'

'Did she really?' I was surprised. 'Why didn't she ask Alicia?'

'Ursula detests her mother-in-law,' Joyce said. 'We have that in common. Ursula and I have become quite good friends.'

Amazing, I thought, and stood up to fetch the refills.

Joyce's eyes suddenly widened in disbelief, looking beyond me.

'I knew you were lying,' she said bitterly. 'There's Malcolm.'

CHAPTER SEVEN

I turned, not knowing whether to be frightened or merely irritated.

Malcolm hadn't seen Joyce, and he wasn't looking for her or for me but solely for a drink. I made my way to the bar to meet him there and took him by the arm.

'Why aren't you bloody upstairs?' I said.

'I was outstaying my welcome, old chap. It was getting very awkward. They had an ambassador to entertain. I've been up there three bloody hours. Why didn't you come and fetch me?'

'Joyce,' I said grimly, 'is sitting over there in the corner. I am buying her a drink, and she saw you come in.'

'Joyce!' He turned round and spotted her as she looked balefully in our direction. 'Damn it.'

'Prowling around outside we also have Donald and Helen, Lucy and Edwin, Ferdinand and Debs, and Serena.'

'Christ,' he said. 'Hunting in pairs.'

144

'You may joke,' I said, 'and you may be right.'

'I couldn't stay up there. They were waiting for me to leave, too polite to tell me to go.'

He looked apprehensive, as well he might.

'Will Joyce tell them all that I'm here?'

'We'll see if we can stop it,' I said. 'What do you want to drink? Scotch?'

He nodded and I squeezed through the throng by the bar and eventually got served. He helped me carry the glasses and bottles back to the table, and sat where I'd been sitting, facing Joyce. I fetched another chair from nearby and joined my ever non-loving parents.

'Before you start shouting at each other,' I said, 'can we just take two things for granted? Joyce wants Malcolm to stop scattering largesse, Malcolm wants to go on living. Both ends are more likely to be achieved if we discover who murdered Moira, in case it is Moira's murderer who wishes also to kill Malcolm.' I paused. 'OK for logic?'

They both looked at me with the sort of surprise parents reserve for unexpected utterances from their young.

Malcolm said, 'Surely it's axiomatic that it's Moira's murderer who's trying to kill me?'

I shook my head. 'Ever heard of copycat crime?'

'My God,' he said blankly. 'One possible murderer in the family is tragedy. Two would be . . .'

'Statistically improbable,' Joyce said.

Malcolm and I looked at her with respect.

'She's right,' Malcolm said, sounding relieved, as if one killer were somehow more manageable than two.

'OK,' I agreed, wondering what the statistical probabilities really were, wondering whether Ferdinand could work them out, 'OK, the police failed to find Moira's murderer although they tried very hard and are presumably still trying . . .'

'Trying to link me with an assassin,' muttered Malcolm darkly.

'We might, as a family,' I said, 'have been able to overcome Moira's murder by making ourselves believe in the motiveless unknown outside-intruder theory . . .'

'Of course we believe it,' Joyce said faintly.

'Not now, we can't. Two unknown outside-intruder motiveless murders – because Malcolm was meant to die – are so statistically improbable as to be out of sight. The police haven't found Moira's murderer, but we have now got to try to do it ourselves. It's no longer safe not to, which is why we engaged Norman West.' I looked directly at Joyce. 'Stop fussing over what Malcolm is spending and start thinking of ways to save his life, if only so that he can make more money, which he can do, but only if he's alive.'

'Ian . . .' She was shocked.

'You roused the whole family this morning on the telephone, telling them where to find me, and now seven of them that we know of are here, and others may be who've kept out of sight. Much though we hate the idea, Moira's murderer may be here.'

'No, no,' Joyce exclaimed.

'Yes,' I said. 'Malcolm's primary defence against being murdered is staying out of reach of lethal instruments, which means people not knowing where to find him. Well, you, my darling mother, brought the whole pack here to the races, so now you'd better help Malcolm to leave before they catch him.'

'I didn't know he'd be here,' she protested.

'No, but he is. It's time to be practical.'

No one pointed out that if she *had* known he'd be there, she would have sent everyone with even more zeal.

'Do you have any ideas?' Malcolm asked me hopefully.

'Yes, I do. But we have to have Joyce's help, plus her promise of silence.'

My mother was looking less than her normal commanding self and gave assurances almost meekly.

'This is not a private bar,' I said, 'and if any of the family have bought Club passes, they may turn up in here at any moment, so we'd best lose no time. I'm going to leave you both here for a few minutes, but I'll be back. Stay in this corner. Whatever happens, stay right here. If the family find you, still stay here. OK?'

They both nodded, and I left them sitting and looking warily at each other in the first tête-à-tête they'd shared for many a long year.

I went in search of the overall catering director whom I knew quite well because one of his daughters rode against me regularly in amateur races, and found him by sending urgent messages via the manager of the Members' bar.

'Ian,' he said ten slow minutes later, coming to the bar from the back, where the bottles were, 'what's the trouble?'

He was a company director, head of a catering division, a capable man in his fifties, sprung from suburbia, upwardly mobile from merit, grown worldly wise.

I said the trouble was private, and he led me away from the crowds, through the back of the bar and into a small area of comparative quiet, out of sight of the customers.

My father, I told him, badly needed an immediate inconspicuous exit from the racecourse and wanted to know if a case of vintage Bollinger would ease his passage.

'Not skipping his bookie, I hope?' the caterer said laconically.

'No, he wants to elope with my mother, his ex-wife, from under the eyes of his family.'

The caterer, amused, agreed that Bollinger might be nice. He also laughed at my plan, told me to put it into operation, he would see it went well, and to look after his Rosemary whenever she raced.

I went back through the bar to collect Malcolm and to ask Joyce to fetch her car and to drive it to where the caterers parked their vans, giving her directions. The two of them were still sitting alone at the table, not exactly gazing into each other's eyes with rapture but at least not drawn apart in frost. They both seemed relieved at my reappearance, though, and Joyce picked up her handbag with alacrity to go to fetch her car.

'If you see any of the others,' I said, 'just say you're going home.'

'I wasn't born yesterday, darling,' she replied with reviving sarcasm. 'Run along and play games, and let me do my part.'

The game was the same one I'd thought of earlier in the changing-room, modified only by starting from a different point. It was just possible that the wrong eyes had spotted Malcolm in his brief passage outside from the exit door of the Directors' rooms to the entrance door of the bar, but even if so, I thought we could fool them.

In the quiet private space at the rear of the bar, the catering director was watching the large chef remove his white coat and tall hat.

'A case of vintage Bollinger for the caterer, a handout for the chef,' I murmured in Malcolm's ear. 'Get Joyce to drop you at a railway station, and I'll see you in the Savoy. Don't move until I get there.'

Malcolm, looking slightly dazed, put on the chef's coat and hat and pulled out his wallet. The chef looked delighted with the result and went back to slicing his turkeys in temporary shirtsleeves. Malcolm and the catering director left through the bar's rear door and set off together through the racecourse buildings to go outside to the area where the caterers' vans were parked. I waited quite a long anxious time in the bar, but eventually the catering director returned, carrying the white disguise, which he restored to its owner.

'Your father got off safely,' he assured me. 'He didn't see anyone he knew. What was it all about? Not really an elopement, was it?'

'He wanted to avoid being assassinated by his disapproving children.'

The caterer smiled, of course not believing it. I asked where he would like the fizz sent and he took out a business card, writing his private address on the back.

'Your father lunched with the Directors, didn't he?' he said. 'I thought I saw him up there.' His voice implied that doing favours for people who lunched with the Directors was doubly vouched for, like backing up a cheque with a credit card, and I did my best to reinforce further his perception of virtue.

'He's just bought a half share in an Arc de Triomphe runner,' I said. 'We're going over for the race.'

'Lucky you,' he said, giving me his card. He frowned suddenly, trying to remember. 'Didn't Rosemary tell me something about your father's present wife being pointlessly murdered some weeks ago? His late wife, I suppose I should say. Dreadful for him, dreadful.'

'Yes,' I said. 'Well . . . some people connected with

her turned up here today unexpectedly, and he wanted to escape meeting them.'

'Ah,' he said with satisfied understanding. 'In that case, I'm glad to have been of help.' He chuckled. 'They didn't really look like elopers.'

He shook my hand and went away, and with a couple of deep breaths I left the Members' bar and walked back to the weighing room to pick up my gear. There was still one more race to be run but it already felt like a long afternoon.

George and Jo were there when I came out carrying saddle, helmet, whip and holdall, saying they'd thought they'd catch me before I left.

'We've decided to run Young Higgins again two weeks tomorrow at Kempton,' Jo said. 'You'll be free for that, won't you?'

'Yes, indeed.'

'And Park Railings, don't forget, at Cheltenham next Thursday.'

'Any time, any place,' I said, and they laughed, conspirators in addiction.

It occurred to me as they walked away, looking back and waving, that perhaps I'd be in Singapore, Australia or Timbuktu next week or the week after; life was uncertain, and that was its seduction.

I saw none of the family on my way to the exit gate, and none between there and my car. With a frank sigh of relief, I stowed my gear in the boot and without much hurry set off towards Epsom, a detour of barely ten miles, thinking I might as well pick up my mail and listen to messages.

The telephone answering machine did have a faculty for listening to messages from afar, but it had never worked well, and I'd been too lazy to replace the remote controller which, no doubt, needed new batteries anyway.

With equally random thoughts I drove inattentively onwards, and it wasn't until I'd gone a fair distance that I realized that every time I glanced in the rear-view mirror I could see the same car two or three cars back. Some cars passed me: it never did, nor closed a gap to catch up.

I sat up, figuratively and literally, and thought, 'What do you know?' and felt my heart beat as at the starting gate.

What I didn't know was whose car it was. It looked much like the hired one I was driving, a middle-rank four-door in underwashed cream; ordinary, inconspicuous, no threat to Formula One.

Perhaps, I thought sensibly, the driver was merely going to Epsom, at my own pace, so at the next traffic lights I turned left into unknown residential territory, and kept on turning left at each crossroads thereafter, reasoning that in the end I would complete the circle and end up facing where I wanted to go. I didn't hurry nor continually look in the rear-view mirror, but when I was back again on a road – a different one – with signposts to Epsom, the similar car was still somewhere on my tail, glimpsed tucked in behind a van.

If he had only a minimal sense of direction, I thought, he would realize what I had done and guess I now knew he was following. On the other hand, the back roads between Sandown Park and Epsom were a maze, like most Surrey roads, and he might possibly not have noticed, or thought I was lost, or....

Catching at straws, I thought. Face facts. I knew he was there and he knew I knew and what should I do next?

We were already on the outskirts of Epsom and almost automatically I threaded my way round corners, going towards my flat. I had no reason not to, I thought. I wasn't leading my follower to Malcolm, if that was what he had in mind. I also wanted to find out who he was, and thought I might outsmart him through knowing some ingenious short cuts round about where I lived.

Many of the houses in that area, having been built in the thirties without garages, had cars parked permanently on both sides of the streets. Only purpose-built places, like my block of flats, had adequate parking, except for two or three larger houses converted to flats which had cars where once there had been lawns.

I drove on past my home down the narrow roadway and twirled fast into the driveway of one of the large houses opposite. That particular house had a narrow exit drive also into the next tree-lined avenue: I drove straight through fast, turned quickly, raced round two more corners and returned to my own road to come up behind the car which had been following me.

He was there, stopped, awkwardly half-parked in too small a space with his nose to the kerb, rear sticking out, brake lights still shining: indecision showing all over the place. I drew to a halt right behind him, blocking his retreat, put on my brakes, climbed out, took three or four swift strides and opened the door on the driver's side.

There was a stark moment of silence.

Then I said, 'Well, well, well,' and after that I nodded up towards my flat and said, 'Come on in,' and after that I said, 'If I'd known you were coming, I'd have baked a cake.'

Debs giggled. Ferdinand, who had been driving, looked sheepish. Serena, unrepentant, said, 'Is Daddy here?'

They came up to my flat where they could see pretty clearly that no, Daddy wasn't. Ferdinand looked down from the sitting room window to where his car was now parked beside mine in neat privacy, and then up at the backs of houses opposite over a nearby fence.

'Not much of a view,' he said disparagingly.

'I'm not here much.'

'You knew I was following you, didn't you?'

'Yes,' I said. 'Like a drink?'

'Well . . . scotch?'

154

I nodded and poured him some from a bottle in the cupboard.

'No ice,' he said, taking the glass. 'After that drive, I'll take it neat.'

'I didn't go fast,' I said, surprised.

'Your idea of fast and mine round those goddam twisty roads are about ten miles an hour different.'

The two girls were poking about in the kitchen and bedrooms and I could hear someone, Serena no doubt, opening doors and drawers in a search for residues of Malcolm.

Ferdinand shrugged, seeing my unconcern. 'He hasn't been here at all, has he?' he said.

'Not for three years.'

'Where is he?'

I didn't answer.

'We'll have to torture you into telling,' said Ferdinand. It was a frivolous threat we'd used often in our childhood for anything from 'Where are the corn-flakes?' to 'What is the time?' and Ferdinand himself looked surprised that it had surfaced.

'Mm,' I said. 'As in the tool shed?'

'Shit,' Ferdinand said. 'I didn't mean . . .'

'I should absolutely hope not.'

We both remembered, though, the rainy afternoon when Gervase had put the threat into operation, trying to make me tell him where I'd hidden my new cricket bat which he coveted. I hadn't told him, out of cussedness. Ferdinand had been there, too frightened of

Gervase to protest, and also Serena, barely four, wide-eyed and uncomprehending.

'I thought you'd forgotten,' Ferdinand said. 'You've never mentioned it.'

'Boys will be bullies.'

'Gervase still is.'

Which of us, I thought, was not as we had been in the green garden? Donald, Lucy, Thomas, Gervase, Ferdinand, Serena – all playing there long ago, children's voices calling through the bushes, the adults we would become already forming in the gangling limbs, smooth faces, groping minds. None of those children . . . *none of us* . . . I thought protestingly, could have killed.

Serena came into the sitting room carrying a white lace negligée and looking oddly shocked.

'You've had a woman here!' she said.

'There's no law against it.'

Debs, following her, showed a more normal reaction. 'Size ten, good perfume, expensive tastes, classy lady,' she said. 'How am I doing?'

'Not bad.'

'Her face cream's in the bathroom,' Serena said. 'You didn't tell us you had a . . . a . . .'

'Girlfriend,' I said. 'And do you have . . . a boy-friend?'

She made an involuntary face of distaste and shook her head. Debs put a sisterly arm round Serena's shoulders and said, 'I keep telling her to go to a sex

156

therapist or she'll end up a dry old stick, but she won't listen, will you love?'

Serena wriggled free of Debs' arm and strode off with the negligée towards the bedrooms.

'Has anyone ever assaulted her?' I asked Ferdinand. 'She has that look.'

'Not that I know of.' He raised his eyebrows. 'She's never said so.'

'She's just scared of sex,' Debs said blithely. 'You wouldn't think anyone would be, these days. Ferdinand's not, are you, bunny?'

Ferdinand didn't react, but said, 'We've finished here, I think.' He drained his scotch, put down his glass and gave me a cold stare as if to announce that any semi-thaw I might have perceived during the afternoon's exchanges was now at an end. The ice-curtain had come down again with a clang.

'If you cut us out with Malcolm,' he said, 'you'll live to regret it.'

Hurt, despite myself, and with a touch of acid, I asked, 'Is that again what Alicia says?'

'Damn you, Ian,' he said angrily, and made for the door, calling, 'Serena, we're going,' giving her no choice but to follow.

Debs gave me a mock gruesome look as she went in their wake. 'You're Alicia's number one villain, too bad, lovey. You keep your hooks off Malcolm's money or you won't know what hit you.'

There was a fierce last-minute threat in her final

words, and I saw, as the jokey manner slipped, that it was merely a façade which hid the same fears and furies of all the others, and her eyes, as she went, were just as unfriendly.

With regret, I watched from the window as the three of them climbed into Ferdinand's car and drove away. It was an illusion to think one could go back to the uncorrupted emotions of childhood, and I would have to stop wishing for it. I turned away, rinsed out Ferdinand's glass, and went into my bedroom to see how Serena had left it.

The white negligée was lying on my bed. I picked it up and hung it in its cupboard, rubbing my cheek in the fabric and smelling the faint sweet scent of the lady who came occasionally for lighthearted interludes away from a husband who was all but impotent but nevertheless loved. We suited each other well: perfectly happy in ephemeral passion, with no intention of commitment.

I checked round the flat, opened a few letters and listened to the answering machine: there was nothing of note. I spent a while thinking about cars. I had arranged on the telephone two days earlier that the hotel in Cambridge would allow my own car to remain in their park for a daily fee until I collected it, but I couldn't leave it there for ever. If I took a taxi to Epsom station, I thought, I could go up to London by train. In the morning, I would go by train to Cambridge, fetch my car, drive back to the flat, change to the hired car and drive that back to London. It might even be a shade safer, I thought, considering that Ferdinand, and through him the others, would know its colour, make and number, to turn that car in and hire a different one.

The telephone rang. I picked up the receiver and heard a familiar voice, warm and husky, coming to the point without delay.

'How about now?' she said. 'We could have an hour.'

I could seldom resist her. Seldom tried.

'An hour would be great. I was just thinking of you.'

'Good,' she said. 'See you.'

I stopped worrying about cars and thought of the white lace negligée instead; more enticing altogether. I put two wine glasses on the table by the sofa and looked at my watch. Malcolm would scarcely have reached the Savoy, I thought, but it was worth a try; and in fact he picked up the telephone saying he had that minute walked into the suite.

'I'm glad you're safely back,' I said. 'I've been a bit detained. I'll be two or three hours yet. Don't get lost.'

'Your mother is a cat,' he said.

'She saved your skin.'

'She called me a raddled old roué done up like a fifth-rate pastrycook.'

I laughed and could hear his scowl down the line.

'What do you want after caviar,' he said, 'if I order dinner?'

'Chef's special.'

'God rot you, you're as bad as your mother.'

I put the receiver down with amusement and waited through the twenty minutes it would take until the doorbell rang.

'Hello,' she said, as I let her in. 'How did the races go?'

I kissed her. 'Finished third.'

'Well done.'

She was older than I by ten or twelve years, also slender, auburn-haired and unselfconscious. I fetched the always-waiting champagne from the refrigerator, popped off the cork and poured our drinks. They were a ritual preliminary, really, as we'd never yet finished the bottle and, as usual, after half a glass, there was no point in sitting around on the sofa making small talk.

She exclaimed over the long black bruise down my thigh. 'Did you fall off a horse?'

'No, hit a car.'

'How careless.'

I drew the bedroom curtains to dim the setting western sun and lay with her naked between the sheets. We were practised lovers and comfortable with each other, philosophical over the fact that the coupling was usually better for one than the other, rarely earth-moving for both simultaneously. That day, like the time before, it turned out ecstatic for her, less so for me, and I thought the pleasure of giving such pleasure enough in itself.

'Was it all right for you?' she said finally.

'Yes, of course.'

'Not one of your great times.'

'They don't come to order. Not your turn, my turn. It's luck.'

'A matter of friction and angles,' she teased me, repeating what I'd once said. 'Who's showering first?'

She liked to return clean to her husband, acknowledging the washing to be symbolic. I showered and dressed, and waited for her in the sitting room. She was an essential part of my life, a comfort to the body, a contentment in the mind, a bulwark against loneliness. I usually said goodbye with regret, knowing she would return, but on that particular afternoon I said, 'Stay,' knowing all the same that she couldn't.

'What's the matter?' she said.

'Nothing.'

'You shivered.'

'Premonition.'

'What of?' She was preparing to go, standing by the door.

'That this will be the last time.'

'Don't be silly,' she said. 'I'll be back.'

She kissed me with what I knew was gratitude, the way I too kissed her. She smiled into my eyes. 'I'll be back.'

I opened the door for her and she went away lightheartedly, and I knew that the premonition had been not for her, but for myself.

*

I ferried the cars in the morning, going from London to Cambridge and Epsom and back to the hire firm, and no one followed me anywhere, as far as I could see.

When I'd departed, Malcolm had been full of rampaging indignation over the non-availability of first-class seats on any flight going to Paris the following day for the Arc de Triomphe.

'Go economy,' I said, 'it's only half an hour.'

It appeared that there were no economy seats either. I left him frowning but returned to find peace. He had chartered a private jet.

He told me that snippet later, because he was currently engaged with Norman West who had called to give a progress report. The detective still seemed alarmingly frail but the grey on-the-point-of-death look had abated to fawn. The dustbin clothes had been replaced by an ordinary dark suit, and the greasy hair, washed, was revealed as almost white and neatly brushed.

I shook his hand: damp, as before.

'Feeling better, Mr West?' I asked.

'Thank you, yes.'

'Tell my son what you've just said,' Malcolm commanded. 'Give him the bad news.'

West gave me a small apologetic smile and then looked down at the notepad on his knee.

'Mrs Vivien Pembroke can't remember what she did on the Friday,' he said. 'And she spent Tuesday alone at home sorting through piles of old magazines.'

'What's bad news about that?' I asked.

'Don't be obtuse,' Malcolm said impatiently. 'She hasn't an alibi. None of the whole damn bunch has an alibi.'

'Have you checked them all?' I said, surprised. 'You surely haven't had time.'

'I haven't,' he agreed.

'Figure of speech.' Malcolm waved a hand. 'Go on telling him, Mr West.'

'I called on Mrs Berenice Pembroke.' West sighed expressively. 'She found me unwelcome.'

Malcolm chuckled sourly. 'Tongue like a rhinoceros-hide whip.'

West made a small squirming movement as if still feeling the lash, but said merely, with restraint, 'She was completely uncooperative.'

'Was Thomas there, when you called?' I asked.

'No, sir, he wasn't. Mrs Pembroke said he was at work. I later telephoned his office, to the number you gave me, hoping he could tell me where both his wife and himself had been at the relevant times, and a young lady there said that Mr Pembroke left the firm several weeks ago, and she knew nothing of his present where-abouts.'

'Well,' I said, stumped. 'I didn't know.'

'I telephoned Mrs Pembroke again to ask where her husband worked now, and she told me to ... er ... drop dead.'

Thomas, I thought, had worked for the same firm of

biscuit makers from the day he'd finished a course in bookkeeping and accountancy. Berenice referred disparagingly to his occupation as 'storekeeping' but Thomas said he was a quantity surveyor whose job it was to estimate the raw materials needed for each large contract, and cost them, and pass the information to the management. Thomas's promotions within the firm had been minor, such as from second assistant to first assistant, and at forty he could see, I supposed, that he would never be boardroom material. How bleak, I thought, to have to face his mid-life limitations with Berenice cramming them down his throat at every turn. Poor old Thomas . . .

'Mrs Joyce Pembroke,' West said, 'is the only one who is definite about her movements. On each relevant day, she was playing bridge. She didn't like me snooping, as she called it, and she wouldn't say who she was playing bridge with as she didn't want those people bothered.'

'You can leave Mrs Joyce Pembroke out,' I said.

'Huh?' Malcolm said.

'You know perfectly well,' I told him, 'that Joyce wouldn't kill you. If you'd had any doubts, you wouldn't have gone off in a car with her yesterday.'

'All right, all right,' he said, grumbling. 'Cross Joyce off.'

I nodded to West, and he put a line through Joyce.

'Yesterday I called on Mrs Alicia Pembroke and then later on Mrs Ursula Pembroke.' West's face showed no joy over the encounters. 'Mrs Alicia Pembroke told me to mind my own business, and Mrs Ursula Pembroke had been crying and wouldn't speak to me.' He lifted his hands out in a gesture of helplessness. 'I couldn't persuade either of them of the advantage of establishing alibis.'

'Did you get any impression,' I asked, 'that the police had been there before you, asking the same questions?'

'None at all.'

'I told you,' Malcolm said. 'They didn't believe I was attacked. They thought I'd just staged the whole thing.'

'Even so . . .'

'They checked everyone out over Moira, as you no doubt remember, and came up with a load of clean slates. They're just not bothering to do it again.'

'Do you happen to have their telephone number with you?'

'Yes I do,' he said, bringing a diary out of an inner pocket and flicking over the pages. 'But they won't tell you anything. It's like talking to a steel door.'

I dialled the number all the same and asked for the superintendent.

'In what connection, sir?'

'About the attempted murder of Mr Malcolm Pembroke a week ago yesterday.'

'One moment, sir.'

Time passed, and a different voice came on the line, plain and impersonal.

'Can I help you, sir?'

'About the attempted murder of Mr Malcolm Pembroke...'

'Who are you, sir?'

'His son.'

'Er... which one?'

'Ian.'

There was a brief rustling of paper.

'Could you tell me your birth date, as proof of identity?' Surprised, I gave it.

Then the voice said, 'Do you wish to give information, sir?'

'I wanted to find out how the investigation was going.'

'It isn't our custom to discuss that.'

'But...'

'But I can tell you, sir, that investigations into the alleged attack are being conducted with thoroughness.'

'*Alleged!*' I said.

'That's right, sir. We can find no evidence at all that there was another party involved.'

'I don't believe it.'

With slightly exaggerated patience but also a first flicker of sympathy, he said, 'I can tell you, sir, that there was no evidence of Mr Pembroke being dragged from the garden to the garage, which he alleged must have happened. No marks on the path. No scrapes on the heels of Mr Pembroke's shoes, which we examined at the time. There were no fingerprints except his own on the door handles of the car, no fingerprints except his anywhere. He showed no signs of carbon monoxide poisoning, which he explained was because he had delayed calling us. We examined the scene thoroughly the following morning, after Mr Pembroke had left home, and we found nothing at all to indicate the presence of an assailant. You can be sure we are not closing the case, but we are not at this time able to find grounds for suspicion of any other person.'

'He was nearly killed,' I said blankly.

'Yes, sir, well I'm sorry, sir, but that's how things stand.' He paused briefly. 'I can understand your disbelief, sir. It can't be easy for you.' He sounded quite human, offering comfort.

'Thank you at least for talking to me,' I said.

'Right, sir. Goodbye.'

'Goodbye,' I said slowly, but he had already gone.

'*Now* what's the matter?' Malcolm asked, watching my face.

I repeated what I'd just heard.

'Impossible!' Malcolm said explosively.

'No.'

'What then?'

'Clever.'

CHAPTER EIGHT

'Which door did you go out of, with the dogs?' I asked.

'The kitchen door, like I always do.'

'The kitchen door is about five steps along that covered way from the rear door into the garage.'

'Yes, of course it is,' Malcolm said testily.

'You told me that you set off down the garden with the dogs, and I suppose you told the police the same thing?'

'Yes, of course I did.'

'But you can't really remember actually going. You remember that you meant to, isn't that what you told me?'

He frowned. 'I suppose it is.'

'So what if you never made it to the garden, but were knocked out right there by the kitchen door? And what if you weren't dragged from there into the garage, but *carried*?'

His mouth opened. 'But I'm . . .'

'You're not too heavy,' I said. 'I could carry you easily in a fireman's lift.'

He was five foot seven, stocky but not fat. He weighed ten stone something, I would have guessed.

'And the fingerprints?' Norman West asked.

'In a fireman's lift,' I said, 'you sling the person you want to carry over your left shoulder, don't you, with his head hanging down your back. Then you grasp his knees with your left arm, and hold his right wrist in your own right hand, to stop him slipping off?'

They both nodded.

'So if you're holding someone's wrist, you can put his hand easily onto any surface you like, including car door handles . . . particularly,' I said, thinking, 'if you've opened the doors yourself first with gloves on, so that your victim's prints will be on top of any smudges you have made.'

'You should have been an assassin,' Malcolm said. 'You'd have been good at it.'

'So now we have Malcolm slumped in the back seat, half lying, like you said. So next you switch on the engine and leave the doors open so that all the nice fumes pour into the car quickly.'

'Doors?' Malcolm interrupted.

'The driver's door and one of the rear doors, at the least.'

'Oh, yes.'

'And then you have,' I said, 'a suicide.'

'And when I woke up,' Malcolm said gloomily, 'I put my prints all over the place. On the ignition key . . . everywhere.'

169

'No one could have counted on that.'

'It just looked bad to the police.'

We contemplated the scenario.

'If it happened like that,' West said, 'as indeed it could have done, whoever attacked you had to know that you would go out of the kitchen door at around that time.'

Malcolm said bleakly, 'If I'm at home, I always go for a walk with the dogs about then. Take them out, bring them back, give them their dinners, pour myself a drink. Routine.'

'And ... er ... is there anyone in your family who doesn't know when you walk the dogs?'

'Done it all my life, at that time,' Malcolm said.

There was a short silence, then I said, 'I wish I'd known all this when that car nearly killed us at Newmarket. We really ought to have told the police.'

'I was fed up with them,' Malcolm said. 'I've spent hours and hours with the suspicious buggers since Moira's death. I'm allergic to them. They bring me out in a rash.'

'You can't blame them, sir. Most murdered wives are killed by their husbands,' West said. 'And frankly, you appeared to have an extremely strong motive.'

'Rubbish,' Malcolm said. 'I don't see how people can kill people they've loved.'

'Unfortunately it's common.' West paused. 'Do you want me to continue with your family, sir, considering how little progress I've been able to make with them?'

'Yes,' Malcolm said heavily. 'Carry on. I'll get Joyce to tell them all to answer your questions. She seems to be able to get them to do what she wants.'

To get them to do what *they* want, I thought. She couldn't stir them into courses they didn't like.

Norman West put his notebook into his jacket pocket and shifted his weight forward on his chair.

'Before you go,' I said, 'I thought you might like to know that I asked the telephonist of the Cambridge hotel if anyone besides yourself had asked if a Mr Pembroke was staying there last weekend. She said they'd definitely had at least three calls asking for Mr Pembroke, two men and a woman, and she remembered because she thought it odd that no one wanted to talk to him, or would leave a message; they only wanted to know if he was there.'

'*Three!*' Malcolm exclaimed.

'One would be Mr West,' I pointed out. To West, I said, 'In view of that, could you tell us who asked you to find my father?'

West hesitated. 'I don't positively know which Mrs Pembroke it was. And ... er ... even if I became sure during these investigations, well, no sir, I don't think I could.'

'Professional ethics,' Malcolm said, nodding.

'I did warn you, sir,' West said to me, 'about a conflict of interests.'

'So you did. Hasn't she paid you yet, then? No name on any cheque?'

'No, sir, not yet.'

He rose to his feet, no one's idea of Atlas, though world-weary all the same. He shook my hand damply, and Malcolm's, and said he would be in touch. When he'd gone, Malcolm sighed heavily and told me to pour him some scotch.

'Don't you want some?' he said, when I gave him the glass.

'Not right now.'

'What did you think of Mr West?'

'He's past it.'

'You're too young. He's experienced.'

'And no match for the female Pembrokes.'

Malcolm smiled with irony. 'Few are,' he said.

We flew to Paris in the morning in the utmost luxury and were met by a chauffeured limousine which took its place with regal slowness in the solid traffic jam moving as one entity towards Longchamp.

The French racecourse, aflutter with flags, seemed to be swallowing *tout le monde* with insatiable appetite, until no one could walk in a straight line through the public areas where the crowds were heavy with guttural vowels and garlic.

Malcolm's jet/limousine package also included, I found, an invitation from the French Jockey Club, passes to everywhere and a Lucullan lunch appointment with the co-owner of Blue Clancy, Mr Ramsey Osborn.

Ramsey Osborn, alight with the *joie de vivre* gripping the whole place, turned out to be a very large sixtyish American who towered over Malcolm and took to him at once. Malcolm seemed to see the same immediate signals. They were cronies within two minutes.

'My son, Ian,' Malcolm said eventually, introducing me.

'Glad to know you.' He shook my hand vigorously. 'The one who fixed the sale, right?' His eyes were light grey and direct. 'Tell you the truth, there's a colt and a filly I want to buy for next year's Classics, and this way Blue Clancy will finance them very nicely.'

'But if Blue Clancy wins the Arc?' I said.

'No regrets, son.' He turned to Malcolm. 'You've a cautious boy, here.'

'Yeah,' Malcolm said. 'Cautious like an astronaut.'

The Osborn grey eyes swivelled back my way. 'Is that so? Do you bet?'

'Cautiously, sir.'

He laughed, but it wasn't unalloyed good humour. Malcolm, I thought, was much more to his liking. I left them sitting down at table together and, confident enough that no assassin would penetrate past the eagle-eyed doorkeepers of the upper citadel of the French Jockey Club, went down myself to ground level, happier to be with the action.

I had been racing in France a good deal, having for

some years been assistant to a trainer who sent horses across the Channel as insouciantly as to York. Paris and Deauville were nearer anyway, he used to say, despatching me from Epsom via nearby Gatwick airport whenever he felt disinclined to go himself. I knew in consequence a smattering of racecourse French and where to find what I wanted, essential assets in the vast stands bulging with hurrying, vociferous, uninhibited French racegoers.

I loved the noise, the smell, the movement, the quick angers, the gesticulations, the extravagance of ground-level French racing. British jockeys tended to think French racegoers madly aggressive, and certainly once I'd actually had to defend with my fists a jockey who'd lost on a favourite I'd brought over. Jockeys in general had been insulted and battered to the extent that they no longer had to walk through crowds when going out or back from races at many tracks, and at Longchamp made the journey from weighing room to horse by going up an escalator enclosed with plastic walls like a tunnel, across a bridge, and down a similar plastic-tunnel escalator on the other side.

I wandered around, greeting a few people, watching the first race from the trainers' stand, tearing up my losing pari-mutuel ticket, wandering some more, and feeling finally, without any work to do, without any horse to saddle, purposeless. It was an odd feeling. I couldn't remember when I'd last gone racing without being actively involved. Racing wasn't my playground, it was my work; without work it felt hollow.

Vaguely depressed, I returned to Malcolm's eyrie and found him blossoming in his new role as racehorse owner. He was referring to Le Prix de l'Arc de Triomphe familiarly as 'the Arc' as if it hadn't swum into his consciousness a bare half-week earlier, and discussing Blue Clancy's future with Ramsey Osborn as if he knew what he was talking about.

'We're thinking of the Breeders' Cup,' he said to me, and I interpreted the glint in his eyes as a frantic question as well as an instant decision.

'If he runs well today,' Osborn put in, qualifying it.

'It's a long way to California,' I said, agreeing with him. 'To the world championships, one might say.'

Malcolm was grateful for the information and far from dismayed by it. Pretty well the opposite, I saw. It would be to California we would go on the way to Australia, I guessed, rather than Singapore.

Lunch seemed to be continuing all afternoon, in the way French lunches do, with tidy circles of chateaubriand appearing, the empty plates to be cleared before small bundles of beans and carrots were served, followed by fresh little cheeses rolled in chopped nuts, and tiny strawberry tartlets with vanilla coulis. According to the menu, I had through my absence missed the *écrevisses*, the consommé, the *crêpes de volaille*, the *salade verte* and the sorbet. Just as well, I thought, eyeing the

175

friandises which arrived with the coffee. Even amateur jockeys had to live by the scales.

Malcolm and Ramsey Osborn passed mellowly to cognac and cigars and watched the races on television. No one was in a hurry: the Arc was scheduled for five o'clock and digestion could proceed until four-thirty.

Ramsey Osborn told us he came from Stamford, Connecticut, and had made his money by selling sports clothes. 'Baseball caps by the million,' he said expansively. 'I get them made, I sell them to retail outlets. And shoes, shirts, jogging suits, whatever goes. Health is big business, we'd be nowhere without exercise.'

Ramsey looked as if he didn't exercise too much himself, having pads of fat round his eyes, a heavy double chin and a swelling stomach. He radiated goodwill, however, and listened with kind condescension as Malcolm said reciprocally that he himself dealt modestly in currency and metal.

Ramsey wasn't grasping Malcolm's meaning, I thought, but then for all his occasional flamboyance Malcolm never drew general attention to his wealth. Quantum was a large comfortable Victorian family house, but it wasn't a mansion: when Malcolm had reached mansion financial status, he'd shown no signs of wanting to move. I wondered briefly whether that would change in future, now that he'd tasted prodigality.

In due course, the three of us went down to the saddling boxes and met both Blue Clancy and his trainer. Blue Clancy looked aristocratic, his trainer more so. Malcolm was visibly impressed with the trainer, as indeed was reasonable, as he was a bright young star, now rising forty, who had already trained six Classic winners and made it look easy.

Blue Clancy was restless, his nostrils quivering. We watched the saddling ritual and the final touches; flick of oil to shine the hooves, sponging of nose and mouth to clean and gloss, tweaking of forelock and tack to achieve perfection. We followed him into the parade ring and were joined by his English jockey who was wearing Ramsey's white, green and crimson colours and looking unexcited.

Malcolm was taking with alacrity to his first taste of big-time ownership. The electricity was fairly sparking. He caught my eye, saw what I was thinking, and laughed.

'I used to think you a fool to choose racing,' he said. 'Couldn't understand what you saw in it.'

'It's better still when you ride.'

'Yes . . . I saw that at Sandown. And about time, I suppose.'

Ramsey and the trainer claimed his attention to discuss tactics with the jockey, and I thought of the summer holidays when we were children, when Gervase, Ferdinand and I had all learned to ride. We'd learned on riding-school ponies, cycling to the nearby stables and spending time there grooming, feeding and mucking out. We'd entered local gymkhanas, and booted the poor animals in pop-the-balloon races. We'd ridden them backwards, bareback and with our knees on the saddle, and Ferdinand, the specialist, standing briefly on his head. The ponies had been docile and no doubt tired to death, but for two or three years we had been circus virtuosi: and Malcolm had paid the bills uncomplainingly, but had never come to watch us. Then Gervase and Ferdinand had been whisked away by Alicia, and in the lonely vacuum afterwards I'd ridden almost every possible morning, laying down a skill without meaning it seriously, not realizing, in the flurry of academic school examinations, that it was the holiday pastime that would beckon me for life.

Blue Clancy looked as well as any of the others, I thought, watching the runners walk round, and the trainer was displaying more confidence than uncertainty. He thanked me for fixing the sale (from which he'd made a commission) and assured me that the two-million-guinea yearling was now settled snugly in a prime box in his yard. He'd known me vaguely until then as another trainer's assistant, a dogsbody, but as son and go-between of a new owner showing all signs of being severely hooked by the sport, I was now worth cultivation.

I was amused and far from minding. Life was like that. I might as well make the most of Malcolm's coat-tails while I was on them, I thought. I asked if I could see round the trainer's yard next time I was in Newmarket, and he said sure, he'd like it, and almost seemed to mean it.

'I'm sometimes there with George and Jo,' I said. 'Schooling their few jumpers. I ride them in amateur 'chases.' Everyone in Newmarket knew who George and Jo were: they were the equivalent of minor royalty.

'Oh, that's you, is it?' He put a few things together. 'Didn't realize that was you.'

'Mm.'

'Then come any time.' He sounded warmer, more positive. 'I mean it,' he said.

The way upwards in racing, I thought, ironic at myself, could lead along devious paths. I thanked him without effusiveness, and said 'Soon.'

Blue Clancy went out to the parade and the rest of us moved to the owners' and trainers' stand, which was near the core of things and buzzing with other similar groups locked in identical tensions.

'What chance has he got?' Malcolm demanded of me. 'Seriously.' His eyes searched my face as if for truth, which wasn't what I thought he wanted to hear.

'A bit better than he had on Thursday, since the second favourite has been scratched.' He wanted me to tell him more, however unrealistic, so I said, 'He's got a good chance of being placed. Anything can happen. He could win.'

Malcolm nodded, not knowing whether or not to believe me, but wanting to. Well and truly hooked, I thought, and felt fond of him.

I thought in my heart of hearts that the horse would finish sixth or seventh, not disgraced but not in the money. I'd backed him on the pari-mutuel but only out of loyalty: I'd backed the French horse Meilleurs Voeux out of conviction.

Blue Clancy moved well going down to the start. This was always the best time for owners, I thought, while the heart beat with expectation and while the excuses, explanations, disappointments were still ten minutes away. Malcolm lifted my binoculars to his eyes with hands that were actually trembling.

The trainer himself was strung up, I saw, however he might try to disguise it. There was only one 'Arc' in a year, of course, and too few years in a lifetime.

The horses seemed to circle for an interminable time at the gate but were finally fed into the slots to everyone's satisfaction. The gates crashed open, the thundering rainbow poured out, and twenty-six of Europe's best thoroughbreds were out on the right-hand circuit straining to be the fastest, strongest, bravest over one and a half miles of grass.

'Do you want your binoculars?' Malcolm said, hoping not.

'No. Keep them, I can see.'

I could see Ramsey Osborn's colours on the rails halfway back in the field, the horse moving easily, as were all the others at that point of the race. In the 'Arc', the essentials were simple: to be in the first ten coming round the last long right-hand bend, not to swing too wide into the straight and, according to the horse's stamina, pile on the pressure and head for home. Sometimes in a slow-starting 'Arc', one jockey would slip the field on the bend and hang on to his lead; in others, there would be war throughout to a whisker verdict. Blue Clancy's 'Arc' seemed to be run at give-no-quarter speed, and he came into the finishing straight in a bunch of flying horses, lying sixth or eighth, as far as I could see.

Malcolm shouted 'Come on,' explosively as if air had backed up in his lungs from not breathing, and the ladies around us in silk dresses and hats, and the men in grey morning suits, infected by the same urgency, yelled and urged and cursed in polyglot babel. Malcolm put down the raceglasses and yelled louder, totally involved, rapt, living through his eyes.

Blue Clancy was doing his bit, I thought. He hadn't blown up. In fact, he was hanging on to fifth place. Going faster. Fourth . . .

The trainer, more restrained than owners, was now saying, 'Come on, come *on*' compulsively under his breath, but two of the horses already in front suddenly came on faster than Blue Clancy and drew away from the field, and the real hope died in the trainer with a sigh and a sag to the shoulders.

The finish the crowd watched was a humdinger which only a photograph could decide. The finish Malcolm, Ramsey, the trainer and I watched was two lengths further back, where Blue Clancy and his jockey, never giving up, were fighting all out to the very end, flashing across the line absolutely level with their nearest rival, only the horse's nose in front taking his place on the nod.

'On the nod,' the trainer said, echoing my thought.

'What does that mean?' Malcolm demanded. He was high with excitement, flushed, his eyes blazing. 'Were we third? Say we were third.'

'I think so,' the trainer said. 'There'll be a photograph.'

We hurried down from the stand to get to the unsaddling enclosure, Malcolm still short of breath and slightly dazed. 'What does on the nod mean?' he asked me.

'A galloping horse pokes his head out forward with each stride in a sort of rhythm, forward, back, forward, back. If two horses are as close as they were, and one horse's nose is forward when it passes the finishing line, and the other horse's happens to be back . . . well, that's on the nod.'

'Just luck, you mean?'

'Luck.'

'My God,' he said, 'I never thought I'd feel like that. I never thought I'd *care*. I only did it for a jaunt.'

He looked almost with wonderment at my face, as if I'd been before him into a far country and he'd now discovered the mystery for himself.

Ramsey Osborn, who had roared with the best, beamed with pleasure when an announcement confirmed Blue Clancy's third place, saying he was sure glad the half-share sale had turned out fine. There were congratulations all round, with Malcolm and Ramsey being introduced to the owners of the winner, who were Italian and didn't understand Ramsey's drawl. Press photographers flashed like popping suns. There were television cameras, enquiring journalists, speeches, presentations. Malcolm looked envious of the Italian owners: third was fine but winning was better.

The four of us went for a celebratory drink; champagne, of course.

'Let's go for it,' Ramsey said. 'The Breeders' Cup. All the way.'

'We'll have to see how he is after today,' the trainer said warningly. 'He had a hard race.'

'He'll be all right,' Ramsey said with hearty confidence. 'Did you see the distance? Two lengths behind the winner. That's world class and no kidding.'

The trainer looked thoughtful but didn't argue. The favourite, undeniably world class, had finished second, victory snatched away no doubt by his earlier exhausting outing. He might not come back at all after his gruelling 'Arc'. The French favourite (and mine), Meilleurs Voeux, had finished fifth which made Blue Clancy better than I'd thought. Maybe he wouldn't be disgraced in the Breeders' Cup, if we went. I hoped we would go, but I was wary of hope.

The afternoon trickled away with the champagne, and Malcolm, almost as tired as his horse, sank euphorically into the limousine going back to the airport and closed his eyes in the jet.

'My first ever runner,' he said sleepily. 'Third in the "Arc". Not bad, eh?'

'Not bad.'

'I'm going to call the yearling Chrysos.'

'Why Chrysos?' I said.

He smiled without opening his eyes. 'It's Greek for gold.'

Malcolm was feeling caged in the Savoy.

On Sunday night, when we returned from Paris, he'd hardly had the energy to undress. By Monday morning, he was pacing the carpet with revitalized energy and complaining that another week in the suite would drive him bonkers.

'I'm going back to Quantum,' he said. 'I miss the dogs.'

I said with foreboding, 'It would take the family half a day at most to find out you were there.'

'I can't help it. I can't hide for ever. You can come and stay close to me there.'

'Don't go,' I said. 'You're safe here.'

'Keep me safe at Quantum.'

He was adamant and began packing, and short of roping him to the bedstead, I couldn't stop him.

Just before we left, I telephoned Norman West and found him at home – which didn't bode well for the investigations. He was happy to tell me, he said, that it was now certain Mrs Deborah Pembroke, Ferdinand's wife, couldn't have been at Newmarket Bloodstock Sales, as on that day she had done a photo-modelling session. He had checked up with the magazine that morning, as Mrs Deborah had told him he could, and they had provided proof.

'Right,' I said. 'What about Ferdinand himself?'

'Mr Ferdinand was away from his office on both those days. Working at home on the Friday. The next week, he attended a course on the statistical possibilities of insurance fraud. He says that after registration on the Monday, they kept no record of attendance. I checked there too, and no one clearly remembers, they're all half strangers to each other.'

I sighed. 'Well . . . my father and I are going back to Quantum.'

'That's not wise, surely.'

'He's tired of imprisonment. Report to us there, will you?'

He said he would, when he had more news.

Cross off Debs, I thought. Bully for Debs.

I drove us down to Berkshire, stopping at Arthur Bellbrook's house in the village to collect the dogs. The two full-grown Dobermanns greeted Malcolm like puppies, prancing around him and rubbing against his legs as he slapped and fondled them. Real love on both sides, I saw. Uncomplicated by greed, envy or rejection.

Malcolm looked up and saw me watching him.

'You should get a dog,' he said. 'You need something to love.'

He could really hit home, I thought.

He bent back to his friends, playing with their muzzles, letting them try to snap at his fingers, knowing they wouldn't bite. They weren't guard dogs as such: he liked Dobermanns for their muscular agility, for their exuberance. I'd been brought up with relays of them around me, but it wasn't the affection of dogs I wanted, and I'd never asked for one of my own.

I thought of the afternoon he'd let them out of the kitchen and then been hit on the head. The dogs must have seen or sensed someone there. Though not guard dogs, they should still have warned Malcolm.

'Do those two dogs bark when strangers call?' I asked.

'Yes, of course.' Malcolm straightened, still smiling, letting the lithe bodies press against his knees. 'Why?'

'Did they bark a week last Friday, when you set out to walk them?'

The smile died out of his face. With almost despair he said, 'No. I don't think so. I don't remember. No . . . not especially. They were pleased to be going out.'

'How many of the family do they know well?' I said.

'Everyone's been to the house several times since Moira died. All except you. I thought at first it was to support me, but . . .' he shrugged with disillusion, 'they were all busy making sure none of the others ingratiated themselves with me and cut them out.'

Every possibility led back to the certainty we couldn't accept.

Malcolm shuddered and said he would walk through the village with the dogs. He would meet people he knew on the way, and there were people in that village who'd been close friends with Vivien, Alicia and Joyce and had sided with them, and had since fed them inflammatory half-lies about Malcolm's doings.

'You know the village grapevine is faster than telex,' I said. 'Put the dogs in the car.'

He wouldn't listen. It was only six days since the second time someone had tried to kill him, but he was already beginning to believe there would be no more attempts. Well, no more that morning, I supposed. He walked a mile and a half with the dogs, and I drove slowly ahead, looking back, making sure at each turn that he was coming into sight. When he reached the house safely, he said I was being over-protective.

'I thought that was what you wanted,' I said.

'It is and it isn't.'

Surprisingly, I understood him. He was afraid and ashamed of it, and in consequence felt urged to bravado. Plain straightforward fear, I thought, would have been easier to deal with. At least I got him to wait outside with the dogs for company while I went into the house to reconnoitre, but no one had been there laying booby traps, no one was hiding behind doors with raised blunt instruments, no one had sent parcel bombs in the post.

I fetched him, and we unpacked. We both took it for granted I would sleep in my old room, and I made up the bed there. I had bought provisions in London to the extent of bread, milk, lemons, smoked salmon and caviar, a diet both of us now considered normal. There was champagne in the cellar and a freezer full of post-Moira TV dinners in cardboard boxes. We weren't going to starve, I thought, inspecting them, though we might get indigestion.

Malcolm spent the afternoon in his office opening letters and talking to his stockbroker on the telephone, and at the routine time proposed to give the dogs their pre-dinner walk.

'I'll come with you,' I said.

He nodded without comment, and in the crisp early October air we set off down the garden, through the gate into the field, and across to the willow-lined stream he had been aiming for ten days earlier.

We had all sailed toy boats down that stream when we'd been children, and picked watercress there, and got thoroughly wet and muddy as a matter of course. Alicia had made us strip, more than once, before she would let us into her bridal-white kitchen.

'Last Monday,' Malcolm said casually, watching the dogs sniff for water rats round the tree roots, 'I made a new will.'

'Did you?'

'I did. In Cambridge. I thought I might as well. The old one left a lot to Moira. And then, after that

188

Friday ... well, I wanted to put things in order, in case ... just in case.'

'What did you do with it?' I asked.

He seemed amused. 'The natural question is surely, "What's in it? What have you left to *me*?" '

'Mm,' I said dryly. 'I'm not asking that, ever. What I'm asking is more practical.'

'I left it with the solicitor in Cambridge.'

We were wandering slowly along towards the stream, the dogs quartering busily. The willow leaves, yellowing, would fall in droves in the next gale, and there was bonfire smoke drifting somewhere in the still air.

'Who knows where your will is?' I asked.

'I do. And the solicitor.'

'Who's the solicitor?'

'I saw his name on a brass plate outside his office and went in on impulse. I've got his card somewhere. We discussed what I wanted, he had it typed up, and I signed it with witnesses in his office and left it there for safekeeping.'

'For a brilliant man,' I said peaceably, 'you're as thick as two planks.'

CHAPTER NINE

Malcolm said explosively, 'You're bloody rude,' and, after a pause, 'In what way am I thick? A new will was essential.'

'Suppose you died without telling me or anybody else you'd made it, or where it could be found?'

'Oh.' He was dismayed, then brightened. 'The solicitor would have produced it.'

'If he knew you by reputation, if he had any idea of the sums involved, if he heard you were dead, if he were conscientious, and if he knew who to get in touch with. If he were lazy, he might not bother, he's under no obligation. Within a month, unless you boasted a bit about your wealth, he'll have forgotten your will's in his files.'

'You seem to know an awful lot about it.'

'Joyce worked for years for the Citizens Advice Bureau, do you remember? I used to hear lurid tales of family squabbles because no one knew where to find a will they were sure had been made. And equally lurid tales of family members knowing where the will was and burning it before anyone else could find it, if they didn't like what was in it.'

'That's why I left it in safekeeping,' Malcolm said. 'Precisely because of that.'

We reached the far boundary of the field. The stream ran on through the neighbour's land, but at that point we turned back.

'What should I do then?' he asked. 'Any ideas?'

'Send it to the probate office at Somerset House.'

'How do you mean?'

'Joyce told me about it, one time. You put your will in a special envelope they'll send you if you apply for it, then you take it or send it to the central probate office. They register your will there and keep it safe. When anyone dies and any solicitor anywhere applies for probate, the central probate office routinely checks its files. If it has ever registered a will for that person, that's the envelope that will be opened, and that's the will that will be proved.'

He thought it over. 'Do you mean, if I registered a will with the probate office, and then changed my mind and wrote a new one, it wouldn't be any good?'

'You'd have to retrieve the old will and re-register the new one. Otherwise the old will would be the one adhered to.'

'Good God. I didn't know any of this.'

'Joyce says not enough people know. She says if people would only register their wills, they couldn't be pressured into changing them when they're gaga or

191

frightened or on their deathbeds. Or at least, wills made like that would be useless.'

'I used to laugh, rather, at Joyce's voluntary work. Felt indulgent.' He sighed. 'Seems it had its uses.'

The Citizens Advice Bureau, staffed by knowledge-able armies of Joyces, could steer one from the cradle to the grave, from marriage to divorce to probate, from child allowance to old age supplements. I'd not always listened attentively to Joyce's tales, but I'd been taken several times to the Bureau, and I seemed to have absorbed more than I'd realized.

'I kept a copy of my new will,' Malcolm said. 'I'll show it to you when we go in.'

'You don't need to.'

'You'd better see it,' he said.

I didn't argue. He whistled to the dogs who left the stream reluctantly, and we made our way back to the gate into the garden.

'Just wait out here while I check the house,' I said.

He was astonished. 'We've only been out for half an hour. And we locked the doors.'

'You regularly go out for half an hour at this time. And how many of the family still have keys to the house?'

He was silent. All of the people who had ever lived there could have kept their keys to the house, and there had never been any need, before now, to change the locks.

'Stay here, then?' I asked, and he nodded sadly.

The kitchen door was still locked. I let myself in and went all through the house again, but it was quiet and undisturbed, and doors that I'd set open at certain angles were still as I'd left them.

I called Malcolm and he came into the kitchen and began getting the food for the dogs.

'Are you going through this checking rigmarole every single time we leave the house?' he said, sounding as if he didn't like it.

'Yes, until we get the locks changed.'

He didn't like that either, but expressed his disapproval only in a frown and a rather too vigorous scraping of dog food out of a tin.

'Fill the water bowls,' he said rather crossly, and I did that and set them down again on the floor.

'It isn't so easy to change the locks,' he said. 'They're all mortice locks, as you know, set into the doors. The one on the front door is antique.'

The front door keys were six inches long and ornate, and there had never been more than three of them, as far as I knew.

'All right,' I said. 'If we keep the front door bolted and the keys in your safe, we won't change that one.'

A little pacified, he put the filled dinner bowls on the floor, wiped his fingers and said it was time for a noggin. I bolted the kitchen door on the inside and then followed him through the hall to the office, where he poured scotch into two glasses and asked if I wanted to desecrate mine with ice. I said yes and went back to the kitchen to fetch some. When I returned, he had taken some sheets of paper from his open briefcase and was reading them.

'Here you are. Here's my will,' he said, and passed the papers over.

He had made the will, I reflected, before he had telephoned me to put an end to our quarrel, and I expected not to figure in it in consequence, but I'd done him an injustice. Sitting in an armchair and sipping the whisky, I read through all the minor bequests to people like Arthur Bellbrook, and all the lawyerly gobbledegook 'upon trust' and without commas, and came finally to the plain language.

'To each of my three divorced wives Vivien Joyce and Alicia I bequeath the sum of five hundred thousand pounds.

'My son Robin being provided for I direct that the residue of my estate shall be divided equally among my children Donald Lucy Thomas Gervase Ian Ferdinand and Serena.'

A long clause followed with provisions for 'if any of my children shall pre-decease me', leaving 'his or her share' to the grandchildren.

Finally came two short sentences:

'I bequeath to my son Ian the piece of thin wire to be found on my desk. He knows what he can do with it.'

Surprised and more moved than I could say, I looked up from the last page and saw the smile in Malcolm's eyes deepen to a throaty chuckle.

'The lawyer chap thought the last sentence quite obscene. He said I shouldn't put that sort of thing in a will.'

I laughed. 'I didn't expect to be in your will at all.'

'Well . . .' He shrugged. 'I'd never have left you out. I've regretted for a long while . . . hitting you . . . everything.'

'Guess I deserved it.'

'Yes, at the time.'

I turned back to the beginning of the document and re-read one of the preliminary paragraphs. In it, he had named me as his sole executor, when I was only his fifth child. 'Why me?' I said.

'Don't you want to?'

'Yes. I'm honoured.'

'The lawyer said to name someone I trusted.' He smiled lopsidedly. 'You got elected.'

He stretched out an arm and picked up from his desk a leather pot holding pens and pencils. From it, he pulled a wire about ten inches long and about double the thickness of the sort used by florists for stiffening flower stalks.

'If this one should get lost,' he said, 'just find another.'

'Yes. All right.'

'Good.' He put the wire back in the pot and the pot back on the desk.

'By the time you pop off,' I said, 'the price of gold

195

might have risen out of sight and all I'd find in the wall would be spiders.'

'Yeah, too bad.'

I felt more at one with him than at any time since he'd telephoned, and perhaps he with me. I hoped it would be a very long time before I would have to execute his will.

'Gervase,' I said, 'suggests that you should distribute some of your money now, to . . . er . . . reduce the estate tax.'

'Does he? And what do you think?'

'I think,' I said, 'that giving it to the family instead of to scholarships and film companies and so on might save your life.'

The blue eyes opened wide. 'That's immoral.'

'Pragmatic.'

'I'll think about it.'

We dined on the caviar, but the fun seemed to have gone out of it.

'Let's have shepherd's pie tomorrow,' Malcolm said. 'There's plenty in the freezer.'

We spent the next two days uneventfully at Quantum being careful, but with no proof that care was needed.

Late on Tuesday afternoon, out with the dogs and having made certain that Arthur Bellbrook had gone home, we walked round behind the kitchen wall and came to the treasure house.

A veritable sea of nettles guarded the door. Malcolm looked at them blankly. 'The damn things grow overnight.'

I pulled my socks over the bottoms of my trousers and assayed the traverse; stamped down an area by the bottom of the door and with fingers all the same stinging felt along to one end of the wooden sill and with some effort tugged it out. Malcolm leaned forward and gave me the piece of wire, and watched while I stood up and located the almost invisible hole. The wire slid through the tiny tube built into the mortar and, under pressure, the latch inside operated as smoothly as it had when I'd installed it. The wire dislodged a metal rod out of a slot, allowing the latch to spring open.

'I oiled it,' Malcolm said. 'The first time I tried, it was as rusty as hell.'

I pushed the edge of the heavy narrow door and it opened inwards, its crenellated edges disengaging from the brick courses on each side with faint grating noises but with no pieces breaking off.

'You built it well,' Malcolm said. 'Good mortar.'

'You told me how to mix the mortar, if you remember.'

I stepped into the small brick room which was barely four feet across at the far end and about eight feet long, narrowing in a wedge-shape towards the door which was set into one of the long walls. The wider end wall was stacked to waist height with flat wooden boxes like those used for château-bottled wines. In front, there were two large cardboard boxes with heavily taped-down tops. I stepped further in and tried to open one of the wine-type boxes, but those were nailed shut. I turned round and took a couple of steps back and stood in the doorway, looking out.

'Gold at the back, treasures in front,' Malcolm said, watching me with interest.

'I'll take your word for it.'

The air in the triangular room smelled faintly musty. There was no ventilation, as I'd told Arthur Bellbrook, and no damp course, either. I reset the rod into the latch on the inside, as it wouldn't shut unless one did, and stepped outside. My teenage design limitations meant that one had to go down on one's knees to close the door the last few inches, hooking one's fingers into a hollow under the bottom row of bricks and pulling hard. The door and walls fitted together again like pieces of jigsaw, and the latch inside clicked into place. I replaced the sill under the door, kicking it home, and tried to encourage the crushed nettles to stand up again.

'They'll be flourishing again by morning,' Malcolm said. 'Rotten things.'

'Those cardboard boxes are too big to come out through the door,' I observed, rubbing stings on my hands and wrists.

'Oh, sure. I took them in empty and flat, then set them up, and filled them bit by bit.'

'You could take those things out again now.'

There was a pause, then he said, 'I'll wait. As things are at present, they might as well stay there.'

I nodded. He whistled to the dogs and we went on with the walk. We had given up referring explicitly to fear of the family, but it still hung around us like grief. On our return from the field, Malcolm waited outside without comment until I checked through the house, and prosaically began feeding the dogs on my report of all clear.

Neither of us discussed how long all the precautions were going to have to go on. Norman West's latest report had been as inconclusive as his first, and by Wednesday evening the pitiful summary I'd been making of his results read as follows:

DONALD:	busy about the golf club. Cannot pinpoint any times.
HELEN:	working at home making Henley souvenirs.
LUCY:	reading, walking, writing, meditating.
EDWIN:	housework, shopping for groceries, going to public library.
THOMAS:	looking for new job, suffering headaches.
BERENICE:	housekeeping, looking after children, uncooperative.
GERVASE:	commuting to London, in and out of his office, home late.

URSULA:	looking after daughters, unhappy.
FERDINAND:	on statistics course, no attendance records.
DEBS:	photo-session vouched for on Newmarket Sales day.
SERENA:	teaching aerobics mornings and most evenings, shopping for clothes afternoons.
VIVIEN:	pottering about, can't remember.
ALICIA:	probably the same, unhelpful.
JOYCE:	playing bridge.

All one could say, I thought, was that no one had made any effort to produce alibis for either relevant time. Only Debs had a firm one, which had been arranged and vouched for by others. All the rest of the family had been moving about without timing their exits and entrances: normal behaviour for innocent people.

Only Joyce and I lived beyond half an hour's drive from Quantum. All of the others, from Donald at Henley to Gervase at Maidenhead, from Thomas near Reading to Lucy near Marlow, from Ferdinand in Wokingham to Serena in Bracknell, and even Vivien in Twyford and Alicia near Windsor, all of them seemed to have put down roots in a ring round the parent house like thistledown blown on the wind and reseeding.

The police had remarked on it when investigating

Moira's murder, and had checked school runs and train timetables until they'd been giddy. They had apparently caught no one lying, but that seemed to me inconclusive in a family which had had a lot of practice in misrepresentation. The fact had been, and still was, that anybody could have got to Quantum and home again without being missed.

I spent a short part of that Wednesday wandering around Moira's greenhouse, thinking about her death.

The greenhouse was invisible from the house, as Arthur Bellbrook had said, set on a side lawn which was bordered with shrubs. I wondered whether Moira had been alarmed to see her killer approach. Probably not. Quite likely, she had herself arranged the meeting, stating time and place. Malcolm had once mentioned that she didn't like casual callers, preferring them to telephone first. Perhaps it had been an unforeseen killing, an opportunity seized. Perhaps there had been a quarrel. Perhaps a request denied. Perhaps one of Moira's specials in acid-sweet triumphs, like picking Arthur Bellbrook's vegetables.

Moira in possession of Quantum, about to take half of everything Malcolm owned. Moira smugly satisfied, oblivious to her danger. I doubted if she had believed in her nightmare death even while it was happening.

Malcolm spent the day reading the *Financial Times* and making phone calls: yen, it appeared from snatches I overheard, were behaving gruesomely from Malcolm's point of view.

Although making calls outward, neither of us was keen to answer inward calls since that morning, when Malcolm had been drenched by a shower of recriminations from Vivien, all on the subject of meanness. He had listened with wry pain and given me a resumé once Vivien had run out of steam.

'One of the cats in the village told her we were here, so now the whole family will know,' he said gloomily. 'She says Donald is bankrupt, Lucy is starving and Thomas got the sack and can't deal with unemployment. Is it all true? It can't be. She says I should give them twenty thousand pounds each immediately.'

'It wouldn't hurt,' I said. 'It's Gervase's idea watered down.'

'But I don't believe in it.'

I explained about Donald's school fees crisis, Lucy's crumbling certainties, Thomas with Berenice chipping away at his foundations. He said their troubles lay in their own characters, which was true enough. He said if he gave those three a hand-out, he would have to do it for us all, or there would be a shooting civil war among Vivien, Joyce and Alicia. He made a joke of it, but he was stubborn. He had provided for us through our trust funds. The rest was up to us. He hadn't changed his mind. He'd thought over Vivien's suggestion, and the answer was no.

He telephoned back to Vivien and to her fury told her so. I could hear her voice calling him wicked, mean, cruel, vindictive, petty, sadistic, tyrannical and evil. He took offence, shouted at her to shut up, shut up, and finally slammed down the receiver while she was still in full flood.

All Vivien had achieved, I thought, was to make him dig his toes in further.

I thought him pig-headed, I thought him asking to be murdered. I looked at the unrelenting blue eyes daring me to argue, and wondered if he thought giving in would be weakness, if he thought baling out his children would diminish his own self-respect.

I said nothing at all. I was in a bad position to plead for the others, as I stood to gain myself. I hoped for many reasons that he would be able to change his mind, but it had to come from inside. I went out to Moira's greenhouse to give him time to calm down, and when I returned neither of us mentioned what had passed.

On the dogs' walk that afternoon, I reminded him that I was due to ride at Cheltenham the following day, and asked if he had any cronies in that direction with whom he could spend the time.

'I'd like to see you ride again,' he said.

He constantly surprised me.

'What if the family come too?'

'I'll dress up as another chef.'

I didn't know that it was wise, but again he had his own way, and I persuaded myself he would come to no harm on a racecourse. When we got there, I introduced him to George and Jo who congratulated him on Blue Clancy and took him off to lunch.

203

I looked around apprehensively all afternoon for brothers, sisters, mother and step-mothers, but saw none. The day was cold and windy with everyone turning up collars and hunching shoulders to keep warm, with hats on every head, felt, tweed, wool and fur. If anyone had wanted to hide inside their clothes, the weather was great for it.

Park Railings gave me a splendid ride and finished fourth, less tired than his jockey, who hadn't sat on a horse for six days. George and Jo were pleased enough, and Malcolm, who had been down the track with them to watch one of the other steeplechases from beside one of the jumps, was thoughtful.

'I didn't realize you went so fast,' he said, going home. 'Such speed over those jumps.'

'About thirty miles an hour.'

'I suppose I could buy a steeplechaser,' he said, 'if you'd ride it.'

'You'd better not. It would be favouritism.'

'Huh.'

We went thirty miles towards Berkshire and came to a hostelry he liked where we stopped for the late afternoon noggins (Arthur Bellbrook was taking the dogs home with him for the night) and waited lazily until dinner.

We talked about racing, or rather Malcolm asked questions and I answered them. His interest seemed inexhaustible, and I wondered if it would die as fast as it had sprung up. He couldn't wait to find out what Chrysos might do next year.

We ate without hurrying, lingering over coffee, and went on home, pulling up yawning outside the garage, sleepy from fresh air and French wine.

'I'll check the house,' I said without enthusiasm.

'Oh, don't bother, it's late.'

'I'd better check it. Honk the horn if you see something you don't like.'

I left him in the car, let myself into the kitchen and switched on the lights. The door to the hall was closed as usual, to keep the dogs, when they were there, from roaming through the house. I opened the door to the hall and switched on the hall lights.

I stopped there briefly, looking round.

Everything looked quiet and peaceful, but my skin began to crawl just the same, and my chest felt tight from suddenly suspended breath.

The door to the office and the door to the sitting room were not as I had left them. The door to the office was more than half open, the door to the sitting room all but closed; neither standing at the precise narrow angle at which I'd set them every time we'd been out.

I tried to remember whether I'd actually set the doors before leaving that morning, or whether I'd forgotten. But I *had* set them. I knew I had. I'd picked up my saddle and other gear in the hall after doing it, and shut the hall-to-kitchen door, and locked the outside door, leaving the dogs with Arthur Bellbrook in the garden.

I hadn't until then thought of myself as a coward, but I felt dead afraid of going further into the house. It was so large, so full of dark corners. There were two cellars, and the several unlit attic bedrooms of long-gone domestic servants, and the boxroom deep with shadows. There were copious cupboards everywhere and big empty wardrobes. I'd been round them all three or four times during the past few days, but not at night, and not with the signals standing at danger.

With an effort, I took a few steps into the hall, listening. I had no weapon. I felt nakedly vulnerable. My heart thumped uncomfortably. The house was silent.

The heavy front door, locked and bolted like a fortress, had not been touched. I went over to the office, reached in with an arm, switched on the light and pushed the half-open door wider.

There was no one in there. Everything was as Malcolm had left it in the morning. The windows shone blackly, like threats. Taking a deep breath, I repeated the procedure with the sitting room, but also checking the bolts on the French windows, and after that with the dining room, and the downstairs cloak-room, and then with worse trepidation went down the passage beside the stairs to the big room that had been our playroom when we were children and a billiard room in times long past.

The door was shut. Telling myself to go on with it, I opened the door, switched on the light, pushed the door open.

There was no one there. It wasn't really a relief, because I would have to go on looking. I checked the storeroom opposite, where there were stacks of garden furniture, and also the door at the end of the passage, which led out into the garden: securely bolted on the inside. I went back to the hall and stood at the bottom of the stairs, looking upward.

It was stupid to be so afraid, I thought. It was home, the house I'd been brought up in. One couldn't be frightened by home.

One was.

I swallowed. I went up the stairs. There was no one in my bedroom. No one in five other bedrooms, nor in the boxroom, no one in the bathrooms, no one in the plum and pink lushness of Malcolm's own suite. By the end, I was still as scared as I'd been at the beginning, and I hadn't started on cellars or attics or small hiding places.

I hadn't looked under the beds. Demons could be waiting anywhere to jump out on me, yelling. Giving in, I switched off all the upstairs lights and went cravenly back to the hall.

Everything was still quiet, mocking me.

I was a fool, I thought.

Leaving the hall and kitchen lights on, I went back to Malcolm who started to get out of the car when he saw me coming. I waved him back and slid in beside him, behind the driving wheel.

'What's the matter?' he said.

'Someone may be here.'

'What do you mean?'

I explained about the doors.

'You're imagining things.'

'No. Someone has used their key.'

We hadn't yet been able to have the locks changed, although the carpenter was due to be bringing replacements the following morning. He'd had difficulty finding good new locks to fit into such old doors, he'd said, and had promised them for Thursday, but I'd put him off until Friday because of Cheltenham.

'We can't stay out here all night,' Malcolm protested. 'It's bound to be the wind or something that moved the doors. Let's go to bed, I'm whacked.'

I looked at my hands. They weren't actually shaking. I thought for a while until Malcolm grew restless.

'I'm getting cold,' he said. 'Let's go in, for God's sake.'

'No ... we're not sleeping here.'

'What? You can't mean it.'

'I'll lock the house, and we'll go and get a room somewhere else.'

'At this time of night?'

'Yes.' I made to get out of the car and he put a hand on my arm to catch my attention.

'Fetch some pyjamas, then, and washing things.'

I hesitated. 'No, I don't think it's safe.' I didn't say I couldn't face it, but I couldn't.

'Ian, all this is crazy.'

'It would be crazier still to be murdered in our beds.'

'But just because two doors . . .'

'Yes. Because.'

He seemed to catch some of my own uneasiness because he made no more demur, but when I was headed again for the kitchen he called after me, 'At least bring my briefcase from the office, will you?'

I made it through the hall again with only a minor tremble in the gut; switched on the office light, fetched his briefcase without incident and set the office door again at its usual precise angle. I did the same to the sitting room door. Perhaps they would tell us in the morning, I thought, whether or not we had had a visitor who had hidden from my approach.

I went back through the hall, switched the lights off, shut the hall-to-kitchen door, let myself out, left the house dark and locked and put the briefcase on the car's back seat.

On the basis that it would be easiest to find a room in London, particularly at midnight, for people without luggage, I drove up the M4 and on Malcolm's instructions pulled up at the Ritz. We might be refugees, he said, but we would be staying in no camp, and he explained to the Ritz that he'd decided to stay over-night in London as he'd been delayed late on business.

'Our name is Watson,' I said impulsively, thinking suddenly of Norman West's advice and picking out of the air the first name I could think of. 'We will pay with travellers' cheques.'

Malcolm opened his mouth, closed it again, and kept blessedly quiet. One could write whatever name one wanted onto travellers' cheques.

The Ritz batted no eyelids, offered us connecting rooms (no double suites available) and promised razors, toothbrushes and a bottle of scotch.

Malcolm had been silent for most of the journey, and so had I, feeling with every heart-calming mile that I had probably over-reacted, that maybe I hadn't set the doors, that if any of the family had let themselves into the house while we were out, they'd been gone long before we returned. We had come back hours later than anyone could have expected, if they were judging the time it would take us to drive from Cheltenham.

I could have sat at the telephone in the house and methodically checked with all the family to make sure they were in their own homes. I hadn't thought of it, and I doubted if I could have done it, feeling as I had.

Malcolm, who held that sleeping pills came a poor second to scotch, put his nightcap theory to the test and was soon softly snoring. I quietly closed the door between our two rooms and climbed between my own sheets, but for a long time lay awake. I was ashamed of my fear in the house which I now thought must have been empty. I had risked my neck without a qualm over big fences that afternoon: I'd been petrified in the house that someone would jump out on me from the dark. The two faces of courage, I thought mordantly: turn one face to the wall.

We went back to Berkshire in the morning and couldn't reach Quantum by car because the whole village, it seemed, was out and blocking the road. Cars and people everywhere: cars parked along the roadsides, people walking in droves towards the house.

'What on earth's going on?' Malcolm said.

'Heaven knows.'

In the end I had to stop the car, and we finished the last bit of the journey on foot.

We had to push through crowds and were unpopular until people recognized Malcolm, and made way for him, and finally we reached the entrance to the drive . . . and there literally rocked to a stop.

To start with there was a rope stretched across it, barring our way, with a policeman guarding it. In front of the house, there were ambulances, police cars, fire engines . . . swarms of people in uniform moving purposefully about.

Malcolm swayed with shock, and I felt unreal,

disconnected from my feet. Our eyes told us: our brains couldn't believe.

There was an immense jagged gaping hole in the centre of Quantum.

People standing near us in the gateway, round-eyed, said, 'They say it was the gas.'

CHAPTER TEN

We were in front of the house, talking to policemen. I couldn't remember walking up the drive.

Our appearance on the scene had been a shock to the assembled forces, but a welcome one. They had been searching for our remains in the rubble.

They told us that the explosion had happened at four-thirty in the morning, the *wumph* and reverberation of it waking half the village, the shockwaves breaking windows and setting dogs howling. Several people had called the police, but when the force had reached the village, everything had seemed quiet. No one knew where the explosion had occurred. The police drove round the extended neighbourhood until daylight, and it was only then that anyone saw what had happened to Quantum.

The front wall of the hall, the antique front door with it, had been blown out flat onto the drive, and the centre part of the upper storey had collapsed into the hall. The glass in all the windows had disappeared.

'I'm afraid it's worse at the back,' a policeman said

phlegmatically. 'Perhaps you'd come round there, sir. We can at least tell everyone there are no bodies.'

Malcolm nodded mechanically and we followed the policeman round to the left, between the kitchen and garage, through to the garden and along past the dining-room wall. The shock when we rounded onto the terrace was, for all the warning, horrific and sickening.

Where the sitting room had been, there was a mountain of jumbled dusty bricks, plaster, beams and smashed furniture spilling outwards onto the grass. Malcolm's suite, which had been above the sitting room, had vanished, had become part of the chaos. Those of the attic rooms that had been above his head had come down too. The roof, which had looked almost intact from the front, had at the rear been stripped of tiles, the old sturdy rafters standing out against the sky like picked ribs.

My own bedroom had been on one side of Malcolm's bedroom: all that remained of it were some shattered spikes of floorboards, a strip of plaster cornice and a drunken mantle clinging to a cracked wall overlooking a void.

Malcolm began to shake. I took off my jacket and put it round his shoulders.

'We don't have gas,' he said to the policeman. 'My mother had it disconnected sixty years ago because she was afraid of it.'

There was a slight spasmodic wind blowing, enough

to lift Malcolm's hair and leave it awry. He looked suddenly frail, as if the swirling air would knock him over.

'He needs a chair,' I said.

The policeman gestured helplessly to the mess. No chairs left.

'I'll get one from the kitchen. You look after him.'

'I'm quite all right,' Malcolm said faintly.

'The outside kitchen door is locked, sir, and we can't allow you to go in through the hall.'

I produced the key, showed it to him, and went along and in through the door before he could stop me. In the kitchen, the shiny yellow walls themselves were still standing, but the door from the hall had blown open, letting in a glacier tongue of bricks and dust. Dust everywhere, like a veil. Lumps of plaster had fallen from the ceiling. Everything glass, everything china in the room had cracked apart. Moira's geraniums, fallen from their shelves, lay in red farewell profusion over her all-electric domain.

I picked up Malcolm's pine armchair, the one thing he had insisted on keeping through all the changes, and carried it out to where I'd left him. He sank into it without seeming to notice it and put his hand over his mouth.

There were firemen and other people tugging at movable parts of the ruins, but the tempo of their work had slowed since they'd seen we were alive. Several of them came over to Malcolm, offering sympathy, but mostly wanting information, such as were we certain there had been no one else in the house?

As certain as we could be.

Had we been storing any gas in the house? Bottled gas? Butane? Propane? Ether?

No.

Why ether?

It could be used for making cocaine.

We looked at them blankly.

They had already discovered, it seemed, that there had been no mains gas connected. They were asking about other possibilities because it nevertheless looked like a gas explosion.

We'd had no gas of any sort.

Had we been storing any explosive substances whatsoever?

No.

Time seemed disjointed.

Women from the village, as in all disasters, had brought hot tea in thermos flasks for the men working. They gave some to Malcolm and me, and found a red blanket for Malcolm so that I could have my jacket back in the chill gusty air. There was grey sheet cloud overhead: the light was grey, like the dust.

A thick ring of people from the village stood in the garden round the edges of the lawn, with more arriving every minute across the fields and through the garden gate. No one chased them away. Many were taking photographs. Two of the photographers looked like Press.

A police car approached, its siren wailing ever louder as it made slow progress along the crowded road. It wailed right up the drive, and fell silent, and presently a senior-looking man not in uniform came round to the back of the house and took charge.

First, he stopped all work on the rubble. Then he made observations and wrote in a notebook. Then he talked to the chief of the firemen. Finally he came over to Malcolm and me.

Burly and black moustached, he said, as to an old acquaintance, 'Mr Pembroke.'

Malcolm similarly said, 'Superintendent,' and everyone could hear the shake he couldn't keep out of his voice. The wind died away for a while, though Malcolm's shakes continued within the blanket.

'And you, sir?' the superintendent asked me.

'Ian Pembroke.'

He pursed his mouth below the moustache, considering me. He was the man I'd spoken to on the telephone, I thought.

'Where were you last night, sir?'

'With my father in London,' I said. 'We've just . . . returned.'

I looked at him steadily. There were a great many things to be said, but I wasn't going to rush into them.

He said noncommittally, 'We will have to call in explosive experts as the damage here on preliminary inspection, and in the absence of any gas, seems to have been caused by an explosive device.'

Why didn't he say bomb, I thought irritably. Why shy away from the word? If he'd expected any reaction from Malcolm or me, he probably got none as both of us had come to the same conclusion from the moment we'd walked up the drive.

If the house had merely been burning, Malcolm would have been dashing about, giving instructions, saving what he could, dismayed but full of vigour. It was the implications behind a bomb which had knocked him into shivering lassitude: the implications and the reality that if he'd slept in his own bed, he wouldn't have risen to bath, read the *Sporting Life*, go to his bank for travellers' cheques and eat breakfast at the Ritz.

And nor, for that matter, would I.

'I can see you're both shocked,' the superintendent said unemotionally. 'It's clearly impossible to talk here, so I suggest you might come to the police station.' He spoke carefully, giving us at least theoretically the freedom of refusing.

'What about the house?' I said. 'It's open to the four winds. Apart from this great hole, all the windows are broken everywhere else. There's a lot of stuff still inside ... silver ... my father's papers in his office ... some of the furniture.'

'We will keep a patrol here,' he said. 'If you'll give the instructions, we'll suggest someone to board up the windows, and we'll contact a construction firm with a tarpaulin large enough for the roof.'

'Send me the bill,' Malcolm said limply.

'The firms concerned will no doubt present their accounts.'

'Thanks anyway,' I said.

The superintendent nodded.

A funeral for Quantum, I thought. Coffin windows, pall roof. Lowering the remains into the ground would probably follow. Even if any of the fabric of the house should prove sound enough, would Malcolm have the stamina to rebuild, and live there, and remember?

He stood up, the blanket clutched around him, looking infinitely older than his years, a sag of defeat in the cheeks. Slowly, in deference to the shaky state of his legs, Malcolm, the superintendent and I made our way along past the kitchen and out into the front drive.

The ambulances had departed, also one of the fire engines, but the rope across the gateway had been overwhelmed, and the front garden was full of people, one young constable still trying vainly to hold them back.

A bunch in front of the rest started running in our direction as soon as we appeared, and with a feeling of unreality I saw they were Ferdinand, Gervase, Alicia, Berenice, Vivien, Donald, Helen . . . I lost count.

'Malcolm,' Gervase said loudly, coming to a halt in front of us, so that we too had to stop. 'You're alive!'

A tiny flicker of humour appeared in Malcolm's eyes at this most obvious of statements, but he had no chance of answering as the others set up a clamour of questions.

Vivien said, 'I heard from the village that Quantum had blown up and you were both dead.' Her strained voice held a complaint about having been given erroneous news.

'So did I,' Alicia said. 'Three people telephoned . . . so I came at once, after I'd told Gervase and the others, of course.' She looked deeply shocked, but then they all did, mirroring no doubt what they could see on my own face but also suffering from the double upset of misinformation.

'Then when we all get here,' Vivien said, 'we find you *aren't* dead.' She sounded as if that too were wrong.

'What did happen?' Ferdinand asked. 'Just look at Quantum.'

Berenice said, 'Where were you both, then, when it exploded?'

'We thought you were dead,' Donald said, looking bewildered.

More figures pushed through the crowd, horror opening their mouths. Lucy, Edwin and Serena, running, stumbling, looking alternately from the wounded house to me and Malcolm.

Lucy was crying, 'You're alive, you're alive!' Tears ran down her cheeks. 'Vivien said you were dead.'

'I was told they were dead,' Vivien said defensively. Dim-witted . . . Joyce's judgement came back.

Serena was swaying, pale as pale. Ferdinand put an arm round her and hugged her. 'It's all right, girl, they're not dead after all. The old house's a bit knocked about, eh?' He squeezed her affectionately.

'I don't feel well,' she said faintly. 'What happened?'

'Too soon to say for certain,' Gervase said assertively. 'But I'd say one can't rule out a bomb.'

They repudiated the word, shaking their heads, covering their ears. Bombs were for wars, for wicked schemes in aeroplanes, for bus stations in far places, for cold-hearted terrorists . . . for other people. Bombs weren't for a family house outside a Berkshire village, a house surrounded by quiet green fields, lived in by an ordinary family.

Except that we weren't an ordinary family. Ordinary families didn't have fifth wives murdered while planting geraniums. I looked around at the familiar faces and couldn't see on any of them either malice or dismay that Malcolm had escaped. They were all beginning to recover from the shock of the wrongly reported death and also beginning to realize how much damage had been done to the house.

Gervase grew angry. 'Whoever did this shall pay for it!' He sounded pompous more than effective.

'Where's Thomas?' I asked.

Berenice shrugged waspishly. 'Dear Thomas went out early on one of his useless job-hunting missions.

I've no idea where he was going. Vivien telephoned after he'd left.'

Edwin said, 'Is the house insured against bombs, Malcolm?'

Malcolm looked at him with dislike and didn't answer.

Gervase said masterfully, 'You'd better come home with me, Malcolm. Ursula will look after you.'

None of the others liked that. They all instantly made counter-proposals. The superintendent, who had been listening with attentive eyes, said at this point that plans to take Malcolm home would have to be shelved for a few hours.

'Oh, really?' Gervase stared down his nose. 'And who are you?'

'Detective Superintendent Yale, sir.'

Gervase raised his eyebrows but didn't back down. 'Malcolm's done nothing wrong.'

'I want to talk to the superintendent myself,' Malcolm said. 'I want him to find out who tried to destroy my house.'

'Surely it was an accident,' Serena said, very upset.

Ferdinand still had his arm round her. 'Face facts, girl.' He hesitated, looking at me. 'Vivien and Alicia told everyone you were both living here again ... so how come you escaped being hurt?'

'Yes,' Berenice said. 'That's what I asked.'

'We went to London for a night out and stayed there,' I said.

'Very lucky,' Donald said heartily, and Helen, who stood at his elbow and hadn't spoken so far at all, nodded a shade too enthusiastically and said, 'Yes, yes.'

'But if we'd been in the office,' I said, 'we would have been all right.'

They looked along the front of the house to the far corner where the office windows were broken but the walls still stood.

'You wouldn't be in the office at four-thirty in the morning,' Alicia said crossly. 'Why should you be?'

Malcolm was growing tired of them. Not one had hugged him, kissed him, or made warm gestures over his survival. Lucy's tears, if they were genuine, had come nearest. The family obviously could have accommodated his death easily, murmuring regrets at his graveside, maybe even meaning them, but looking forward also with well-hidden pleasure to a safely affluent future. Malcolm dead could spend no more. Malcolm dead would free them to spend instead.

'Let's go,' he said to the superintendent, 'I'm cold.'

An unwelcome thought struck me. 'Did any of you,' I asked the family, 'tell Joyce . . . about the house?'

Donald cleared his throat. 'Yes, I . . . er . . . broke it to her.'

His meaning was clear. 'You told her we were dead?'

'Vivien said you were dead,' he said, sounding as defensive as she had. 'She said I should tell Joyce, so I did.'

'My God,' I said to the superintendent, 'Joyce is my mother. I'll have to phone her at once.'

I turned instinctively back to the house, but the superintendent stopped me, saying the telephones weren't working.

He, I and Malcolm began to move towards the gate, but we had gone only halfway when Joyce herself pushed through the crowd and ran forward, frantically, fearfully distraught.

She stopped when she saw us. Her face went white and she swayed as Serena had done, and I sprinted three or four long strides and caught her upright before she fell.

'It's all right,' I said, holding her. 'It's all right. We're alive.'

'Malcolm . . .'

'Yes, we're both fine.'

'Oh, I thought . . . Donald said . . . I've been crying all the way here, I couldn't see the road . . .' She put her face against my jacket and cried again with a few deep gulps, then pushed herself off determinedly and began searching her tailored pockets for a handkerchief. She found a tissue and blew her nose. 'Well, darling,' she said, 'as you're alive, what the hell's been going on?'

She looked behind Malcolm and me and her eyes widened.

'The whole bloody tribe come to the wake?' To

Malcolm she said, 'You've the luck of the devil, you old bugger.'

Malcolm grinned at her, a distinct sign of revival.

The three ex-wives eyed each other warily. Any mushy idea that the near-death of the man they'd all married and the near-destruction of the house they'd all managed might have brought them to sisterly sympathy was a total non-starter.

'Malcolm can come and stay with me,' Joyce said.

'Certainly not,' Alicia said instantly, clearly alarmed. 'You can take your precious Ian. Malcolm can go with Gervase.'

'I won't have it,' Vivien said sharply. 'If Malcolm's going anywhere, it's fitting he should stay with Donald, his eldest son.'

Malcolm looked as if he didn't know whether to laugh or scream.

'He's staying with me,' I said. 'If he wants to.'

'In your flat?' Ferdinand asked.

I had an appalling vision of my flat disintegrating like Quantum but, unlike Quantum, killing people above and below.

'No, not there,' I said.

'Then where, darling?' Joyce asked.

'Wherever we happen to be.'

Lucy smiled. It was the sort of thing she was happy with. She pulled her big brown cloak closer round her large form and said that it sounded a thoroughly sensible proposal. The others looked at her as if she were retarded instead of the brains of the tribe.

'I'll go wherever I want to,' Malcolm said flatly, 'and with Ian.'

I collected a battery of baleful glares, all of them as ever afraid I would scoop their shares of the pool: all except Joyce, who wanted me to.

'As that's settled,' she said with a hint of maternal smugness which infuriated all the others, 'I want to see just how bad the damage is to the house.' She looked at me briefly. 'Come along, darling, you can show me.'

'Run along, mummy's boy,' Gervase said spitefully, smarting from having been spurned by Malcolm.

'Poor dear Ian, tied to mummy's apron strings.' Berenice's effort came out thick with detestation. 'Greedy little Ian.'

'It isn't fair,' Serena said plaintively. 'Ian gets everything, always. I think it's beastly.'

'Come on, darling,' Joyce said. 'I'm waiting.'

I felt rebellious, tried to smother it, and sought for a different solution.

'You can all come,' I said to them. 'Come and see what really happened here.'

The superintendent had in no way tried to break up the family party but had listened quietly throughout. I happened to catch his eye at that point, and he nodded briefly and walked back beside Malcolm as everyone slowly moved round to the rear of the house.

The extent and violence of the damage there

silenced even Gervase. All of the mouths gaped: in all eyes, horrified awe.

The chief fireman came over and with a certain professional relish began in a strong Berkshire accent to point out the facts.

'Blast travels along the lines of least resistance,' he said. 'This is a good strong old house, which I reckon is why so much of it is still standing. The blast, see, travelled outwards, front and back from a point somewhere near the centre of the main upper storey. Some of the blast went upwards into the roof, bringing down some of those little attic bedrooms, and a good bit of blast, I'd reckon, blew downwards, making a hole that the upper storey and part of the attic just collapsed into, see what I mean?'

Everyone saw.

'There's this wall here,' he pointed to the one between what had been the sitting room and what was still the dining room, 'this wall here, with the chimney built into it, this is one of the main load-bearing walls. It goes right up to the roof. Same the other side, more or less. Those two thick walls stopped the blast travelling sideways, except a bit through the doorways.' He turned directly to Malcolm. 'I've seen a lot of wrecked buildings, sir, mostly burned, it's true, but some gas explosions, and I'd say, and mind you, you'd have to get a proper survey done, but I'd say, on looking at this house, that although it got a good shaking you could think of rebuilding it. Good solid Victorian house, otherwise it would have folded up like a pack of cards.'

'Thank you,' Malcolm said faintly.

The fireman nodded. 'Don't you let any fancy demolition man tell you different, sir. I don't like people being taken advantage of when they're overcome by disasters. I've seen too much of that, and it riles me. What I'm telling you is a straight opinion. I've nothing to gain one way or the other.'

'We're all grateful,' I said.

He nodded, satisfied, and Gervase finally found his voice.

'What sort of bomb was it?' he asked.

'As to that, sir, I wouldn't know. You'd have to wait for the experts.' The fireman turned to the superintendent. 'We shut off the electricity at the meter switch in the garage when we got here, and likewise turned off the mains water under a man-hole cover out by the gate. The storage tank in the roof had emptied through the broken pipes upstairs and water was still running when we got here, and all that water's now underneath the rubble. There's nothing I can see can start a fire. If you want to go into the upper storey at the sides, you'll need ladders, the staircase is blocked. I can't vouch for the dividing walls up there, we looked through the windows but we haven't been inside, you'd have to go carefully. We didn't go up to the attic much, bar a quick look from up the ladder. But down here, you should be all right in the dining room and in that big room the other side of this mess, and also in the kitchen and the front room on the far side.'

'My office,' Malcolm said.

The superintendent nodded, and I reflected that he already knew the layout of the house well from earlier repeated visits.

'We've done as much as we can here,' the fireman said. 'All right if we shove off now?'

The superintendent, agreeing, went a few steps aside with him in private consultation and the family began to come back from suspended animation.

The Press photographers moved in closer, and took haphazard pictures of us, and a man and a woman from different papers approached with insistent questions. Only Gervase seemed to find those tolerable and did all the answering. Malcolm sat down again on the pine chair, which was still there, and gathered his blanket around him, retreating into it up to his eyes like a Red Indian.

Vivien, spotting him, went over and told him she was tired of standing and needed to sit down and it was typically selfish of him to take the only seat, and an insult to her, as she was the senior woman present. Glancing at her with distaste, Malcolm got to his feet and moved a good distance away, allowing her to take his place with a self-satisfied smirk. My dislike of Vivien rose as high as her cheekbones and felt as shrewish as her mouth.

Alicia, recovered, was doing her fluttery feminine act

for the reporters, laying out charm thickly and eclipsing Serena's little-girl ploy. Seeing them together, I thought that it must be hard for Serena to have a mother who refused to mature, who in her late fifties still dressed and behaved like an eighteen-year-old, who for years had blocked her daughter's natural road to adulthood. Girls needed a motherly mother, I'd been told, and Serena didn't have one. Boys needed one too, and Joyce wasn't one, but I'd had a father all the time and in the end I'd also had Coochie, and Serena hadn't had either, and there lay all the difference in the world.

Edwin was having as hard a time as Donald in putting on a show of rejoicing over Malcolm's deliverance.

'It's all very well for you,' he said to me bitterly, catching my ironic look in his direction. 'Malcolm despises me – and don't bother to deny it, he makes it plain enough – and I don't see why I should care much for him. Of course, I wouldn't wish him dead . . .'

'Of course not,' I murmured.

' . . . but, well, if it had happened . . .' he stopped, not actually having the guts to say it straight out.

'You'd have been glad?' I said.

'No.' He cleared his throat. 'I could have faced it,' he said.

I almost laughed. 'Bully for you, Edwin,' I said. 'Hang in there, fellow.'

'I could have faced your death, too,' he said stuffily.

Oh well, I thought. I asked for that.

'How much do you know about bombs?' I asked.

'That's a ridiculous question,' he said, and walked off, and I reflected that Norman West had reported Edwin as spending an hour most days in the public library, and I betted one could find out how to make bombs there, if one persevered.

Berenice said to me angrily, 'It's all your fault Thomas is out of work.'

I blinked. 'How do you make that out?'

'He's been so worried about Malcolm's behaviour that he couldn't concentrate and he made mistakes. He says you could get Malcolm to help us, but of course I tell him you won't, why should you, you're Malcolm's pet.' She fairly spat the last word, the rage seething also in her eyes and tightening all the cords in her neck.

'You told Thomas that?' I said.

'It's true,' she said furiously. 'Vivien says you've always been Malcolm's favourite and he's never been fair to Thomas.'

'He's always been fair to all of us,' I said positively, but of course she didn't believe it.

She was older than Thomas by four or five years and had married him when she was well over thirty and (Joyce had said cattily) desperate for any husband that offered. Ten years ago, when I'd been to their wedding, she had been a thin, moderately attractive woman lit up by happiness. Thomas had been proud of himself and proprietary. They had looked, if not an exciting couple, stable and full of promise, embarking on a good adventure.

Ten years and two daughters later, Berenice had put on weight and outward sophistication and lost whatever illusions she'd had about marriage. I'd long supposed it was basic disappointment which had made her so destructive of Thomas, but hadn't bothered to wonder about the cause of it. Time I did, I thought. Time I understood the whole lot of them, because perhaps in that way we might come to know who could and who couldn't murder.

To search through character and history, not through alibis. To listen to what they said and didn't say, to learn what they could control, and what they couldn't.

I knew, as I stood there looking at the bunch of them, that only someone in the family itself could go that route, and that if I didn't do it, no one else would.

Norman West and Superintendent Yale could dig into facts. I would dig into the people. And the problem with that, I thought, mocking my own pretension, was that the people would do anything to keep me out.

I had to recognize that what I was going to do could produce more trouble than results. Spotting the capability of murder could elude highly-trained psychiatrists, who had been known to advise freedom for reformed characters only to have them go straight out and kill. A highly-trained psychiatrist I was not. Just someone who could remember how we *had* been, and could learn how we were now.

I looked at the monstrously gutted house and shivered. We had returned unexpectedly on Monday; today was Friday. The speed of planning and execution was itself alarming. Never again were we likely to be lucky. Malcolm had survived three attacks by sheer good fortune, but Ferdinand wouldn't have produced healthy statistics about a fourth. The family looked peacefully normal talking to the reporters, and I was filled with a sense of urgency and foreboding.

CHAPTER ELEVEN

One of Malcolm's dogs came bounding across the grass towards him, followed a few seconds later by the other. Malcolm put a hand out of his blanket and patted them, but with more absentmindedness than welcome. After them came Arthur Bellbrook with a face of consternation and concern which lightened considerably when he set eyes on Malcolm. In his grubby trousers and ancient tweed jacket, he came at a hobbling run in old army boots and fetched up very out of breath at Malcolm's side.

'Sir! You're alive! I went to Twyford to fetch some weedkiller. When I got back, they told me in the village ...'

'Gross exaggeration,' Malcolm said, nodding.

Arthur Bellbrook turned to me, panting. 'They said you were both dead. I couldn't get down the road ... had to come across the fields. Look at the house!'

I explained about our going to London, and asked him what time he'd gone home the previous day.

'Four o'clock, same as always. Say three-forty, then.

About then.' He was beginning to get his breath back, his eyes round with disbelief as he stared at the damage.

Nearer to three-thirty, I privately reckoned, if he was admitting to going home early at all.

'Did you go in the house at any time during the day?' I asked.

He switched his gaze from the ruins to me and sounded aggrieved. 'No, I didn't. You know I couldn't have. You've been locking the place like it's a fortress since you came back, and I didn't have a key. Where could I have got a key from?'

I said placatingly, 'It's just that we're anxious . . . someone got in, they must have.'

'Not me.' He was slightly mollified. 'I was working in the kitchen garden all day, digging potatoes and such like. I had the two dogs with me, tied up on their leads. If anyone had tried to get in the house, they'd have barked for sure, but they didn't.'

Malcolm said, 'Arthur, could you keep the dogs with you for another day or two?'

'Yes, I . . .' He looked helplessly at the heap of rubble spilling out across the terrace and onto the lawn. 'What do you want me to do about the garden?'

'Just . . . carry on,' Malcolm said. 'Keep it tidy.' It didn't seem incongruous to him to polish the setting, though I thought that perhaps, left to its own, nature would scatter leaves and grow longer grass and soften the raw brutality of the jagged edges.

The superintendent, seeing Arthur Bellbrook, came

across to him and asked the same questions that I had. Again, they seemed to know each other well, undoubtedly from Moira's investigations, and if there didn't seem to be friendship, there was clearly a mutual respect.

The reporters, having sucked the nectar from Gervase, advanced on Malcolm and on the gardener and the superintendent. I moved away, leaving them to it, and tried to talk to Ferdinand.

He was unfriendly and answered with shrugs and monosyllables.

'I suppose,' I said bitterly, 'you would rather I was lying in shreds and bloody tatters under all that lot.'

He looked at the tons of fallen masonry. 'Not really,' he said coolly.

'That's something.'

'You can't expect us to like it that you've an inside edge with Malcolm.'

'You had three years,' I pointed out, 'during which he wouldn't speak to me. Why did you waste them? Why didn't you get an inside edge yourself?'

'We couldn't get past Moira.'

I half smiled. 'Nor could I.'

'It's now we're talking about,' he said. He looked greatly like Malcolm, right down to the stubbornness in the eyes.

'What do you want me to do, walk away and let him be murdered?' I said.

'Walk away . . .?'

'That's why he wants me with him, to try to keep him safe. He asked me to be his bodyguard, and I accepted.'

Ferdinand stared. 'Alicia said . . .'

'Alicia is crazy,' I interrupted fiercely. 'So are you. Take a look at yourself. Greed, jealousy and spite, you've let them all in. I won't cut you out with Malcolm, I'd never attempt it. Try believing that instead, brother, and save yourself a lot of anxiety.'

I turned away from him in frustration. They were all illogical, I thought. They had almost begged me to use any influence I had with Malcolm to stop him spending and bale them out, and at the same time they believed I would ditch them to my own advantage. But then people had always been able to hold firmly to two contradictory ideas at the same time, as when once, in racing's past, Stewards, Press and public alike had vilified one brilliant trainer as 'most crooked', and elected one great jockey as 'most honest', blindly and incredibly ignoring that it was the self-same trusted jockey who for almost all of his career rode the brilliant trainer's horses. I'd seen a cartoon once that summed it up neatly: 'Entrenched belief is never altered by the facts.'

I wished I hadn't lashed out at Ferdinand. My idea of detection from the inside wasn't going to be a riotous success if I let my own feelings get in the way so easily. I might think the family unjust, they might think me conniving: OK, I told myself, accept all that and forget it. I'd had to put up with their various resentments for much of my life and it was high time I developed immunity.

Easier said than done, of course.

Superintendent Yale had had enough of the reporters. The family had by this time divided into two larger clumps, Vivien's and Alicia's, with Joyce and I hovering between them, belonging to neither. The superintendent went from group to group asking that everyone should adjourn to the police station. 'As you are all here,' he was saying, 'we may as well take your statements straight away, to save you being bothered later.'

'Statements?' Gervase said, eyebrows rising.

'Your movements yesterday and last night, sir.'

'Good God,' Gervase said. 'You don't think any of us would have done this, do you?'

'That's what we have to find out.'

'It's preposterous.'

None of the others said anything, not even Joyce.

The superintendent conferred with a uniformed colleague who was busy stationing his men round the house so that the ever-increasing spectators shouldn't get too close. The word must have spread, I thought. The free peepshow was attracting the next villages, if not Twyford itself.

Much of the family, including Malcolm, Joyce and myself, packed into the three police cars standing in the front drive, and Gervase, Ferdinand and Serena set off on foot to go back to the transport they had come in.

'I wouldn't put it past Alicia,' Joyce said darkly to the superintendent as we drove past them towards the gate, 'to have incited that brood of hers to blow up Quantum.'

'Do you have any grounds for that statement, Mrs Pembroke?'

'Statement? It's an opinion. She's a bitch.'

In the front passenger seat, Yale's shoulders rose and fell in a sigh.

The road outside was still congested with cars, with still more people coming on foot. Yale's driver stopped beside Joyce's car, which she'd left in the centre of the road in her haste, and helped to clear room for her to turn in. With her following, we came next to the hired car Malcolm and I had arrived in, but as it was hopelessly shut in on three sides by other locked vehicles, we left it there and went on in the police car.

In his large modern police station with its bullet-proofed glass enquiry desk, the superintendent ushered us through riot-proofed doors to his office and detailed a policewoman to take Joyce off for some tea. Joyce went protestingly, and Yale with another sigh sat us down in his bare-looking Scandinavian-type place of business.

He looked at us broodingly from behind a large desk. He looked at his nails. He cleared his throat. Finally he said to Malcolm, 'All right. You don't have to say it. I do not believe you would blow up your house just to make me believe that someone is trying to kill you.'

There was a long pause.

'That being so,' he said, as we both sat without speaking, 'we must take the attack in the garage more seriously.'

He was having a hard time, I thought. He ran a finger and thumb down his large black moustache and waited for comments from us that still didn't come.

He cleared his throat again. 'We will redouble our efforts to find Mrs Moira Pembroke's killer.'

Malcolm finally stirred, brought out his cigar case, put a cigar in his mouth and patted his pockets to find matches. There was a plastic notice on Yale's desk saying NO SMOKING. Malcolm, his glance resting on it momentarily, lit the match and sucked the flame into the tobacco.

Yale decided on no protest and produced a glass ashtray from a lower drawer in his desk.

'I would be dead twice over,' Malcolm said, 'if it weren't for Ian.'

He told Yale about the car roaring straight at us at Newmarket.

'Why didn't you report this, sir?' Yale said, frowning.

'Why do you think?'

Yale groomed his moustache and didn't answer.

Malcolm nodded. 'I was tired of being disbelieved.'

'And ... er ... last night?' Yale asked.

Malcolm told him about our day at Cheltenham, and

about Quantum's inner doors. 'I wanted to sleep in my own bed. I was tired. Ian absolutely wouldn't have it, and drove us to London.'

Yale looked at me steadily. 'Did you have a premonition?'

'No, I don't think so.' I hadn't felt a shiver, as I had in my flat. Perhaps the premonition in the flat had been for the house. 'I was just . . . frightened,' I said.

Malcolm glanced at me with interest.

Yale said, 'What of?'

'Not of bombs,' I said. 'I never considered that. Frightened there was someone in the house. I couldn't have slept there, that's all.' I paused. 'I saw the way the car drove at my father at Newmarket – it hit my leg, after all – and I believed him, of course, about being attacked and gassed in the garage. I knew he wouldn't have murdered Moira, or have had her murdered by anyone else. I believe absolutely in his extreme danger. We've been moving around, letting no one know where to find us, until this week.'

'My fault,' Malcolm said gloomily. 'I insisted on coming back here. Ian didn't want to.'

'When the doors were moved,' I said, 'it was time to go.'

Yale thought it over without comment for a while and then said, 'When you were in the house looking round, did you see anything unusual except for the doors?'

'No, nothing.'

'Nothing where it shouldn't be? Or absent from where it should have been?'

I thought back to that breathless heart-thumping search. Whoever had moved the doors must at least have looked into the office and the sitting room. I hadn't bothered with the position of any of the other doors except closing the one from the kitchen to the hall. Someone could have looked into all the rooms in the house, for all I knew.

'No,' I said in the end. 'Nothing else seemed out of place.'

Yale sighed again. He sighed a lot, it seemed to me. 'If you think of anything later, let me know.'

'Yes, all right.'

'The time-frame we're looking at,' he said, 'is between about three-forty p.m., when the gardener went home taking the dogs, and ten-thirty p.m., when you returned from Cheltenham.' He pursed his lips. 'If you hadn't stayed out to dinner, what time would you have been home?'

'We meant to stay out to dinner,' Malcolm said. 'That's why Arthur had the dogs.'

'Yes, but if . . .'

'About six-thirty,' I said. 'If we'd gone straight home after the last race.'

'We had a drink at the racecourse after the last race,' Malcolm said. 'I had scotch, Ian had some sort of fizzy gut-rot.' He tapped ash into the ashtray. He was enjoying having Yale believe him at last, and seemed to be feeling expansive.

'Ian thinks,' he said, 'that I was probably knocked out just outside the kitchen door that day, and that I was carried from there straight into the garage, not dragged, and that it was someone the dogs knew, as they didn't bark. They were jumping up and down by the kitchen door, I can remember that, as they do if someone they know has come. But they do that anyway when it's time for their walk, and I didn't give it a thought.' He inhaled a lot of smoke and let it out into the superintendent's erstwhile clean air. 'Oh yes, and about the fingerprints . . .' He repeated what I'd said about firemen's lifts.

Yale looked at me neutrally and polished his moustache. He was difficult to read, I thought, chiefly because he didn't want to be read. All policemen, I supposed, raised barriers and, like doctors and lawyers, tended not to trust what they were told, which could be bitterly infuriating to the truthful.

He must have been forty or forty-five, I supposed, and had to be competent to have reached that rank. He looked as if he habitually had too little exercise and too many sandwiches, and gave no impression of wallowing in his own power. Perhaps now he'd dropped his over-smart suspicions of Malcolm, he could actually solve his case, though I'd heard the vast majority of criminals were in jail because of having been informed on, not detected. I did very much want him to succeed.

I wished he could spontaneously bring himself to share what he was thinking, but I supposed he'd been trained not to. He kept his counsel anyway on that occasion, and I kept mine, and perhaps it was a pity.

A policewoman came in and said, looking harassed, that she didn't know where to put the Pembroke family.

Yale thought briefly and told her to show them all to his office. Malcolm said, 'Oh God,' and dragged on his cigar, and presently the whole troop arrived.

I got to my feet and Alicia immediately sat on my chair. Vivien and Joyce both glared at Malcolm, still seated, willing him to rise, which he didn't. Which of them could he possibly give his chair to, I thought, stifling laughter, without causing exmarital bloodshed?

With a straight face, Yale asked the policewoman to fetch two more chairs, and I couldn't even tell if he were amused or simply practical. When Vivien and Joyce were suitably enthroned, he looked around and counted us all: thirteen.

'Who's missing?' he asked.

He got various answers: 'My wife, Debs', 'Thomas, my husband', 'Ursula, of course.'

'Very well. Now, if any of you know anything or guess anything about the explosion at Quantum House, I want to hear about it.'

'Terrorists,' Vivien said vaguely.

Everyone ignored her and no one else made any suggestion.

'While you are here,' Yale said, 'I'll ask you all to

answer certain questions. I'll have my personnel write down your answers, and of course after that you can leave. The questions are, what were you doing yesterday between three in the afternoon and midnight, what were you doing a week last Tuesday between the same hours, and what were you doing two weeks ago today, Friday, also between three p.m. and midnight?'

Edwin said crossly, 'We've already answered most of those questions for that wretched man, West. It's too much to go over it all again.'

Several of the others nodded.

Yale looked blank. 'Who is West?'

'A detective,' Berenice said. 'I sent him away with a flea in his ear, I can tell you.'

'He was awfully persistent,' Helen said, not liking the memory. 'I told him I couldn't possibly remember exactly, but he went on prying.'

'Dreadful little man,' Serena said.

'He said I was illegitimate,' Gervase complained sourly. 'It's thanks to Joyce that he knew.'

Yale's mouth opened and closed again and he took a deep breath. 'Who is West?' he asked intensely.

'Fellow I hired,' Malcolm said. 'Private detective. Hired him to find out who was trying to kill me, as I reckoned the police weren't getting anywhere.'

Yale's composure remained more or less intact. 'All the same,' he said, 'please answer the questions again. And those of you without husband and wife here, please answer for them as best you can.' He looked around at all the faces, and I would have sworn he was puzzled. I looked to see what he had seen, and I saw the faces of ordinary people, not murderers. Ordinary people with problems and hang-ups, with quirks and grievances. People anxious and disturbed by the blasting of the house that most had lived in and all had visited. Not one of them could possibly be a murderer, I thought. It had after all to be someone from outside.

I felt a lot of relief at this conclusion until I realized I was raising any excuse not to have to find a murderer among ourselves; yet we did have to find one, if Malcolm were to live. The dilemma was permanent.

'That's all for now,' Yale said, rising to his feet. 'My staff will take your statements in the interview rooms. And Mr Pembroke senior, will you stay here a moment? And Mr Ian Pembroke also? There are the arrangements to be made about the house.'

The family left me behind with bad grace. 'It's my job, not Ian's, to see to things. I am the eldest.' That was Donald. 'You need someone with know-how.' That was Gervase, heavily. 'It's not Ian's house.' Petulance from Edwin.

Yale managed however to shovel them all out, and immediately the door had closed, I said, 'While they're all in the interview rooms, I'm taking my father out of here.'

'The house . . .' Malcolm began.

'I'll see to the house later. We're leaving here now,

246

this minute. If Superintendent Yale will lend us a police car, fine; otherwise we'll catch buses or taxis.'

'You can have a police car within reason,' Yale said.

'Great. Then ... um ... just take my father to the railway station. I'll stay here.'

'All right.'

To Malcolm, I said, 'Go to London. Go to where we were last night. Use the same name. Don't telephone anyone. Don't for God's sake let anyone know where you are.'

'You're bloody arrogant.'

'Yes. This time, listen to me.'

Malcolm gave me a blue glare, stubbed out his cigar, stood up and let the red blanket drop from his shoulders to the floor.

'Where will you be?' Yale asked him.

'Don't answer,' I said brusquely.

Malcolm looked at me, then at the superintendent. 'Ian will know where I am. If he doesn't want to tell you, he won't. Gervase tried to burn some information out of him once, and didn't succeed. He still has the scars ...' he turned to me ' ... don't you?'

'Malcolm!' I protested.

Malcolm said to Yale, 'I gave Gervase a beating he'll never forget.'

'And he's never forgiven me,' I said.

'Forgiven you? For what? You didn't snitch to me. Serena did. She was so young she didn't really understand what she'd been seeing. Gervase could be a proper bully.'

'Come on,' I said, 'we're wasting time.'

Superintendent Yale followed us out of his office and detailed a driver to take Malcolm.

'I'll come in the car, once I can move it,' I said to him. 'Don't go shopping, I'll buy us some things later. Do be sensible, I beg you.'

'I promise,' he said; but promises with Malcolm weren't necessarily binding. He went out with the driver and I stood on the police station steps watching his departure and making sure none of the family had seen him or could follow.

Yale made no comment but waved me back to his office. Here he gave me a short list of reputable building contractors and the use of his telephone. I chose one of the firms at random and explained what was needed, and Yale took the receiver himself and insisted that they were to do minimum weather-proofing only, and were to move none of the rubble until the police gave clearance.

'When the driver returns from taking your father,' he said to me, disconnecting, 'we can spare him to ferry you back to your car.'

'Thank you.'

'I'm trusting you, you know, to maintain communications between me and your father.'

'I'll telephone here every morning, if you like.'

'I'd much rather know where he is.'

I shook my head. 'The fewer people know, the safer.'

He couldn't exactly accuse me of taking unreasonable precautions, so he left it, and asked instead, 'What did your half-brother burn you with?'

'A cigarette. Nothing fancy.'

'And what information did he want?'

'Where I'd hidden my new cricket bat,' I answered: but it hadn't been about cricket bats, it had been about illegitimacy, which I hadn't known at the time but had come to understand since.

'How old were you both?'

'I was eleven. Gervase must have been thirteen.'

'Why didn't you give him the bat?' Yale asked.

'It wasn't the bat I wouldn't give him. It was the satisfaction. Is this part of your enquiries?'

'Everything is,' he said laconically.

The hired car was movable when I got back to it and as it was pointing in that direction I drove it along to Quantum. There were still amazing numbers of people there, and I couldn't get past the now more substantial barrier across the drive until the policeman guarding it had checked with Superintendent Yale by radio.

'Sorry, sir,' one of them said, finally letting me in. 'The superintendent's orders.'

I nodded and drove on, parking in front of the house beside two police cars which had presumably returned from taking the many family members to their various cars.

I had already grown accustomed to the sight of the house; it still looked as horrific but held no more shocks. Another policeman walked purposefully towards me as I got out of the car and asked what I wanted. To look through the downstairs windows, I said.

He checked by radio. The superintendent replied that I could look through the windows as long as the constable remained at my side, and as long as I would point out to him anything I thought looked wrong. I readily agreed to that. With the constable beside me, I walked towards the place where the hall could still be discerned, skirting the heavy front door, which had been blown outwards, frame and all, when the brick-work on either side of it had given way.

QUANTUM IN ME FUIT lay face downwards on the gravel. I did the best I could. Someone's best, I thought, grateful to be alive, hadn't quite been good enough.

'Don't go in, sir,' the young constable said warningly. 'There's more could come down.'

I didn't try to go in. The hall was full of ceilings and floors and walls from upstairs, though one could see daylight over the top of the heap, the daylight from the back garden. Somewhere in the heap were all of Malcolm's clothes except the ones he'd worn to Chel-tenham, all his vicuna coats and handmade shoes, all of the gold-and-silver brushes he'd packed on his flight to Cambridge, and somewhere, too, the portrait of Moira.

Jagged arrows of furniture stuck up from the devastation like the arms of the drowning, and pieces of dusty unrecognizable fabric flapped forlornly when a gust of wind took them. Tangled there, too, was everything I'd brought with me from my flat, save only my racing kit – saddle, helmet and holdall – which was still in the boot of the car along with Malcolm's briefcase. Everything was replaceable, I supposed; and I felt incredibly glad I hadn't thought of bringing the silver-framed picture of Coochie and the boys.

There was glass everywhere along the front of the house, fallen from the shattered windows. With the constable in tow, I crunched along towards the office, passing the ruins of the downstairs cloakroom on the way, where a half-demolished wall had put paid to the plumbing.

The office walls themselves, like those of the kitchen, were intact, but the office door that I'd set at such a careful angle was wide open with another brick and plaster glacier spilling through it. The shockwave that must have passed through the room to smash its way out through the windows had lifted every unweighted sheet of paper and redistributed it on the floor. Most of the pictures and countless small objects were down there also, including, I noticed, the pen pot holding the piece of wire. Apart from the ancient bevelled glass of a splendid breakfront bookcase which stood along one wall, everything major looked restorable, though getting rid of the dust would be a problem in itself.

I spent a good deal of time gazing through the open spaces of the office windows, but in the end had to admit defeat. The positions of too much had been altered for me to see anything inexplicably wrong. I'd seen nothing significant in there the previous evening when I'd fetched Malcolm's briefcase, when I'd been wide awake with alarm to such things.

Shaking my head I moved on round the house, passing the still shut and solidly bolted garden door which marked the end of the indoor passage. The blast hadn't shifted it, had dissipated on nearer targets. Past it lay the long creeper-covered north wall of the old playroom, and I walked along there and round into the rear garden.

The police had driven stakes into the lawn and tied ropes to them, making a line for no one to cross. Behind the rope the crowd persisted, open-eyed, chattering, pointing, coming to look and moving away to trail back over the fields. Among them Arthur Bellbrook, the dogs at his side, was holding a mini-court in a semi-circle of respectful listeners. The reporters and Press photographers seemed to have vanished but other cameras still clicked in a barrage. There was a certain restrained orderliness about everything which struck me hard as incongruous.

Turning my back to the gawpers, I looked through

the playroom window, seeing it, like the office, from the opposite angle to the previous night. Apart from the boxroom and my bedroom, it was the only room unmetamorphosed by Moira, and it still looked what it had been for forty years, the private domain of children.

The old battered armchairs were still there, and the big table that with a little imagination had been fort, boat, spaceship and dungeon in its time. The long shelves down the north wall still bore generations of train sets, building sets, board games and stuffed toys. Robin and Peter's shiny new bicycles were still propped there, that had been the joy of their lives in the week before the crash. There were posters of pop groups pinned to the walls and a bookcase bulging with reprehensible tastes.

The explosion on the other side of the thick load-bearing wall had done less damage to the playroom than to anywhere else I'd seen; only the broken windows and the ubiquitous dust, which had flooded in from the passage, showed that anything had happened. A couple of teddy bears had tumbled off the shelves, but the bicycles were still standing.

Anything there that shouldn't be there, anything not there that should be, Yale had said. I hadn't seen anything the night before in those categories, and I still couldn't.

With a frustrated shrug, I skirted the poured-out guts of the house and on the far side looked through the dining-room windows. Like the playroom, the dining room was relatively undamaged, though here the blast had blown in directly from the hall, leaving the now familiar tongue of rubble and covering everything with a thick grey film. For ever after, I would equate explosions with dust.

The long table, primly surrounded by high-backed chairs, stood unmoved. Some display plates held in wires on the wall had broken and fallen off. The sideboard was bare, but then it had been before. Malcolm had said the room had hardly been used since he and Moira had taken to shouting.

I continued round to the kitchen and went in through the door, to the agitation of the constable. I told him I'd been in there earlier to fetch the pine chair, which someone had since brought back, and he relaxed a very little.

'That door,' I said, pointing to one in a corner, 'leads to the cellars. Do you know if anyone's been down there?'

He didn't think so. He was pretty sure not. He hadn't heard anyone mention cellars.

The two underground rooms lay below the kitchen and dining room, and without electric lights I wasn't keen to go down there. Still . . . what excuse did I have not to?

Malcolm kept some claret in racks there, enough to grieve him if the bottles were broken. Coochie had used the cellars romantically for candlelit parties with red-checked tablecloths and gypsy music, and the folding tables and chairs were still stacked there, along with the motley junk of ages that was no longer used but too valuable to throw away.

'Do you have a torch, constable?' I asked.

No, he hadn't. I went to fetch the one I'd installed by habit in the hired car and, in spite of his disapproval, investigated downstairs. He followed me, to do him justice.

To start with, the cellars were dry, which was a relief as I'd been afraid the water from the storage tank and the broken pipes would have drained down and flooded them.

None of Malcolm's bottles was broken. The chimney wall, continuing downwards as sturdy foundations, had sheltered everything on its outer side as stalwartly below as it had above.

The dire old clutter of pensioned-off standard lamps, rocking chair, pictures, tin trunk, tiger skin, bed head-board, tea trolley, all took brief life in the torchlight and faded back to shadow. Same old junk, undisturbed.

All that one could say again was that nothing seemed to be there in the cellar that shouldn't be, and nothing not there that should. Shrugging resignedly, I led the way upstairs and closed the door.

Outside again, I looked into the garage, which seemed completely untouched, and walked round behind it to the kitchen garden. The glass in the old greenhouse was broken, and I supposed Moira's little folly, away on the far side of the garden, would have suffered the same fate.

I dearly wanted to go down to the far end of the kitchen garden to make sure the gold store was safe, but was deterred by the number of interested eyes already swivelled my way, and particularly by Arthur Bellbrook's.

The wall itself looked solid enough. The crowds were nowhere near it, as it was away to the left, while they were coming in from the fields on the right.

The constable stood by my side, ready to accompany me everywhere.

Shrugging, I retreated. Have faith, I thought, and drove away to London.

CHAPTER TWELVE

Malcolm had achieved a double suite at the Ritz with views of Green Park. He had lunched on Strasbourg pâté and Dover sole, according to the remains on the white-clothed room-service table, and had reached the lower half of a bottle of Krug.

'How are the shakes?' I said, putting his briefcase down beside him.

'Were you followed here?' he asked.

'I was not.'

He was doing his best to pretend he had regained total command of himself, yet I guessed the train journey had been an anxious and lonely ordeal. It was difficult for me to imagine the escalating trauma within him. How could anyone be the target of deadly unrelenting virulence and not in the end break down? I'd got to invent something better for him, I thought, than cooping him up in millionaire cells. Make him safe, give him back his lightheartedness, set him free.

'Um,' I said. 'I hope your passport's still in your briefcase.'

'Yes, it is.' He had taken it in his briefcase to Paris.

'Good.'

An unfortunate thought struck him. 'Where's yours?' Malcolm asked.

'In the rubble. Don't worry, I'll get a replacement. Do you have a visa for America?'

'Yes. I also had one for Australia once, but they only last a year. If we go, we'll have to get new visas from Australia House.'

'How about if you go to America tomorrow?' I said.

'*Tomorrow*? How can I?'

'I'll take you safely to Heathrow and see you off.'

'Dammit, that's not what I meant.'

'No,' I said. 'Well ... the Breeders' Cup races are three weeks tomorrow at Santa Anita. Why don't we phone Ramsey Osborn? Why don't we phone Blue Clancy's trainer? Why don't you fly to Los Angeles tomorrow and have a fine old time at the races for three weeks? They have racing every day on the same track. If I know you, you'll be cronies with the racetrack committee immediately. Ramsey Osborn will send introductions. You can stay where the Breeders' Cup organizers do, at the Beverly Wilshire hotel which I've heard is right at the end of Rodeo Drive where there's a man's shop so expensive you have to make an appointment to be let in. Buy a few shirts there, it'll make a nice dent in your bankroll. Forget Quantum. Forget the bloody family. They won't know where you are and they'll never find you.'

I stopped only a fraction for breath, not long enough for him to raise objections. 'On the Tuesday after the Breeders' Cup, they're running the Melbourne Cup in Melbourne, Australia. That's their biggest race. The whole country stops for it. A lot of the people from the Breeders' Cup will go on to Australia. You'll have made cronies among them by the dozen. I've heard it's all marvellous. I've never been, and I'd love to. I'll join you as soon as my passport's renewed and I'll go on minding your back – if you still want me to.'

He had listened at first with apathy, but by the end he was smiling. I'd proposed the sort of impulsive behaviour that had greatly appealed to him in the past, and it still did, I was grateful to see.

'A damn sight better than rotting at the Ritz,' he announced.

'Great,' I said. 'Get out your diary for the numbers.'

It was soon settled. Blue Clancy would go over for the Breeders' Cup as long as he was fit. Ramsey Osborn, booming away in Stamford, Connecticut, promised introductions galore to a score of very dear friends he'd met a couple of times out West. Why didn't Malcolm stop off at Lexington on the way and feast his eyes on some real bloodstock? Ramsey had some very good friends in Lexington who would be delighted to have Malcolm stay with them. Ramsey would call them and fix it. Stay by the phone, you guys, he said. He would fix it and call back. It was breakfast time in Connecticut, he said. It would be an hour earlier in Lexington. He would see if the lazy so and so's were out of bed.

Whether they were or they weren't, Ramsey phoned back within twenty minutes. As before, Malcolm talked on the sitting-room telephone, I on the extension in my bedroom.

'All set,' Ramsey said. 'They're expecting you, Malcolm, tomorrow, and I'm flying down Sunday. They're real sweet guys, you'll love them. Dave and Sally Cander. Dogwood Drift Farm, outside of Lexington.' He read out the telephone number. 'You got that?'

Malcolm had got it.

Ramsey asked where Malcolm was planning to stay for the Breeders' Cup. 'Beverly Wilshire? Couldn't be better. Centre of the universe. I'll make reservations right away.'

Malcolm explained he needed a two-bedroom suite for himself and me. Sure thing, Ramsey agreed. No problem. See you, he said. We had made his day, he said, and to have a good one.

The sitting room seemed smaller and quieter when he'd gone off the line, but Malcolm had revitalized remarkably. We went at once by taxi to Australia House where Malcolm got his visa without delay, and on the way back stopped first at his bank for more travellers' cheques and then in Piccadilly a little short of the Ritz to shop in Simpson's for replacement clothes from the skin up, not forgetting suitcases to pack them in.

Malcolm paid for all of mine with his credit card, which was a relief. I hardly liked to ask him outright for my fare to California, but he'd thought of my other finances himself already and that evening gave me a bumper cheque to cover several additional destinations.

'Your fare and so on. Pay Arthur Bellbrook. Pay Norman West. Pay the contractors for weatherproofing Quantum. Pay for the hired car. Pay your own expenses. Anything else?'

'Tickets to Australia?'

'We'll get those in the morning. I'll pay for them here, with mine to Lexington. If we can get you a Los Angeles ticket without a date on, I can pay for that too.'

We made plans about telephone calls. He was not to phone me, I would phone him.

We dined in good spirits, the dreadful morning at least overlaid. He raised his glass: 'To Blue Clancy' and 'To racing' and 'To life.'

'To life,' I said.

I drove him to Heathrow in the morning safely as promised, and saw him on his way to Lexington via New York and Cincinnati. He was fizzing at least at half strength and gave me a long blue look before he departed.

'Don't think I don't know what I owe you,' he said.

'You owe me nothing.'

261

'Bloody Moira,' he said unexpectedly, and looked back and waved as he went.

Feeling good about him, I telephoned from the airport to Superintendent Yale but got one of his assistants: his chief was out at Quantum and had left a message that if I phoned I was to be asked if I could join him. Yes, I could, I agreed, and arrived in the village about forty minutes later.

The road to the house wasn't as congested as the day before, but fresh waves of sightseers still came and went continuously. I drove up to the gate and after radio consultation the constable there let me pass. Another policeman was at my side the moment I stopped in front of the house. Different men, both of them, from the day before.

Superintendent Yale appeared from the direction of the kitchen, having been alerted by the gateman, I surmised.

'How is Mr Pembroke?' he asked, shaking hands with every sign of having adopted humanity as a policy.

'Shaken,' I said.

He nodded understandingly. He was wearing an overcoat and looked cold in the face, as if he'd been out of doors for some time. The mild wind of yesterday had intensified rawly and the clouds looked more threatening, as if it would rain. Yale glanced with anxiety at the heavens and asked me to go round with him to the back garden.

The front of the house looked sad and blind, with

light brown plywood hammered over all the windows and a heavy black tarpaulin hanging from under the roof to hide the hole in the centre. At the rear, the windows were shuttered and the bare roof rafters were covered but the devastated centre was still open to the elements. Several men in hard hats and overalls were working there, slowly picking up pieces from the huge jumble and carrying them to throw them into a rubbish skip which stood a short distance away across the lawn.

'Do they propose to move all that by hand?' I asked.

'As much as is necessary,' Yale said. 'We've got a surprise for you.' He waved to a man in beige overalls with a blue hard hat who came over to us and asked me my name.

'Ian Pembroke,' I said obligingly.

He unzipped the front of his overalls, put a hand inside and drew out a battered navy-blue object which he held out to me with a small satisfied smile. 'You may need this,' he said.

Never a truer word. It was my passport.

'Where on earth did you find it?' I said, delighted.

He shrugged and pointed to the mess. 'We always come across a few things unharmed. We're making a pile of them for you, but don't get your hopes up.'

I zipped the passport into my new Simpson's Barbour and thought gratefully that I wouldn't have to trail around getting a new one.

'Have you found any gold-and-silver-backed brushes?'
I asked.

'Not so far.'

'They're my father's favourite things.'

'We'll look out for them,' he said. 'Now, we'd like
you to help us in return.'

'Anything I can.'

He was a lean, highly professional sort of man, late
forties I guessed, giving an impression of army. He said
his name was Smith. He was an explosives expert.

'When you first came here yesterday morning,' he
said, 'did you smell anything?'

I was surprised. I thought back.

'Brick dust,' I said. 'The wind was stirring it up. It
was in my throat.'

He grunted. 'This looks like a gas explosion, but
you're quite certain, aren't you, that there was no gas
in the house?'

'Absolutely certain.'

'Do you know what cordite smells like?' he asked.

'Cordite? Like after a gun's been fired, do you
mean?'

'That's right.'

'Well, yes, I know what it smells like.'

'And you didn't smell that here yesterday morning?'

I looked at him, puzzled. 'No one was shot,' I said.

He smiled briefly. 'Do you know what cordite is?'
he asked.

'Not really.'

'It was used very commonly as a general explosive,' he said, 'before Nobel invented dynamite in 1867. It's less fierce than dynamite. It's sort of high-grade gunpowder, and it's still used in some types of quarries. It explodes comparatively slowly, at about two thousand five hundred metres per second, or a little over. It explodes like a gas. It doesn't punch small holes through walls like a battering ram. It's rather like an expanding balloon that knocks them flat.'

I looked at the house.

'Yes, like that,' Smith said.

'Cordite . . .' I frowned. 'It means nothing.'

'Its strong smell lingers,' he said.

'Well . . . we didn't get here until ten, and the explosion was at four-thirty in the morning, and it was fairly windy, though not as rough as today. I should think any smell had blown away.' I paused. 'What about all the people who were here before us? What do they say?'

'They're not here today,' Smith said succinctly. 'I haven't asked them.'

'No one said anything to me about a smell,' I said.

Smith shrugged. 'We'll do microscopic tests. We would do, anyway. But it looks to me as if cordite is a strong possibility.'

'Can you buy cordite?' I asked vaguely. 'Can anyone?'

'No, they definitely can't,' Smith said with decision. 'Twenty years or so ago, maybe, but not now. Since terrorism became a part of life, most sorts of explosives are highly regulated. It's extremely difficult for the general public to get hold of them. There are a few explosive substances on the open market, but detonators to set them off are not.'

I found I was thinking of cordite in terms of the small quantities used in firearms, whereas to knock down half a house . . .

'How much cordite would that have taken?' I asked, gesturing to the results.

'I haven't yet worked it out. A good deal.'

'What would it have been in?'

'Anything.'

'What does it look like? Is it like jelly?'

'No, you're thinking of high-explosive TNT. That's liquid when it's fed into bomb cases, then it gels inside. Bombs dropped from aircraft are that sort. Cordite is loose grains, like gunpowder. To get a useful result, you have to compress it. Confine it. Then you need heat to start off the chemical reaction, which proceeds at such a rate that the ingredients appear to explode.'

'Appear!' I said, and added hastily, 'OK, I take your word for it, don't explain.'

He gave me a slightly pitying look but let up on the lecture and went back to searching in the ruins. Superintendent Yale asked if any of the Pembrokes had ever had any connection whatever with quarries. None that I knew of, I said. It was most improbable.

'Or had friends who had quarries, or who worked in quarries?'

I didn't know. I'd never heard of any.

My gaze wandered away from Smith and his fellow diggers after truth, and I became more aware of the audience beyond the rope in the garden. There weren't anything like as many as the day before, but clearly the work in progress was a draw in itself.

Arthur Bellbrook was there again, talking away. He must enjoy the celebrity, I thought. He'd been the one who'd found Moira, and now there was the house ... Arthur was talking as if he owned the news, rocking back on his heels and sticking his stomach out. The dogs on their leads patiently waited. It didn't matter to them, I supposed, that Arthur was into maybe the twentieth account of life and death with the Pembrokes.

A stray piece of memory connected Arthur to the smell of cordite, and I couldn't think why that should be until I remembered him carrying his shotgun into the house on the day he'd thought I was a burglar.

I cast the stray thought out but it sauntered back, telling me it was nothing to do with Arthur and shotguns.

What then?

I frowned, trying to remember.

'What's the matter?' Yale said, watching me.

'Nothing, really.'

'You've thought of something. One of your family does have a quarry connection, is that it?'

267

'Oh no,' I half laughed. 'Not that. The smell of cordite . . .'

The smell of cordite on a misty morning, and the gardener . . . not Arthur, but old Fred before him . . . telling us children to keep out of the way, to go right back out of the field, he didn't want our heads blown off . . .

I remembered abruptly, like a whole scene springing to life on a film screen. I walked across to where Smith in his hard blue hat bent to his task and said, without preamble, 'Does cordite have another name?'

He straightened, with a piece of brick and plaster in his hand.

'I suppose so,' he said. 'It's commonly called "black powder".'

Black powder.

'Why?' he said.

'Well, we had some here once. But long ago, when we were children. Twenty years ago at least, probably more. But I suppose . . . some of the family could have remembered . . . as I just have.'

Yale, who had followed me to listen, said, 'Remember what?'

'There used to be four or five great old willow trees down by the stream, across the field.' I pointed. 'Those you can see now are only twenty years old or so. They grow very fast . . . they were planted after they took the old trees down. They were splendid old trees, huge, magnificent.'

Yale made hurrying-up motions with his hands, as if to say the state of long-gone willows, however patrician, was immaterial.

'They were at the end of their lives,' I said. 'If there was a gale, huge branches would crack off. Old Fred, who was the gardener for years here before Arthur, told my father they weren't safe and they'd have to come down, so he got some foresters to come and fell them. It was dreadful seeing them come down . . .' I didn't think I'd tell Yale that half the family had been in tears. The trees had been friends, playground, climbing frames, deepest purple imaginary rain forests: and, afterwards, there was too much daylight and the dead bodies being sawn up for firewood and burned on bonfires. The stream hadn't looked the same when open to bright sunshine; rather ordinary, not running through dappled mysterious shade.

'Go on,' Yale said with half-stifled impatience. 'What's all this about trees?'

'The stumps,' I said. 'The tree men sawed the trees off close to the ground but left the stumps, and no one could get them out. A tractor came from a nearby farm and tried . . .' We'd had a great time then, having rides all day. 'Anyway, it failed. Nothing else would move the stumps, and Fred didn't want to leave them there to rot, so he decided to blow them up . . . with black powder.'

'Ah,' Yale said.

Black powder had sounded, somehow, as if it ought

to belong to pirates. We'd been most impressed. Fred had got his powder and he'd dug a hole down below the stubborn roots of the first stump, and filled it and set off one enormous explosion. It was just as well he'd cleared us out of the field first because the blast had knocked Fred himself flat although he'd been about a hundred feet away. The first tree stump had come popping out of the ground looking like a cross between an elephant and an octopus, but Malcolm, who came running in great alarm to see what had happened, forbade Fred to blow up the others.

As I told the gist of this to Yale and Smith, the second reel of the film was already unrolling in my mind, and I stopped fairly abruptly when I realized what I was remembering.

'Fred,' I said, 'carried the box of black powder back to the tool shed and told us never to touch it. We were pretty foolish but not that crazy. We left it strictly alone. And there the box stayed until it got covered over with other junk and we didn't notice it or think of it any more . . .' I paused, then said, 'Wouldn't any explosive be useless after all this time?'

'Dynamite wouldn't last much more than a year in a tool shed,' Smith said. 'One hot summer would ruin it. But black powder – cordite – is very stable, and twenty years is immaterial.'

'What are we waiting for?' Yale said, and walked towards the tool shed which lay behind the garage on the near side of the kitchen garden.

The tool shed was a place I hadn't thought of looking into the day before: but even if I had, I doubted if I would have remembered the black powder. Its memory had been too deep.

'Where is this box?' Yale asked.

I looked at the contents of the tool shed in perplexity. I hadn't been in there for years, and in that time it had passed from Fred to Arthur. Fred had had an upturned orange box to sit on while he waited through heavy showers: Arthur had an old fireside chair. Fred had had a tray with a cracked mug and a box of sugar cubes and had come indoors to fetch his tea: Arthur had an electric kettle. Fred had tended old tools lovingly: Arthur had shiny new ones with paint still on the handles.

Beyond the tools and the chair, in the centre section of the spacious shed, were things like mowers, chainsaws and hedgeclippers and, at the furthest shadowy end, the flotsam by-passed by time, like the stuff in the cellar, stood in forgotten untidy heaps.

It all looked unpromisingly undisturbed, but Yale called up a pair of young policemen and told them to take everything out of the tool shed and lay each object separately on the ground. Smith went back to the rubble, but Yale and I watched the policemen and so did Arthur Bellbrook, who came hurrying across the moment he saw what was happening.

'What's going on?' he said suspiciously.

271

'When did you last clean out the tool shed?' Yale asked.

Arthur was put out and beginning to bridle.

'Just say,' I said to him. 'We just want to know.'

'I've been meaning to,' he said defensively. 'That's Fred's old rubbish, all that at the back.'

The superintendent nodded, and we all watched the outgoing procession of ancient, rusting, broken and neglected tat. Eventually one of the men came out with a dirty wooden box which I didn't recognize at first because it was smaller than I'd seen in my memory. He put it on the ground beside other things, and I said doubtfully, 'I think that's it.'

'Mr Smith,' Yale called.

Mr Smith came. Yale pointed at the box, which was about the size of crates used for soft drink bottles, and Smith squatted beside it.

The lid was nailed shut. With an old chisel, Smith prised it open and peeled back the yellowish paper which was revealed. Inside the paper, half-filling the box, there was indeed black powder.

Smith smelled it and poked it around. 'It's cordite, all right, and in good condition. But as it's here, it obviously hasn't been used. And anyway, there wouldn't have been anything like enough in this box to have caused that much damage to the house.'

'Well,' I said weakly, 'it was only an idea.'

'Nothing wrong with the idea,' Smith said. He looked

around at the growing collection of discards. 'Did you find any detonators?'

He had everyone open every single packet and tin: a lot of rusty staples and nails saw daylight, and old padlocks without keys and rotting batteries, but nothing he could identify as a substance likely to set off an explosion.

'Inconclusive,' he said, shrugging, and returned to his rubble.

Yale told Arthur to leave the cordite where it was and do what he liked with the rest, and Arthur began throwing the decaying rubbish into the skip.

I tried to apologize for all the waste of time, but the superintendent stopped me.

'When you saw the tree stump blown up, which of your brothers and sisters were there?'

I sighed, but it had to be faced. 'Gervase, Ferdinand and I were always together at that time, but some of the older ones were there too. They used to come for weekends still after they were grown up. Vivien used to make them, so that Malcolm wouldn't cut them out. Alicia hated it. Anyway, I know Lucy was there, because she wrote a poem about roots shrieking blindly to the sky.'

Yale looked sceptical.

'She's a poet.' I said lamely. 'Published.'

'The roots poem was published?'

'Yes.'

'All right, then. She was there. Who else?'

'Someone was carrying Serena on his shoulders when we had to leave the field for the explosion. I think it must have been Thomas. He used to make her laugh.'

'How old were you all at that time?' Yale asked.

'I don't know exactly.' I thought back. Alicia had swept out not very long after. 'Perhaps I was thirteen. Gervase is two years older, Ferdinand one year younger. Lucy would have been ... um ... twenty-two, about, and Thomas nineteen. Serena must have been six, at that rate, and Donald ... I don't know if he was there or not ... he would have been twenty-four.'

Yale thoughtfully pulled out his notebook and asked me to repeat the ages, starting with Donald.

'Donald twenty-four, Lucy twenty-two, Thomas nineteen, Gervase fifteen, myself thirteen, Ferdinand twelve, Serena six.'

'Right,' he said, putting a full-stop.

'But what does it matter, if the cordite is still here?' I said.

'They all saw the force of the explosion,' he said. 'They all saw it knock the gardener over from a hundred feet away, isn't that what you said?'

I looked at the shattered house and said forlornly, 'None of them could have done it.'

Yale put his notebook away. 'You might be right,' he said.

Smith again came over to join us. 'You've given me an idea,' he said to me. 'You and your tree roots. Can you draw me a plan of where the rooms were, exactly, especially those upstairs?'

I said I thought so, and the three of us went into the garage out of the wind, where I laid a piece of paper on the bonnet of Moira's car and did my best.

'The sitting room stretched all the way between the two thick walls, as you know,' I said. 'About thirty feet. Above that . . .' I sketched, 'there was my room, about eight feet wide, twelve deep, with a window on the short side looking out to the garden. Malcolm's bedroom came next, I suppose about fifteen feet wide and much deeper than mine. The passage outside bent round it . . . and then his bathroom, also looking out to the garden, with a sort of dressing room at the back of it which also led out of the bedroom . . .' I drew it. 'Malcolm's whole suite would have been about twenty-two feet wide facing the garden, by about seventeen or eighteen feet deep.'

Yale studied the drawing. 'Your room and the suite together were more or less identical with the sitting room, then?'

'Yes, I should think so.'

'A big house,' he commented.

'It used to be bigger. The kitchen was once a morning room, and where the garage is now there were kitchens and servants' halls. And on the other side, where the passage now goes out into the garden, there were gun rooms and flower rooms and music rooms, a bit of a rabbit warren. I never actually saw the wings, only photographs of them. Malcolm had them pulled down when he inherited the house, to make it easier to deal with without the droves of servants his mother had.'

'Hm,' he said. 'That explains why there are no side-ways-facing windows on the ground floor.'

'Yes,' I agreed.

He borrowed my pen and did some calculations and frowned.

'Where exactly was your father's bed?'

I drew it in. 'The bed was against the wall between his room and the large landing, which was a sort of upstairs place to sit in, over the hall.'

'And your bed?'

'Against the wall between my room and Malcolm's.'

Smith considered the plan for some time and then said, 'I think the charge here was placed centrally. Did your father by any chance have a chest, or anything, at the foot of his bed?'

'Yes, he did,' I said, surprised. 'A long box with a padded top for a seat. He kept his tennis things in it, when he used to play.'

'Then I'd think that would be where the explosion occurred. Or under your father's bed. But if there was a box at the foot, I'd bet on that.' Smith borrowed the pen again for some further calculations and looked finally undecided.

'What's the matter?' I asked.

'Mm . . . well, because of your tree roots, I was

thinking of an explosive that farmers and landowners use sometimes which is safer than cordite. They blow up tree trunks, clear blocked ditches, that sort of thing. You can buy the ingredients anywhere without restrictions and mix it yourself.'

'That sounds extraordinary,' I said.

He smiled slightly. 'It's not so easy to get the detonators to set it off.'

'What is it, then?' I asked.

Yale, too, was listening with great interest.

'Fertilizer and diesel oil,' Smith said.

'What?' I sounded disappointed and Smith's smile expanded.

'Ammonium nitrate,' he said. 'You can buy it in fine granules from seed merchants and garden centres, places like that. Mix it with fuel oil. Dead simple. As far as I remember, but I'd have to look it up to be sure, it would be sixteen parts fertilizer to one part oil. The only problem is,' he scratched his nose, 'I think you'd need a good deal of it to do the sort of damage we have here. I mean, again I'd have to look it up, but I seem to remember it'll be volume in cubic metres over three, answer in kilos.'

'What volume?' I asked.

'The volume of the space you want cleared by the explosion.'

He looked at the mixed emotions I could feel on my face and dealt at least with the ignorance.

'Say you want effective destruction of everything

within a space three metres by three metres by three metres. Twenty-seven cubic metres, OK? Volume of your bedroom, near enough. Divide by three, equals nine. Nine kilos of explosive needed.'

'Is that,' I said slowly, 'why reports of terrorist attacks are often so definite about the weight of the bomb used?'

'Absolutely. The area cleared directly relates to the size of the ... er ... bomb. If you can analyse the type of explosive and measure the area affected, you can tell how much explosive was needed.'

Superintendent Yale was nodding as if he knew all that.

'But you don't think this bomb went off in my bedroom,' I said.

'No, I don't. Nine kilos of ammonium nitrate in your bedroom would have annihilated it and made a nasty hole all round, but I wouldn't have thought it would bring half a house down. So if we locate the device in that foot-of-the-bed box, we are looking at something in the region of ...' he did some more calculations ' ... say at least seventy-five cubic metres for your father's bedroom ... that's twenty-five kilos of explosive.'

'That's heavy,' I said blankly.

'Yes. A large suitcaseful. But then you'd need a suitcaseful also if you were using cordite. For demolishing this whole house, you'd have needed four times that amount, placed in about four places on the ground floor right against the thickest walls. People often think a small amount of explosive will do a tremendous lot of damage, but it doesn't.'

'What sets it off, then?' I asked.

'Ah.' He smiled the professional smile that wasn't about to give away its secrets. 'Let's just say fulminate of mercury, plus, I should say, an electrical circuit.'

'Please do explain,' I said.

He hesitated, then shrugged. 'ANFO won't explode on its own, it's very stable.'

'What's ANFO?' I interrupted.

'Ammonium nitrate fuel oil. The first letters. ANFO for short.'

'Oh yes. Sorry.'

'So you stick into it a package of something that explodes fast: the detonator, in fact. Then you arrange to heat the detonating substance, either with a burning fuse, or by an electrical circuit which can be achieved by ordinary batteries. The heat sets off the detonator, the detonator detonates the ANFO. And bingo . . .'

'Bang, you're dead.'

'Quite right.'

'At four-thirty in the morning,' I said, 'it would probably be a time-bomb, wouldn't it?'

Mr Smith nodded happily. 'That's what we're looking for. If it was an alarm clock, for instance, we'll probably find the pieces. We usually do if we look hard enough. They don't vaporize in the explosion, they scatter.'

CHAPTER THIRTEEN

I drove unhurriedly to Epsom but as soon as I let myself into my flat, I knew I wouldn't stay there. It was too negative, too empty, too boring. I wouldn't live there much longer, I thought.

There were a few letters, a few bills, a few messages on the answering machine, but nothing of great interest. If I'd been blown up at Quantum along with Malcolm, it wouldn't have made any vital difference to anybody, and I didn't like that thought very much.

I went into the bedroom to see what I'd got left in the way of clothes and came to the white lace negligée. Well, maybe *she* would have been sorry for a while. I wished I could phone her, but it was forbidden: her husband would answer as he had once before when I'd tried, and too many 'sorry, I've got the wrong number' messages would raise the suspicions of the dimmest of men, which he reputedly wasn't.

Apart from her, I thought, making a mental inventory, I mostly knew a lot of racing people on the borderline between acquaintance and friend. Enough to be asked to parties, enough for contentment at work. I knew I wasn't in general unpopular. It was enough, I guessed. Or it had seemed enough, up to now.

I had enjoyed being with Malcolm more than I'd realized. I missed him already, and in the twelve days I'd spent with him, I'd developed a taste for spontaneity which made sitting around in my flat impossible. I packed a pair of breeches and a sweater, added some limp old shirts to the new ones in the Simpson's suitcase, closed up the flat and went down to the car park.

My own car stood there, but I took the hired one again, meaning to turn it in some time and return for my own by train. First stop was at the bank to drop through the letter box an envelope containing Malcolm's cheque, with a paying-in slip to lodge it in my account. After that, I set off again in the overall direction of Quantum, but without really knowing where I was going.

I felt an awful aversion to the task of searching the psyches of the family, but I ended up in a place from where visiting them all would be easy, taking by impulse a turn onto the road to the village of Cookham and booking a room there in an old inn friendly with dark oak beams and log fires.

Norman West was out. I phoned him on the hour at four and five and reached him at six. He said apologetically that he had stopped working on the Pembroke case, there was nothing else he could do. He was sorry he hadn't been able to solve the ... er ... problem, and should he send his account to Mr Pembroke at the Savoy, or at Quantum House?

'Neither,' I said. 'We'd like you to carry on working.' And I told him what had happened to Quantum and very nearly to ourselves.

'Dear me,' he said.

I laughed internally, but I supposed 'dear me' was as apt a comment as any.

'So would you mind traipsing all the way round again to ask what everyone was doing the day before yesterday between three p.m. and midnight?'

He was silent for an appreciable interval. Then, he said, 'I don't know that it would be useful, you know. Your family were unhelpful before. They would be doubly unhelpful again. Surely this time the police will make exhaustive enquiries? I think I must leave it to them.'

I was more dismayed than I expected. 'Please do reconsider,' I said. 'If the police go asking the family their movements, and then you do also, I agree they won't like it. But if after that I too go and ask, they may be upset enough or angry enough to let out things that could tell us . . . one way or another.' I paused. 'I suppose I'm not making much sense.'

'Do you remember what you said to me about stepping on a rattlesnake?' he said.

'Well, yes.'

'You're proposing to stir up one with a stick.'

'We absolutely have to know who the rattlesnake is.'

I heard him sigh and could feel his disinclination.

'Look,' I said, 'could you just meet me somewhere? You gave my father and me summaries of what all the family were doing on those two days we asked about, but there must be much more you could tell me. If you don't want to visit them again, could you just . . . help me?'

'I don't mind doing that,' he said. 'When?'

'Tonight? Tomorrow?'

Tonight he was already working. Tomorrow he was taking his wife to visit their grandchildren all day as it was Sunday, but his evening would be free. He knew the pub I was staying in, he would come there, he said; he would meet me in the bar at seven.

I thanked him for that anyway, and next telephoned two stables along on the Downs to ask the trainers if I could ride exercise on their horses for several mornings, if it would be useful to them. The first said no, the second said yes, he was a couple of lads short and he'd be glad of the free help. Start Monday, first lot, pull out at seven-thirty, could I be there by seven-fifteen?

'Yes,' I said appreciatively.

'Stay to breakfast.'

Sanity lay in racing stables, I thought, thanking him. Their brand of insanity was my sort of health. I couldn't stay away for long. I felt unfit, not riding.

I spent the evening in the bar in the pub, mostly listening to a lonely man who felt guilty because his wife was in hospital having her guts rearranged. I never did discover the reason for the guilt but while he grew slowly drunk, I learned a lot about their financial troubles and about his anxieties over her illness. Not a riotously amusing evening for me, though he said he felt better himself from being able to tell a perfect stranger all the things he'd been bottling up. Was there anyone at all, I wondered, going to bed, who went through life feeling happy?

I dawdled Sunday away pleasurably enough, and Norman West, true to his word, appeared at seven.

His age was again very apparent from the grey-white hair downwards, and when I remarked that he looked tired, he said he'd been up most of the previous night but not to worry, he was used to it. Had he been to see his grandchildren? Yes, he had: lively bunch. He accepted a double scotch with water and, under its reviving influence, opened the large envelope he was carrying and pulled out some papers.

'Your photographs of the family are in here,' he said, patting the envelope, 'and I've also brought these copies of all my notes.' He laid the notes on the small table between us. 'You can have them to keep. The originals are in my files. Funny thing,' he smiled fleetingly, 'I used to think that one day I'd write a book about all my cases, but there they are, all those years of work, sitting in their files, and there they'll stay.'

'Why don't you write it?' I asked.

'I'm better at following people.'

I reflected that following people was what he'd been

good at when Joyce had first employed him, and that probably we'd expected too much of him, setting him to unravel attempted murders.

He said, 'You'll find there's a definite pattern about the movements of your family, and at the same time an absence of pattern. The murder of Mrs Moira and the gassing of Mr Pembroke both took place at about five in the evening, and at five almost all your family are habitually on the move. Mind you, so is most of the working population. It's a time of day when it's easy to lose an hour or so without anyone noticing. Traffic jams, left work late, stopped for a drink, watched television in shop windows . . . I've heard all those from erring husbands. The list is limitless of things people think up as excuses for getting home late. With a family like yours, where practically no one has a set time for leaving a place of work, it's even easier. That's why it's been almost hopeless establishing alibis, and I'm pretty sure the police found the same thing over Mrs Moira. When there's no expectation of anyone arriving at a regular time, no one looks at the clock.'

'I do understand,' I said thoughtfully.

'Newmarket was a bit different,' he said, 'because it meant someone being away from their normal environment for a whole day, assuming that Mr Pembroke was followed from his hotel when he left at lunchtime for Newmarket. And one has to assume that a follower would be in position much earlier than that, because he wouldn't know when Mr Pembroke would leave, or where he would go.' He cleared his throat and sipped his whisky. 'I thought it would be simple in those circumstances to discover which family member had been away all of that Tuesday, but in fact it wasn't, as you'll read. Now, if the explosive device was planted in Quantum House between four when the gardener usually left and six, when you might have returned from the races, we're back to the ... er ...'

'Five o'clock shadow,' I said.

He looked mildly shocked. It wasn't a laughing matter. 'I've no doubt the same pattern will be found,' he said. 'No one will be able, or willing, to say exactly where they were or where anyone else was during that period.'

'We may be lucky,' I said.

He said maybe, and looked unconvinced.

'Couldn't you please tell me,' I said, 'which Mrs Pembroke got you to find Malcolm? I know all about your ethics, but after this bomb ... can't you? Whose name was on the cheque?'

He considered, staring at his drink as if to find wisdom in the depths. He sighed heavily, and shrugged.

'I didn't get paid,' he said. 'The cheque never came. I'm not sure, but I think ... I think it was the voice of Mrs Alicia Pembroke.' He shook his head. 'I asked her if it was her, when I interviewed her. She said it wasn't but I think she was lying. But two other people found out on their own account, don't forget, by doing exactly as I did, telephoning around.'

'I won't forget.'

He looked at me sombrely. 'I hope Mr Pembroke can't be found as easily at this moment.'

'I don't think so,' I said.

'Can I give you some advice?'

'Please do.'

'Carry a weapon with you.'

'Mr West!'

'Even if it's only a pot of pepper,' he said, 'or a can of spray paint. There's a good deal of enmity towards you in your family because of your favoured status with Mr Pembroke. You were supposed to die with him in the house, I should imagine. So don't go unprepared.'

I swallowed and thanked him. He nodded and prosaically produced a smaller envelope from an inner pocket, which contained his account. I wrote him his cheque. He took it, inspected it, and put it away.

He rose wearily to his feet and shook my hand. 'Any time you want to,' he said, 'phone me. I don't mind talking, if it will help.'

I thanked him again and he went greyly away, leaving me on my own with his notes and a feeling of nakedness.

I began reading the notes. It so happened that he had reversed his original working order, or perhaps the order had become reversed during the copying: in any event, the eldest-to-youngest progression had been transposed, and it was Serena's notes which came first.

Norman West had written all his notes in longhand

with aides-mémoire to himself, and I could almost hear his radio-announcer voice in my head as I read.

Miss Serena Pembroke (26) unmarried, lives at 14 Mossborough Court, Bracknell, a block of flats just off the Easthampstead Road, turn left by the pub. Flats built during Bracknell's new-town expansion, middle-income, business people tenants, keep themselves to themselves. Pretty girl, one of the neighbours said (No. 12) but don't know her name. Miss S. has lived there three months. One bedroom, one sitting room, kit, bath, all small.

Miss S. works at Deanna's Dance and Aerobics Studio, High Street, Bracknell, teaching aerobics. Private business, sloppily run (my opinion), owned by Mrs Deanna Richmond (45?) whose mind is on a younger gent with a hairy chest, gold chain showing, rubbish.

Miss S. works mornings Monday to Friday 8.00 to 1.30 pm, taking classes, first office workers, then housewives. Miss S. and another girl (Sammy Higgs) work in rotation, half hour on, half off. Miss S.'s times are 8–8.30, 9–9.30, 10–10.30, 11–11.30, 12–12.30, 1–1.30 most days.

Miss S. and Sammy H. are both good workers. The clients I spoke to said classes v. good. Continuous, therefore popular. A girl can drop in on way to office, on way home after taking children to school, etc. Sign in, pay on way out. Clients come from all over – large clientele.

Evening classes, Monday to Friday, 7 pm–8.30 only. Miss S. does these alone. (S. Higgs does afternoons 1.30–4 pm.) Evenings quite social – rests for clients' drinks etc. Well attended.

Miss S. has bad menstrual cramps every month. Can't dance or exercise. Always two days off. The Tuesday of Newmarket Sales was one of these days – the second. Miss S. called in Monday morning in pain, didn't work, no one expected her Tuesday, she returned Wednesday. Mrs Deanna Richmond's daughter stands in on these occasions and also if either girl especially asks for time off otherwise. No records kept of these times.

Miss S. leads sober, hard-working, regulated life.

Likes pretty clothes, a bit immature (my opinion), has few friends. Goes to her brother's house (Mr Ferdinand) a good deal at weekends, or to her mother's (Mrs Alicia).

No ascertainable love life.

Miss S. likes shopping and window-shopping. On the Friday of attack on Mr Pembroke she says she bought food and frilly white blouse at Marks and Spencers, she thinks. (Not sure of the day.) She buys something to wear about four times a week probably – tights, leotards, sweaters, etc. 'Has to look nice for her clients.'

Miss S. owns two-year-old grey/silver Ford Escort,

but usually jogs one mile to work to warm up. Drives only if cold or wet. Car clean from automatic car wash: Miss S. goes through same car wash approx every two weeks. Car wash people corroborate, but can't remember exact dates.

Miss S. says Mr Ian must have killed Mrs Moira because she (Mrs Moira) took away both Mr Pembroke and his (Mr Ian's) inheritance, and he hated her. She says Mr Ian must have tried to kill Mr Pembroke for the money. The police are fools not to arrest him, she says. I told her Mr Ian couldn't have killed Moira or attacked his father as he was seeing round a racehorse training stable forty miles away at both times, with thirty or more witnesses. I said he obviously hadn't been driving the car which nearly ran him down. She says he could have arranged it. In my opinion, Miss S. doesn't want to be convinced of Mr Ian's innocence. She wants the killer to be Mr Ian because she doesn't want to find any others in her family guilty. If it is Mr Ian, she can bear it, she says, because it would serve him right for being Daddy's pet. (Muddled thinking!)

End of enquiry.

The three pages of notes on Serena were held together with a paperclip. I shuffled Serena to the bottom of the pack and came to the next paperclip, holding notes on Debs and Ferdinand.

Norman West used grey paperclips, not silver. Most appropriate, I thought.

The first page read:

Mrs Deborah Pembroke (27) second wife of Mr Ferdinand, lives with him at Gables Cottage, Reading Road, Wokingham, Berkshire.

Mrs Deborah works as a photographic model chiefly for mail-order catalogues, and was engaged in London on the Tuesday of Newmarket Sales modelling a succession of swimsuits. There were two other models there, also a photographer and two assistants, also a dresser, a representative of the mail-order firm and a notetaker. The swimsuit session went on until 6 pm. Mrs D. was there until the end. Vouched for without possibility of doubt. Mrs Debs has no firm alibi for the previous Friday evening. She finished work early in London at 3.30 (corroborated by mail-order people) and drove home. No witness to arrival (Mr Ferdinand was out).

Owing to her Tuesday engagement Mrs Debs could not have been at Newmarket. Friday, inconclusive.

Mrs Debs drives her own car, a scarlet Lancia. When I inspected it, it was dusty overall, with no sign of contact with Mr Ian.

Mrs Debs appeared undisturbed in the main by my questions and gave the following answers. She says her husband is the only good one in the

Pembroke family, the only one with any sense of humour. She says he listens to his mother too much, but she'll change that in time. She says they'll be well off one day as long as Mr Ian doesn't queer their pitch. She said that she was happy enough and is in no hurry to have children. She objected to my asking about such a personal matter.

End of enquiry.

I turned over the page and on the next one found:

Mr Ferdinand Pembroke (32) married to Deborah (2nd wife), lives at Gables Cottage, Reading Road, Wokingham, Berks.

Mr Ferdinand is a statistician/actuary for the Merchant General Insurance Company, head office in Reading, Berks. He works about a third of the time at home, where he has a computer with a link to the one in the insurance company offices. Both he and his company like the arrangement which means he can do exacting work without constant interruption. In addition, his company arranged for him to go on an anti-fraud course, as they are pleased with his ability.

I visited his office and explained to his boss that Mr Pembroke senior wanted to prove his children couldn't have been implicated in attacking him. Mr Ferdinand's boss wanted to be helpful, but in the end couldn't satisfy me.

Mr F. was not in the office on Friday afternoon, nor on the following Tuesday. On the Friday he'd worked at home, on Tuesday he was on the course.

I checked with the course at the Bingham Business Institute, City of London. Mr F. signed in on the first day, Monday, but after that no stringent attendance records were kept. Mr F. couldn't suggest anyone on the course who knew him well enough to swear he was there on Tuesday. I asked if he had made notes on the lectures. He said he didn't take any: the Tuesday lectures were about statistical probabilities and how to calculate them; basic stuff which he knew about. I checked this on the course schedule. The Tuesday lectures were as he said.

Mr Ferdinand drives a cream/grey Audi. It was clean when I saw it. Mr F. says he washes it himself with a brush on a hose (he showed it to me) and he does it frequently. He says he likes things to be clean.

Although he was working at home on the Friday afternoon, he was not in when Mrs Debs arrived from London. He says he had finished the job he'd been working on and decided to drive over to Henley and feed the ducks on the Thames. He found it peaceful. He liked the fresh air. He often did it, had done all his life, he said. He didn't know Mrs Debs was finishing work as early as 3.30 that day, but he said that wouldn't have stopped him going out. They were independent people and not accountable to each other for every minute.

I stopped reading and lifted my head. It was true that Ferdinand had always been attracted to the ducks. I couldn't count the number of times we'd walked along the Henley towpath, scattering bread and listening to the rude laughter of the mallards. Malcolm was the one who took us, whenever Alicia started throwing plates. She squawked rather like the ducks, I'd thought, and had had enough sense not to say so.

I went on reading:

Mr Ferdinand is hard working and successful, going to be more so. (My opinion and his boss's.) He has planning ability and energy. He is physically like his father, stocky and strong. (I remember Mr Pembroke 28 years ago. He threatened to throw me over his car when he found out I'd been following him, and I believed he could do it. Mr Ferdinand is the same.)

Mr F. can be very funny and good company, but his moods change to black disconcertingly fast. He is casual with his wife, not possessive. He is protective of his sister Serena. He is attentive to his mother, Mrs Alicia. He seems to have ambivalent feelings about Mr Pembroke and Mr Ian; I gathered from his inconsistent attitude that he liked them both in the past but no longer trusts them. Mr F. is capable of hate, I think.

End of enquiry.

I put Debs and Ferdinand to the back of the pile but had no mental stamina left for the next section on Ursula and Gervase. I put all the notes into the envelope and ate some pub steak instead and decided I would see the family in the age-reversed order Norman West had handed me, taking the easy ones first. Where was the bravado that had led me to tell Malcolm at Cambridge that I would stay with him just because it was dangerous?

Where indeed.

Somewhere under the rubble of Quantum.

In the morning, I rode out on the windy Downs, grateful for the simplicity of horses and for the physical pleasure of using one's muscles in the way they were trained for. Vigour seemed to flow of its own accord in my arms and legs, and I thought that maybe it was the same for a pianist sitting down after a few days to play; there was no need to work out what to do with one's fingers, it was easy, it was embedded in one's brain, the music came without thought.

I thanked my host sincerely after breakfast and drove towards Quantum thinking of the telephone call I'd made to Malcolm the evening before. It had been nearly midnight for me: nearly six, early evening, for him.

He had arrived safely, he said, and Dave and Sally Cander were true blue cronies. Ramsey Osborn had flown down. The Canders were giving a party, starting in five minutes. He'd seen some good horses. He'd had some great new ideas for spending money (wicked chuckle). How were things in England?

He sounded satisfactorily carefree, having shed depression with the miles, and I said things were the same as when he left except that the house was wrapped up in tarpaulins. The state of the house troubled him for roughly ten seconds, and after that he said he and Ramsey might be leaving Lexington on Tuesday or Wednesday; he wasn't sure.

'Wherever you go,' I said, 'will you please give the Canders a telephone number where I can reach you?'

'I promise,' he said blithely. 'Hurry up with your passport, and come over.'

'Soon.'

'I've got used to you being with me. Keep looking round for you. Odd. Must be senile.'

'Yes, you sound it.'

He laughed. 'It's a different world here, and I like it.'

He said goodbye and disconnected, and I wondered how many horses he would have bought by the time I reached him.

Back at the pub in Cookham, I changed out of riding clothes and dutifully telephoned Superintendent Yale.

He had nothing to tell me, nor I to tell him: the call
was short.

'Where is your father?' he asked conversationally.

'Safe.'

He grunted. 'Phone me,' he said, and I said, 'Yes.'

With a heavy lack of enthusiasm I returned to the
car and pointed its nose towards Bracknell, parking in
one of the large featureless car parks and walking
through to the High Street.

The High Street, long before, had been the main
road through a minor country town; now it was a ped-
estrian backwater surrounded by the factories, offices
and convoluted ring roads of mushroom progress.
'Deanna's Dance and Aerobics Studio' looked like a
wide shop front flanked by a bright new shiny news-
agent on one side and on the other a photographic
shop whose window display seemed to consist chiefly
of postcard-sized yellow fluorescent labels with prices
on, mostly announcing '20% OFF'.

Deanna's studio consisted firstly of a reception area
with a staircase on one side leading upwards. A young
girl sitting behind the reception desk looked up and
brightened when I pushed open the glass entrance door
and stepped onto some thick grey carpet, but lost
interest when I asked for Serena, explaining I was her
brother.

'Back there,' she said. 'She's taking class at the
moment.'

Back there was through white-painted double doors.

I went through and found myself in a windowless but brightly lit and attractive area of small tables and chairs, where several women sat drinking from polystyrene cups. The air vibrated with the pulse of music being played somewhere else, and when I again asked for Serena and was directed onwards, I came to its source.

The studio itself ran deeply back to end in a wall of windows overlooking a small strip of garden. The floor was of polished wood, sprung somehow so that it almost bounced underfoot. The walls were white except for the long left-hand one, which was entirely of looking-glass. The music, warm and insistent, invited rhythmic response.

Serena herself danced with her back to the mirror. Facing her, in three spread-out rows, was a collection of clients, all female, bouncing in unison on springy ankles, arms and legs swinging in circles and kicks. On every face, concentration and sweat. 'Go for the burn,' Serena commanded, looking happy, and her class with an increase of already frenetic energy, presumably went.

'Great, ladies, that's great,' Serena said eventually, stopping jumping and switching off the music machine which stood in a corner near where I'd come in. She gave me an unfriendly glance but turned with radiance back to the customers. 'If any of you want to continue, Sammy will be here within a minute. Take a rest, ladies.'

A few of the bodies stayed. Most looked at the

clock on the wall and filed panting into a door marked 'changing rooms'.

Serena said, 'What do you want?'

'Talk.'

She looked colourful but discouraging. She wore a bright pink long-sleeved body stocking with white bouncing shoes, pink and white leg-warmers and a scarlet garment like a chopped off vest. 'I'll give you five minutes,' she said.

She was hardly out of breath. A girl who was apparently Sammy Higgs came in in electric blue and started taking charge, and Serena with bad grace led me back through the refreshment area and the entrance hall and up the stairs.

'There are no classes up here just now. Say what you've come for and then go.'

Upstairs, according to a notice on the wall, Deanna offered ballroom dancing tuition, also 'ballet and posture'. Serena stood with her hands on her skinny pink hips and waited.

'Malcolm wants me to find out who bombed Quantum,' I said.

She glowered at me. 'Well, I didn't.'

'Do you remember the day old Fred blew up the tree stump?'

'No,' she said. She didn't bother to think, hadn't tried to remember.

'Thomas gave you a ride on his shoulders out of the

field, and the blast of the explosion knocked old Fred over.'

'I don't know what you're talking about.'

'Why are you so hostile?'

'I'm not. Where's Daddy?'

'With friends,' I said. 'It saddens him that you're hostile.'

She said bitterly, 'That's a laugh. He's rejected all of us except you. And I'll bet you killed Moira.'

'He hasn't rejected you,' I said. 'And I didn't.'

'He kicked us all out. I loved him when I was little.' Tears appeared suddenly in her eyes and she shook them angrily away. 'He couldn't wait to get rid of me.'

'He tried to keep you, but Alicia wouldn't have it. She fought him in the courts for custody, and won.'

'He didn't want me,' she said fiercely. 'He only said so to spite Mummy, to make her suffer. I know all about it.'

'Alicia told you?'

'Of course she did. Daddy couldn't wait to get rid of us, to get rid of Mummy, to get married again, to ... to ... throw everything about us out of the house, to tear out all the pretty rooms ... blot us out.'

She was deeply passionate with the old feelings, still smouldering after twenty years. I remembered how upset I'd been when Alicia tore out my own mother's kitchen, how I'd felt betrayed and dispossessed. I had been six, as Serena had been, and I still remembered it clearly.

'Give him a chance,' I suggested.

'I did give him a chance. I offered to help him after Moira died and he still didn't want me. And look at the way he's behaving,' she said. 'Throwing money away. If he thinks I care a tuppenny damn about his stupid scholarships, he's a fool. You can toady up to him all you like, but I'm not going to. He can keep his damned money. I can manage without it.'

She looked hard-eyed and determinedly stubborn. The old man in all of us, I thought.

'You've had your five minutes,' she said. She side-stepped me in swift movements and made for the stairs. 'See you at the funeral.'

'Whose funeral?' I asked, following her.

'Anyone's,' she said darkly, and ran weightlessly down the stairs as if skimming were more normal than walking.

When I reached the entrance hall, she was vanishing through the white double doors. It was pointless to pursue her. I left Deanna's studio feeling I had achieved nothing, and with leaden spirits went back to the car and drove to Wokingham to call on Ferdinand.

I half-hoped he wouldn't be in, but he was. He came to the door frowning because I had interrupted him at his computer, and grudgingly let me in.

'We've nothing to say,' he said, but he sounded more resigned than forbidding; half-relaxed, as he'd been in my flat.

He led the way into the front room of the bungalow

he and Debs had bought on the road to Reading. The front room was his office, a perfectly natural arrangement to Ferdinand, since Malcolm's office had always been at home.

The rest of the bungalow, which I'd visited two or three times before, was furnished sparsely in accordance with Debs' and Ferdinand's joint dislike of dirt and clutter. One of the three bedrooms was completely empty, one held a single bed and a chest of drawers (for Serena's visits), and in the third, the couple's own, there was a mattress on a platform and a wall of cupboards and enclosed shelves that Ferdinand had put together himself. The sitting room held two chairs, a standard lamp, a lot of floor cushions and a television set. In the tidy kitchen, there was a table with four stools. All visible life was in the office, though even there, in direct contrast to Malcolm's comfortable shambles, a spartan order of neatness ruled.

Ferdinand's computer bore a screenful of graphics. He glanced at it and then looked with some impatience back to me.

'What do you want?' he asked. 'I've a lot to do after being away on a course.'

'Can't you save all that,' I gestured to the screen, 'or whatever it is you do? Record it, and come out to a pub for lunch.'

He shook his head and looked at his watch. Then, in indecision, said, 'I suppose I have to eat,' and fiddled about with the computer. 'All right. Half an hour, max.'

I drove us to the town centre and he pointed out a pub with a car park. The bar was full of business people similarly out for lunch breaks, and I bought scotch and sandwiches after a good deal of polite elbowing. Ferdinand had secured a table from which he was clearing the past customer's detritus with a finicky expression.

'Look,' I said, handing him his drink as we sat down, 'Malcolm wants me to find out who's trying to kill him.'

'It isn't me,' he said. He took a swallow, unconcerned.

'Do you remember old Fred blowing up the tree roots, that time? When we were about twelve or thirteen? When the blast blew old Fred flat?'

He stared. 'Yes, I do,' he said slowly, 'but that's years ago. It can't have anything to do with the house.'

'Why not?' I asked. 'That bang made a big impression on us. Memories last more or less for ever, they just need digging up. The explosives expert working at Quantum asked if I knew what cordite was, and I remembered old Fred.'

Ferdinand did his own digging. 'Black powder ... in a box.'

'Yes, it's still there in the tool shed. Still viable, but not used on the house. They're working now on its being a homemade explosive called ANFO.'

Ferdinand was visibly shaken and after a minute said, 'I suppose I hadn't considered ... what it was.'

'Do you know what ANFO is?' I asked.

He said no uncertainly, and I thought he wasn't being truthful. Perhaps he felt that knowing could be considered guilt. I needed to jolt him into being more positive. Into being an ally, if I could.

'Malcolm's made a new will,' I said.

'And left you the lot, I suppose,' he sneered bitterly.

'No,' I said. 'If he dies from normal causes, we all inherit equally.' I paused, and added an invention. 'If someone murders him, it all goes to charities. So how about you getting on the telephone and telling the whole tribe to help me find out who's trying to do them out of their future?'

CHAPTER FOURTEEN

In my room at Cookham in the evening, I read Norman West's notes on Gervase and Ursula.

Gervase first:

Mr Gervase Pembroke (35) lives with Mrs Ursula at 14 Grant St, Maidenhead, a detached house with a quarter-acre garden in good residential neighbourhood. They have been married for 11 years and have 2 daughters (8 and 6) both attending a private school.

Mr G. is a stockbroker who commutes to the City firm of Wells, Gibson & Cathcart. (Wells, Gibson and Cathcart have all died or retired long ago, but the respected name is kept.) Mr Gervase works for his own commission within the firm: each partner does. He has flexible working hours; he's his own boss to a great extent. He used to work harder than he does now but has become erratic of late, according to the firm's lady receptionist. She didn't like to say outright, but I gathered Mr G. sometimes returns from lunch the worse for drink, and sometimes doesn't return at all.

She didn't of course note down such times. She said she'd heard two of the other partners discussing Mr G., saying he'd lost his nerve and was selling his clients only gilts. They thought that too much playing safe was bad stockbroking. She had no qualms in denigrating Mr G., who she said has a filthy temper when things don't go his way, and never appreciates how hard she works (!)

I requested to interview Mr G. at his place of work. I was shown into his office and explained who I was. He said he knew. I said as a preliminary that I understood he was the illegitimate son of Mrs Alicia Pembroke, and the interview ended immediately. He physically hustled me out (bruise on left arm). He said I'd insulted him. Perhaps I did! I managed to say that if he could produce office records – letters written, brokerage transactions – for the Tuesday in question, he would be in the clear. He said to consult his secretary, which I did. Mr G. went into the office that morning, she confirmed, and dictated two letters. Mr G. told her he was going to see a new client, and left at 10.30 am. She didn't know who the client was, he was not listed on Mr G.'s office diary. It was more usual for new clients to come to the office, but not invariable. Mr G. didn't return to the office that day, but returned Wednesday in bad mood (with a hangover?).

Mr G. left the office the previous Friday (secretary's notes) at midday, didn't return. (Mr G. worked normally all day Monday.)

Mr G. commutes by train, leaves off-white Rover in station car park. His car clean and unmarked when I saw it.

Visited Mr G. at his home to ask about the client on Tuesday re solid alibi. Mr G. said none of my business. Guess: client was either a mistress or a bottle, or else Mr G. wants me to believe that.

Mr G.'s alcohol problem is serious (my opinion) but not incapacitating. He has strong masterful manner, but must have insecurities (illegitimacy??) to make him drink and treat people badly. (His secretary does not love him.) Mr G. appears to make good income, no sign of financial straits.

Attentive to Mrs Alicia. Bossy and possessive with his wife and children. Jealous of Mr Ian and (my judgement) fears him. (I don't know why this is. Something in the past? Mr Pembroke's preference?) Despises but also fears Mr Pembroke. (A lot of bluster when he talked of him.)

Mr G. is physically strong but getting less so, I'd think. Takes little exercise, somewhat overweight. Difficult personality. A bully.

End of enquiry.

I paperclipped Gervase together with a sigh. Norman West, for all his ineffective appearance, had a way of getting to the heart of things pretty smartly.

What had he made of Ursula, I wondered. Ursula, the quiet wife, who had talked in tears to Joyce. Pretty enough in an insipid way, she was like an unfinished painting, without highlights. Pleasant enough to me whenever Gervase allowed, she had never told me her thoughts. I turned with unexpected interest to the West view of Gervase's wife.

Mrs Ursula Pembroke (35) wife of Mr Gervase, lives with him at 14 Grant St, Maidenhead. She has no employment beyond looking after children and household. A cleaner comes in Monday to Friday mornings, 9 am to 1 pm, stays Tuesdays and Thursdays until 4 pm, also babysits whenever asked. (I had to make two visits to Mrs U. On the first occasion she had been crying and wouldn't talk. On the second she was cooperative.)

The daughters' school is at the other end of Maidenhead. Mrs U. shares the school run with a family nearby; Mrs U.'s mornings are Tuesday and Thursday; afternoons Mon., Wed. and Fri. Mrs U.'s car is a cream Austin. Clean.

On the Friday of the attack on Mr Pembroke, the daughters were invited to tea by the other school run family (the mother corroborates). Mrs U. left the daughters there after school (4 pm). Picked them up about 6.30.

On the following Tuesday, Mrs U. arranged for the cleaner to stay and give the daughters their tea as she wanted a day out in London. The cleaner told me Mrs U. did the school run, came back and changed, and drove away to the station to catch the train. She (Mrs U.) said she would be back late as she would go to the cinema after she'd done her shopping. Mrs U. has done this several times lately. She returned at 10 pm. Cleaner went home. (Mrs U. gave me permission to consult the cleaner.) Mrs U. says she didn't go to the cinema, she didn't like the look of the films, she just had dinner in a steak house. She also said she had been into a church to pray. She hadn't bought anything (nothing fitted).

Mrs U. nervous and evasive about trip to London. Did she go to Newmarket? Possible (my opinion) that she goes to London to meet someone, doesn't want cleaner or husband to know. Who? Lover? Not possible, she hasn't the air, they can't hide that inner excitement. Priest? Friend unacceptable to Mr G.? Doctor? Some sort of solace, I would say.

Mrs U. unhappy woman but wouldn't unbutton. Loyal. Any wife of Mr G. liable to be unhappy (my opinion). Mrs U. doesn't like having the cleaner around for so long. Mr G. insists on cleanliness. Mrs U. gets tired of the cleaner's incessant chatter. All adds to Mrs U.'s stress. Mrs U. would like a job or to do voluntary work. Mr G. won't have it. 'The children come first.' (Mrs U. obviously very fond of the children.)

Mrs U. wishes Mr Pembroke would give all the family a lot of money now so that they would stop griping about it. She sees nothing wrong in Mr Ian, but her husband won't let her talk to him. She could like Mr Pembroke, she thinks he's funny and generous, but her husband ditto. She can't go against her husband. She has no money of her own, I'd say. She's in a trap. (Can't support children herself, couldn't leave without them.)

Does she believe killing Mr Pembroke could solve her problems? Does she believe if Mr G. becomes richer it will make things right? I could tell her it won't.

End of enquiry.

Poor Mrs U. Poor Ursula. Could she have blown up Quantum? Perhaps, if she'd wanted to. She sounded desperate enough for anything, but if she had any sense, her desperation should drive her to beg from Malcolm, not to kill him.

I clipped Ursula behind Gervase: forever in his shadow.

I wondered why she'd married him, but then I'd attended their wedding also, and if one hadn't in the past been on the wrong end of his glowing cigarette, one could have taken him as he seemed on the surface, confident, good looking, positive and strong. A rising young stockbroker. A catch.

I put Gervase and Ursula back in the envelope but they wouldn't stay there, they stuck like burrs in my mind.

There must be thousands, hundreds of thousands of sad marriages like that, I thought, where the unhappiness came from inside. Probably one could more easily withstand disasters that came from without, survive wars, poverty, illness, grief. Much harder to find any good way forward when personality disintegrated. Each of them was disintegrating, Ursula because of Gervase, Gervase because of . . .

Because of Malcolm? Because of Malcolm's boredom with Vivien, his affair with Alicia, his quick marriage to Joyce? Because of illegitimacy? But Ferdinand had been a product of the same process, and Ferdinand was whole.

There were questions without answers. The most likely answers were often wrong. I didn't know why Gervase was disintegrating: I thought only that the process had already begun when we both lived at Quantum; had maybe begun in the womb.

I slept with troubled dreams and went to ride the next morning as if for therapy and release. Solace, Norman West's word, met the case. The raw morning, the moving horses, the filthy language and the crude jokes, a daily fix of the sort of reality I'd chosen at eighteen. I didn't know why I'd liked horses so much.

Choice sprang from deep needs, but where did the needs come from?

I wasn't accustomed to thinking in that way. I usually coasted along, not worrying much, doing my job, enjoying riding in races, making love without strings. Lazy in many respects, I dared say, but uncomplicated. An opt-out that had come to an abrupt end with meeting Malcolm at Newmarket.

It was Tuesday.

Ursula's cleaner, I thought, driving back to Cookham, would currently be chatting away with no respite for Ursula until the girls got back from school. I wondered if Ursula was quietly going bananas at 14 Grant St, Maidenhead. I changed into ordinary clothes and went along there to find out.

The cleaner came to the door; middle-aged, in a flowered overall, with an inquisitive face. Mrs Pembroke was lying down with a headache, she said, and yes, perhaps she could go upstairs and ask her if her brother-in-law might take her out to lunch. Perhaps I would like to wait in the hall.

I waited, and presently Ursula came downstairs looking wan and wearing a coat and gloves.

'Oh!' she said faintly when she saw me. 'I thought it was Ferdinand.'

I'd hoped she would. I said, 'Where would you best like to go?'

'Oh.' She was irresolute. She looked back up the stairs and saw the cleaner watching interestedly from the landing. If she didn't come out with me, she'd be stuck with explaining.

'Come on,' I said persuasively. 'The car's warm.'

It sounded a silly thing to say, but I suppose she listened to the intention, not the words. She continued across the hall and came with me out of the front door, closing it behind us.

'Gervase won't like this,' she said.

'Why should he know?'

'She'll find a way of telling him.' She gestured back to the house, to the cleaner. 'She likes to make trouble. It brightens up her life.'

'Why do you keep her?'

She shrugged. 'I hate housework. If I sack her, I'd have to do it. Gervase thinks she's thorough, and he pays her. He said he wouldn't pay anyone else.'

She spoke matter-of-factly, but I was startled by the picture of domestic tyranny. We got into the car and I drove out of the town and towards the village of Bray, and twice more on the way she said, 'Gervase won't like this.' We stopped at a small roadside restaurant and she chose homemade soup and moussaka, several times looking over her shoulder as if her husband would materialize and pounce.

I ordered a carafe of red wine. Not for her, she protested, but when it came she drank it almost absent-mindedly. She had removed the coat and gloves to reveal a well-worn grey skirt topped by a blue sweater with a cream shirt underneath. She wore a string of

313

pearls. Her dark hair was held back at one side by a tortoiseshell slide, and there was no lipstick on her pale mouth. The sort of appearance, I supposed, that Gervase demanded.

When the soup came, she said, 'Ferdinand phoned last night and told Gervase that Malcolm had made a new will, according to you.'

'Yes, he made one,' I agreed. 'He showed it to me.'

'Gervase didn't tell me,' she said. 'He phoned Alicia and told her, and I listened. That's what usually happens. He doesn't tell me things, he tells his mother.'

'How do you get on with Alicia?' I asked.

She very carefully drank the soup already in her spoon. She spoke as if picking her way through a minefield.

'My mother-in-law,' she said intensely, 'has caused more trouble than anyone since Eve. I can't talk about her. Drink your soup.'

I had the impression that if she once started talking about Alicia, she would never stop. I wondered how to start her, but when I tentatively asked what she meant about trouble, she shook her head vehemently.

'Not here,' she said.

I left it. She talked about her children, which she could do without strain, looking almost animated, which saw us through to the moussaka.

'What do you do on your trips to London?' I asked casually.

She looked amazed, then said, 'Oh yes, that

wretched Mr West. Gervase was furious with him. Then Gervase was annoyed with me also, and wanted to know where I'd been. I'd been wandering around, that's all.' She ate her moussaka methodically. 'Ferdinand told Gervase and Gervase told Alicia something about a tree stump. What was that all about?'

I explained about the cordite.

She nodded. 'Gervase told Alicia he'd had a good laugh when old Fred was knocked flat.'

She seemed undisturbed by the thought of explosives. We finished the lunch, I paid the bill, and we set off on the short road back to Maidenhead. A little way along there, I stopped the car in a lay-by and switched off the engine.

She didn't ask why we'd stopped. After a pause she said, 'Alicia is ruining our marriage, I suppose you know that?'

I murmured an assent.

'I'd known Gervase for only four months when we got married. I didn't realize . . . She's twisted him from birth, hasn't she? With her awful lies and spite. She sets him against you all the time. Gervase says terrible things about you sometimes . . . I mean, violent . . . I hate it. I try to tell him not to, but he doesn't listen to me, he listens to her. She says you sneer at him, you think you're much superior, because you're legitimate. I know you don't. Gervase believes her though. She tells him over and over that Malcolm threw them out and never loved them. She's wicked. And look what

315

she's done to Serena. Gervase says she was a bright girl, but Alicia wouldn't let her stay on at school, Alicia wanted her to be a little girl, not to grow up. And Serena hates all men, and it's Alicia's fault. The only men Serena will let touch her are Ferdinand and Gervase. It's such a waste. Alicia got rid of Ferdinand's first wife, did you know? Went on and on at her until she couldn't stand it and left. I don't know how Debs puts up with her. It's driving me insane, you know, her drip, drip, drip. She's the worst enemy you'll ever have. If it was you that had been murdered, she would have done it.'

'She wasn't always like that,' I said, as she paused. 'When she lived at Quantum, she treated me the same as Ferdinand and Gervase.'

'Then it must have started when Malcolm kept you there on your own, and as she's got older it's got worse. She's much worse now than she was when we got married, and she was bad enough then. She hated Coochie, you know, and Coochie was nice, wasn't she? I was sorry when Coochie died. But Coochie banned all the family from staying in the house except you, and I should think that's when Alicia turned against you. Or let it all out. I bet it was there inside all the time. Like Gervase keeps things in and lets them out violently . . . so does Serena, and Ferdinand too . . . they're all like that. I wish Alicia would die. I can understand people wanting to kill. I would like to kill Alicia.'

She stopped abruptly, the raw truth quivering in her voice.

'Drive me home,' she said. 'I shouldn't have said that.'

I didn't immediately restart the engine. I said, 'Is it Alicia that's causing Gervase to drink?'

'Oh!' Ursula gulped, the flow of anger ending, the misery flooding back. 'It's just . . . everything. I can see he's unhappy, but he won't let me help him, he won't talk to me, he just talks to *her*, and she makes it worse.'

I sighed and set off towards Grant Street. Alicia hadn't quite reached sixty: the worst of the witches could outlive them all.

'I shouldn't have told you all this,' Ursula said, when I stopped at the door. 'Gervase won't like it.'

'Gervase won't know what you've said.'

She fished a handkerchief out of her handbag and blew her nose.

'Thank you for the lunch. Did your mother tell you we've had lunch a few times in London, she and I? She gives me good advice. I can't tell Gervase, he'd be furious.'

I nodded. 'Joyce told me you were friends.'

'She's awfully catty about Alicia. It cheers me up no end.' She gave me a wan smile and got out of the car. She waved as she opened her front door: I waved back and drove away, and covered the few miles to Cookham.

I thought it might be interesting to see what Norman West had made of Alicia, and I searched through the notes until I came to her.

West had written:

Mrs Alicia Pembroke (59) refused to speak to me at all on my first visit and was ungracious and edgy on my second.

Mrs Alicia lives at 25 Lions Court, London Road, Windsor, a block of flats. She still maintains she can't remember what she was doing on the Friday or the Tuesday: she was pottering about, she says. 'One day is much like another.' I think she's being obstructive for the sake of it.

Mrs A. drives a big silver/grey Fiat. Clean, no damage.

Mrs A. antagonistic to me personally because of my following her in Mrs Joyce's divorce case, although in the end she benefited.

Twenty-eight years ago! She remembers every detail of that time. Can't remember last Tuesday . . .

I asked her if she had ever engaged me to work for her. She said no. (?)

Mrs A. has changed from the Miss A. I followed. Miss A. was full of giggles, very little-girl. Mrs A. still dresses very young, acts young, but is embittered. Odd how some women flower in love affairs and wither in marriage. Seen it often. Seems as if the spice of secrecy and naughtiness is what they love, not the man himself.

Mrs A. very bitter on subject of Mr Pembroke spending money. Mr Ian's name brought angry looks. Mrs A. turned me out.

End of enquiry.

Short and unsweet, I thought.

I couldn't face going to see Alicia at that moment. I didn't think her physically capable of carrying Malcolm while he was unconscious, and I didn't think her efficient enough to construct a bomb: good enough reasons for avoiding something I wanted to do as much as jump into a crocodile-infested swamp.

I didn't want to talk to Gervase either, but that couldn't be as easily avoided.

I drove back to Grant Street in the early evening and parked along the road from No 14 waiting for the master to return. It wasn't until I was sitting there that I remembered Norman West's advice about defence. Pepper... paint... I couldn't see myself throwing either in Gervase's eyes, or anyone else's for that matter. Gervase was, goddammit, my brother. Half-brother. Cain killed Abel. Abel hadn't had his pepper ready, or his paint.

Upon that sober reflection, Gervase came home.

His Rover turned into his house's short driveway and pulled up outside the garage. Gervase, carrying a briefcase, let himself in through the front door. Five minutes later, I walked along the road and rang the bell.

The door was opened by one of the children, who called over her shoulder, 'It's Ian.'

Gervase, still in his City suit, came immediately into the hall from his sitting room, looking inhospitable and carrying a cut-glass tumbler half filled with what I expected was scotch.

'Ferdinand phoned me,' he said authoritatively. 'It's the police's business to look into the bombing of Quantum, not yours.'

'Malcolm asked me to,' I said.

'You'd better come in, I suppose.' He was grudging, but pointed me to the room he'd left. 'Do you want a drink?'

'Yes, please.'

He poured from the scotch bottle into a duplicate tumbler, and handed me the glass, gesturing to the matching jug of water which stood on a silver tray. I diluted my drink and sipped it, and said, 'Thanks.'

He nodded, busy with his own.

There was no sign of Ursula, but I could hear the two girls' high voices in the kitchen and supposed she was with them. They would tell her I had come, and she would be worrying about her lunch.

'Ferdinand told me about Malcolm's new will,' Gervase said with annoyance. 'It's ridiculous putting in that clause about being murdered. What if some random mugger bumps him off? Do we all lose our inheritance?'

'Some random mugger is unlikely. A paid assassin might not be.'

Gervase stared. 'That's rubbish.'

'Who killed Moira?' I said. 'Who's tried three times to kill Malcolm?'

'How should I know?'

'I think you should put your mind to it.'

'No. It's for the police to do that.' He drank. 'Where is he now?'

'Staying with friends.'

'I offered him a bed here,' he said angrily, 'but I'm not good enough, I suppose.'

'He wanted to be away from the family,' I said neutrally.

'But he's with you.'

'No, not any more.'

He seemed to relax a little at the news. 'Did you quarrel again?' he said hopefully.

We were still standing in the centre of the room, as the offer of a drink hadn't extended to a chair also. There were fat chintz-covered armchairs in a stylized flower pattern on a mottled grey carpet, heavy red curtains and a brick fireplace with a newly-lit fire burning. I'd been in his house about as seldom as in Ferdinand's, and I'd never been upstairs.

'We haven't quarrelled,' I said. 'Do you remember when old Fred blew up the tree stump?'

He found no difficulty in the change of subject.

'Ferdinand said you'd asked that,' he said. 'Yes, of course I remember.'

'Did Fred show you how he set off the explosive?'

'No, he damn well didn't. You're not trying to make out that I blew up the house, are you?' His anger, always near the surface, stoked up a couple of notches.

'No,' I said calmly. 'I should have said, did Fred show you or anyone else how he set off the explosive.'

'I can only speak for myself,' he said distinctly, 'and the answer is no.'

Gervase was heavy and, I thought, getting heavier. His suit looked filled. I had never quite grown to his height. He was the tallest and biggest of all Malcolm's children and easily the most forceful. He looked a strong successful man, and he was cracking up for lack of a piece of paper that no one gave a damn about except himself.

Perhaps, I thought, there was something of that obsessiveness in us all. In some it was healthy, in others destructive, but the gene that had given Malcolm his Midas obsession with gold had been a dominant strain.

Gervase said, 'Will Malcolm ante up anything before he dies?'

His voice was as usual loud and domineering, but I looked at him speculatively over my glass. There had been an odd sub-note of desperation, as if it weren't just of academic interest to him, but essential. Norman West's notes recycled themselves: ' . . . lost his nerve and was selling only gilts. Too much playing safe was bad stockbroking...' Gervase, who had seemed comfortably fixed, might all of a sudden not be.

I answered the words of the question, not the implications. 'I did ask him to. He said he would think about it.'

'Bloody old fool,' Gervase said violently. 'He's playing bloody games with us. Chucking the stuff away just to spite us. Buying bloody *horses*. I could strangle him.' He stopped as if shocked at what he'd more or less shouted with conviction. 'Figure of speech,' he said, hard-eyed.

'I'll try again,' I said, ignoring it, 'but Vivien tried, and rubbed him up the wrong way so that he stuck his toes in. Malcolm's obstinate, the way we all are, and the more anyone tries to push him, the harder he'll resist.'

'It's you that got him to buy horses. He wouldn't have thought of it on his own.' He was glaring at me. 'Two million pounds for a bloody *colt*. Do you realize what two million pounds means? Have you any idea? *Two million pounds* for a four-legged nothing? He's raving mad. Two million pounds invested in any one of us would give us freedom from worry for the rest of our lives, and he goes and spends it on a *horse*. Retarded children are bad enough, half a million for retarded children ... but that's not enough for him, is it? Oh no. He buys that bloody horse Blue Clancy, and how many more millions did that cost him? How many?' He was insistent, belligerent, demanding, his chin thrust aggressively forward.

'He can afford it,' I said. 'I think he's very rich.'

'Think!' Gervase grew even angrier. 'How do you know he isn't flinging away every penny? I'll find a way of stopping him. He's *got* to be stopped.'

He suddenly stretched out his free hand and plucked my half-full glass from my grasp.

'Go on, get out of here,' he said. 'I've had enough.'

I didn't move. I said, 'Throwing me out won't solve any problems.'

'It'll make a bloody good start.' He put both glasses on the table and looked ready to put thought into action.

'When Malcolm fled to Cambridge,' I said, 'did Alicia tell you where he was?'

'What?' It stopped him momentarily. 'I don't know what you're talking about. Go on, get out.'

'Did you telephone to Malcolm's hotel in Cambridge?'

He hardly listened. He embarked on a heartfelt tirade. 'I'm fed up with your sneers and your airs and graces. You think you're better than me, you always have, and you're *not*. You've always weaselled into Malcolm's good books and set him against us and he's blind and stupid about you . . . and get out.' He stepped forward threateningly, one hand in a fist.

'But you still want me to plead your case,' I said, standing still.

His mouth opened but no words came out.

'Alicia tells you I sneer at you,' I said, 'but I don't. She tells you lies, you believe them. I've never set Malcolm against you. You hit me now, and I might think of it. If you want me to try to get him to cough up, you'll put that fist down and give me my scotch back, and I'll drink it and go.'

After a long staring pause, he turned his back on me. I took it as agreement to the terms and picked up one of the glasses, not sure whether it was mine or his.

It was his. The drink was much stronger, hardly any water in it at all. I put it down and picked up the other. He didn't turn round, didn't notice.

'Gervase,' I said dispassionately, 'try a psychiatrist.'

'Mind your own bloody business.'

I drank a mouthful of scotch but as a token only, and put the glass down again.

'Goodbye,' I said.

He still showed me his back, and was silent. I shrugged wryly and went out into the hall. Ursula and the two girls stood in the kitchen doorway looking anxious. I smiled at them lopsidedly and said to Ursula, 'We'll get through it somehow.'

'I hope so.' Forlorn hope, she was saying.

'I'll be back,' I said, not knowing if I meant it, but meaning anyway that anything I could do to help her or Gervase, I would do.

I let myself out of the front door quietly, and back

at Cookham telephoned to the Canders in Lexington. I talked to Mrs Cander; Sally.

Malcolm had gone to Stamford, Connecticut with Ramsey, she said. She thought they were fixing some kind of deal. She and Dave had really enjoyed Malcolm's visit and Malcolm had just loved the horse farms. Yes, of course she had Ramsey's phone number, he was an old friend. She read it out to me. I thanked her and she said sure thing and to have a nice day.

Ramsey and Malcolm were out. A woman who answered said to try at five-thirty. I tried at five-thirty Connecticut time and they were still out. The woman said Mr Osborn was a busy man and would I like to leave a message. I asked her to tell Mr Pembroke that his son Ian had phoned, but that there was no special news. She would do that, she said.

I went to bed and in the morning rode out on the Downs, and afterwards, from the house of the trainer whose horses I was riding, got through to Superintendent Yale's police station. He was there and came on the line.

'Where are you?'

'At the moment in a racing stable near Lambourn.'

'And your father?'

'I don't know.'

He made a disbelieving grunt. 'What time could you meet me at Quantum House?'

I looked at my watch. 'In riding clothes,' I said, 'in

326

forty-five minutes. If you want me to change, add on an hour.'

'Come as you are,' he said. 'Mr Smith says there's something to see.'

CHAPTER FIFTEEN

At Quantum, the heap of rubble had reduced to merely a mess.

I walked round to the back of the house and found two men in hard hats barely ankle deep as they methodically removed debris brick by brick from house to rubbish skip. The wind had abated and the clouds had relented to the extent that a pale sunshine washed the scene, making it to my eyes more of a wasteland than ever.

Superintendent Yale stood beside a trestle table that had been erected on the lawn, with the explosives expert Smith in his beige overalls and blue hat standing close beside him, heads bent in conference. There were no spectators any more on the far side of the rope across the lawn, not even Arthur Bellbrook. I walked over to the experts and said good morning.

'Good morning,' they said, looking up. 'Glad you came,' Smith said.

He stretched out a casual hand and picked up an object from the table, holding it out to me.

'We've found this,' he said. 'What do you think?'

I took the thing from him. It had been a coil of thin plastic-coated wire, but the coils had been stretched so that the wire was straighter, but still curled. It was about eighteen inches long. The plastic coating had been white, I thought. About an inch of bare wire stuck out of the plastic at each end. Onto the plastic, near one end, someone had bonded a hand from a clock. The hand pointed to the bare wire, so that the wire was an extension of the hand.

I looked at it with despair, though not with shock. I'd been fearing and hoping . . . trying not to believe it possible.

When I didn't ask what it was, Yale said with awakening suspicion, 'Does your silence mean that you know what it is?'

I looked up at the two men. They hadn't expected me to know, were surprised by my reaction, even astonished.

'Yes,' I said drearily. 'I do know. Did you find any other bits?'

Smith pointed to a spot on the table. I took a step sideways and stared down. There were some pieces of metal and plastic, but not those I'd expected. No cogwheels or springs. A grey plastic disc with a small hole in the centre.

'Was this a clock?' I said dubiously.

'A battery-driven clock,' Smith said. 'There's the coil from the electric motor.'

The coil was tiny, about a centimetre in diameter.

'How did you find it in all this rubbish?' I asked.

'We found various remains of the padded box which used to stand at the foot of Mr Pembroke's bed. These small pieces became embedded in the lid when the box blew apart. The wire with the clock's hand on it, and this . . .' he picked up the flat plastic disc ' . . . were in the same area.' He turned the plastic disc over to reveal a clock face on the other side. 'There should also be at least one other piece of wire somewhere, and some of the clock case and a battery or two, but we haven't found those yet. This was not actually an alarm clock, I don't think. We've found no sign of an alarm mechanism.'

'No, it won't have been an alarm clock,' I said.

The superintendent had been growing restive during Smith's account and could contain himself no longer.

'Will you please explain your familiarity with this device,' he said formidably. 'Did the gardener use this sort of thing for blowing up the tree trunk?'

'No, I don't think so. This device wasn't meant for setting off bombs. It was a toy.'

'What sort of toy?'

'Well . . . it was for switching things on. Torch bulbs, mostly. Like the lights we had on a station in a train set. A buzzer, sometimes. It was incredibly simple.'

'Explain,' Yale commanded.

I glanced at Smith. He was nodding resignedly.

'You get an old or cheap clock,' I said. 'We had

wind-up clocks, not a battery clock. You fix a length of wire to one of the hands, like this, so that a bare bit of wire sticks out and makes the hand much longer.'

'The hands are still on the clock, I take it?'

'Oh yes. Though sometimes we'd pull the minute hand off and just use the hour hand, because it's stronger, even though it's shorter. All you need is for the bare wire to reach out beyond the edge of the clock face. We used glue to stick the wire to the hand. Then you have a long bit of wire coming out from the centre of the front of the clock, and you fasten the free end of that to a battery. One of those nine-volt batteries with things like press-studs at the end.'

Smith was still nodding. Yale looked very much as if I shouldn't know such things.

'We made quite a lot of other gadgets,' I said, hearing the defensiveness in my voice. 'Buzzers for morse codes. Rudimentary telephones. Not just time switches. I made a lock once which could only be operated with a straight piece of wire.' And it still worked fine, although I wasn't going to show him.

Yale sighed. 'So in this case, we've got the wire fixed to the clock's hand at one end and to a battery at the other, right? Go on from there.'

'You need two more lengths of wire. One goes from the battery to whatever you want to activate. In our case, it was usually a torch bulb screwed into a metal holder. We fastened a bare end of wire to the metal holder. Then the third wire went back from

331

the metal holder to the clock. We fixed this wire with glue to the clock case itself, not to the hands, in such a way that the bare end of wire was pointing out forwards, towards you if you were facing the clock like this.' I demonstrated with the clock face. 'We usually stuck it on over the number twelve, at the top, but you could fix it anywhere you liked. Then you wind up the clock and set the hand with the wire where you want it, and just wait. The wired hand travels round towards the jutting out wire and eventually hits against it at right angles. The circuit is thus complete from the clock wires to the battery to the light and back to the clock, so the light goes on. The clock hand keeps on trying to go round and the jutting wire keeps stopping it, so the light stays on. Well . . .' I finished lamely, 'that's what happened when we made them.'

'Them?' Yale said with apprehension.

'They were easy to make. They were interesting. I don't know how many we had, but quite a few.'

'My God.'

'There might be one still in the playroom,' I said. 'The old train sets are there.'

Yale looked at me balefully. 'How many of your family saw these devices?' he asked.

'Everyone.'

'Who made them?'

'I did, Gervase did, and Ferdinand. Thomas did. I don't remember who else.'

'But your whole family knows how to make a simple time switch?'

'Yes, I should think so.'

'And why,' he said, 'haven't you mentioned this before?'

I sighed and twisted the wired clock hand round in my fingers. 'Because,' I said, 'for starters I didn't think of it until after I'd left here the other day. After we'd been digging out the black powder and so on, and I'd been looking back to the past. I didn't want you to find this. I wanted you to find something sophisticated, that no one in the family could have thought up.'

'Hm,' he said, seeming to accept it. 'How many people outside your family knew about these clocks?'

'Several did, I suppose, but it was such a long time ago. No one would remember, would they?'

'They might.' Yale turned to Smith. 'This toy, is this really what set off the bomb?'

Smith nodded. 'It sounds just right. Wire in a detonator where the Pembroke children had a torch bulb . . .' He spread his hands. 'It wouldn't need more current than that.'

Not surprisingly, they decided to take a look in the playroom. They picked their way cautiously across the ankle-twisting rubble and headed for the passage which was comparatively clear by this time. The playroom, when we reached it, was shadowy inside, with the windows boarded up. Light of sorts seeped in through the door, but it took a few minutes for eyes to acclimatize, during which Yale bumped into the bicycles, knocking them over. I helped him pick them up. He wanted to know whose they were, and I told him about Peter and Robin.

He made no especial comment but watched while I went over to the shelves and began peering into boxes. I hadn't been in the room at all since the twins had gone, and their own playthings had overlaid those outgrown and abandoned by their elder brothers and sisters so that most of what I was looking at was unfamiliar and seemed to belong to strangers. It took several minutes to locate the box I thought I wanted, and to pick it off the shelves and put it on the table.

Someone, Coochie I dared say, had packed the trains away for good after Gervase and Ferdinand had left and I'd been busy with school and horses. At one time, the tracks had run permanently round half the room, but Peter and Robin had been television-watchers more than the rest of us, and hadn't dragged them out again. I opened the box and found the old treasures undisturbed, looking more battered than I'd thought, with rust on the much-used wheels.

I lifted out a couple of engines and some coaches, then followed them with a tunnel, a signal box with green and red bulbs and a brown plastic railway station adorned with empty bulb-holders among the advertisement stickers. I suppose to any adult, his childhood's rediscovered toys look smaller, deader, less appealing than he remembers. The trains were dusty and sad, relics ready for the skip outside, melancholic. The little lights had long gone out.

I took everything out of the box, but there were no clocks.

'Sorry,' I said. 'They could be in anything, really. If they're here.'

Smith began looking into any box whose contents weren't easily identifiable by the picture on top. Yale, with a no-hope expression, followed suit. I packed the trains back into oblivion with regret.

'Well, just look here,' Smith said suddenly. 'Gold mine.'

He had produced from a jumble of Lego constructions a bright new-looking clock with a Mickey Mouse face in unfaded technicolour. Mickey's hands in fat white gloves were the hands of the clock. To the minute hand was fixed a coil of white plastic-covered wire. A second white coil was stuck to the scarlet clock casing, its bared end jutting out over noon. When Smith held it all up, the white coils stretched out and down like curling streamers.

I looked at it blankly.

'I've never seen that one before,' I said. 'We didn't make them decorative. Ours were . . .' I sought for the word ' . . . utilitarian.'

Smith picked away among the Lego. 'Can't find a battery,' he reported. 'Nor a torch bulb, for that matter.' A pause. 'Wait a minute . . .' He rattled around and, finally, triumphantly produced a red and white Lego tower with a bulb-holder lodged inside near the top.

'A lighthouse, wouldn't you say?' he asked, standing it upright. 'Neat.'

'Someone made this for your twin brothers,' Yale said. 'Are you sure you never saw it?'

I shook my head. 'I didn't live here then, only visited. The twins had a short attention span, anyway. They tired of new toys pretty quickly. Always wanted to get on with the next thing.'

'I'll find out who made it,' Yale said. 'Can you sort out a box to put it in? I'll give you a receipt, of course.'

Smith found him an empty Lego box and into it they packed the bright co-star of an act that had brought half the house down. There was room in the box for the lighthouse, so they took that, too. Yale solemnly wrote a receipt on a page of his notebook and gave it to me, and with him carrying the box we went out into the daylight, blinking as our eyes adjusted after the gloom.

As we walked back in the general direction of the trestle table, Smith said, 'We've put all the clothes we've found on a table in the garage. I'm afraid they're mostly torn and unwearable, but you might want to see. All the personal things we've salvaged are in a cardboard carton. Do you want to take those today, or wait until we're finished?'

'Look now, take later,' I said.

Smith half smiled. 'They're in that box under the table.'

I squatted down beside the brown cardboard carton and opened the top flaps. Inside there was quite a good collection of dusty bits and pieces, more than I would have imagined. I picked out one of Malcolm's precious brushes and ran my finger over the gold and silver chased backing. The dust came off and the metal shone in the sunlight. He would be pleased, I thought.

'We've found five of those,' Smith observed. 'Two are badly dented, the others look all right.'

'There were eight,' I said. 'In his dressing room.'

He shrugged. 'We might find more.'

I turned over a few things in the box. Mostly they were uninteresting, like a bottle of aspirins from the bathroom. At the bottom, I came across one or two things of my own – an empty spongebag and the tape recorder.

I lifted the recorder out, straightened up and put it on the table. Pressed the start button. Absence of results.

'It was just a chance you might want it,' Smith said philosophically. 'It doesn't work as it is, but you might want to get it mended.'

'Probably cheaper to buy a new one,' I said. I pressed the rewind and fast-forward buttons pointlessly, and then the eject button, which worked. The plastic lid staggered open, revealing a tape within. I had to think for a minute which tape it was and then remembered it was only the one from my answering machine; nothing interesting. I shut the lid and put the recorder back in the box under the table.

'If you find my camera, now that would be good news,' I said, straightening again.

Yale had lost interest and was preparing to leave.

'Was it yours?' said Mr Smith. 'It's in the skip, I'm afraid. Badly smashed.'

'Oh well . . .'

'Were you insured?'

I shook my head. 'Never thought of it.'

Smith made sympathetic gestures and went back to the rubble. The superintendent said I should telephone him the following morning without fail. He ran his thumb and finger down his moustache and asked me if I now knew who had bombed the house.

'No,' I said. 'I don't. Do you?'

He wouldn't say he didn't, but he didn't. He picked up the Lego box and marched off with it, and I went to look at the clothes in the garage.

Nothing was worth saving, I thought. All highly depressing. My jodhpur boots with the toes flattened, Malcolm's vicuna coats with triangular tears. I left it all as it lay and started out on a quick hike round the garden to make sure all was well with the gold, and came upon Arthur Bellbrook digging potatoes within six feet of it. My heart jumped a bit. His was undisturbed.

We exchanged good mornings and remarks about

the weather. He asked what he should do with the potatoes and I told him to take them home. He nodded his thanks. He complained that the pick-up trucks for the rubbish skips were ruining the lawn. He said souvenir hunters had stripped Mrs Pembroke's fancy greenhouse of every single geranium, including the cuttings, but not to worry, without glass in the windows they would have died in the first frost. It had been a mild autumn, but frost would come soon.

He looked along the length of the kitchen garden, his back towards the end wall. He would dig everything over, he said, ready for winter.

I left him bending again to his task, not sure whether he was a guardian of the gold or a threat to it. Malcolm had a nerve, I thought, hiding his stockpile in that place and seeing Arthur work close to it day after day. Malcolm had more nerve than was good for him.

I drove to the pub in Cookham, where they were getting used to my hours, took a bath, put on trousers, shirt and jersey and, accompanied by Norman West's notes, went down to the bar for a drink before lunch. I read:

Mr Thomas Pembroke (39) lives with his wife Berenice at 6 Arden Haciendas, Sonning, Nr. Reading, in the strip of new townhouses where old Arden House used to be. Two daughters (9 and 7) go to comprehensive school.

Mr T. used to work as quantity surveyor for

Reading firm of biscuit makers, Shutleworth Digby Ltd. He got sacked for wrong estimates several weeks ago. I was told unofficially at the firm that he'd cost them thousands by ordering six times the glacé cherries needed for a run of 'dotted pinks'. (Had to laugh!) No laughing matter when tons of sliced almonds turned up after 'nut fluffs' had been discontinued. Mr T. didn't contest sacking, just left. Firm very relieved. Mr T. had been getting more and more useless, but had long service.

Mr T. didn't tell his wife he'd lost his job, but went off as if to work every day. (Common reaction.) On Newmarket Sales Tuesday he was 'walking about', same as the previous Friday. Pressed, he says he probably went to the public library in Reading, he did that most days; also sat around wherever there were seats, doing nothing. He read the job-offer pages in newspapers, but apparently did little to find work. No heart. (My opinion.)

Mr T. on brink of nervous breakdown (my opinion). I interviewed him in coffee shop. His hands trembled half the time, rattling cup against teeth, and he's not yet forty. Alcohol? Don't think so. Nerves shot to hell.

Mr T. drives old grey Austin 1100. Has slight dent in front wing. Mr T. says it's been there weeks. Car dirty, could do with wash, Mr T. says he has no energy for things like that.

Mr T.'s opinion of Mr Ian is very muddled (like

the rest of him). Mr Ian is 'best of bunch, really', but also Mr T. says Mr Ian is Mr Pembroke's favourite and it isn't fair. (!)

End of enquiry.

With a sigh, I put Thomas to the back and read about Berenice; no happy tale.

Mrs Berenice Pembroke (44 according to Mrs Joyce), wife of Mr Thomas, lives at 6 Arden Haciendas. No job. Looks after daughters, spends her days doing housework and reading trashy romances (according to Mrs Joyce again!).

Mrs B. very hard to interview. First visit, nothing. Second visit, a little, not much. She couldn't produce alibi for either day.

I asked about children and school journeys. Mrs B. doesn't drive them, they go by bus. They walk alone along pavement in residential side road to and from bus stop, which is about one-third of mile away, on the main thoroughfare. Mrs B.'s mother lives actually on the bus route. The girls get off the bus there most afternoons and go to their grandmother's for tea.

Interviewed Mrs B.'s mother. Not helpful. Agreed girls go there most days. Sometimes (if cold, wet or dark) she drives them home at about 7 pm. Other days, they finish journey by bus. I asked why they go there for tea so often and stay so late. Told to mind my own business. Younger girl said Granny makes better teas, Mummy gets cross. Told to shut up by older girl. Mrs B.'s mother showed me out.

Mrs B. drives old white Morris Maxi, clean, no marks on it.

Mrs B. gave no opinion of Mr Ian when asked, but looked as if she could spit. Says Mr Pembroke is wicked. Mrs B. slammed her front door (she hadn't asked me in!).

End of enquiry.

I put Berenice, too, back in the packet, and cheered myself up just a fraction with a slice of pork pie and a game of darts.

From the outside, Arden Haciendas were dreadful: tiny houses of dark brown-red brick set at odd angles to each other, with dark-framed windows at odd heights and dark front doors leading from walled front gardens one could cross in one stride. Nevertheless, Arden Haciendas, as Joyce had informed me a year earlier when Thomas had moved there, were socially the in thing, as they had won a prize for the architect.

God help architecture, I thought, ringing the bell of No 6. I hadn't been to this house before: had associated Thomas and Berenice always with the rather ordinary bungalow they'd bought at the time of their wedding.

Berenice opened the door and tried to close it again

when she saw me, but I pushed from my side and put my shoe over the threshold, and finally, with ill grace, she stepped back.

'We don't want to see you,' she said. 'Dear Thomas isn't well. You've no right to shove your way in here. I hate you.'

'Well, hate or not, I want to talk to Thomas.'

She couldn't say he wasn't there, because I could see him. Inside, the Haciendas were open plan with rooms at odd angles to each other, which explained the odd-angled exteriors. The front door led into an angled off-shoot of the main room, which had no ceiling where one would expect it, but soared to the rafters. Windows one couldn't see out of let daylight in at random points in the walls. Horrible, I thought, but that was only, as Mr West would say, my opinion.

Thomas rose to his feet from one of the heavily-stuffed armchairs brought from the bungalow, old comfortable chairs looking incongruous in all the aggressive modernity. There was no carpet on the woodblock floor; Thomas's shoes squeaked on it when he moved.

'Come in, old chap,' he said.

'We don't want him,' Berenice objected.

Thomas was looking haggard and I was shocked. I hadn't seen him, I realized, for quite a long time. All youth had left him, and I thought of him as he had been at eighteen or nineteen, laughing and good-humoured, coming for weekends and making Serena giggle.

Twenty years on, he looked middle-aged, the head balder than when I'd last taken his photograph, the ginger moustache less well tended, the desperation all-pervading. Norman West's assessment of early breakdown seemed conservative. It looked to me as if it had already happened. Thomas was a lot further down the line to disintegration than Gervase.

Ferdinand, he confirmed in answer to my question, had told him about Malcolm's will and about Malcolm's wish that I should try to find out who wanted to kill him. Thomas couldn't help, he said.

I reminded him of the day old Fred blew up the tree stump. Ferdinand had mentioned that too, he said. Thomas had been there. He remembered it clearly. He had carried Serena on his shoulders, and Fred had been blown flat.

'And do you remember the time switches we used to make, with wire on the clocks' hands?'

He stared, his eyes gaunt. After a long pause, he said, 'Yes.'

'Thomas, after Gervase and Ferdinand left Quantum, did you or they make any more of them?'

Berenice interrupted, 'Dear Thomas couldn't make a time switch to save his life, could you, darling?' Her voice was pitying, sneering, unkind. Thomas sent her a haunted look but no protest.

'Someone gave Robin and Peter a Mickey Mouse clock with white plastic-covered wires stuck on it,' I said. 'Very bright and attractive.'

Thomas shook his head helplessly.

'In the rubble at Quantum, they've found a clock hand stuck onto some white plastic-covered wire.'

'Oh, my God,' Thomas said miserably.

'So what?' Berenice demanded. 'Dear Thomas does overact so.'

'So,' I said, 'someone who knew how to make these time switches blew up Quantum.'

'What of it?' she said. 'I can't see Thomas doing it. Not enough nerve, have you, darling?'

Thomas said to me, 'Have a drink?'

Berenice looked disconcerted. Asking me to have a drink had been for Thomas an act of rebellion against her wishes. There hadn't been many of them, I guessed. I accepted with thanks, although it was barely five-thirty and to my mind too early. I'd chosen the hour on purpose, hoping both that Thomas would have returned from his day's wanderings and that the daughters would stop at their grandmother's house on their way home from school.

Thomas squeaked across the floor to the kitchen, which was divided from the main room only by a waist-high counter, and began opening cupboards. He produced three tumblers which he put clumsily on the counter, and then sought in the fridge interminably for mixers. Berenice watched him with her face screwed into an expression of long-suffering impatience and made no move to help.

'We have some gin somewhere,' he said vaguely,

having at last found the tonic. 'I don't know where Berenice puts things. She moves them about.'

'Dear Thomas couldn't find a book in a library.'

Thomas gave her a look of black enmity which she either didn't see or chose to ignore. He opened another cupboard, and another, and in his wife's continued unhelpful silence finally found a nearly full bottle of Gordon's gin. He came round into the main room and poured from the bottle into three glasses, topping up inadequately from a single bottle of tonic.

He handed me a glass. I didn't much care for gin, but it was no time to say so.

He held out the second glass to Berenice.

'I don't want any,' she said.

Thomas's hand was trembling. He made an awkward motion as if to raise the glass to his own lips, then put it down with a bang on the counter, and in an uncoordinated movement accidentally knocked the gin bottle over so that it fell to the floor, smashing into green shiny pieces, the liquid spreading in a pool.

Thomas bent down to pick up the bits. Berenice didn't help.

She said, 'Thomas can't get anything right, can you, darling?' The words were no worse than others, but the acid sarcasm in her voice had gone beyond scathing to unbearable.

Thomas straightened with a face filled with passionate hatred, the worm turning at last, and by the neck he held the top part of the green bottle, the broken edges jagged as teeth.

He came up fast with his hand rising. Berenice, cushioned in complacency, wasn't even looking at him and seemed not to begin to understand her danger.

Malcolm said I had fast reactions . . . I dropped my own drink, grasped Berenice by both arms and swung her violently round and out of the slicing track of the razor-sharp weapon. She was furiously indignant, protesting incredulously, sprawling across the floor where I'd almost thrown her, still unaware of what had been happening.

Thomas looked at the damage he'd done to me for a long blank second, then he dropped the fearsome bottle and turned to stumble off blindly towards his front door. I took two strides and caught him by the arm.

'Let me go . . .' He struggled, and I held on. 'Let me go . . . I can't do anything right . . . she's right.'

'She's bloody wrong.'

I was stronger than he. I practically dragged him across the room and flung him into one of the armchairs.

'I've cut you,' he said.

'Yes, well, never mind. You listen to me. You both listen to me. You're over the edge. You're going to have to face some straight facts.'

Berenice had finally realized how close she'd come to needing stitches. She looked with anger at the point of my left shoulder where jersey and shirt had been ripped away, where a couple of cuts were bleeding. She turned to Thomas with a bitterly accusing face and opened her mouth.

'Shut up,' I said roughly. 'If you're going to tell him he's incompetent, don't do it. If you're going to complain that he could have cut you instead, yes he could, he was trying to. Sit down and *shut up.*'

'Trying to?' She couldn't believe it. She sat down weakly, her hair awry, her body slack, eyes shocked.

'You goaded him too far. Don't you understand what you've been doing to him? Putting him down, picking him to pieces every time you open your mouth? You have now completely succeeded. He can't function any more.'

'Dear Thomas – ' she began.

'Don't say that. You don't mean it.'

She stared.

'If he were your dear Thomas,' I said, 'you would help him and encourage him, not sneer.'

'I'm not listening to this.'

'You just think what you stirred up in Thomas today, and if I were you, I'd be careful.' I turned to Thomas, 'And it's not all her fault. You've let her do it, let her carp all this time. You should have stopped her years ago. You should have walked out. You've been loyal to her beyond reason and she's driven you to want to kill her, because that's what I saw in your face.'

Thomas put a hand over his eyes.

'You were dead lucky you didn't connect with her mouth or her throat or whatever you were going for. There would have been no going back. You just think what would have happened, both of you. The consequences to yourselves, and to your girls. *Think!*' I paused. 'Well, it's beyond facing.'

'I didn't mean it,' Thomas mumbled.

'I'm afraid you did,' I said.

'He couldn't have done,' Berenice said.

'He did mean it,' I said to her. 'It takes quite a force to tear away so much woollen jersey. Your only hope is to believe to the depths of your soul that he put all his goaded infuriated strength behind that blow. I'll tell you, I was lucky too. I was moving away fast trying to avoid being cut, and it can have been only the points of the glass that reached my skin, but I'll remember the speed of them . . .' I broke off, not knowing how else to convince her. I didn't want to say, 'It bloody hurts,' but it did.

Thomas put his head in his hands.

'Come on,' I said to him, 'I'm taking you out of here. On your feet, brother.'

'Don't be ridiculous,' Berenice said.

'If I leave him here, will you cuddle him?'

The negative answer filled her whole face. She wouldn't have thought of it. She was aggrieved. It would have taken little time for her to stoke up the recriminations.

'When the firemen have gone,' I said, 'fires often start again from the heat in the embers.'

I went over to Thomas. 'Come on. There's still life ahead.'

Without looking up, he said in a dull sort of agony, 'You don't know . . . It's too late.'

I said 'No' without great conviction, and then the front door opened with a bang to let in the two girls.

'Hello,' they said noisily, bringing in swirls of outside air. 'Granny turned us out early. What's going on? What's all this glass on the floor? What's all the blood on your arm?'

'A bottle got broken,' I said, 'and I fell on it.'

The young one looked at the bowed head of her father, and in a voice that was a devastating mimic of her mother's, vibrating with venom and contempt, she said, 'I'll bet it was Dear Thomas who broke it.'

Berenice heard for herself what she'd been doing to her husband. Heard what she was implanting in her own children. The revelation seemed to overwhelm her, and she sought for excuses.

'If we had more money . . . If only Malcolm . . . It's not fair . . .'

But they had two cars, thanks to their trust fund, and a newly-built townhouse, and Thomas's unemployment had brought no immediate financial disaster: money wasn't their trouble, nor would it cure it.

'Why didn't you get a job?' I said. 'What did you

350

ever expect of Thomas? That he'd set the world alight?
He did the best he could.'

Quantum in me fuit . . .

'I wanted a son,' she said flatly. 'Thomas got a vasec-
tomy. He said two children were enough, we couldn't
afford any more. It wasn't fair. Malcolm should have
given us more money. *I always wanted a son.*'

Dear God, I thought: flat simple words at the
absolute heart of things, the suppurating disappointment that she had allowed to poison their lives. Just
like Gervase, I thought. So much unhappiness from
wanting the unobtainable, so much self-damage.

I could think of nothing to say. Nothing of help. It
was too late.

I went across to Thomas and touched him on the
shoulder. He stood up. He didn't look at his family, or
at me. I put my hand lightly under his elbow and
steered him to the front door, and in unbroken silence
we left the wasteland of his marriage.

CHAPTER SIXTEEN

I took Thomas to Lucy's house.

It seemed to me, as I drove away from the pretentious Haciendas, that Lucy's particular brand of peace might be just what Thomas needed. I couldn't take him to Vivien, who would demolish him further, and Joyce, who was fond of him, would be insufferably bracing. I frankly didn't want him with me in Cookham; and Donald, influenced by Berenice, tended to despise him.

Lucy was in, to my relief, and opened the front door of the farm cottage where she and Edwin led the simple life near Marlow.

She stared at us. At my red arm. At Thomas's hanging head.

'Sister, dear,' I said cheerfully. 'Two brothers needing succour come knocking at thy gate. Any chance of hot sweet tea? Loving looks? A sticking plaster?'

Edwin appeared behind her, looking peevish. 'What's going on?'

To Lucy, I said, 'We cracked a bottle of gin, and I fell on it.'

'Are you drunk?' she said.

'Not really.'

'You'd better come in.'

'Ferdinand has been on the telephone,' Edwin said without welcome, staring with distaste at my blood as we stepped over his threshold. 'He warned us you'd be turning up some time. You might have had the courtesy to let us know in advance.'

'Sorry,' I said dryly.

Lucy glanced swiftly at my face. 'This is trouble?'

'Just a spot.'

She took Thomas by the arm and led him out of the tiny entrance hall into her book-filled sitting room. Edwin's and Lucy's cottage consisted of two rooms downstairs, which had been partly knocked into one, with a modern bathroom tacked on at the back. The stairs, which were hidden behind a latched door, led up to three rooms where one had to inch round the beds, bending one's head so as not to knock it on the eaves. Laura Ashley wallpaper everywhere covered uneven old plaster, and rag rugs provided warmth underfoot. Lucy's books were stacked in columns on the floor along one wall in the sitting room, having overflowed the bookcases, and in the kitchen there were wooden bowls, pestles and mortar, dried herbs hanging.

Lucy's home was unselfconscious, not folksy. Lucy herself, large in dark trousers and thick handknitted

353

sweater, sat Thomas in an armchair and in a very short time thrust a mug of hot liquid into his unwilling hand.

'Drink it, Thomas,' I said. 'How about some gin in it?' I asked Lucy.

'It's in.'

I smiled at her.

'Do you want some yourself?' she said.

'Just with milk.' I followed her into the kitchen. 'Have you got any tissues I could put over this mess?'

She looked at my shoulder. 'Are tissues enough?'

'Aspirins?'

'I don't believe in them.'

'Ah.'

I drank the hot tea. Better than nothing. She had precious few tissues, when it came to the point, and far too small for the job. I said I would leave it and go along to the hospital later to get it cleaned up. She didn't argue.

She said, 'What's all this about?' and dipped into a half-empty packet of raisins and then offered me some, which I ate.

'Thomas has left Berenice. He's in need of a bed.'

'Not here,' she protested. 'Take him with you.'

'I will if you won't keep him, but he'd be better off here.'

She said her son, my nephew, was up in his bedroom doing his homework.

'Thomas won't disturb him,' I said.

She looked at me doubtfully. 'There's something you're not telling me.'

'The last straw,' I said, 'has just broken Thomas. If someone doesn't treat him kindly, he'll end up in the nut house or the suicide statistics and I am not, repeat not, joking.'

'Well . . .'

'That's my girl.'

'I'm not your girl,' she said tartly. 'Perhaps I'm Thomas's.' Her face softened slightly. 'All right, he can stay.'

She ate another handful of raisins and went back to the sitting room, and I again followed. Edwin had taken the second armchair. Lucy lowered her bulk onto a leather stool beside Thomas, which left me on my feet looking around. There were no other seats. Resignedly I sat on the floor and rested my back against a wall. Neither Lucy nor Edwin commented. Neither had invited me to sit.

'As I'm here,' I said, 'I may as well ask the questions I was going to come and ask tomorrow.'

'We don't want to answer,' Edwin said. 'And if you get blood on the wallpaper you can pay for redecorating.'

'The police will come,' I said, twisting slightly out of harm's way. 'Why not practise on me? They'll ask about the timing device that set off the bomb at Quantum.'

Thomas stirred. 'I made it, you know. The Mickey Mouse clock.'

It was the first time he'd spoken since we'd left his house. Lucy looked as if she thought him delirious, then raised her eyebrows and started to concentrate.

'Not that,' she said, troubled.

'Do you remember those clocks?' I asked.

'Of course I do. We've got one upstairs, that Thomas made for our son.'

'What sort of face has it got?'

'A sailing ship. Did the Mickey Mouse clock explode . . .?'

'No,' I said. 'The one actually used had a grey plastic dial with white numbers. The Mickey Mouse clock was intact, in the playroom.'

Thomas said dully, 'I haven't made one for years.'

'When did you make the Mickey Mouse for Robin and Peter?' I asked.

'I didn't make it for them. I made it a long time ago for Serena. She must have given it to them. It made her laugh, when I made it.'

'You were a nice boy, Thomas,' Lucy said. 'Funny and kind.'

Edwin said restlessly, 'I would have thought any timing device would have been blown to unrecognizable fragments by such a big bomb.'

'It seems they often find pieces,' I said.

'Do you mean,' he demanded, 'that they've actually sifted through all those tons of rubbish?'

'More or less. They know it was a battery clock. They found part of the motor.'

'It serves Malcolm right the house was blown up,' Edwin said with barely suppressed violence. 'Flinging money about on ridiculous scholarships. Keeping us poor. I suppose *you're* all right, aren't you?' There was a sneer there for me, openly. 'He's never been fair to Lucy. You've always been in the way, smarming him up, taking the lion's share. He gives you whatever you ask for while we have to struggle along on a pittance.'

'Is that the authentic voice of Vivien?' I asked.

'It's the truth!'

'No,' I said. 'It's what you have been told over and over again, but it's not the truth. Most people believe a lie if they're told it often enough. It's easy enough after all to believe a lie if you've heard it only once. Especially if you want to believe it.'

Lucy looked at me intently. 'You care about this, don't you?'

'About being cast perpetually as the family villain? Yes, I dare say I do. But I was thinking also of Thomas. He's been told ad infinitum that he's useless, and now he believes it. I'm going now, Lucy.' I stood up without haste. 'You tell Thomas over and over that he's a worth-while person, and maybe he'll begin to believe that instead. You have to believe in yourself to get anywhere.'

'Oh yes,' she said quietly. 'You do.'

'What you've written,' I said, 'is for ever.'

Her eyes widened. 'How do you know ... that I've lost ...'

'I guessed.' I bent and kissed her cheek, to her surprise. 'Are you seriously in need?'

'Financially?' She was startled. 'No worse than usual.'

'Of course we are,' Edwin said to her waspishly. 'You're earning almost nothing now and you still spend a fortune on books.'

Lucy looked only mildly embarrassed, as if she'd heard that often before.

'If I held the purse-strings,' Edwin complained, 'you'd use the public library, as I do.'

'Why don't you work, Edwin?' I asked.

'Lucy doesn't like bustle.' He seemed to think it explanation enough. 'We'd be perfectly happy if Malcolm trebled Lucy's trust fund, as he ought to. He has millions, we live in a hovel. It's not fair.'

'Doesn't Lucy despise money?' I asked. 'And people who have it? Do you want her to become what she despises?'

Edwin glared.

Lucy looked at me blandly. 'There's no such state as perfection,' she said.

I drove back to Reading, to the hospital that had an emergency room open all evening, and there got my shoulder and upper arm cleaned and stitched. There were three cuts, it seemed, variously deep but nothing frightful, and they had long stopped bleeding: with the stitches, they would heal almost instantly. The staff advised pain-killers pro tem. I thanked them and eventually drove to Cookham feeling more than slightly tired but chiefly hungry, and having remedied both conditions satisfactorily, set off again next morning to ride. There was no problem there with the stitches: they were tender to the touch and stiff when I lifted my arm, but that was all.

Restored yet again in spirit by the dose of fresh air, I took a lazy day off from the emotional battering of the family and went to London to get my American and Australian visas. It was only a week since I'd ridden Park Railings at Cheltenham and it felt like eternity. I bought a new sweater and had my hair cut and thought about Ursula 'wandering about' through days of escape. One could wander for hours in London, thinking one's thoughts.

On an impulse, I telephoned Joyce, not expecting her to be in.

'Darling,' she yelled. 'I'm going out. Bridge. Where are you?'

'In a phone box.'

'Where's your father?'

'I don't know.'

'Darling, you're *infuriating*. What did you ring for?'

'I suppose . . . just to hear your voice.'

It seemed to stump her entirely. 'Are you out of your head? You tell that old bugger . . . tell him . . .' She choked on it.

'That you're glad he's alive?' I suggested.

'Don't let the old sod get blown up.'

'No,' I said.

'Must rush, darling. Don't break your neck. 'Bye . . .'

''Bye now,' I said.

I wondered if she ever talked on the telephone except at the top of her voice. The decibels were comforting, somehow. At least she never sounded bored. I would rather infuriate her than bore her, I thought.

I went unhurriedly back to Cookham and in the evening bent again to Norman West's notes.

Of Edwin, he had said:

Mr Edwin Pembroke (53) née Bugg, lives with his wife Lucy in No 3 Wrothsay Farm Cottages, near Marlow. One son (15), attends state school, bicycles to school, has latchkey, gets his own tea, goes upstairs, does homework, working for exams, conscientious, doesn't know if his parents were around on the Friday or Tuesday at specified hours, doesn't expect so. He comes downstairs about 8 or 9 pm, they all eat vegetarian meal then. (No TV!) Mrs L. cooks in a wok. Mr E. washes up.

Mr E. does the housework (not much) and shopping, mostly vegetables. He spends hours reading in public library (librarians agree). Goes to pub, spends more hours over one beer (barman indignant). Takes laundry to laundromat. Listens to radio.

Spends hours doing crossword puzzles. (The garden's untidy. Mr E. doesn't like gardening. They grow only runner beans, they're easy.)

Mr E. and Mrs L. share an old Hillman, which Mr E. mostly drives. (Mrs L. has licence.) Car dusty and rusty, no dents.

Mr E. good-looking man, complete drone (my opinion). Idle life suits him. Mr E.'s idle life seems to suit Mrs L. also – no accounting for people. She does less than he does, come to think. Mr E. has sharp sarcastic manner on occasions. Detests Mr Ian, curses Mr Pembroke but at same time wants money from him (!). Definitely thinks of Mr Pembroke's money too much, broods on it, talked about it all the time.

End of enquiry.

Of Lucy, among other things, he had written:

Mrs L. spends large parts of the day unaware of what's going on around her (my opinion). I had to repeat several questions. It seemed she didn't hear me, but nothing wrong with her ears. She listens to things going on in her own head (can't put it very well). Has no alibis for Friday or Tuesday. Can't remember where she was. (I believe it.) Goes for rambling walks. Mrs L. very troubled over something, but wouldn't say what. She ate a tinful of peanuts while I was there, looked surprised when they'd gone.

So much for Lucy and Edwin, I thought. What about Donald and Helen?

Donald Pembroke (44) eldest of Mr Pembroke's offspring, lives at Marblehill House, detached chalet-style house which goes with his job, Secretary, Marblehill Golf Club (rich club, high fees) near Henley-on-Thames. Long waiting list for membership, rich members.

Mr D. has staff (green keeper, club steward, etc). He himself oversees and runs the whole place, is said to be good at it, members like him, say he gets things done, runs tight ship, decent bar, club rooms, tournaments etc, always listens to and deals with complaints, seen as friend, authority figure, social equal. Mr D. likes his work. His social standing extremely important to him (my opinion). Keeps up high appearances.

As to alibis for the Friday and Tuesday in question: no alibis ascertainable. Is always 'round the place', never at any place at set hours except first thing in the mornings (9 am) to see to post with office staff. Has Mondays off, works Saturdays and Sundays.

Walks to work (barely 100 yds). Usually returns home at 7 pm (much earlier in winter), sometimes stays until bar closes. Often walks round later to see all is well everywhere. Dedicated.

Mr D. has daughter in art school, high fees. Also twin sons who have started this term at Eton, previously at good prep. school. (How does he afford it?)

Mr D. drives silver Mercedes, 2 years old. Clean. No marks of collision with Mr Ian.

Mr D. thinks it's very bad news Mr Ian is back in Mr Pembroke's favour. Certain to mean less inheritance for him (Mr D.). He's angry about that. But he also thinks Mr Ian the only one who can persuade Mr Pembroke to distribute some wealth now. Sees no inconsistency in these beliefs. (He'll use Mr Ian, doesn't have to trust him, he said.) Thinks Mr Pembroke's recent expenditure unreasonable, 'insane' (!). Says he's senile.

Mr D. gave me rapid answers; busy. Says his financial affairs were none of my business, edgy on subject. Is he in debt? (My opinion, considering his expenses, probably.) Champagne lifestyle.

End of enquiry.

And Helen?

Mrs Helen Pembroke (43) wife of Mr D. Very good-looking lady. Very worried, wouldn't say what about.

I interviewed her in Marblehill House – big name

for fairly ordinary-sized three-bedroom, nice sitting room, though, over-looking golf course. Good furniture, appearance of wealth.

Mrs H. works at home (on dustsheet in dining room) painting views of Henley by hand onto plates, jugs, boxes; all china. Very quick, very good (to my eyes), nice pictures. They go off to be glazed, she said, then sell in local shops. Reasonably paid, she says. (What's reasonable? She says her work was to be seen as a hobby. Mr D. refers to it in that way.)

Mrs H. works alone nearly every day, no alibis for Friday or Tuesday. Sometimes drives into Henley to shop, no regular pattern. Mrs H. has white Cavalier, clean, no dents.

No children at home. Daughter shares flat with friends near art school (more expense).

Mrs H. ultra-loyal to Mr D. Says my enquiries unnecessary. Says it's ridiculous to suppose Mr D. would attack his father. Out of the question. (My opinion, she wasn't too sure.) They need more cash badly (my opinion).

Mrs H. mostly shares Mr D.'s opinion of Mr Ian, but doesn't seem to dislike him personally.

End of enquiry.

On Friday morning, I called in on a public library and looked up 'explosives' in encyclopaedias. Ammonium nitrate was there, also the proportion of fertilizer to diesel oil needed, also the formula for relating volume to kilos. The knowledge was available to anyone who sought it.

On Friday after lunch I went to the Marblehill Golf Club and found Donald in the clubroom placating a foursome who had arrived late and missed their game.

'Go over to the house,' he said when he saw me. 'I can't talk here.' He turned decisively back to the problem in hand and I did what I was told, like a good little brother.

Helen was resigned more than annoyed to see me. 'Ferdinand said you would come, and we had the police here yesterday. Not that we could tell them anything, or you either.'

She was wearing a painter's smock over jeans and looked dressed by Dior. She took me into the sitting room and pointed to a chair, and with unconscious grace sat herself half-on, half-off a polished table, raising her wrists to keep her paint-smudged hands away from the furniture.

Donald came bustling in, telling me he could give me ten minutes. 'Don't see what you can do,' he said. 'Leave it to the police.'

'What did they ask you?'

'About Fred blowing up the tree stump. I said yes, of course we'd been there. Helen and I weren't then married. It was the first time she'd met Malcolm, she was staying the weekend.'

'Saturday morning,' she said, nodding. 'The gardener came in specially to blow up the tree trunks. Not something one would forget, seeing him knocked flat. I took a photograph of the tree roots afterwards. It's still in one of our albums.'

'And the time switch clocks, do you remember those?' I asked.

'Naturally,' Donald said.

Helen added, 'Dear Thomas made two for our boys for their birthday once, when they could just tell the time.' She had said Dear Thomas, I noticed, as if she had meant it, not as Berenice said it. 'They got lost in one of our moves.'

'Where's Malcolm?' Donald asked brusquely.

'I don't know.'

'You're lying,' he said, but for once I wasn't. Malcolm and Ramsey Osborn had left the Osborn residence, according to the female voice on the line the evening before, and had given her no number at which they could be reached. I could try again tomorrow, she said. Mr Osborn should have let her know by then; he usually did.

'Did either of you,' I asked, 'trace Malcolm to Cambridge the weekend he was put in the car?'

I hadn't expected any answer but negative, but the question came at them unexpectedly and Helen practically jumped.

'Did you?' I said to her.

'No, of course not,' Donald said quickly. 'We had no

way of knowing he would go to Newmarket Sales, if that's what you're inferring.'

'The hotel at Cambridge said three people – two men and a woman – had asked if Malcolm was staying there,' I said. 'One was Norman West, who were the others? I'm not saying you went to Newmarket Sales, just did one of you trace Malcolm?'

They looked at me glumly. Then Helen said, 'I suppose so.'

'Why?' I asked.

Donald cleared his throat. 'I needed his signature on a guarantee.'

'Go on, what guarantee?'

'For a temporary bank loan.' He swallowed. 'I thought he might . . .'

'We had to have the money in a hurry,' Helen said. 'The bank manager told Donald we could borrow it if Malcolm would guarantee it. Then we couldn't get hold of Malcolm. We had to think where he might be, and he's always going to Cambridge. Donald and I just talked about it, guessing, wondering . . . And then, well, Donald went over to the club house and I just picked up the AA book and found those hotels in Cambridge, and without really believing in it I tried two . . . only two . . . and he was there, at the second. When Donald came home I told him and the extraordinary thing was, he'd had the same idea and got the same result.' She paused. 'We were pretty desperate, you see.'

'Don't say that,' Donald said. ' "Desperate" gives the wrong picture.'

'What did you need the money for?' I asked.

They looked at each other, foreheads wrinkled in worry. Finally, reluctantly, but as if coming to a decision, Donald said, 'We had some interest to pay unexpectedly. I had negotiated three months' deferment of interest on a loan, or at least I thought I had, and then I got a threatening demand. I had to pay at once or they'd start proceedings.' The desperation he said wasn't there, definitely had been; it still echoed in his voice. 'I couldn't have it getting around the golf club, could I?' he demanded. 'No one in the family could lend me a large sum in a hurry. Our ordinary bank overdraft is always at maximum. The finance company was inflexible. I knew Malcolm wouldn't *give* me the money, he has those stupid warped views, but I did think he might guarantee . . . just for a short while . . .'

To save the whole pack of cards collapsing, perhaps he might. Malcolm wasn't cruel. He'd lent Edwin money sometimes in the past. Donald, I thought, had stood a good chance.

'But when you'd found where he was, you didn't get in touch with him, did you?'

'No,' Donald said. 'I didn't relish telling Malcolm our troubles. I didn't want to look a fool, and Helen thought of a different way out.'

I looked at her enquiringly.

'Popped my baubles,' she said with a brave attempt

at lightness. 'Took them to London. All my lovely rocks.' She held her head high, refusing to cry.

'Pawned them?' I said.

'We'll get them back,' she said valiantly, trying to believe it.

'What day did you pop them?'

'Wednesday. Donald took the money in cash to the finance company, and that gives us a three-months' breather.'

Wednesday, I thought. The day after someone had failed to kill Malcolm at Newmarket.

'When did the finance company start threatening you?'

'The Thursday before,' Helen said. 'They gave us a week. They were utterly beastly, Donald said.'

'Vivien tried to get Malcolm to give us some money,' Donald said with resentment, 'and he flatly refused.'

'Well,' I said, half-smiling, 'she called him an evil, wicked, vindictive tyrant, and that's not the best way in the world to persuade Malcolm to be generous. If she'd used honey, she might have succeeded.'

Helen said, 'You're the only one he'll listen to. I don't care if you get millions more than us. All the others are furious about it, they don't believe it about equal shares in his will, but I don't care. If you could just . . . I mean . . .'

'I'll try,' I promised, 'but the equal shares are true.'

It fell on deaf ears. They believed what they believed, the whole lot of them, feeding and reinforcing their fears every time they consulted.

I left Donald and Helen among their antique furniture and behind their shaky façade and trundled along to Quantum to see how things were developing.

Not fast, was the answer. The place was abandoned except for a solitary uniformed policeman sitting in a police car outside what had been the front door. One could see right through the house now. The tarpaulin that had hung from the roof had come down. The policeman was the one who had accompanied me on my tour of peering in through the windows, and I gathered he was pleased to have a visitor to enliven a monotonous stint.

He picked up his car radio and spoke into it to the effect that Mr Ian Pembroke had come by. A request came back, which he relayed to me: would Mr Pembroke please drop in at the police station when he left? Mr Pembroke would.

The policeman and I walked round to the back of the house. Mr Smith had gone, also his helpers. The last of the rubble was away from the house and overflowing a skip. A flat black plastic sheet, the sort used for roofing hayricks, lay where a week ago the walls of my bedroom had come tumbling down. The interior doors had been sealed with plywood, like the windows, to deter looters, and the broken end of the staircase had been barred off. A house with its centre torn out; a thirty-foot yawn between surviving flanks.

'It looks terrible,' I said, and the policeman agreed.

Arthur Bellbrook was cleaning his spades, getting

ready to leave. I gave him a cheque for his wages for that week and the next, and added a chunk for the care of the dogs. He gave me dignified thanks. He hoped Mr Pembroke was all right, poor man, and I said I thought so.

'I had my picture in the paper,' he said. 'Did you see it?'

I said I was sorry I hadn't.

'Oh, well. I did.' He shrugged disappointedly and set off homewards, and I walked down to where he'd earlier been digging potatoes, and then further, to check that the nettles were still untrampled on the far side of the wall.

The green sea looked dusty and ageing but upright. They too, I supposed, would die with the frost.

The policeman was watching me incuriously. I stopped and stared at the house from a distance, giving the impression that that's why I had gone as far as I had, and then walked back and took my leave. The house from a distance looked just as bad, if not worse.

Superintendent Yale shook my hand. Things were almost friendly at the police station but they were no nearer discovering who had planted the bomb. Enquiries were proceeding, the superintendent said and perhaps I could help.

'Fire away,' I said.

'We interviewed the former gardener, Fred Perkins,' Yale said. 'We asked him about the tree stump and what he used to blow it up. Besides cordite, that is. What sort of a fuse.'

I was interested. 'What did he say? Does he remember?'

'He said he'd got the black powder and some detonators and some fuse cord from a quarryman friend of his. The black powder was in the box which we saw, the detonators were in a separate tin with the cord and the instructions.'

'The instructions!' I repeated incredulously.

'Yes.' He sighed. 'Fred Perkins says he followed the instructions because he'd never blown anything up before. He said he used a bit of extra black powder just to make sure.'

'It was quite an explosion.'

'Yes. We asked him what he'd done with the other detonators. He says Mr Pembroke took them away from him that morning, when he came running out of the house. We need to ask Mr Pembroke what he did with them, so . . . er . . . where is he?'

'I really don't know,' I said slowly, 'and that's the truth. I can probably find him, but it'll take a day or two.' I thought for a moment, then said, 'Surely he would have thrown away those detonators years ago.'

'If he had any sense he wouldn't have thrown them anywhere,' Yale said. 'Mr Smith says you handle detonators with extreme caution if you don't want to lose a finger or an eye. They can explode if you knock or drop them or make them too warm. Mr Pembroke's correct course would have been to turn them over to the police.'

'Maybe he did,' I said.

'We'd like to find out.'

'But would detonators still detonate after twenty years?' I asked.

'Mr Smith thinks it possible, perhaps likely. He wouldn't take any liberties, he said.'

'What does a detonator look like?' I asked.

He hesitated, but said, 'Mr Smith said we might be looking for a small aluminium tube about the thickness of a pencil or slightly less, about six centimetres long. He says that's what the army used. He used to be in the Royal Engineers. He says the tube contains fulminate of mercury, and the word "fulminate" means to flash like lightning.'

'He should know.'

'Fred Perkins can't clearly remember what his detonators looked like. He remembers he had to fasten the cord into the end of the tube with pliers. Crimp it in. Mr Smith says civilians who touch explosives should be certified.'

I reflected. 'Did Mr Smith find out exactly what the Quantum bomb was made of?'

'Yes. ANFO, as he thought. He said the whole thing was amateur in the extreme.'

'Amateurs,' I said dryly, 'run faster than anyone else.'

As an amateur, I went to Kempton Park the next day and on Young Higgins beat the hell out of a lot of professionals.

I didn't know what possessed me. It seemed that I rode on a different plane. I knew it was the horse who had to be fast enough; the jockey, however determined, couldn't do it on his own. Young Higgins seemed inspired and against more formidable opponents than at Sandown produced a totally different race.

There were no aunts riding this time, no lieutenant colonels falling off. No earl's son to chat to. No journalist to make it look easy. For some reason, George and Jo had entered Young Higgins in a high-class open three-mile steeplechase, and I was the only amateur in sight.

I'd ridden against an all-professional field of top jockeys a few times before, and it was usually a humbling experience. I had the basic skills and a good deal of touch. I could get horses settled and balanced. I liked speed, I liked the stretch of one's spirit: but there was always a point against top professionals at which that wasn't enough.

George and Jo were unfussed. Young Higgins was fitter than at Sandown, they thought, and at Kempton there was no hill to tire him. They were bright-eyed and enthusiastic, but not especially hopeful. 'We didn't want to change you for a professional,' they said in explanation. 'It wouldn't have been fair.'

Maybe not fair, but prudent, I thought. The top pros raced with sharper eyes, better tactics, more strength, quicker reactions. Theirs was an intenser determination, a fiercer concentration. Humour was for before and after, not during. Race-riding was their business, besides their pleasure, and some of them thought of amateur opponents as frivolous unfit nuisances who caused accidents and endangered lives.

Perhaps because of an arrogant desire to prove them wrong, perhaps because of the insights and realities I'd faced in a traumatic week, perhaps because of Young Higgins himself: I rode anyway with a new sharp revelationary perception of what was needed for winning, and the horse and I came home in front by four lengths to a fairly stunned silence from the people on the stands who'd backed everything else on the card but us.

George and Jo were vindicated and ecstatic. Young Higgins tossed his head at the modest plaudits. A newspaperman labelled the result as a fluke.

I'd cracked it, I thought. I'd graduated. That had been real professional riding. Satisfactory. But I was already thirty-three. I'd discovered far too late the difference between enjoyment and fire. I'd needed to know it at nineteen or twenty. I'd idled it away.

'This is no time,' Jo said laughing, 'to look sad.'

CHAPTER SEVENTEEN

I flew to New York two days later, still not knowing where to find Malcolm.

The voice at Stamford, Connecticut, always helpful but uninformed, had thought, the previous evening, that the gentlemen might have gone back to Kentucky: they'd been talking of buying a horse that they'd seen there a week earlier. Another horse, not the one they'd bought yesterday.

It was just as well, I thought, that Donald and Helen and Thomas and Berenice and Edwin and Lucy and Vivien and Joyce didn't know. That Gervase, Ursula, Alicia, Ferdinand, Debs and Serena hadn't heard. All fourteen of them would have fallen upon Malcolm and torn him apart.

I chose New York for the twin reasons that Stamford, Connecticut, was barely an hour and a half's drive away (information from the voice) and that everyone should see New York some time. My journeys before that had been only in Europe, to places like Paris,

Rome, Athens and Oslo. Beaches and race-meetings and temples. Horses and gods.

I was heading for a hotel on 54th Street, Manhattan, that the voice had recommended: she would tell Mr Pembroke I would be there, as soon as she knew where Mr Pembroke was. It seemed as good an arrangement as any.

Superintendent Yale didn't know I'd left England, nor did any of the family. I sighed with deep relief on the aeroplane and thought about the visits I'd made the day before to Alicia and Vivien. Neither had wanted to see me and both had been abrasive, Alicia in the morning, Vivien in the afternoon.

Alicia's flat outside Windsor was spacious and over-looked the Thames, neither of which pleasures seemed to please her. She did reluctantly let me in, but was unplacated by my admiration of her view.

She was, in fact, looking youthfully pretty in a white wool dress and silver beads. Her hair was pulled high in a velvet bow on the crown, and her neat figure spoke of luck or dieting. She had a visitor with her already when I called, a fortyish substantial-looking man introduced coquettishly as Paul, who behaved with unmistakable lordliness, the master in his domain. How long, I wondered, had this been going on?

'You might have said you were coming,' Alicia complained. 'Ferdinand said you would, some time. I told him to tell you not to.'

'It seemed best to see everyone,' I said neutrally.

'Then hurry up,' she said. 'We're going out to lunch.'

'Did Ferdinand tell you about Malcolm's new will?'

'He did, and I don't believe a word of it. You've always been Malcolm's wretched little pet. He should have sent you back to Joyce when I left. I told him to. But would he listen? No, he wouldn't.'

'That was twenty years ago,' I protested.

'And nothing's changed. He does what he likes. He's utterly selfish.'

Paul listened to the conversation without stirring and with scant apparent interest but he did, it seemed, have his influence. With an arch look at him, Alicia said, 'Paul says Gervase should force Malcolm to give him power of attorney.'

I couldn't offhand think of anything less likely to happen.

'Have you two known each other long?' I asked.

'No,' Alicia said, and the look she gave Paul was that of a flirt of sixteen.

I asked her if she remembered the tree stump. 'Of course. I was furious with Malcolm for letting Fred do anything so ridiculous. The boys might have been hurt.'

And did she remember the switches? How could she forget them, she said, they'd been all over the house. Not only that, Thomas had made another one for Serena some time later. It had sat in her room gathering dust. Those clocks had all been a pest.

'You were good to me in those old days,' I said.

She stared. There was almost a softening round her

eyes, but it was transitory. 'I had to be,' she said acidly. 'Malcolm insisted.'

'Weren't you ever happy?' I asked.

'Oh, yes.' Her mouth curled in a malicious smile. 'When Malcolm came to see me, when he was married to Joyce. Before that weaselly detective spoiled it.'

I asked her if she had engaged Norman West to find Malcolm in Cambridge.

She looked at me with wide empty eyes and said blandly, 'No, I didn't. Why would I want to? I didn't care where he was.'

'Almost everyone wanted to find him to stop him spending his money.'

'He's insane,' she said. 'Paranoid. He should hand control over to Gervase, and make sure that frightful Ursula isn't included. She's the wrong wife for Gervase, as I've frequently told him.'

'But you didn't ask Norman West to find Malcolm?'

'No, I didn't,' she said very sharply. 'Stop asking that stupid question.' She turned away from me restlessly. 'It's high time you went.'

I thought so too, on the whole. I speculated that perhaps the presence of Paul had inhibited her from saying directly to my face the poison she'd been spreading behind my back. They would dissect me when I'd gone. He nodded coolly to me as I left. No friend of mine, I thought.

If my visit to Alicia had been unfruitful, my call on Vivien was less so. Norman West's notes had been minimal: name, address, sorting magazines, no alibis. She wouldn't answer any of my questions either, or discuss any possibilities. She said several times that Malcolm was a fiend who was determined to destroy his children, and that I was the devil incarnate helping him. She hoped we would both rot in hell. (I thought devils and fiends might flourish there, actually.)

Meanwhile, I said, had she employed Norman West to find Malcolm in Cambridge? Certainly not. She wanted nothing to do with that terrible little man. If I didn't remove myself from her doorstep she would call in the police.

'It can't be much fun,' I said, 'living with so much hatred in your head.'

She was affronted. 'What do you mean?'

'No peace. All anger. Very exhausting. Bad for your health.'

'Go away,' she said, and I obliged her.

I drove back to Cookham and spent a good deal of the evening on the telephone, talking to Lucy about Thomas and to Ferdinand about Gervase. 'We are all our brothers' keepers,' Lucy said, and reported that Thomas was spending most of the time asleep. 'Retreating,' Lucy said.

Lucy had spoken to Berenice. 'Whatever did you say to her, Ian? She sounds quite different. Subdued.

Can't see it lasting long, can you? I told her Thomas was all right and she started blubbing.'

Lucy said she would keep Thomas for a while, but not for his natural span.

Ferdinand, when he heard my voice, said, 'Where the hell have you been? All I get is your answering machine. Did you find out who killed Moira?' There was anxiety, possibly, in his voice.

'I found out a few who didn't,' I said.

'That's not what I asked.'

'Well,' I said, 'like you with your computer, I've fed in a lot of data.'

'And the result?'

'The wheels are turning.'

'Computers don't have wheels. Come to think of it, though, I suppose they do. Anyway, you've left a whole trail of disasters behind you, haven't you? I hear Thomas has left Berenice, and as for Gervase, he wants your guts for taking Ursula out to lunch. Did you do that? Whatever for? You know how possessive he is. There's a hell of a row going on.'

'If you want to hang on to Debs,' I said, 'don't listen to Alicia.'

'What the hell's that got to do with Gervase and Ursula having a row?' he demanded.

'Everything.'

He was furious. 'You've always got it in for Alicia.'

'The other way round. She's a dedicated trouble-maker who's cost you one wife already.' He didn't immediately answer. I said, 'Gervase is knocking back a fortune in scotch.'

'What's that got to do with anything?'

'How do you cope so well with illegitimacy?'

'*What?*'

'Everything's linked. So long, pal. See you.' I put the receiver down with a sigh, and ate dinner, and packed.

In the morning, having paid a few bills, I took the hired car to Heathrow and turned it in there and, with a feeling of shackles dropping off, hopped into the air.

I spent four nights in New York before I found Malcolm; or before he found me, to be more precise.

In daily consultations, the Stamford voice assured me that I wasn't forgotten, that the message would one day get through. I had a vision of native bearers beating through jungles, but it wasn't like that, it transpired. Malcolm and Ramsey had simply been moving from horse farm to horse farm through deepest Kentucky, and it was from there he finally phoned at eight-ten in the morning.

'What are you doing in New York?' he demanded.

'Looking at skyscrapers,' I said.

'I thought we were meeting in California.'

'Well, we are,' I said. 'When?'

'What's today?'

'Friday.'

'Hang on.'

I heard him talking in the background, then he returned. 'We're just going out to see some horses breeze. Ramsey reserved the rooms from tomorrow through Saturday at the Beverly Wilshire, he says, but he and I are going to spend a few more days here now. You go to California tomorrow and I'll join you, say, on Wednesday.'

'Couldn't you please make it sooner? I do need to talk to you.'

'Did you find something out?' His voice suddenly changed gear, as if he'd remembered almost with shock the world of terrors he'd left behind.

'A few things.'

'Tell me.'

'Not on the telephone. Not in a hurry. Go and see the horses breeze and meet me tomorrow.' I paused. 'There are horses in California. Thousands of them.'

He was quiet for a few moments, then he said, 'I owe it to you. I'll be there,' and disconnected.

I arranged my air ticket and spent the rest of the day as I'd spent all the others in New York, wandering around, filling eyes and ears with the city . . . thinking painful private thoughts and coming to dreadful conclusions.

Malcolm kept his word and, to my relief, came without Ramsey who had decided Stamford needed him if Connecticut were to survive. Ramsey, Malcolm said, would be over on Wednesday, we would all have three days at the races and go to Australia on Saturday night.

He was crackling with energy, the eyes intensely blue. He and Ramsey had bought four more horses in partnership, he said in the first three minutes, and were joining a syndicate to own some others down under.

A forest fire out of control, I thought, and had sympathy for my poor brothers.

The Beverly Wilshire gave us a suite with brilliant red flocked wallpaper in the sitting room and vivid pink and orange flowers on a turquoise background in the bedrooms. There were ornate crimson curtains, filmy cream inner curtains, a suspicion of lace, an air of Edwardian roguishness brought up to date. Rooms to laugh in, I thought. And with little wrought-iron balconies outside the bowed windows looking down on a pool with a fountain and gardens and orange trees, not much to complain of.

We dined downstairs in a bar that had tables at one end and music, and Malcolm said I looked thinner.

'Tell me about the horses,' I said; and heard about them through the smoked salmon, the salad, the veal and the coffee.

'Don't worry,' he said, near the beginning. 'They're not all as expensive as Blue Clancy and Chrysos. We got all four for under a million dollars, total, and they're two-year-olds ready to run. Good breeding; the best. One's by Alydar, even.'

I listened, amused and impressed. He knew the

breeding of all his purchases back three generations, and phrases like 'won a stakes race' and 'his dam's already produced Group I winners' came off his tongue as if he'd been saying them all his life.

'Do you mind if I ask you something?' I said eventually.

'I won't know until you ask.'

'No ... um ... just how rich *are* you?'

He laughed. 'Did Joyce put you up to that question?'

'No. I wanted to know for myself.'

'Hm.' He thought. 'I can't tell you to the nearest million. It changes every day. At a rough estimate, about a hundred million pounds. It would grow now of its own accord at the rate of five million a year if I never lifted a finger again, but you know me, that would be boring, I'd be dead in a month.'

'After tax?' I said.

'Sure.' He smiled. 'Capital gains tax usually. I've spent a year's investment income after tax on the horses, that's all. Not as much as that on all those other projects that the family were going bananas about. I'm not raving mad. There'll be plenty for everyone when I pop off. More than there is now. I just have to live longer. You tell them that.'

'I told them you'd said in your will that if you were murdered, it would all go to charity.'

'Why didn't I think of that?'

'Did you think any more of letting the family have some of the lucre before you ... er ... pop off?'

'You know my views on that.'

'Yes, I do.'

'And you don't approve.'

'I don't disapprove in theory. The trust funds were generous when they were set up. Many fathers don't do as much. But your children aren't perfect and some of them have got into messes. If someone were bleeding, would you buy them a bandage?'

He sat back in his chair and stared moodily at his coffee.

'Have they sent you here to plead for them?' he asked.

'No. I'll tell you what's been happening, then you can do what you like.'

'Fair enough,' he said, 'but not tonight.'

'All right.' I paused. 'I won a race at Kempton, did you know?'

'Did you really?' He was instantly alive with interest, asking for every detail. He didn't want to hear about his squabbling family with its latent murderer. He was tired of being vilified while at the same time badgered to be bountiful. He felt safe in California although he had, I'd been interested to discover, signed us into the hotel as Watson and Watson.

'Well, you never know, do you?' he'd said. 'It may say in the British papers that Blue Clancy's coming over, and Ramsey says this hotel is the centre for the Breeders' Cup organizers. They're having reception rooms here, and buffets. By Wednesday, he says, this place will be teeming with the international racing crowd. So where, if someone wanted to find me, do you think they'd look first?'

'I think Norman West gave us good advice.'

'So do I.'

The Watsons, father and son, breakfasted the following morning out in the warm air by the pool, sitting in white chairs beside a white table under a yellow sun umbrella, watching the oranges ripen amid dark green leaves, talking of horrors.

I asked him casually enough if he remembered Fred and the tree roots.

'Of course I do,' he said at once. 'Bloody fool could have killed himself.' He frowned. 'What's that got to do with the bomb at Quantum?'

'Superintendent Yale thinks it may have given someone the idea.'

He considered it. 'I suppose it might.'

'The superintendent, or some of his men, asked old Fred what he'd used to set off the cordite . . .' I told Malcolm about the cordite still lying around in the tool shed ' . . . and Fred said he had some detonators, but after that first bang, you came out and took them away.'

'Good Lord, I'd forgotten that. Yes, so I did. You were all there, weren't you? Pretty well the whole family?'

'Yes, it was one of those weekends. Helen says it

was the first time she met you, she was there too, before she was married to Donald.'

He thought back. 'I don't remember that. I just remember there being a lot of you.'

'The superintendent wonders if you remember what happened to the detonators after you'd taken them away.'

He stared. 'It's twenty years ago, must be,' he protested.

'It might be the sort of thing you wouldn't forget.'

He shook his head doubtfully.

'Did you turn them over to the police?'

'No.' He was definite about that, anyway. 'Old Fred had no business to have them, but I wouldn't have got him into trouble, or the friend he got them from, either. I'll bet they were nicked.'

'Do you remember what they looked like?' I asked.

'Well, yes, I suppose so.' He frowned, thinking, pouring out more coffee. 'There was a row of them in a tin, laid out carefully in cotton wool so that they shouldn't roll about. Small silverish tubes, about two and a half inches long.'

'Fred says they had instructions with them.'

He laughed. 'Did he? A do-it-yourself bomb kit?' He sobered suddenly. 'I suppose it was just that. I don't remember the instructions, but I dare say they were there.'

'You did realize they were dangerous, didn't you?'

'I probably did, but all those years ago ordinary

people didn't know so much about bombs. I mean, not terrorist bombs. We'd been bombed from the air, but that was different. I should think I took the detonators away from Fred so he shouldn't set off any more explosions, not because they were dangerous in themselves, if you see what I mean?'

'Mm. But you did know you shouldn't drop them?'

'You mean if I'd dropped them, I wouldn't be here talking about it?'

'According to the explosives expert working at Quantum, quite likely not.'

'I never worked with explosives, being an adjutant.' He buttered a piece of croissant, added marmalade and ate it. His service as a young officer in his war had been spent in arranging details of troop movements and as assistant to camp commanders, often near enough to the enemy but not seeing the whites of their eyes. He never spoke of it much: it had been history before I was born.

'I remembered where the cordite was, even after all this time,' I said. 'If you imagine yourself going into the house with this tin of detonators, where would you be likely to put it? You'd put it where you would think of looking for it first, wouldn't you?'

'Yes,' he nodded, 'always my system.' A faraway unfocused look appeared in his eyes, then he suddenly sat bolt upright.

'I know where they are! I saw the tin not so very long ago, when I was looking for something else. I didn't pay much attention. It didn't even register what was in it, but I'm pretty sure now that that's what it was. It's a sort of sweet tin, not very big, with a picture on top.'

'Where was it, and how long ago?'

'Surely,' he said, troubled, 'they'd be duds by this time?'

'Quite likely not.'

'They're in the office.' He shrugged self-excusingly. 'You know I never tidy that place up. I'd never find anything ever again. I'm always having to stop people tidying it.'

'Like Moira?'

'She could hardly bear to keep her hands off.'

'Where in the office?' I remembered the jumble in his desk drawer when I'd fetched his passport. The whole place was similar.

'On top of some of the books in the breakfront bookcase. Bottom row, right over on the right-hand side, more or less out of sight when the door's closed. On top of the Dickens.' His face suddenly split into a huge grin. 'I remember now, by God. I put it there because the picture on the tin's lid was The Old Curiosity Shop.'

I rubbed my hand over my face, trying not to laugh. Superintendent Yale was going to love it.

'They're safe enough there,' Malcolm said reasonably, 'behind glass. I mean, no one can pick them up accidentally, can they? That's where they are.'

I thought it highly likely that that's where they weren't, but I didn't bother to say so. 'The glass in the breakfront is broken,' I said.

He was sorry about that. It had been his mother's, he said, like all the books.

'When did you see the tin there?' I asked.

'Haven't a clue. Not all that long ago, I wouldn't have thought, but time goes so quickly.'

'Since Moira died?'

He wrinkled his forehead. 'No, probably not. Then, before that, I was away from the house for a week or ten days when I couldn't stand being in the same place with her and she obdurately wouldn't budge. Before that, I was looking for something in a book. Not in Dickens, a shelf or two higher. Can't remember what book, though I suppose I might if I went back and stood in front of them and looked at the titles. Altogether, over three months ago, I should say.'

I reflected a bit and drank my coffee. 'I suppose the bookcase must have been moved now and then for redecorating. The books taken out . . .'

'Don't be ridiculous,' Malcolm interrupted with amusement. 'It weighs more than a ton. The books stay inside it. Redecorating goes on around it, and not at all if I can help it. Moira tried to make me take everything out so she could paint the whole office dark green. I stuck my toes in. She had the rest of the house. That room is mine.'

I nodded lazily. It was pleasant in the sunshine. A

few people were sunbathing, a child was swimming, a waiter in a white jacket came along with someone else's breakfast. All a long way away from the ruins of Quantum.

From that quiet Sunday morning and on until Wednesday, Malcolm and I led the same remote existence, being driven round Los Angeles and Hollywood and Beverly Hills in a stretch-limousine Malcolm seemed to have hired by the yard, neck-twisting like tourists, going out to Santa Anita racetrack in the afternoons, dining in restaurants like Le Chardonnay.

I gradually told him what was happening in the family, never pressing, never heated, never too much at one time, stopping at once if he started showing impatience.

'Donald and Helen should send their children to state schools,' he said moderately.

'Maybe they should. But you sent Donald to Marlborough, and you went there yourself. Donald wants the best for his boys. He's suffering to give them what you gave him effortlessly.'

'He's a snob to choose Eton.'

'Maybe, but the Marlborough fees aren't much less.'

'What if it was Donald and Helen who've been trying to kill me?'

'If they had plenty of money they wouldn't be tempted.'

'You've said that before, or something like it.'

'Nothing has changed.'

Malcolm looked out of the long car's window as we were driven up through the hills of Bel Air on the way to the racetrack.

'Do you see those houses perched on the cliffs, hanging out over space? People must be mad to live like that, on the edge.'

I smiled. 'You do,' I said.

He liked Santa Anita racetrack immediately and so did I; it would have been difficult not to. Royal palms near the entrances stretched a hundred feet upward, all bare trunks except for the crowning tufts, green fronds against the blue sky. The buildings were towered and turreted, sea-green in colour, with metal tracery of stylized palm leaves along the balconies and golden shutters over rear-facing windows. It looked more like a château than a racecourse, at first sight.

Ramsey Osborn had given Malcolm fistfuls of instructions and introductions and, as always, Malcolm was welcomed as a kindred spirit upstairs in the Club. He was at home from the first minute, belonging to the scene as if he'd been born there. I envied him his ease and didn't know how to acquire it. Maybe time would do it. Maybe millions. Maybe a sense of achievement.

While he talked easily to almost strangers (soon to be cronies) about the mixing of European and American bloodlines in thoroughbreds, I thought of the phone call I'd made at dawn on Monday morning to Superintendent Yale. Because of the eight-hour time difference, it was already afternoon with him, and I thought it unlikely I would reach him at first try. He was there, however, and came on the line with unstifled annoyance.

'It's a week since you telephoned.'

'Yes, sorry.'

'Where are you?'

'Around,' I said. His voice sounded as clear to me as if he were in the next room, and presumably mine to him, as he didn't at all guess I wasn't in England. 'I found my father,' I said.

'Oh. Good.'

I told him where Malcolm had stored the detonators. 'On top of *The Old Curiosity Shop*, as appropriate.'

There was a shattered silence. 'I don't believe it,' he said.

'The books are all old and leatherbound classics standing in full editions. Poets, philosophers, novelists, all bought years ago by my grandmother. We were all allowed to borrow a book occasionally to read, but we had to put it back. My father had us well trained.'

'Are you saying that anyone who borrowed a book from that bookcase could have seen the detonators?'

'Yes, I suppose so, if they've been there for twenty years.'

'Did you know they were there?'

'No. I didn't read those sort of books much. Spent my time riding.'

Lucy, I thought, had in her teens plunged into poets as a fish into its native sea, but twenty years ago she had been twenty-two and writing her own immortality. None of the rest of us had been scholars. Some of grandmother's books had never been opened.

'It is incredible that when someone thought of making a bomb, the detonators were to hand,' Yale complained.

'Other way round, wouldn't you think?' I said. 'The availability of the detonators suggested the bomb.'

'The pool of common knowledge in your family is infuriating,' he said. 'No one can be proved to have special access to explosives. No one has a reliable alibi . . . except Mrs Ferdinand . . . Everyone can make a timing device and nearly all of you have a motive.'

'Irritating,' I agreed.

'That's the wrong word,' he said sourly. 'Where's your father?'

'Safe.'

'You can't stay in hiding for ever.'

'Don't expect to see us for a week or two. What chance is there of your solving the case?'

Enquiries were proceeding, he said with starch. If I came across any further information, I would please give it to him.

Indeed, I said, I would.

'When I was younger,' he said to my surprise, 'I used to think I had a nose for a villain, that I could always tell. But since then, I've met embezzlers I would have trusted my savings to, and murderers I'd have let marry my daughter. Murderers can look like harmless ordinary people.' He paused. 'Does your family know who killed Moira Pembroke?'

'I don't think so.'

'Please enlarge,' he said.

'One or two may suspect they know, but they're not telling. I went to see everyone. No one was even guessing. No one accusing. They don't want to know, don't want to face it, don't want the misery.'

'And you?'

'I don't want the misery either, but I also don't want my father killed, or myself.'

'Do you think you're in danger?'

'Oh, yes,' I said. '*In loco* Moira.'

'As chief beneficiary?'

'Something like that. Only I'm not chief, I'm equal. My father made a new will saying so. I've told the family but they don't believe it.'

'Produce the will. Show it to them.'

'Good idea,' I said. 'Thank you.'

'And you,' he paused, 'do you know, yourself?'

'I don't know.'

'Guess, then.'

'Guessing is one thing, proof is another.'

'I might remind you it's your duty . . .'

'It's not my duty,' I interrupted without heat, 'to go off half-cocked. My duty to my family is to get it right or do nothing.'

I said goodbye to him rather firmly and concluded, from his tone as much as his words, that the police had no more information than I had, and perhaps less: that they hadn't managed (if they'd tried) to find out where the grey plastic clock had come from or who had bought it, which was their only lead as far as I could see and a pretty hopeless proposition. It had been a cheap mass-production clock, probably on sale in droves.

Malcolm said on one of our car journeys, after I'd been telling him about Berenice, 'Vivien, you know, had this thing about sons.'

'But she had a boy first. She had two.'

'Yes, but before Donald was born, she said she wouldn't look at the baby if it was a girl. I couldn't understand it. I'd have liked a girl. Vivien's self-esteem utterly depended on having a boy. She was obsessed with it. You'd have thought she'd come from some dreadful tribe where it really mattered.'

'It did matter,' I said. 'And it matters to Berenice. All obsessions matter because of their results.'

'Vivien never loved Lucy, you know,' he said thoughtfully. 'She shoved her away from her. I always thought that was why Lucy got fat and retreated into poetic fantasies.'

'Berenice shoves off her daughters onto her mother as much as she can.'

'Do you think Berenice murdered Moira?' he said doubtfully.

'I think she thinks that having more money would make her happier, which it probably would. If you were going to think of any ... er ... distribution, I'd give it to the wives as well as the husbands. Separately, I mean. So they had independence.'

'Why?' he said.

'Gervase might value Ursula more if she didn't need him financially.'

'Ursula's a mouse.'

'She's desperate.'

'They're all desperate,' he said with irritation. 'It's all their own faults. The fault, dear Brutus, is not in our stars but in ourselves, that we are underlings.'

'I dare say,' I said.

'The bell captain at the hotel gave me a tip for the fourth race.'

Back to horses.

Another day, another journey.

Malcolm said, 'What did Serena say, when you saw her?'

'She said you could stuff your money, or words to that effect.'

Malcolm laughed.

'She also said,' I went on, 'that Alicia told her you'd only tried to get custody of her that time so as to be cruel to Alicia.'

'Alicia's a real bitch.'

'She's got a lover, did you know?' I said.

He was thunderstruck. 'Who is he?'

'Someone else's husband, I should think. That's what she likes, isn't it?'

'Don't be so bloody accurate.'

Further down the road we were talking about the time switch clocks, which had been an unwelcome piece of news to him also.

'Thomas was best at making them, wasn't he?' Malcolm said. 'He could do them in a jiffy. They were his idea originally, I think. Serena brought one over for Robin and Peter which Thomas had made for her years ago.'

I nodded. 'A Mickey Mouse clock. It's still there in the playroom.'

'Serena made them a lighthouse of Lego to go with it, I remember.' He sighed deeply. 'I miss Coochie still, you know. The crash happened not long after that.' He shook his head to rid it of sadness. 'What race shall we choose for the Coochie Memorial Trophy? What do you think?'

On another day, I asked why Ferdinand didn't mind being illegitimate when Gervase did, to the brink of breakdown.

'I don't know,' Malcolm said. 'Gervase always thinks people are sneering and laughing, even now. Someone rubbed his nose in it when he was young, you know. Told him he was rubbish, a mistake, should have been aborted. Boys can be bloody cruel. Gervase got aggressive to compensate, I suppose. Nothing ever worried Ferdinand very much. He's like me in more than looks.'

'Only two wives so far,' I said incautiously.

'Why don't you get married?' he asked.

I was flippant. 'Haven't met the one and only. Don't want five.'

'Don't you trust yourself?' he said.

Christ, I thought, that was sharp, that was penetrating. That was unfair. It was because of him that I didn't trust myself: because in inconstancy, I felt I was very much his son.

His imprint, for better or worse, was on us all.

CHAPTER EIGHTEEN

On Wednesday, the Beverly Wilshire came alive as Ramsey had prophesied and Ramsey himself blew in with gusto and plans. We would go to parties. We would go round the horse barns. We would go to a Hollywood Gala Ball.

The Breeders' Cup organizers opened their reception room where everyone concerned with the races could have breakfast and cocktails (together if they liked) and talk about horses, could arrange cars and tickets and talk about horses, could meet the people they'd met at Epsom and Longchamp and talk about horses. Well-mannered people in good suits and silk dresses, owners whose enthusiasm prompted and funded the sport. Big bucks, big business, big fun.

Malcolm adored it. So did I. Life in high gear. Early on Friday, we went out to the racecourse to see Blue Clancy in his barn and watch him breeze round the track in his last warm-up before the big one. His English trainer was with him, and his English lad. There was heady excitement, a lot of anxiety. The orderly bustle of stable life, the smells, the swear words, the earthy humour, the pride, the affection, the jealousies, the injustices, the dead disappointments, all the same the world over.

Blue Clancy looked fine, worked well, threw Malcolm and Ramsey into back-slapping ecstasies. 'Wait until tomorrow,' the trainer said cautiously, watching them. 'We're taking on the best in the world, don't forget. The hot money is for a California-bred horse.'

'What's hot money?' Malcolm demanded.

'The bets made by people in the know. People with inside information.'

Who cared, Malcolm said. He couldn't remember ever having more fun in his life: and I thought his euphoria was at least partly due to his three close approaches to losing it.

Along with a thousand others, we went to the ball, though in the stretch-limo, not a converted pumpkin, and in the vast sound stage which had lately held a split-open aeroplane for filming cabin dramas, Malcolm danced with several ladies he'd known well for two days. He spent his time laughing. He was infectious. Everyone around him lit up like nightlights, banishing gloom.

We slept, we ate breakfast, we went to the races. The smog that all week had covered the mountains everyone swore were there on the far side of the track, relented and evaporated and disclosed a sunlit rocky backdrop worthy of the occasion. Tables with table-cloths had appeared overnight throughout the Club stands, and overworked black-coated waiters sweated under huge trays of food, threading through ever-moving racegoers, never dropping the lot.

There were seven Breeders' Cup races; various distances, variously aged horses. The first five each offered a total purse (for first, second, third and so on) of one million dollars. Blue Clancy's race, the one-and-a-half-mile Turf, had a purse of two million, and the climactic event, the Breeders' Cup Classic, promised three. They weren't racing for peanuts. The owner of the winner of Blue Clancy's race would be personally richer by six hundred and twenty-nine thousand dollars, enough to keep him in Bollinger for weeks.

We cheered home the first five winners. We went down to the saddling stalls and saw Blue Clancy prepared. We went up to the stands and bit our nails.

Five of the seven races were run on the dirt track, two on grass, of which this was the second; and most of the European horses were running on grass, the green stuff of home. Blue Clancy was taking on the Epsom Derby winner, the Arc de Triomphe winner and the winner of the Italian Derby. On paper, he looked to have an outside chance of coming fourth. In Malcolm's and Ramsey's eyes, he was a shoo-in. (Malcolm had learned the local jargon.)

Blue Clancy broke cleanly from the gate away on the far side of the course and his English jockey held

403

him handily in sixth place all down the far side. Ramsey and Malcolm were looking through binoculars and muttering encouragements. Blue Clancy, not hearing them, swung into the long left-hand bottom bend in no better position and was still lying sixth when the field crossed the dirt track as they turned for home. Malcolm's muttering grew louder. 'Come on, you bugger. Come on.'

There was no clear leader. Three horses raced together in front, followed by a pair together, then Blue Clancy alone. Too much to do, I thought: and the agile colt immediately proved me wrong. His jockey swung him wide of the others to allow him a clear run and gave him unmistakable signals that now was the time that mattered, now, this half-minute, if never again.

Blue Clancy accelerated. Malcolm was shouting, Ramsey was speechless. Blue Clancy in third place, all the crowds roaring. Blue Clancy still faster, second now. Malcolm silent, mouth open, eyes staring. The incredible was happening, awesome, breathtaking . . . and Blue Clancy had definitely, indubitably won.

Malcolm's eyes were like sapphires lit from inside. He still couldn't speak. Ramsey grabbed him by the arm and pulled him, and the two of them ran, almost dancing, weaving through slowcoaches, making their way down to greet their champion's return. I followed close on their heels, marvelling. Some owners were always lucky, some owners always weren't; it was an inexplicable fact of racing life. Malcolm's luck was stupendous. It always had been, in everything except wives. I should have known, I supposed, that it would come with him onto the track. King Midas had touched him, and Blue Clancy was his latest gold.

I wondered ironically what the family would say. The fortune he'd flung away on horses had already come back: Blue Clancy was worth at least double what he'd been before the Arc.

Chrysos, I daydreamed, would win the Derby. The tadpole film (about sharks actually, Malcolm had told me) would win at Cannes. The Pol Roger would appreciate. Everyone would see the point of not murdering the golden goose (Wrong sex, never mind. It was a lightheaded day.) We could return home to welcomes and safety.

Only it wasn't like that. We would return home to an unassessable danger, and it was essential to be aware of it, and to plan.

Sobered as always by what lay ahead, I nevertheless went to a post-race party in fine spirits, and after that to Los Angeles airport to fly through the night to Australia. The party, the people came with us. Melbourne took up the impetus, pressing forward to its own Cup, always held on the first Tuesday in November. Everything, they told us there, stopped for the race. Schoolchildren had a holiday and the Melbourne shops closed. The Hyatt Hotel, where we stayed (Watson and Watson), had a lobby criss-crossed by people known better in Newmarket, all with the ready grins of kids out of school.

Ramsey had surpassed himself in the matter of reservations. Even to reach our floor, we had to use a special key in the elevator, and there was a private lounge up there for cocktails and breakfast (but separately). Malcolm appreciated it, took it all in his stride, ordered champagne, breathed Melbourne air and became an instant Australian.

Out at Flemington racecourse (no château), there was less sophistication than at Santa Anita, just as much enthusiasm, very good food, a much better parade ring. Malcolm found the day's racing less compulsive than Paris or California through not owning a runner. He'd tried to remedy this on arrival, but no one would sell one of the top bunch, and he wanted nothing less. Instead, he set about gambling with method but only in tens and soon tired of it, win or lose. I left him and Ramsey in the Committee rooms and wandered down to the crowd as in Paris, and wondered how many in the throng struggled with intractable problems in their shirtsleeves, no shirts, carnival hats. When the party was over, Malcolm would grow restless and want to move on, and I wasn't ready. Under the shade of trees, surrounded by beer cans, listening to the vigorous down-under language, I searched for the solution that would cause us least grief.

There was no truly easy way out. No overlooking or dodging what had been done to Moira. But if someone could plead guilty and plead diminished responsibility owing to stress, there might be a quiet trial and a lifetime for us of visiting a sort of hospital instead of a rigorous prison. Either way, any way, there were tears in our future.

On top of that I had to be right, and I had to convince Malcolm beyond any doubt that I was. Had to convince all the family, and the police, without any mistake. Had to find a way of doing it that was peaceful and simple, for all our sakes.

I watched the Melbourne Cup from ground level, which meant in effect that I didn't see much of it because of the other thousands doing the same. On the other hand, I was closer to the horses before and after, watching them walk, listening to comments, mostly unflattering, from knowledgeable elbowers striving for a view.

The Melbourne Cup runners were older and more rugged than stars back home. Some were eight or nine. All raced far more often, once a week not being unusual. The favourite for that day's race had won on the course three days earlier.

They were racing for a purse of a million Australian dollars, of which sixty-five per cent went to the winner, besides a handsome gold cup. Thwarted this year, Malcolm, I imagined, would be back next year. He'd met in Paris and California several of the owners now standing in the parade ring and I could guess the envy he was feeling. No one was as passionate as a new convert.

When the race was finally off, I couldn't hear the commentary for the exhortations around me, but it didn't much matter: the winner was owned by one of the international owners and afterwards I found Malcolm beside the winner's enclosure looking broody and thinking expensive thoughts.

'Next year,' he said.

'You're addicted.'

He didn't deny it. He and Ramsey slapped each other on the back, shook hands and promised like blood brothers to meet regularly on every major racecourse in the world. Ramsey, the bulky manufacturer of millions of baseball caps, had somewhere along the line realized what 'metal' really meant in Malcolm's vocabulary and from cronies they had become comfortable friends, neither feeling at an advantage over the other.

They discussed staying on in Australia but Ramsey said the baseball caps needed guidance. Malcolm wavered about going to see some gold mines in Kalgoorlie but decided on a gold share broker in Melbourne instead. We spent Melbourne Cup night in a farewell dinner, and when Ramsey had departed in the morning and left us alone in the quiet breakfast room upstairs, Malcolm looked at me as if coming down to earth for the first time since we'd left England. With a touch of despondency, he asked for how long he was to be exiled for safety's sake.

'But you've enjoyed it,' I said.

'God, yes.' The remembrance flashed in his eyes. 'But it's not real life. We have to go back. I know I've avoided talking about it, it's all dreadful. I know you've been thinking about it all this time. I could see it in your face.'

'I've come to know them all so much better,' I said, 'my brothers and my sisters. I didn't care for them all that much, you know, before Moira died. We've always met of course from time to time, but I'd forgotten to a great extent what we had been like as children.' I paused for a bit, but he didn't comment. 'Since the bomb went off at Quantum,' I said, 'a great deal of the past has come back. And I've seen, you know, how the present has grown out of that past. How my sisters-in-law and my brother-in-law have been affected by it. How people easily believe lies, old and new. How destructive it is to yearn for the unobtainable, to be unsatisfied by anything else. How obsessions don't go away, they get worse.'

He was silent for a while, then said, 'Bleak.' Then he sighed and said, 'How much do they need, then? How much should I give them? I don't believe in it, but I see it's necessary. Their obsessions have got worse as I've grown richer. If the money wasn't there, they'd have sorted themselves out better. Is that what you're saying?'

'Yes, partly.' It hadn't been, entirely, but as it had

produced a reaction I'd wanted but hadn't expected, I kept quiet.

'All right, then,' he said. 'I've had a bloody good holiday and I'm feeling generous, so draw up a list of who's to get what.'

'All equal,' I said.

He began to protest, but sighed instead. 'What about you, then?'

'I don't know. We'll decide about that later.'

'I thought you wanted half a million to set up as a trainer.'

'I've changed my mind. For now, anyway. There's something else I want to do first.'

'What's that?'

I hesitated. I'd barely admitted it to myself, had certainly told no one else.

'Go on,' he urged.

'Be a jockey. Turn professional.'

'Good Lord,' he said, astonished, 'haven't you left it too late?'

'Maybe. We'll see. I'll have three or four years, perhaps. Better than not trying.'

'You amaze me.' He reflected. 'Come to think of it, you've constantly amazed me since you came to Newmarket Sales. It seems I hardly knew you before.'

'That's how I feel about you,' I said, 'and about all of the family.'

*

We set off homewards later the same day, travelling west via Singapore. Malcolm's gold share broker happened to be going there at the same time, so I changed places with him on the aeroplane and let the two of them say things like 'percussion and rotary air blast drilling to get a first idea' and 'diamond core drilling is necessary for estimating reserves accurately', which seemed to entertain them for hours.

I thought meantime about invitations. About invitations like meat over bear pits. The right invitation would bring the right visitor. The problem was how to make the invitation believable.

Part of the trouble was time. When we reached England, Malcolm would have been out of harm's way for four weeks, and I for almost three. We'd been safe, and I'd had time to reflect: those on the plus side. On the minus, as far as the invitation was concerned, was the fact that it would be six weeks since Malcolm had survived in the garage, and ten since Moira had died. Would a classic trap invitation work after so long an interval? Only one thing to do: try it and see.

Malcolm's voice was saying, ' . . . a section assaying five point eight grams per tonne' and a bit later, ' . . . Big Bell's plant milling oxide and soft rock', and ' . . . the future is good in Queensland, with those epithermal gold zones at Woolgar'. The broker listened and nodded and looked impressed. My old man, I thought, really knows his stuff. He'd told me at one point on our journeyings that there were roughly twenty-five hundred active gold mines in Australia and that it would soon rival or even surpass Canada as a producer. I hadn't known gold was big in Canada. I was ignorant, he said. Canada had so far come regularly second to South Africa in the non-communist world.

We'd taught each other quite a lot, I thought, in one way and another.

I would need someone to deliver the invitation. Couldn't do it myself.

'Market capitalization per ounce ...' I heard the broker saying in snatches, and ' ... in situ reserves based on geological interpretation ...'

I knew who could deliver the invitation. The perfect person.

'As open-cut mining cost as little as two hundred Australian dollars an ounce ...'

Bully for open-cut mining, I thought, and drifted to sleep.

We left spring behind in Australia on Wednesday and came home to winter on Friday in England. Malcolm and I went back to the Ritz as Mr and Mr Watson and he promised with utmost sincerity that he wouldn't telephone anyone, not even his London broker. I went shopping in the afternoon and then confounded him at the brandy and cigar stage late that evening by getting through to Joyce.

'But you said...' he hissed as he heard her voice jump as usual out of the receiver.

'Listen,' I hissed back. 'Hello, Joyce.'

'Darling! Where are you? What are you doing? Where's your father?'

'In Australia,' I said.

'*What?*' she yelled.

'Looking at gold mines,' I said.

It made sense to her, as it would make sense to them all.

'He went to California, I saw it in the paper,' she said. 'Blue Clancy won a race.'

'We went to Australia afterwards.'

'*We?* Darling, where are you now?'

'It doesn't matter where I am,' I said. 'To make it safe for us to come home, will you help to find out who killed Moira?'

'But darling, the police have been trying for weeks... and anyway, Ferdinand says it has to be Arthur Bellbrook.'

'It's not Arthur Bellbrook,' I said.

'Why not?' She sounded argumentative, still wanting it to be Arthur, wanting it to be the intruder from outside. 'He could have done it easily. Ferdinand says he could have done everything. It has to be him. He had a shotgun, Ferdinand says.'

I said, 'Arthur didn't use his shotgun. More importantly, he wouldn't have made a timing device exactly like we'd made as children, and he hadn't a motive.'

413

'He could have detested Moira.'

'Absolutely,' I said, 'but why should he want to kill Malcolm, whom he liked? I saw his face when he found Malcolm was alive that morning after the bomb, and he was genuinely glad.'

'Everyone wants it to be Arthur Bellbrook,' she said obstinately. 'He found her body.'

'If the police thought he'd done it, they wouldn't have been so suspicious of Malcolm.'

'You've got an answer for everything,' she complained.

I had myself for a while wished it to be Arthur. After all, there had been the affair of the prize vegetables (but he'd sounded philosophical about them, and would anyone kill for so little?) and he'd been in the army and might know about explosives. But he stood to lose rather than gain from Malcolm's death, and it was beyond believing that he would trace Malcolm to Cambridge, follow him to Newmarket Sales and try to run him down. That was the work of obsession. Arthur placidly digging potatoes; Arthur enjoying the temporary fame; Arthur looking after the dogs. Arthur had been the personification of stolid, sensible balance.

Besides, whoever had tried to run Malcolm down at Newmarket had guessed Malcolm would leave the sales with me and would come to the car park, and at that point Arthur would have had no reason to think so. He didn't know me. Hadn't met me until he came into the house with his shotgun, thinking I was a burglar. I'd had to exclude Arthur, although with regret.

Joyce said, 'Darling, how do you expect to succeed where the police have failed?'

'The police can't do what we can do.'

'What do you mean? What can we do?'

I told her. Malcolm's mouth opened and there was a long silence from Joyce.

'Let me get this straight,' she said eventually. 'You want me to telephone to everyone in the family . . .'

'*Everyone*,' I said emphatically. 'If a husband answers, tell him, then ask to speak to the wife, and tell her too. And vice versa.'

'Yes,' she said. 'I'm to say you're in Australia, both of you. Right?'

'Yes.'

'I'm to gush. Dreadful word, where *did* you learn it? I'm to let all this drip out as if it were of absolutely no importance but something I've just thought of? Darling, you can't mean I have to ring up *Alicia*?'

'Especially Alicia. Tell her I told you she has a boy-friend. That should stir her up nicely.'

'Darling, you don't mean it!'

'Ask her. And . . . er . . . do you know if the police are still guarding Quantum?'

'They told Donald that if he wanted constant guards, he'd have to get his own now. No one in the family wants to spend the money, so the police just have it on their occasional surveillance list, apparently.'

415

'And has anything else much happened in the family since we've been away?'

'No, nothing new. Thomas left Berenice, did you know that?'

'Yes ... Is he still with Lucy?'

'Yes, darling, I think so. Do you want me to tell him too?'

'You might as well.'

'I'm to think of something to phone them about and gossip a bit, and then I'm to say that I don't really care who killed Moira, but I don't think the police were thorough. Is that right? They never thought of looking for her notepad, the one she used to keep in the kitchen, in one of the drawers of those dazzling white cabinets. When anyone telephoned when she was in the kitchen, which was a lot of the time, she doodled their names with stars and things round it and wrote notes like "Donald, Sunday, noon" when people were coming to visit. I'm to say the police could never have found it but I've just remembered it, and I wonder if it's still there. I'm thinking of telling the police about it after the weekend. Is that right?'

'That's right,' I said.

'And I'm to say, what if she wrote down the name of her murderer?'

'Yes,' I said.

'Darling, why do you think her murderer telephoned? To make an appointment to kill her? You don't mean that, do you?'

'To make an appointment to see her, yes. To kill her, I don't know.'

'But why, darling? Why do you think the killer telephoned?'

'Because Malcolm told me she didn't like people just dropping in,' I said. 'She preferred people to telephone first. And because Moira's greenhouse can't be seen from the road, the drive, or from any windows of Quantum. Malcolm made her put it where it was well out of sight on that patch of lawn surrounded by shrubs, because he didn't like it. If anyone had come to see Moira unannounced that evening, they'd have found the house empty. If they'd telephoned first, she'd have said to come round to the greenhouse, that's where she'd be.'

'I suppose that's logical, darling. The police always did say she knew her killer, but I didn't want to believe it unless it was Arthur Bellbrook. He knew her. He fits all round, darling.'

'If Arthur had killed her, why would he go back later and find her body?'

'Darling, are you *sure* it wasn't Arthur Bellbrook?'

'Positive.'

'Oh dear. All right then, darling. You want me to start those phone calls tomorrow but definitely not before ten o'clock, and to go on all day until I've reached everyone? You do realize, I hope, that I'm playing in a sort of exhibition bridge game tomorrow evening?'

'Just keep plugging along.'

'What if they're out, or away?'

'Same thing. If nothing happens and we get no results, I'll phone you on Monday evening.'

'Darling, let me go to Quantum with you.'

'No, definitely not.' I was alarmed. 'Joyce, promise me you'll stay in Surrey. Promise!'

'Darling, don't be so vehement. All right, I promise.' She paused. 'Was that old bugger in good nick when you last saw him?'

'In excellent nick,' I said.

'Can't help being fond of him, darling, but don't bloody tell him I said so. Can't go back, of course. But well, darling, if there's one thing I regret in my life it's getting that frightful man West to catch him with Alicia. If I'd had any bloody *sense*, darling, I'd have turned a blind eye and let him have his bit on the side. But there it is, I was too young to know any better.'

She said goodbye cheerfully, however, promising to do all the phone calls in the morning, and I put the receiver down slowly.

'Did you hear any of that last bit?' I asked Malcolm.

'Not a lot. Something about if she'd had any sense, she wouldn't have done something or other.'

'Wouldn't have divorced you,' I said.

He stared incredulously. 'She insisted on it.'

'Twenty-seven years later, she's changed her mind.'

He laughed. 'Poor old Joyce.' He spent no more

thought on it. 'Moira didn't doodle on notepads that I know of.'

'I dare say she didn't. But if you were a murderer, would you bet on it?'

He imagined it briefly. 'I'd be very worried to hear from Joyce. I would think long and hard about going to Quantum to search for the notepad before she told the police.'

'And would you go? Or would you think, if the police didn't find it when Moira was first murdered, then it isn't there? Or if it is there, there's nothing incriminating on it?'

'I don't know if I would risk it. I think I would go. If it turned out to be a silly trap of Joyce's, I could say I'd just come to see how the house was doing.' He looked at me questioningly. 'Are we both going down there?'

'Yes, but not until morning. I'm jet-lagged. Don't know about you. I need a good sleep.'

He nodded. 'Same for me.'

'And that shopping you were doing?' he eyed the several Fortnum & Mason carrier bags with tall parcels inside. 'Essential supplies?'

'Everything I could think of. We'll go down by train and . . .'

He waved his cigar in a negative gesture. 'Car and chauffeur.' He fished out his diary with the phone numbers. 'What time here?'

419

Accordingly, we went in the morning in great comfort and approached Quantum circumspectly from the far side, not past the eyes of the village.

The chauffeur goggled a bit at the sight of the house, with its missing centre section and boarded-up windows and large new sign saying: 'Keep out. Building unsafe.'

'Reconstructions,' Malcolm said.

The chauffeur nodded and left, and we carried the Fortnum & Mason bags across the windy central expanse and down the passage on the far side of the staircase, going towards the playroom.

Black plastic sheeting still covered all the exposed floor space, not taut and pegged down, but wrinkled and slack. Our feet made soft crunching noises on the grit under the plastic and there were small puddles here and there as if rain had blown in. The boarded-up doors and the barred stairs looked desolate, and far above, over the roof, the second black plastic sheet flapped like sails between the rafters.

Sad, sad house. Malcolm hadn't seen it like that, and was deeply depressed. He looked at the very solid job the police had made of hammering the plywood to the door frame of the playroom and asked me politely how I proposed to get in.

'With your fingernails?' he suggested.

I produced a few tools from one of the bags. 'There are other shops in Piccadilly,' I said. 'Boy scouts come prepared.'

I'd thought it likely that I wouldn't be able to get

the plywood off easily as I understood they'd used four-inch nails, so I'd brought a hammer and chisel and a saw, and before Malcolm's astonished gaze proceeded to dig a hole through the plywood and cut out a head-high, body-wide section instead. Much quicker, less sweat.

'You didn't think of all this since yesterday, did you?' he asked.

'No. On the plane. There were a lot of hours then.'

I freed the cut-out section and put it to one side, and we went into the playroom. Nothing had changed in there. Malcolm fingered the bicycles when his eyes had adjusted to the partial light, and I could see the sorrow in his body.

It was by that time nine-thirty. If Joyce by any chance phoned the right person first, the earliest we could have a visitor was about half past ten. After that, anything was possible. Or nothing.

Malcolm had wanted to know what we would do if someone came.

'All the family have keys to the outside kitchen door,' I said. 'We never had the locks changed, remember? Our visitor will go into the kitchen that way and we will go round and ... er ...'

'Lock him in,' Malcolm said.

'Roughly, yes. And then talk about confessing. Talk about what to do with the future.'

I went round myself to the kitchen door and made sure it did still unlock normally, which it did. I locked it again after a brief look inside. Still a mess in there, unswept.

I returned to the playroom and from the bags produced two stick-on mirrors, each about eight inches by ten.

'I thought you'd brought champagne,' Malcolm grumbled. 'Not saws and bloody looking-glasses.'

'The champagne's there. No ice.'

'It's cold enough without any bloody ice.' He wandered aimlessly round the playroom, finally slumping into one of the armchairs. We had both worn layers of the warmest clothes we had, leaving the suitcases in the Ritz, but the raw November air looked as if it would be a match for the Simpson's vicuna overcoat and my new Barbour, and the gloves I had bought for us in the same shop the day before. We were at least out of the wind which swirled round and through the house, but there was no heat but our own.

I stuck one of the mirrors onto the cut-out piece of plywood, and the other at the same height onto the wall which faced the playroom door, the side wall of the staircase: stuck it not exactly opposite the door but a little further along towards the hall.

'What are you doing?' Malcolm asked.

'Just making it possible for us to see anyone come up the drive without showing ourselves. Would you mind sitting in the other chair, and telling me when the mirrors are at the right angle? Look into the one on the stair wall. I'll move the other. OK?'

He rose and sat in the other chair as I'd asked, and I moved the plywood along and angled it slightly until he said, 'Stop. That's it. I can see a good patch of drive.'

I went and took his place and had a look for myself. It would have been better if the mirrors had been bigger, but they served the purpose. Anyone who came to the house that way would be visible.

If they came across the fields we'd have to rely on our ears.

By eleven, Malcolm was bored. By eleven-thirty, we'd temporarily unbolted and unlocked the door at the end of the passage and been out into the bushes to solve the problem posed by no plumbing. By twelve, we were into Bollinger in disposable glasses (disgusting, Malcolm said) and at twelve-thirty ate biscuits and pâté.

No one came. It seemed to get colder. Malcolm huddled inside his overcoat in the armchair and said it had been a rotten idea in the first place.

I had had to promise him that we wouldn't stay overnight. I thought it unlikely anyway that someone would choose darkness rather than daylight for searching for a small piece of paper that could be anywhere in a fairly large room, and I'd agreed to the chauffeur returning to pick us up at about six. Left to myself, I might have waited all night, but the whole point of the exercise was that Malcolm himself should be there. We would return in the morning by daybreak.

He said, 'This person we're waiting for . . . you know who it is, don't you?'

'Well . . . I think so.'

'How sure are you, expressed as a percentage?'

'Um . . . ninety-five.'

'That's not enough.'

'No, that's why we're here.'

'Edwin,' he said. 'It's Edwin, isn't it?'

I glanced across at him, taking my gaze momentarily off the mirrors. He wanted it to be Edwin. He could bear it to be Edwin. In Edwin's own words, he could have faced it. Edwin might possibly have been capable of killing Moira, I thought: an unplanned killing, shoving her head into the potting compost because the open bag of it gave him the idea. I didn't think he had the driving force, the imagination or the guts to have attempted the rest.

When I didn't contradict him, Malcolm began saying, 'If Edwin comes . . .' and it was easier to leave it that way.

Time crept on. It was cold. By two-thirty, to stoke our internal fires, we were eating rich dark fruit cake and drinking claret. (Heresy, Malcolm said. We should have had the claret with the pâté and the champagne with the cake. As at weddings? I asked. God damn you, he said.)

I didn't feel much like laughing. It was a vigil to which there could be no good end. Malcolm knew as well as I did that he might be going to learn something

e fervently didn't want to know. He didn't deep down
want anyone to come. And I wanted it profoundly.

By three-thirty, he was restless. 'You don't really
mean to go through all this again tomorrow, do you?'

I watched the drive. No change, as before. 'The Ritz
might give us a packed lunch.'

'And Monday? Not Monday as well.' He'd agreed
on three days before we'd started. The actuality was
proving too much.

'We'll give up on Monday when it gets dark,' I said.

'You're so bloody persistent.'

I watched the mirrors. Come, I thought. *Come.*

'Joyce might have forgotten the phone calls,'
Malcolm said.

'She wouldn't forget.'

'Edwin might have been out.'

'That's more likely.'

A light-coloured car rolled up the drive, suddenly
here.

No attempt at concealment. No creeping about,
looking suspicious. All confidence. Not a thought given
to entrapment.

I sat still, breathing deeply.

She stood up out of the car, tall and strong. She
went round to the passenger side, opened the door,
and lifted out a brown cardboard box which she held
in front of her, with both arms round it, as one holds
groceries. I'd expected her to go straight round to the
kitchen door, but she didn't do that, she walked a few

steps into the central chasm, looking up and around her as if with awe.

Malcolm noticed my extreme concentration, rose to his feet and put himself between me and the mirrors so that he could see what I was looking at. I thought he would be stunned and miserably silent, but he was not in the least.

'Oh, no,' he said with annoyance. 'What's *she* doing here?'

Before I could stop him, he shot straight out of the playroom and said, 'Serena, do go away, you're spoiling the whole thing.'

I was on his heels, furious with him. Serena whirled round when she heard his voice. She saw him appear in the passage. I glimpsed her face, wide-eyed and scared. She took a step backwards, and tripped on a fold of the black plastic floor covering, and let go of the box. She tried to catch it . . . touched it . . . knocked it forward.

I saw the panic on her face. I had an instantaneous understanding of what she'd brought.

I yanked Malcolm back with an arm round his neck, twisting and flinging us both to find shelter behind the wall of the staircase.

We were both still falling when the world blew apart.

CHAPTER NINETEEN

I lay short of the playroom door trying to breathe. My lungs felt collapsed. My head rang from the appalling noise, and the smell of the explosive remained as a taste as if my mouth were full of it.

Malcolm, on his stomach a few feet away, was unconscious.

The air was thick with dust and seemed to be still reverberating, though it was probably my concussion. I felt pulped. I felt utterly without strength. I felt very lucky indeed.

The house around us was still standing. We weren't under tons of new rubble. The tough old load-bearing walls that had survived the first bomb had survived the second – which hadn't anyway been the size of a suitcase.

My chest gave a heave, and breath came back. I moved, struggled to get up, tried things out. I felt bruised and unwell, but there were no broken bones; no blood. I rolled to my knees and went on them to Malcolm. He was alive, he was breathing, he was not bleeding from ears or nose: at that moment, it was enough.

I got slowly, weakly, to my feet, and walked shakily into the wide centre space. I could wish to shut my eyes, but one couldn't blot it out. One had to live through terrible things if they came one's way.

At the point where the bomb had exploded, the black floor covering had been ripped right away, and the rest was doubled over and convoluted in large torn pieces. Serena – the things that had been Serena – lay among and half under the black folds of plastic: things in emerald and frilly white clothes, pale blue leg-warmers, dark blue tights; torn edges of flesh, scarlet splashes . . . a scarlet pool.

I went round covering the parts of her completely with the black folds, hiding the harrowing truth from anyone coming there unprepared. I felt ill. I felt as if my head were full of air. I was trembling uncontrollably. I thought of people who dealt often with such horrors and wondered if they ever got hardened.

Malcolm groaned in the passage. I went back to him fast. He was trying to sit up, to push himself off the floor. There was a large area already beginning to swell on his forehead, and I wondered if he'd simply been knocked out through hitting the wood floor at high speed.

'God,' he said in anguish. 'Serena . . . oh dear God.'

I helped him to his groggy feet and took him out into the garden through the side door, and round past

the office to the front of the house. I eased him into the
passenger seat of Serena's car.

Malcolm put his head in his hands and wept for his
daughter. I stood with my arms on top of the car
and my head on those, and felt wretched and sick and
unutterably old.

I'd hardly begun to wonder what to do next when a
police car came into the drive and rolled slowly, as if
tentatively, towards us.

The policeman I'd looked through the windows with
stopped the car and stepped out. He looked young,
years younger than I was.

'Someone in the village reported another
explosion . . .' He looked from us to the house questioningly.

'Don't go in there,' I said. 'Get word to the superintendent. Another bomb has gone off here, and this
time someone's been killed.'

Dreadful days followed, full of questions, formalities,
explanations, regrets. Malcolm and I went back to the
Ritz where he grieved for the lost child who had tried
hard to kill him.

'But you said . . . she didn't care about my money.
Why . . . why did she do it all?'

'She wanted . . .' I said. 'To put it at its simplest, I
think she wanted to live at Quantum with you. That's
what she's longed for since she was six, when Alicia

took her away. She might perhaps have grown up sweet and normal if the courts had given you custody, but courts favour mothers, of course. She wanted to have back what had been wrenched away from her. I saw her cry about it, not long ago. It was still sharp and real to her. She wanted to be your little girl again. She refused to grow up. She dressed very often like a child.'

He was listening with stretched eyes, as if seeing familiar country haunted by devils.

'Alicia was no help to her,' I said. 'She filled her with stories of how you'd rejected her, and she actively discouraged her from maturing, because of her own little-girl act.'

'Poor Serena.' He looked tormented. 'She didn't have much luck.'

'No, she didn't.'

'But Moira . . .?' he said.

'I think Serena made herself believe that if she got rid of Moira, you would go back to Quantum and she would live there with you and look after you, and her dream would come true.'

'It doesn't make sense . . .'

'Murder has nothing to do with sense. It has to do with obsession. With compulsion, irresistible impulse, morbid drive. An act beyond reason.'

He shook his head helplessly.

'It's impossible to know,' I said, 'whether she intended to kill Moira on that day. I wish we could know, but we can't . . . she can't have meant to kill her the way she did, because no one could know there'd be a slit-open nearly full sack of potting compost waiting there, handy. If she meant to kill Moira that day, she'd have taken some sort of weapon. I've been wondering, you know, if she meant to hit her over the head and put her in the car, the way she did you.'

'God . . .'

'Anyway, after Moira was out of the way, Serena offered to live with you at Quantum and look after you, but you wouldn't have it.'

'But it wouldn't have worked, you know. I didn't even consider it seriously. It was nice of her, I thought, but I didn't want her, it's true.'

'And I expect you made it clear in a fairly testy way?'

He thought about it. 'I suppose in the end I did. She kept on about it, you see. Asked me several times. Came to Quantum to beg me. I got tired of it and said no pretty definitely. I told her not to keep bothering me . . .' He looked shattered. 'She began to hate me then, do you think?'

I nodded unhappily. 'I'd think so. I think she finally believed she would never have what she craved for. You could have given it to her, and you wouldn't. The rejection was ultimate. Absolute. Extreme. She believed it, as she'd never really believed it before. She told me she'd given you a chance, but you'd turned her down.'

He put a hand over his eyes.

431

'So she set out to kill you, and finally to kill the house as well . . . to destroy what she couldn't have.'

I still wondered, as I'd wondered in New York, whether it was because I, Ian, had gone back to live at Quantum with Malcolm that she'd come to that great violent protest. I had too often had what she'd yearned for. The bomb had been meant as much for me as for Malcolm, I thought.

'Do you remember that morning when she found we weren't dead?' I asked. 'She practically fainted. Everyone supposed it was from relief, but I'll bet it wasn't. She'd tried three times to kill you and it must have seemed intolerable to her that you were still alive.'

'She must have been . . . well . . . insane.'

Obsessed . . . insane. Sometimes there wasn't much difference.

Malcolm had given up champagne and gone back to scotch. The constant bubbles, I saw, had been a sort of gesture, two fingers held up defiantly in the face of danger, a gallant crutch against fear. He poured a new drink of the old stuff and stood by the window looking over Green Park.

'You knew it was Serena . . . who would come.'

'If anyone did.'

'How did you know?'

'I saw everyone, as you know. I saw what's wrong with their lives. Saw their desperations. Donald and Helen are desperate for money, but they were coping the best way they could. Bravely, really, pawning her

432

jewellery. They thought you might help them with guaranteeing a loan, if they could find you. That's a long way from wanting to kill you.'

Malcolm nodded and drank, and watched life proceeding outside.

'Lucy,' I said, 'may have lost her inspiration but not her marbles. Edwin is petulant but not a planner, not dynamic. Thomas . . .' I paused. 'Thomas was absolutely desperate, but for peace in his house, not for the money itself. Berenice has made him deeply ineffective. He's got a long way to go, to climb back. He seemed to me incapable almost of tying his shoelaces, let alone making a time bomb, even if he did invent the wired-up clocks.'

'Go on,' Malcolm said.

'Berenice is obsessed with herself and her desires, but her grudge is against Thomas. Money would make her quieter, but it's not money she really wants, it's a son. Killing Moira and you wouldn't achieve that.'

'And Gervase?'

'He's destroying himself. It takes all his energies. He hasn't enough left to go around killing people for money. He's lost his nerve. He drinks. You have to be courageous and sober to mess with explosives. Ursula's desperation takes her to churches and to lunches with Joyce.'

He grunted in his throat, not quite a chuckle.

Joyce had been thanked by us on the telephone on the Saturday night when we'd come back exhausted.

She'd been devastated to the point of silence about what had happened and had put the phone down in tears. We phoned her again in the morning. 'I got Serena first,' she said sorrowfully. 'She must have gone out and bought all the stuff ... I can't bear it. That dear little girl, so sweet when she was little, even though I hated her mother. So *awful*.'

'Go on, then,' Malcolm said. 'You keep stopping.'

'It couldn't have been Alicia or Vivien, they're not strong enough to carry you. Alicia's new boyfriend would be, but why should he think Alicia would be better off with you dead? And I couldn't imagine any of them constructing a bomb.'

'And Ferdinand?'

'I really couldn't see it, could you? He has no particular worries. He's good at his job. He's easy-going most of the time. Not him. Not Debs. That's the lot.'

'So did you come to Serena just by elimination?' He turned from the window, searching my face.

'No,' I said slowly. 'I thought of them all together, all their troubles and heart-aches. To begin with, when Moira died, I thought, like everyone else did, that she was killed to stop her taking half your money. I thought the attacks on you were for money, too. It was the obvious thing. And then, when I'd seen them all, when I understood all the turmoils going on under apparently normal exteriors, I began to wonder whether the money really mattered at all ... And when I was in New York,

I was thinking of them all again but taking the money out . . . and with Serena . . . everything fitted.'

He stirred restlessly and went to sit down.

'It wouldn't have convinced the police,' he said.

'Nor you either,' I agreed. 'You had to see for yourself.' We fell silent, thinking what in fact he had seen, his daughter come to blast out the kitchen rather than search it for a notepad.

'But didn't you have any proof?' he said eventually. 'I mean, any real reason to think it was her? Something you could put your finger on.'

'Not really. Nothing that would stand up in court. Except that I think it was Serena who got Norman West to find you in Cambridge, not Alicia, as West himself thought.'

He stared. 'Why do you think that?'

'Alicia said she hadn't done it. Both West and I thought she was lying, but I think now she was telling the truth. Do you remember the tape from my telephone answering machine? Do you remember Serena's voice? "Mummy wants to know where Daddy is. I told her you wouldn't know, but she insisted I ask." That's what she said. Alicia told me positively that she herself hadn't wanted to know where you were. If Alicia's telling the truth, it was *Serena* who wanted to know, and she wanted to know because she'd lost us after failing to run you over. Lost us because of us scooting up to London in the Rolls.'

435

'My God,' he said. 'What happened to the tape? I suppose it got lost in the rubble.'

'No, it's in a box in the garage at Quantum. A few things were saved. Several of your gold-and-silver brushes are there too.'

He waved the thought away, although he was pleased enough. 'I suppose Serena did sound like Alicia on the telephone. I sometimes thought it was Alicia, when she phoned. Breathless and girlish. You know. Norman West just got it wrong.'

'She did call herself Mrs Pembroke,' I pointed out. 'Just to confuse matters. Or maybe she said Ms and he didn't hear clearly.'

'It doesn't much matter.' He was quiet for a while. 'Although it was terrible yesterday, it was the best thing, really. We'll grieve and get over this. She couldn't have borne to be locked up, could she, not with all that energy . . . not in drab clothes.'

On that Sunday morning also, we began telephoning to the family to tell them what had happened. I expected to find that Joyce had already told them, but she hadn't. She'd talked to them all the day before, they said, but that was all.

We left a lot of stunned silences behind us. A lot of unstoppable tears.

Malcolm told Alicia first, and asked if she'd like him to come to see her, to comfort her. When she could speak, she said no. She said Serena didn't kill Moira, Ian did. Everything was Ian's fault. Malcolm put the receiver down slowly, rubbed his hand over his face, and told me what she'd said.

'It's very hard,' he said, excusing her, 'to face that you've given birth to a murderer.'

'She helped to make her a murderer,' I said.

I spoke to my four brothers and to Lucy. Malcolm told Vivien last.

They all asked where we were: Joyce had told them we were in Australia. In London, we said, but didn't add where. Malcolm said he couldn't face having them all descend on him before he was ready. By the end, I was dropping with fatigue and Malcolm had finished off half a bottle. Long before bedtime, we were asleep.

We went back to Quantum on Monday, as we'd promised the police, and found Mr Smith poking around like old times.

All physical signs of Serena had mercifully been taken away, and all that remained were the torn flaps of black plastic that hadn't been near her.

Mr Smith shook hands with us dustily and after a few commiserating platitudes came out with his true opinions.

'Anyone who carries a fully-wired explosive device from place to place is raving mad. You don't connect the battery until the device is where you want it to go

437

off. If you're me, you don't insert the detonator, either.
You keep them separate.'

'I don't suppose she meant to drop it,' I said.

'Mind you, she was also unlucky,' Mr Smith said
judiciously. 'It is possible, but I myself wouldn't risk it,
to drop ANFO with a detonator in it and have it not
explode. But maybe dropping it caused the clock wires
to touch.'

'Have you found the clock?' I asked.

'Patience,' he said, and went back to looking.

A policeman fending away a few sensation seekers
told us that Superintendent Yale had been detained,
and couldn't meet us there: please would we go to the
police station. We went, and found him in his office.

He shook hands. He offered sympathy.

He asked if we knew why Serena had gone to
Quantum with a second bomb, and we told him. Asked
if we knew why she should have killed Moira and tried
to kill Malcolm. We told him my theories. He listened
broodingly.

'There will be an inquest,' he said. 'Mr Ian can formally identify the remains. You won't need to see
them ... her ... again, though. The coroner's verdict
will be death by misadventure, I've no doubt. You may
be needed to give an account of what happened.
You'll be informed of all that in due course.' He paused.
'Yesterday, we went to Miss Pembroke's flat and conducted a search. We found a few items of interest. I

am going to show you some objects and I'd be glad if you'd say whether you can identify them or not.'

He reached into a carton very like the one Serena had been carrying, which stood on his desk. He brought out a pile of twenty or thirty exercise books with spiral bindings and blue covers and after that a tin large enough to contain a pound of sweets, with a picture on top.

'*The Old Curiosity Shop*,' Malcolm said sadly.

'No possibility of doubt,' Yale nodded. 'The title's printed across the bottom of the picture.'

'Are there any detonators in it?' I asked.

'No, just cotton wool. Mr Smith wonders if she used more than one detonator for each bomb, just to make sure. He says amateurs are mad enough to try anything.'

I picked up one of the notebooks and opened it.

'Have you seen those before, sirs?' Yale asked.

'No,' I said, and Malcolm shook his head.

In Serena's looping handwriting, I read:

'Daddy and I had such fun in the garden this morning. He was teaching the dogs to fetch sticks and I was throwing the sticks. We picked a lot of beautiful daffodils and when we went indoors I put them all in vases in all the rooms. I cooked some lamb chops for lunch and made mint sauce and peas and roast potatoes and gravy and for pudding we had ice cream and peaches. Daddy is going to buy me some white boots with zips and silver tassels.

He calls me his princess, isn't that lovely? In the afternoon, we went down to the stream and picked some watercress for tea. Daddy took his socks off and rolled up his trousers and the boys *no* the boys weren't there I won't have them in my stories it was Daddy who picked the watercress and we washed it and ate it with brown bread. This evening I will sit on his lap and he will stroke my hair and call me his little princess, his little darling, and it will be lovely.'

I flicked through the pages. The whole book was full. Speechlessly I handed it to Malcolm, open where I'd read.

'All the notebooks are like that,' Yale said. 'We've had them all read right through. She's been writing them for years, I would say.'

'But you don't mean . . . they're recent?' I said.

'Some of them are, certainly. I've seen several sets of books like these in my career. Compulsive writing, I believe it's called. These of your sister's are wholesome and innocent by comparison. You can't imagine the pornography and brutality I've read. They make you despair.'

Malcolm, plainly moved, flicking over pages, said, 'She says I bought her a pretty red dress . . . a white sweater with blue flowers on it . . . a bright yellow leotard – I hardly know what a leotard is. Poor girl. Poor girl.'

'She bought them herself,' I said. 'Three or four times a week.'

Yale tilted the stack of notebooks up, brought out the bottom one and handed it to me. 'This is the latest. It changes at the end. You may find it interesting.'

I turned to the last entries in the book and with sorrow read:

'Daddy is going away from me and I don't want him any more. I think perhaps I will kill him. It isn't so difficult. I've done it before.'

There was a space on the page after that, and then, lower down: 'Ian is back with Daddy.'

Another space, and then,

'IAN IS AT QUANTUM WITH DADDY. I CAN'T BEAR IT.'

After yet another space, she had written my name again in larger-still capitals 'IAN' and surrounded it with a circle of little lines radiating outwards: an explosion with my name in the centre.

That was the end. The rest of the notebook was empty.

Malcolm read the page over my arm and sighed deeply. 'Can I have them?' he said to Yale. 'You don't need them, do you? There won't be a trial.'

Yale hesitated but said he saw no reason to retain them. He pushed the pile of books towards Malcolm and put the sweet tin on top.

'And the lighthouse and clock,' I said. 'Could we have those?'

He produced the Lego box from a cupboard, wrote

a list of what we were taking on an official-looking receipt and got Malcolm to sign it.

'All very upsetting, Mr Pembroke,' he said, again shaking hands, 'but we can mark our case closed.'

We took the sad trophies back to the Ritz, and that afternoon Malcolm wrote and posted cheques that would solve every financial problem in the Pembrokes' repertoire.

'What about the witches?' he said. 'If Helen and that dreadful Edwin and Berenice and Ursula and Debs are all having their own share, what about those other three?'

'Up to you,' I said. 'They're your wives.'

'*Ex*-wives.' He shrugged and wrote cheques for them also. 'Easy come, easy go,' he said. 'Bloody Alicia doesn't deserve it.'

'Engines work better with a little oil,' I said.

'Greasing their palms, you mean.' He still didn't believe in it. Still felt he was corrupting them by giving them wealth. Still thinking that *he* could stay sane and reasonably sensible when he had millions, but nobody else could.

He wrote a final cheque and gave it to me. I felt awkward taking it, which he found interesting.

'You should have had double,' he said.

I shook my head, reeling at noughts. 'You've post-dated it,' I said.

'Of course I have. I've post-dated all of them. I don't have that much in readies lying around in the bank.

442

Have to sell a few shares. The family can have the promise now and the cash in a month.'

He licked the envelopes. Not a cruel man, I thought.

On Tuesday, because I wished it, we went to see Robin.

'He won't remember Serena,' Malcolm said.

'No, I don't expect so.'

We went in the car I'd hired the day before for going to Quantum, and on the way stopped again to buy toys and chocolate and a packet of balloons.

I had taken with us the Lego lighthouse and the Mickey Mouse clock, thinking they might interest Robin, over which Malcolm shook his head.

'He won't be able to make them work, you know.'

'He might remember them. You never know. They used to be his and Peter's, after all. Serena gave them the clock and made them the lighthouse.'

Robin's room was very cold because of the open French windows. Malcolm tentatively went across and closed them, and Robin at once flung them open. Malcolm patted Robin's shoulder and moved away from the area, and Robin looked at him searchingly, in puzzlement, and at me the same way, as he sometimes did: trying, it seemed, to remember, and never quite getting there.

We gave him the new toys which he looked at and put down again, and after a while I opened the Lego box and brought out the old ones.

He looked at them for only a moment and then went on a long wander round and round the room, several times. Then he came to me, pointed at the packet of balloons and made a puffing noise.

'Good Lord,' Malcolm said.

I opened the packet and blew up several balloons, tying knots in the necks, as I always did. Robin went on making puffing noises until I'd blown up every balloon in the packet. His face looked agitated. He puffed harder to make me go faster.

When they were all scattered round the room, red, yellow, blue, green and white, bobbing about in stray air currents, shiny and festive, he went round bursting them with furious vigour, sticking his forefinger straight into some, pinching others, squashing the last one against the wall with the palm of his hand, letting out the anger he couldn't express.

Most times, after this ritual, he was released and at peace, and would retreat into a corner and sit staring into space or huddled up, rocking.

This time, however, he went over to the table, picked up the lighthouse, pulled it roughly apart into four or five pieces and threw them forcefully out of the wide-open window. Then he picked up the clock and with violence yanked the wires off, including the Mickey Mouse hands.

Malcolm was aghast. Docile Robin's rage shouted out of his mute body. His strength was a revelation.

He took the clock in his hand and walked round the

room smashing it against the wall at each step. Step, *smash*, step, *smash*, step, *smash*.

'Stop him,' Malcolm said in distress.

'No . . . he's talking,' I said.

'He's not talking.'

'He's telling us . . .'

Robin reached the window and threw the mangled clock far and high into the garden. Then he started shouting, roaring without words, his voice rough from disuse and hoarse with the change taking place from boy into man. The sound seemed to excite him until his body was reverberating, pouring out sound, the dam of silence swept away. 'Aaah . . . aaah . . . aaah . . .' and then real words, 'No . . . No . . . No . . . Serena . . . No . . . Serena . . . No . . . Serena . . . No . . .' He shouted to the skies, to the fates, to the wicked unfairness of the fog in his brain. Shouted in fury and frenzy. 'Serena . . . No . . . Serena . . . No . . .' and on and on until it became mindless, without meaning, just words.

I stepped close beside him in the end and yelled in his ear, 'Serena's dead.'

He stopped shouting immediately. 'Serena's dead,' I repeated. 'Like the clock. Smashed. Finished. Dead.'

He turned and looked at me vaguely, his mouth open, no sound coming out, the sudden silence as unnerving as the shouting had been.

'Serena-is-dead,' I said, making each word separate, giving it weight.

'He doesn't understand,' Malcolm said: and Robin went away and sat in a corner with his arms round his knees and his head down, and began rocking.

'The nurses think he understands quite a lot,' I said. 'Whether he understands that Serena is dead, I don't know. But at least we've tried to tell him.' Robin went on rocking as if we weren't there.

'What does it matter?' Malcolm said helplessly.

'It matters because if he does understand, it may give him rest. I brought the lighthouse and the clock because I wondered if Robin remembered anything at all. I thought it worth trying... didn't expect quite these results... but I think he smashed the clock Serena gave him because it reminded him of her, because she gave it to him and Peter shortly before the car crash. Somewhere in that woolly head, things sometimes connect.'

Malcolm nodded, puzzled and instinctively alarmed.

'One could almost think it was that afternoon,' I said, 'seeing the twins happy at Quantum where she hungered to be, seeing you there with them, loving them; perhaps it was that afternoon which finally tipped her over into the insanity of trying to make her fantasy come true. It didn't come true... you met Moira... but I'm certain she tried.'

Malcolm was staring saying 'No! Don't say it! *Don't!*'

I said it anyway. 'I think Robin saw the hit-and-run driver who forced their car off the road. In whatever mangled dreamlike way, he knows who it was. No

Serena, no Serena, no . . . You heard him. I've thought ever since New York that it could possibly have happened that way. Serena's obsession was full-blown a long time ago, long before she got rid of Moira. I think she killed Peter . . . and Coochie.'

EPILOGUE

We all went back to Quantum a year later for the Grand Reopening Ceremony, the house bedecked with garlands and champagne corks popping.

After much soul-searching, Malcolm had decided to rebuild. Without Quantum as its centre, the family would have fallen apart, and he didn't want that to happen. When he told everyone of his intention, there was great communal relief, and he saw without question that it was the right thing to do.

The rancour level lessened dramatically after the arrival of the cheques and the production of his will for inspection, and I was suddenly not everyone's villain, though still and forever Alicia's. Malcolm, having deleted Serena by codicil, sent his will to the Central Probate Office for registration and let everyone know it.

Malcolm still felt that he had pampered and corrupted his children, but he had to admit they were happier because of it. Dramatically happier in some cases, like Donald and Helen whose problems had all been financial. Helen redeemed her baubles and stopped painting china, and Donald paid off the finance company and the bank and ran the golf club with a light heart.

A few weeks after Serena's death, Helen asked me over to Marblehill House. 'A drink before dinner,' she said. I went on a freezing evening in December and she surprised me by kissing me in greeting. Donald was standing with his back to a roaring fire, looking contentedly pompous.

'We wanted to thank you,' Helen said. 'And I suppose . . . to apologize.'

'There's no need.'

'Oh, yes. We all know there is. Not everyone will say so, but they know.'

'How's Malcolm?' Donald asked.

'He's fine.'

Donald nodded. Even the fact that Malcolm and I were still together seemed no longer to worry him, and later, when we'd sat round the fire drinking for a while, he asked me to stay on for dinner. I stayed, and although we were never going to be in and out of each other's houses every five minutes, at least on that evening we reached a peaceful plateau as brothers.

Some time later, I went to see Lucy. She and Edwin had made no changes to their cottage and had no plans to move, much to Edwin's disgust.

'We should live somewhere more *suitable*,' he said

to her crossly. 'I never thought we would stay here when you inherited.'

Lucy looked at him with affection. 'If you want to leave, Edwin, you can, now that you have money of your own.'

He was disconcerted; open mouthed. 'I don't want to leave,' he said, and it was clearly the truth.

Lucy said to me, 'I'll find a good use for my money: keep the capital, give away most of the income. We have no anxieties now, and that's a relief, I agree, but I haven't changed altogether. I don't believe in luxurious living. It's bad for the soul. I'm staying here.' She ate a handful of raisins determinedly, the old man looking out of her eyes.

Thomas was no longer her guest. Thomas, against all advice, had gone back to Berenice.

I called at Arden Haciendas one dark cold afternoon and Thomas opened the front door himself, looking blank when he saw me.

'Berenice is out,' he said, letting me in.

'I came to see you. How are you doing?'

'Not so bad,' he said, but he still looked defeated.

He gave me a drink. He knew where the gin was, and the tonic. He said Berenice and he had been going to marriage guidance sessions, but he didn't know that they were doing much good.

'You can get vasectomies reversed sometimes,' I said.

'Yes, but I don't really want to. Suppose I did, and

we had another girl? Unless Berenice can get over not having sons, I'm going to leave her again. I told her.'

I gazed at him, awestruck. 'What did she say?'

'Nothing much. I think she's afraid of me, really.'

As long as it didn't go to his head, I thought that might not be at all a bad thing.

I went to see Gervase and Ursula soon after. The change in Ursula, who let me in, was like unwrapping a brown paper parcel and finding Christmas inside. The old skirt, shirt, pullover and pearls had vanished. She wore narrow scarlet trousers, a huge white sweater and a baroque gold chain. She smiled at me like a shy conspirator and came with me into the sitting room. Gervase, if not overpoweringly friendly, seemed ready for neutrality and a truce.

'I told Gervase,' Ursula said sweetly, 'that now that I can afford to leave him and take the girls with me, I'm staying because I want to, not because I have to. I'm staying as long as he gets help with this ridiculous fixation about his birth. Who *cares* that Malcolm wasn't married to Alicia at the time? I certainly don't. No one does. Ferdinand doesn't. Ferdinand's been very good, he's been over here several times giving Gervase advice.'

Gervase, who in the past would have shouted her down, listened almost with gratitude. The bear that had run himself into a thicket was being led out by compassionate hands.

Ferdinand, when I called, was in rocketing good

spirits. He and Debs had moved immediately from their small bare bungalow into a large bare bungalow with a tennis court, a swimming pool and a three-car garage. Affluence was fun, he said; but one of the new house's rooms was also his office. He was going on with his job.

'I took your remarks to heart, you know,' he said. 'Took a look at what Alicia had done to us. I don't listen to her any more. She won't get rid of Debs and she won't get rid of Ursula. Have you seen Ursula? Transformation! I've told Gervase he has a wife in a million and a mother who's nothing but trouble. I've been talking to him about illegitimacy... isn't that what you wanted?' He punched my arm lightly. 'Stay to dinner?' he said.

I didn't go to see either Alicia or Vivien. I stayed a few nights with Joyce.

'Darling, how's that old fool getting along?'

'He spends a lot of time at Quantum with the builders.'

'Don't let him catch pneumonia. It's bitter outside.'

'He does what he likes,' I said.

'Darling, when did he not?'

Joyce rushed busily away to a bridge tournament in Paris, kissing my cheek, patting me with approval, telling me to be careful not to break my neck in those frightful races I insisted on riding.

I gave her the assurances and went back to Lambourn, now my home instead of Epsom. I'd asked the trainer I'd been riding exercise for if he knew of anyone needing a second-string stable jockey, if I should take the giant step of turning professional.

He stared. 'I heard you don't need to. Didn't you come into money?'

'Forget the money. What chance would I have?'

'I saw you win that race at Kempton,' he said. 'If you turn pro, if you come to Lambourn, I'll give you plenty of rides.'

He was as good as his word, and George and Jo, astonished but happy, entered their few horses to fit in.

I bought a house in Lambourn and Malcolm came to live in it while Quantum was rebuilt. Malcolm loved Lambourn. He went often up to the Downs with the trainer I was riding for to watch the horses work, and far from losing interest in racing, grew more and more involved. When I won my first professional race, the Bollinger ran through Lambourn like a river.

By the day the following November that we all went to the house for the Grand Reopening (with embossed invitation cards and an army of caterers), everyone's lives had settled into the new patterns.

Malcolm had been to the 'Arc' again, and round the world with Ramsey Osborn. Chrysos had won the Futurity at Doncaster and was tipped for the next year's Derby. Blue Clancy had gone to stud, syndicated for millions.

I had ended my first professional season with a respectable score and at the start of my second had become the chief retained jockey for the stable. I would be a trainer in the end, I supposed. Meantime, I felt alive and fulfilled as never before.

Lucy and Edwin were still eating healthily in the cottage. Lucy, coming to terms with not writing more poetry herself, had started on a scholarly biography and commentary on the Life and Work of Thomas Stearns Eliot. Edwin was still doing the shopping.

Donald and Helen, arm in arm, wandered round the garden like lovers.

Ferdinand fussed over Debs, who was pregnant.

Gervase had recovered most of his bullishness, which seemed to reassure Ursula rather than cow her. She came in a mink coat, laughing with pleasure.

In Berenice, the fire had gone out: in Thomas, it had been faintly rekindled. No longer needing a job, he was learning to play golf. Berenice was house-hunting, with Thomas's approval.

Alicia came looking girlish, trilling away in a voice like an echo of Serena's, and everyone made polite remarks to her with closed teeth.

Vivien complained that Malcolm had re-done the house too much in Coochie's taste. Joyce made diplomatic friends with the married couple he had engaged to look after him. He – and they – had been living in the house for a week.

All of the grandchildren were there, re-exploring the place: children's voices again in the garden. Robin, far away, had fallen silent once more and had never since that violent day wanted me to blow up balloons.

Malcolm and I walked out through the new sitting-room windows and from the lawn looked up at the house. It felt whole again, not just physically, but at peace.

'I don't feel Serena's here, do you?' Malcolm said.

'No, she isn't.'

'I was afraid she might be. I'm glad she's not.'

We went further down the lawn.

'Did you notice I'd taken the golden dolphin and the amethyst tree and so on out of the wall and put them in the sitting room?' he asked casually.

'Yes, I did.'

'I sold the gold too.'

I glanced at him. He looked quizzically back.

'The price rose sharply this year, as I thought it would. I took the profit. There's nothing in the wall now except spiders and dust.'

'Never mind.'

'I'm leaving the clause in the will though.' The family had been curious about his leaving me the piece of wire, and he'd refused to explain. 'I'll buy more gold, and sell it. Buy and sell. Forward and backward. One of these days . . .' his blue eyes gleamed ' . . . you may win on the nod.'